Witchy

Ariel Slamet Ries

Edited by Hazel Newlevant and Steenz
Lettered by Andworld Design
Designed by Leigh Luna

Witchy, published 2019 by The Lion Forge, LLC.

Witchy is a member of thehiveworks.com
Visit witchycomic.com to read the comic as it updates.

ISBN: 978-1-5493-0481-1
LCCN: 2019937430
10 9 8 7 6 5 4 3 2 1

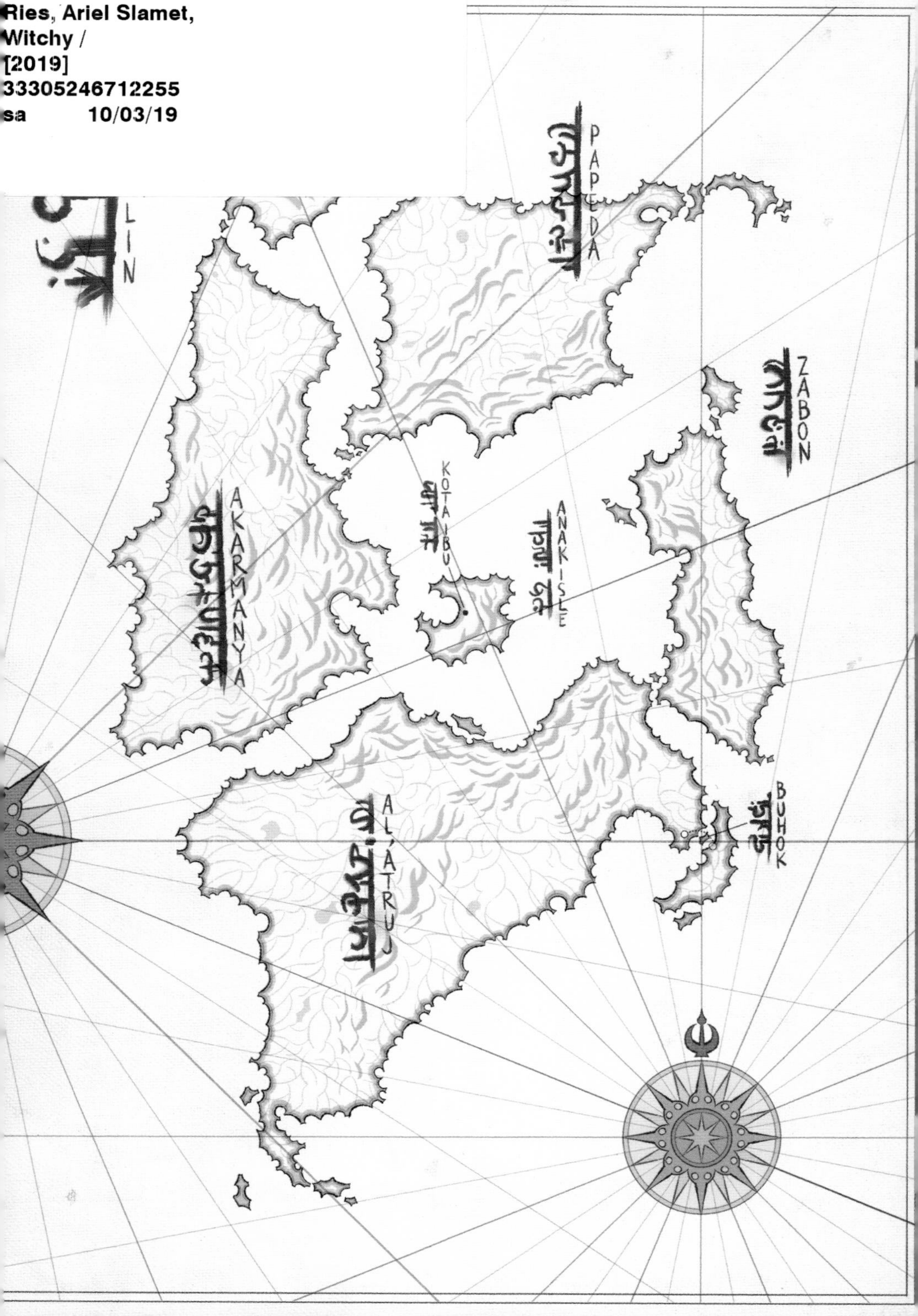
LIN
PAPEDA
ZABON
AKARMANYA
KOTA IBU
ANAKISLE
AL'ATRUJ
BUHOK

For Eyang and Papi;
Inna Lillahi wa inna ilayhi raji'un

WITCHY
CHAPTER ONE

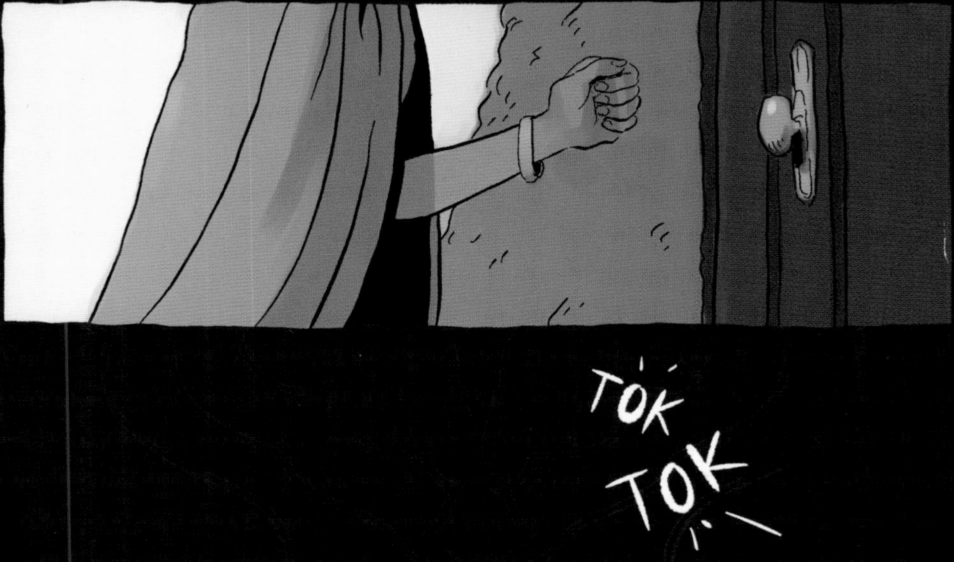
TOK TOK

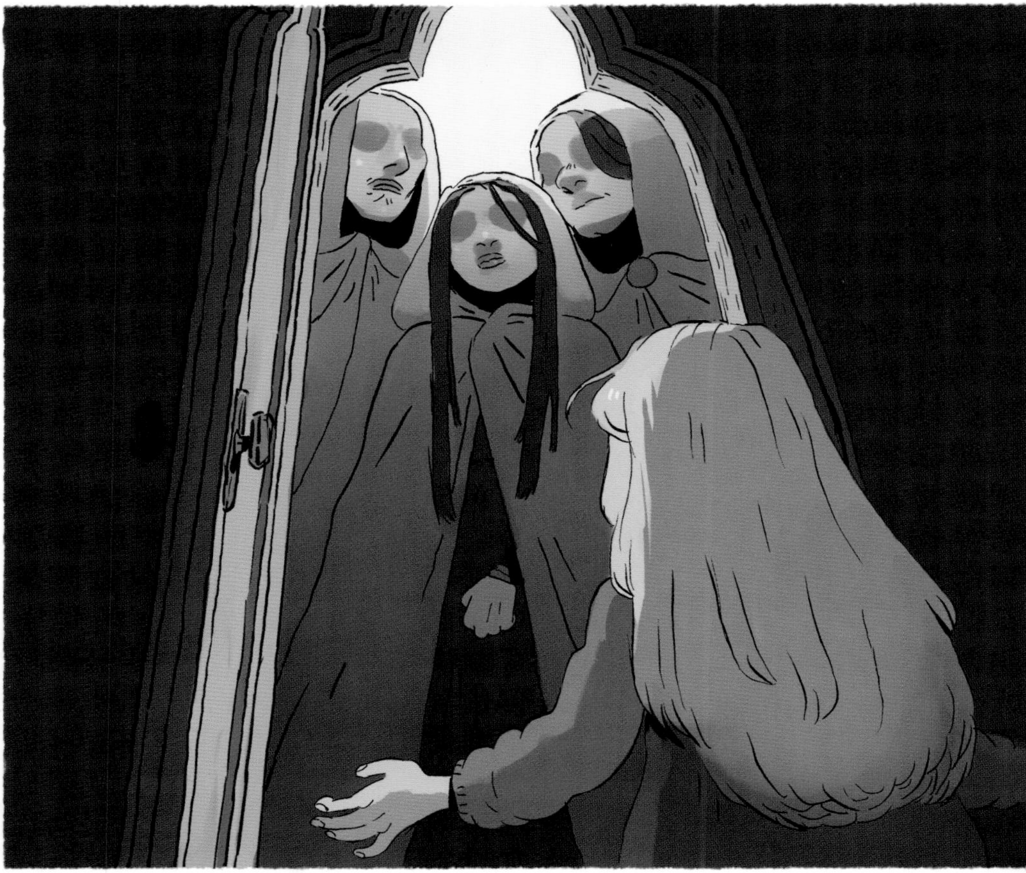

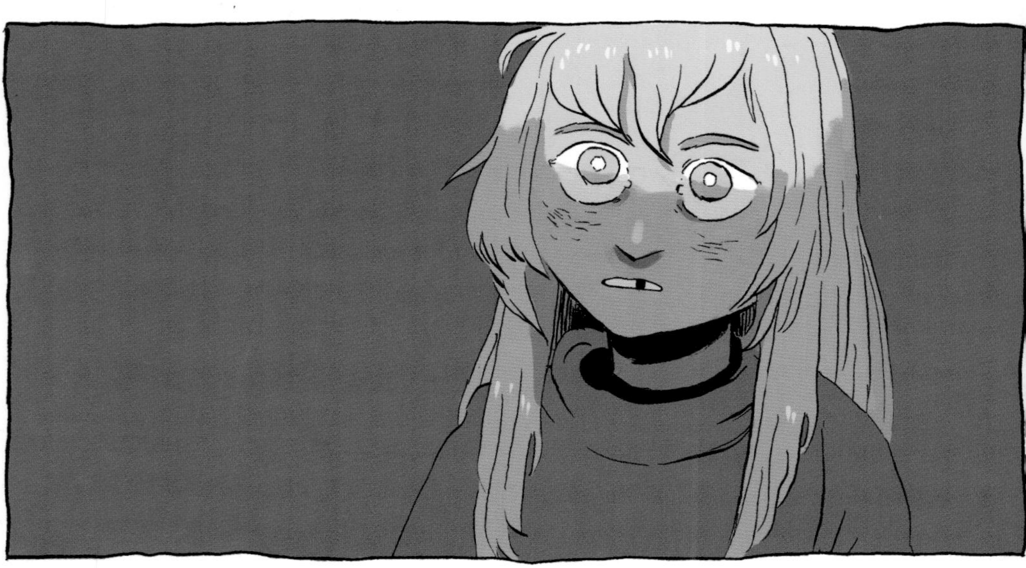

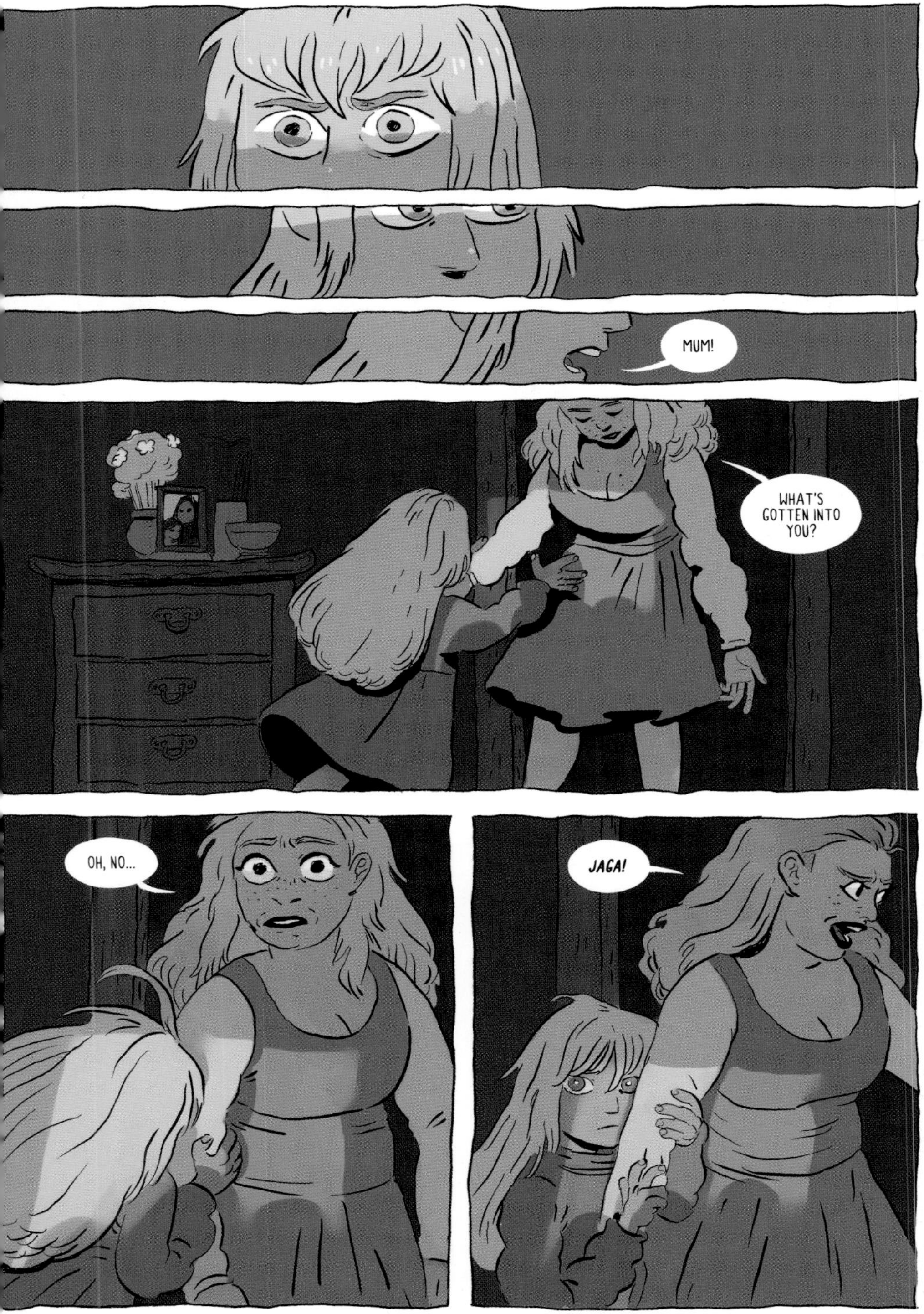
MUM!
WHAT'S GOTTEN INTO YOU?
OH, NO...
JAGA!

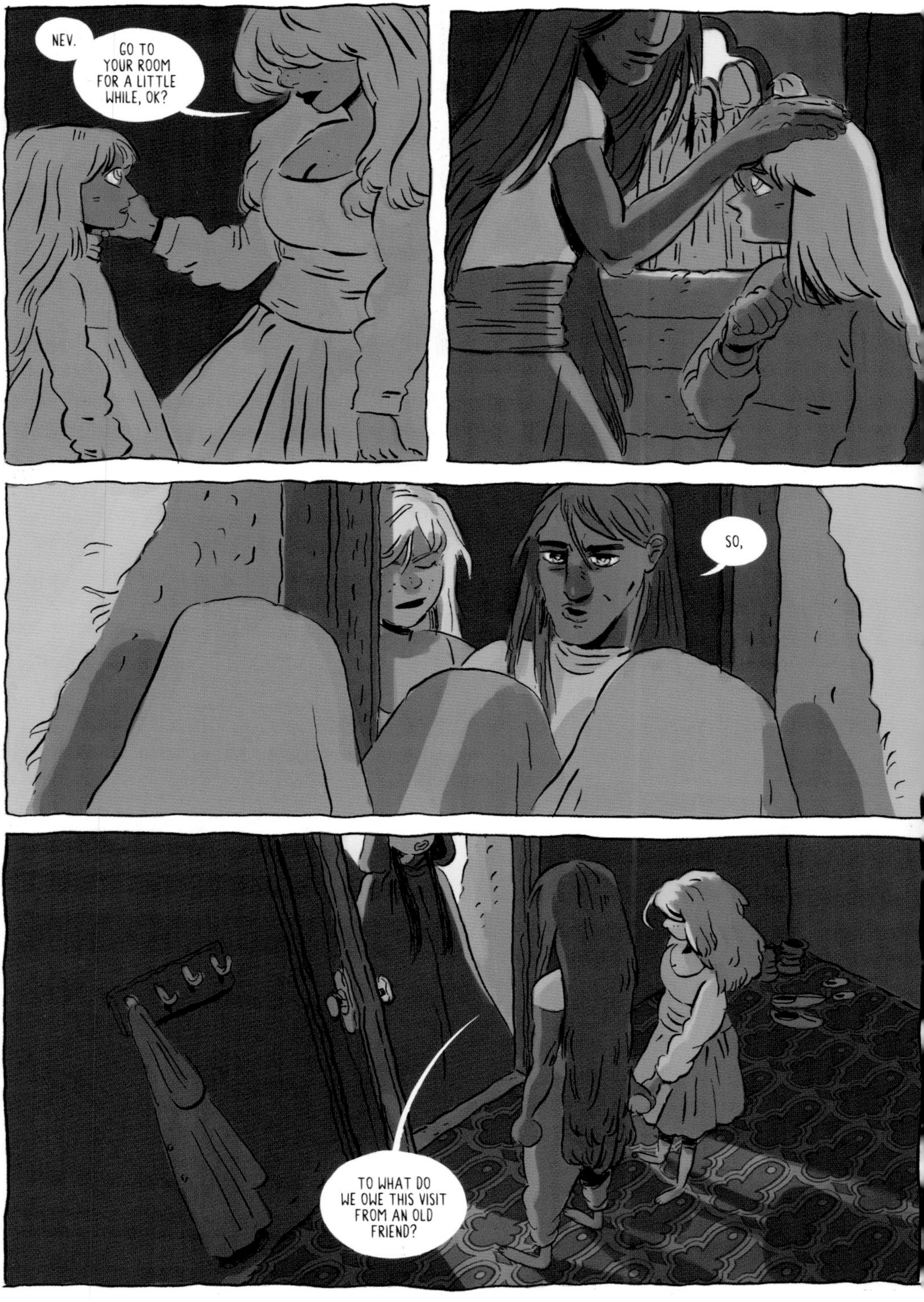
NEV.
GO TO YOUR ROOM FOR A LITTLE WHILE, OK?
SO,
TO WHAT DO WE OWE THIS VISIT FROM AN OLD FRIEND?

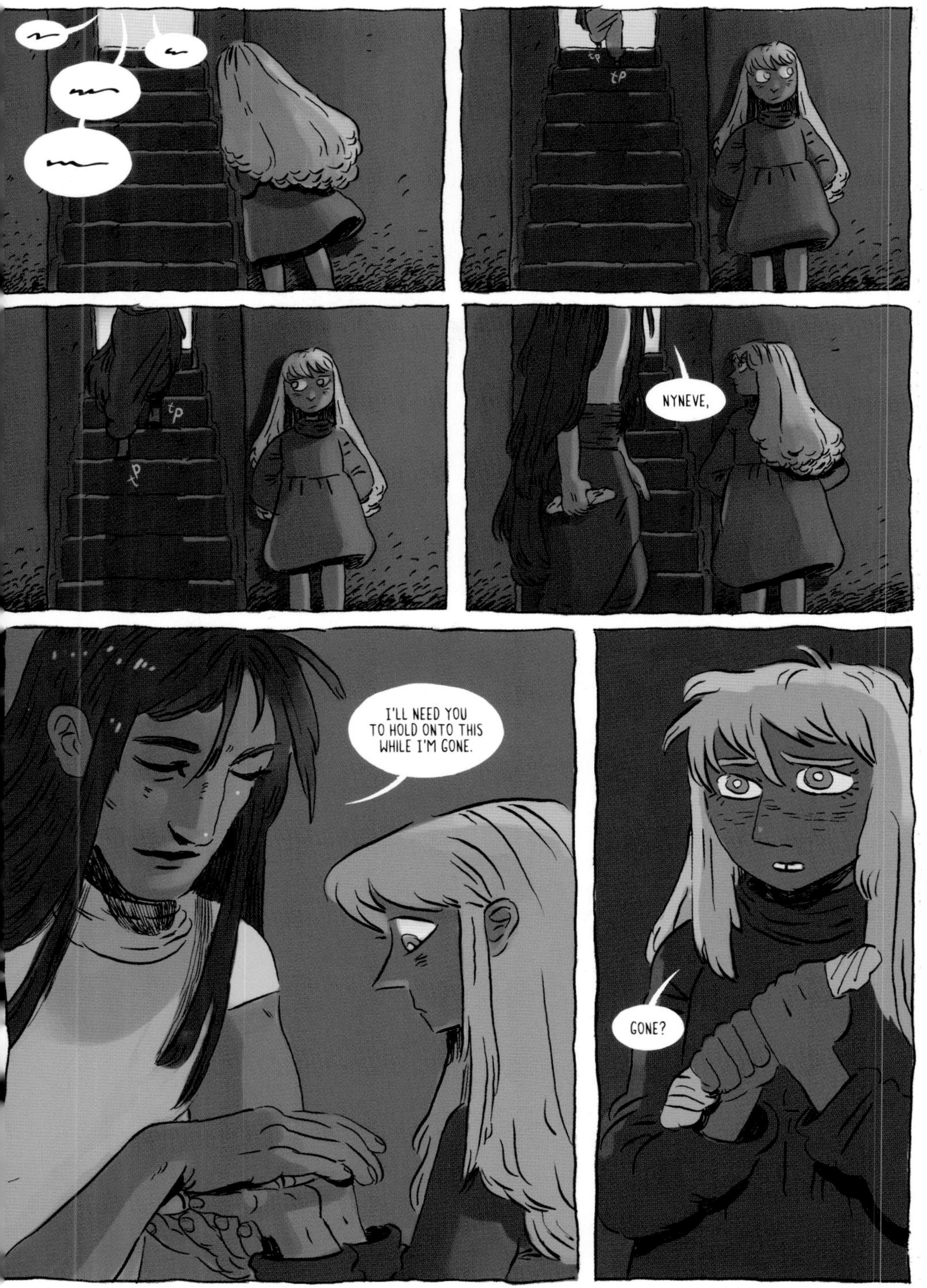
NYNEVE,
I'LL NEED YOU TO HOLD ONTO THIS WHILE I'M GONE.
GONE?

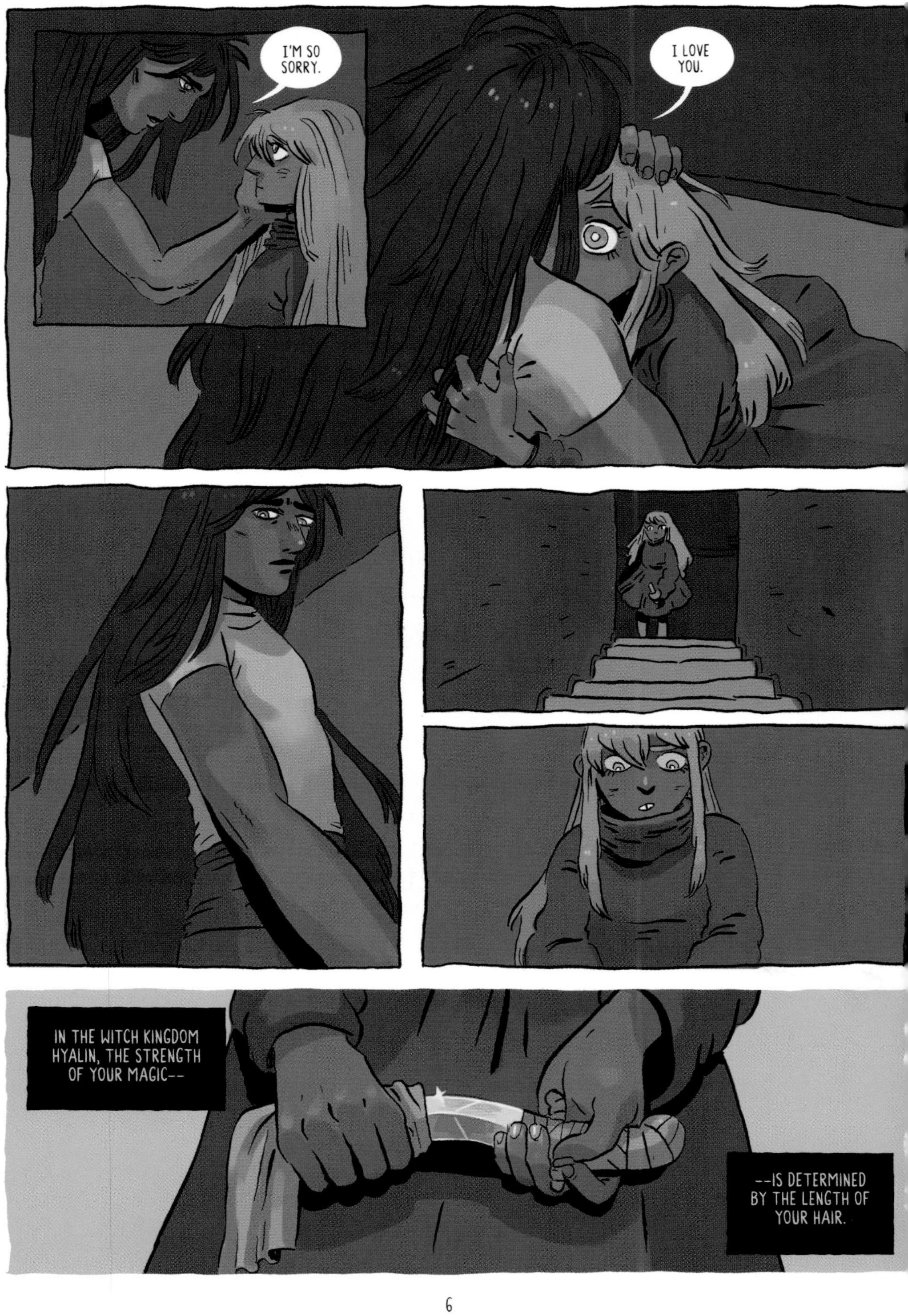
I'M SO SORRY.
I LOVE YOU.
IN THE WITCH KINGDOM HYALIN, THE STRENGTH OF YOUR MAGIC--
--IS DETERMINED BY THE LENGTH OF YOUR HAIR.

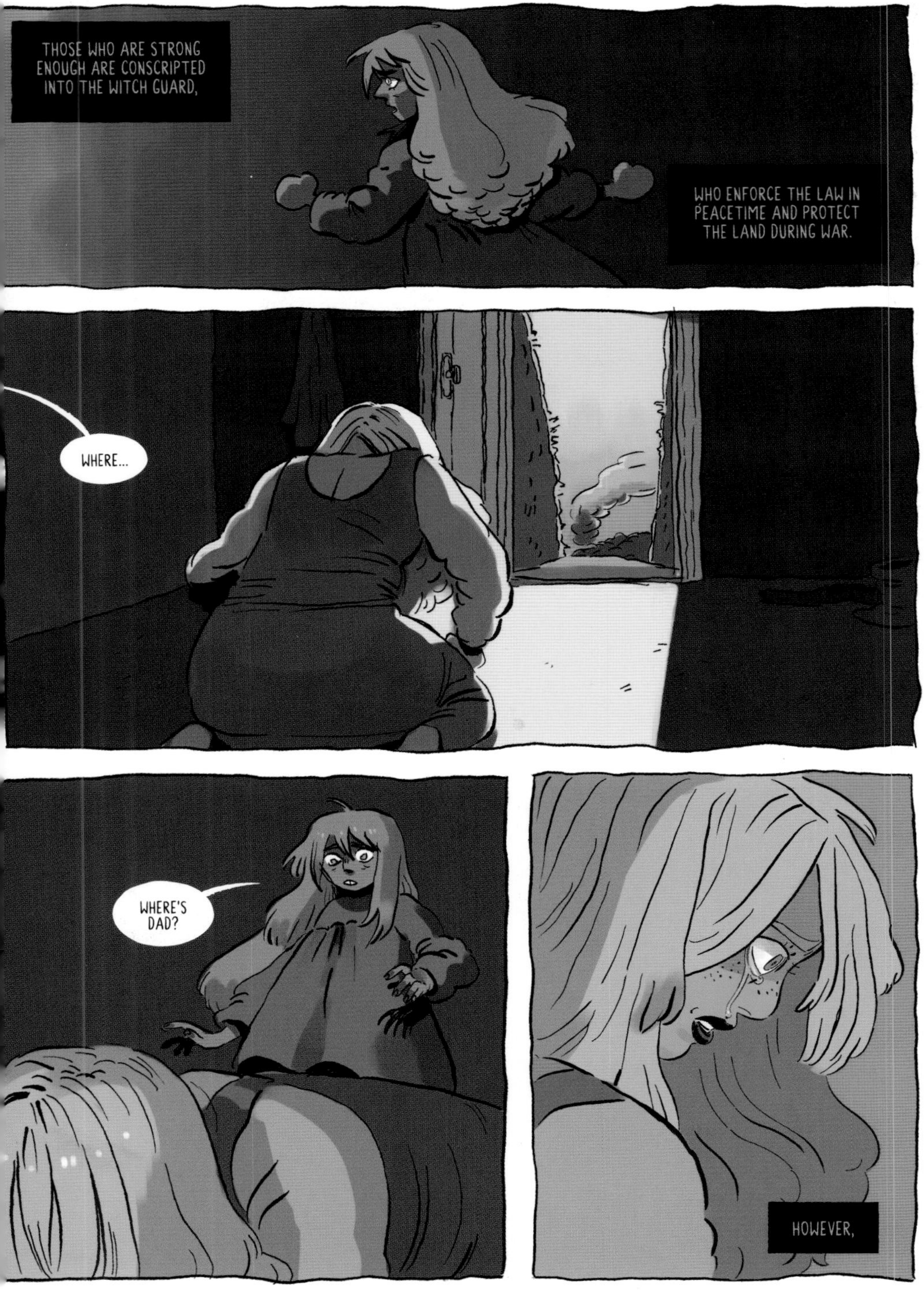
THOSE WHO ARE STRONG ENOUGH ARE CONSCRIPTED INTO THE WITCH GUARD,
WHO ENFORCE THE LAW IN PEACETIME AND PROTECT THE LAND DURING WAR.
WHERE...
WHERE'S DAD?
HOWEVER,

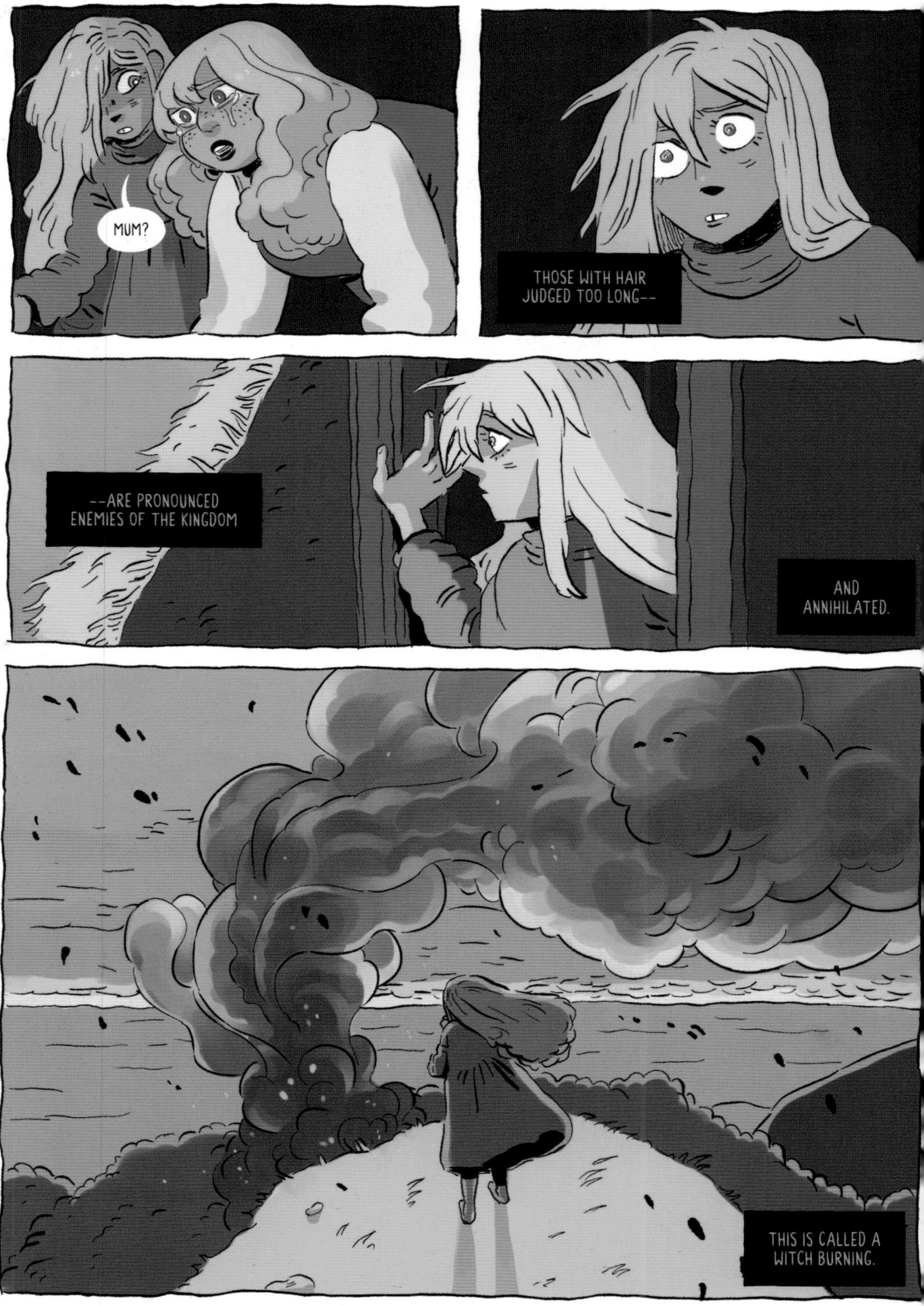
MUM?
THOSE WITH HAIR JUDGED TOO LONG--
--ARE PRONOUNCED ENEMIES OF THE KINGDOM
AND ANNIHILATED.
THIS IS CALLED A WITCH BURNING.

WITCHY
CHAPTER TWO

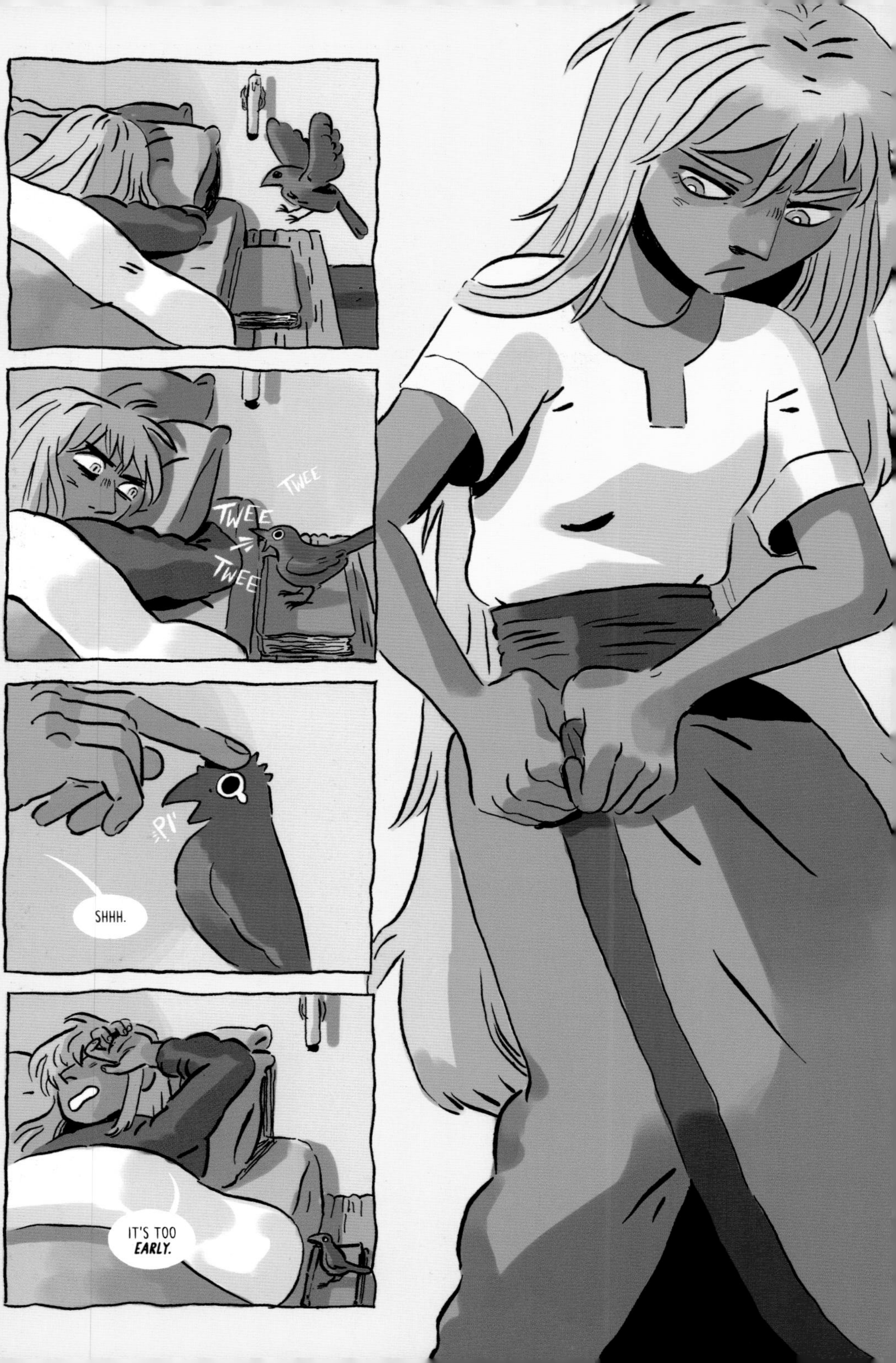
TWEE
TWEE
TWEE
PI
SHHH.
IT'S TOO EARLY.

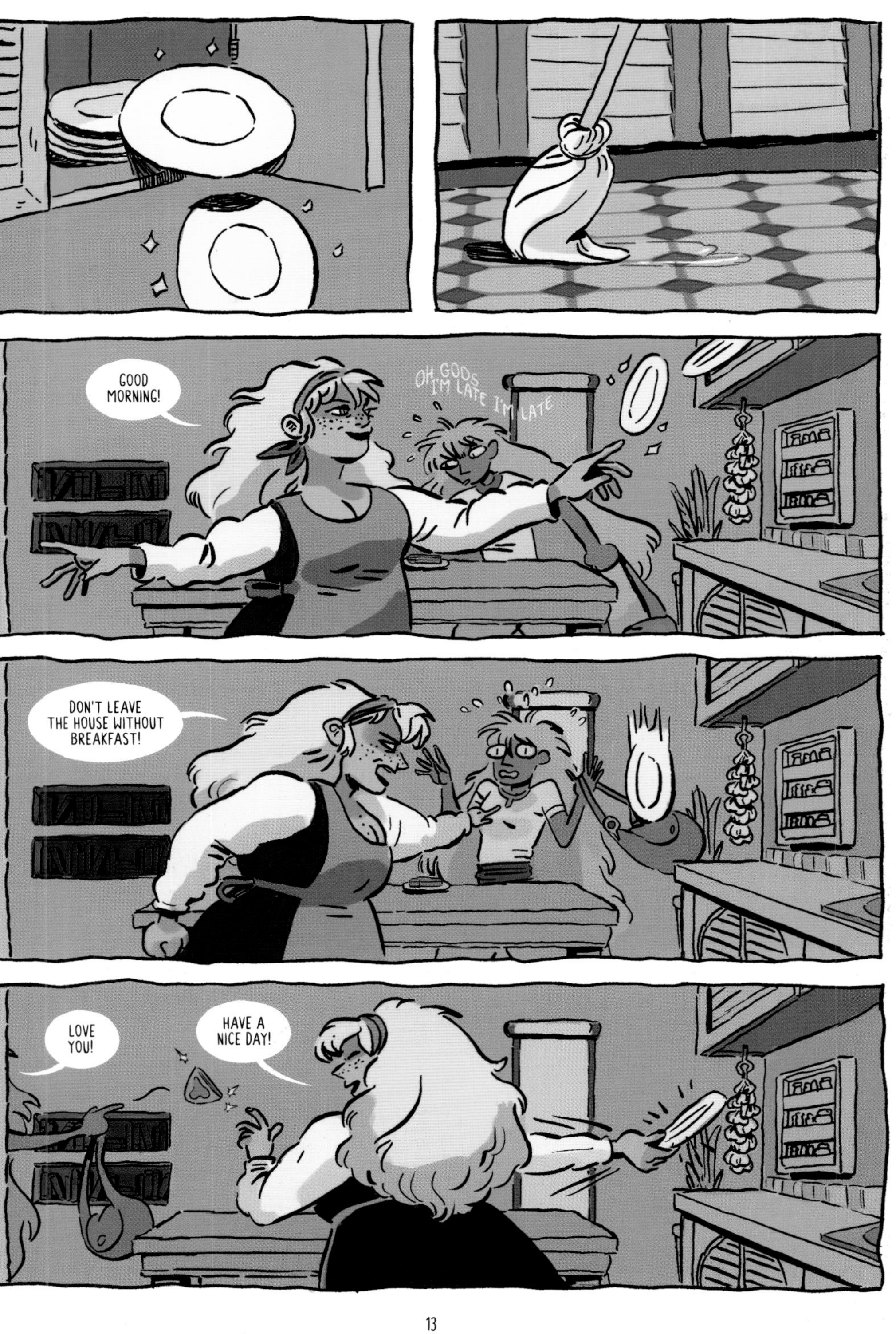
GOOD MORNING!
OH GODS I'M LATE I'M LATE
DON'T LEAVE THE HOUSE WITHOUT BREAKFAST!
LOVE YOU!
HAVE A NICE DAY!

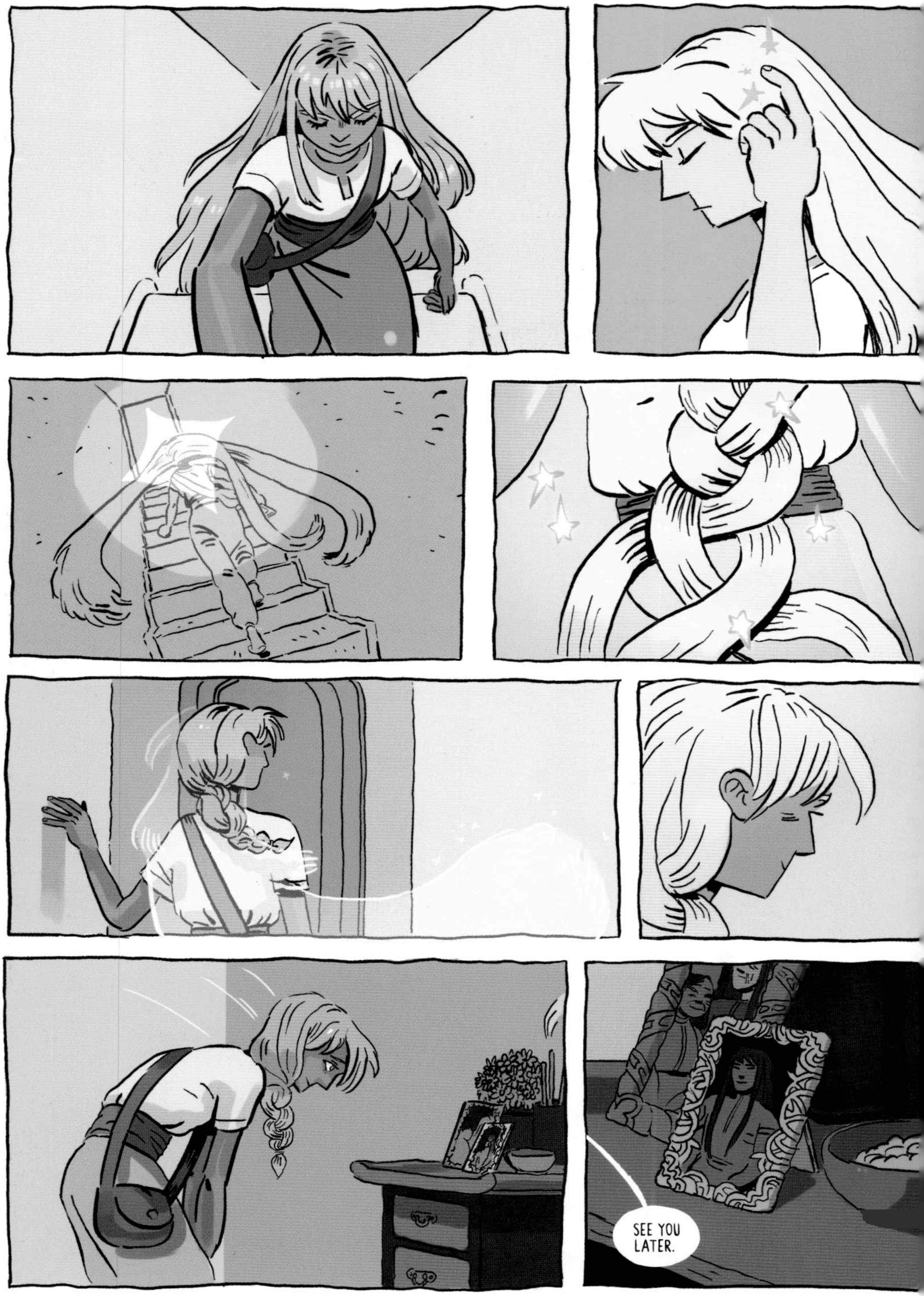
SEE YOU LATER.

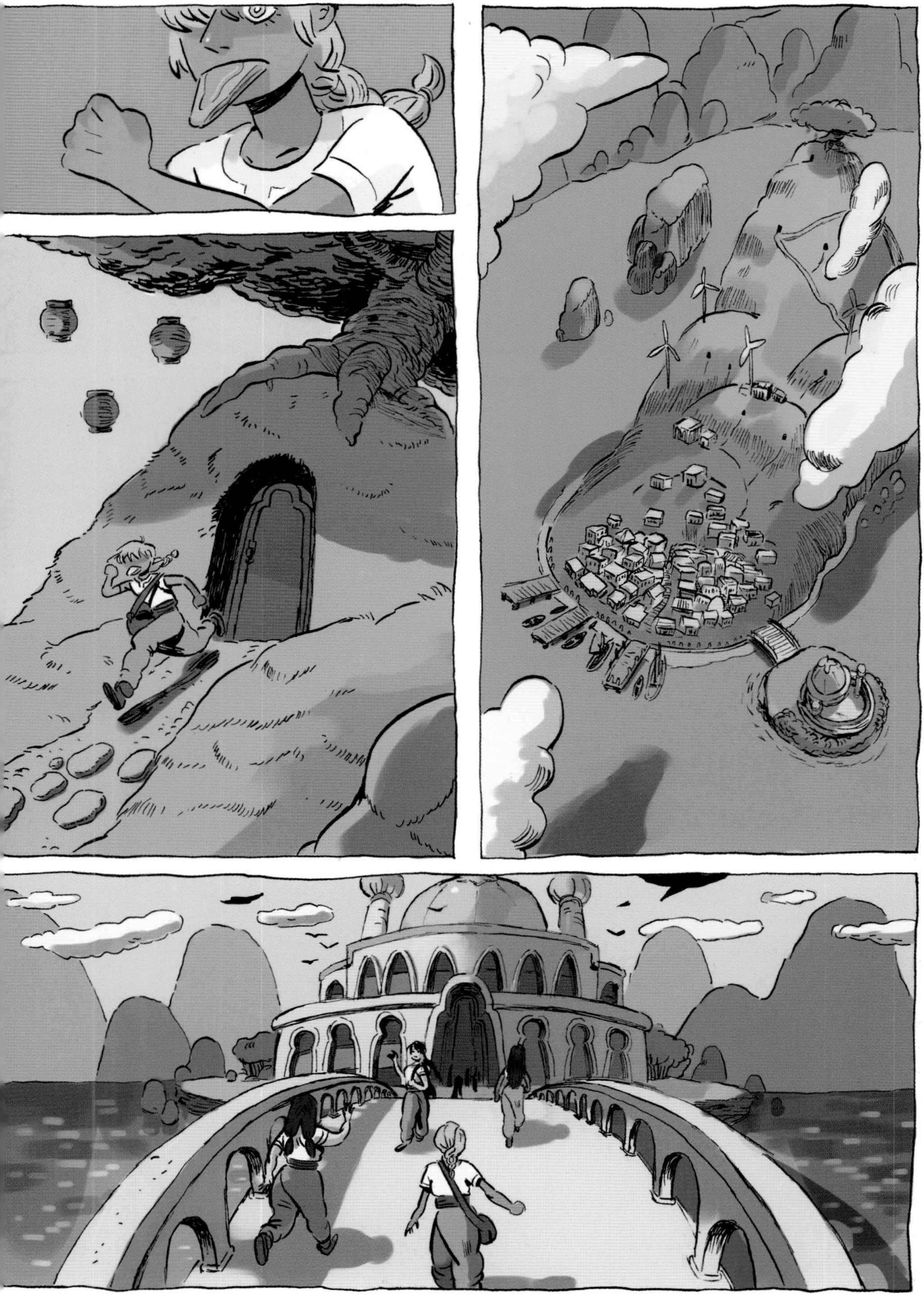

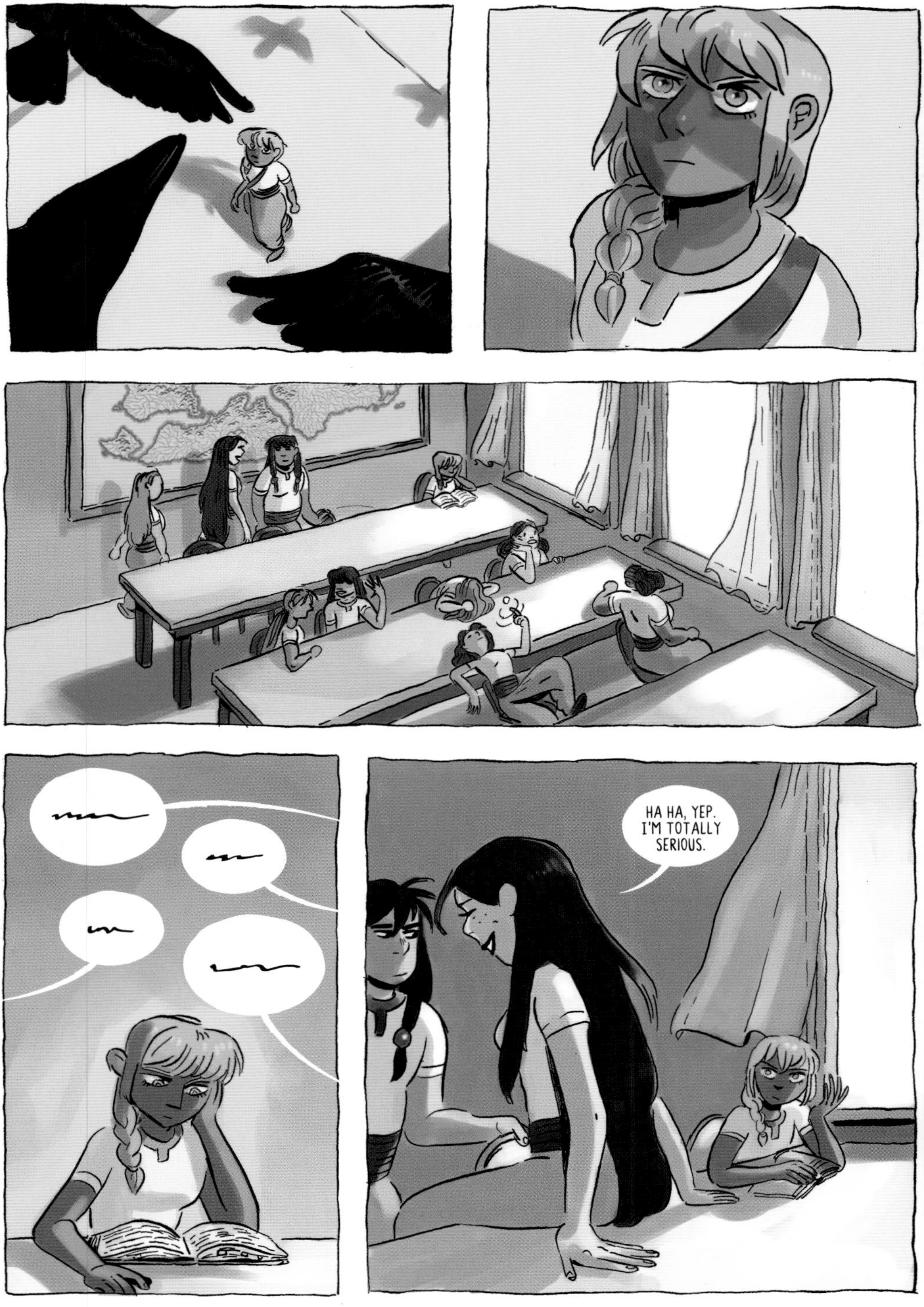
HA HA, YEP. I'M TOTALLY SERIOUS.

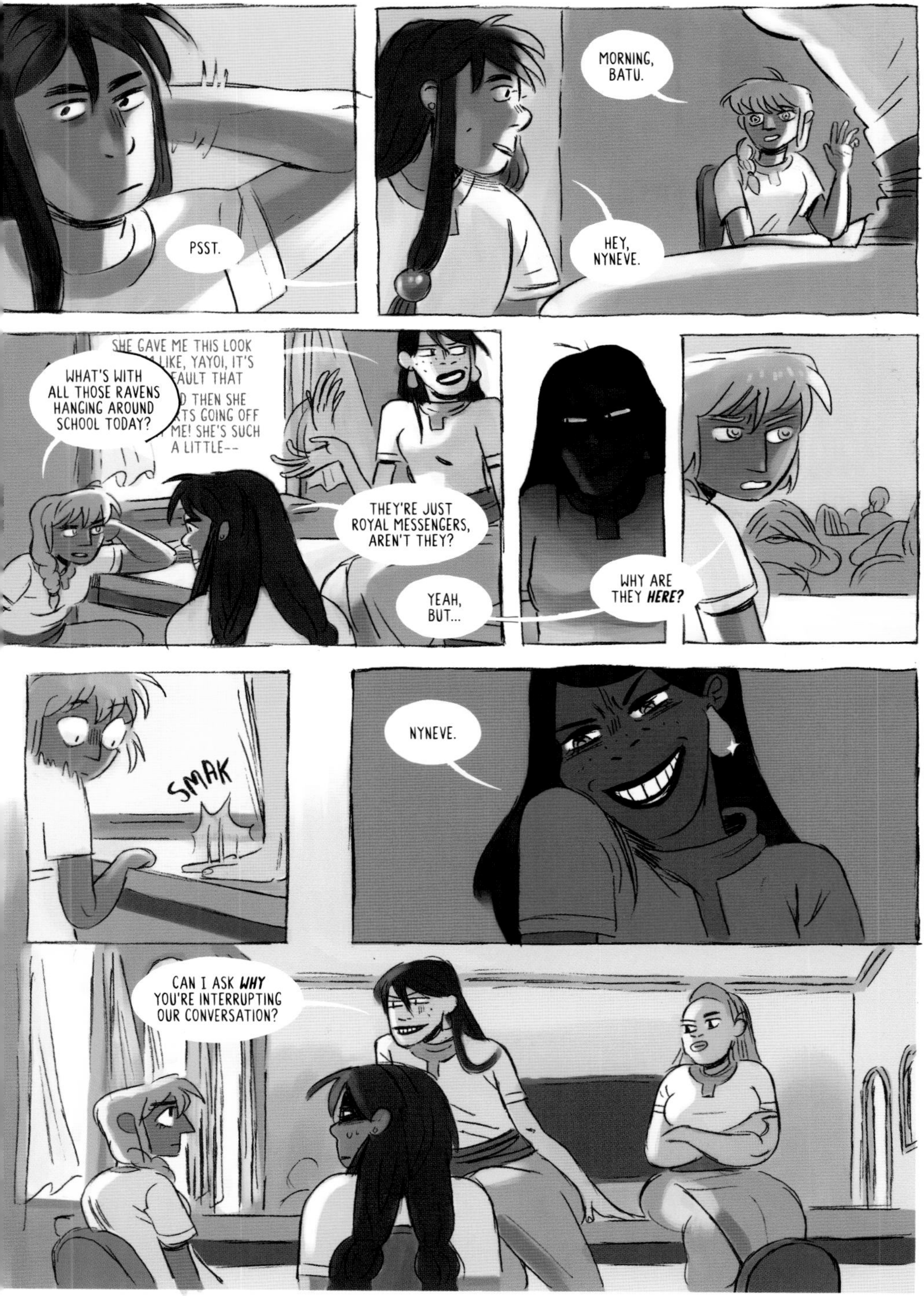
SMAK
PSST.
MORNING, BATU.
HEY, NYNEVE.
WHAT'S WITH ALL THOSE RAVENS HANGING AROUND SCHOOL TODAY?
SHE GAVE ME THIS LOOK
LIKE, YAYOI, IT'S
FAULT THAT
THEN SHE
GOING OFF
ME! SHE'S SUCH
A LITTLE--
THEY'RE JUST ROYAL MESSENGERS, AREN'T THEY?
YEAH, BUT...
WHY ARE THEY **HERE?**
SMAK
NYNEVE.
CAN I ASK **WHY** YOU'RE INTERRUPTING OUR CONVERSATION?

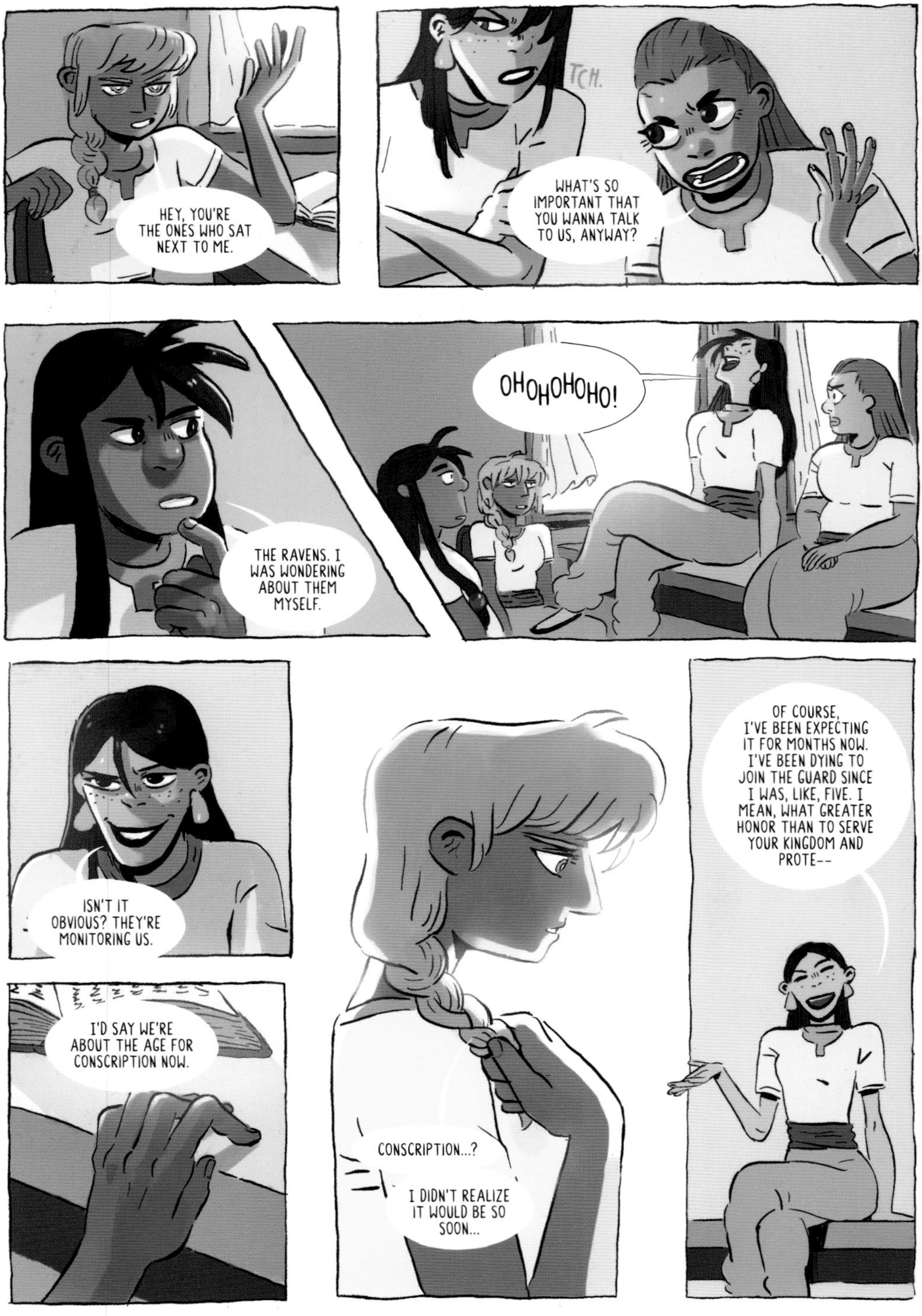
HEY, YOU'RE THE ONES WHO SAT NEXT TO ME.
TCH.
WHAT'S SO IMPORTANT THAT YOU WANNA TALK TO US, ANYWAY?
THE RAVENS. I WAS WONDERING ABOUT THEM MYSELF.
OHOHOHOHO!
ISN'T IT OBVIOUS? THEY'RE MONITORING US.
I'D SAY WE'RE ABOUT THE AGE FOR CONSCRIPTION NOW.
CONSCRIPTION...?
I DIDN'T REALIZE IT WOULD BE SO SOON...
OF COURSE, I'VE BEEN EXPECTING IT FOR MONTHS NOW. I'VE BEEN DYING TO JOIN THE GUARD SINCE I WAS, LIKE, FIVE. I MEAN, WHAT GREATER HONOR THAN TO SERVE YOUR KINGDOM AND PROTE--

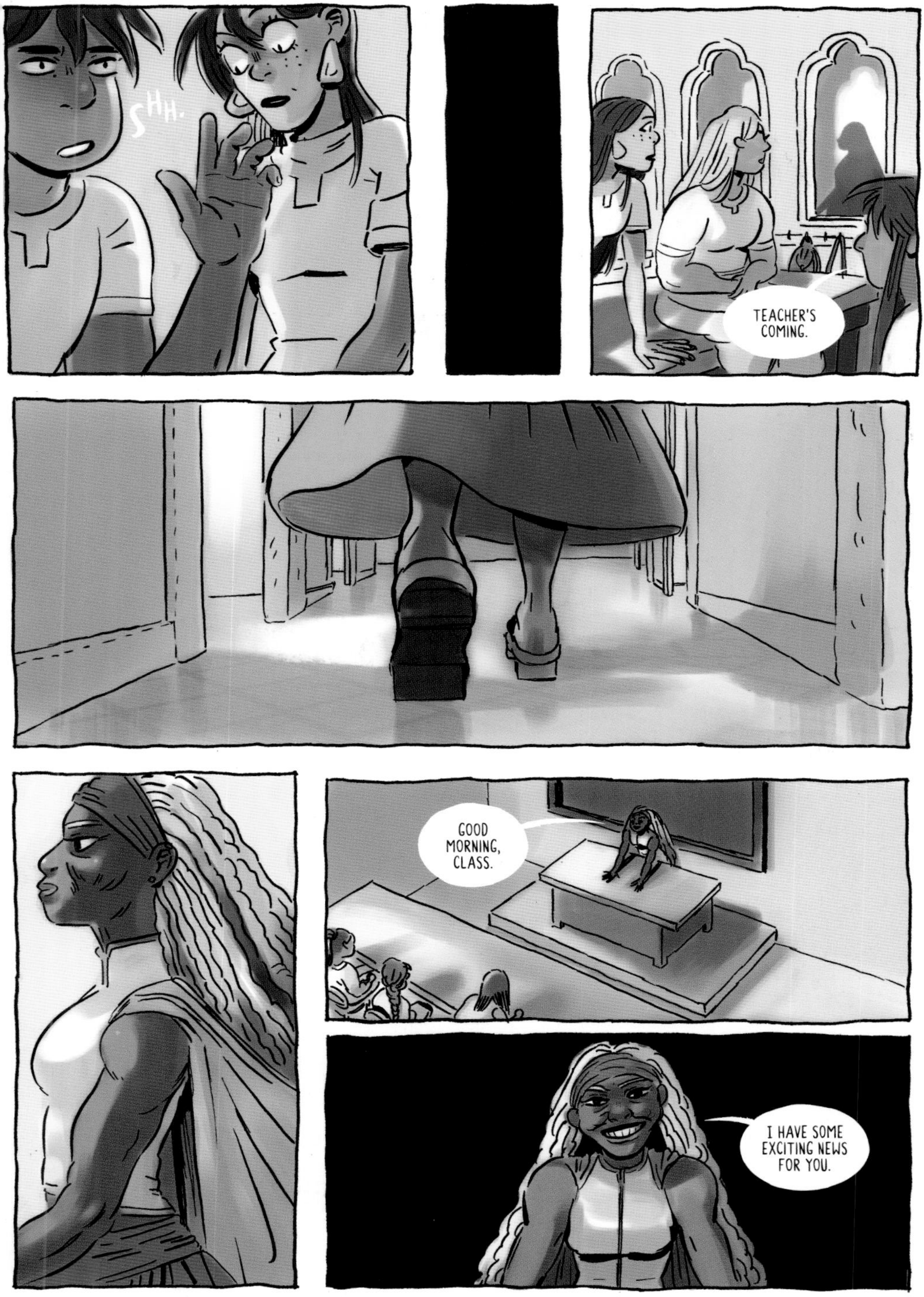
SHH.
TEACHER'S COMING.
GOOD MORNING, CLASS.
I HAVE SOME EXCITING NEWS FOR YOU.

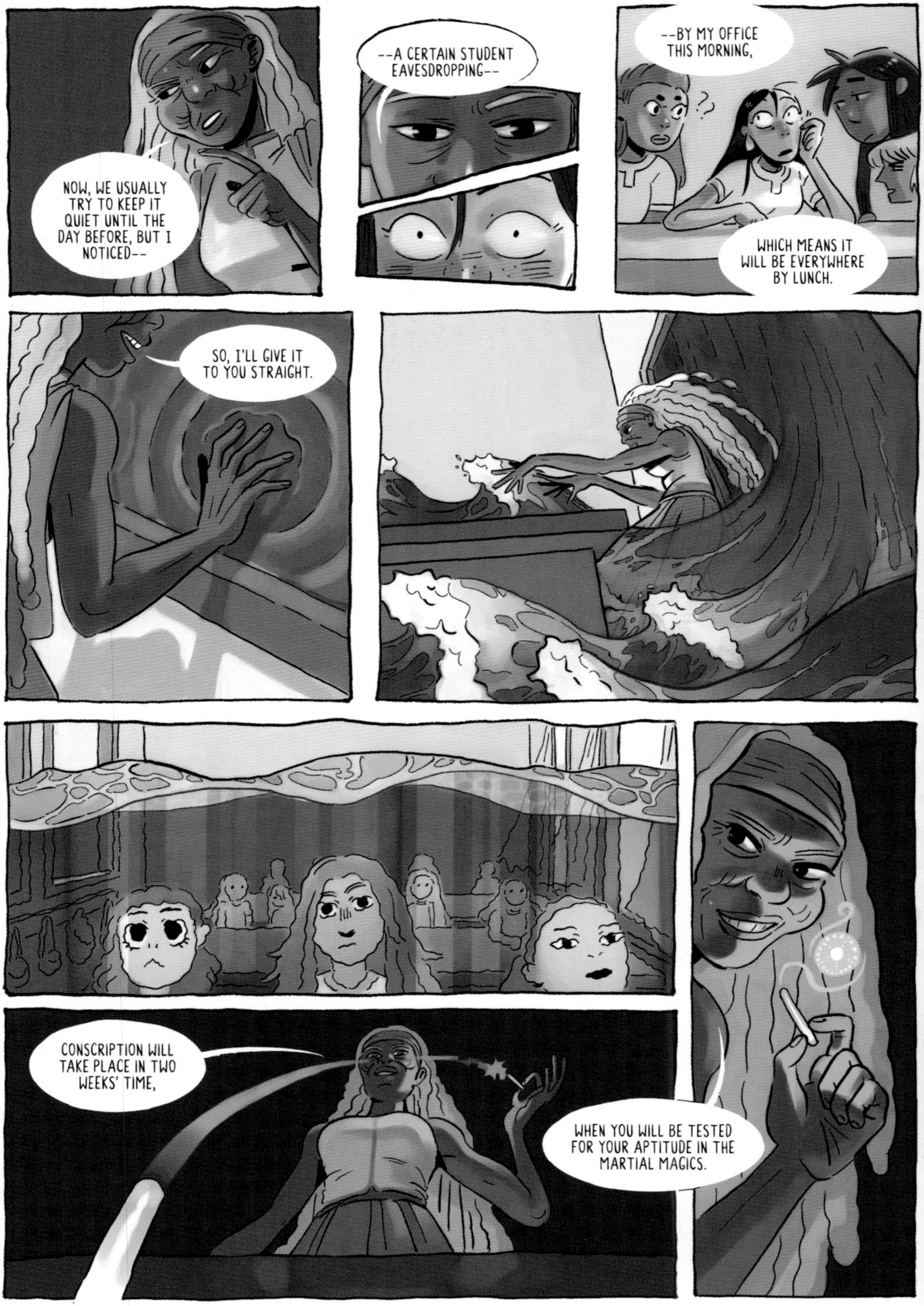
NOW, WE USUALLY TRY TO KEEP IT QUIET UNTIL THE DAY BEFORE, BUT I NOTICED--
--A CERTAIN STUDENT EAVESDROPPING--
--BY MY OFFICE THIS MORNING,
WHICH MEANS IT WILL BE EVERYWHERE BY LUNCH.
SO, I'LL GIVE IT TO YOU STRAIGHT.
CONSCRIPTION WILL TAKE PLACE IN TWO WEEKS' TIME,
WHEN YOU WILL BE TESTED FOR YOUR APTITUDE IN THE MARTIAL MAGICS.

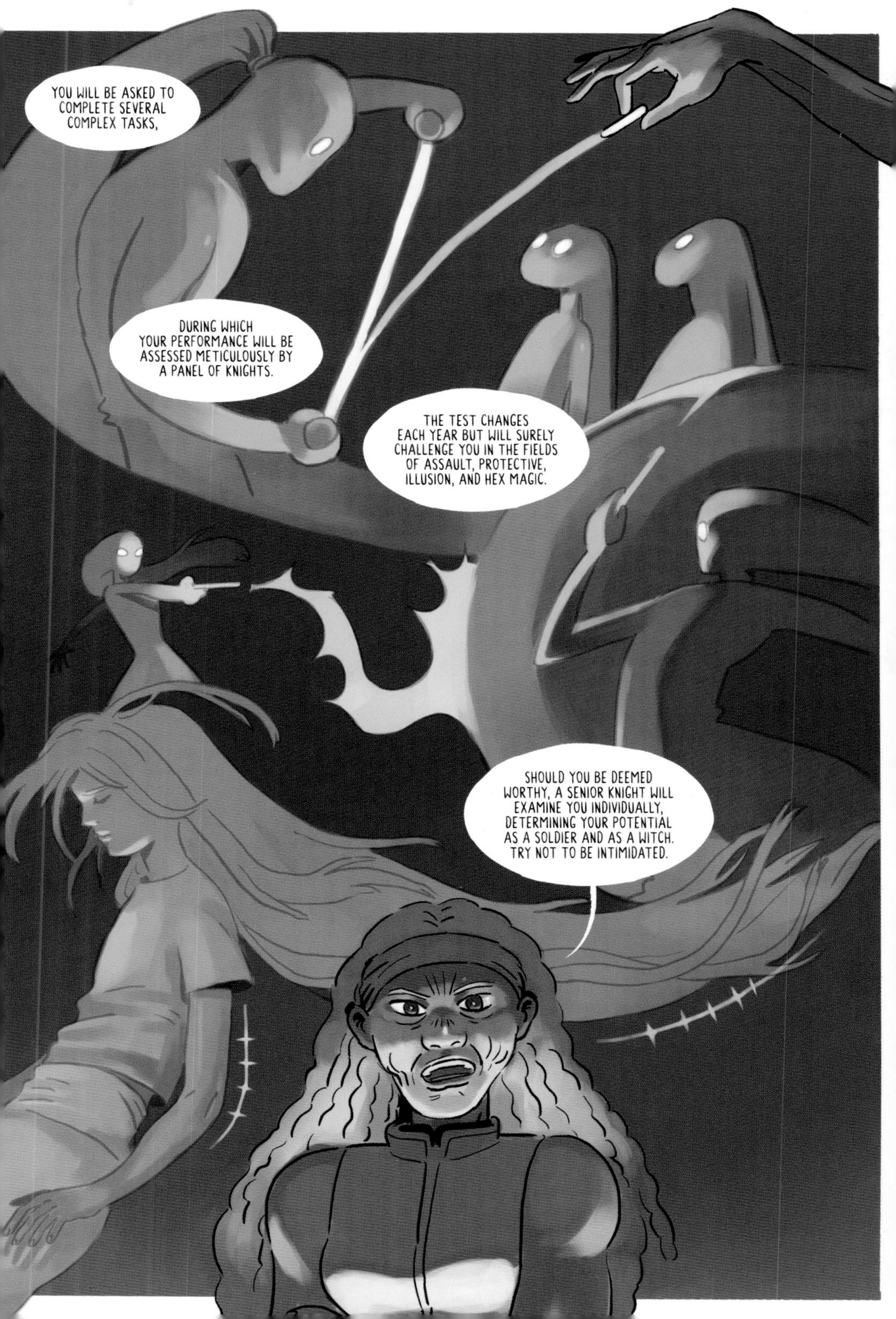
YOU WILL BE ASKED TO COMPLETE SEVERAL COMPLEX TASKS,
DURING WHICH YOUR PERFORMANCE WILL BE ASSESSED METICULOUSLY BY A PANEL OF KNIGHTS.
THE TEST CHANGES EACH YEAR BUT WILL SURELY CHALLENGE YOU IN THE FIELDS OF ASSAULT, PROTECTIVE, ILLUSION, AND HEX MAGIC.
SHOULD YOU BE DEEMED WORTHY, A SENIOR KNIGHT WILL EXAMINE YOU INDIVIDUALLY, DETERMINING YOUR POTENTIAL AS A SOLDIER AND AS A WITCH. TRY NOT TO BE INTIMIDATED.

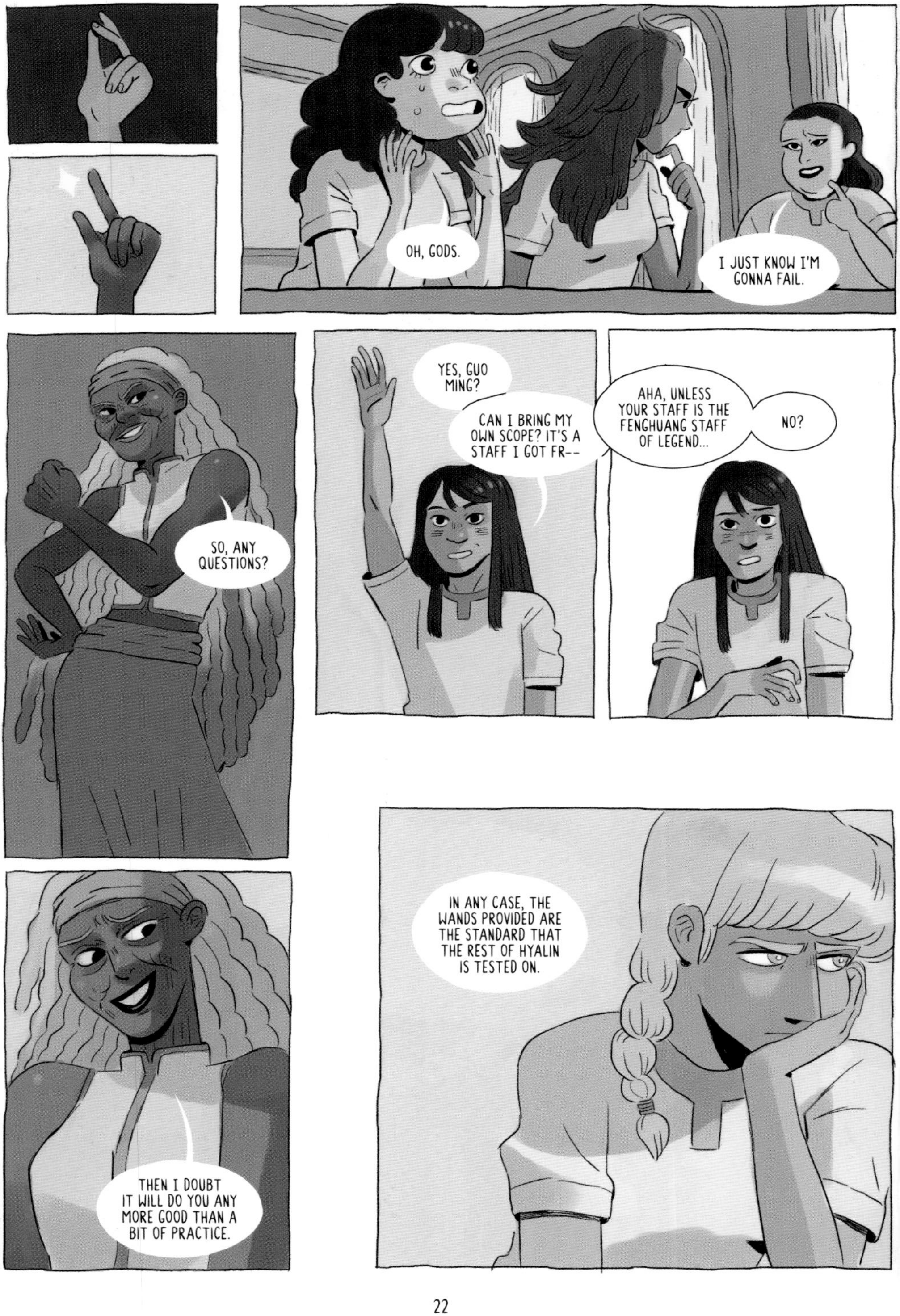
OH, GODS.
I JUST KNOW I'M GONNA FAIL.
SO, ANY QUESTIONS?
YES, GUO MING?
CAN I BRING MY OWN SCOPE? IT'S A STAFF I GOT FR--
AHA, UNLESS YOUR STAFF IS THE FENGHUANG STAFF OF LEGEND...
NO?
THEN I DOUBT IT WILL DO YOU ANY MORE GOOD THAN A BIT OF PRACTICE.
IN ANY CASE, THE WANDS PROVIDED ARE THE STANDARD THAT THE REST OF HYALIN IS TESTED ON.

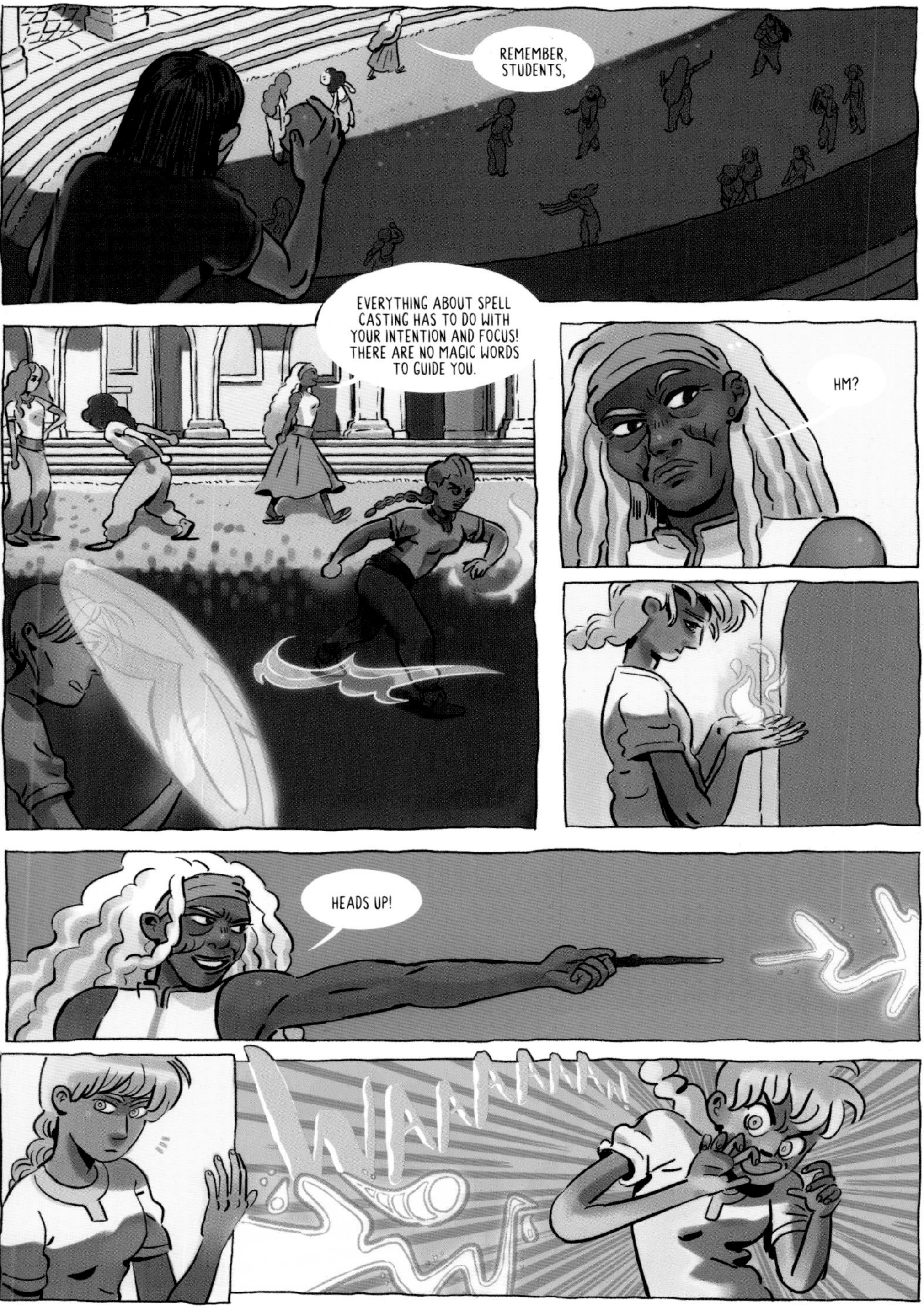
REMEMBER, STUDENTS,
EVERYTHING ABOUT SPELL CASTING HAS TO DO WITH YOUR INTENTION AND FOCUS! THERE ARE NO MAGIC WORDS TO GUIDE YOU.
HM?
HEADS UP!
WAAAAAAH!

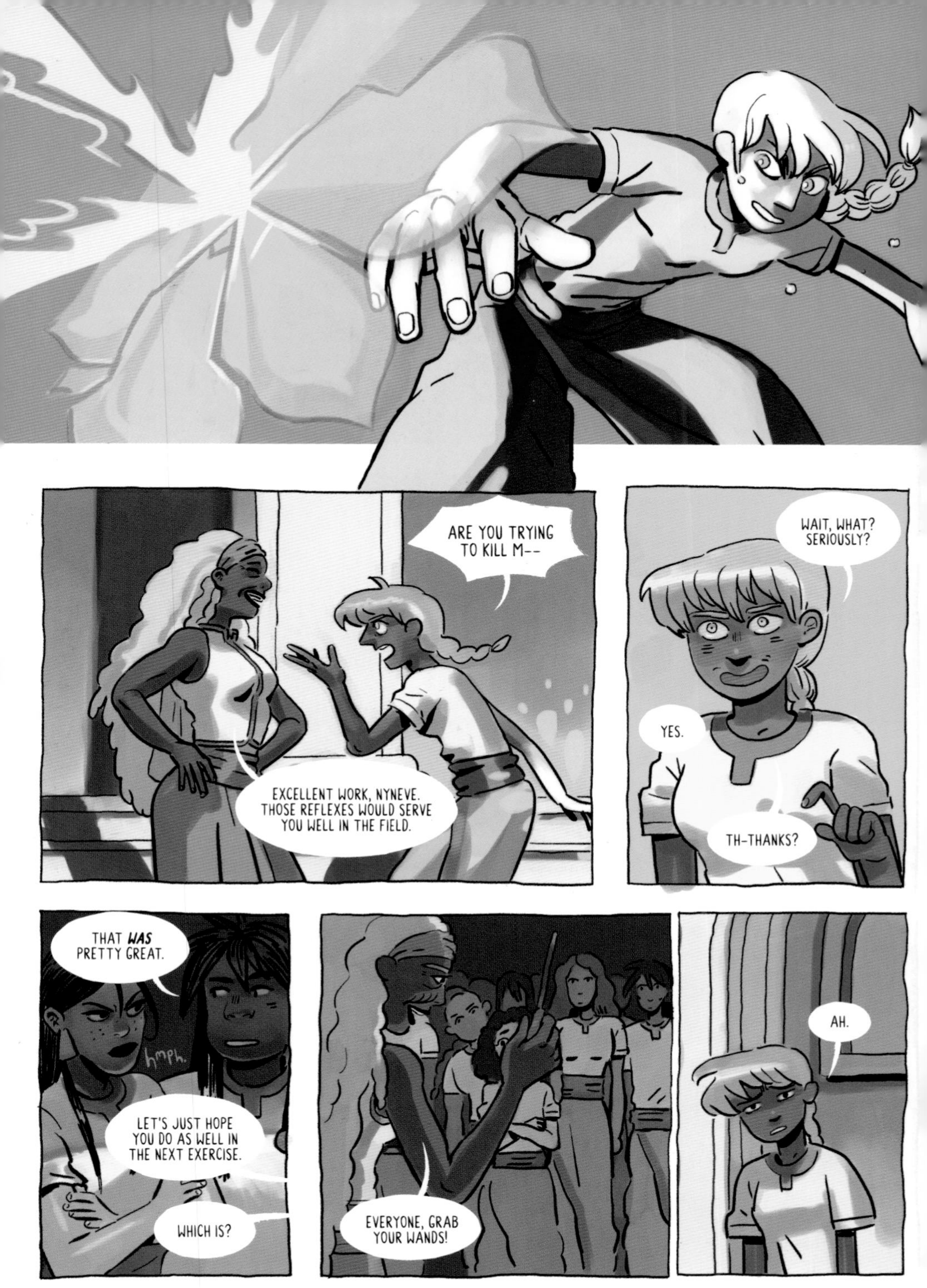

ARE YOU TRYING TO KILL M--
EXCELLENT WORK, NYNEVE. THOSE REFLEXES WOULD SERVE YOU WELL IN THE FIELD.
WAIT, WHAT? SERIOUSLY?
YES.
TH-THANKS?
THAT **WAS** PRETTY GREAT.
hmph.
LET'S JUST HOPE YOU DO AS WELL IN THE NEXT EXERCISE.
WHICH IS?
EVERYONE, GRAB YOUR WANDS!
AH.

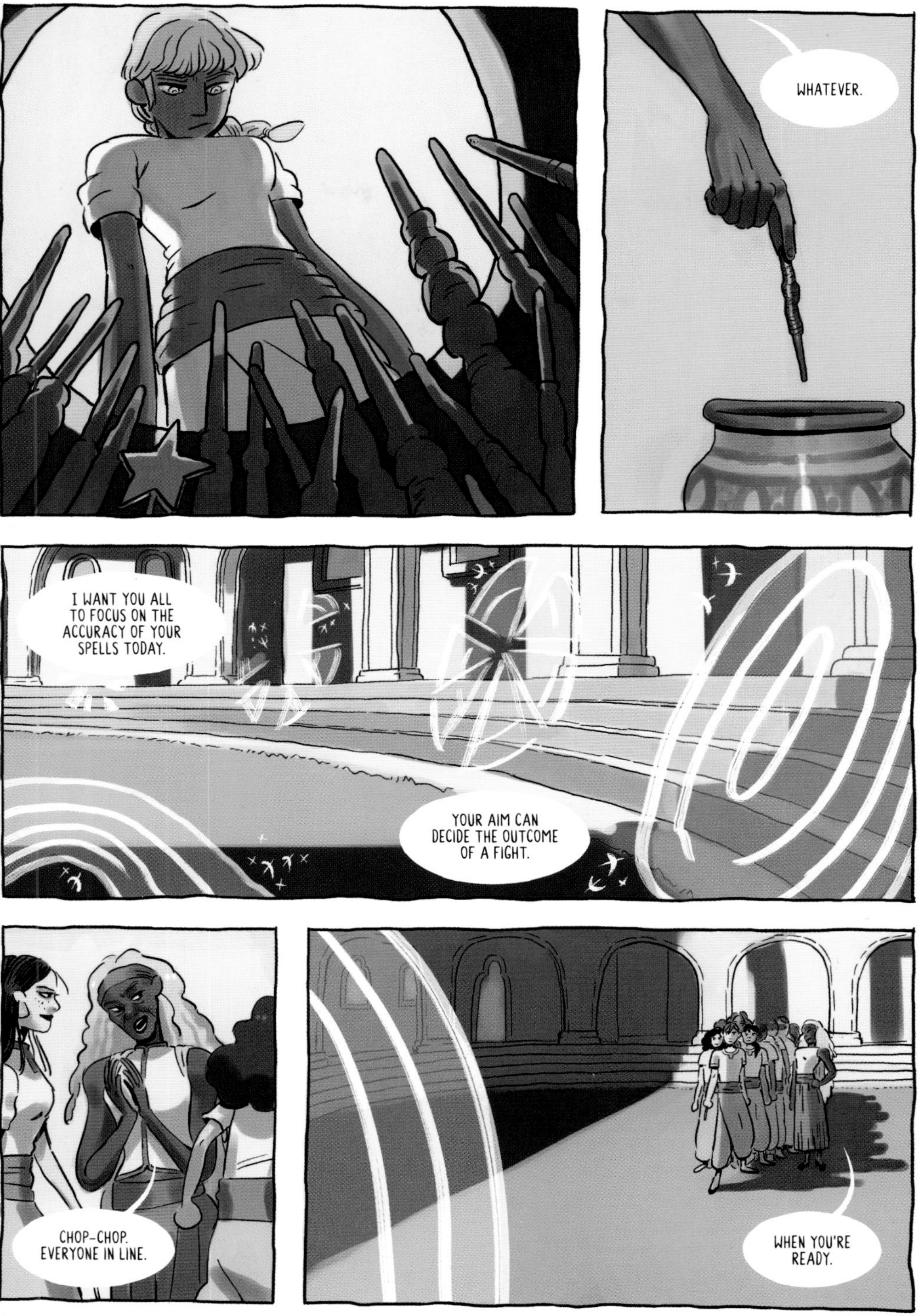
WHATEVER.
I WANT YOU ALL TO FOCUS ON THE ACCURACY OF YOUR SPELLS TODAY.
YOUR AIM CAN DECIDE THE OUTCOME OF A FIGHT.
CHOP-CHOP. EVERYONE IN LINE.
WHEN YOU'RE READY.

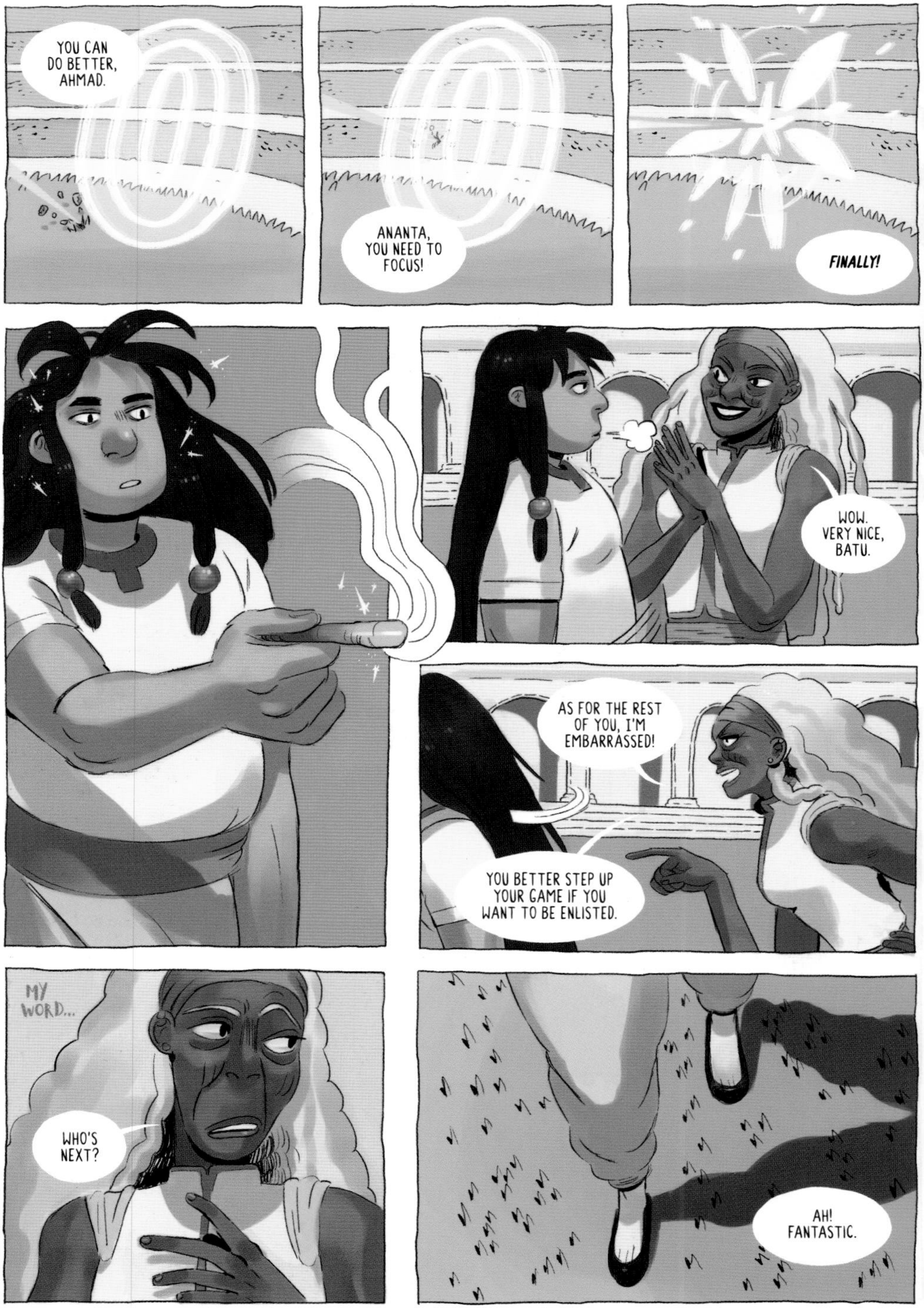
YOU CAN DO BETTER, AHMAD.
ANANTA, YOU NEED TO FOCUS!
FINALLY!
WOW. VERY NICE, BATU.
AS FOR THE REST OF YOU, I'M EMBARRASSED!
YOU BETTER STEP UP YOUR GAME IF YOU WANT TO BE ENLISTED.
MY WORD...
WHO'S NEXT?
AH! FANTASTIC.

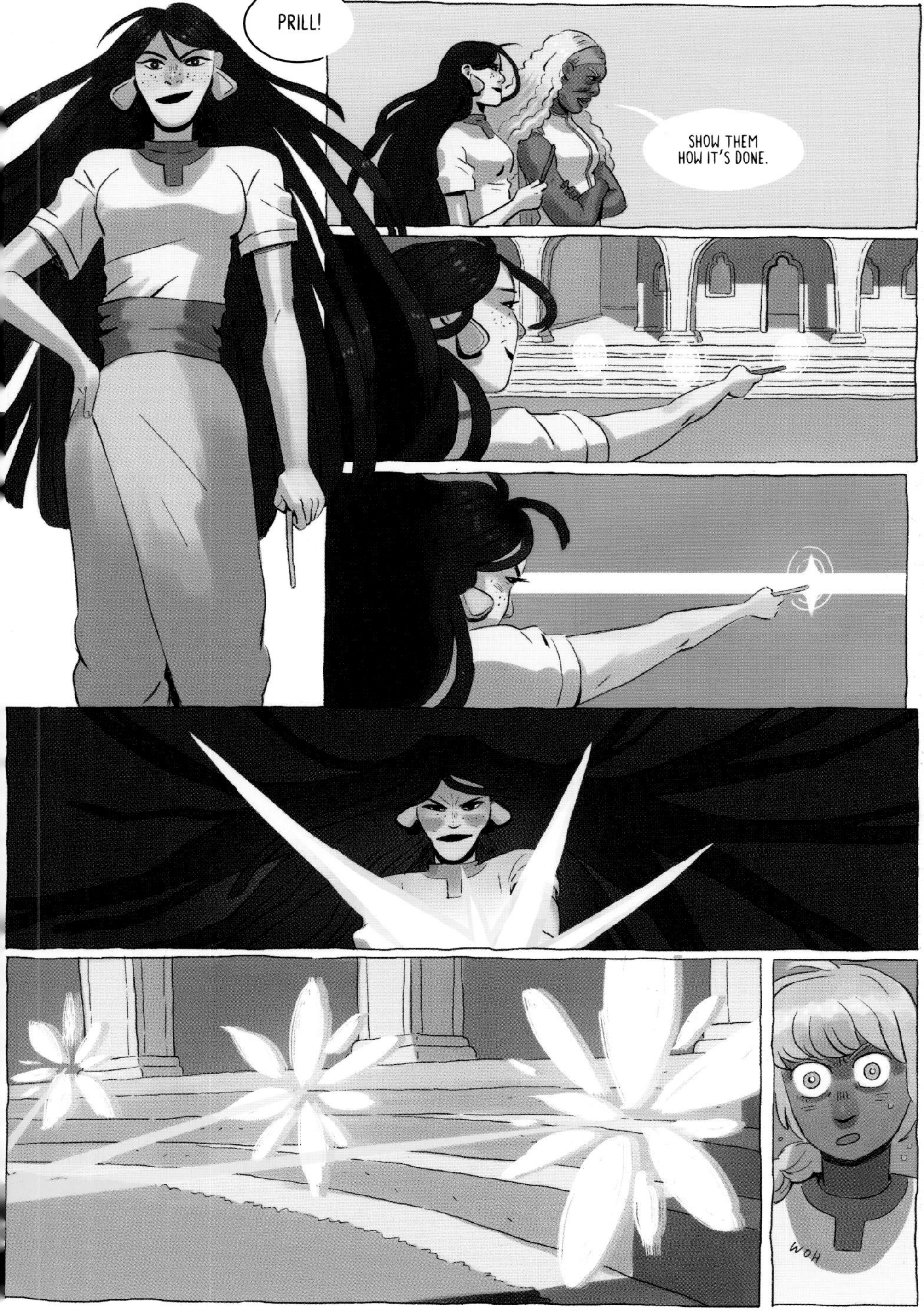
PRILL!
SHOW THEM HOW IT'S DONE.
WOH

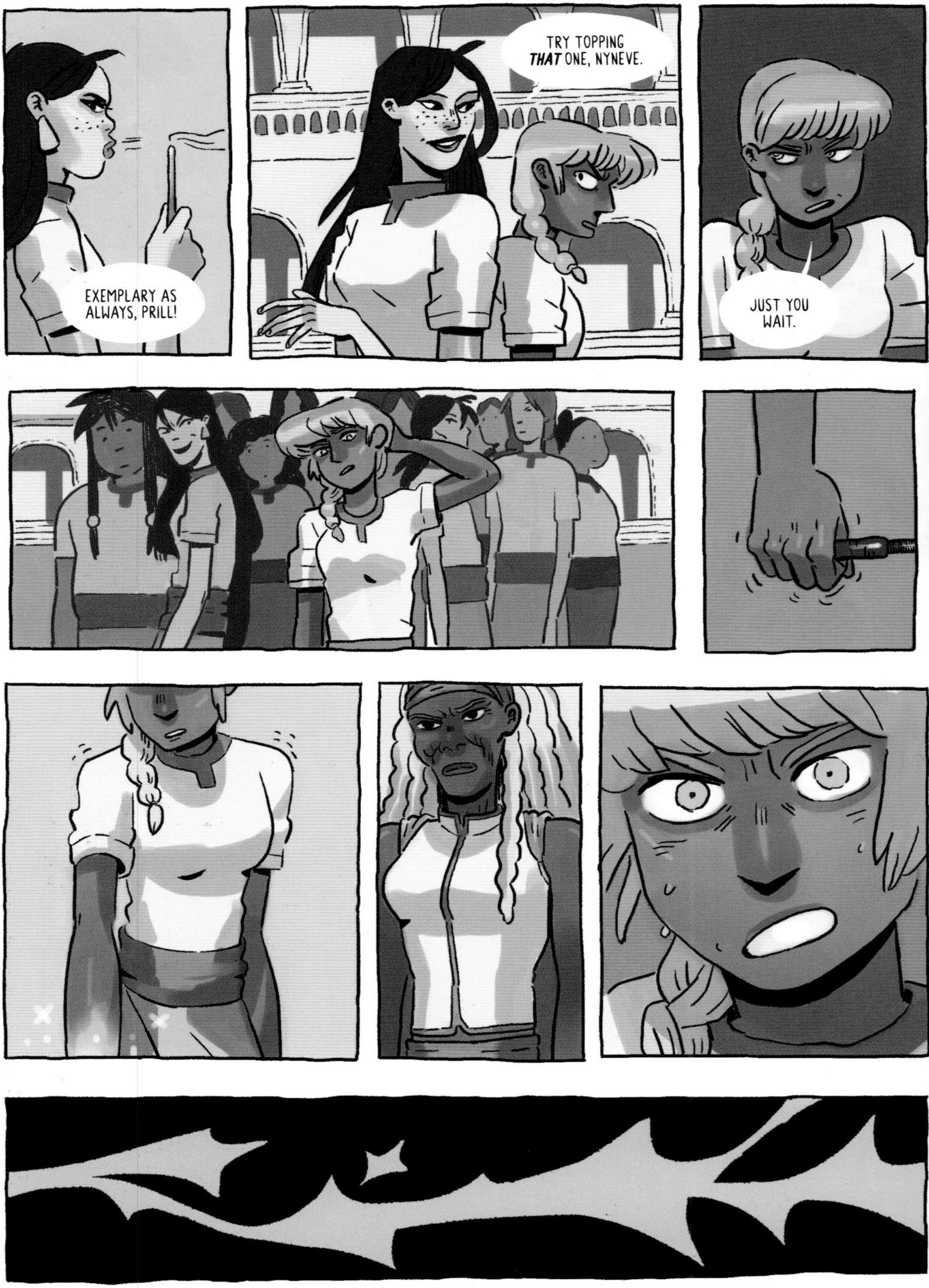

EXEMPLARY AS ALWAYS, PRILL!
TRY TOPPING *THAT* ONE, NYNEVE.
JUST YOU WAIT.

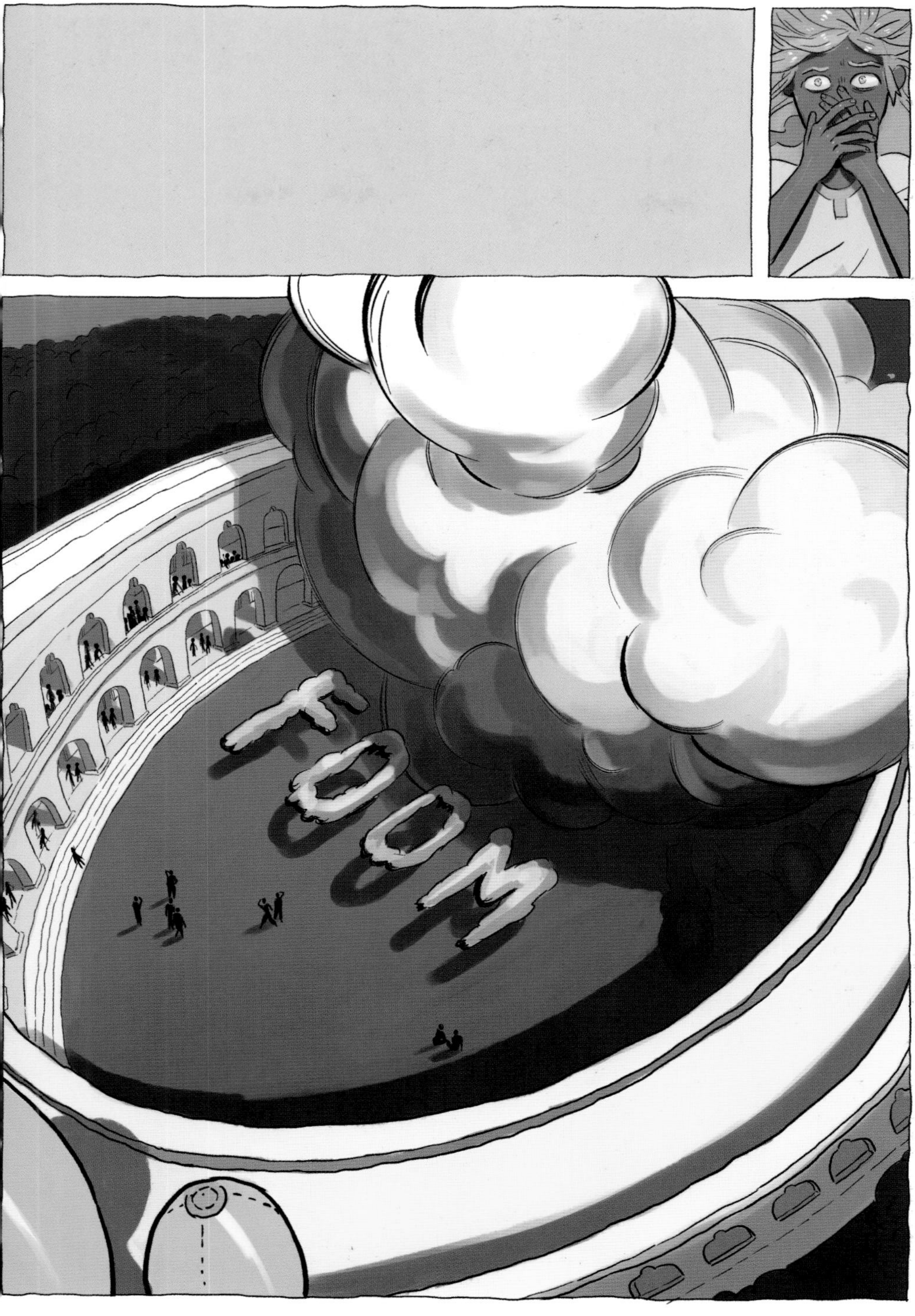
FOOOM

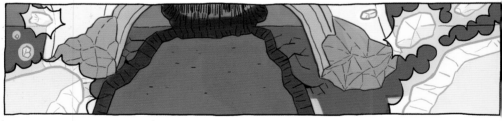

NYNEVE.

TO MY OFFICE, PLEASE.

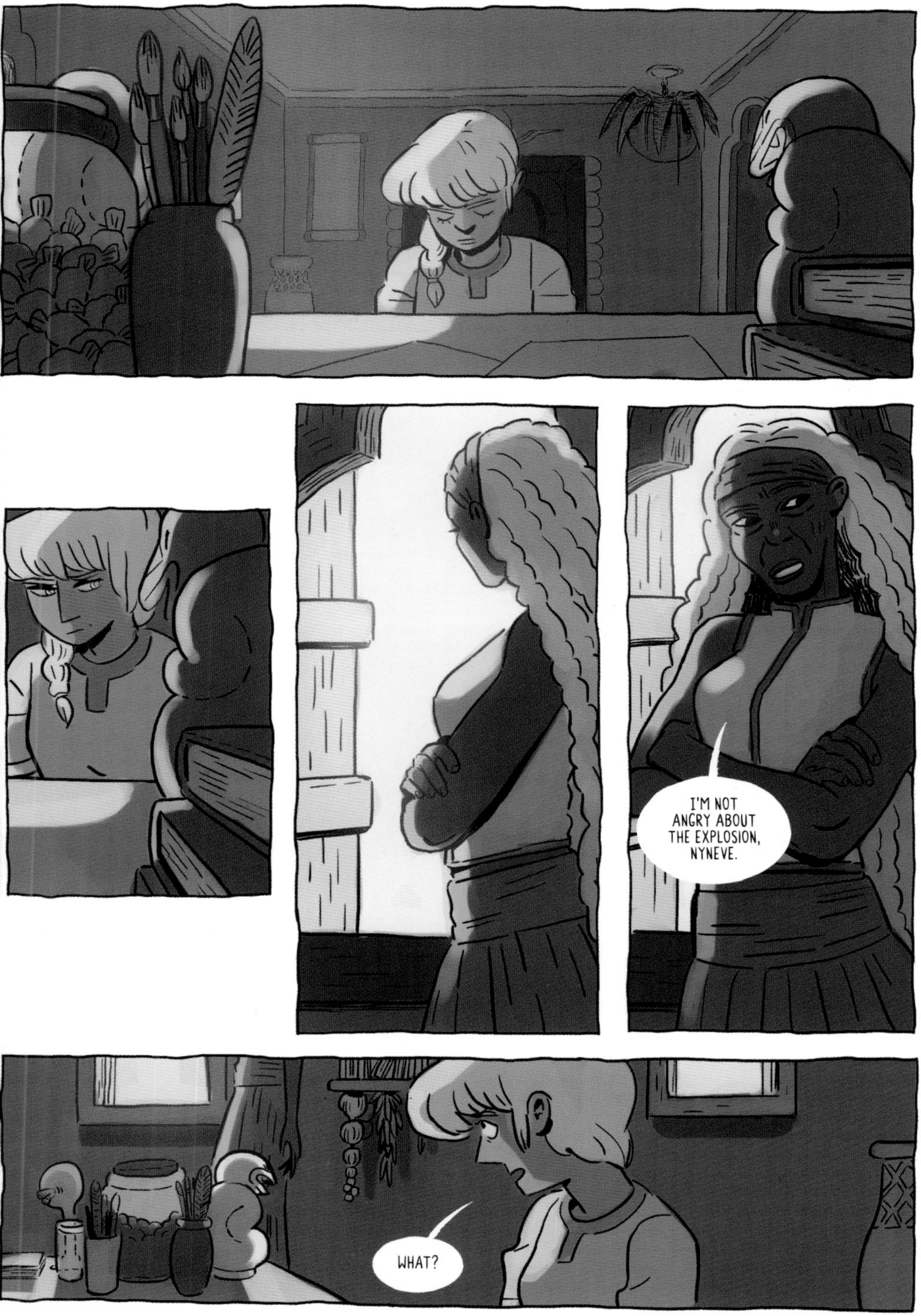
I'M NOT ANGRY ABOUT THE EXPLOSION, NYNEVE.
WHAT?

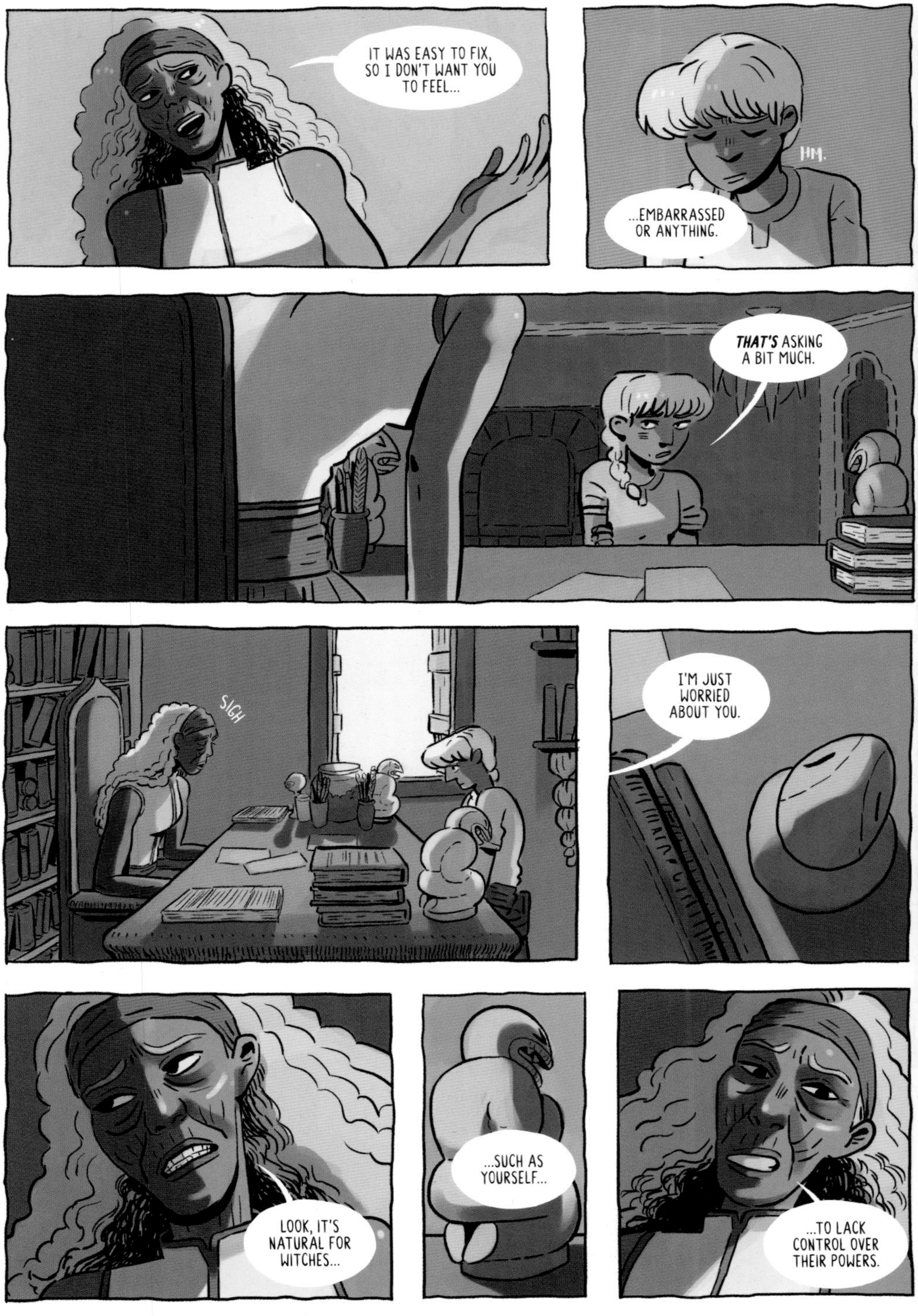
IT WAS EASY TO FIX, SO I DON'T WANT YOU TO FEEL...
HM.
...EMBARRASSED OR ANYTHING.
THAT'S ASKING A BIT MUCH.
SIGH
I'M JUST WORRIED ABOUT YOU.
LOOK, IT'S NATURAL FOR WITCHES...
...SUCH AS YOURSELF...
...TO LACK CONTROL OVER THEIR POWERS.

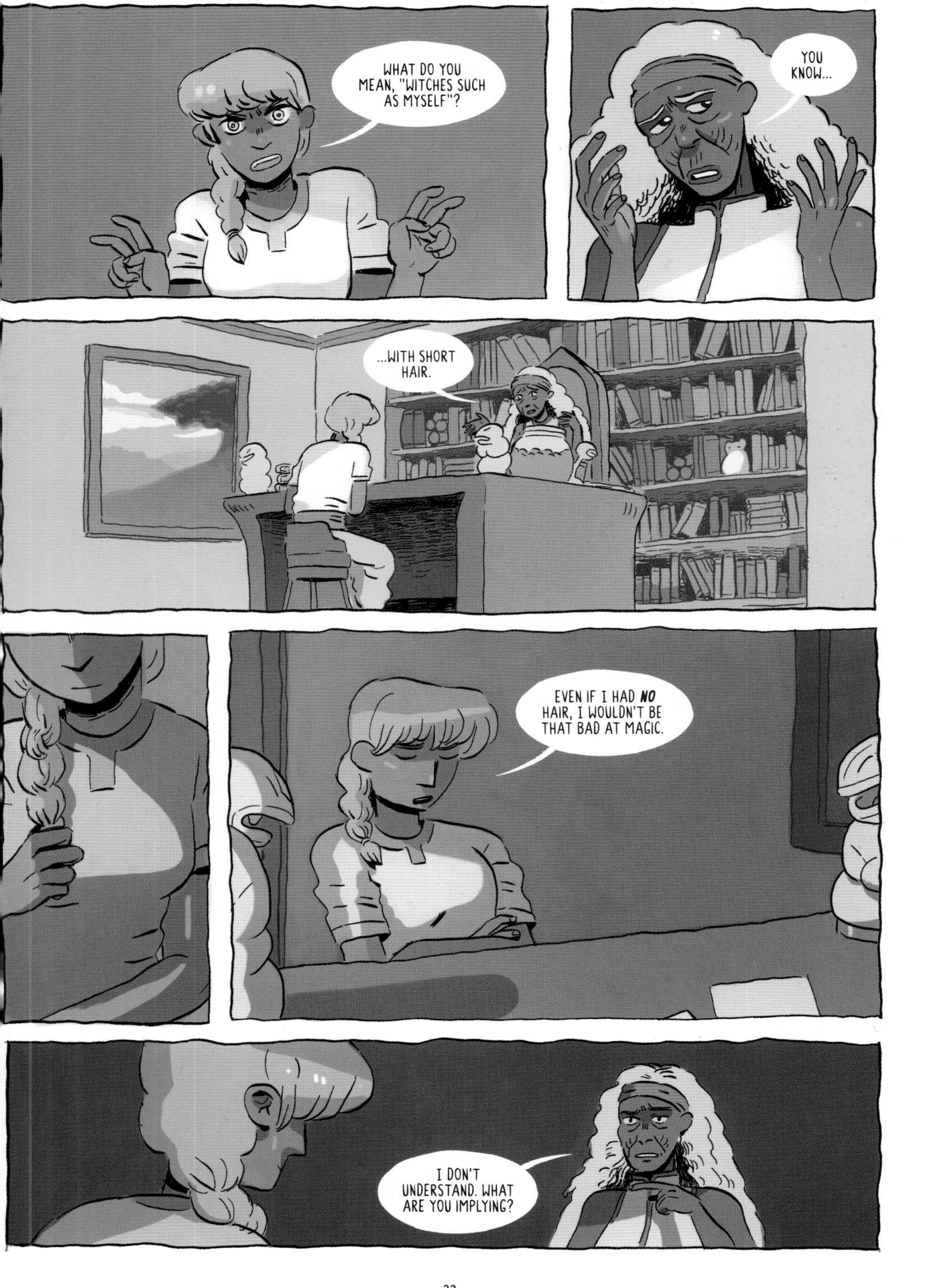
WHAT DO YOU MEAN, "WITCHES SUCH AS MYSELF"?
YOU KNOW...
...WITH SHORT HAIR.
EVEN IF I HAD **NO** HAIR, I WOULDN'T BE THAT BAD AT MAGIC.
I DON'T UNDERSTAND. WHAT ARE YOU IMPLYING?

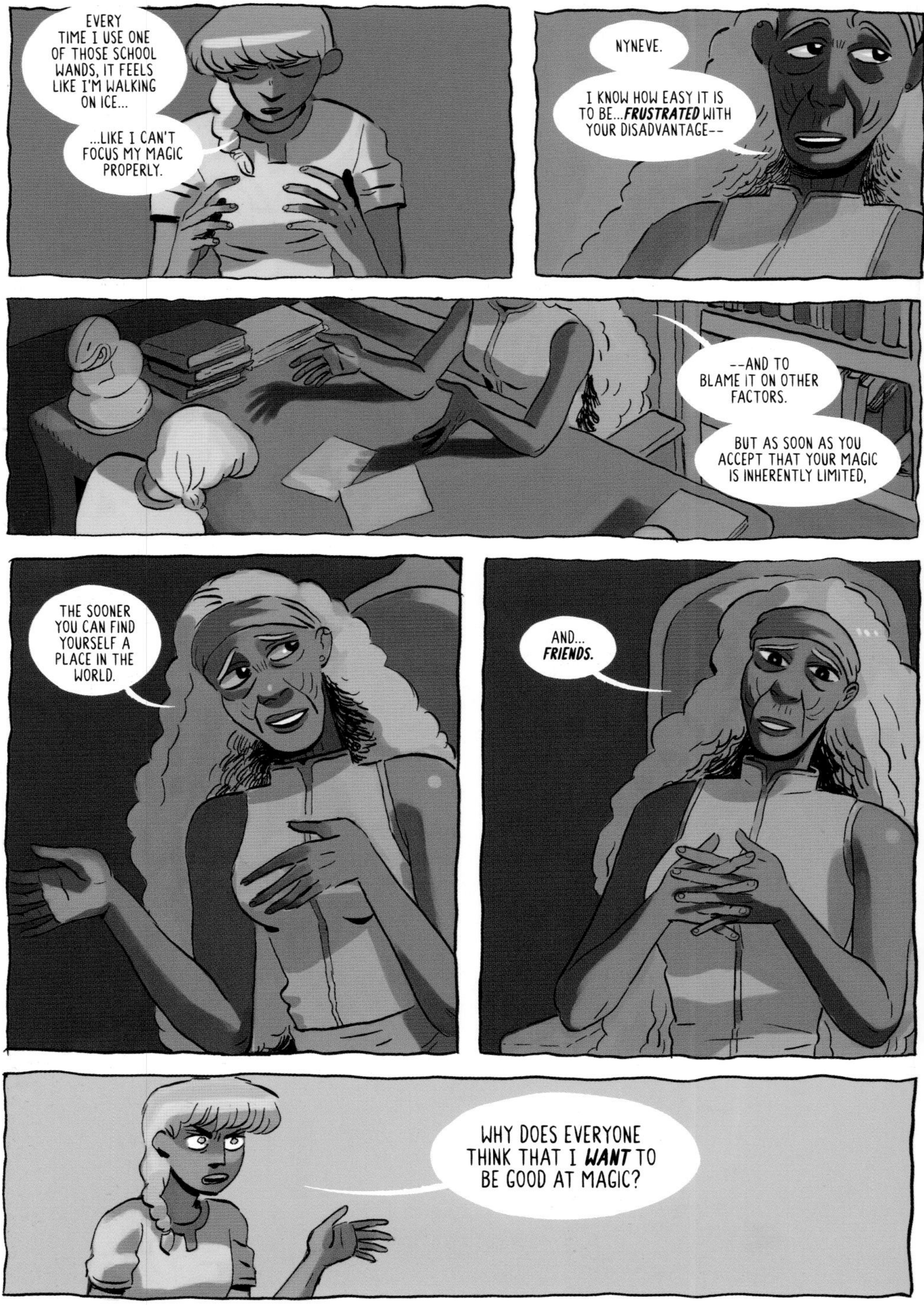
EVERY TIME I USE ONE OF THOSE SCHOOL WANDS, IT FEELS LIKE I'M WALKING ON ICE...
...LIKE I CAN'T FOCUS MY MAGIC PROPERLY.
NYNEVE.
I KNOW HOW EASY IT IS TO BE...**FRUSTRATED** WITH YOUR DISADVANTAGE--
--AND TO BLAME IT ON OTHER FACTORS.
BUT AS SOON AS YOU ACCEPT THAT YOUR MAGIC IS INHERENTLY LIMITED,
THE SOONER YOU CAN FIND YOURSELF A PLACE IN THE WORLD.
AND... **FRIENDS.**
WHY DOES EVERYONE THINK THAT I **WANT** TO BE GOOD AT MAGIC?

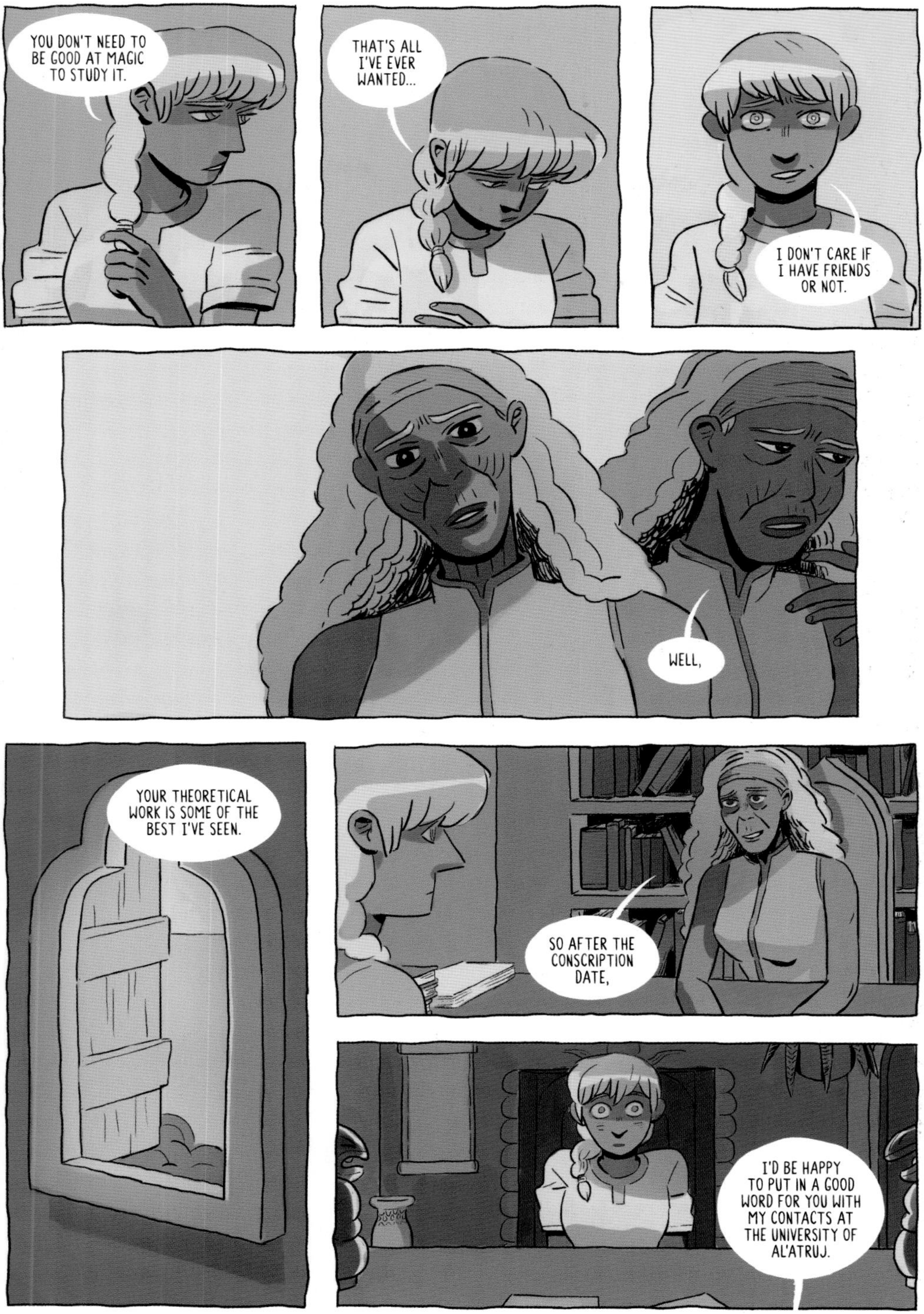

YOU DON'T NEED TO BE GOOD AT MAGIC TO STUDY IT.
THAT'S ALL I'VE EVER WANTED...
I DON'T CARE IF I HAVE FRIENDS OR NOT.
WELL,
YOUR THEORETICAL WORK IS SOME OF THE BEST I'VE SEEN.
SO AFTER THE CONSCRIPTION DATE,
I'D BE HAPPY TO PUT IN A GOOD WORD FOR YOU WITH MY CONTACTS AT THE UNIVERSITY OF AL'ATRUJ.

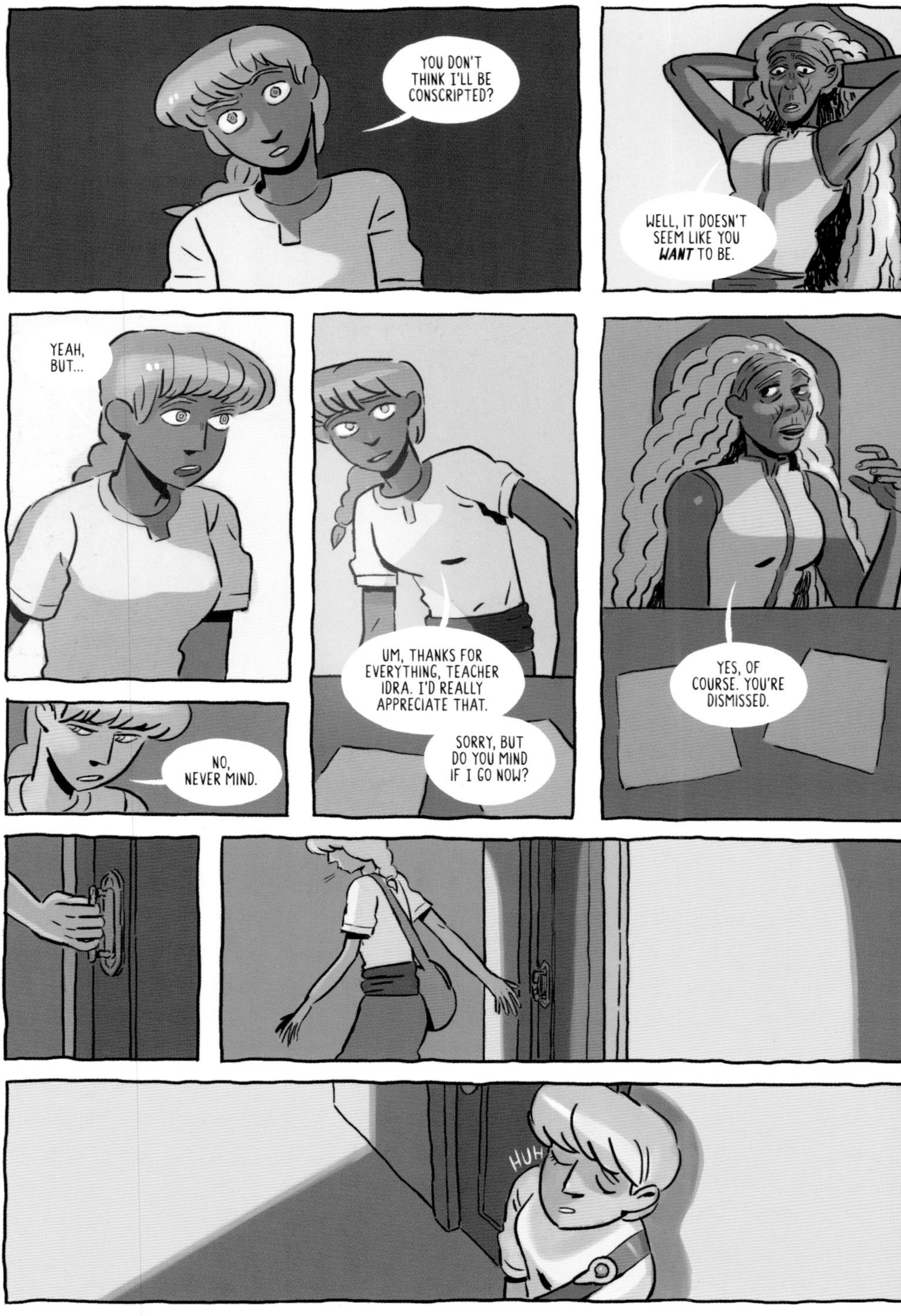
YOU DON'T THINK I'LL BE CONSCRIPTED?
WELL, IT DOESN'T SEEM LIKE YOU **WANT** TO BE.
YEAH, BUT...
NO, NEVER MIND.
UM, THANKS FOR EVERYTHING, TEACHER IDRA. I'D REALLY APPRECIATE THAT.
SORRY, BUT DO YOU MIND IF I GO NOW?
YES, OF COURSE. YOU'RE DISMISSED.
HUH

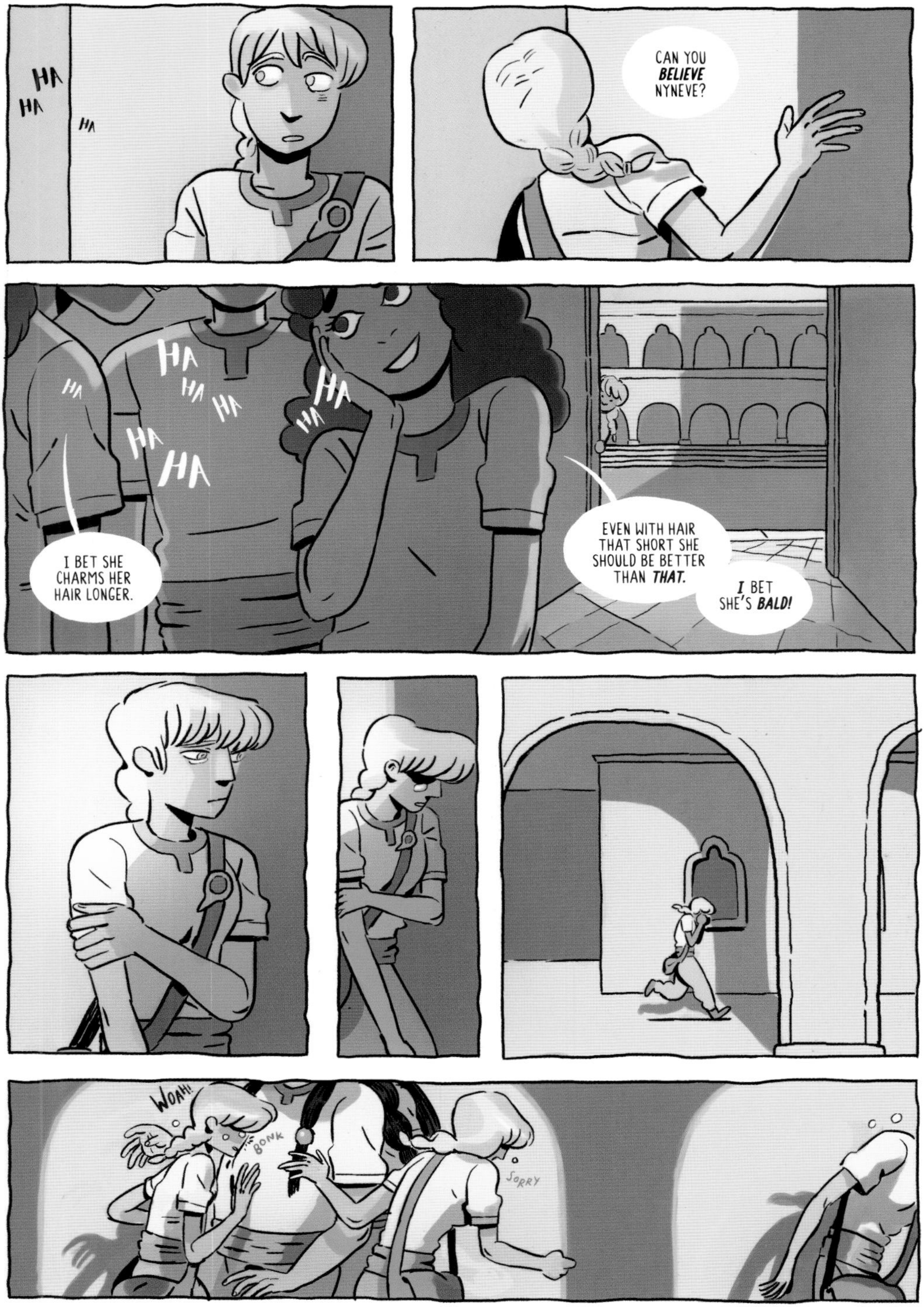
HA
HA
HA
CAN YOU **BELIEVE** NYNEVE?
HA
HA
HA
HA
HA
HA
HA
HA
I BET SHE CHARMS HER HAIR LONGER.
EVEN WITH HAIR THAT SHORT SHE SHOULD BE BETTER THAN **THAT.**
I BET SHE'S **BALD!**
WOAH!
BONK
SORRY

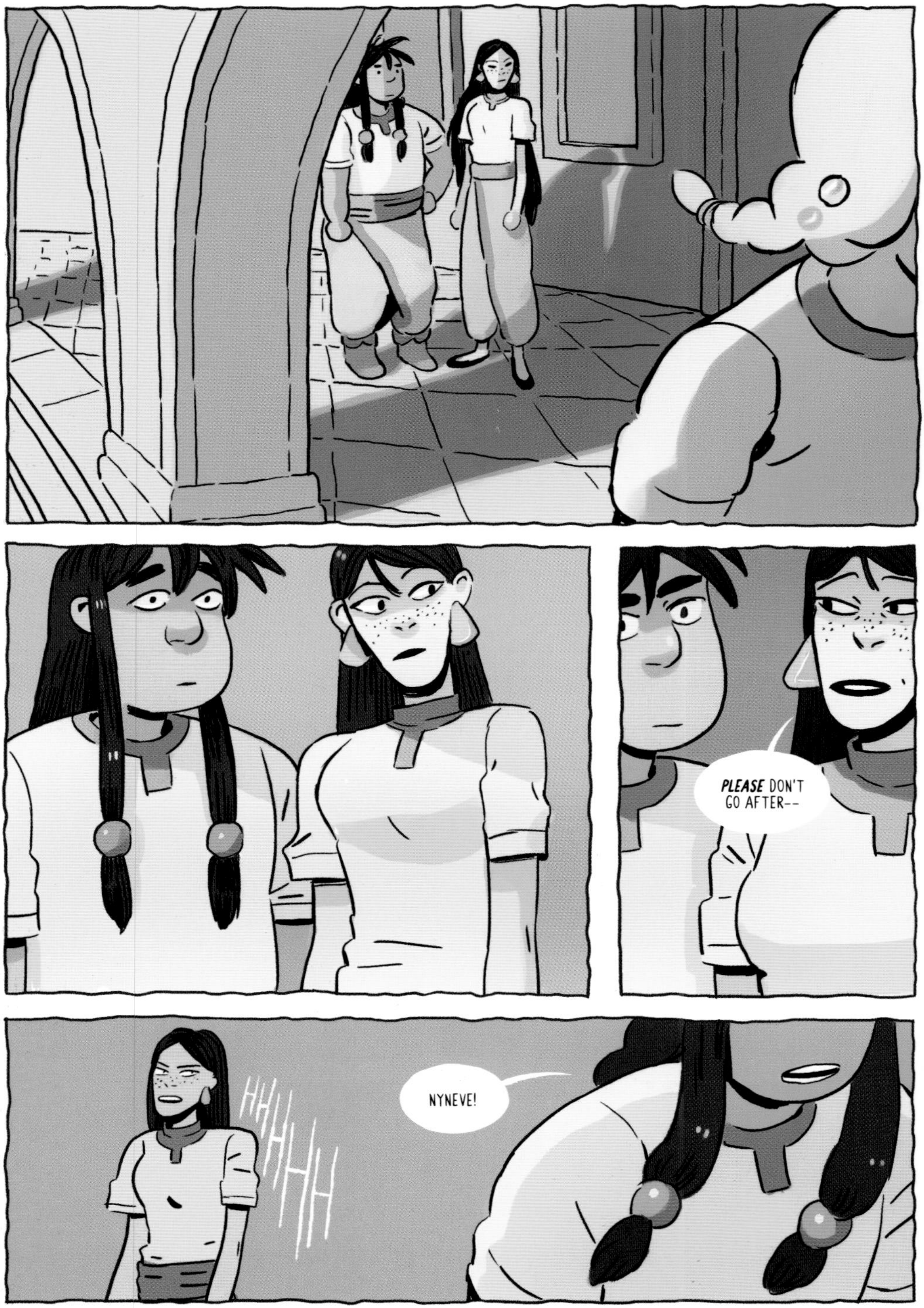

PLEASE DON'T GO AFTER--
HHHHHHH
NYNEVE!

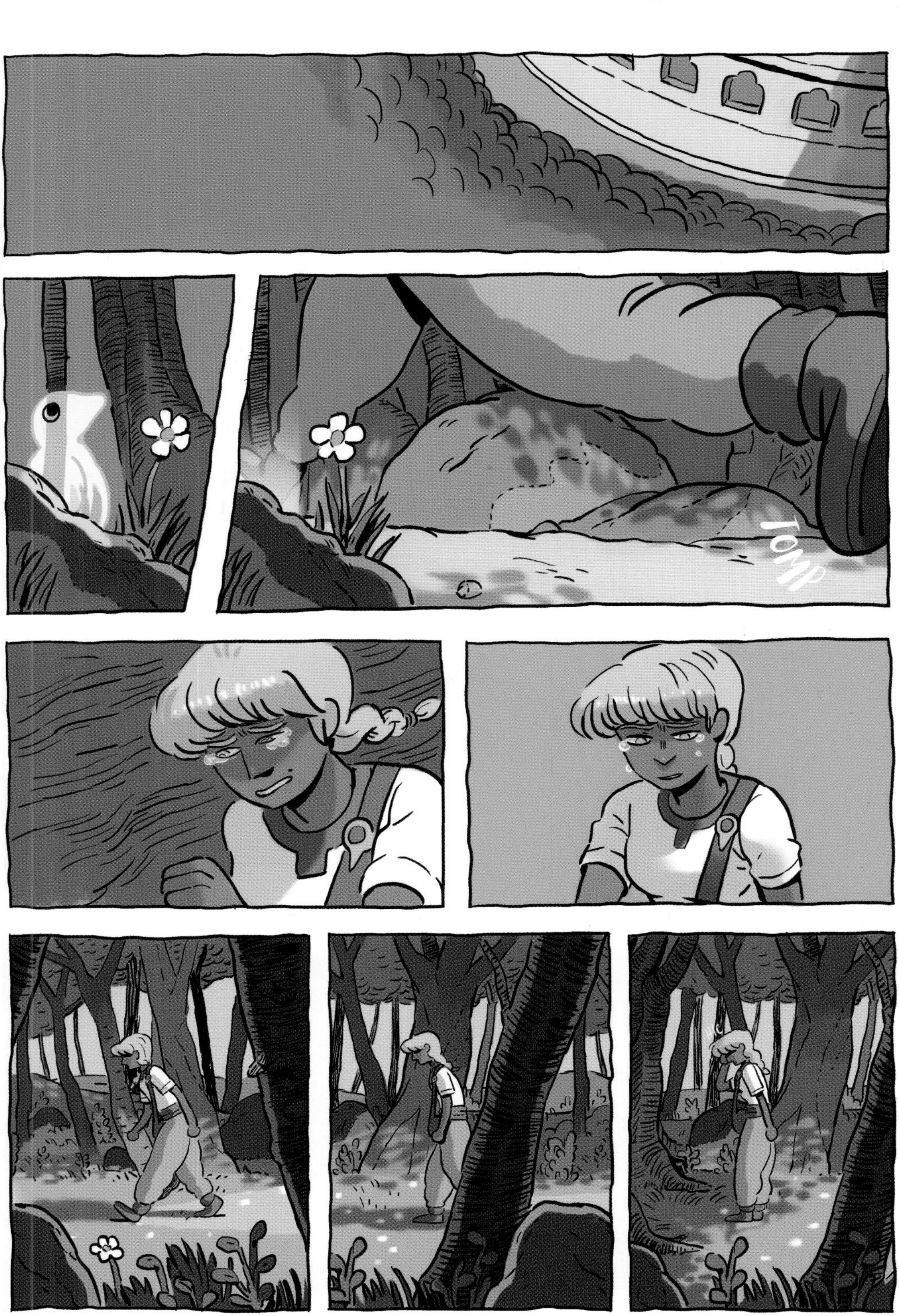
TOMP

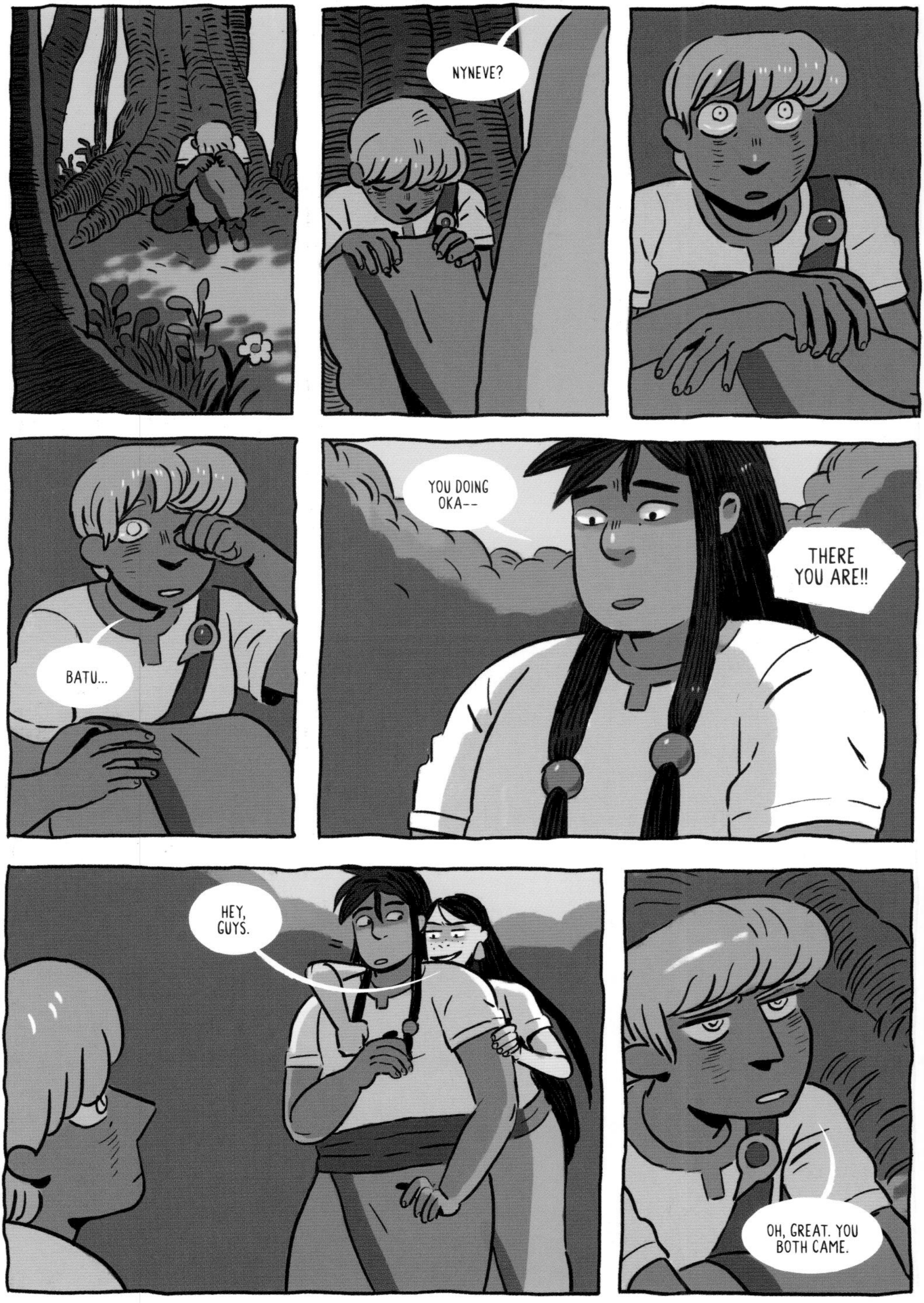
NYNEVE?
BATU...
YOU DOING OKA--
THERE YOU ARE!!
HEY, GUYS.
OH, GREAT. YOU BOTH CAME.

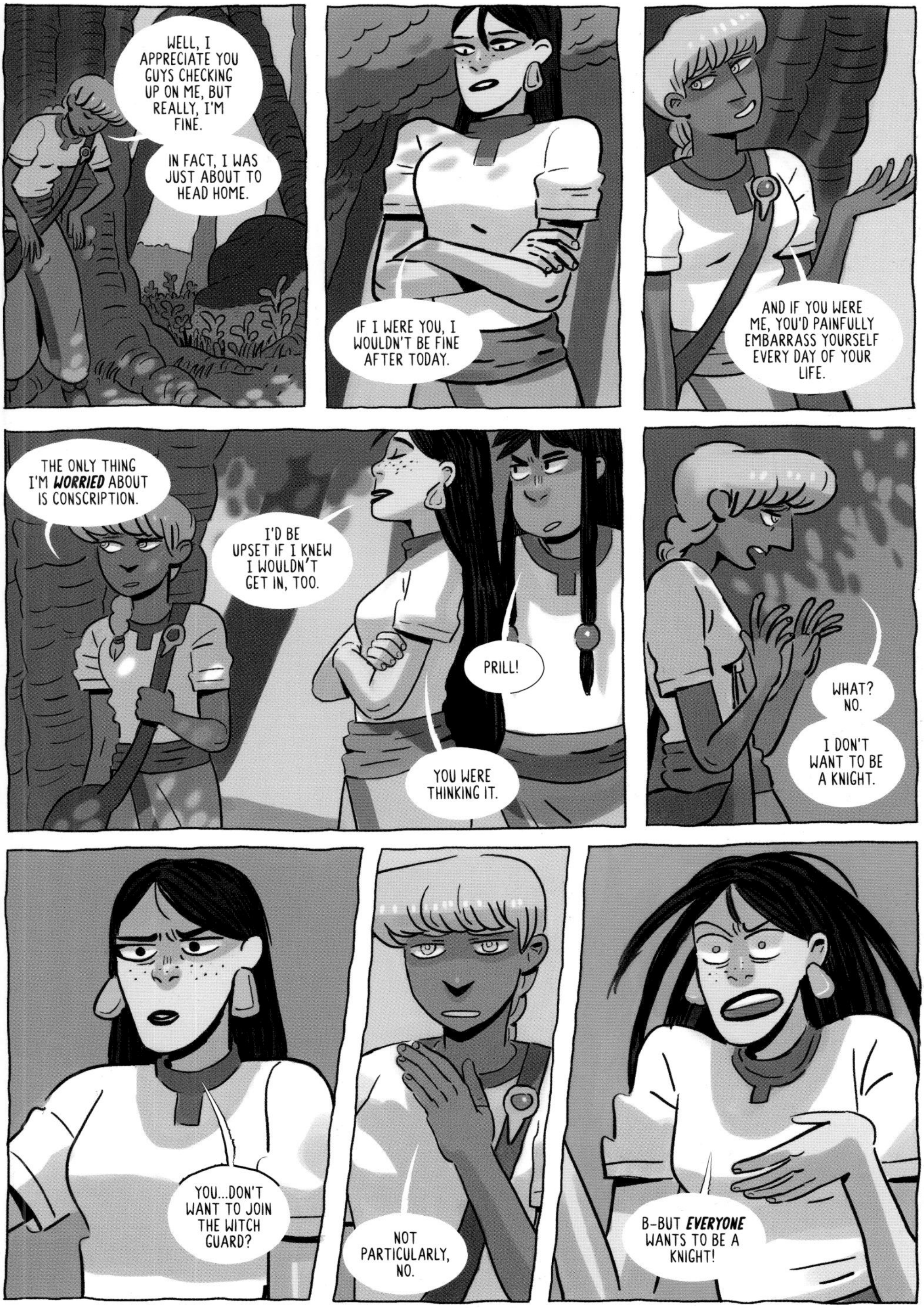
WELL, I APPRECIATE YOU GUYS CHECKING UP ON ME, BUT REALLY, I'M FINE.
IN FACT, I WAS JUST ABOUT TO HEAD HOME.
IF I WERE YOU, I WOULDN'T BE FINE AFTER TODAY.
AND IF YOU WERE ME, YOU'D PAINFULLY EMBARRASS YOURSELF EVERY DAY OF YOUR LIFE.
THE ONLY THING I'M **WORRIED** ABOUT IS CONSCRIPTION.
I'D BE UPSET IF I KNEW I WOULDN'T GET IN, TOO.
PRILL!
YOU WERE THINKING IT.
WHAT? NO.
I DON'T WANT TO BE A KNIGHT.
YOU...DON'T WANT TO JOIN THE WITCH GUARD?
NOT PARTICULARLY, NO.
B-BUT **EVERYONE** WANTS TO BE A KNIGHT!

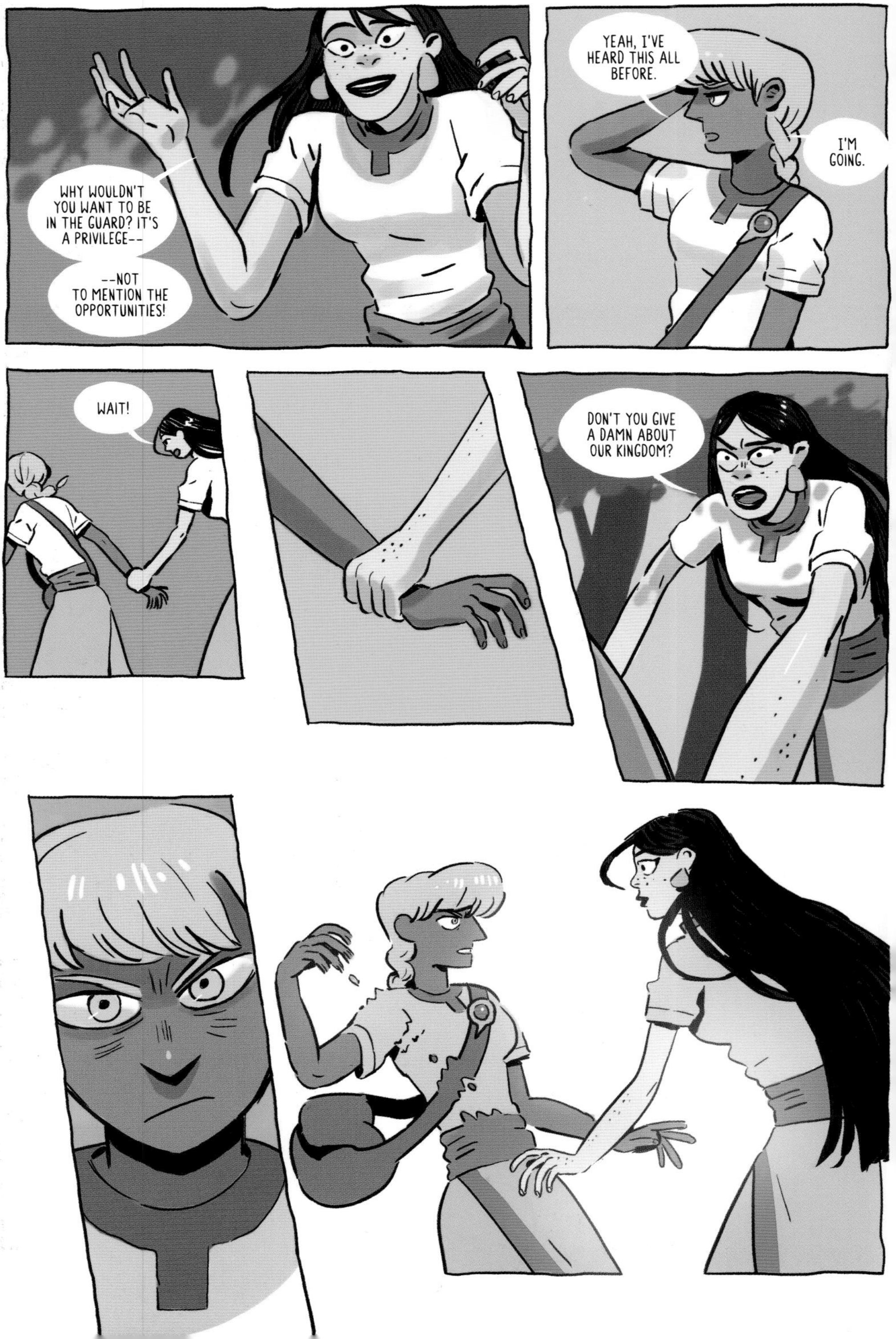
WHY WOULDN'T YOU WANT TO BE IN THE GUARD? IT'S A PRIVILEGE--
--NOT TO MENTION THE OPPORTUNITIES!
YEAH, I'VE HEARD THIS ALL BEFORE.
I'M GOING.
WAIT!
DON'T YOU GIVE A DAMN ABOUT OUR KINGDOM?

THIS **KINGDOM** IS THE REASON MY FATHER'S **DEAD!**

IF IT WEREN'T FOR THE WITCH BURNERS, HE'D STILL BE...

NYNEVE... I DIDN'T KNOW.

SIGH.

IT'S NOT THAT I'M AFRAID OF CONSCRIPTION--

--BECAUSE I THINK I WON'T BE CHOSEN.

I'M AFRAID...

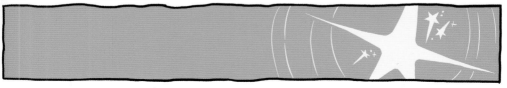

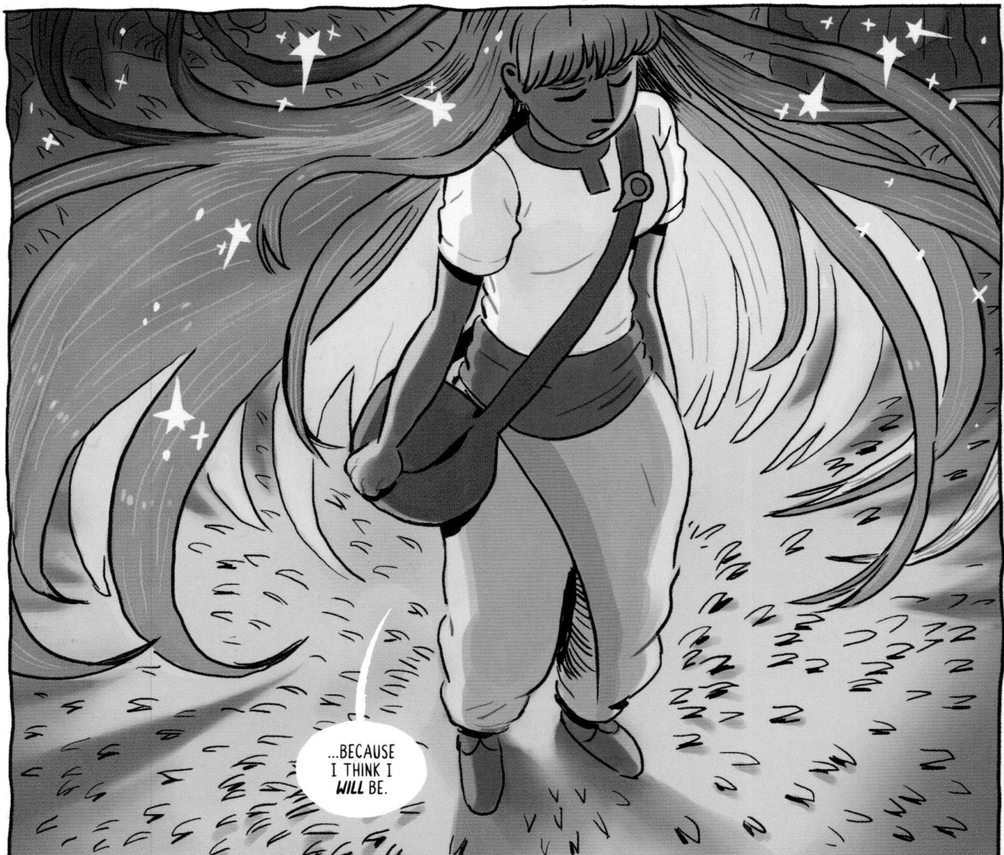
...BECAUSE I THINK I WILL BE.

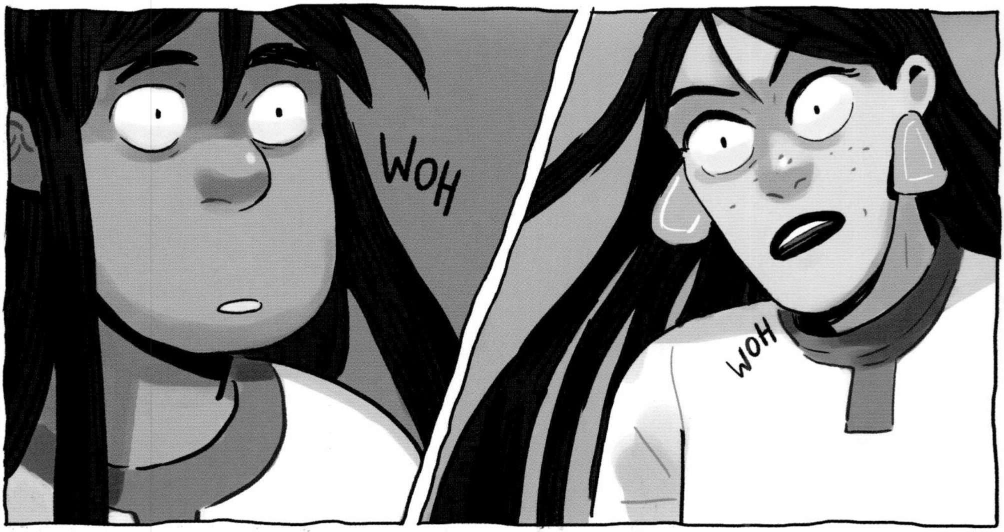
WOH
WOH

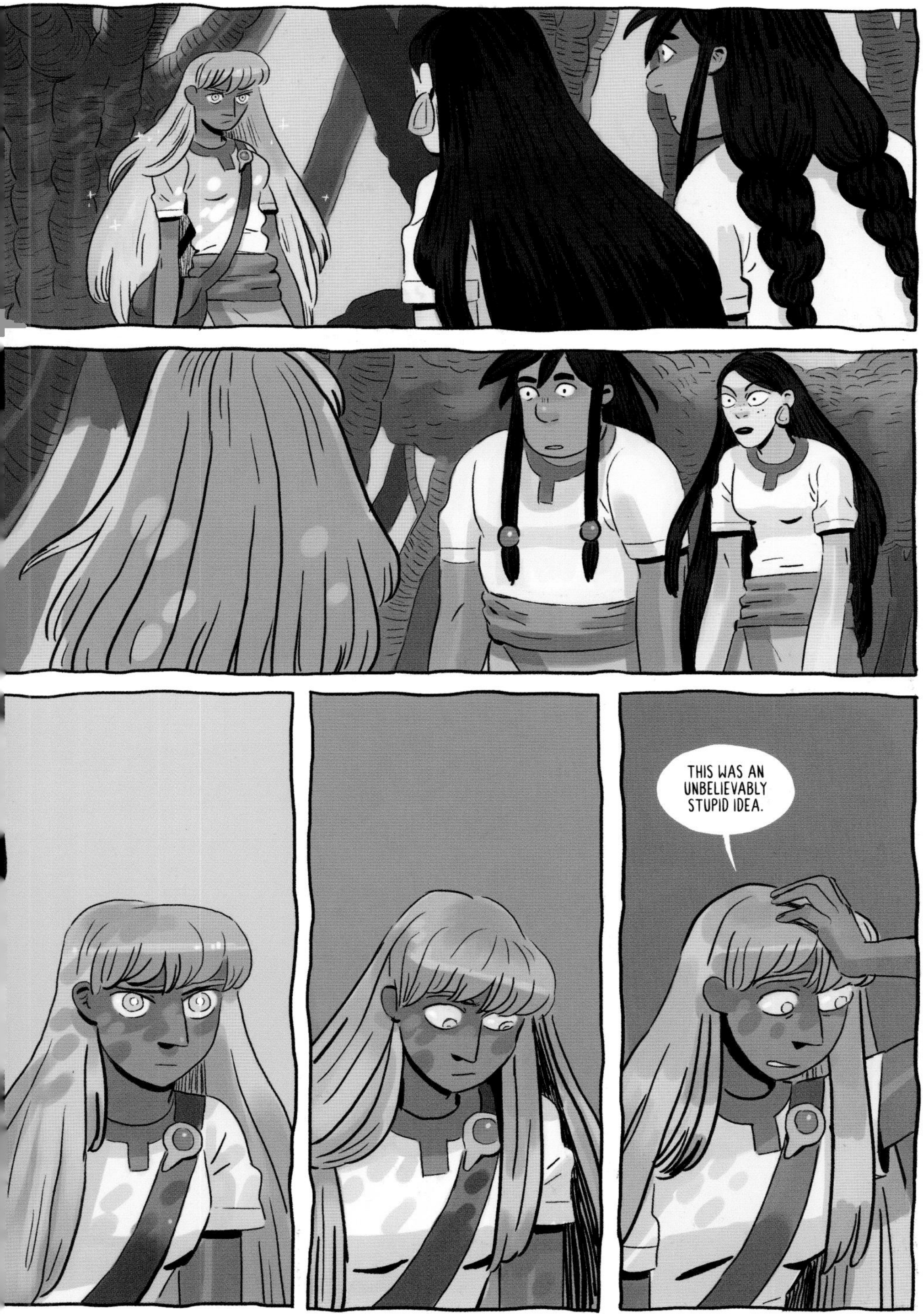
THIS WAS AN UNBELIEVABLY STUPID IDEA.

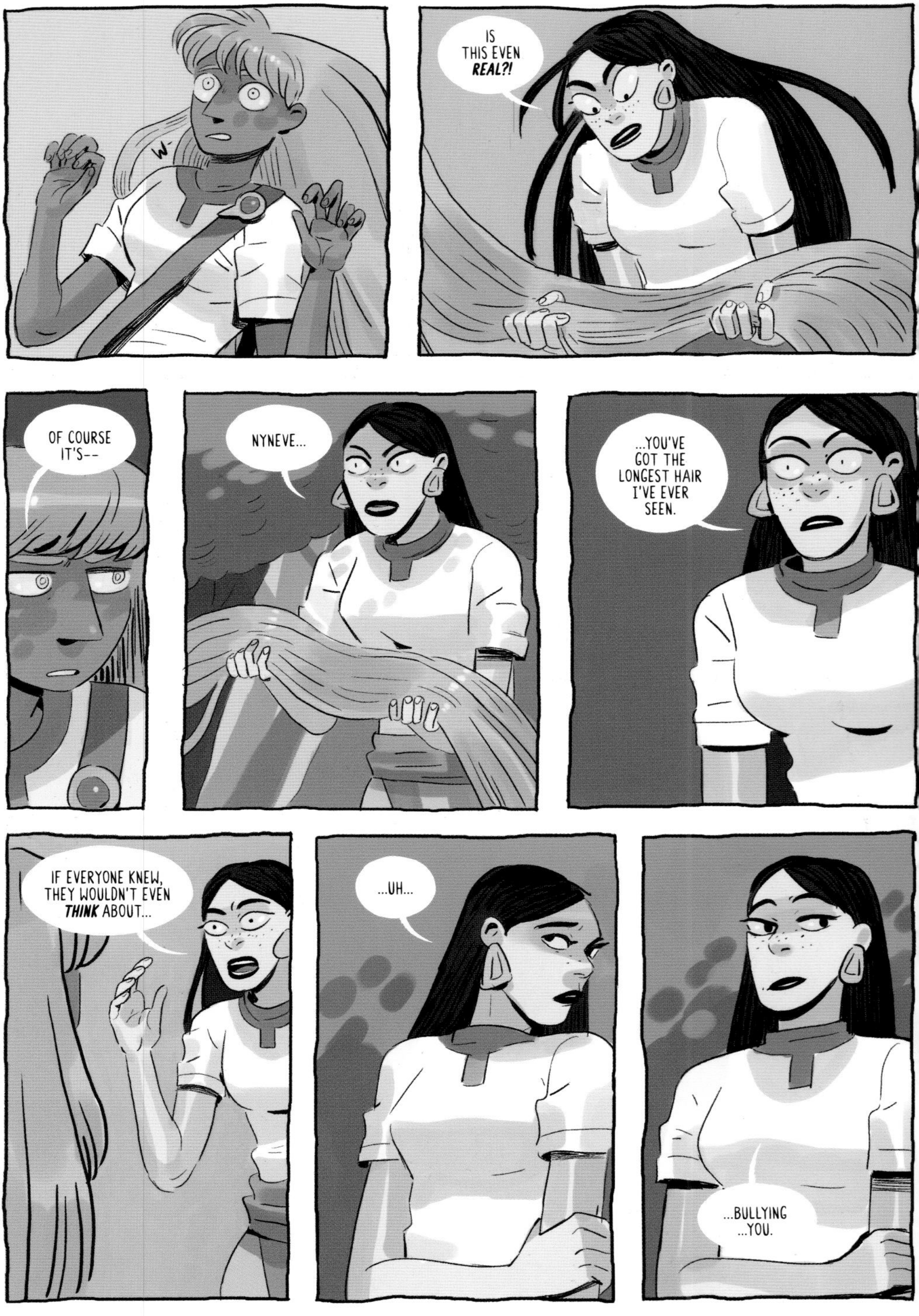
W-
IS THIS EVEN **REAL?!**
OF COURSE IT'S--
NYNEVE...
...YOU'VE GOT THE LONGEST HAIR I'VE EVER SEEN.
IF EVERYONE KNEW, THEY WOULDN'T EVEN **THINK** ABOUT...
...UH...
...BULLYING ...YOU.

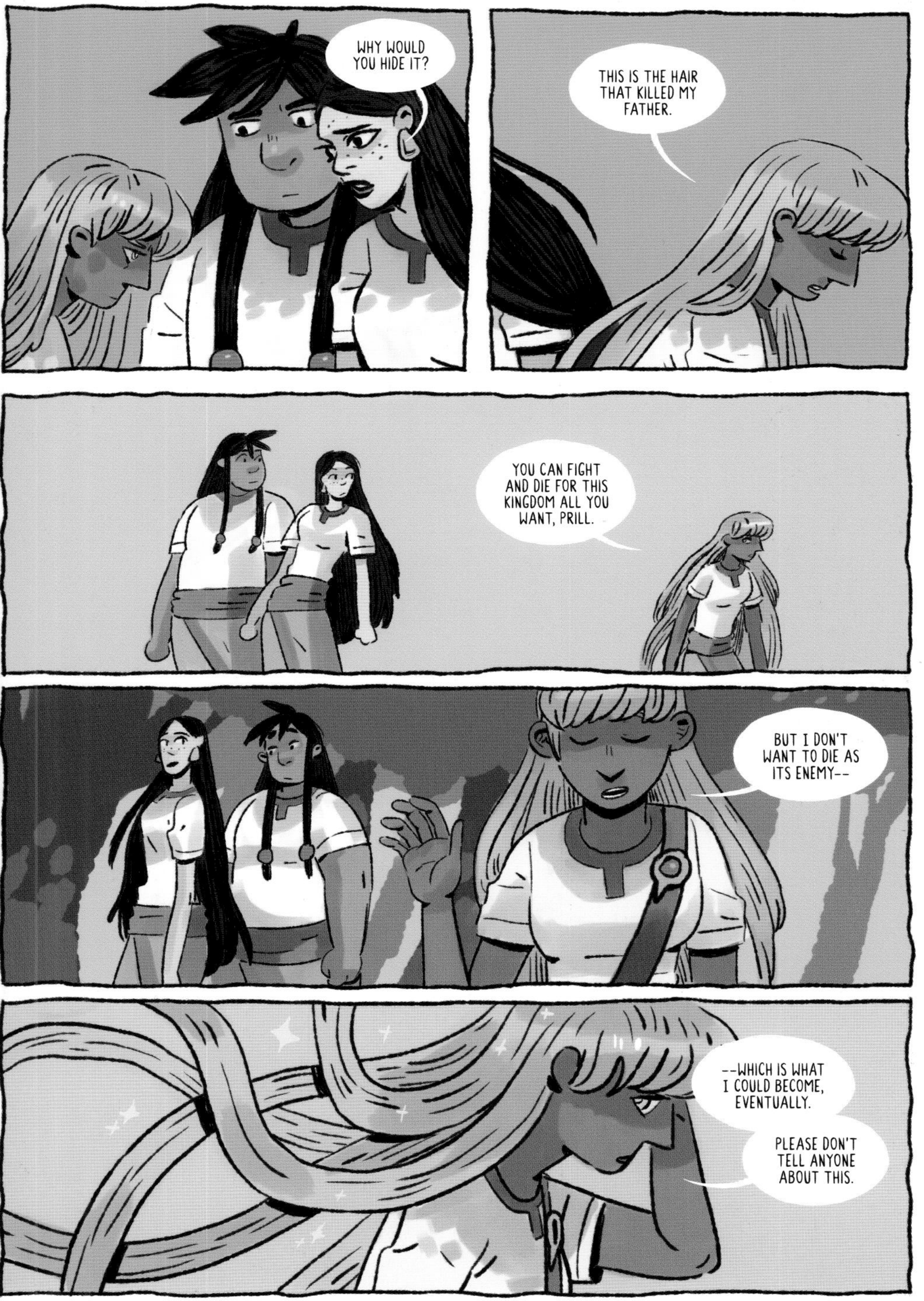
WHY WOULD YOU HIDE IT?
THIS IS THE HAIR THAT KILLED MY FATHER.
YOU CAN FIGHT AND DIE FOR THIS KINGDOM ALL YOU WANT, PRILL.
BUT I DON'T WANT TO DIE AS ITS ENEMY--
--WHICH IS WHAT I COULD BECOME, EVENTUALLY.
PLEASE DON'T TELL ANYONE ABOUT THIS.

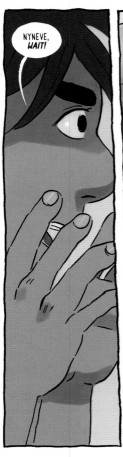

NYNEVE, *WAIT!*

YOUR MAGIC-- WAS THAT A LIE TOO?

HA.

WHO KNOWS WHAT'S WRONG WITH ME, BUT I'VE *NEVER* BEEN GOOD AT MAGIC.

MY HAIR'S AS MUCH A BURDEN AS IT IS USELESS.

48

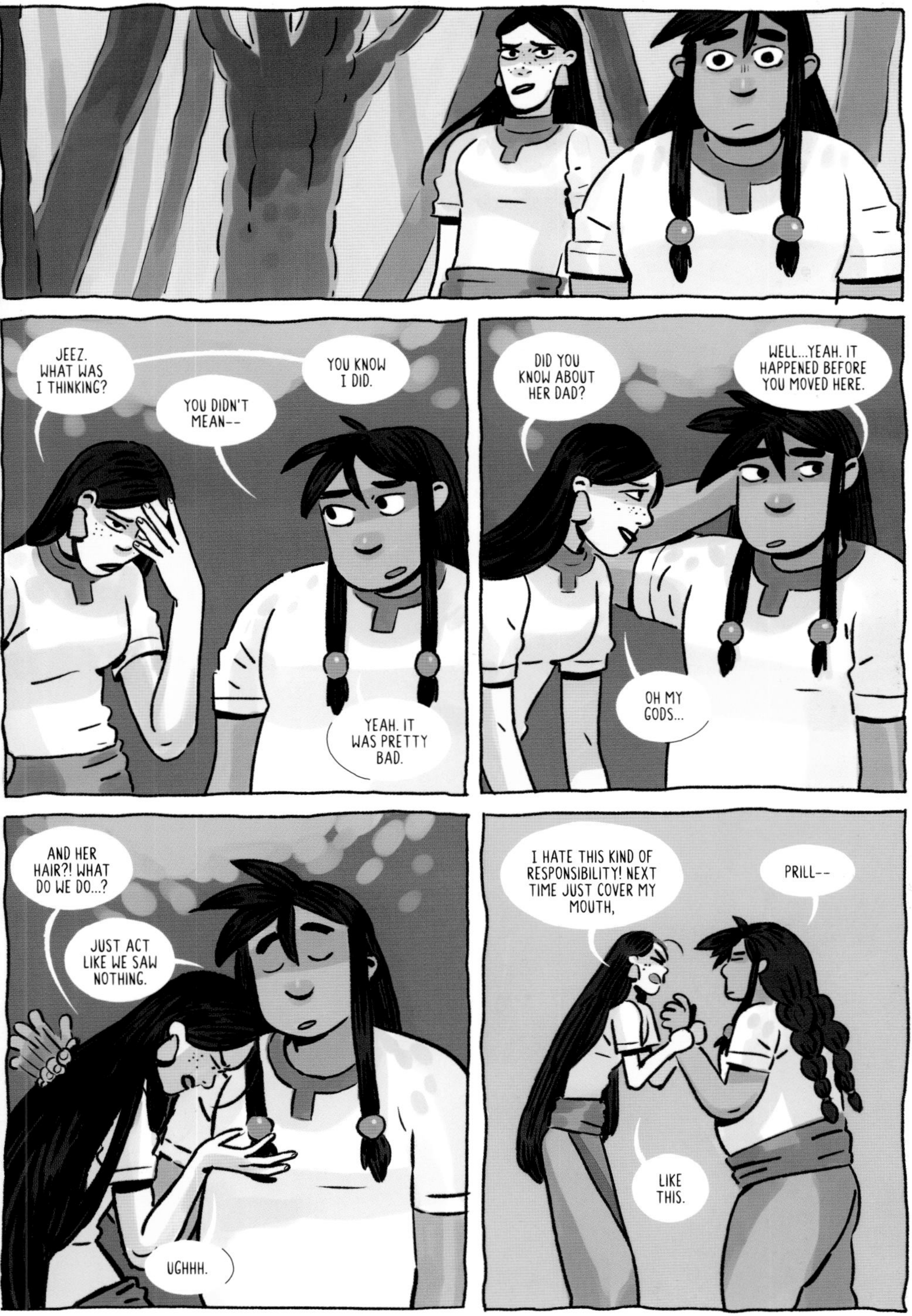

JEEZ. WHAT WAS I THINKING?
YOU DIDN'T MEAN--
YOU KNOW I DID.
YEAH. IT WAS PRETTY BAD.
DID YOU KNOW ABOUT HER DAD?
WELL...YEAH. IT HAPPENED BEFORE YOU MOVED HERE.
OH MY GODS...
AND HER HAIR?! WHAT DO WE DO...?
JUST ACT LIKE WE SAW NOTHING.
UGHHH.
I HATE THIS KIND OF RESPONSIBILITY! NEXT TIME JUST COVER MY MOUTH,
PRILL--
LIKE THIS.

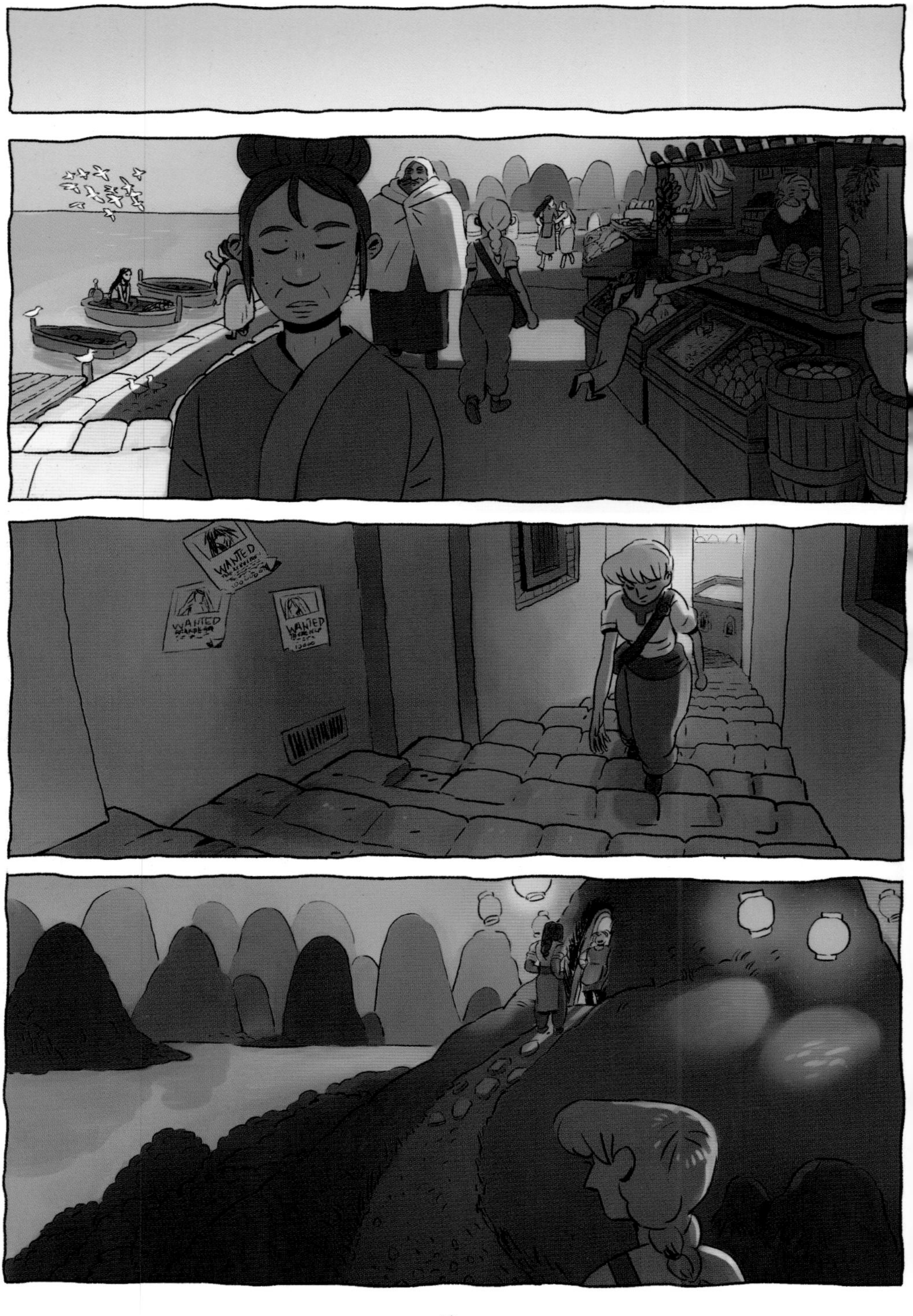
WANTED
WANTED
WANTED

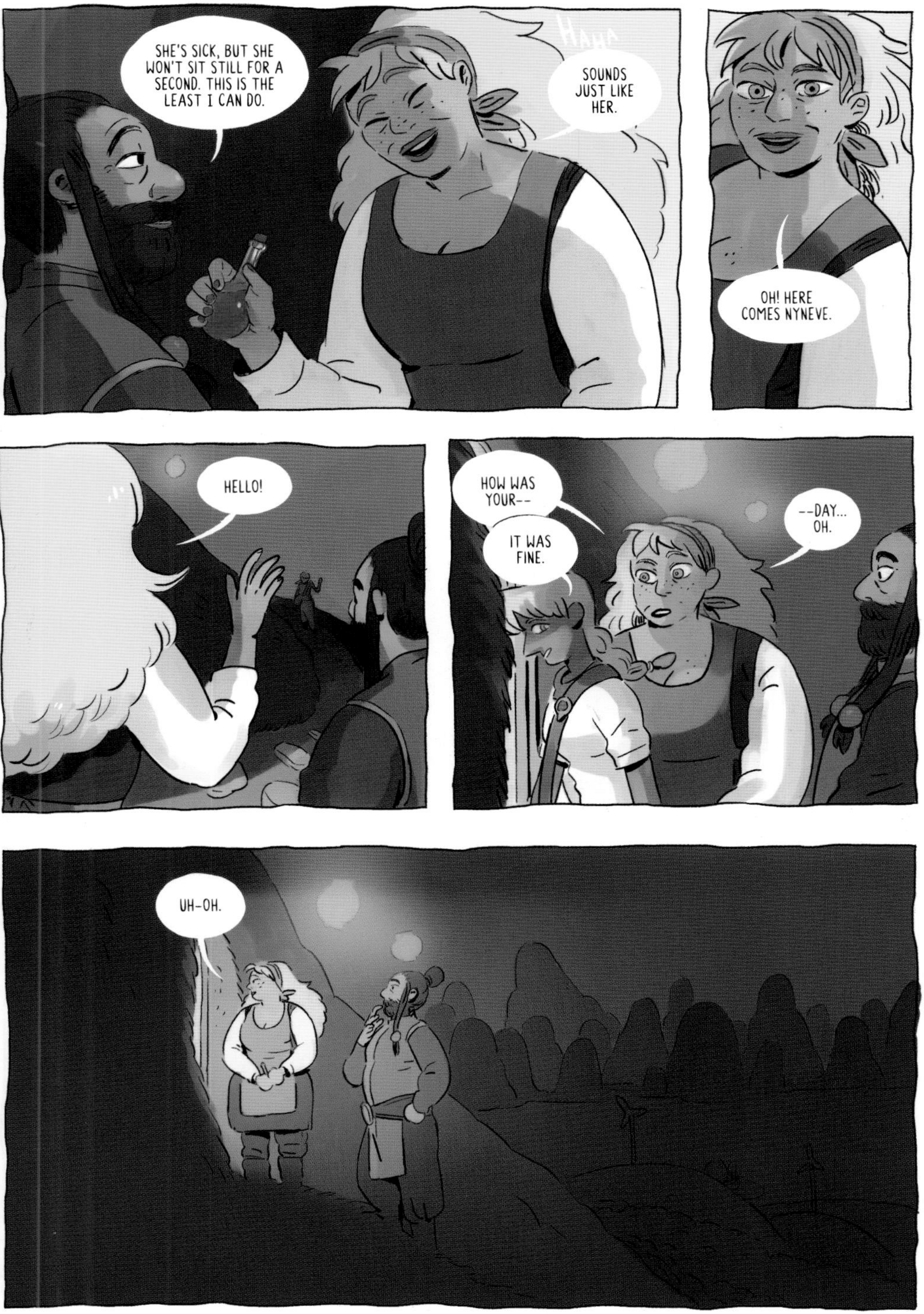
SHE'S SICK, BUT SHE WON'T SIT STILL FOR A SECOND. THIS IS THE LEAST I CAN DO.
SOUNDS JUST LIKE HER.
OH! HERE COMES NYNEVE.
HELLO!
HOW WAS YOUR--
IT WAS FINE.
--DAY... OH.
UH-OH.

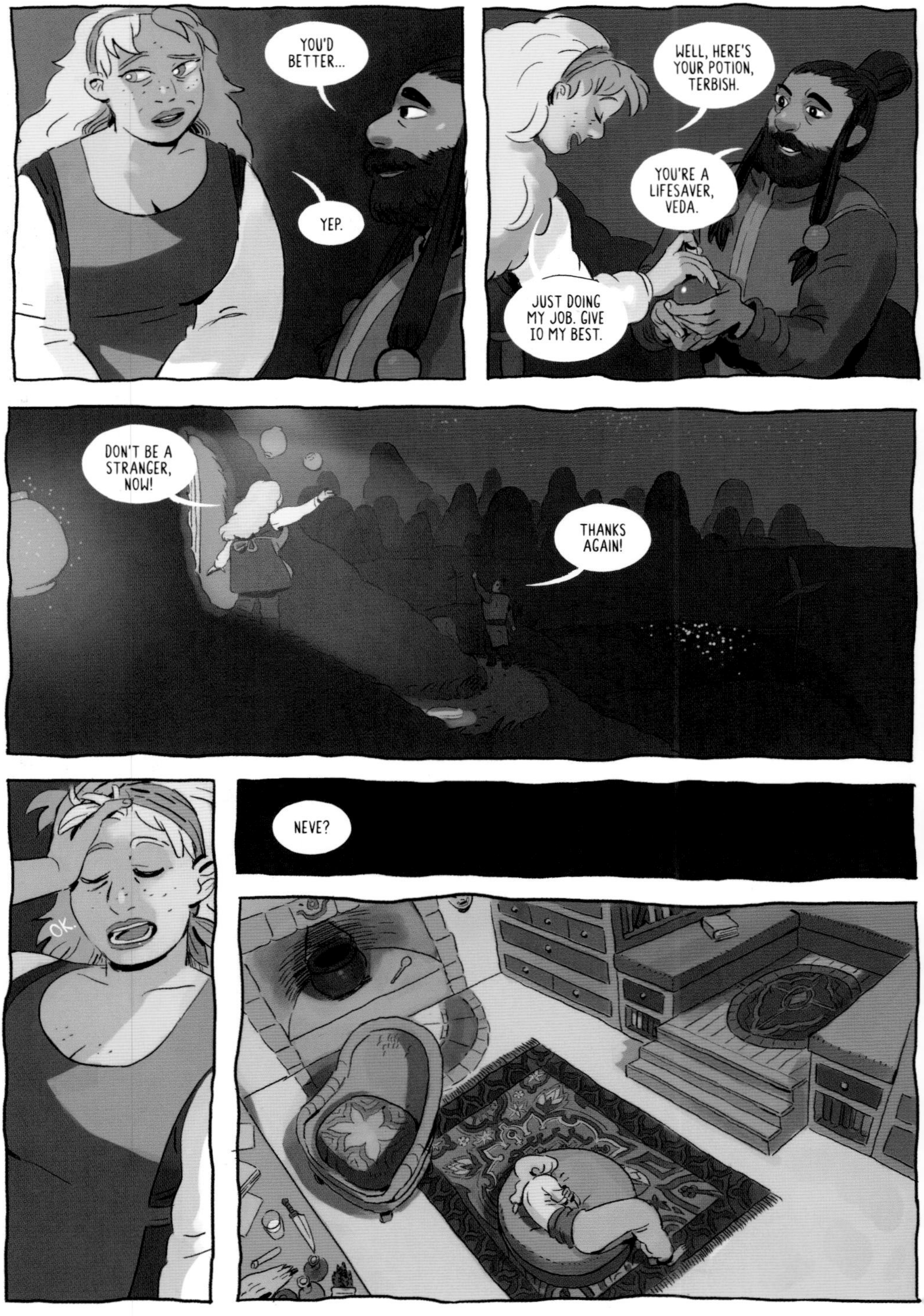

YOU'D BETTER...
YEP.
WELL, HERE'S YOUR POTION, TERBISH.
YOU'RE A LIFESAVER, VEDA.
JUST DOING MY JOB. GIVE IO MY BEST.
DON'T BE A STRANGER, NOW!
THANKS AGAIN!
OK.
NEVE?

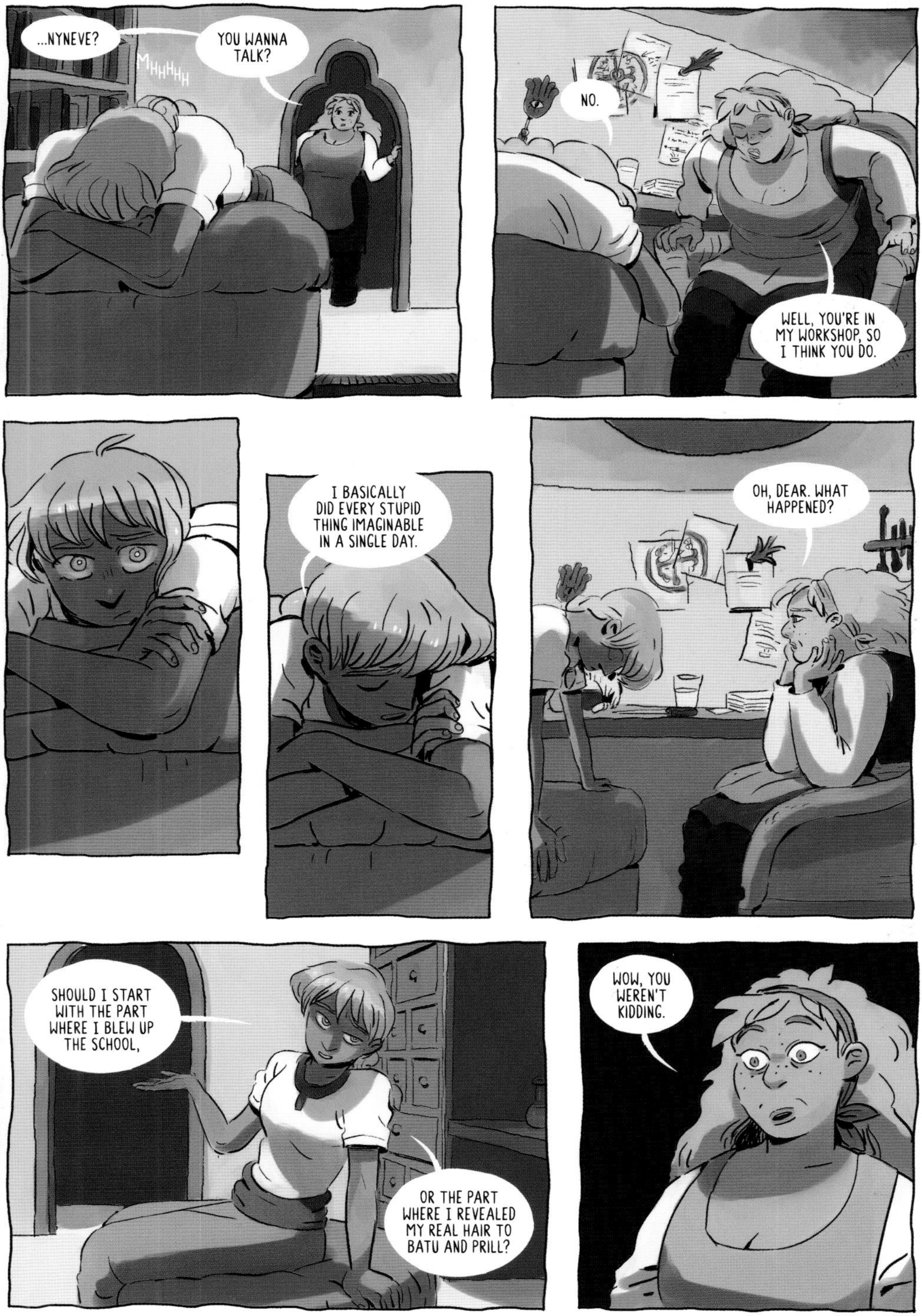
...NYNEVE?
YOU WANNA TALK?
MHHHHH
NO.
WELL, YOU'RE IN MY WORKSHOP, SO I THINK YOU DO.
I BASICALLY DID EVERY STUPID THING IMAGINABLE IN A SINGLE DAY.
OH, DEAR. WHAT HAPPENED?
SHOULD I START WITH THE PART WHERE I BLEW UP THE SCHOOL,
OR THE PART WHERE I REVEALED MY REAL HAIR TO BATU AND PRILL?
WOW, YOU WEREN'T KIDDING.

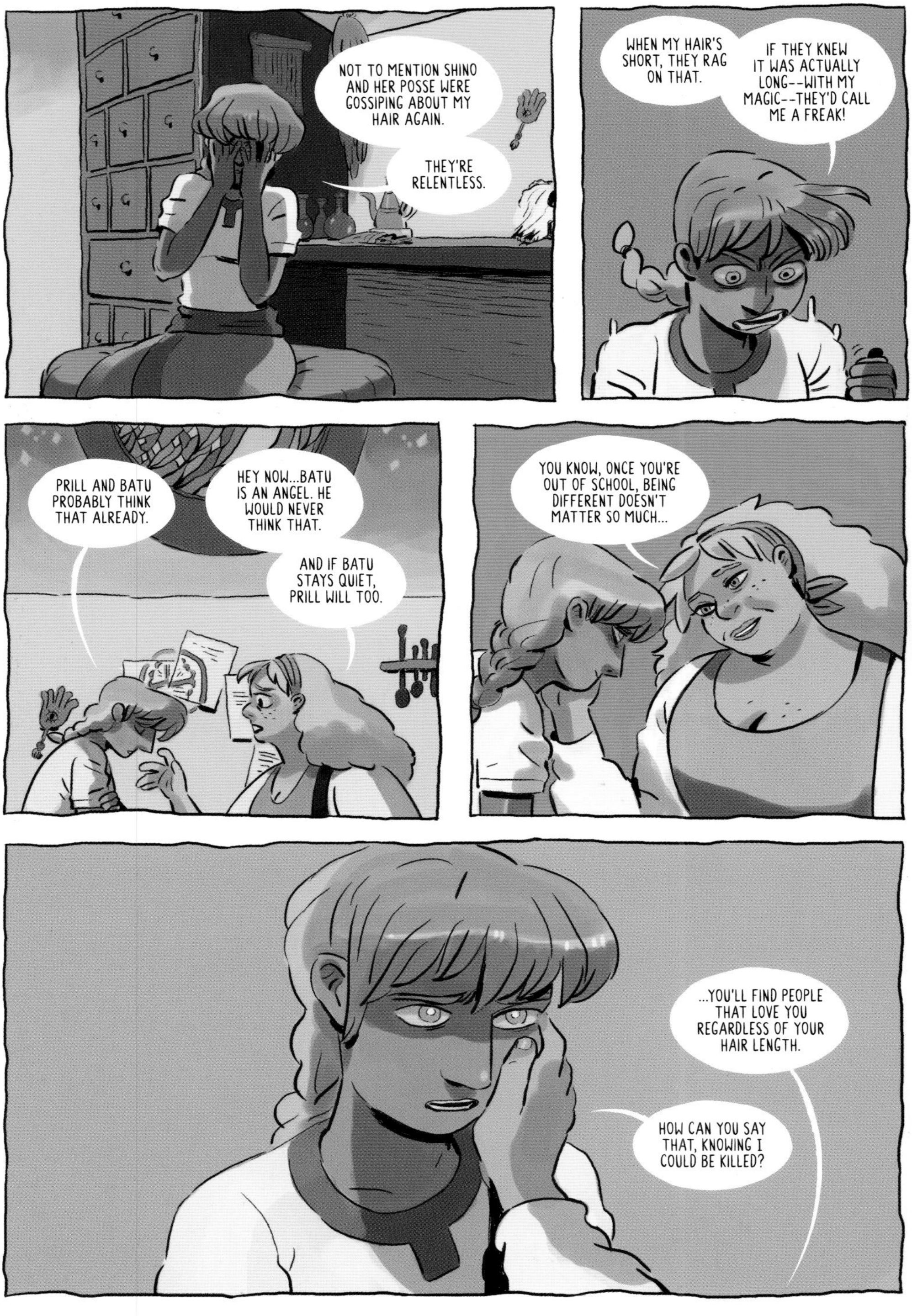
NOT TO MENTION SHINO AND HER POSSE WERE GOSSIPING ABOUT MY HAIR AGAIN.
THEY'RE RELENTLESS.
WHEN MY HAIR'S SHORT, THEY RAG ON THAT.
IF THEY KNEW IT WAS ACTUALLY LONG--WITH MY MAGIC--THEY'D CALL ME A FREAK!
PRILL AND BATU PROBABLY THINK THAT ALREADY.
HEY NOW...BATU IS AN ANGEL. HE WOULD NEVER THINK THAT.
AND IF BATU STAYS QUIET, PRILL WILL TOO.
YOU KNOW, ONCE YOU'RE OUT OF SCHOOL, BEING DIFFERENT DOESN'T MATTER SO MUCH...
...YOU'LL FIND PEOPLE THAT LOVE YOU REGARDLESS OF YOUR HAIR LENGTH.
HOW CAN YOU SAY THAT, KNOWING I COULD BE KILLED?

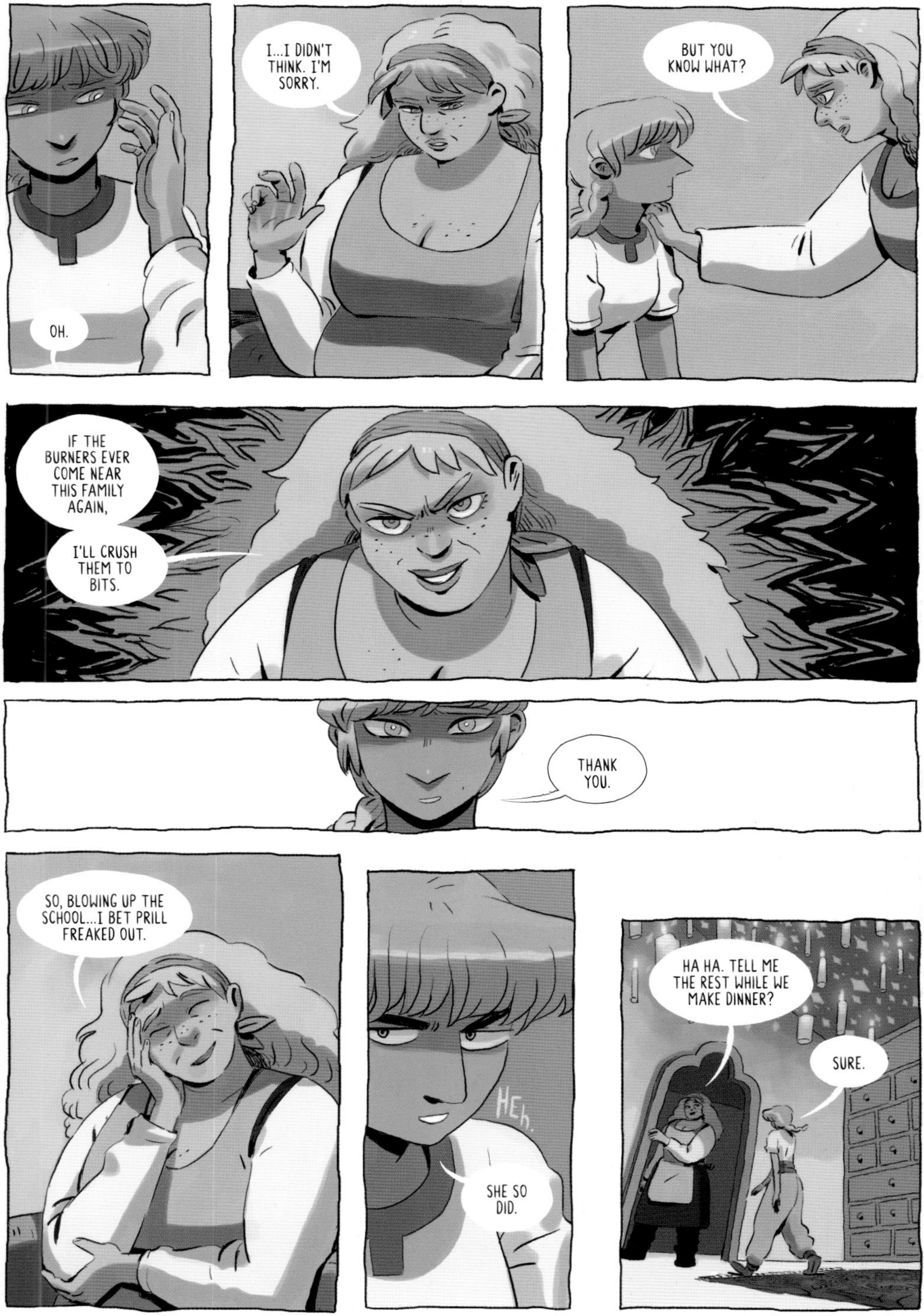
OH.
I...I DIDN'T THINK. I'M SORRY.
BUT YOU KNOW WHAT?
IF THE BURNERS EVER COME NEAR THIS FAMILY AGAIN,
I'LL CRUSH THEM TO BITS.
THANK YOU.
SO, BLOWING UP THE SCHOOL...I BET PRILL FREAKED OUT.
HEh.
SHE SO DID.
HA HA. TELL ME THE REST WHILE WE MAKE DINNER?
SURE.

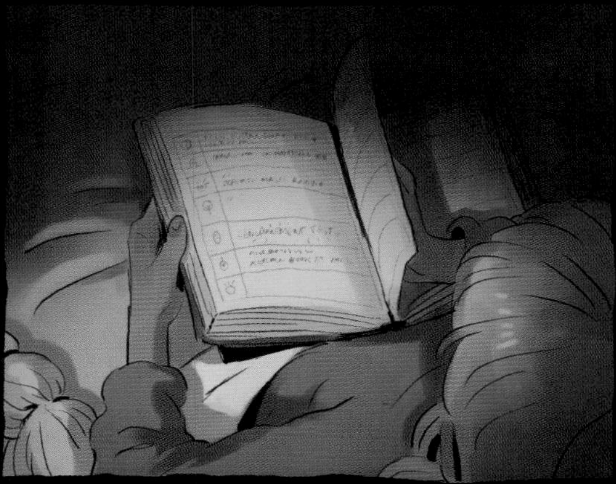

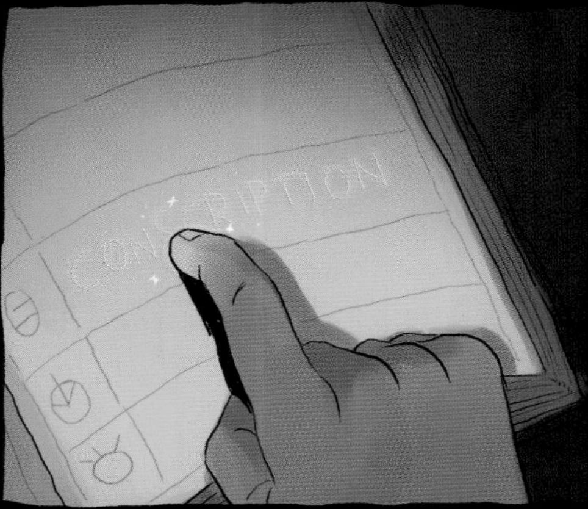

WITCHY
CHAPTER THREE

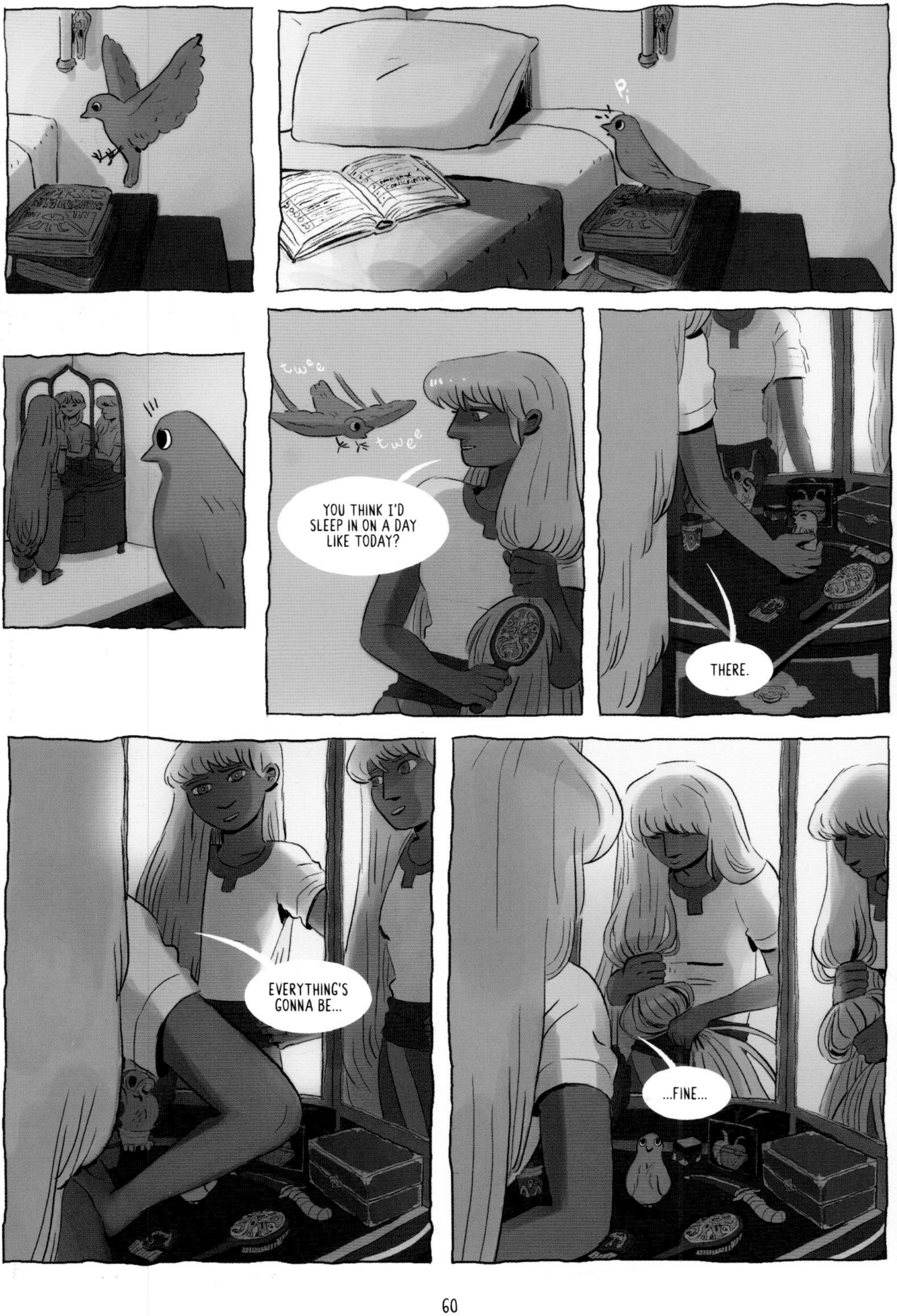
Pi
'''
tweee
tweee
"...
YOU THINK I'D SLEEP IN ON A DAY LIKE TODAY?
THERE.
EVERYTHING'S GONNA BE...
...FINE...

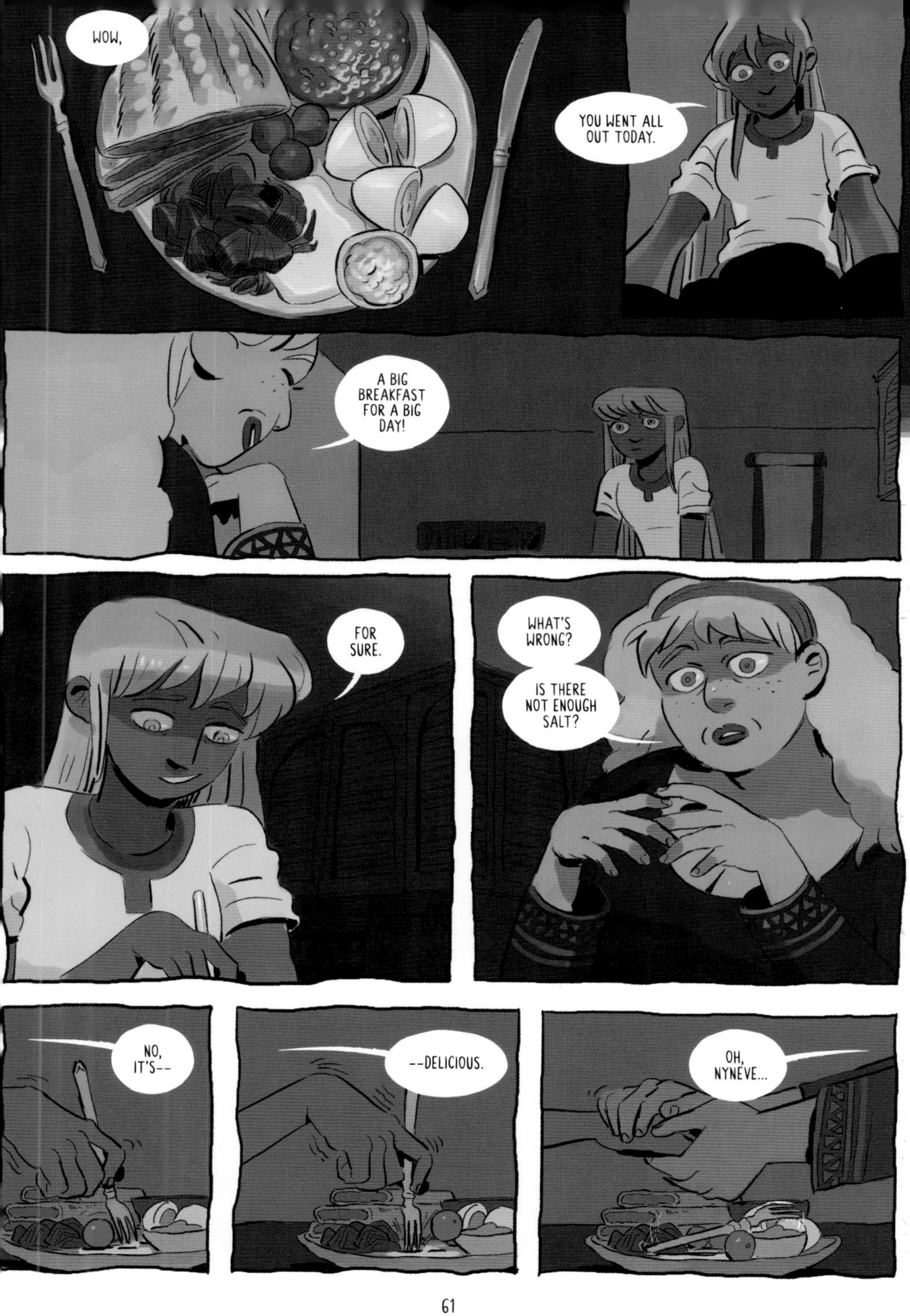
WOW,
YOU WENT ALL OUT TODAY.
A BIG BREAKFAST FOR A BIG DAY!
FOR SURE.
WHAT'S WRONG?
IS THERE NOT ENOUGH SALT?
NO, IT'S--
--DELICIOUS.
OH, NYNEVE...

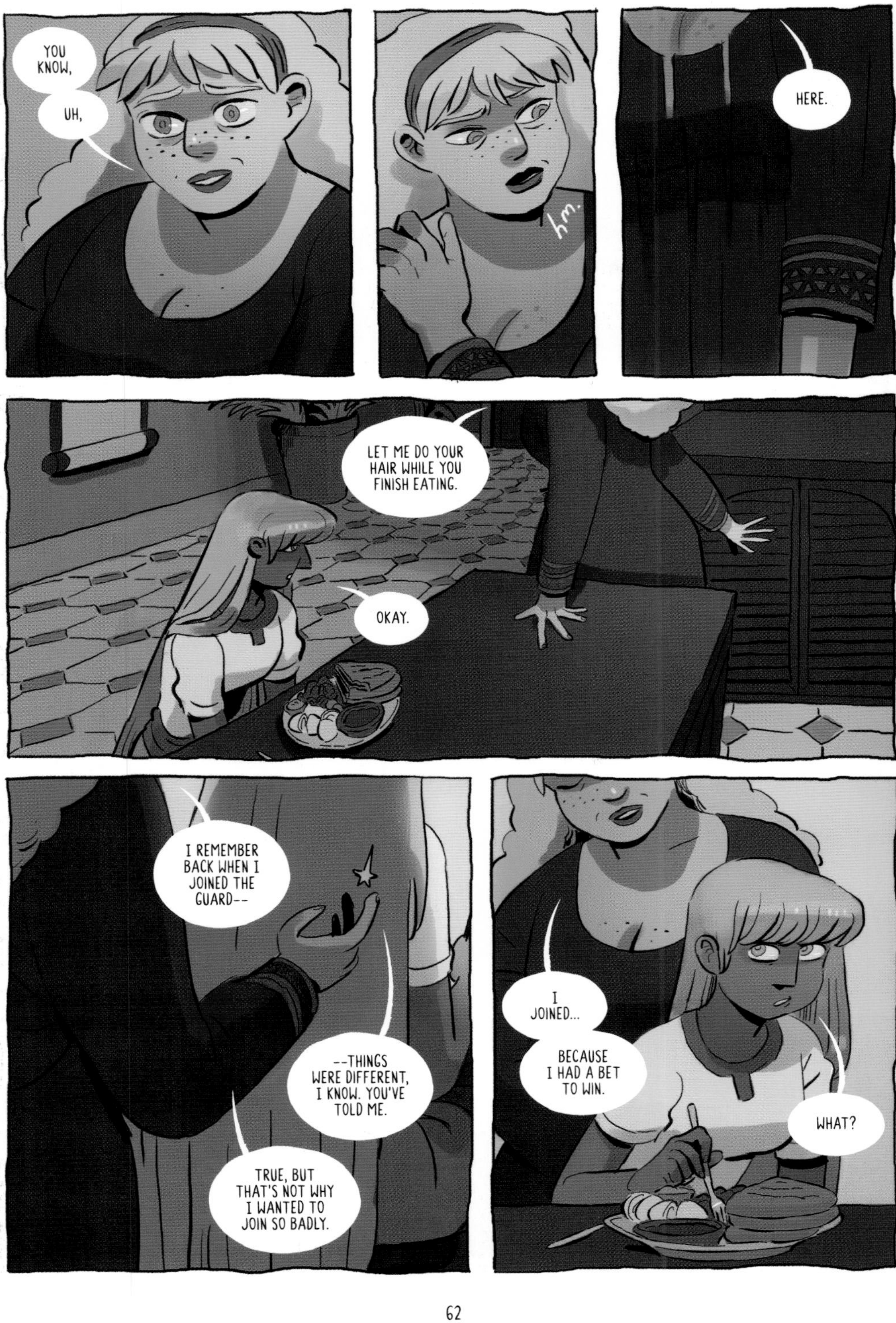
YOU KNOW,
UH,
hm.
HERE.
LET ME DO YOUR HAIR WHILE YOU FINISH EATING.
OKAY.
I REMEMBER BACK WHEN I JOINED THE GUARD--
--THINGS WERE DIFFERENT, I KNOW. YOU'VE TOLD ME.
TRUE, BUT THAT'S NOT WHY I WANTED TO JOIN SO BADLY.
I JOINED...
BECAUSE I HAD A BET TO WIN.
WHAT?

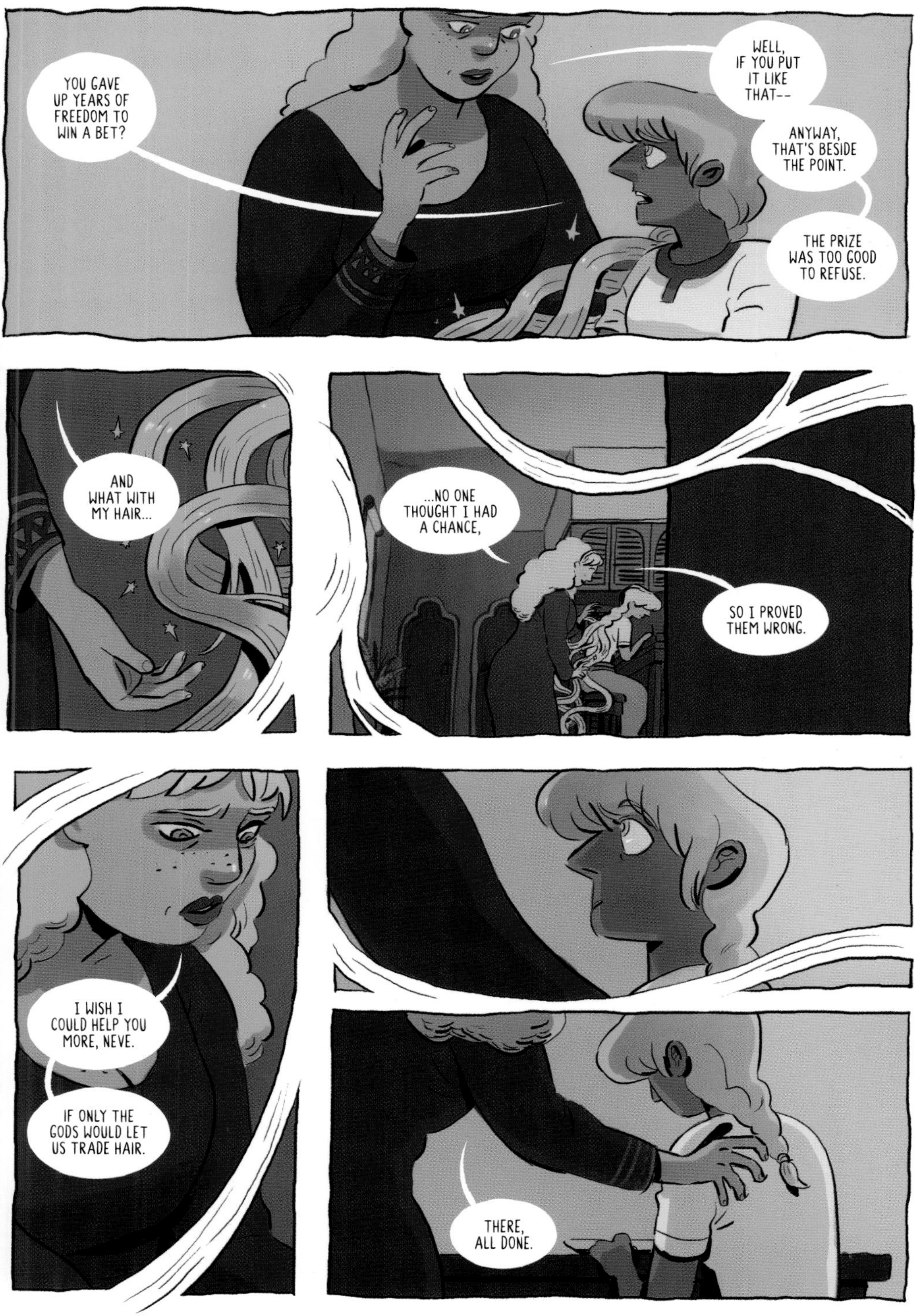
YOU GAVE UP YEARS OF FREEDOM TO WIN A BET?
WELL, IF YOU PUT IT LIKE THAT--
ANYWAY, THAT'S BESIDE THE POINT.
THE PRIZE WAS TOO GOOD TO REFUSE.
AND WHAT WITH MY HAIR...
...NO ONE THOUGHT I HAD A CHANCE,
SO I PROVED THEM WRONG.
I WISH I COULD HELP YOU MORE, NEVE.
IF ONLY THE GODS WOULD LET US TRADE HAIR.
THERE, ALL DONE.

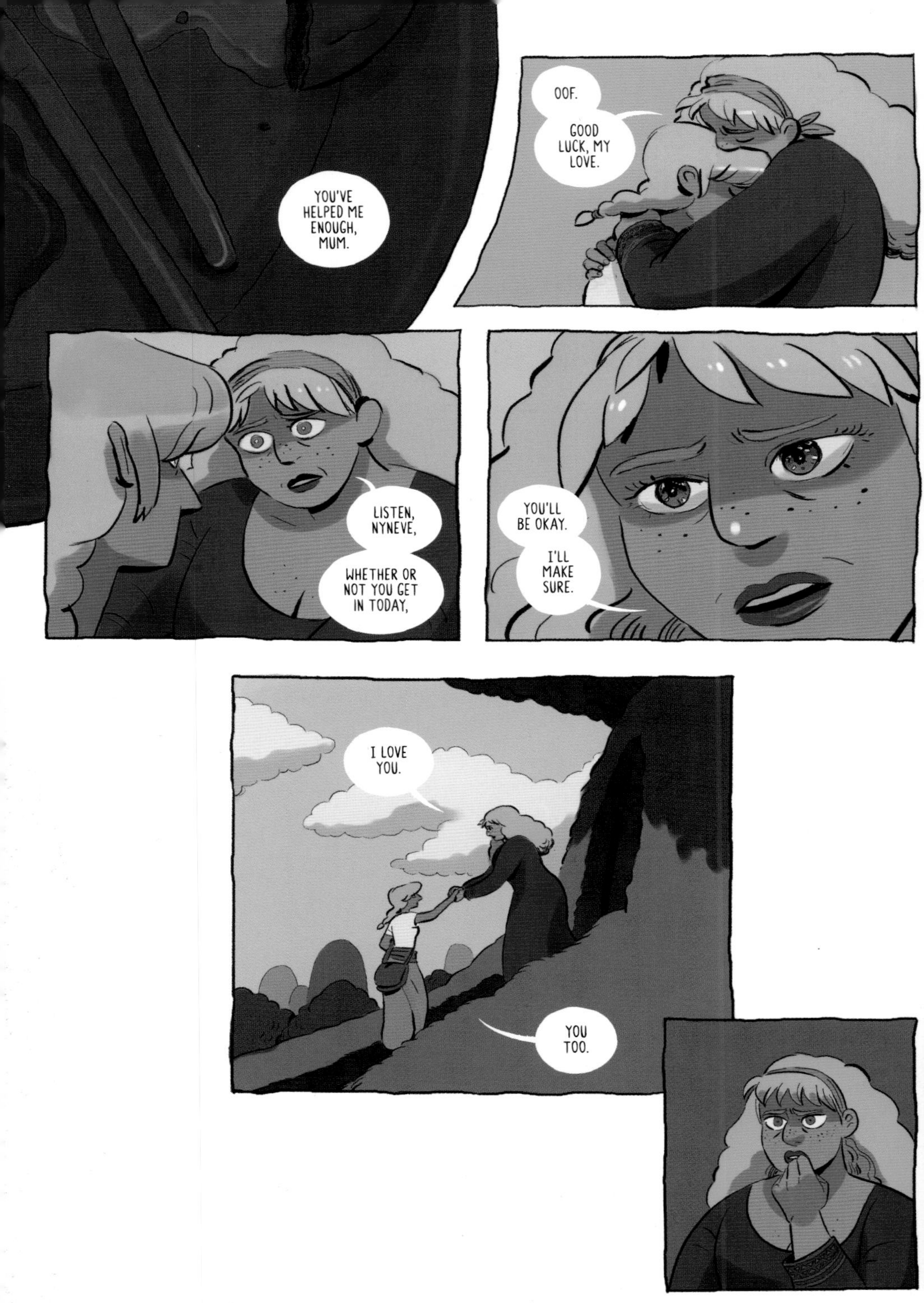
YOU'VE HELPED ME ENOUGH, MUM.
OOF.
GOOD LUCK, MY LOVE.
LISTEN, NYNEVE,
WHETHER OR NOT YOU GET IN TODAY,
YOU'LL BE OKAY.
I'LL MAKE SURE.
I LOVE YOU.
YOU TOO.

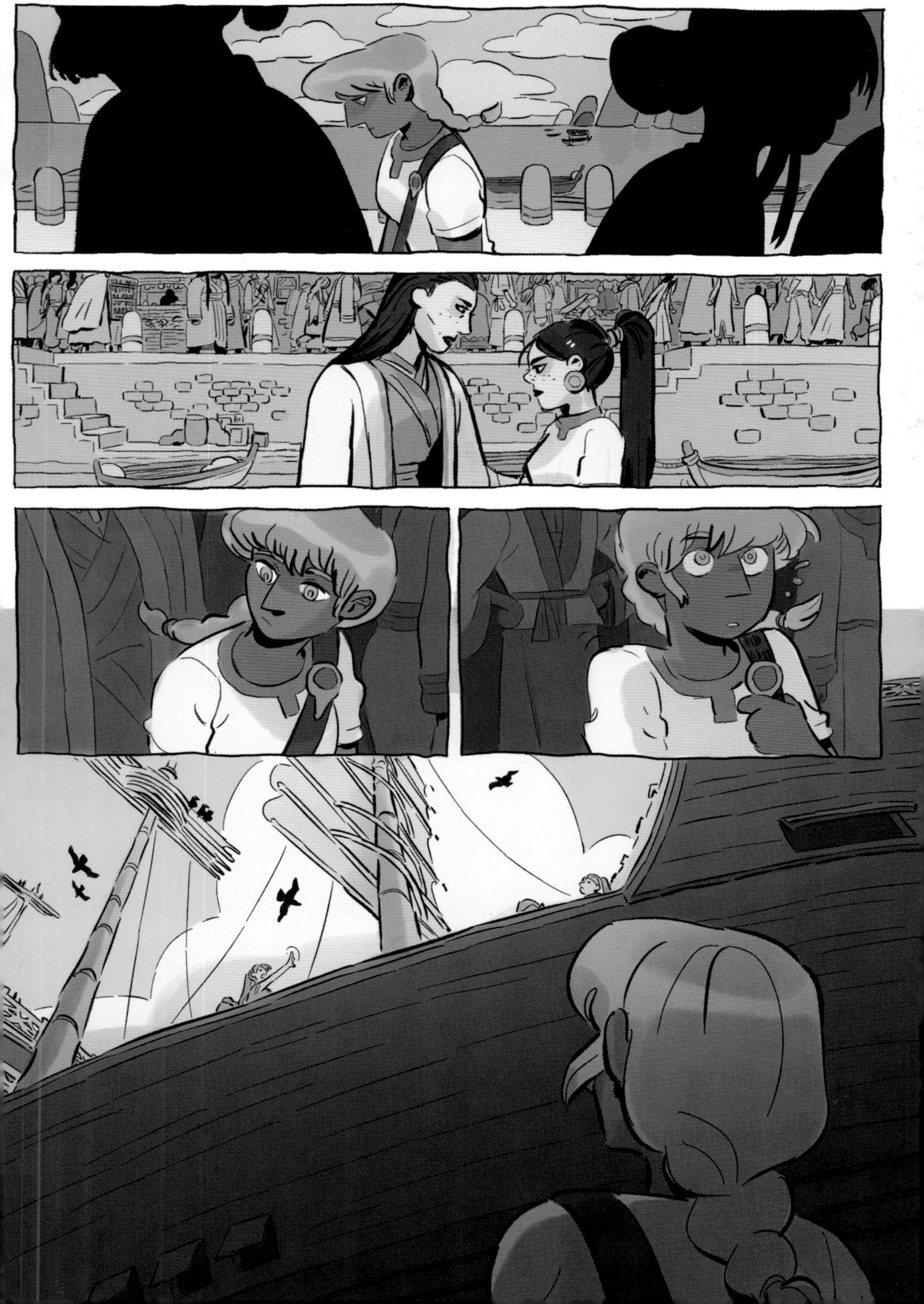

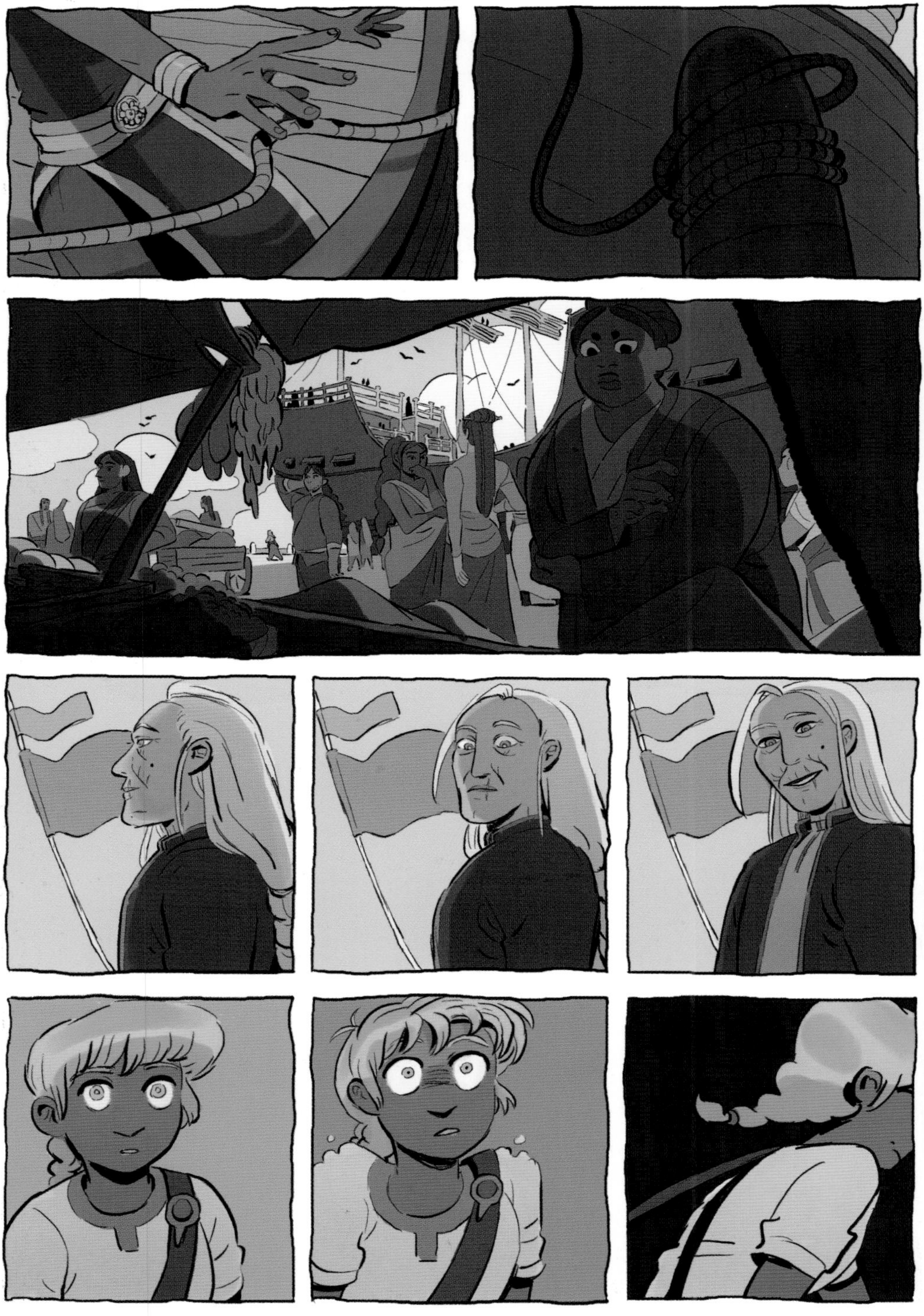

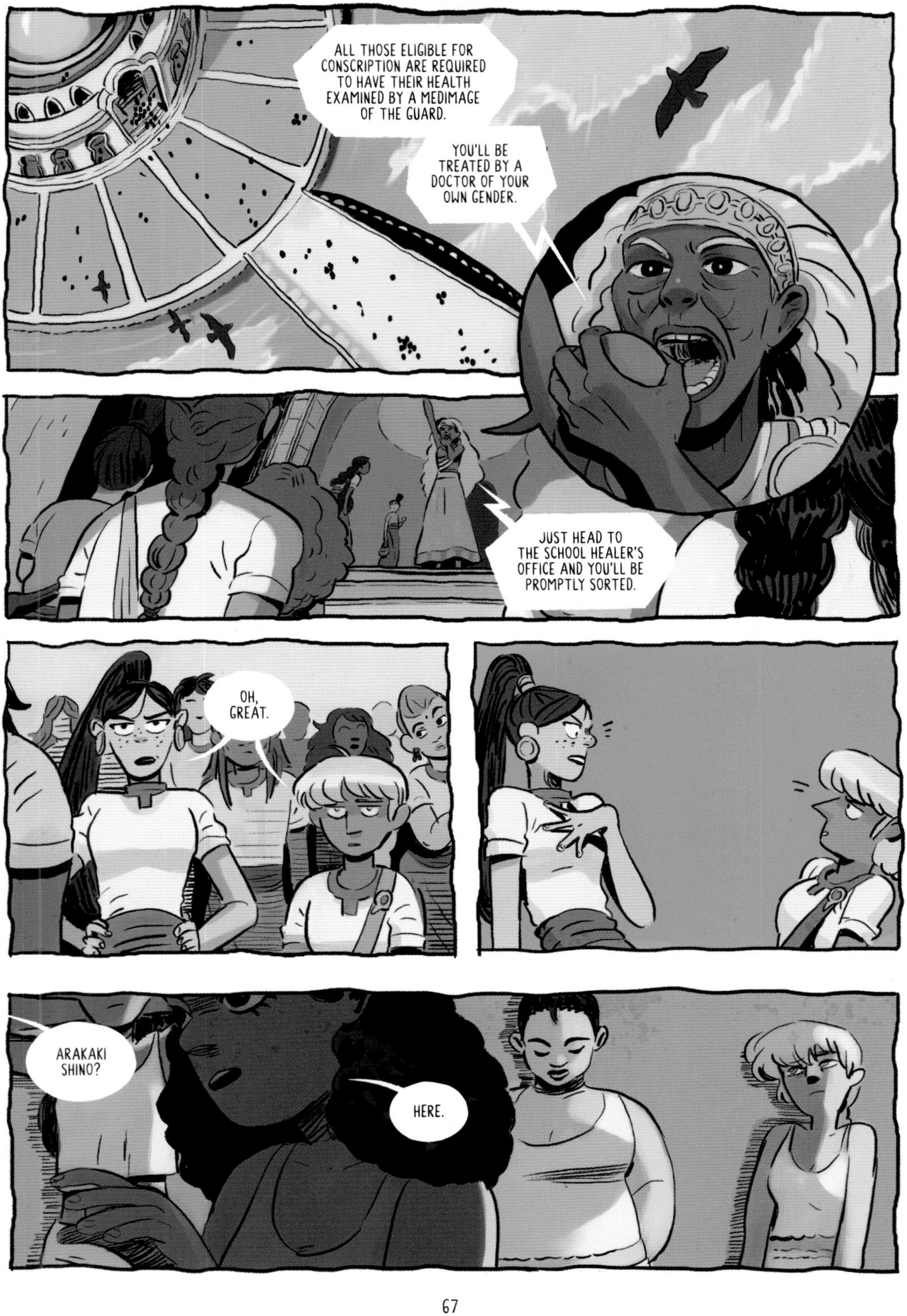
ALL THOSE ELIGIBLE FOR CONSCRIPTION ARE REQUIRED TO HAVE THEIR HEALTH EXAMINED BY A MEDIMAGE OF THE GUARD.
YOU'LL BE TREATED BY A DOCTOR OF YOUR OWN GENDER.
JUST HEAD TO THE SCHOOL HEALER'S OFFICE AND YOU'LL BE PROMPTLY SORTED.
OH, GREAT.
ARAKAKI SHINO?
HERE.

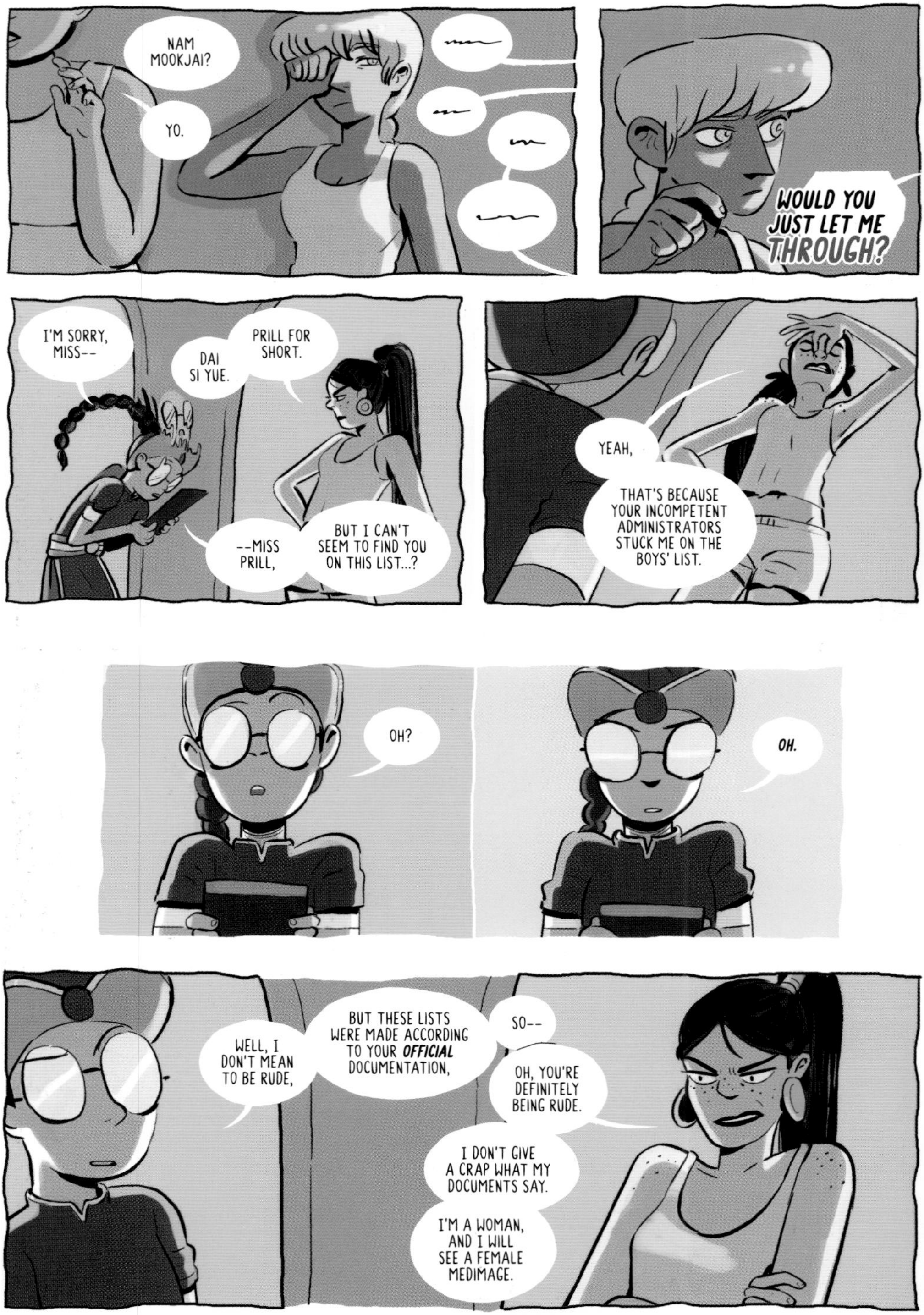
NAM MOOKJAI?
YO.
WOULD YOU JUST LET ME THROUGH?
I'M SORRY, MISS--
DAI SI YUE.
PRILL FOR SHORT.
--MISS PRILL,
BUT I CAN'T SEEM TO FIND YOU ON THIS LIST...?
YEAH,
THAT'S BECAUSE YOUR INCOMPETENT ADMINISTRATORS STUCK ME ON THE BOYS' LIST.
OH?
OH.
WELL, I DON'T MEAN TO BE RUDE,
BUT THESE LISTS WERE MADE ACCORDING TO YOUR *OFFICIAL* DOCUMENTATION,
SO--
OH, YOU'RE DEFINITELY BEING RUDE.
I DON'T GIVE A CRAP WHAT MY DOCUMENTS SAY.
I'M A WOMAN, AND I WILL SEE A FEMALE MEDIMAGE.

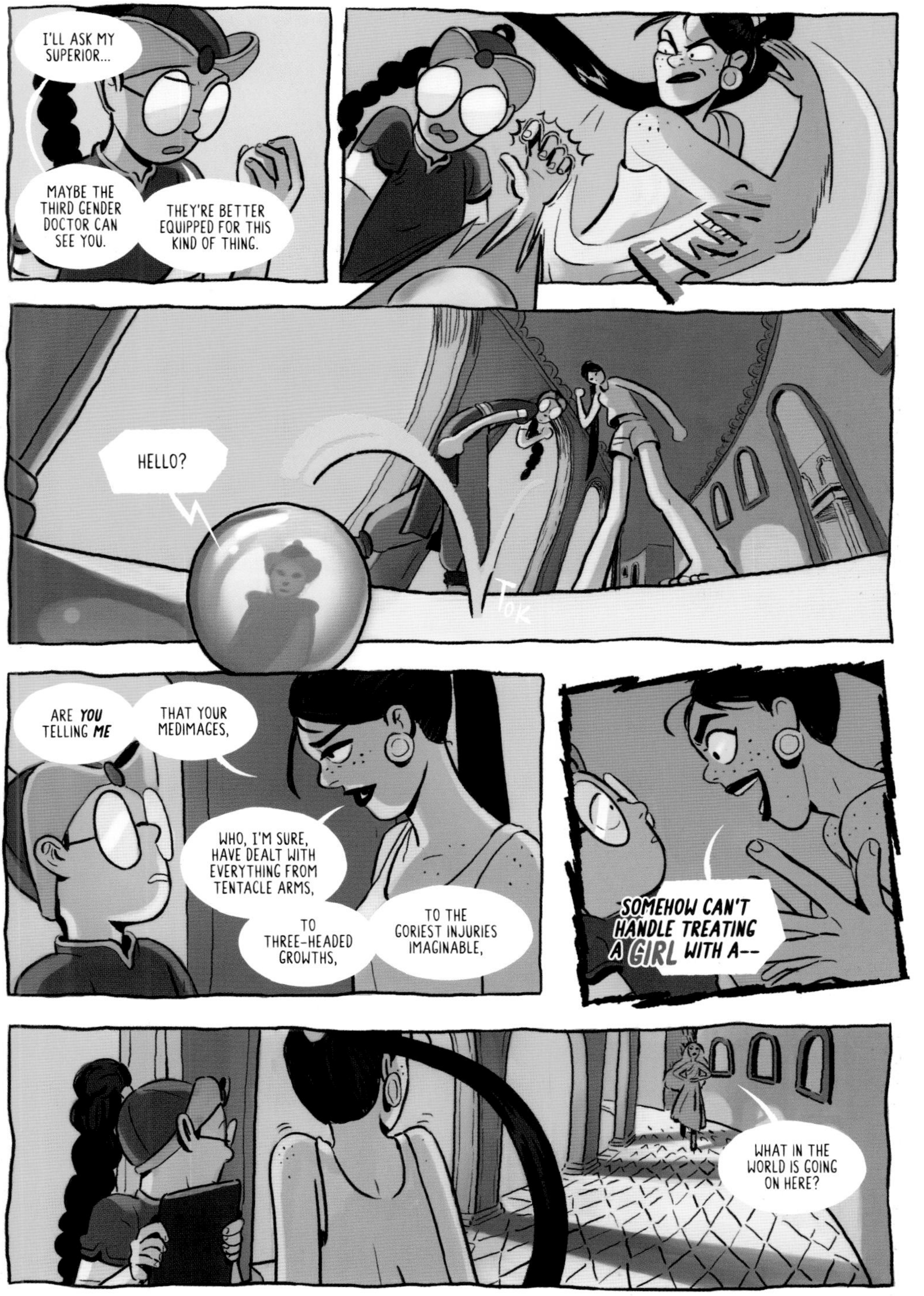
I'LL ASK MY SUPERIOR...
MAYBE THE THIRD GENDER DOCTOR CAN SEE YOU.
THEY'RE BETTER EQUIPPED FOR THIS KIND OF THING.
HELLO?
TOK
ARE YOU TELLING ME
THAT YOUR MEDIMAGES,
WHO, I'M SURE, HAVE DEALT WITH EVERYTHING FROM TENTACLE ARMS,
TO THREE-HEADED GROWTHS,
TO THE GORIEST INJURIES IMAGINABLE,
SOMEHOW CAN'T HANDLE TREATING A GIRL WITH A--
WHAT IN THE WORLD IS GOING ON HERE?

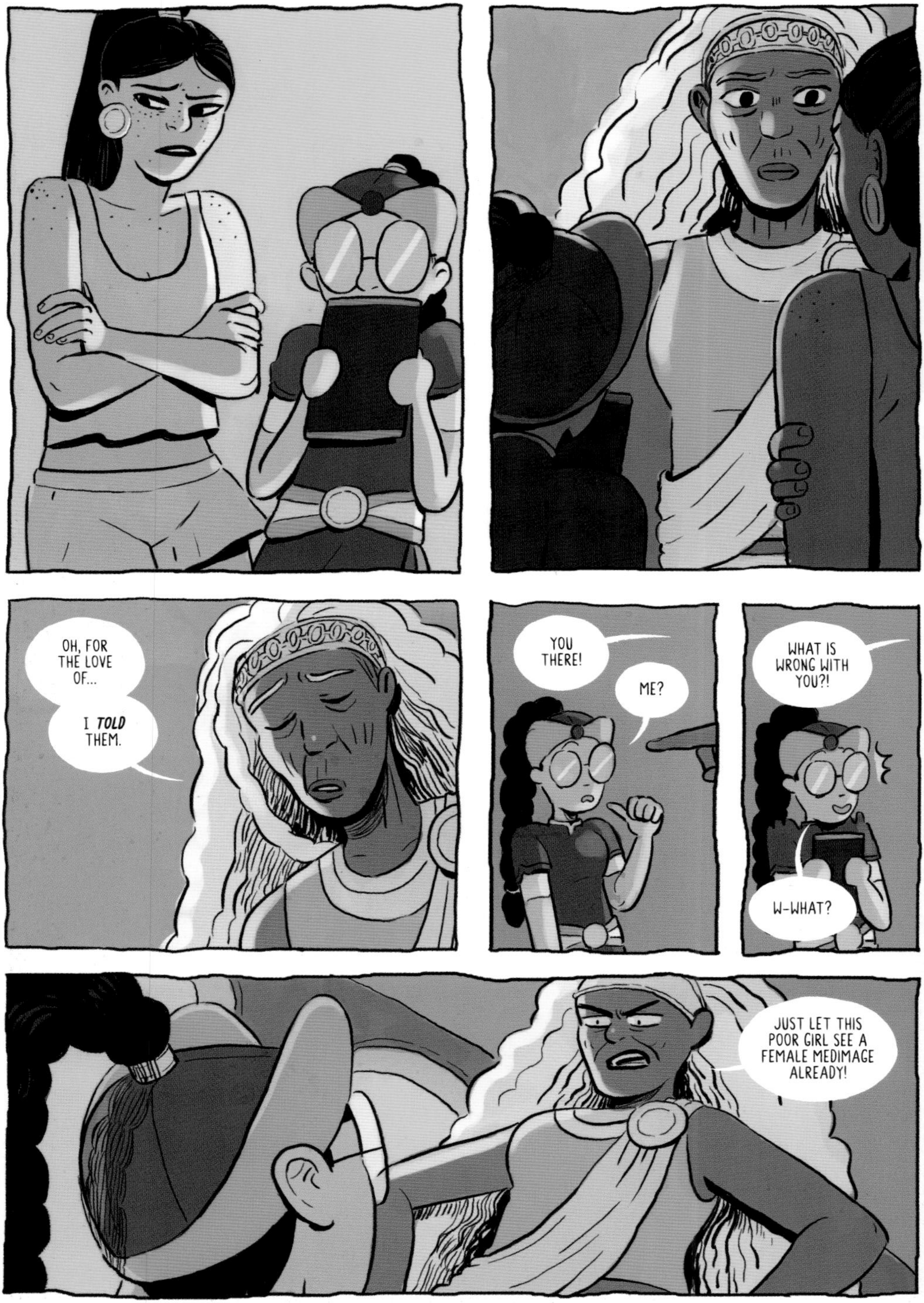
OH, FOR THE LOVE OF...
I *TOLD* THEM.
YOU THERE!
ME?
WHAT IS WRONG WITH YOU?!
W-WHAT?
JUST LET THIS POOR GIRL SEE A FEMALE MEDIMAGE ALREADY!

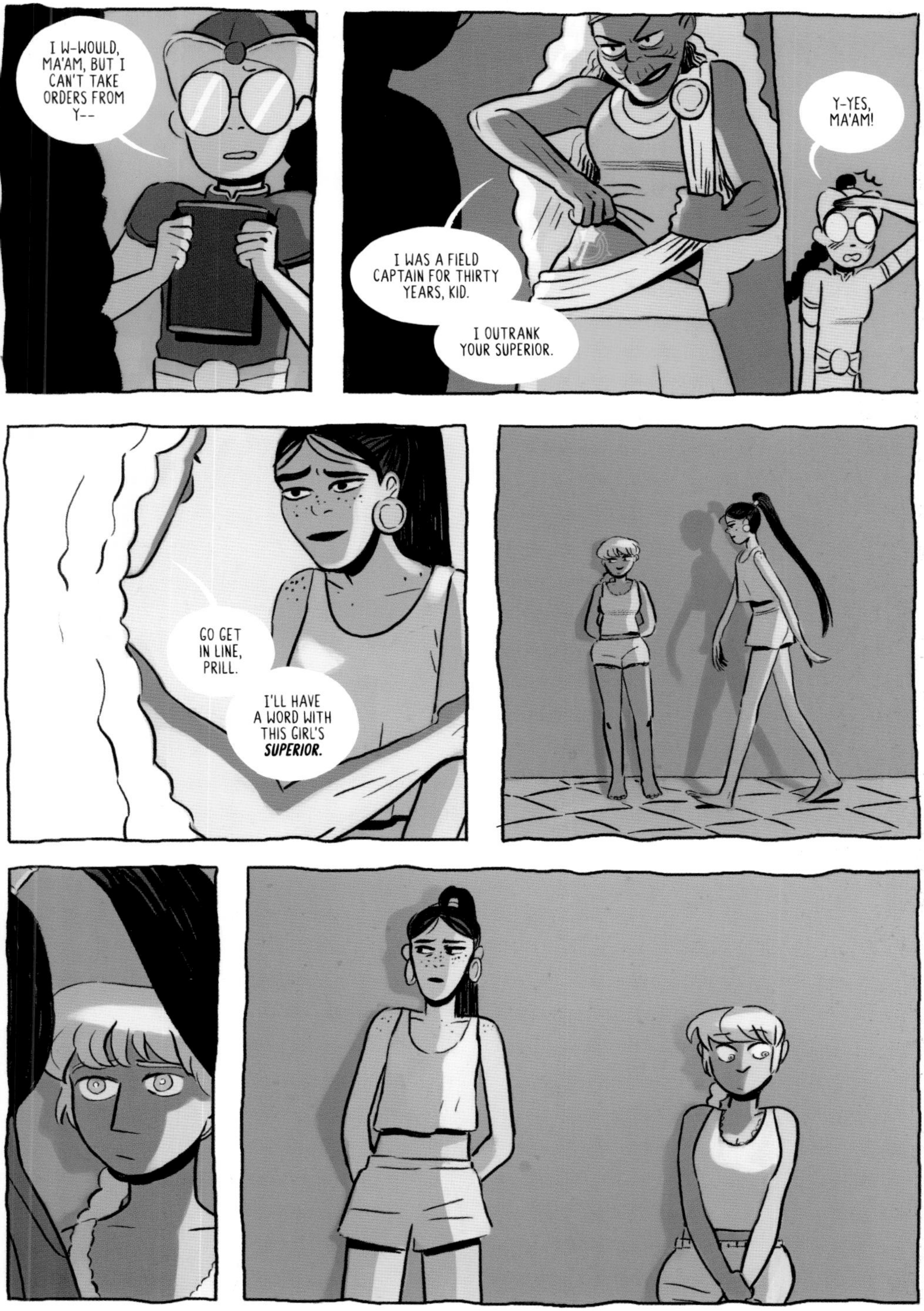
I W-WOULD, MA'AM, BUT I CAN'T TAKE ORDERS FROM Y--
I WAS A FIELD CAPTAIN FOR THIRTY YEARS, KID.
I OUTRANK YOUR SUPERIOR.
Y-YES, MA'AM!
GO GET IN LINE, PRILL.
I'LL HAVE A WORD WITH THIS GIRL'S ***SUPERIOR.***

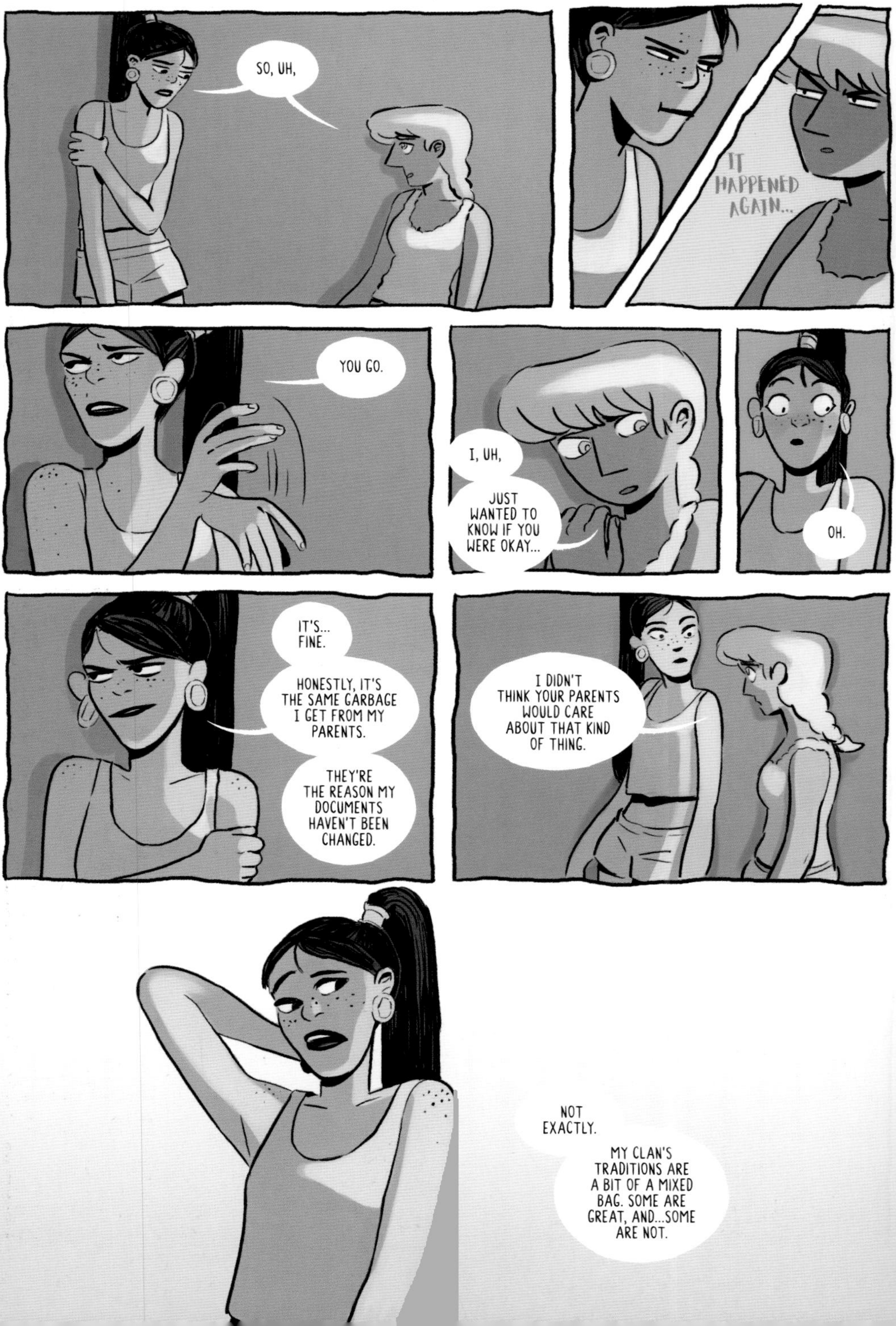

SO, UH,
IT HAPPENED AGAIN...
YOU GO.
I, UH,
JUST WANTED TO KNOW IF YOU WERE OKAY...
OH.
IT'S... FINE.
HONESTLY, IT'S THE SAME GARBAGE I GET FROM MY PARENTS.
THEY'RE THE REASON MY DOCUMENTS HAVEN'T BEEN CHANGED.
I DIDN'T THINK YOUR PARENTS WOULD CARE ABOUT THAT KIND OF THING.
NOT EXACTLY.
MY CLAN'S TRADITIONS ARE A BIT OF A MIXED BAG. SOME ARE GREAT, AND...SOME ARE NOT.

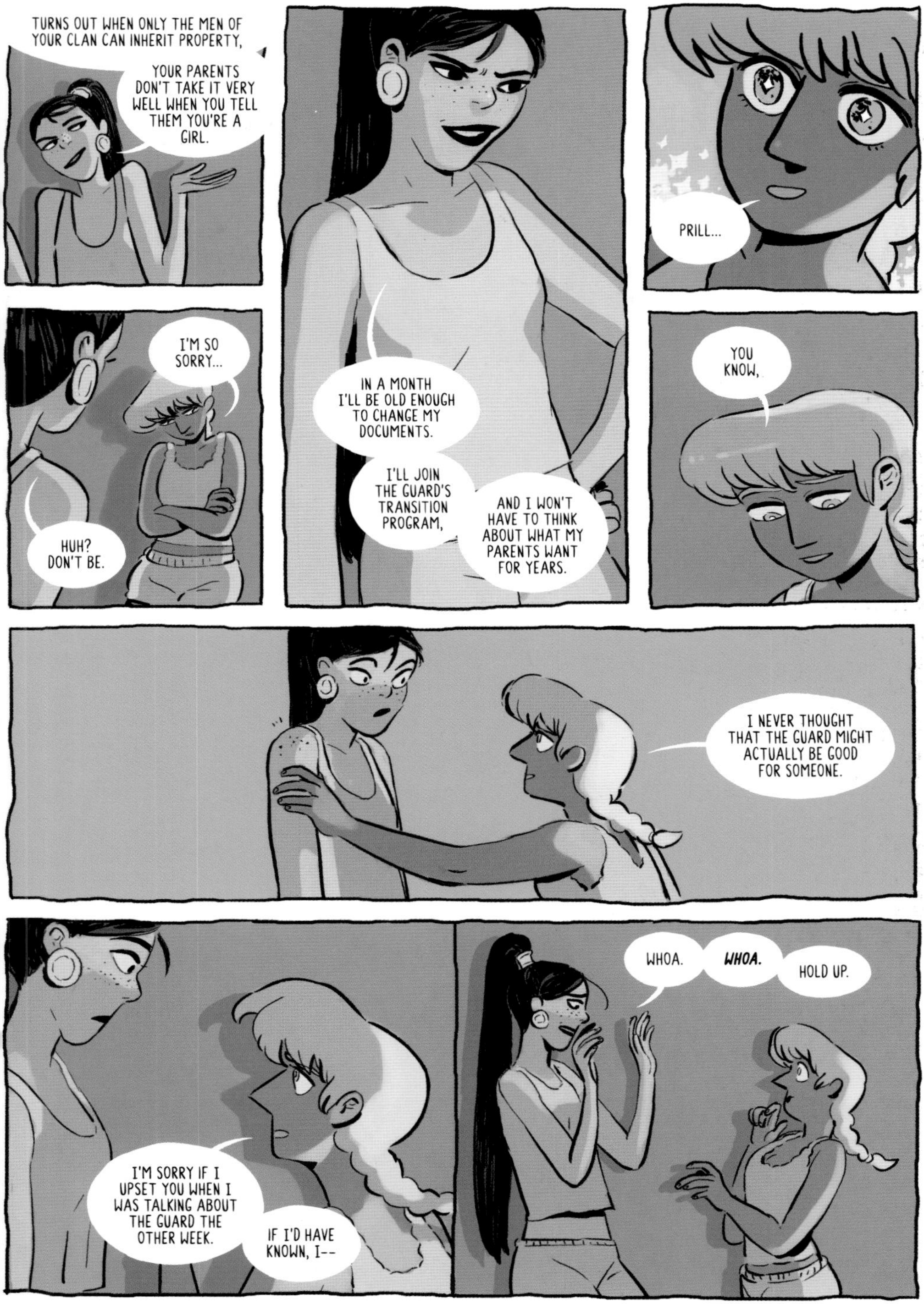

TURNS OUT WHEN ONLY THE MEN OF YOUR CLAN CAN INHERIT PROPERTY,
YOUR PARENTS DON'T TAKE IT VERY WELL WHEN YOU TELL THEM YOU'RE A GIRL.
PRILL...
I'M SO SORRY...
HUH? DON'T BE.
IN A MONTH I'LL BE OLD ENOUGH TO CHANGE MY DOCUMENTS.
I'LL JOIN THE GUARD'S TRANSITION PROGRAM,
AND I WON'T HAVE TO THINK ABOUT WHAT MY PARENTS WANT FOR YEARS.
YOU KNOW,
I NEVER THOUGHT THAT THE GUARD MIGHT ACTUALLY BE GOOD FOR SOMEONE.
I'M SORRY IF I UPSET YOU WHEN I WAS TALKING ABOUT THE GUARD THE OTHER WEEK.
IF I'D HAVE KNOWN, I--
WHOA.
WHOA.
HOLD UP.

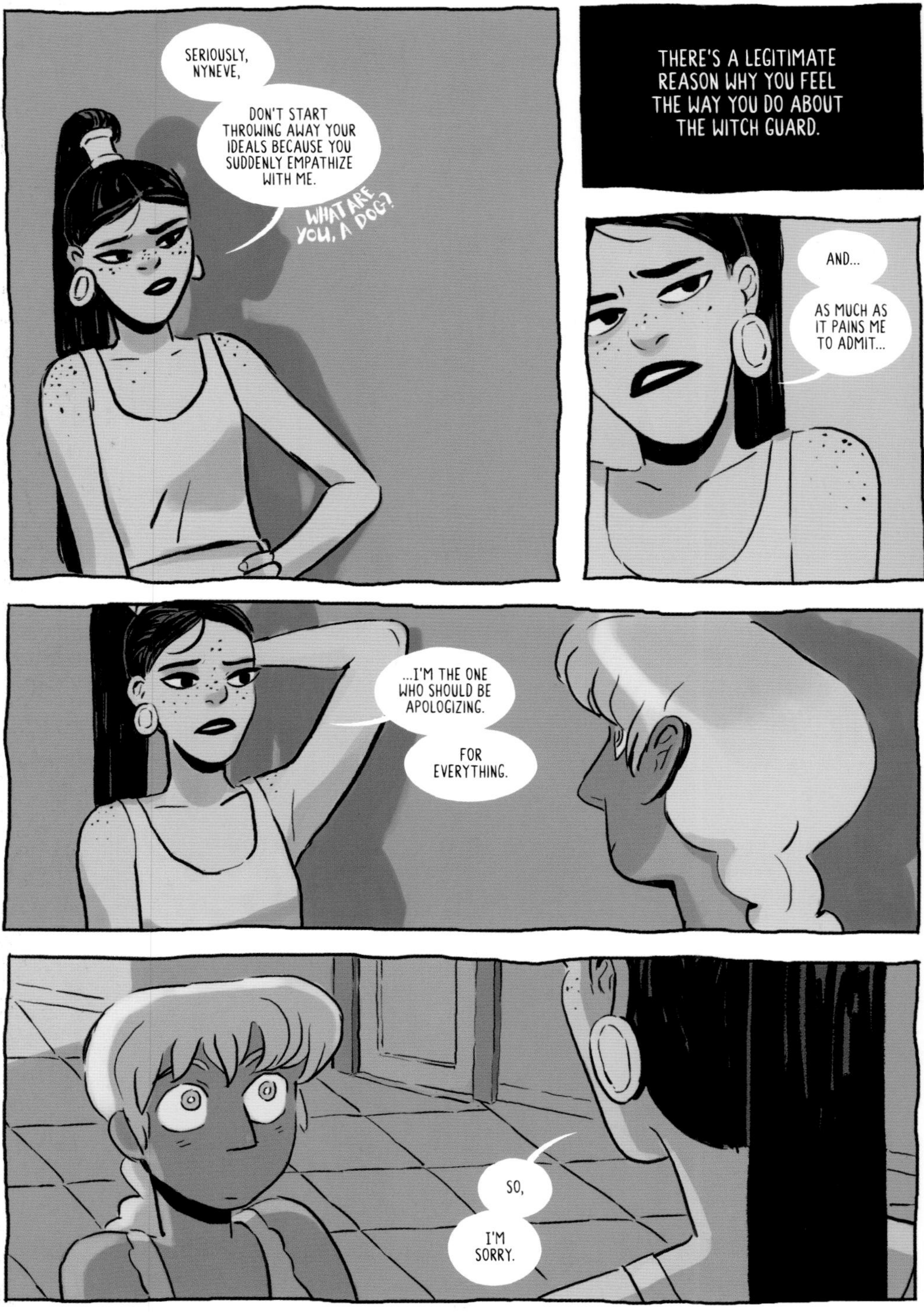
SERIOUSLY, NYNEVE,
DON'T START THROWING AWAY YOUR IDEALS BECAUSE YOU SUDDENLY EMPATHIZE WITH ME.
WHAT ARE YOU, A DOG?
THERE'S A LEGITIMATE REASON WHY YOU FEEL THE WAY YOU DO ABOUT THE WITCH GUARD.
AND...
AS MUCH AS IT PAINS ME TO ADMIT...
...I'M THE ONE WHO SHOULD BE APOLOGIZING.
FOR EVERYTHING.
SO,
I'M SORRY.

HAHA.
WHAT ARE YOU LAUGHING ABOUT?
I DON'T GIVE OUT APOLOGIES TO JUST ANYONE.
AHHA, I DON'T KNOW!
YOU'VE JUST NEVER ACTED THIS NICE TO ME BEFORE.
IT KINDA MAKES ME NERVOUS.
WELL...
I NEVER KNEW HOW MUCH WE HAD IN COMMON BEFORE.
HERE.
YOUR HAND?
YOU'RE SUPPOSED TO SHAKE IT!

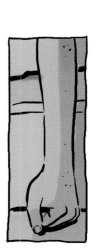

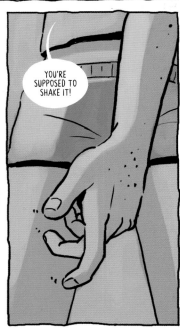

I'M OFFERING A TRUCE BETWEEN OLD RIVALS.

WHAT DO YOU SAY?

FRIENDS?

SURE. FRIENDS...

OR SOMETHING LIKE IT.

YOU REALLY THOUGHT OF ME AS A RIVAL?

PLEASE JUST SHAKE MY HAND.

HEH.

NYNEVE AHMADZAI?

YEP, COMING.

SHOOT.

HEY,

GOOD LUCK.

THANKS.

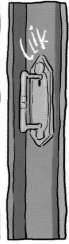

CLIK

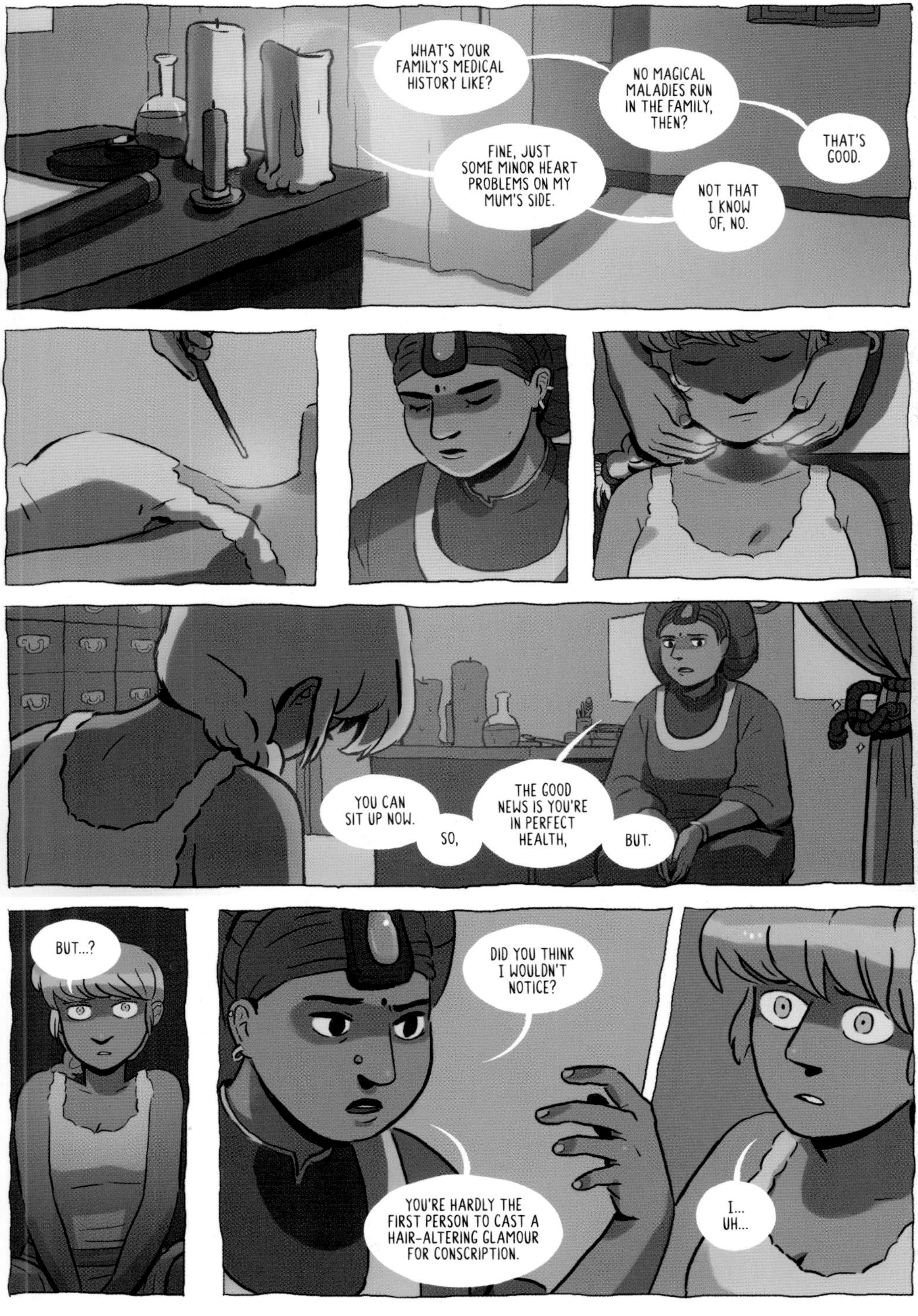
WHAT'S YOUR FAMILY'S MEDICAL HISTORY LIKE?
FINE, JUST SOME MINOR HEART PROBLEMS ON MY MUM'S SIDE.
NO MAGICAL MALADIES RUN IN THE FAMILY, THEN?
NOT THAT I KNOW OF, NO.
THAT'S GOOD.
YOU CAN SIT UP NOW.
SO,
THE GOOD NEWS IS YOU'RE IN PERFECT HEALTH,
BUT.
BUT...?
DID YOU THINK I WOULDN'T NOTICE?
YOU'RE HARDLY THE FIRST PERSON TO CAST A HAIR-ALTERING GLAMOUR FOR CONSCRIPTION.
I... UH...

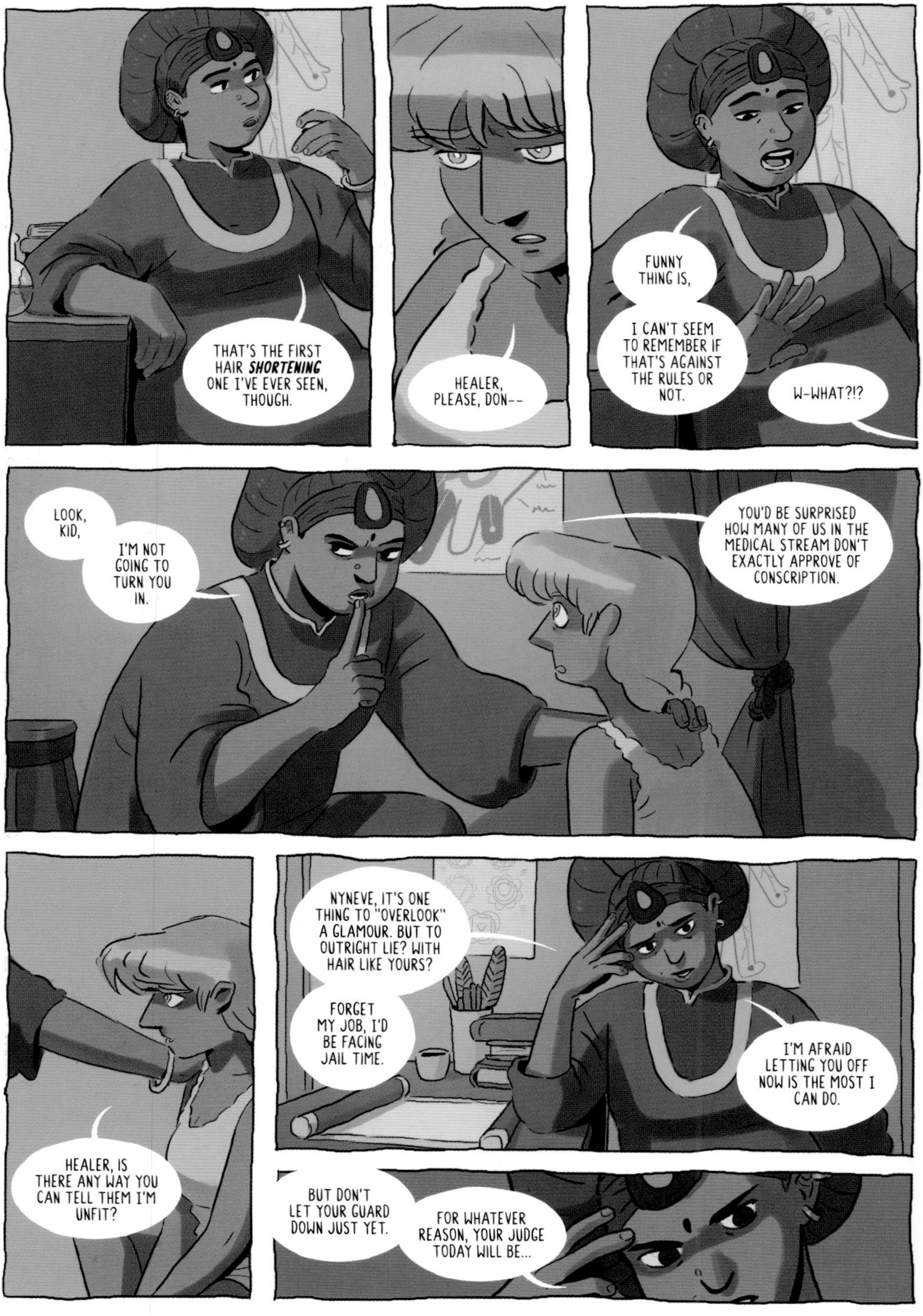
THAT'S THE FIRST HAIR **SHORTENING** ONE I'VE EVER SEEN, THOUGH.
HEALER, PLEASE, DON--
FUNNY THING IS,
I CAN'T SEEM TO REMEMBER IF THAT'S AGAINST THE RULES OR NOT.
W-WHAT?!?
LOOK, KID,
I'M NOT GOING TO TURN YOU IN.
YOU'D BE SURPRISED HOW MANY OF US IN THE MEDICAL STREAM DON'T EXACTLY APPROVE OF CONSCRIPTION.
HEALER, IS THERE ANY WAY YOU CAN TELL THEM I'M UNFIT?
NYNEVE, IT'S ONE THING TO "OVERLOOK" A GLAMOUR. BUT TO OUTRIGHT LIE? WITH HAIR LIKE YOURS?
FORGET MY JOB, I'D BE FACING JAIL TIME.
I'M AFRAID LETTING YOU OFF NOW IS THE MOST I CAN DO.
BUT DON'T LET YOUR GUARD DOWN JUST YET.
FOR WHATEVER REASON, YOUR JUDGE TODAY WILL BE...

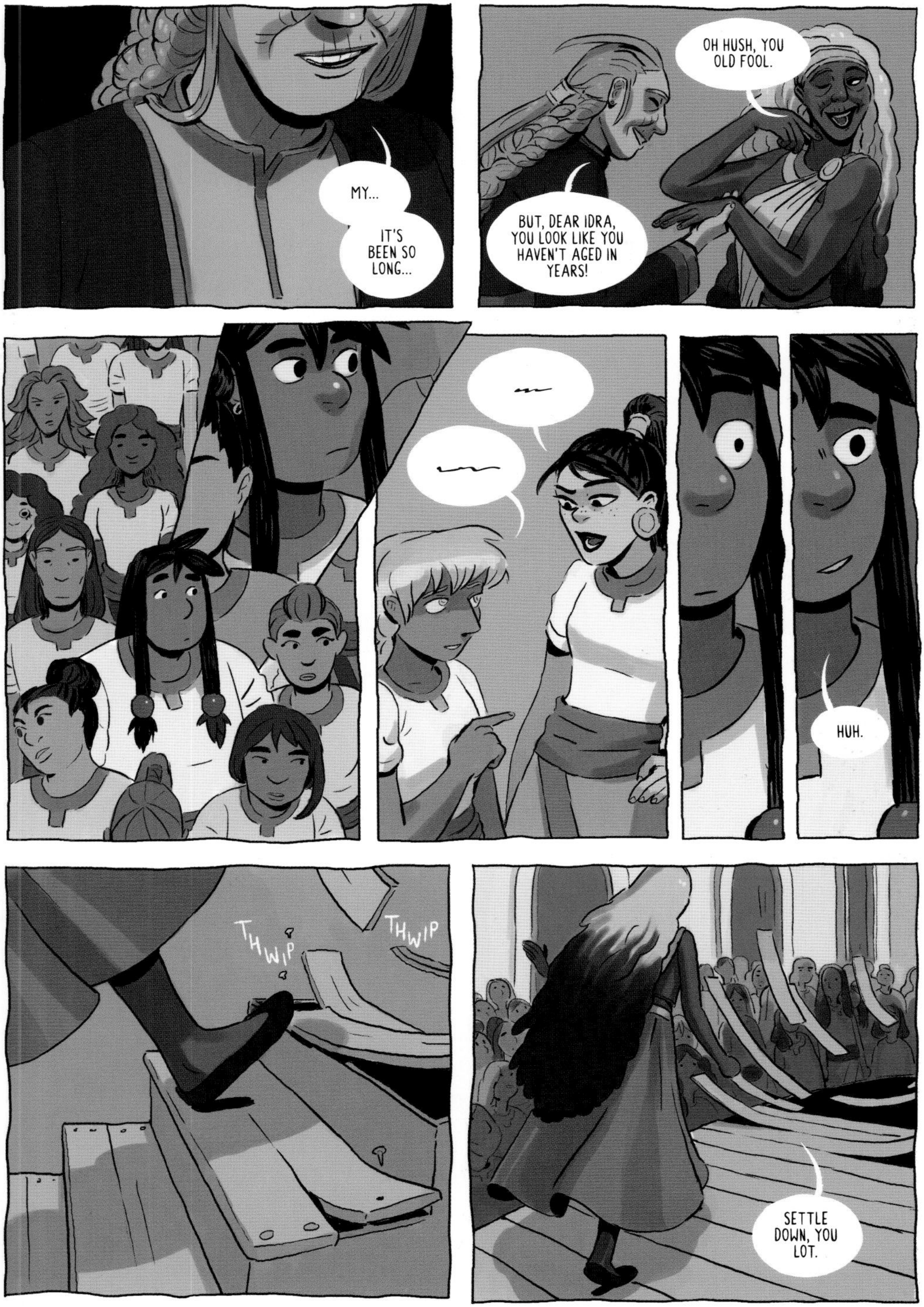
MY...
IT'S BEEN SO LONG...
OH HUSH, YOU OLD FOOL.
BUT, DEAR IDRA, YOU LOOK LIKE YOU HAVEN'T AGED IN YEARS!
HUH.
THWIP
THWIP
SETTLE DOWN, YOU LOT.

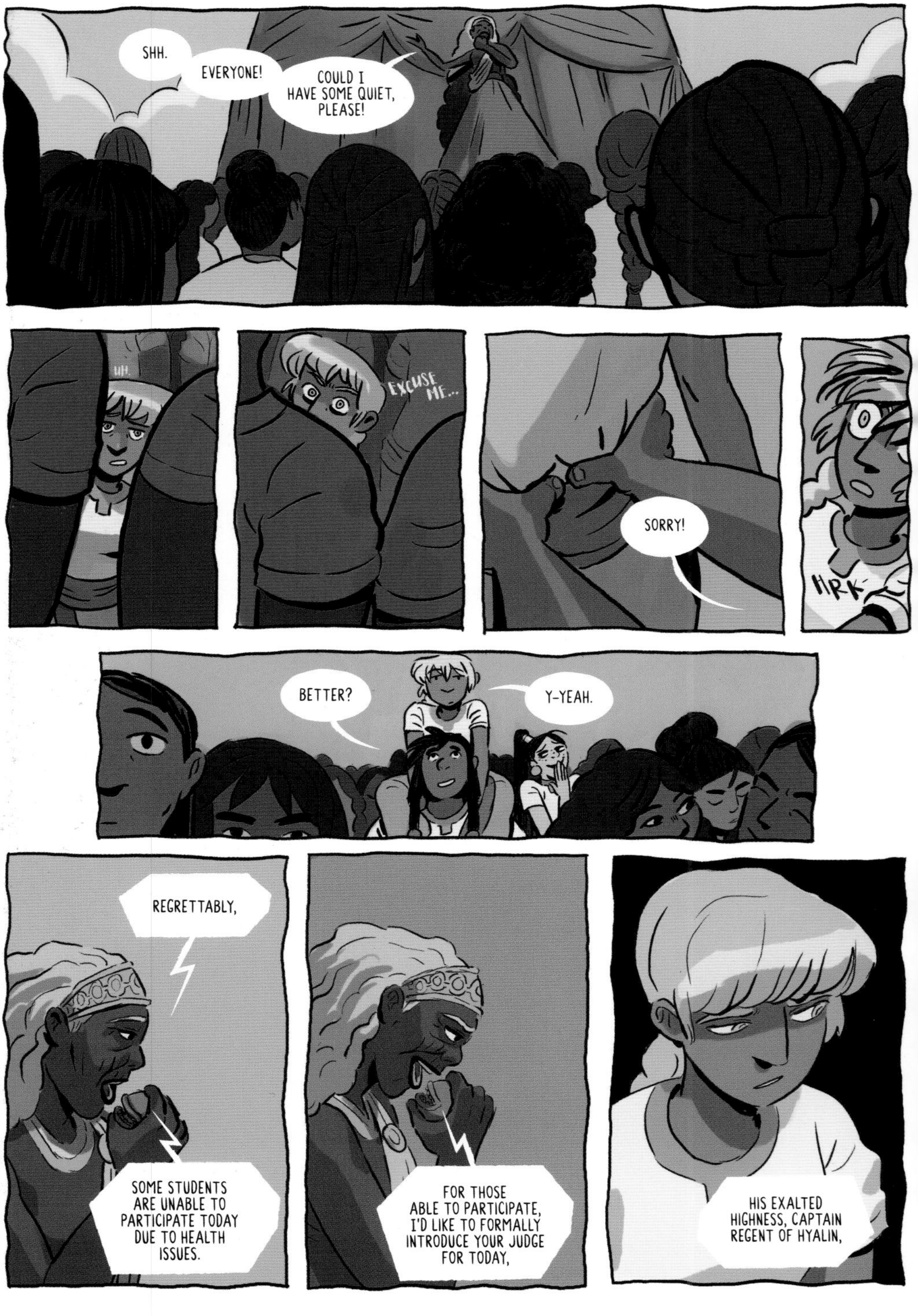
SHH.
EVERYONE!
COULD I HAVE SOME QUIET, PLEASE!
UH.
EXCUSE ME...
SORRY!
HRK
BETTER?
Y-YEAH.
REGRETTABLY,
SOME STUDENTS ARE UNABLE TO PARTICIPATE TODAY DUE TO HEALTH ISSUES.
FOR THOSE ABLE TO PARTICIPATE, I'D LIKE TO FORMALLY INTRODUCE YOUR JUDGE FOR TODAY,
HIS EXALTED HIGHNESS, CAPTAIN REGENT OF HYALIN,

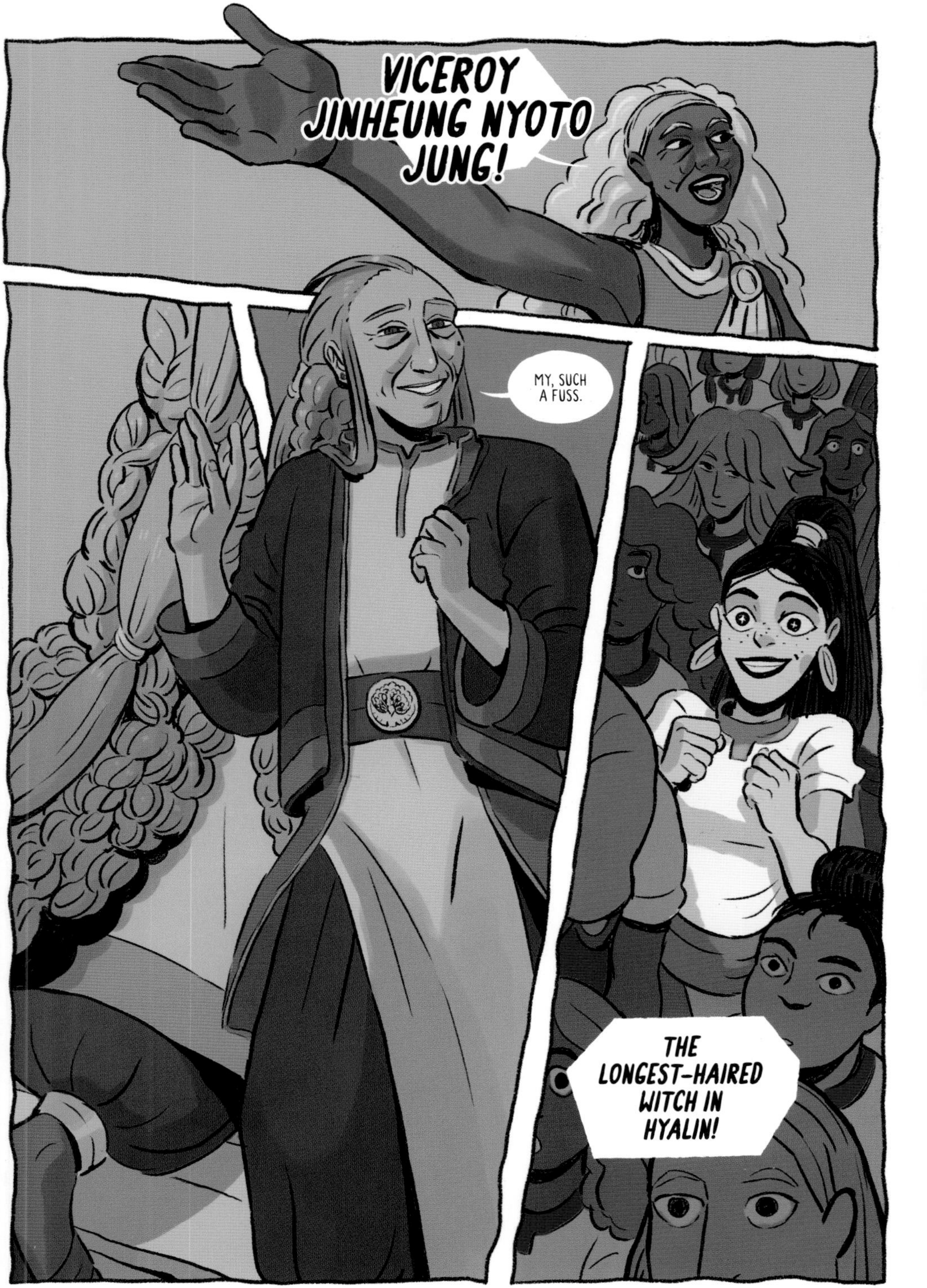
VICEROY JINHEUNG NYOTO JUNG!
MY, SUCH A FUSS.
THE LONGEST-HAIRED WITCH IN HYALIN!

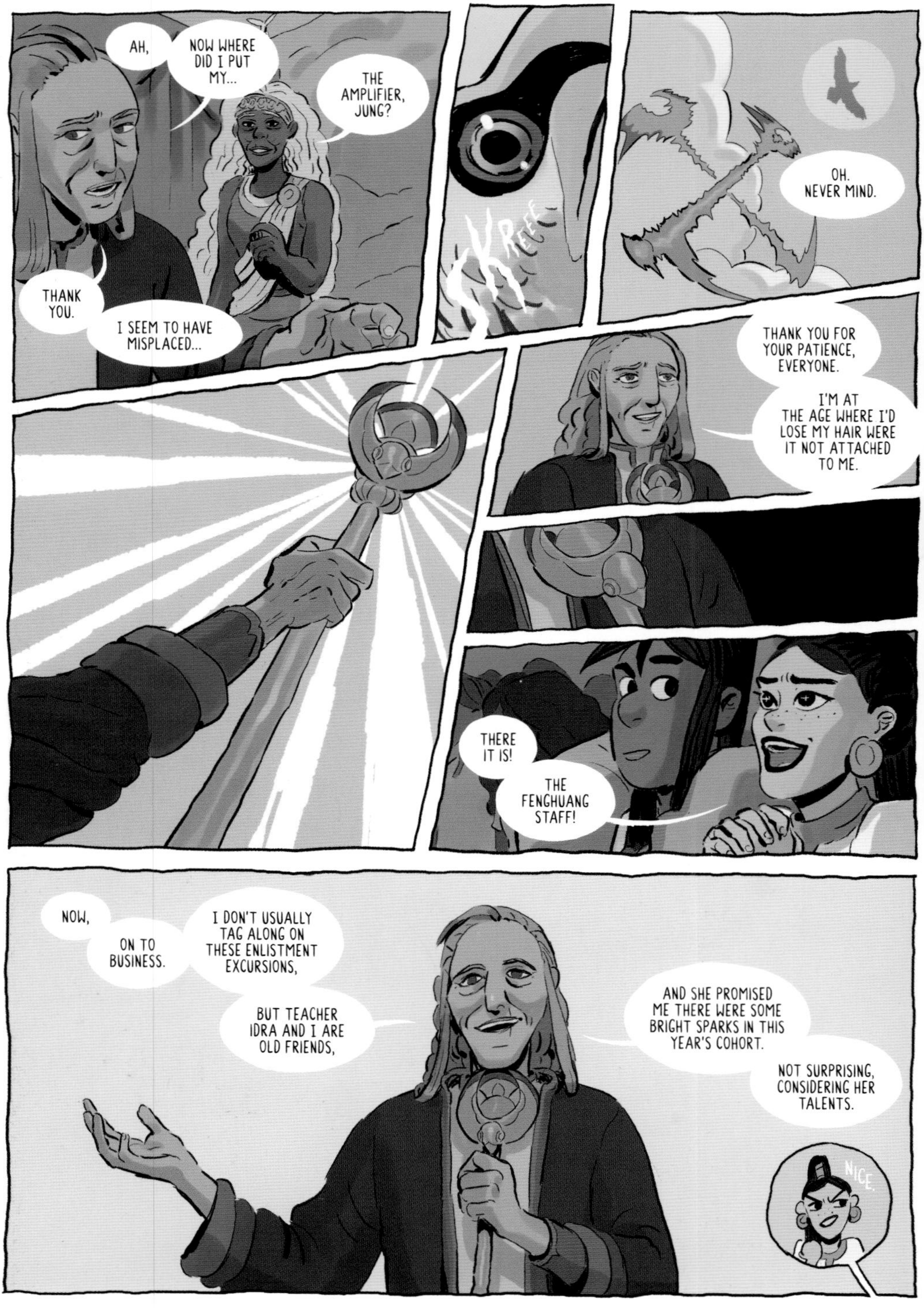
AH,
NOW WHERE DID I PUT MY...
THE AMPLIFIER, JUNG?
THANK YOU.
I SEEM TO HAVE MISPLACED...
SKREEE
OH. NEVER MIND.
THANK YOU FOR YOUR PATIENCE, EVERYONE.
I'M AT THE AGE WHERE I'D LOSE MY HAIR WERE IT NOT ATTACHED TO ME.
THERE IT IS!
THE FENGHUANG STAFF!
NOW,
ON TO BUSINESS.
I DON'T USUALLY TAG ALONG ON THESE ENLISTMENT EXCURSIONS,
BUT TEACHER IDRA AND I ARE OLD FRIENDS,
AND SHE PROMISED ME THERE WERE SOME BRIGHT SPARKS IN THIS YEAR'S COHORT.
NOT SURPRISING, CONSIDERING HER TALENTS.
NICE.

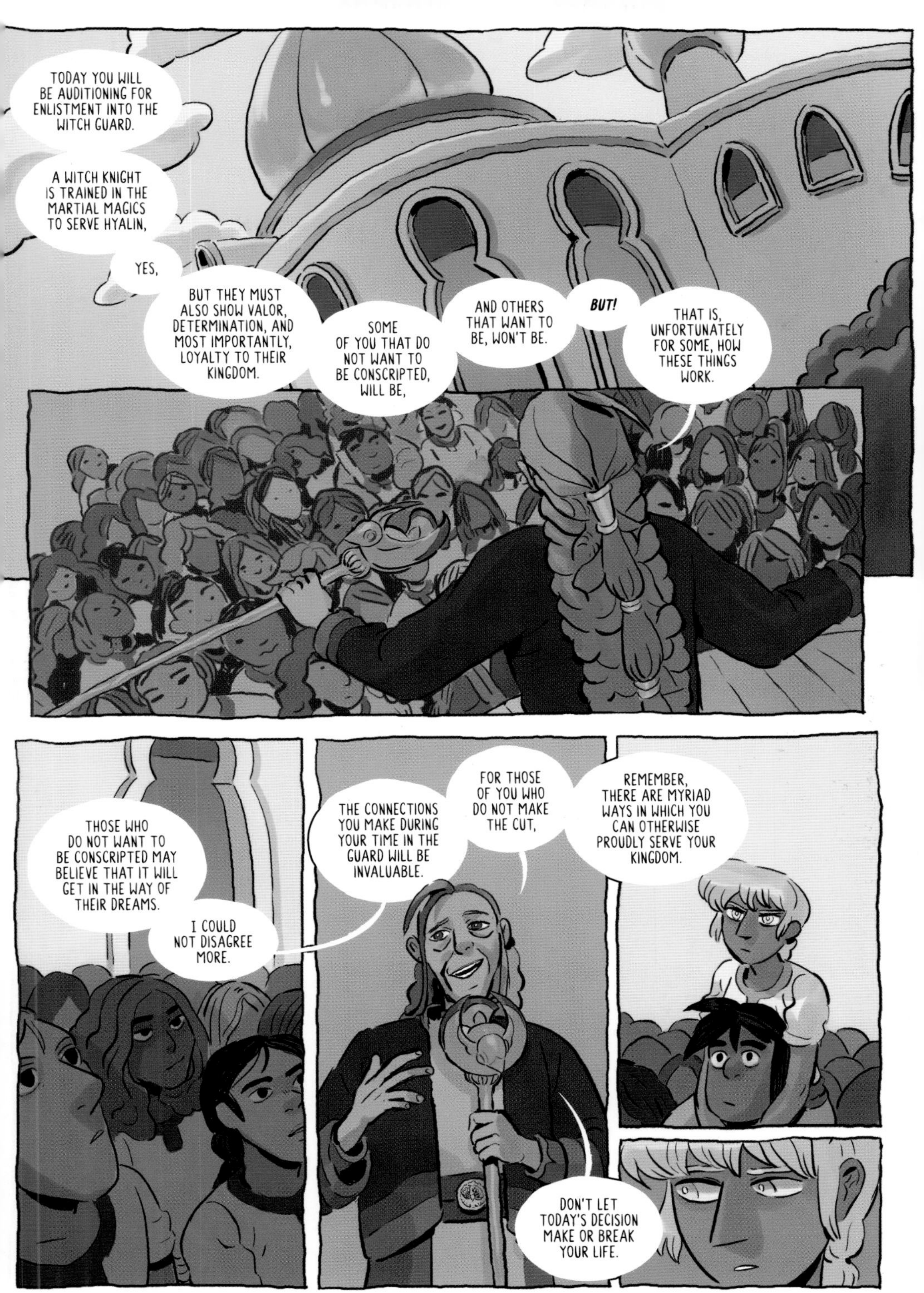
TODAY YOU WILL BE AUDITIONING FOR ENLISTMENT INTO THE WITCH GUARD.
A WITCH KNIGHT IS TRAINED IN THE MARTIAL MAGICS TO SERVE HYALIN,
YES,
BUT THEY MUST ALSO SHOW VALOR, DETERMINATION, AND MOST IMPORTANTLY, LOYALTY TO THEIR KINGDOM.
SOME OF YOU THAT DO NOT WANT TO BE CONSCRIPTED, WILL BE,
AND OTHERS THAT WANT TO BE, WON'T BE.
BUT!
THAT IS, UNFORTUNATELY FOR SOME, HOW THESE THINGS WORK.
THOSE WHO DO NOT WANT TO BE CONSCRIPTED MAY BELIEVE THAT IT WILL GET IN THE WAY OF THEIR DREAMS.
I COULD NOT DISAGREE MORE.
THE CONNECTIONS YOU MAKE DURING YOUR TIME IN THE GUARD WILL BE INVALUABLE.
FOR THOSE OF YOU WHO DO NOT MAKE THE CUT,
REMEMBER, THERE ARE MYRIAD WAYS IN WHICH YOU CAN OTHERWISE PROUDLY SERVE YOUR KINGDOM.
DON'T LET TODAY'S DECISION MAKE OR BREAK YOUR LIFE.

AH,

I'M SORRY.

I MAY HAVE PRATTLED ON TOO LONG.

WELL THEN,

WITHOUT FURTHER ADO, I PRESENT TO YOU THIS YEAR'S TEST:

A HIGH STAKES GAME...

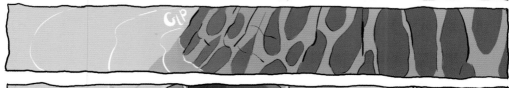

GIP

...OF ***ROBIN'S NEST.***

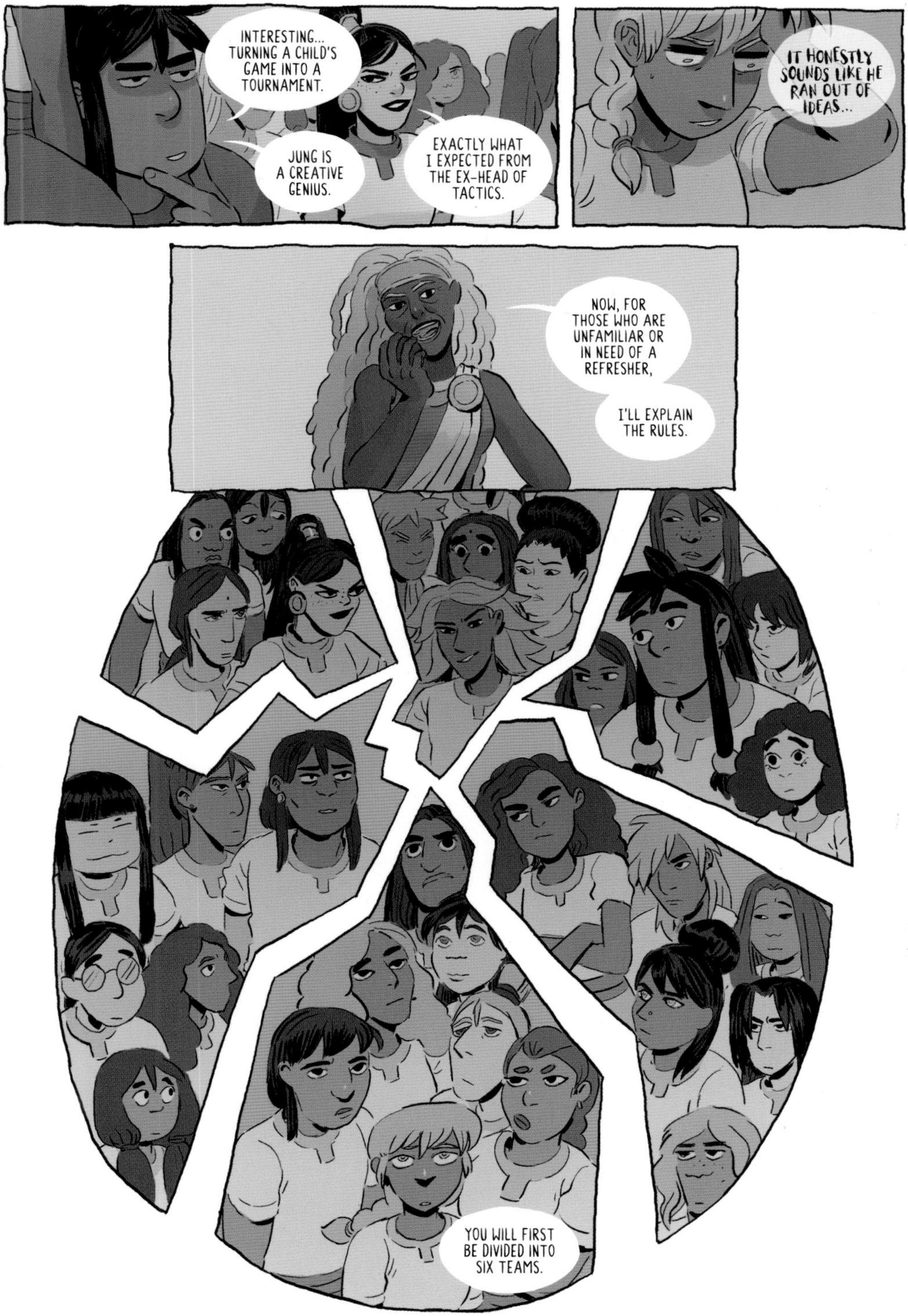

INTERESTING... TURNING A CHILD'S GAME INTO A TOURNAMENT.
JUNG IS A CREATIVE GENIUS.
EXACTLY WHAT I EXPECTED FROM THE EX-HEAD OF TACTICS.
IT HONESTLY SOUNDS LIKE HE RAN OUT OF IDEAS...
NOW, FOR THOSE WHO ARE UNFAMILIAR OR IN NEED OF A REFRESHER,
I'LL EXPLAIN THE RULES.
YOU WILL FIRST BE DIVIDED INTO SIX TEAMS.

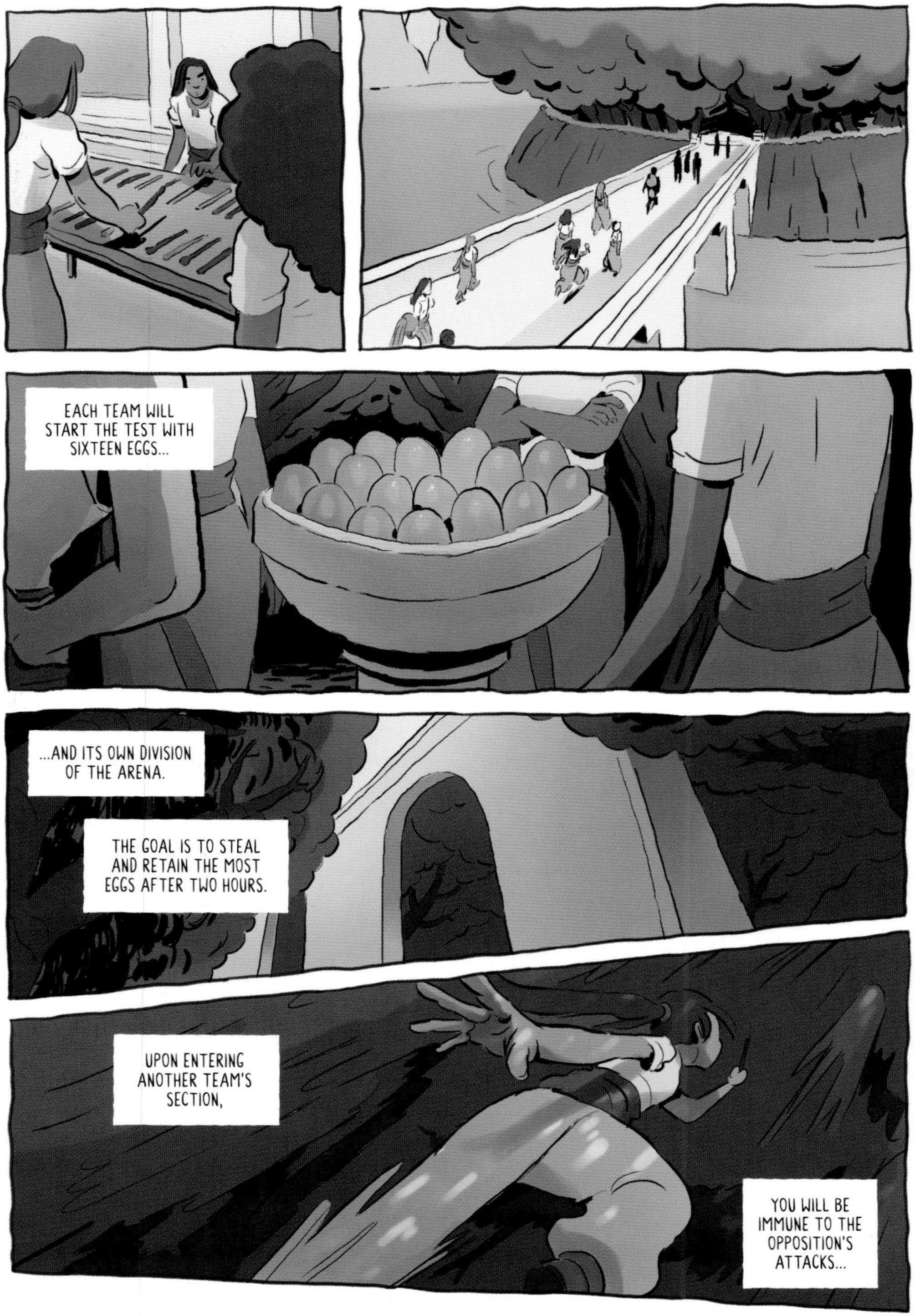
EACH TEAM WILL START THE TEST WITH SIXTEEN EGGS...
...AND ITS OWN DIVISION OF THE ARENA.
THE GOAL IS TO STEAL AND RETAIN THE MOST EGGS AFTER TWO HOURS.
UPON ENTERING ANOTHER TEAM'S SECTION,
YOU WILL BE IMMUNE TO THE OPPOSITION'S ATTACKS...

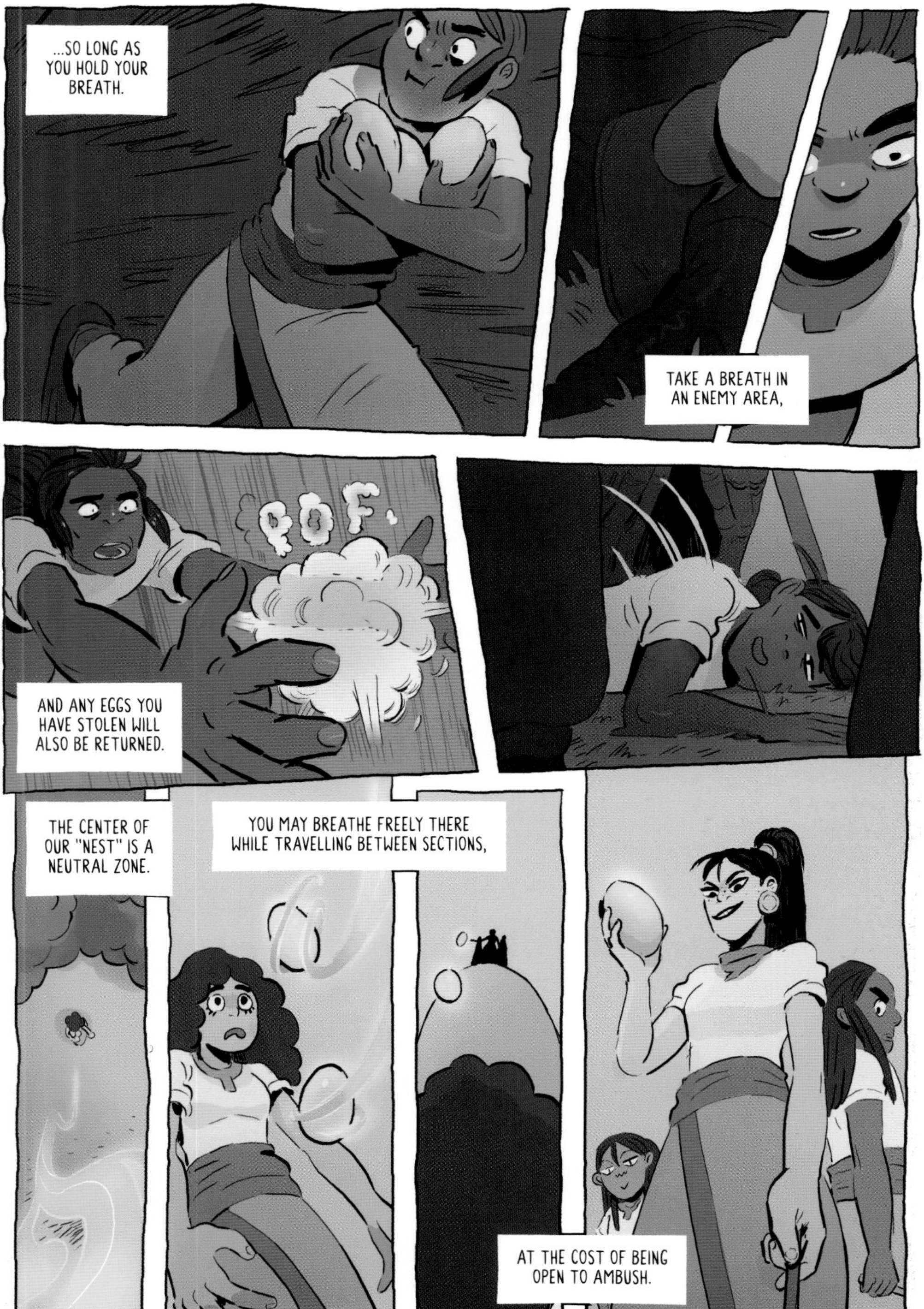
...SO LONG AS YOU HOLD YOUR BREATH.
TAKE A BREATH IN AN ENEMY AREA,
POF
AND ANY EGGS YOU HAVE STOLEN WILL ALSO BE RETURNED.
THE CENTER OF OUR "NEST" IS A NEUTRAL ZONE.
YOU MAY BREATHE FREELY THERE WHILE TRAVELLING BETWEEN SECTIONS,
AT THE COST OF BEING OPEN TO AMBUSH.

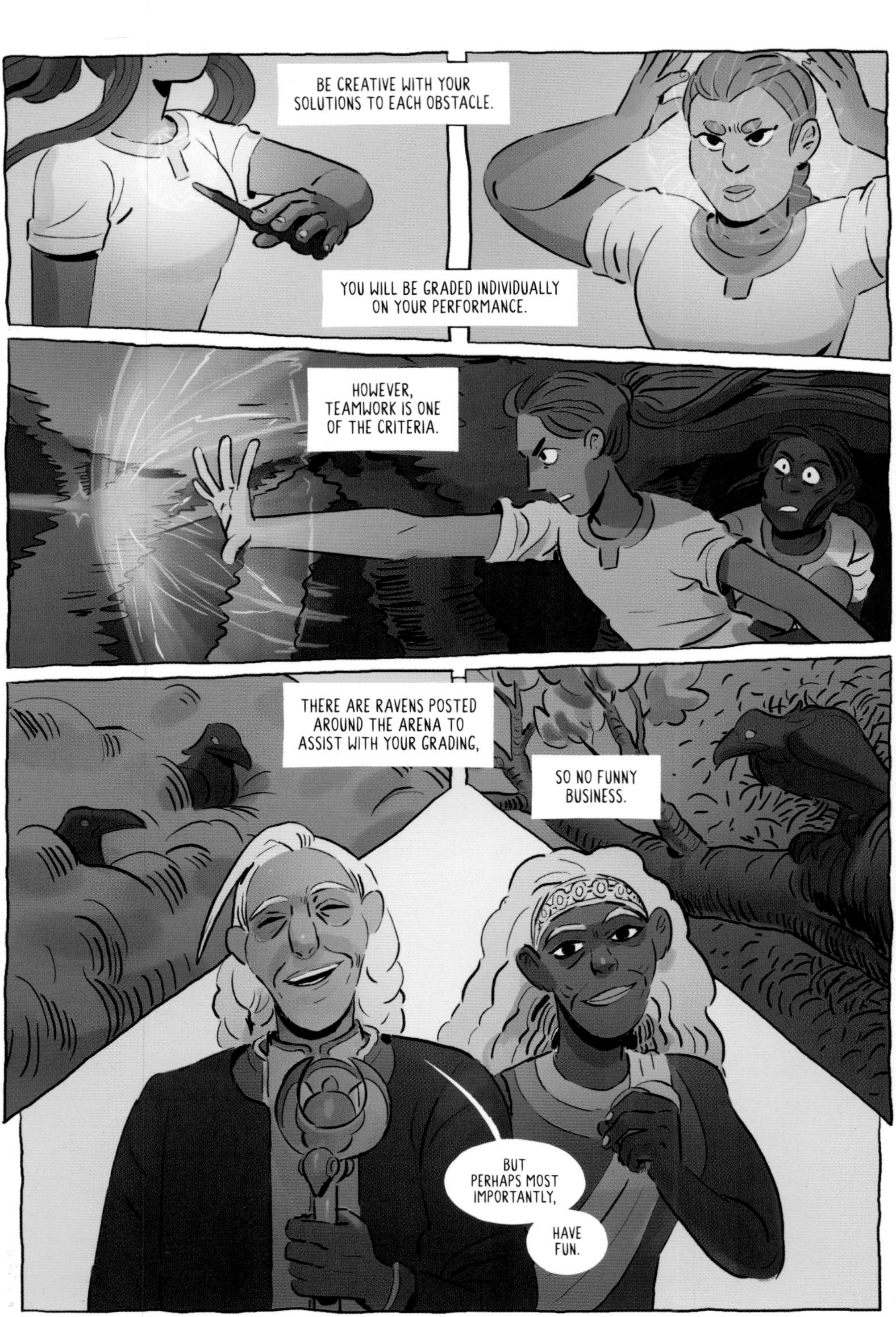
BE CREATIVE WITH YOUR SOLUTIONS TO EACH OBSTACLE.
YOU WILL BE GRADED INDIVIDUALLY ON YOUR PERFORMANCE.
HOWEVER, TEAMWORK IS ONE OF THE CRITERIA.
THERE ARE RAVENS POSTED AROUND THE ARENA TO ASSIST WITH YOUR GRADING,
SO NO FUNNY BUSINESS.
BUT PERHAPS MOST IMPORTANTLY,
HAVE FUN.

JAGA,

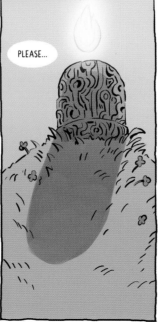

PLEASE...

LOOK OUT FOR NYNEVE TODAY,

WON'T YOU?

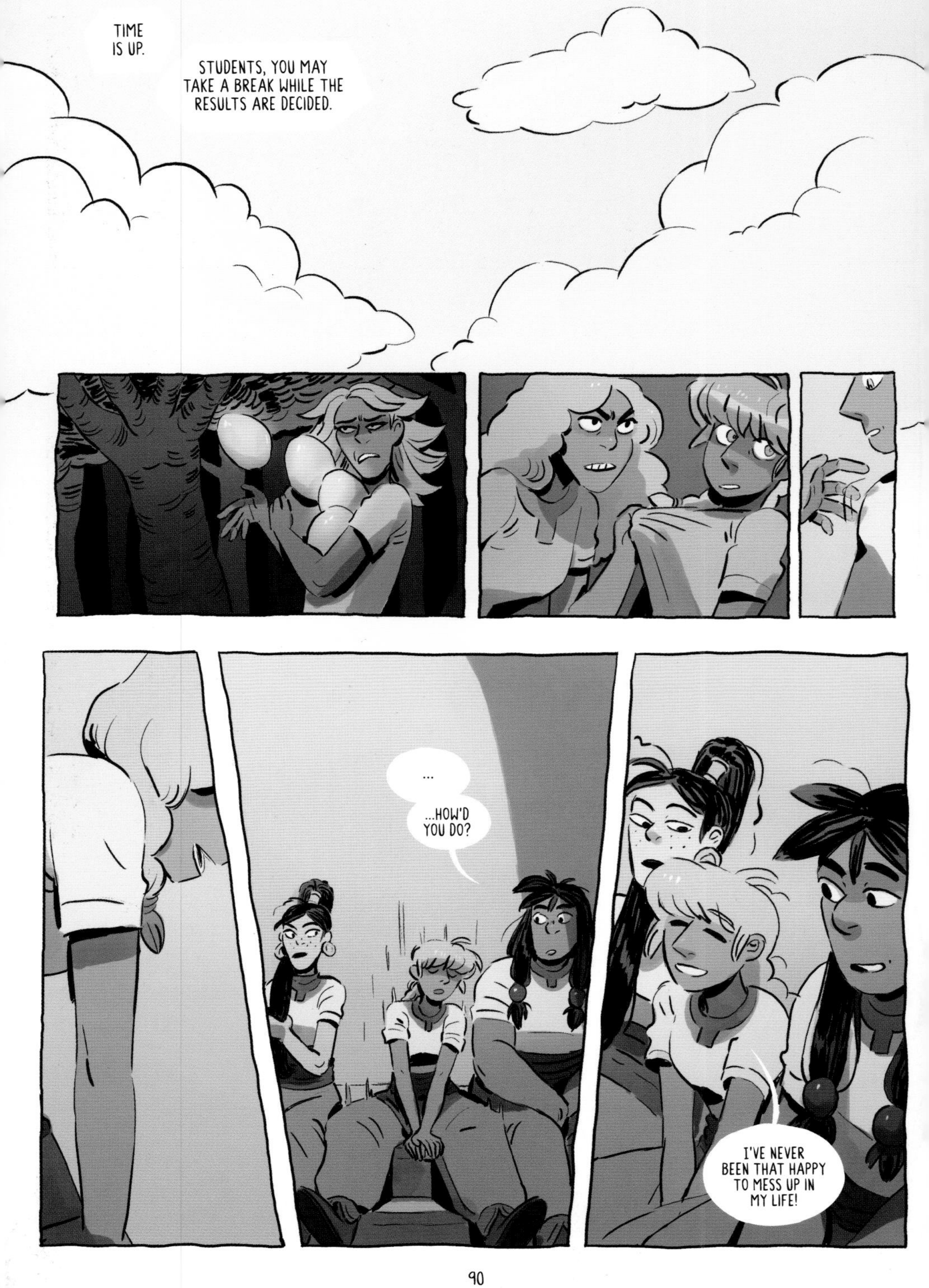
TIME IS UP.
STUDENTS, YOU MAY TAKE A BREAK WHILE THE RESULTS ARE DECIDED.
...
...HOW'D YOU DO?
I'VE NEVER BEEN THAT HAPPY TO MESS UP IN MY LIFE!

IS THAT WHY YOUR TEAMMATES LOOK LIKE THEY'RE GONNA KILL YOU?

WELL, IF EVERYTHING PANS OUT FINE, I WON'T BE SEEING ANY ONE OF THEM IN THE NEAR FUTURE.

HOW'D YOU GUYS DO?

NYNEVE,

DO YOU EVEN NEED TO ASK?

AH, YOUR EXCELLENCY!

VICEROY JUNG,

YOU'RE HERE FOR THE HIGHLIGHT REEL?

YES, THANK YOU.

WALK ME THROUGH THE PROSPECTS.

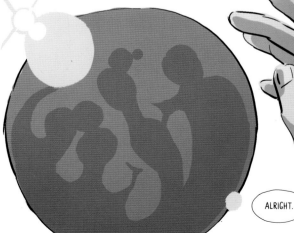

ALRIGHT.

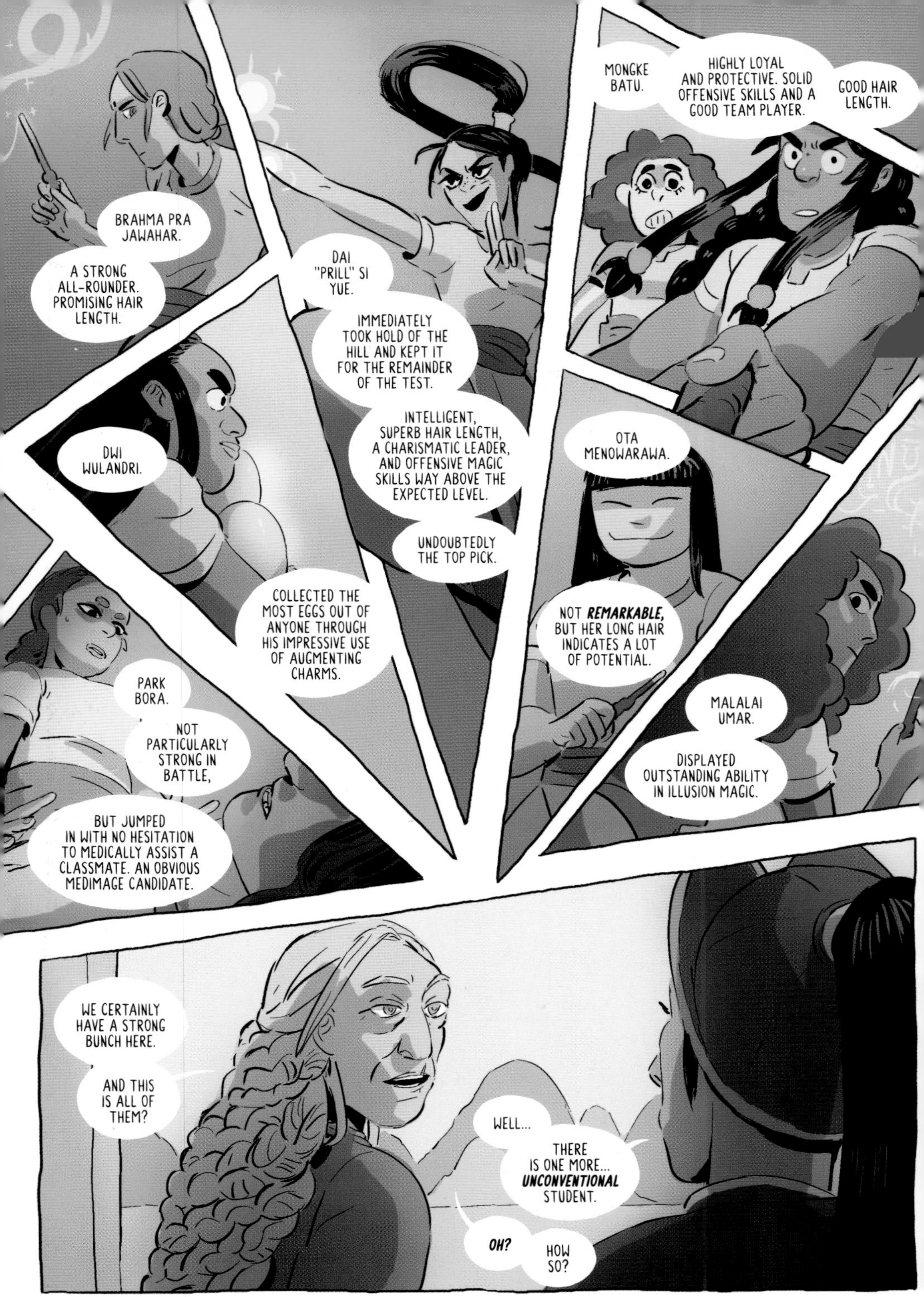
BRAHMA PRA JAWAHAR.
A STRONG ALL-ROUNDER. PROMISING HAIR LENGTH.
DAI "PRILL" SI YUE.
IMMEDIATELY TOOK HOLD OF THE HILL AND KEPT IT FOR THE REMAINDER OF THE TEST.
INTELLIGENT, SUPERB HAIR LENGTH, A CHARISMATIC LEADER, AND OFFENSIVE MAGIC SKILLS WAY ABOVE THE EXPECTED LEVEL.
UNDOUBTEDLY THE TOP PICK.
MONGKE BATU.
HIGHLY LOYAL AND PROTECTIVE. SOLID OFFENSIVE SKILLS AND A GOOD TEAM PLAYER.
GOOD HAIR LENGTH.
DWI WULANDRI.
COLLECTED THE MOST EGGS OUT OF ANYONE THROUGH HIS IMPRESSIVE USE OF AUGMENTING CHARMS.
OTA MENOWARAWA.
NOT ***REMARKABLE,*** BUT HER LONG HAIR INDICATES A LOT OF POTENTIAL.
PARK BORA.
NOT PARTICULARLY STRONG IN BATTLE,
BUT JUMPED IN WITH NO HESITATION TO MEDICALLY ASSIST A CLASSMATE. AN OBVIOUS MEDIMAGE CANDIDATE.
MALALAI UMAR.
DISPLAYED OUTSTANDING ABILITY IN ILLUSION MAGIC.
WE CERTAINLY HAVE A STRONG BUNCH HERE.
AND THIS IS ALL OF THEM?
WELL...
THERE IS ONE MORE... ***UNCONVENTIONAL*** STUDENT.
OH?
HOW SO?

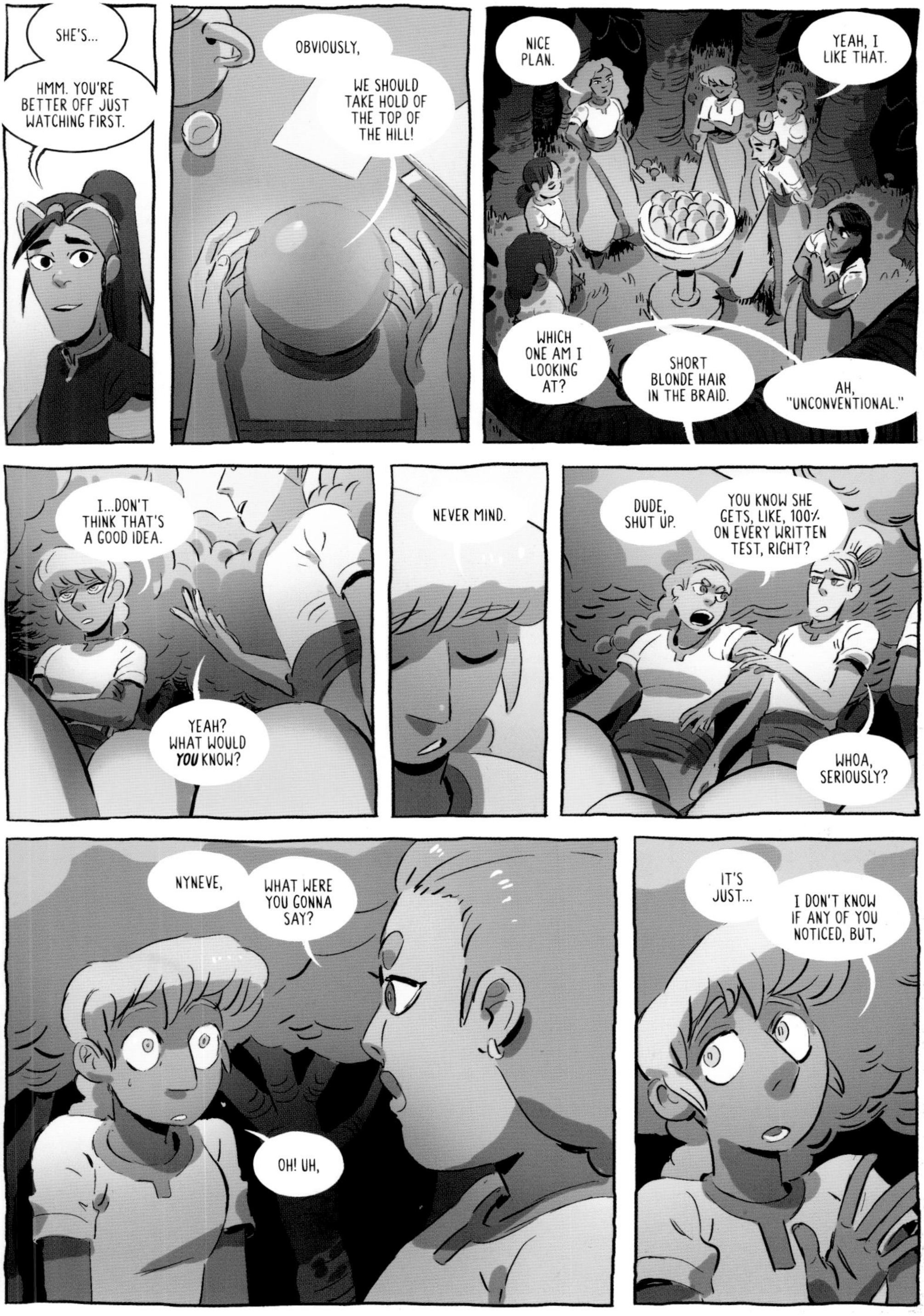
SHE'S...
HMM. YOU'RE BETTER OFF JUST WATCHING FIRST.
OBVIOUSLY,
WE SHOULD TAKE HOLD OF THE TOP OF THE HILL!
NICE PLAN.
YEAH, I LIKE THAT.
WHICH ONE AM I LOOKING AT?
SHORT BLONDE HAIR IN THE BRAID.
AH, "UNCONVENTIONAL."
I...DON'T THINK THAT'S A GOOD IDEA.
YEAH? WHAT WOULD *YOU* KNOW?
NEVER MIND.
DUDE, SHUT UP.
YOU KNOW SHE GETS, LIKE, 100% ON EVERY WRITTEN TEST, RIGHT?
WHOA, SERIOUSLY?
NYNEVE,
WHAT WERE YOU GONNA SAY?
OH! UH,
IT'S JUST...
I DON'T KNOW IF ANY OF YOU NOTICED, BUT,

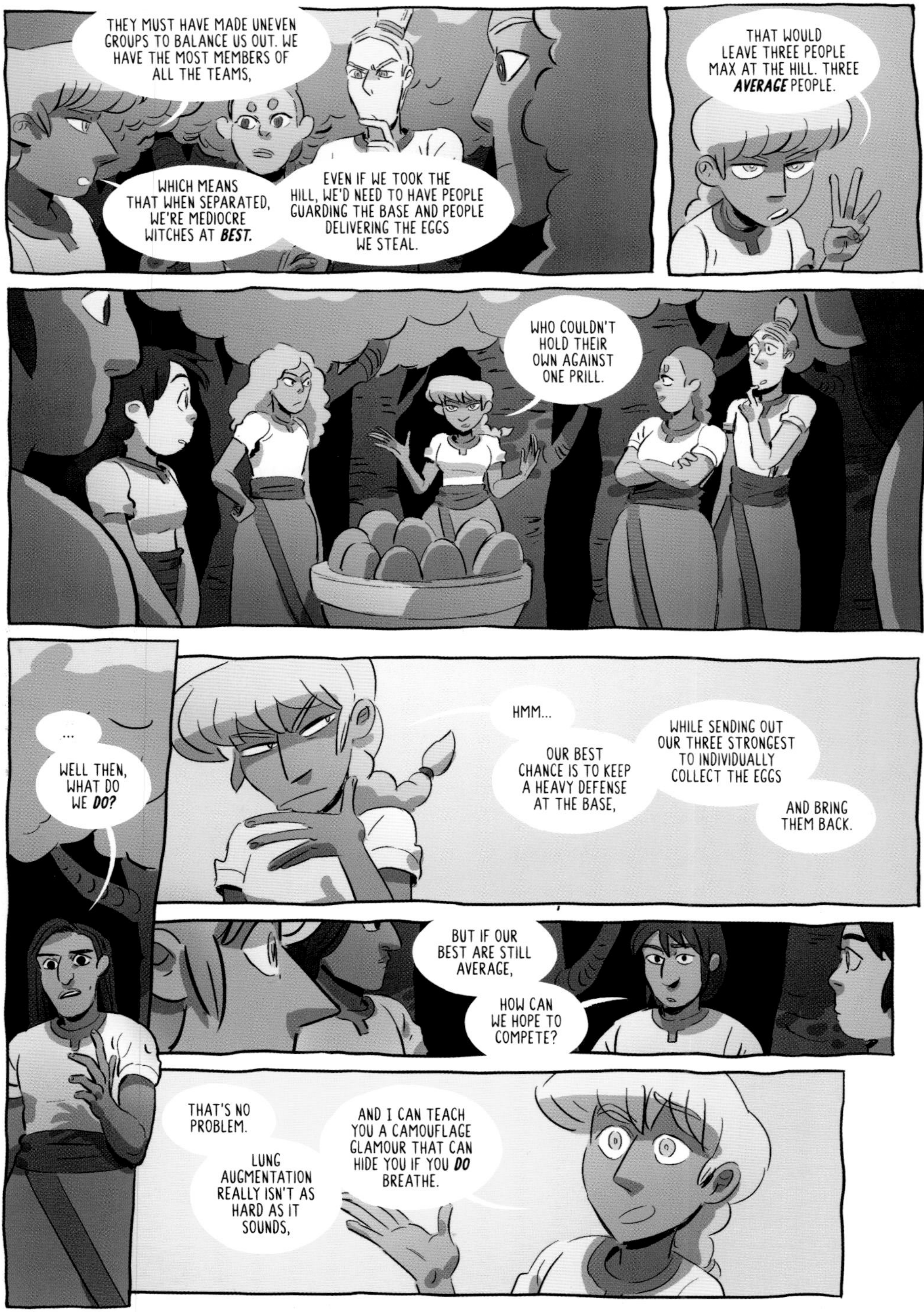
THEY MUST HAVE MADE UNEVEN GROUPS TO BALANCE US OUT. WE HAVE THE MOST MEMBERS OF ALL THE TEAMS,
WHICH MEANS THAT WHEN SEPARATED, WE'RE MEDIOCRE WITCHES AT **BEST.**
EVEN IF WE TOOK THE HILL, WE'D NEED TO HAVE PEOPLE GUARDING THE BASE AND PEOPLE DELIVERING THE EGGS WE STEAL.
THAT WOULD LEAVE THREE PEOPLE MAX AT THE HILL. THREE ***AVERAGE*** PEOPLE.
WHO COULDN'T HOLD THEIR OWN AGAINST ONE PRILL.
...
WELL THEN, WHAT DO WE ***DO?***
HMM...
OUR BEST CHANCE IS TO KEEP A HEAVY DEFENSE AT THE BASE,
WHILE SENDING OUT OUR THREE STRONGEST TO INDIVIDUALLY COLLECT THE EGGS
AND BRING THEM BACK.
BUT IF OUR BEST ARE STILL AVERAGE,
HOW CAN WE HOPE TO COMPETE?
THAT'S NO PROBLEM.
LUNG AUGMENTATION REALLY ISN'T AS HARD AS IT SOUNDS,
AND I CAN TEACH YOU A CAMOUFLAGE GLAMOUR THAT CAN HIDE YOU IF YOU ***DO*** BREATHE.

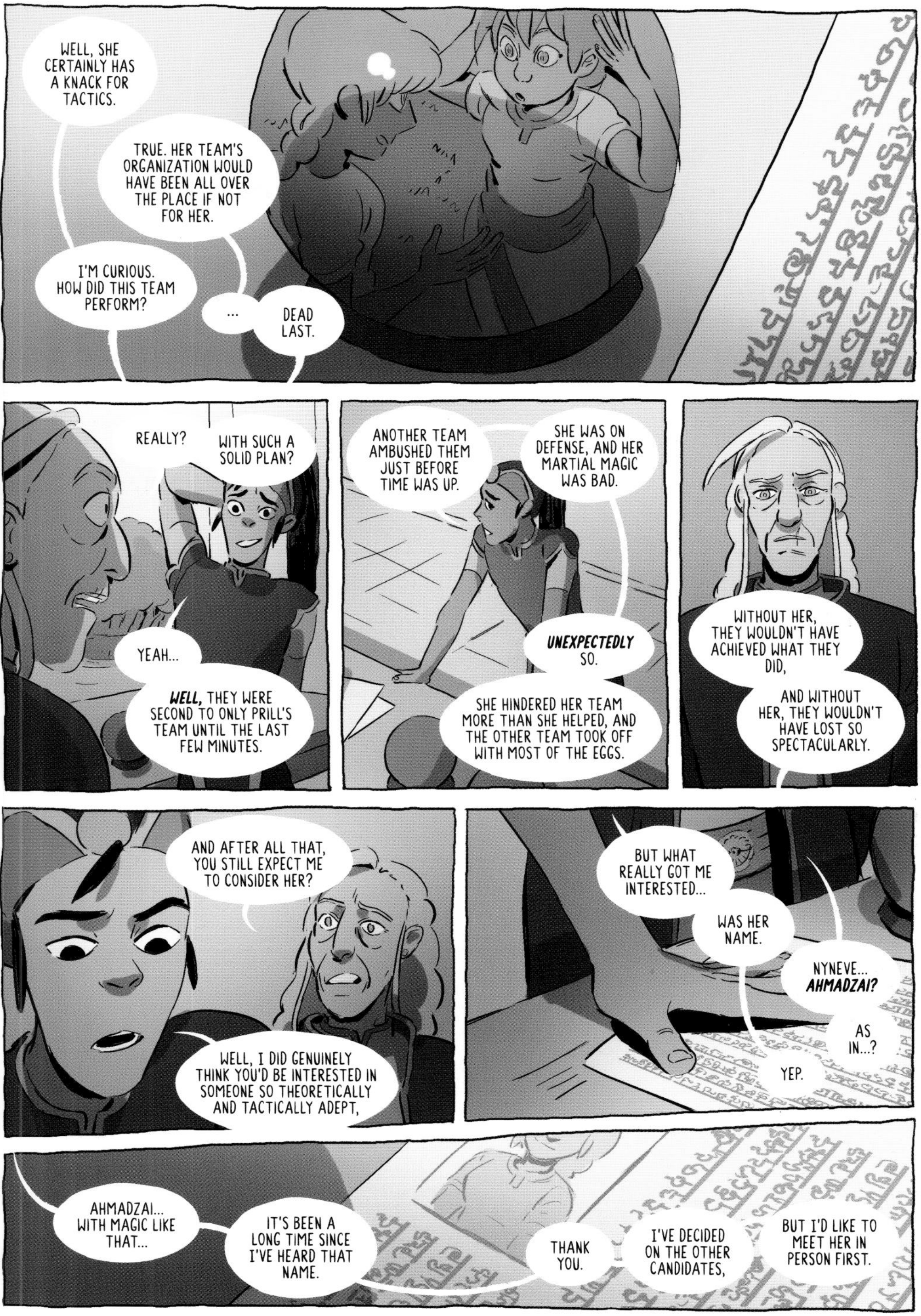
WELL, SHE CERTAINLY HAS A KNACK FOR TACTICS.
TRUE. HER TEAM'S ORGANIZATION WOULD HAVE BEEN ALL OVER THE PLACE IF NOT FOR HER.
I'M CURIOUS. HOW DID THIS TEAM PERFORM?
...
DEAD LAST.
REALLY?
WITH SUCH A SOLID PLAN?
YEAH...
WELL, THEY WERE SECOND TO ONLY PRILL'S TEAM UNTIL THE LAST FEW MINUTES.
ANOTHER TEAM AMBUSHED THEM JUST BEFORE TIME WAS UP.
SHE WAS ON DEFENSE, AND HER MARTIAL MAGIC WAS BAD.
UNEXPECTEDLY SO.
SHE HINDERED HER TEAM MORE THAN SHE HELPED, AND THE OTHER TEAM TOOK OFF WITH MOST OF THE EGGS.
WITHOUT HER, THEY WOULDN'T HAVE ACHIEVED WHAT THEY DID,
AND WITHOUT HER, THEY WOULDN'T HAVE LOST SO SPECTACULARLY.
AND AFTER ALL THAT, YOU STILL EXPECT ME TO CONSIDER HER?
WELL, I DID GENUINELY THINK YOU'D BE INTERESTED IN SOMEONE SO THEORETICALLY AND TACTICALLY ADEPT,
BUT WHAT REALLY GOT ME INTERESTED...
WAS HER NAME.
NYNEVE... AHMADZAI?
AS IN...?
YEP.
AHMADZAI... WITH MAGIC LIKE THAT...
IT'S BEEN A LONG TIME SINCE I'VE HEARD THAT NAME.
THANK YOU.
I'VE DECIDED ON THE OTHER CANDIDATES,
BUT I'D LIKE TO MEET HER IN PERSON FIRST.

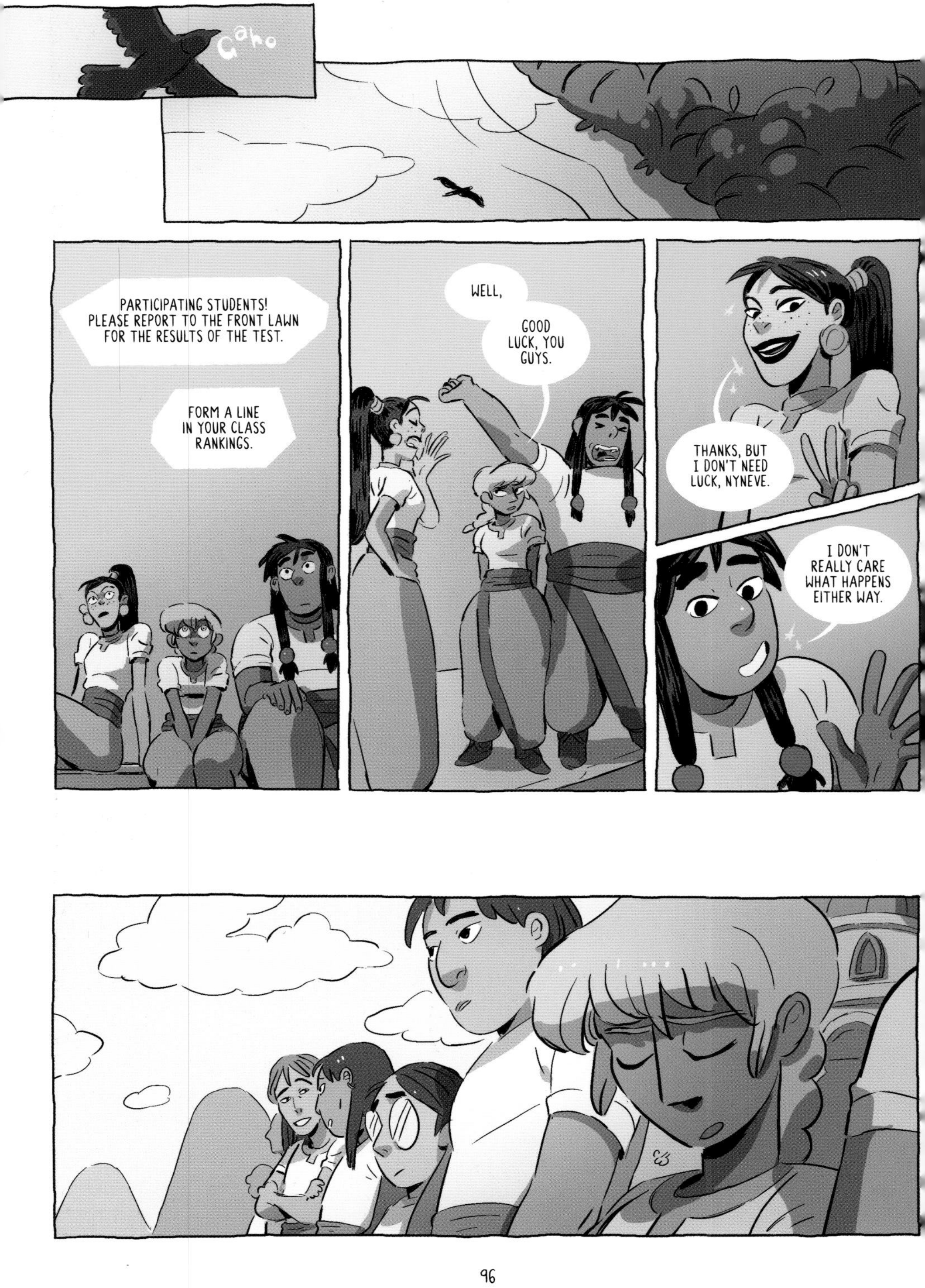
CAHO
PARTICIPATING STUDENTS! PLEASE REPORT TO THE FRONT LAWN FOR THE RESULTS OF THE TEST.
FORM A LINE IN YOUR CLASS RANKINGS.
WELL,
GOOD LUCK, YOU GUYS.
THANKS, BUT I DON'T NEED LUCK, NYNEVE.
I DON'T REALLY CARE WHAT HAPPENS EITHER WAY.

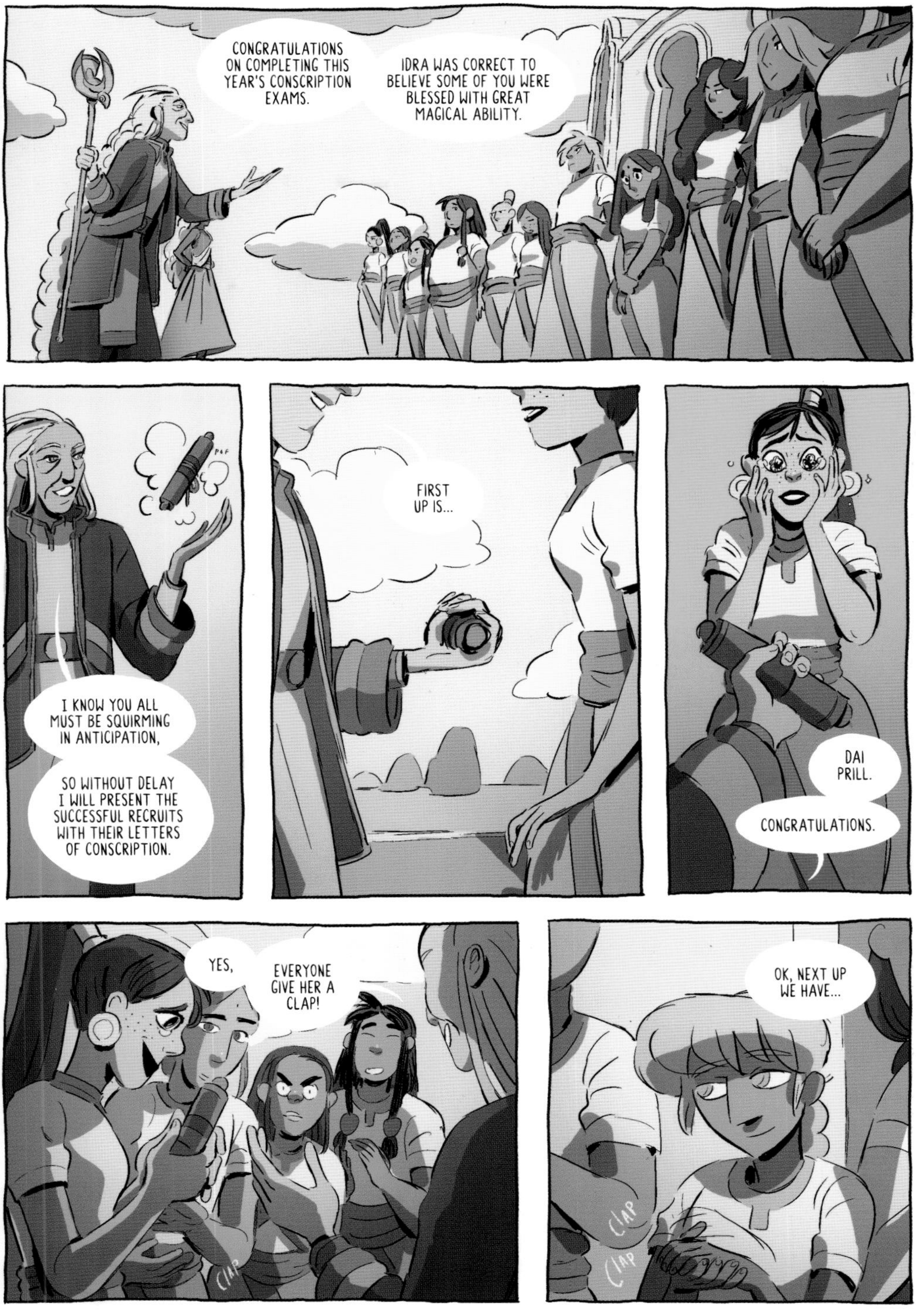
CONGRATULATIONS ON COMPLETING THIS YEAR'S CONSCRIPTION EXAMS.
IDRA WAS CORRECT TO BELIEVE SOME OF YOU WERE BLESSED WITH GREAT MAGICAL ABILITY.
POF
I KNOW YOU ALL MUST BE SQUIRMING IN ANTICIPATION,
SO WITHOUT DELAY I WILL PRESENT THE SUCCESSFUL RECRUITS WITH THEIR LETTERS OF CONSCRIPTION.
FIRST UP IS...
DAI PRILL.
CONGRATULATIONS.
YES,
EVERYONE GIVE HER A CLAP!
CLAP
OK, NEXT UP WE HAVE...
CLAP
CLAP

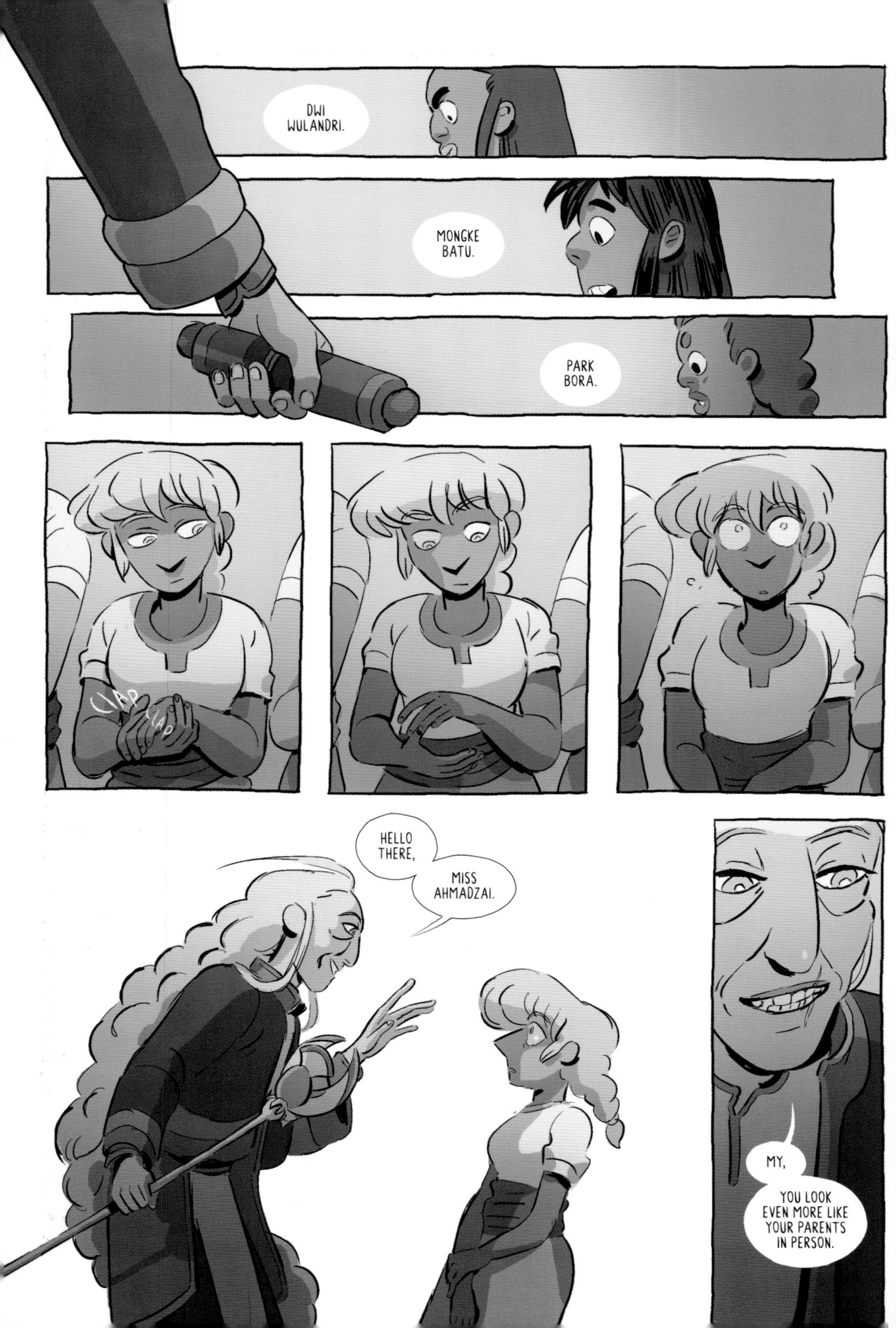
DWI WULANDRI.
MONGKE BATU.
PARK BORA.
CLAP CLAP
HELLO THERE,
MISS AHMADZAI.
MY,
YOU LOOK EVEN MORE LIKE YOUR PARENTS IN PERSON.

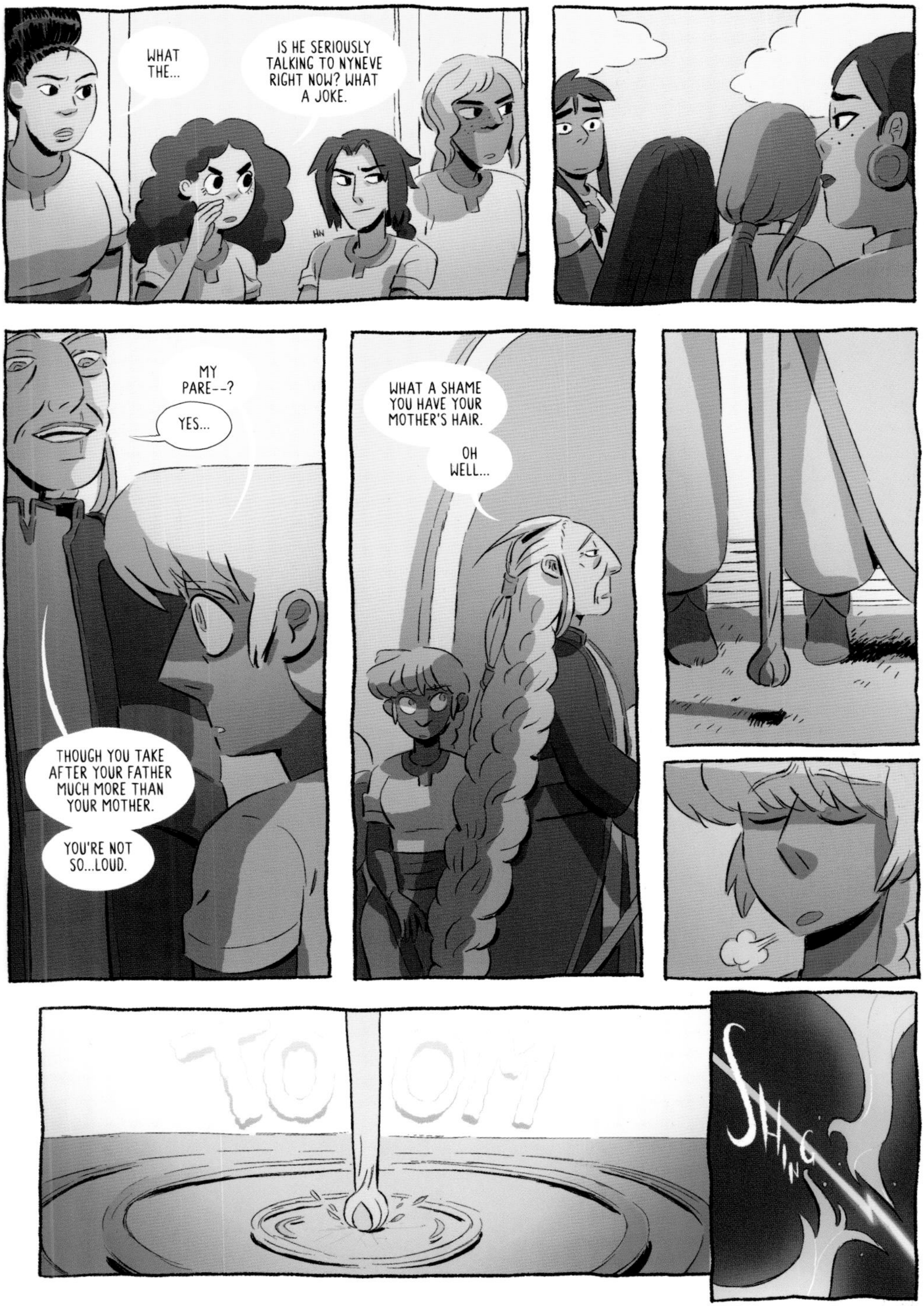
WHAT THE...
IS HE SERIOUSLY TALKING TO NYNEVE RIGHT NOW? WHAT A JOKE.
HN
MY PARE--?
YES...
THOUGH YOU TAKE AFTER YOUR FATHER MUCH MORE THAN YOUR MOTHER.
YOU'RE NOT SO...LOUD.
WHAT A SHAME YOU HAVE YOUR MOTHER'S HAIR.
OH WELL...
TOOM
SHING

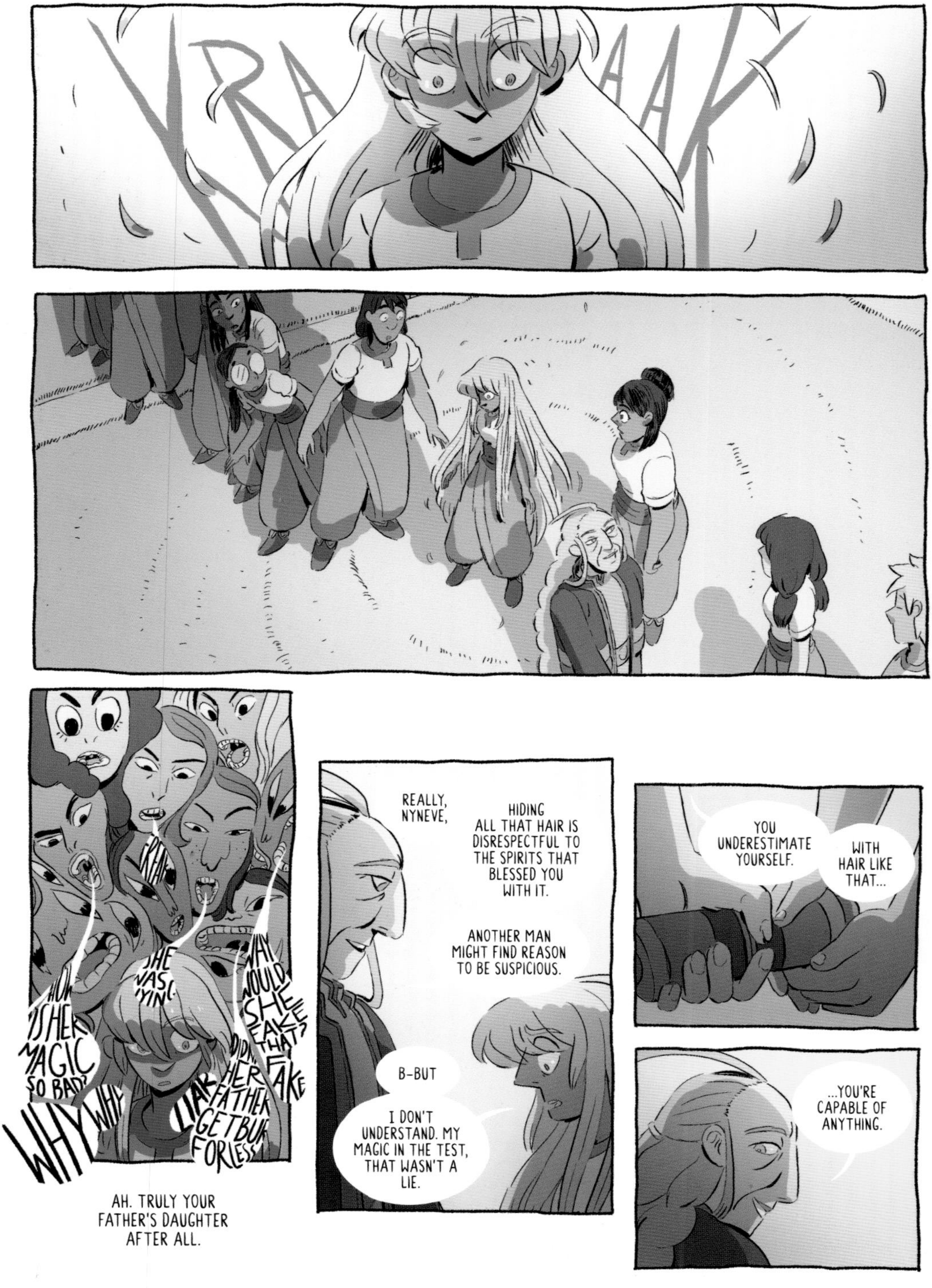
VRAAAK
WHY
WHY
LIAR
FAKE
AH. TRULY YOUR FATHER'S DAUGHTER AFTER ALL.
REALLY, NYNEVE,
HIDING ALL THAT HAIR IS DISRESPECTFUL TO THE SPIRITS THAT BLESSED YOU WITH IT.
ANOTHER MAN MIGHT FIND REASON TO BE SUSPICIOUS.
B-BUT
I DON'T UNDERSTAND. MY MAGIC IN THE TEST, THAT WASN'T A LIE.
YOU UNDERESTIMATE YOURSELF.
WITH HAIR LIKE THAT...
...YOU'RE CAPABLE OF ANYTHING.

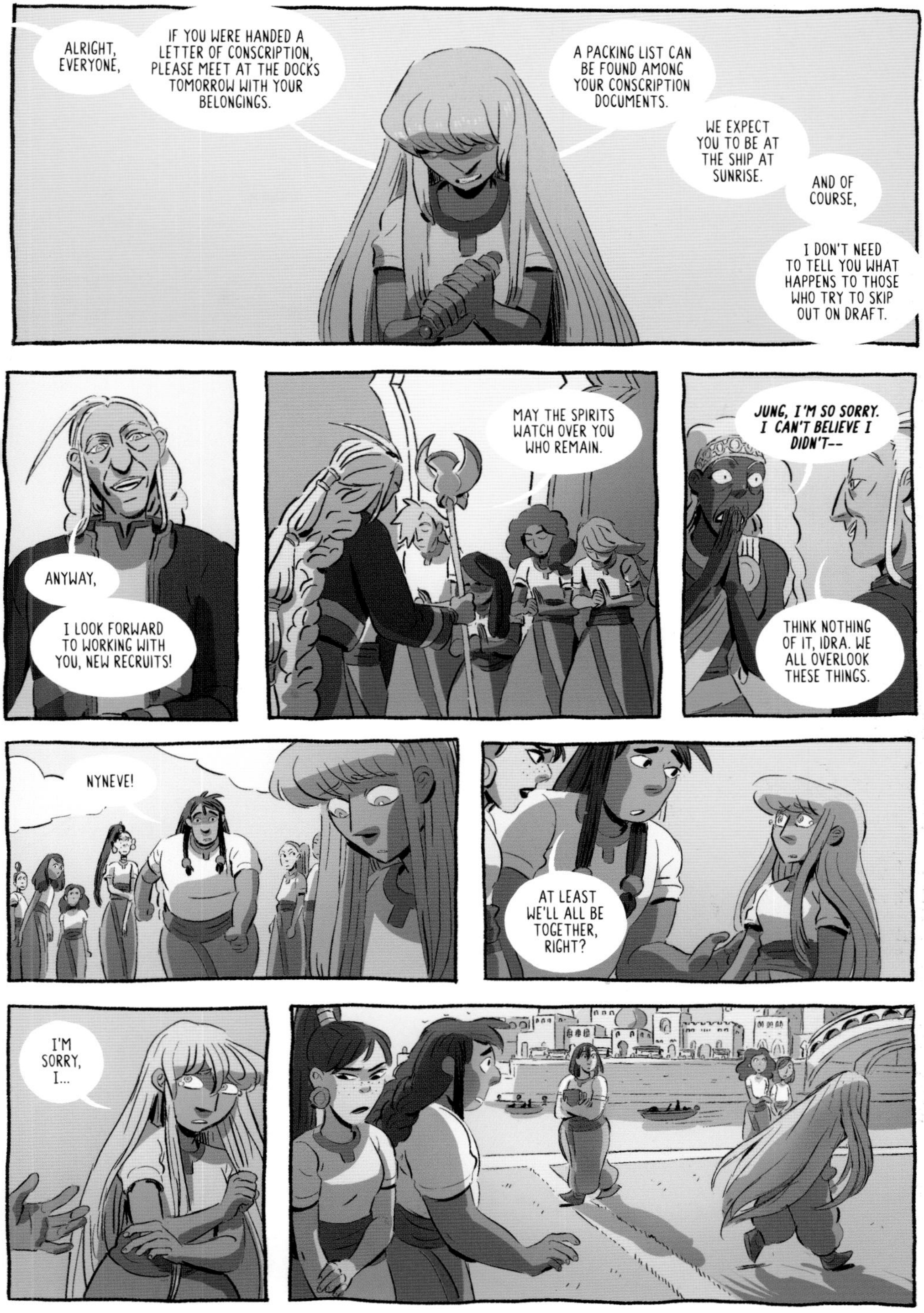
ALRIGHT, EVERYONE,
IF YOU WERE HANDED A LETTER OF CONSCRIPTION, PLEASE MEET AT THE DOCKS TOMORROW WITH YOUR BELONGINGS.
A PACKING LIST CAN BE FOUND AMONG YOUR CONSCRIPTION DOCUMENTS.
WE EXPECT YOU TO BE AT THE SHIP AT SUNRISE.
AND OF COURSE,
I DON'T NEED TO TELL YOU WHAT HAPPENS TO THOSE WHO TRY TO SKIP OUT ON DRAFT.
ANYWAY,
I LOOK FORWARD TO WORKING WITH YOU, NEW RECRUITS!
MAY THE SPIRITS WATCH OVER YOU WHO REMAIN.
JUNG, I'M SO SORRY. I CAN'T BELIEVE I DIDN'T--
THINK NOTHING OF IT, IDRA. WE ALL OVERLOOK THESE THINGS.
NYNEVE!
AT LEAST WE'LL ALL BE TOGETHER, RIGHT?
I'M SORRY, I...

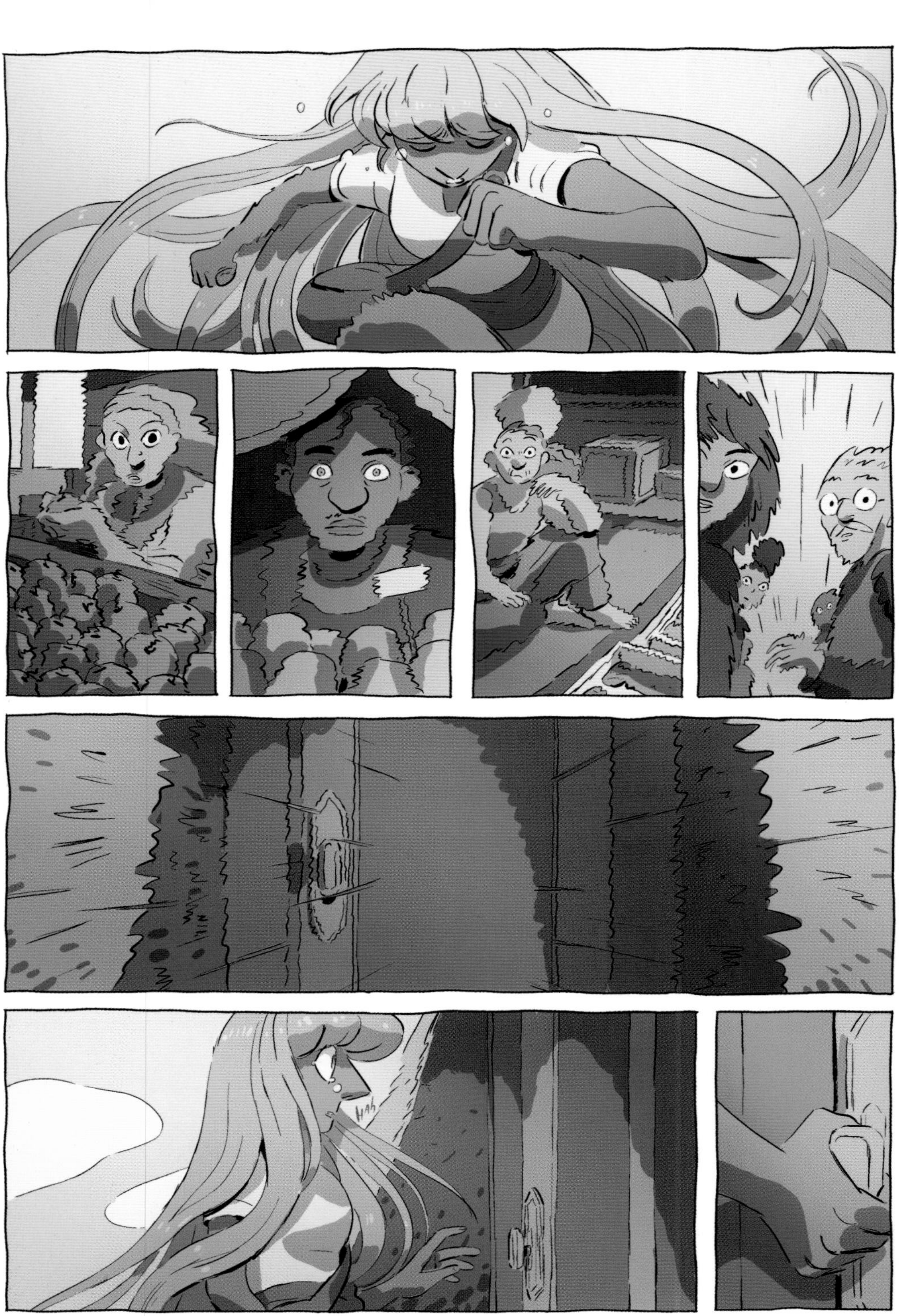
Hah

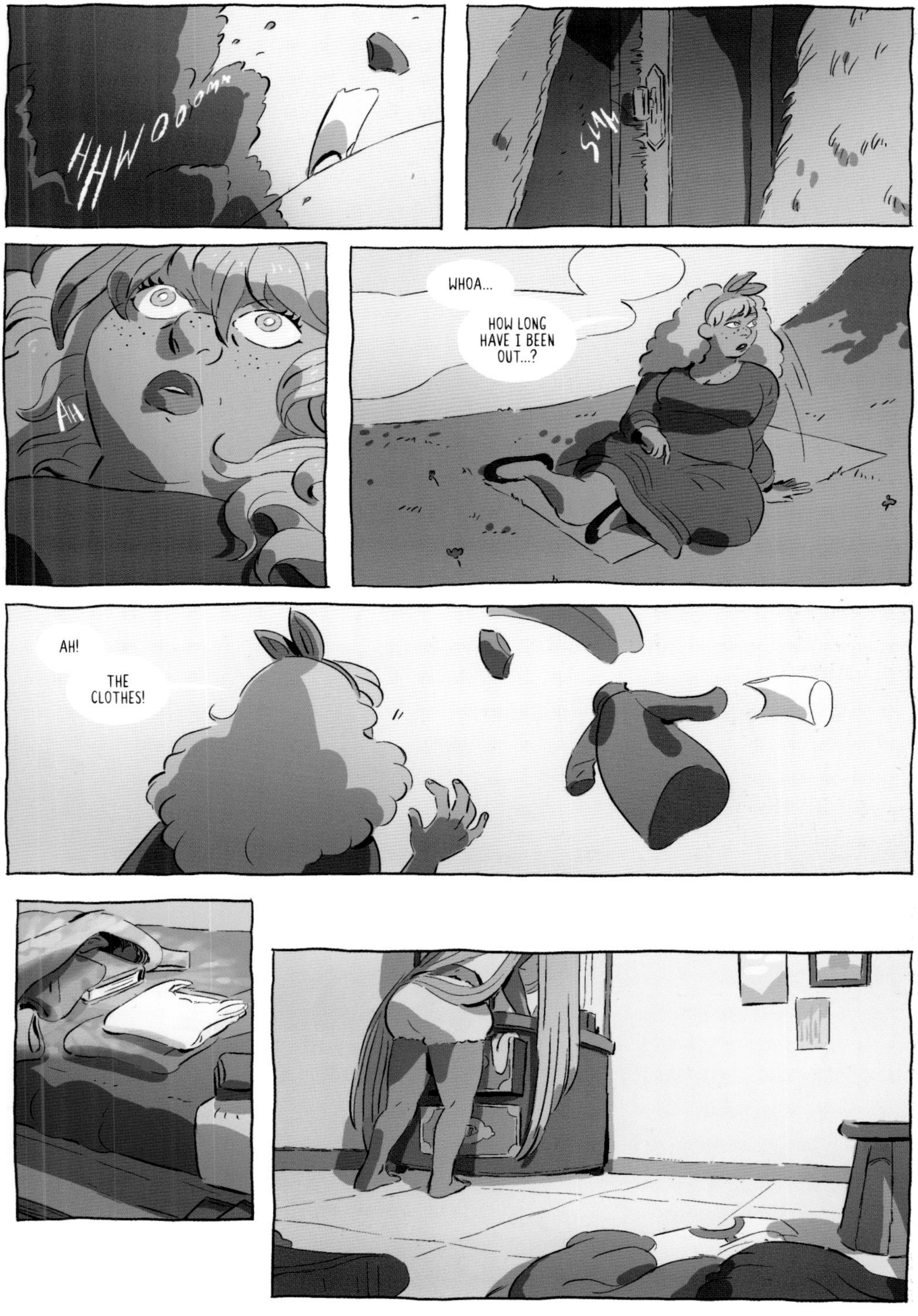
HHWOOOMMM
SLAM
AH
WHOA...
HOW LONG HAVE I BEEN OUT...?
AH!
THE CLOTHES!

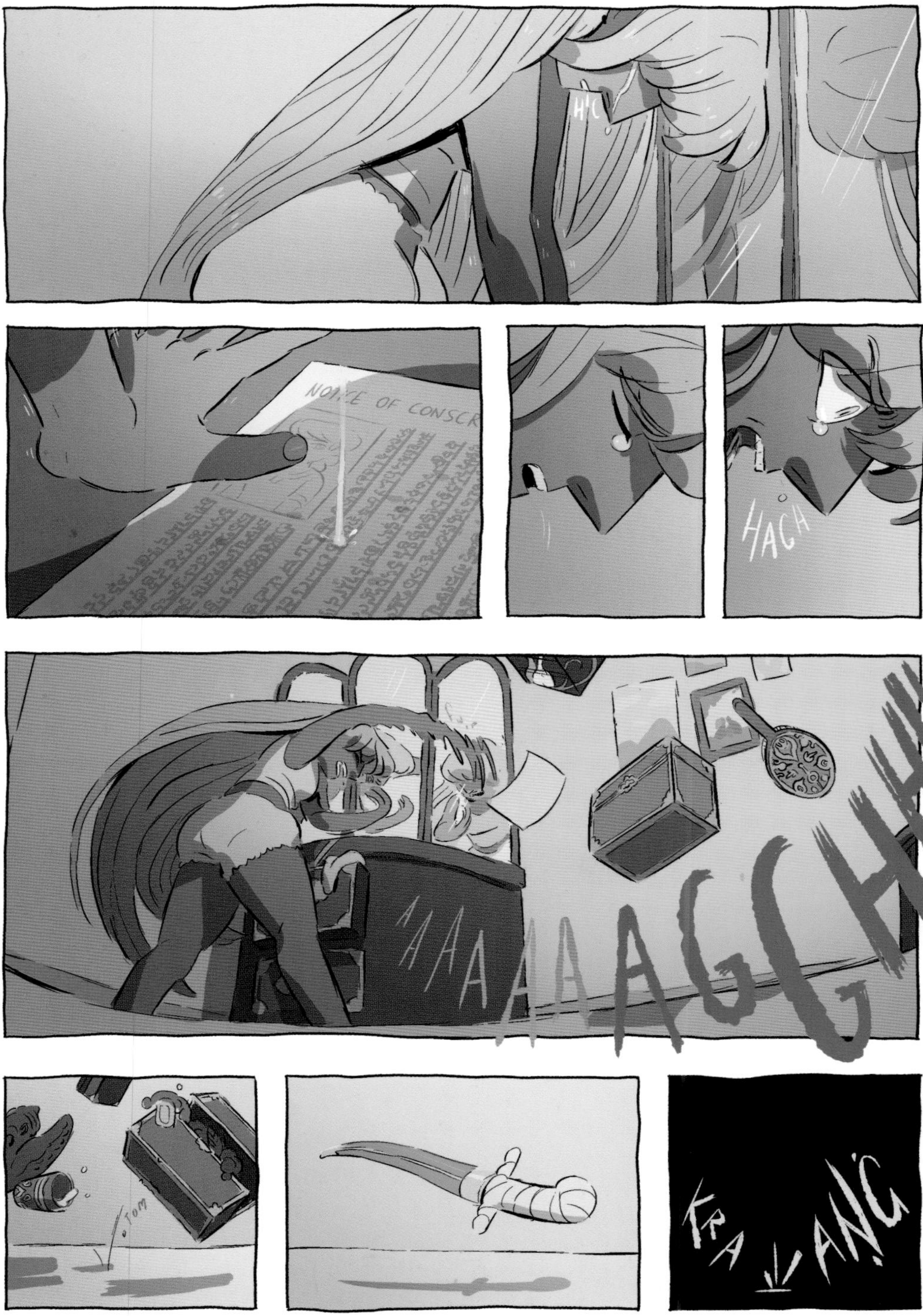
H'C
NOTICE OF CONSCR
HACH
AAAAAAGGHH
TOM
KRA ANG

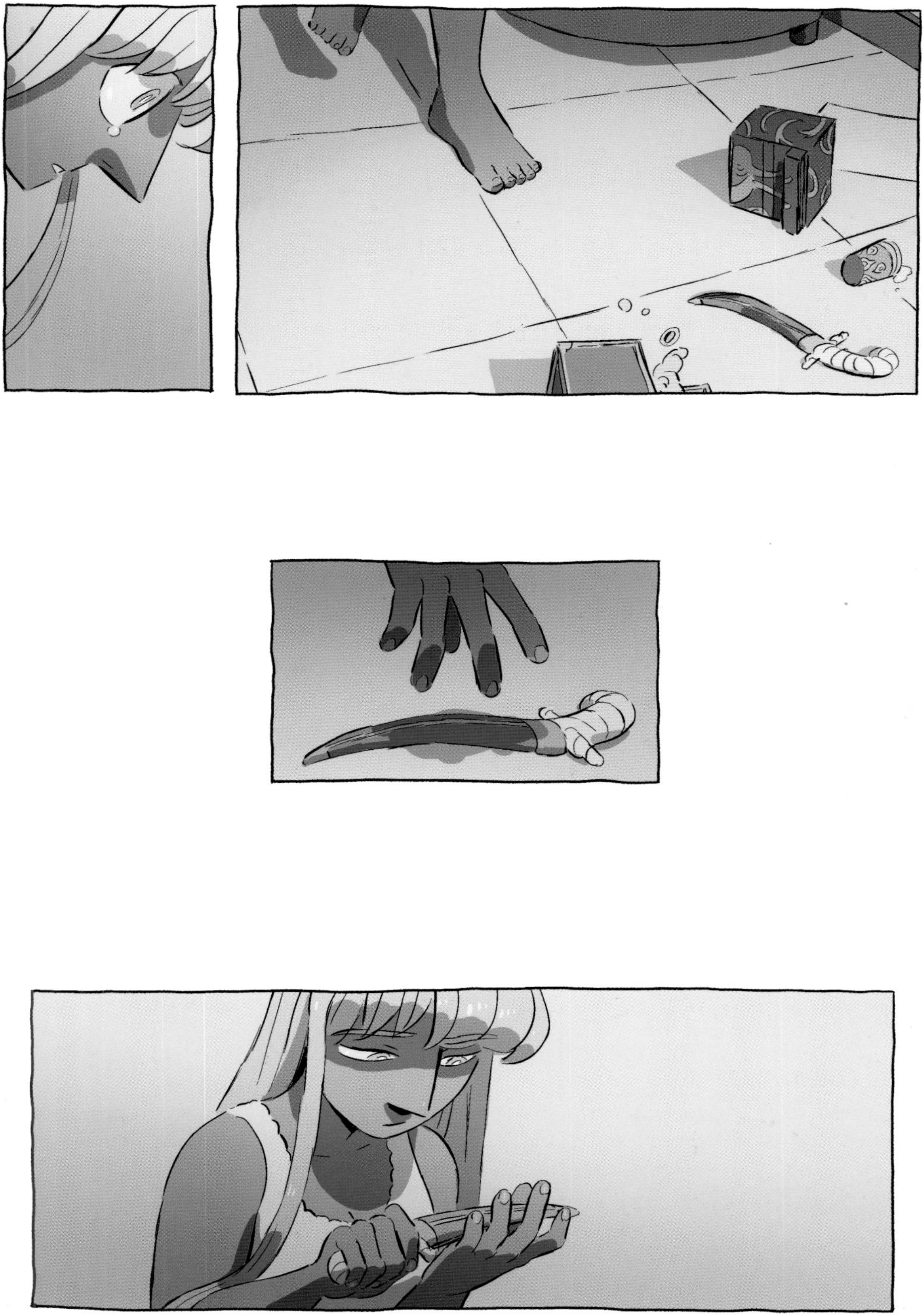

SHIN

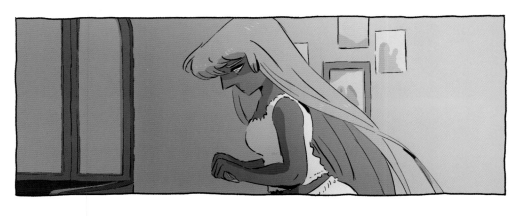

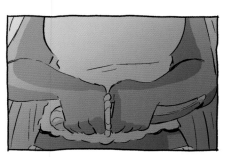

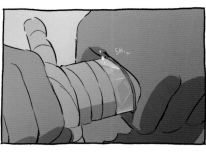

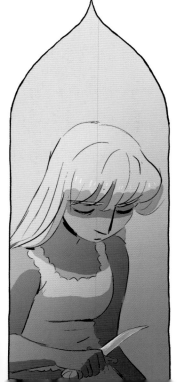

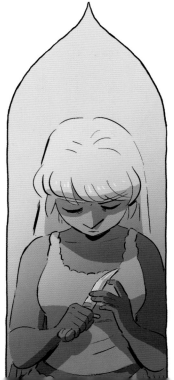

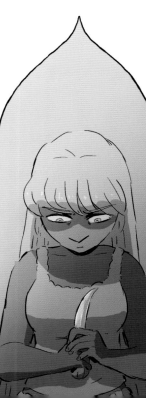

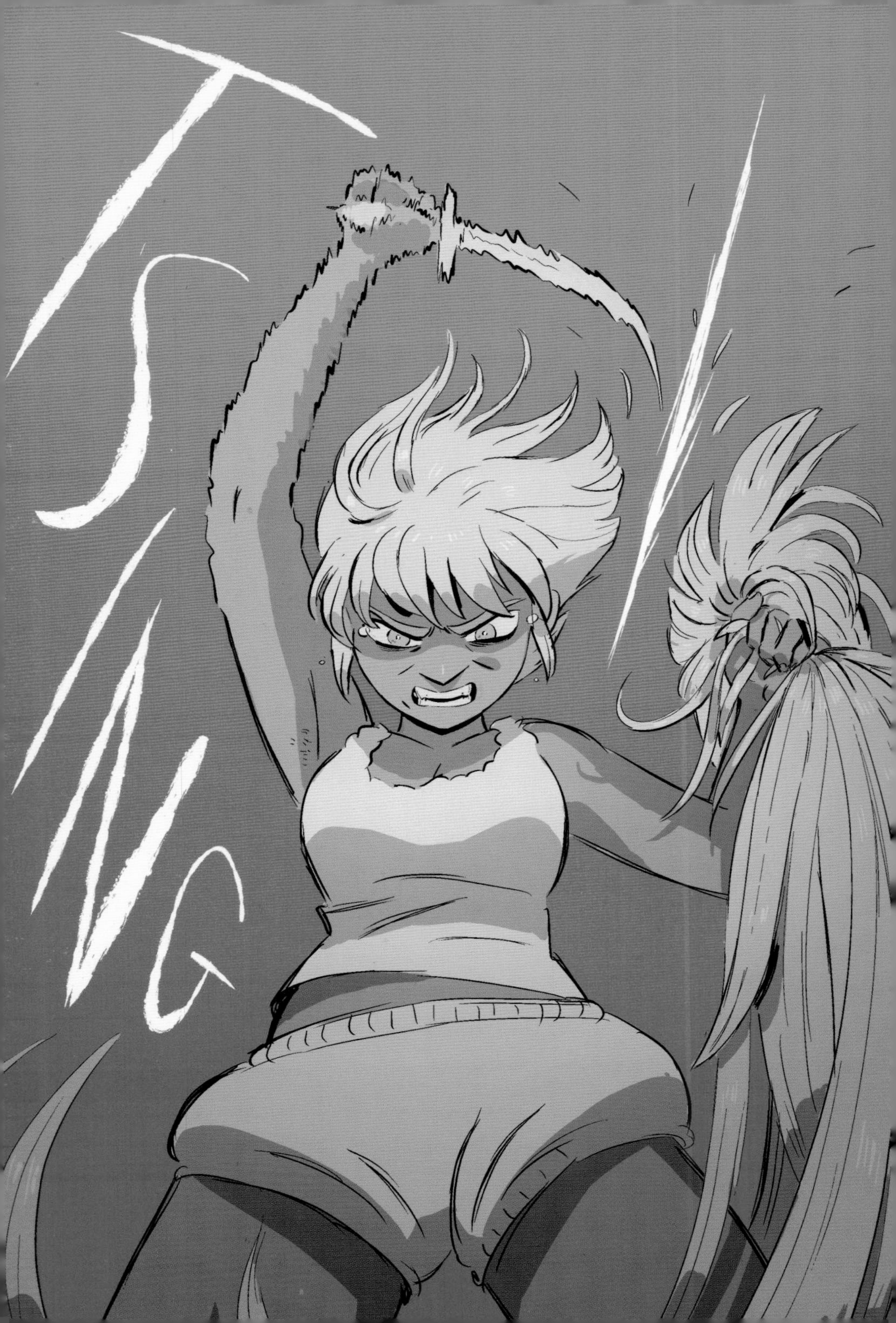
TSNG

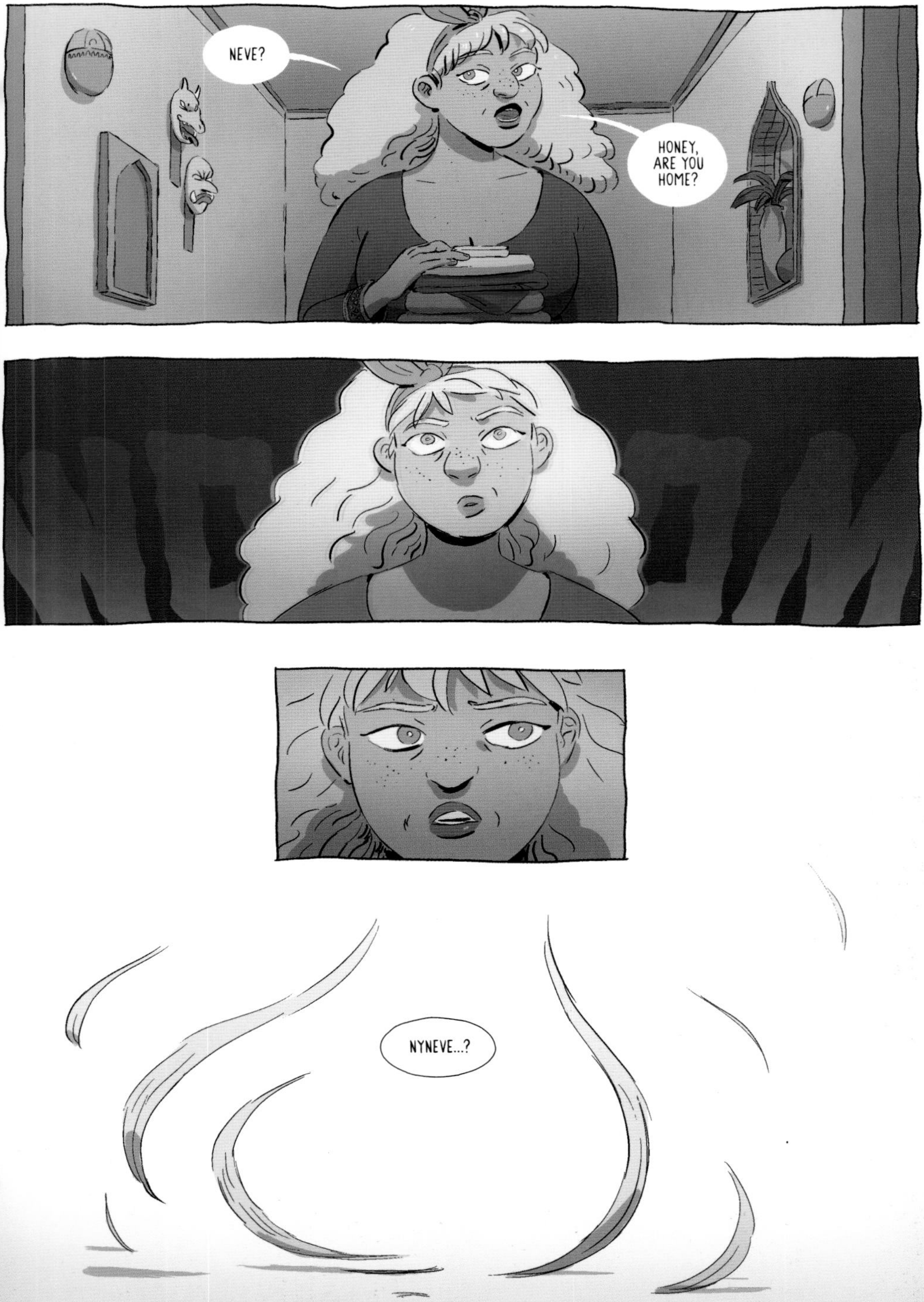
NEVE?
HONEY, ARE YOU HOME?
NYNEVE...?

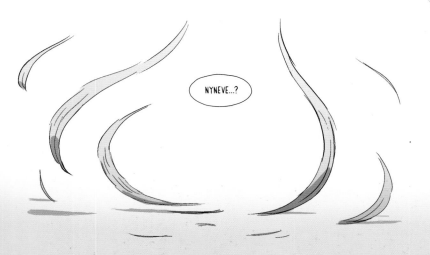

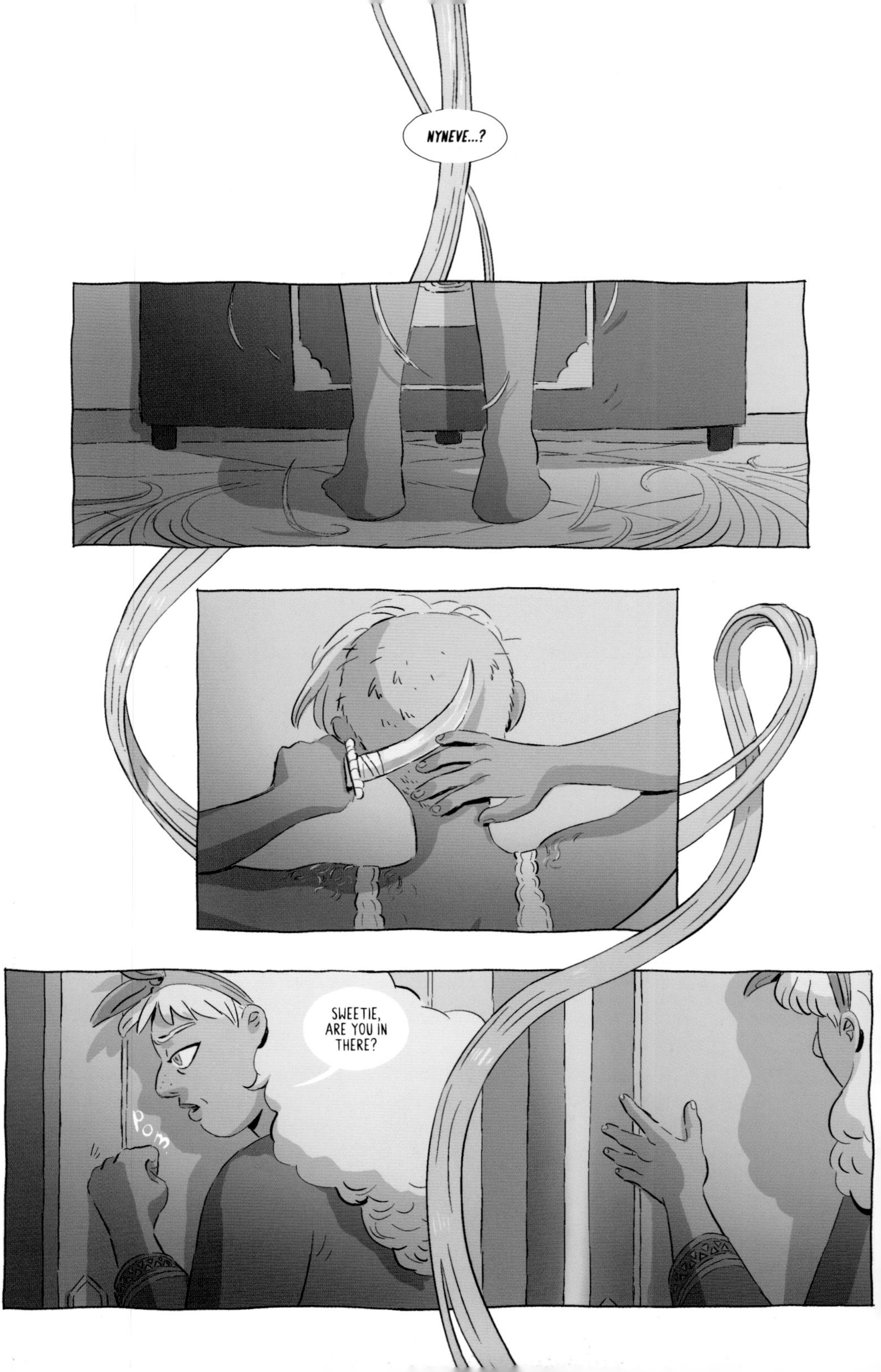
NYNEVE...?
SWEETIE, ARE YOU IN THERE?
POM

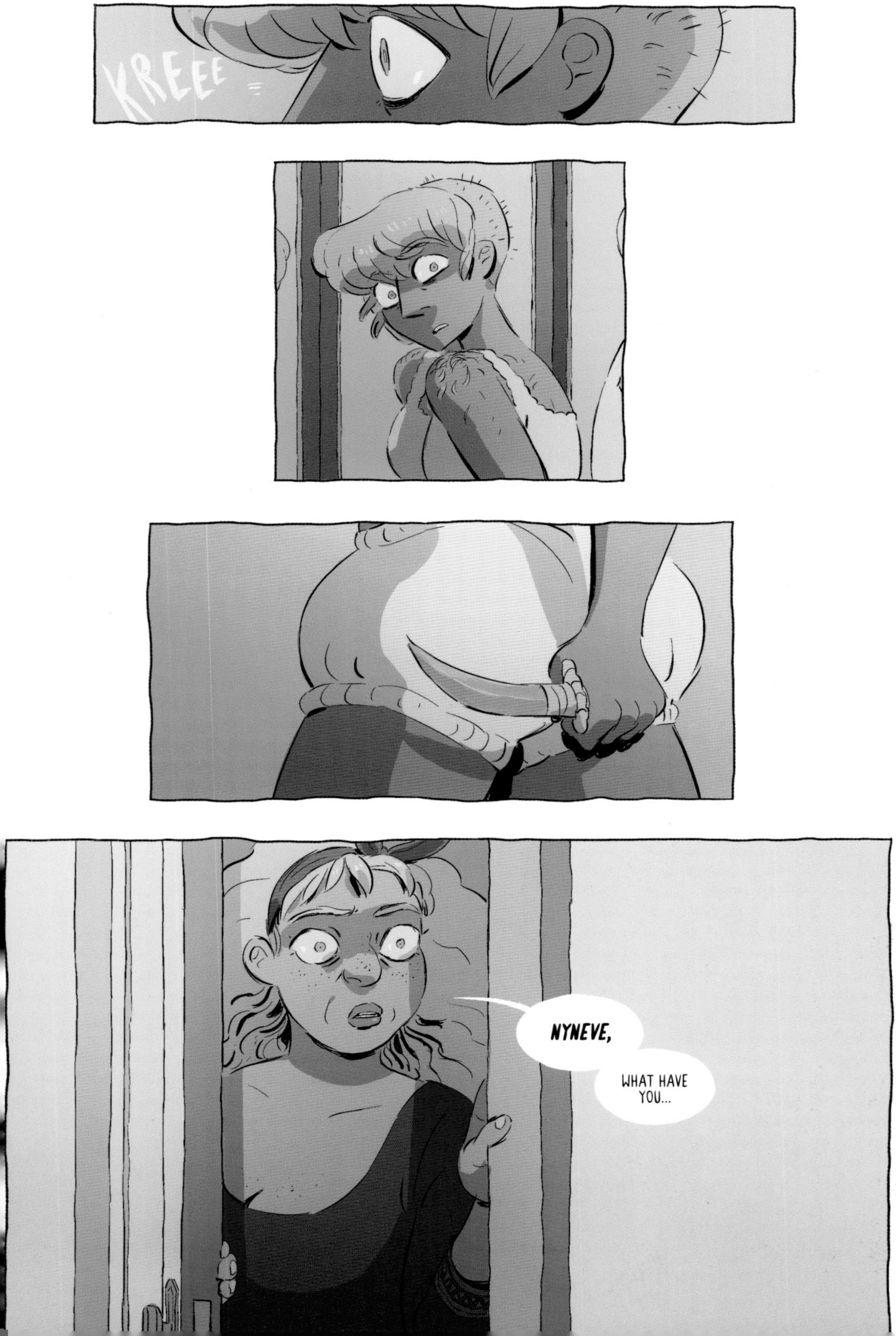
KREEE
NYNEVE,
WHAT HAVE YOU...

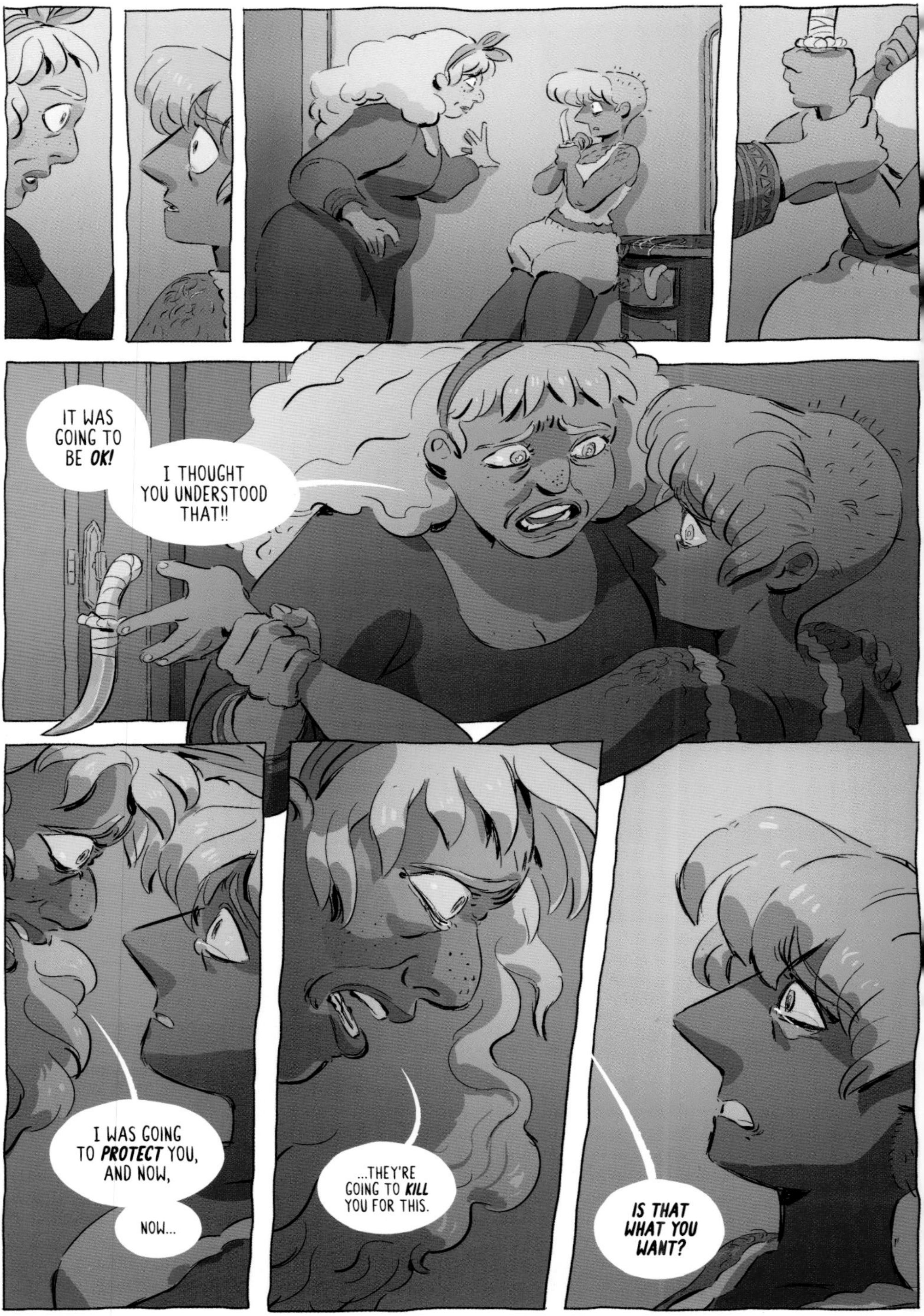
IT WAS GOING TO BE **OK!**
I THOUGHT YOU UNDERSTOOD THAT!!
I WAS GOING TO **PROTECT** YOU, AND NOW,
NOW...
...THEY'RE GOING TO **KILL** YOU FOR THIS.
IS THAT WHAT YOU WANT?

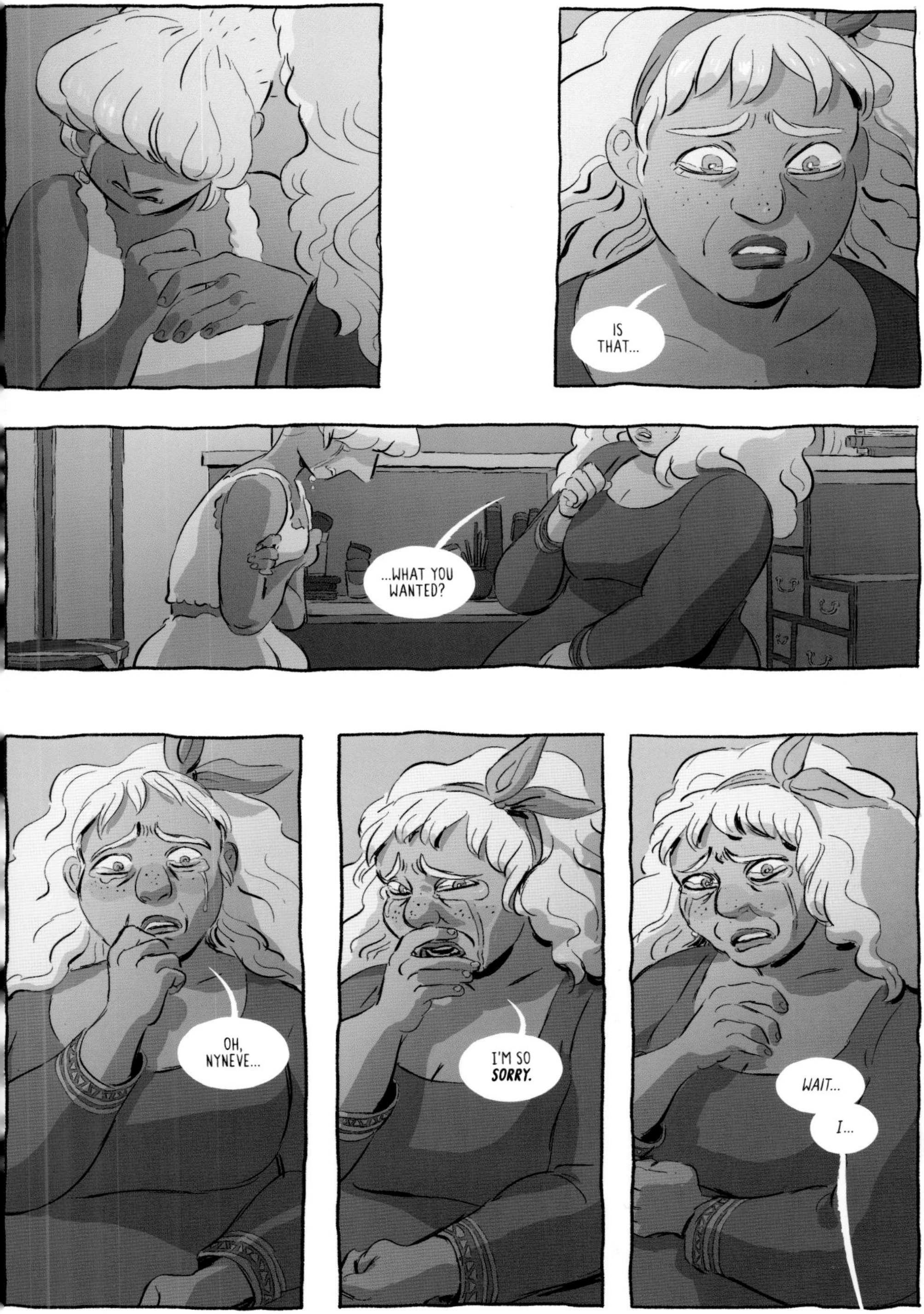
IS THAT...
...WHAT YOU WANTED?
OH, NYNEVE...
I'M SO **SORRY.**
WAIT...
I...

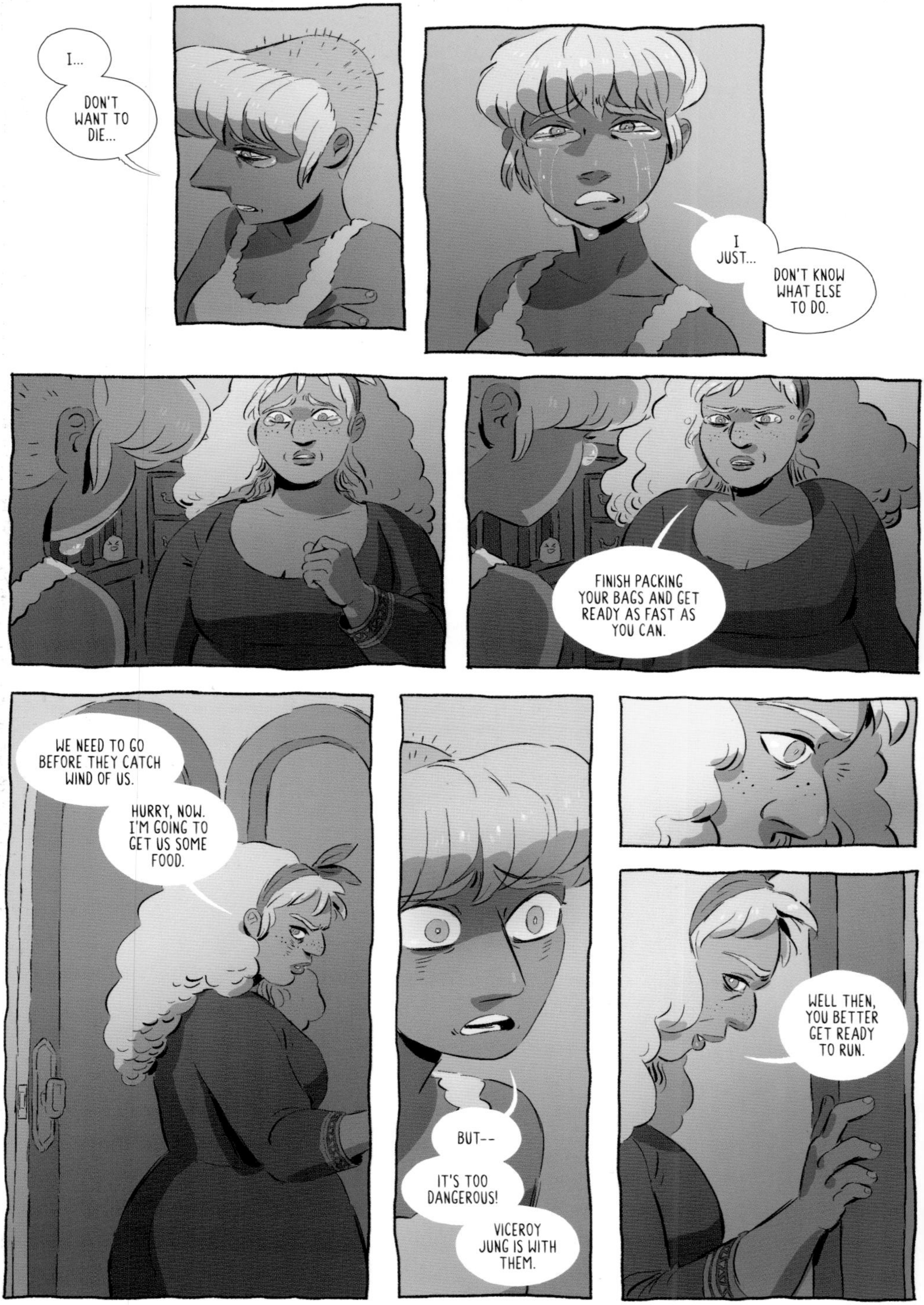
I...
DON'T WANT TO DIE...
I JUST...
DON'T KNOW WHAT ELSE TO DO.
FINISH PACKING YOUR BAGS AND GET READY AS FAST AS YOU CAN.
WE NEED TO GO BEFORE THEY CATCH WIND OF US.
HURRY, NOW. I'M GOING TO GET US SOME FOOD.
BUT--
IT'S TOO DANGEROUS!
VICEROY JUNG IS WITH THEM.
WELL THEN, YOU BETTER GET READY TO RUN.

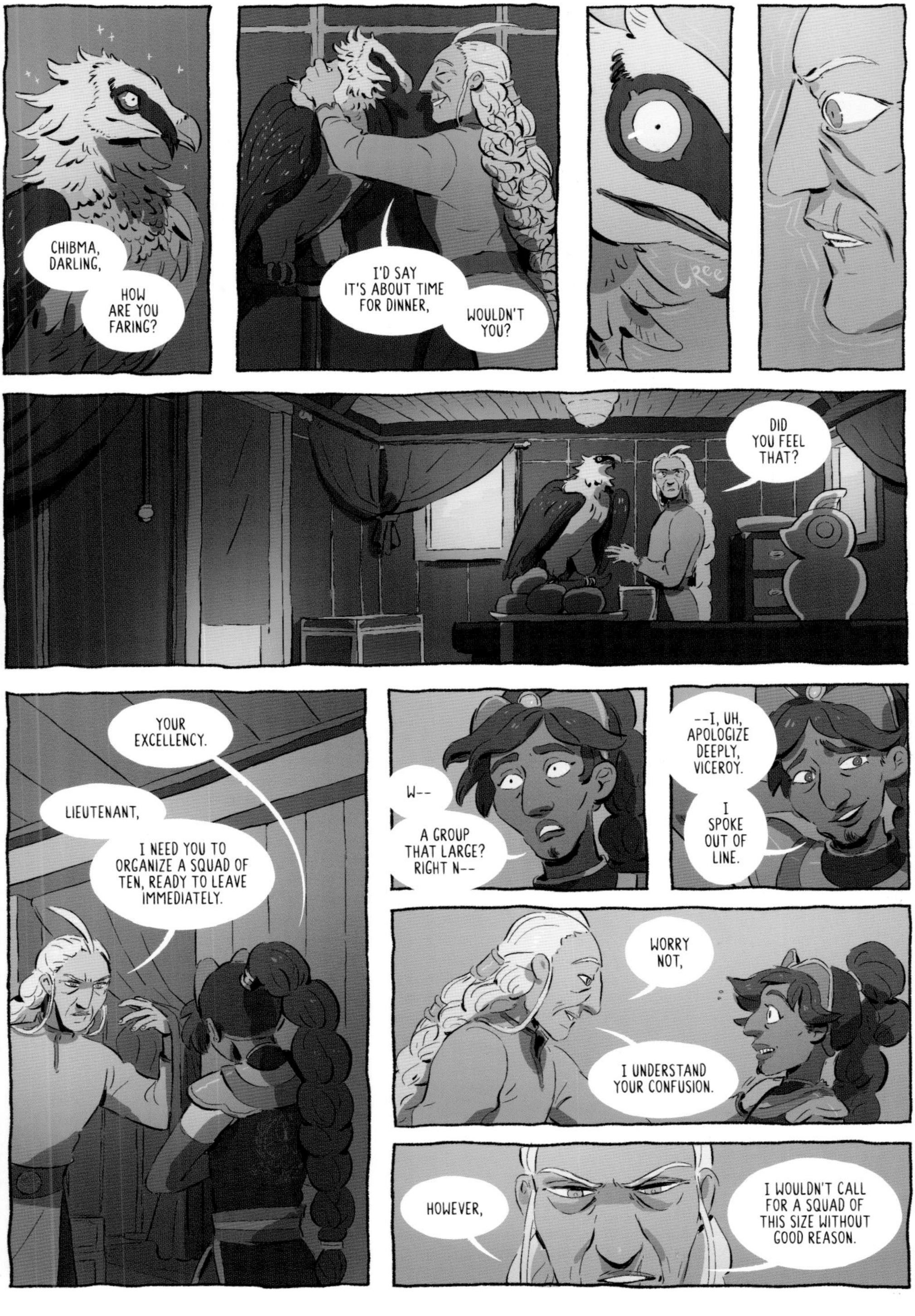
CHIBMA, DARLING,
HOW ARE YOU FARING?
I'D SAY IT'S ABOUT TIME FOR DINNER,
WOULDN'T YOU?
Cree
DID YOU FEEL THAT?
YOUR EXCELLENCY.
LIEUTENANT,
I NEED YOU TO ORGANIZE A SQUAD OF TEN, READY TO LEAVE IMMEDIATELY.
W--
A GROUP THAT LARGE? RIGHT N--
--I, UH, APOLOGIZE DEEPLY, VICEROY.
I SPOKE OUT OF LINE.
WORRY NOT,
I UNDERSTAND YOUR CONFUSION.
HOWEVER,
I WOULDN'T CALL FOR A SQUAD OF THIS SIZE WITHOUT GOOD REASON.

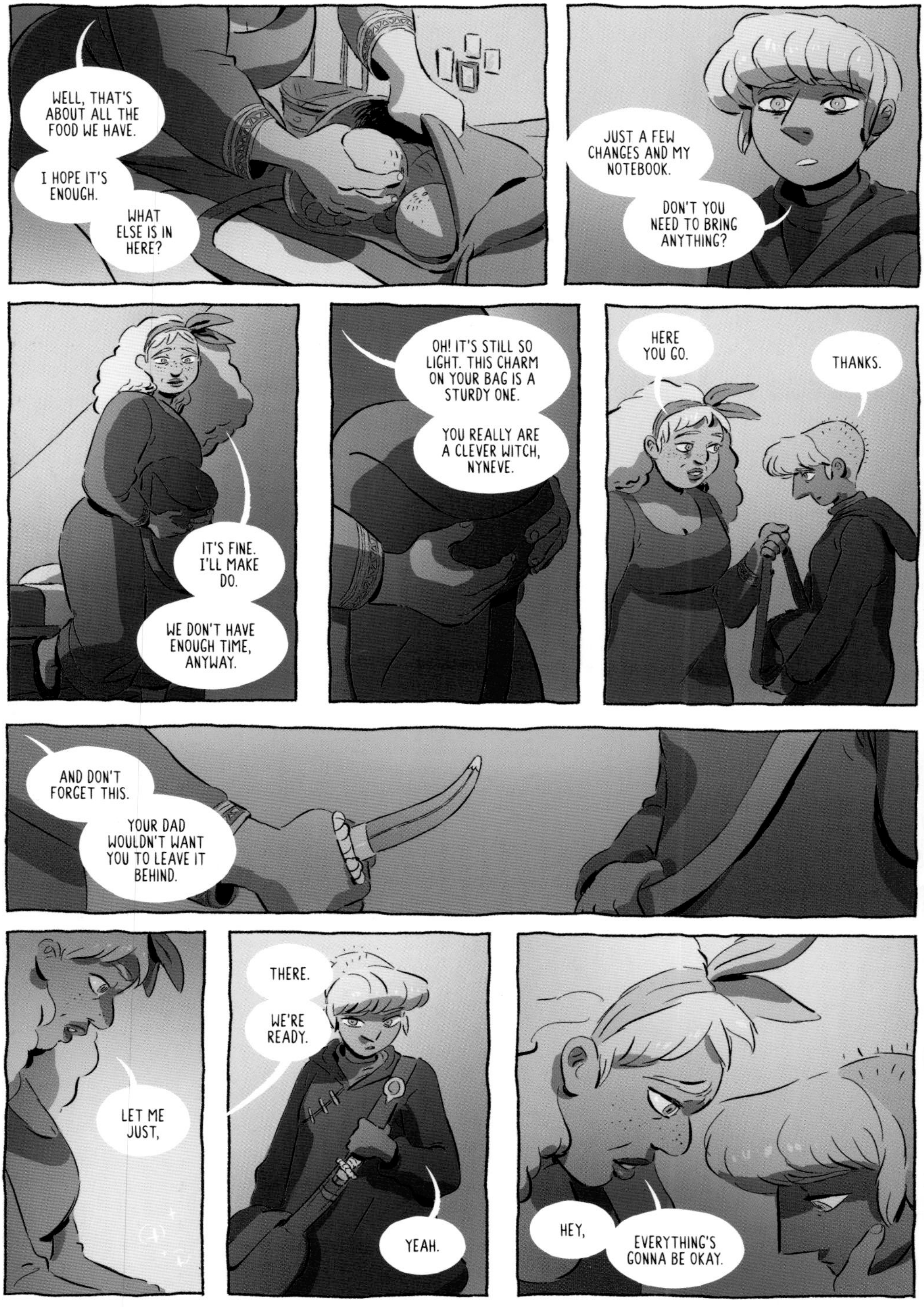

WELL, THAT'S ABOUT ALL THE FOOD WE HAVE.
I HOPE IT'S ENOUGH.
WHAT ELSE IS IN HERE?
JUST A FEW CHANGES AND MY NOTEBOOK.
DON'T YOU NEED TO BRING ANYTHING?
IT'S FINE. I'LL MAKE DO.
WE DON'T HAVE ENOUGH TIME, ANYWAY.
OH! IT'S STILL SO LIGHT. THIS CHARM ON YOUR BAG IS A STURDY ONE.
YOU REALLY ARE A CLEVER WITCH, NYNEVE.
HERE YOU GO.
THANKS.
AND DON'T FORGET THIS.
YOUR DAD WOULDN'T WANT YOU TO LEAVE IT BEHIND.
LET ME JUST,
THERE.
WE'RE READY.
YEAH.
HEY,
EVERYTHING'S GONNA BE OKAY.

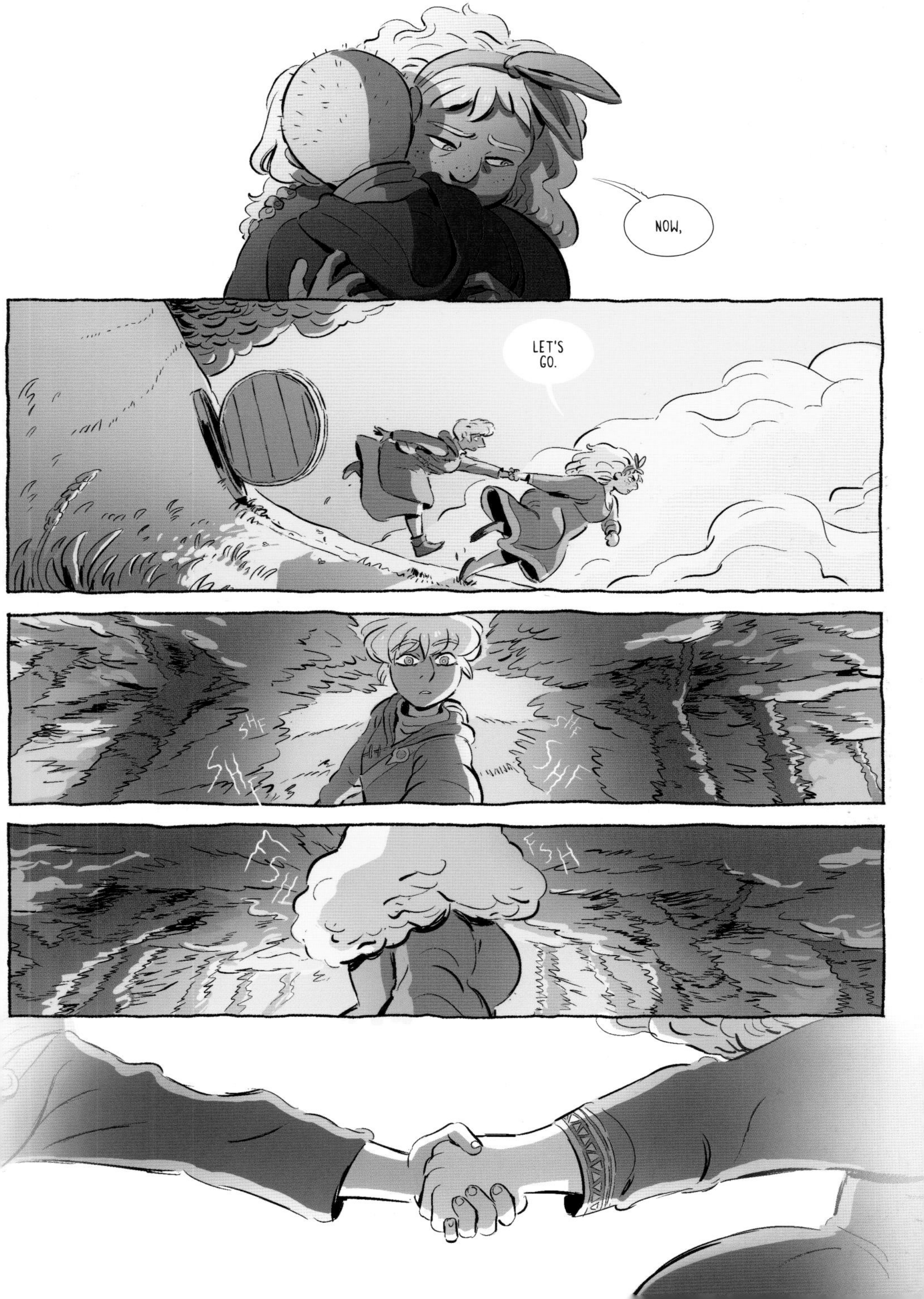
NOW,
LET'S GO.
SHF
SHF
SHF
SHF
FSH
FSH

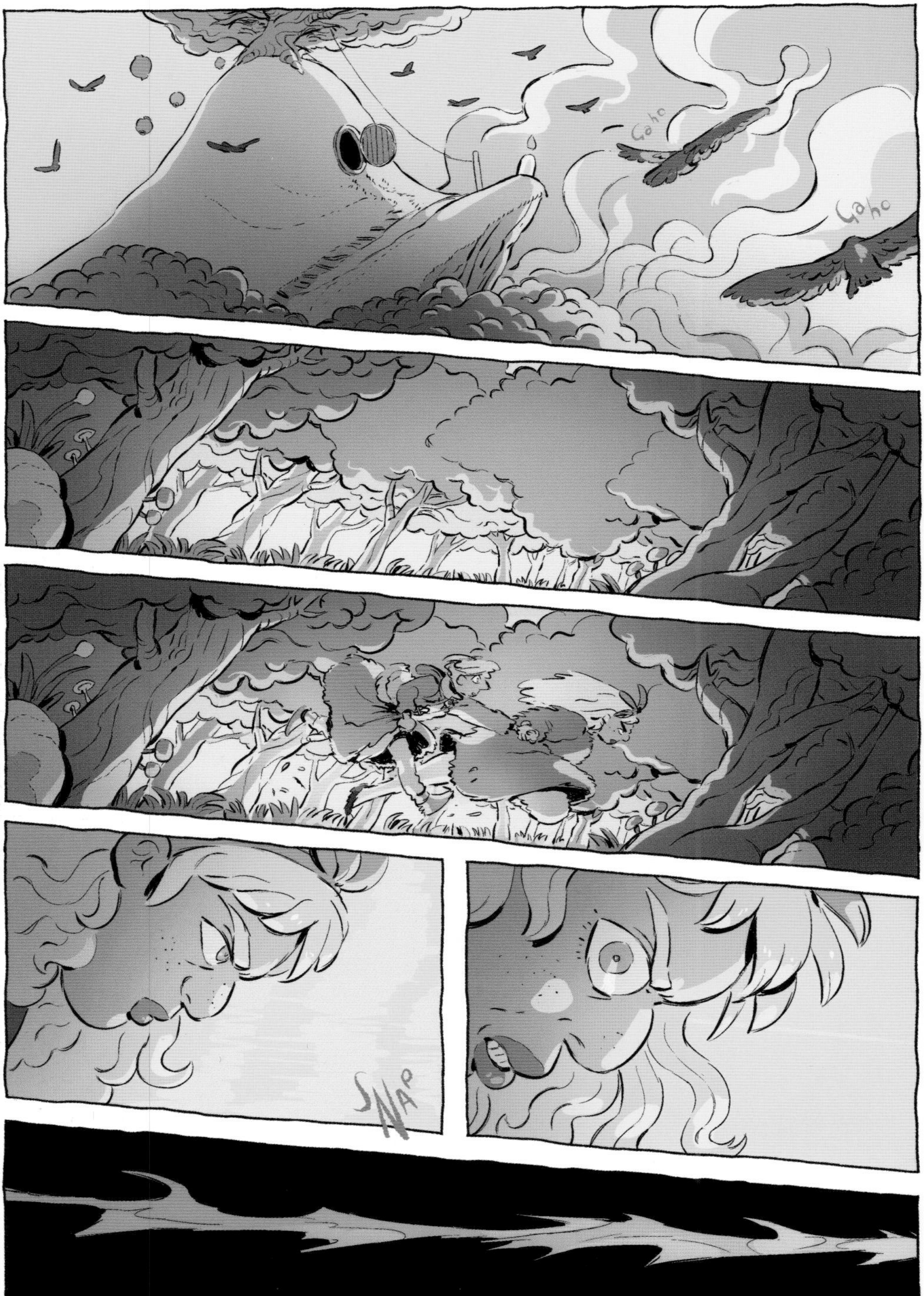
Gaho
Gaho
SNAP

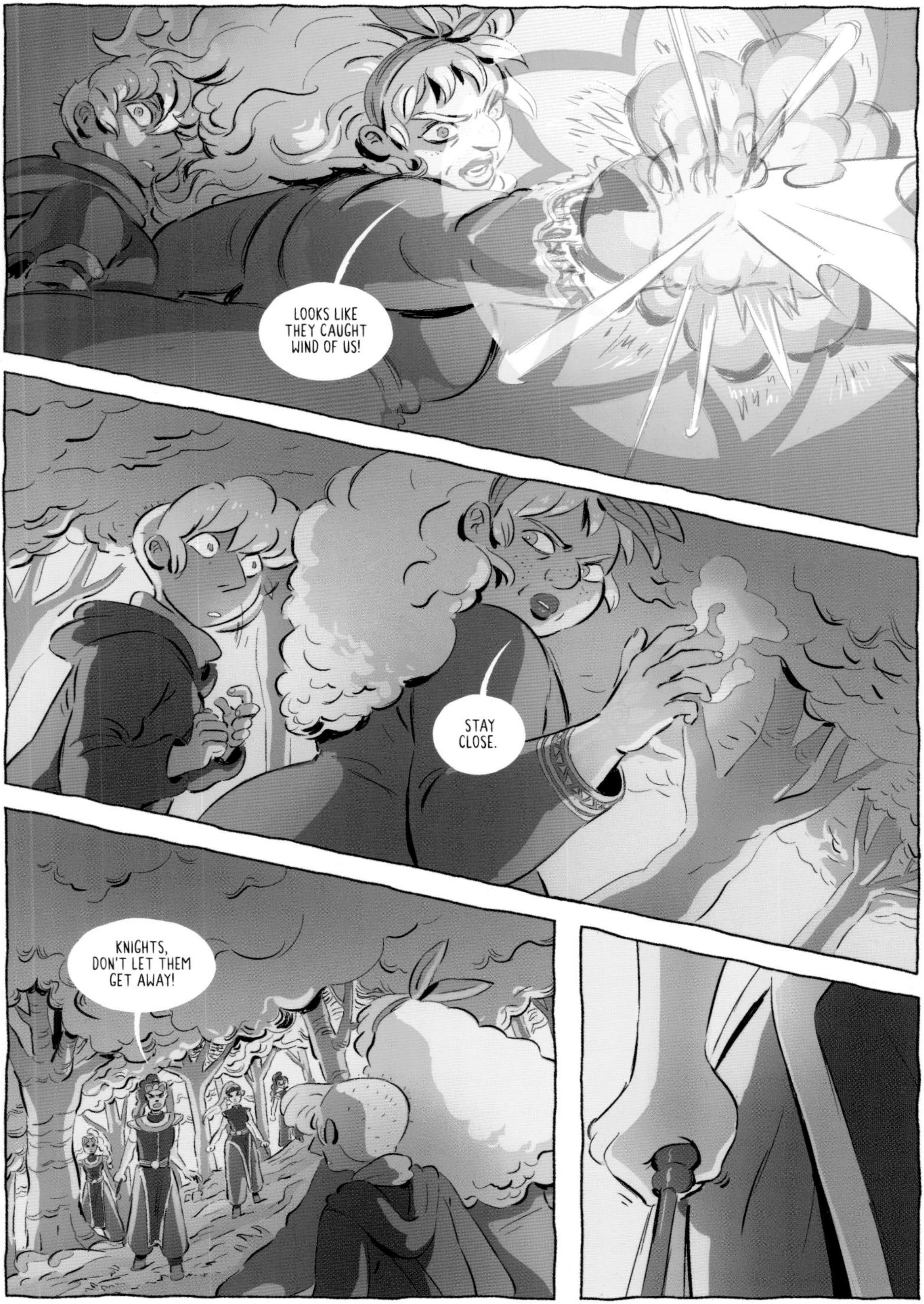
LOOKS LIKE THEY CAUGHT WIND OF US!
STAY CLOSE.
KNIGHTS, DON'T LET THEM GET AWAY!

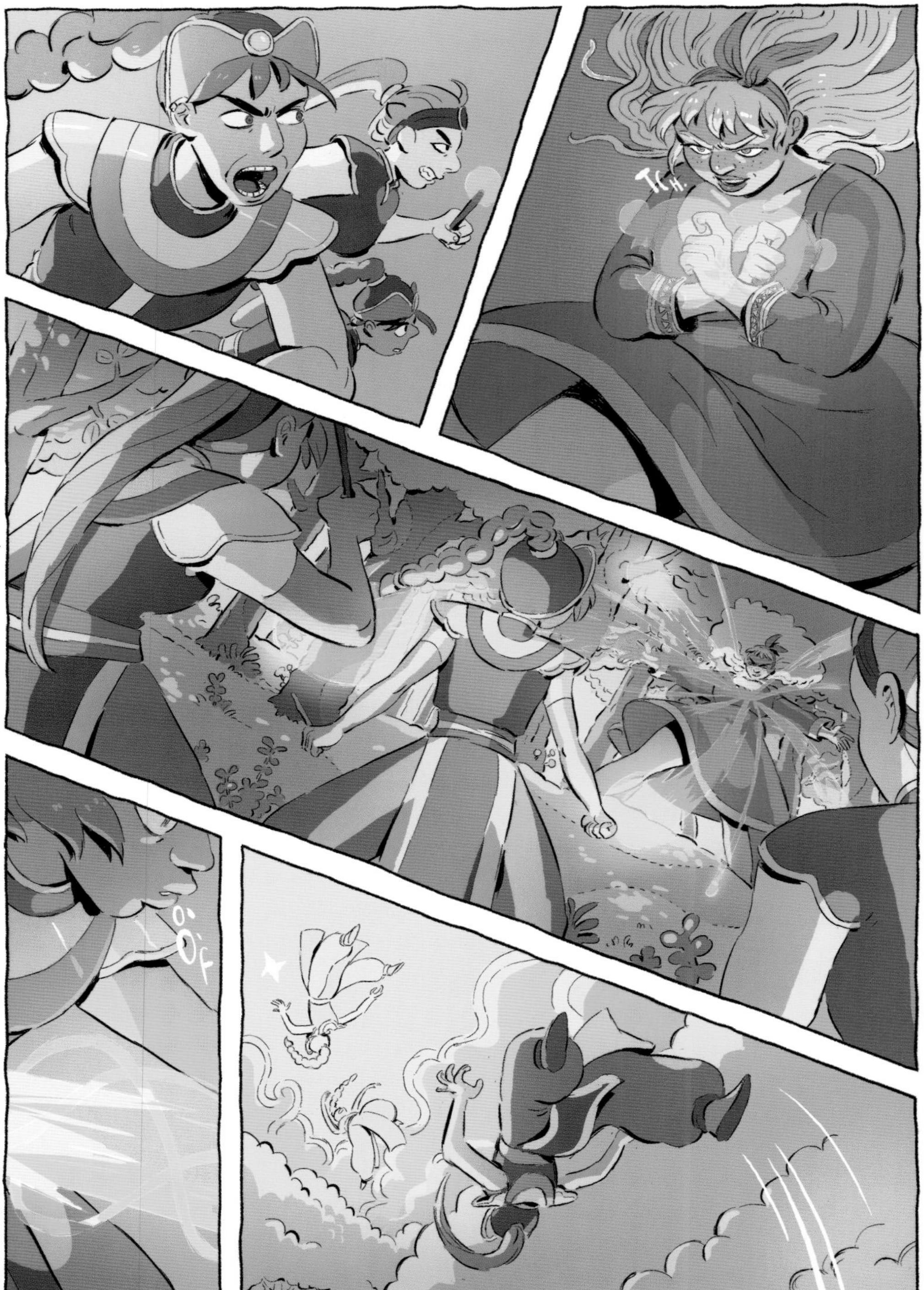
TCH.
OOF

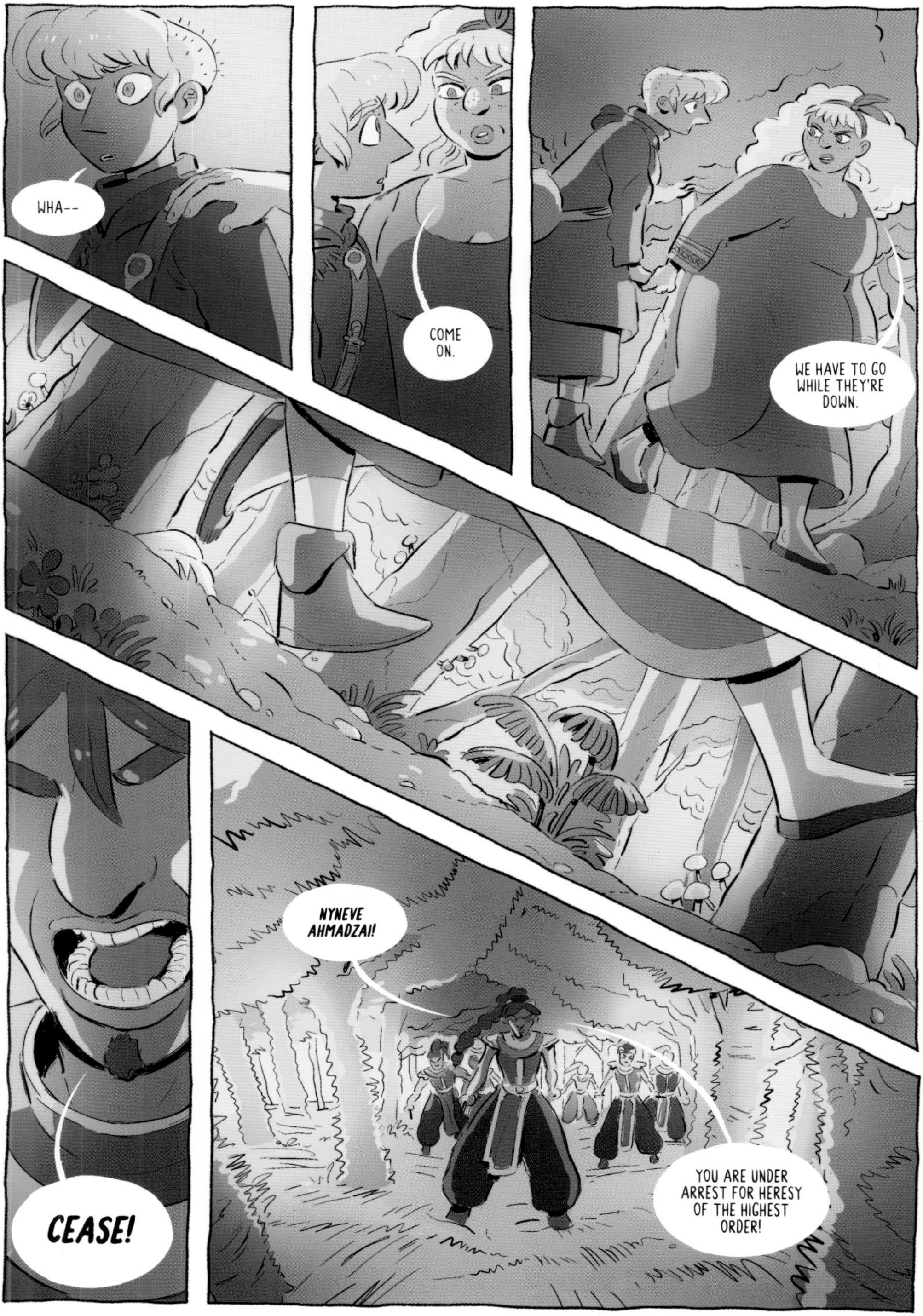
WHA--
COME ON.
WE HAVE TO GO WHILE THEY'RE DOWN.
CEASE!
NYNEVE AHMADZAI!
YOU ARE UNDER ARREST FOR HERESY OF THE HIGHEST ORDER!

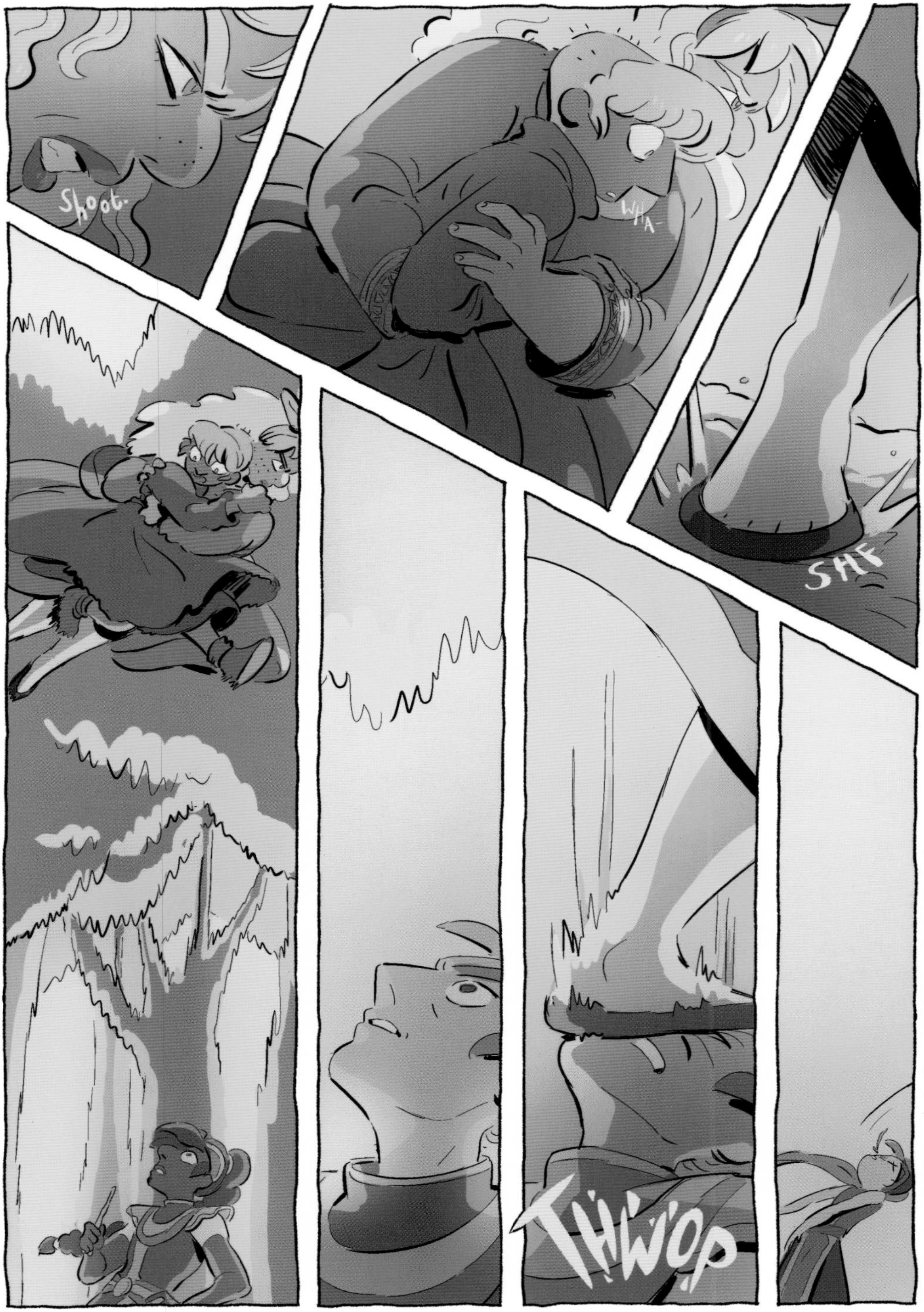
Shoot.
WHA-
SHF
THWOP

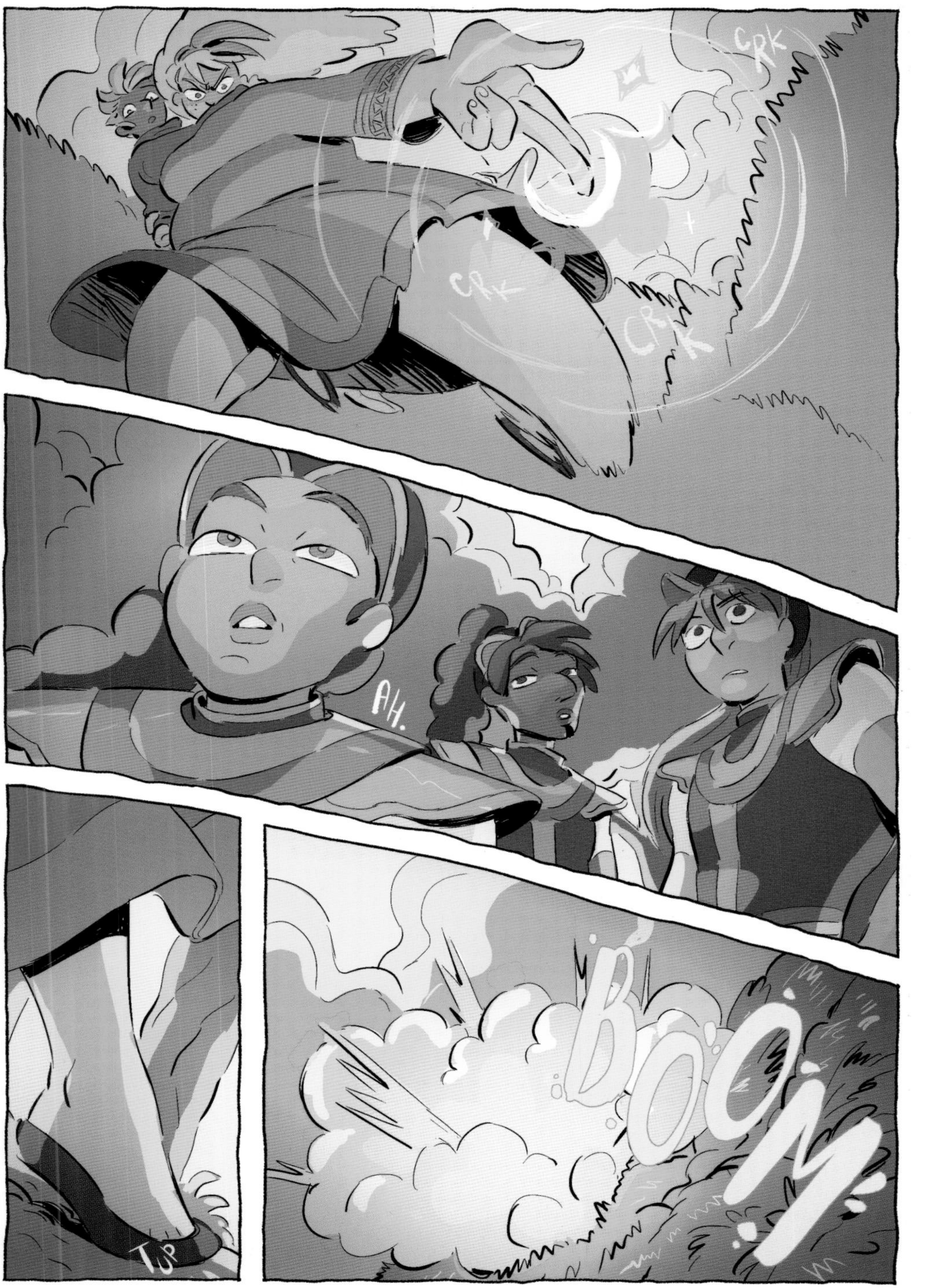
CRK
CRK
CRK
AH.
TUP
BOOM

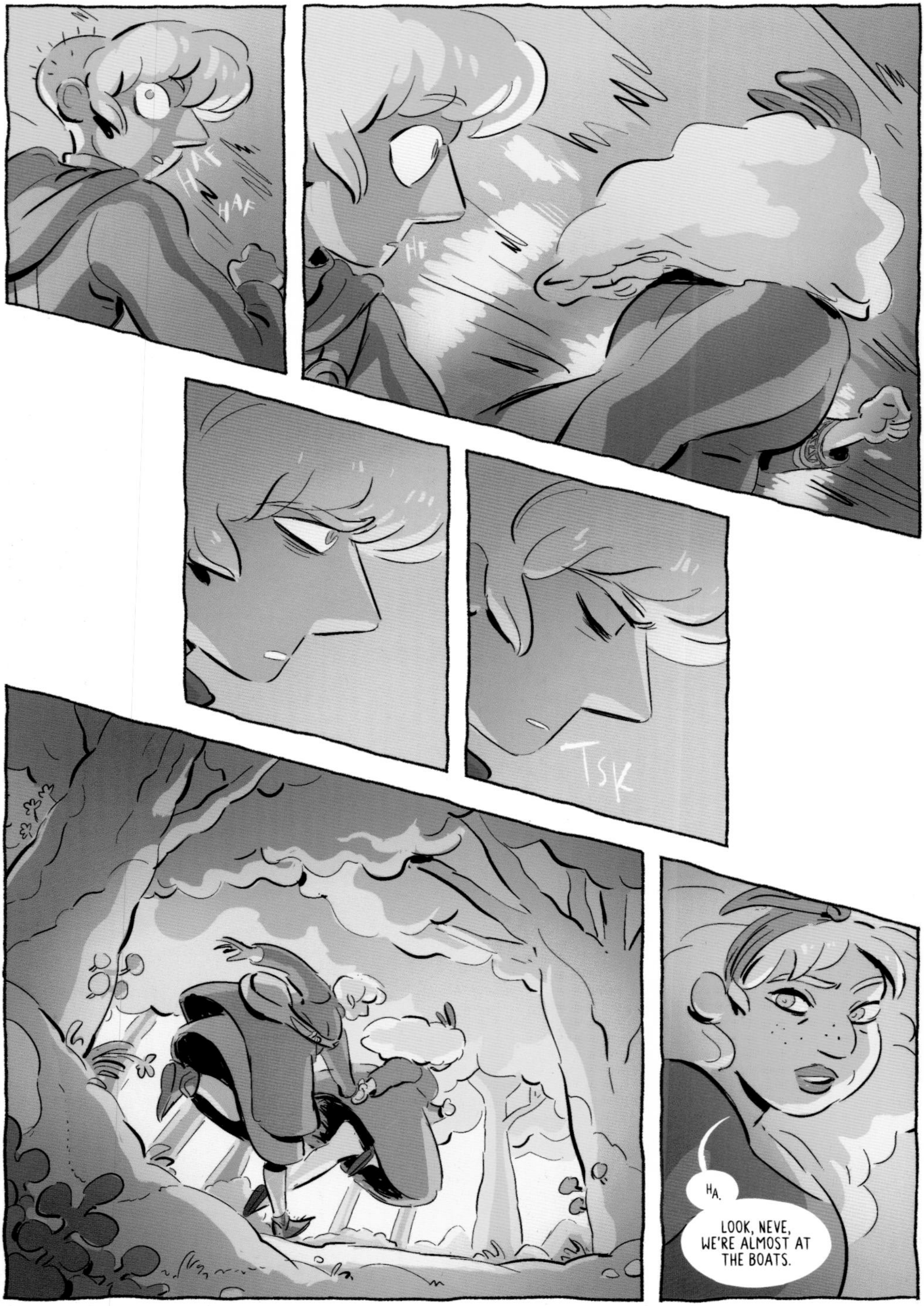
HAF
HAF
HAF
HF
TSK
HA.
LOOK, NEVE, WE'RE ALMOST AT THE BOATS.

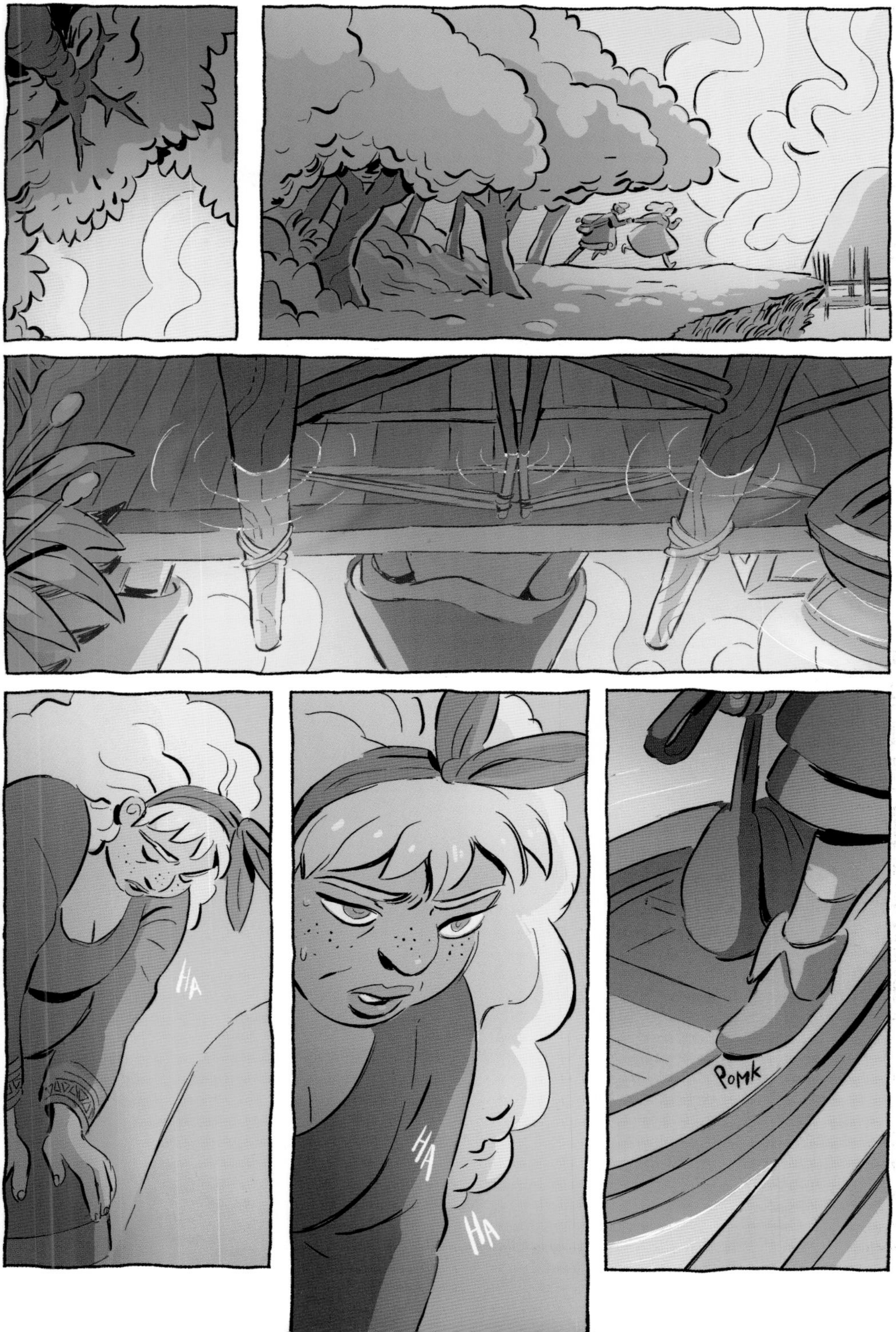
HA
HA
HA
POMK

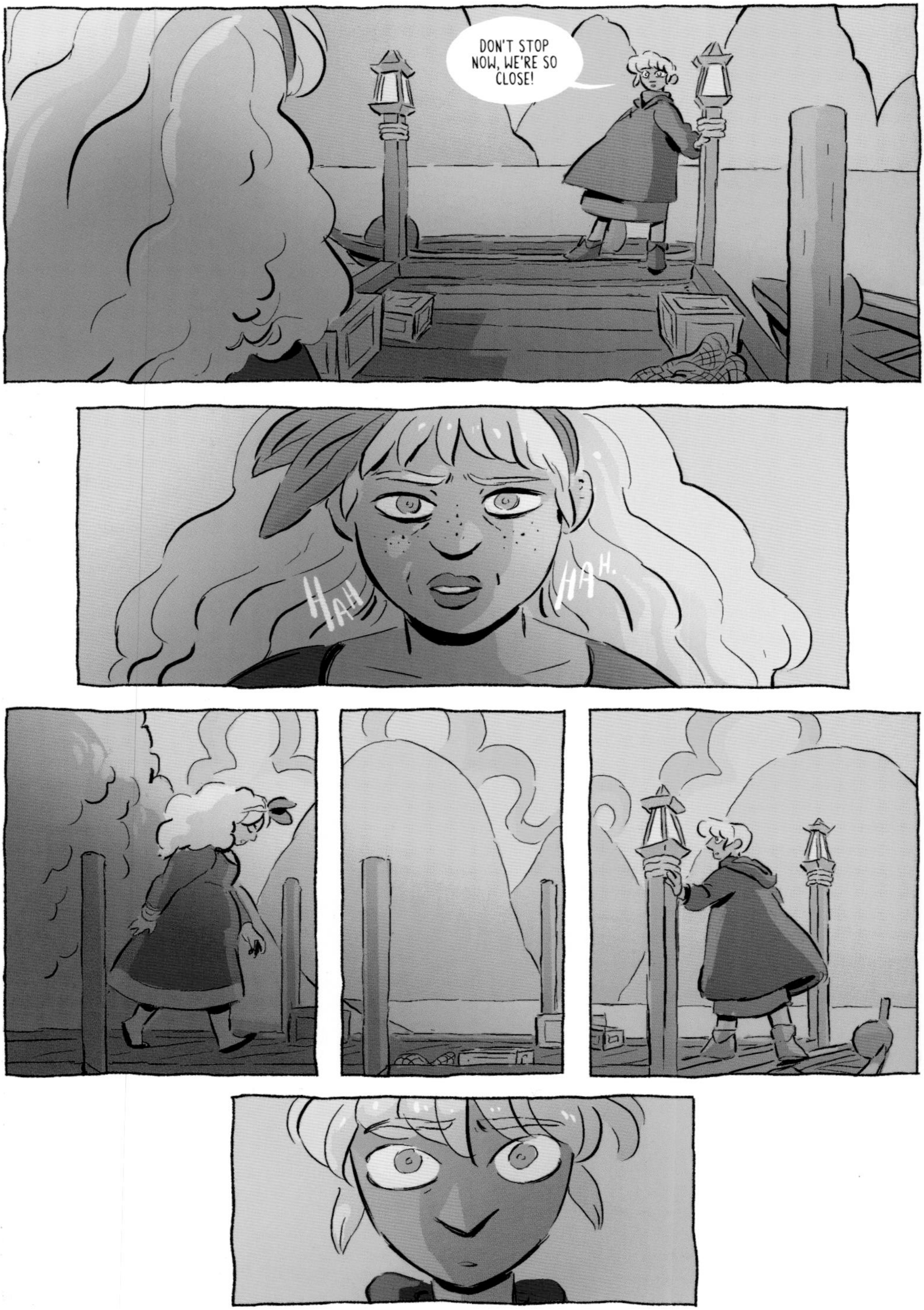
DON'T STOP NOW, WE'RE SO CLOSE!
HAH
HAH.

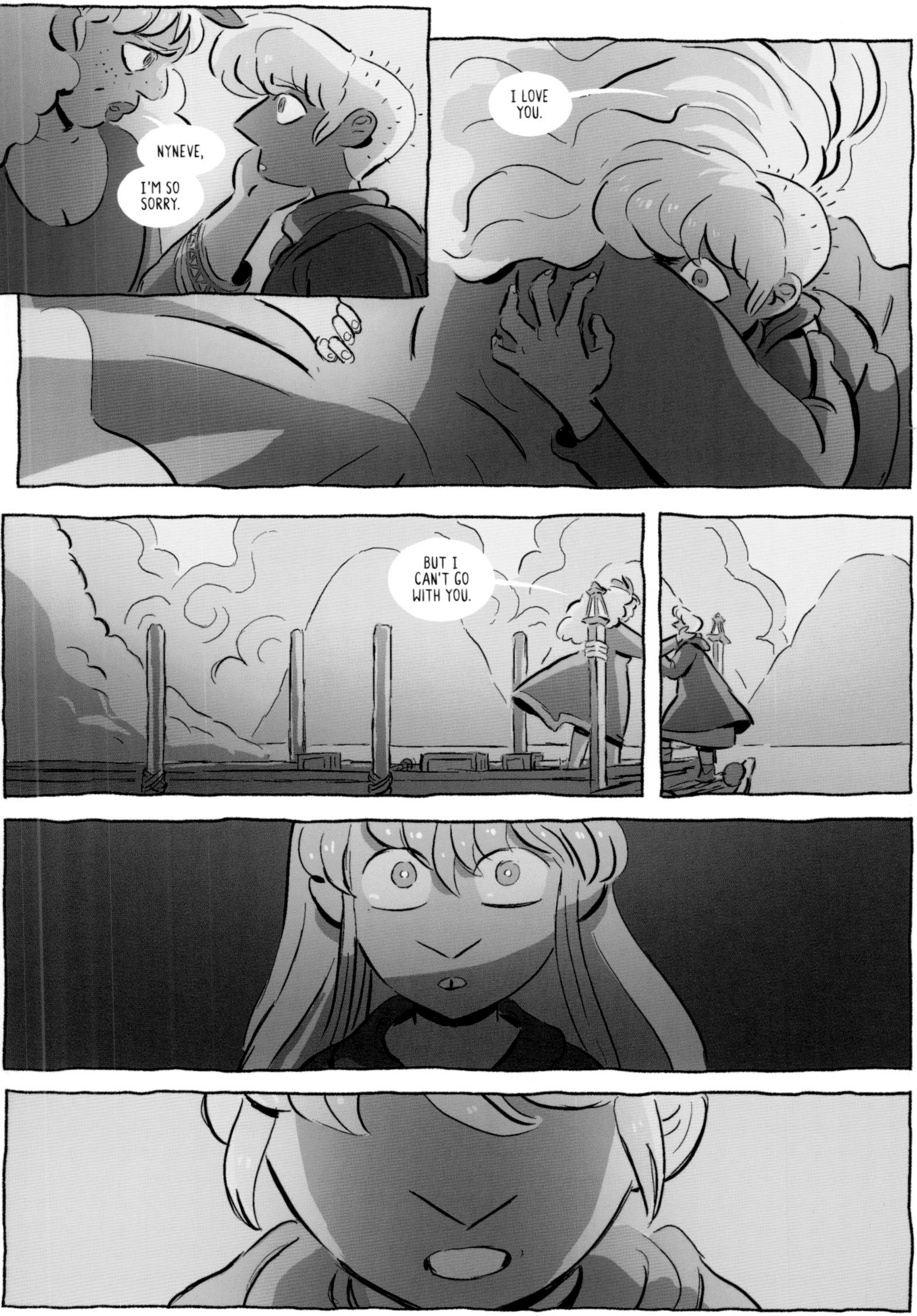
NYNEVE,
I'M SO SORRY.
I LOVE YOU.
BUT I CAN'T GO WITH YOU.

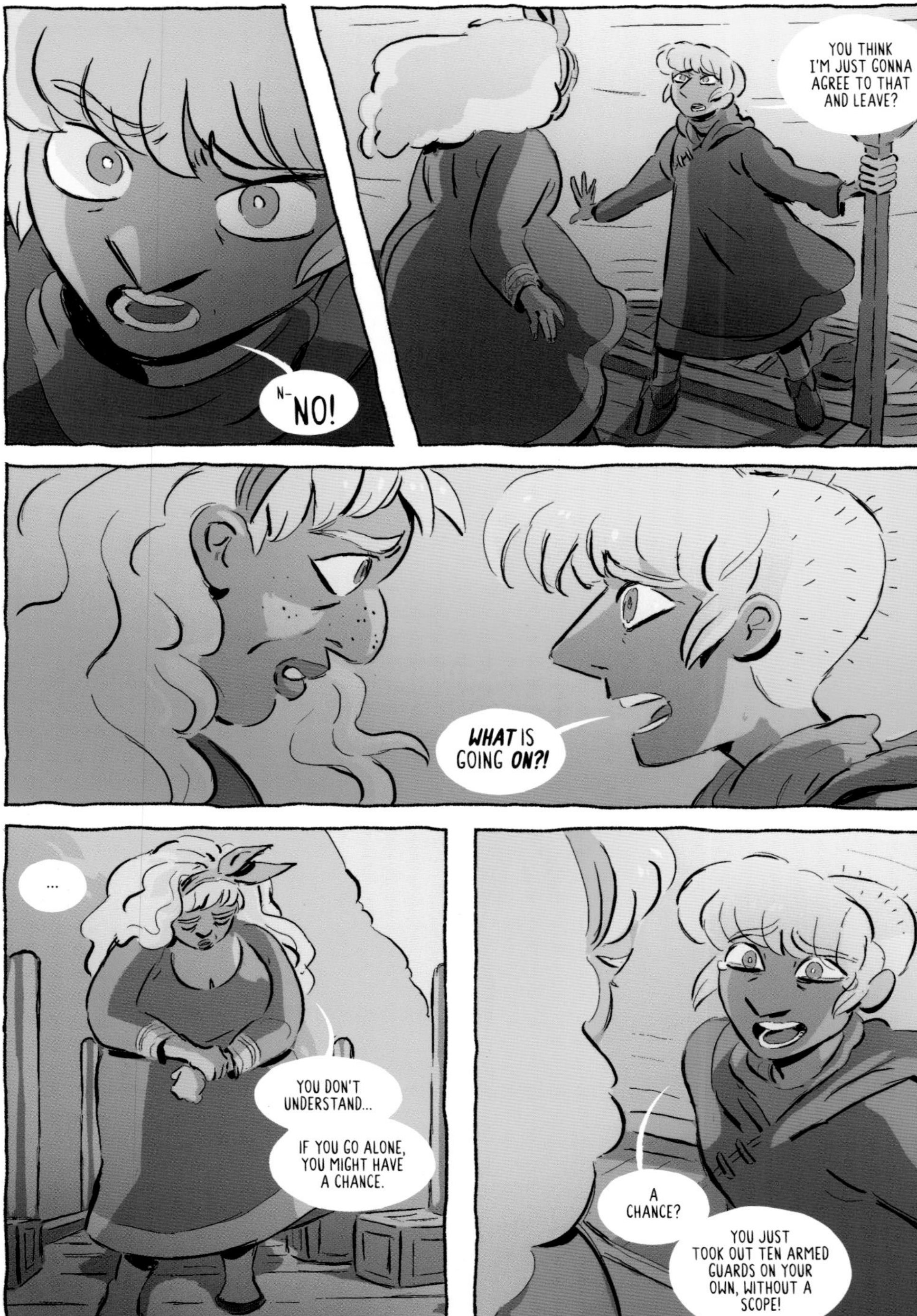
N-NO!
YOU THINK I'M JUST GONNA AGREE TO THAT AND LEAVE?
WHAT IS GOING ON?!
...
YOU DON'T UNDERSTAND...
IF YOU GO ALONE, YOU MIGHT HAVE A CHANCE.
A CHANCE?
YOU JUST TOOK OUT TEN ARMED GUARDS ON YOUR OWN, WITHOUT A SCOPE!

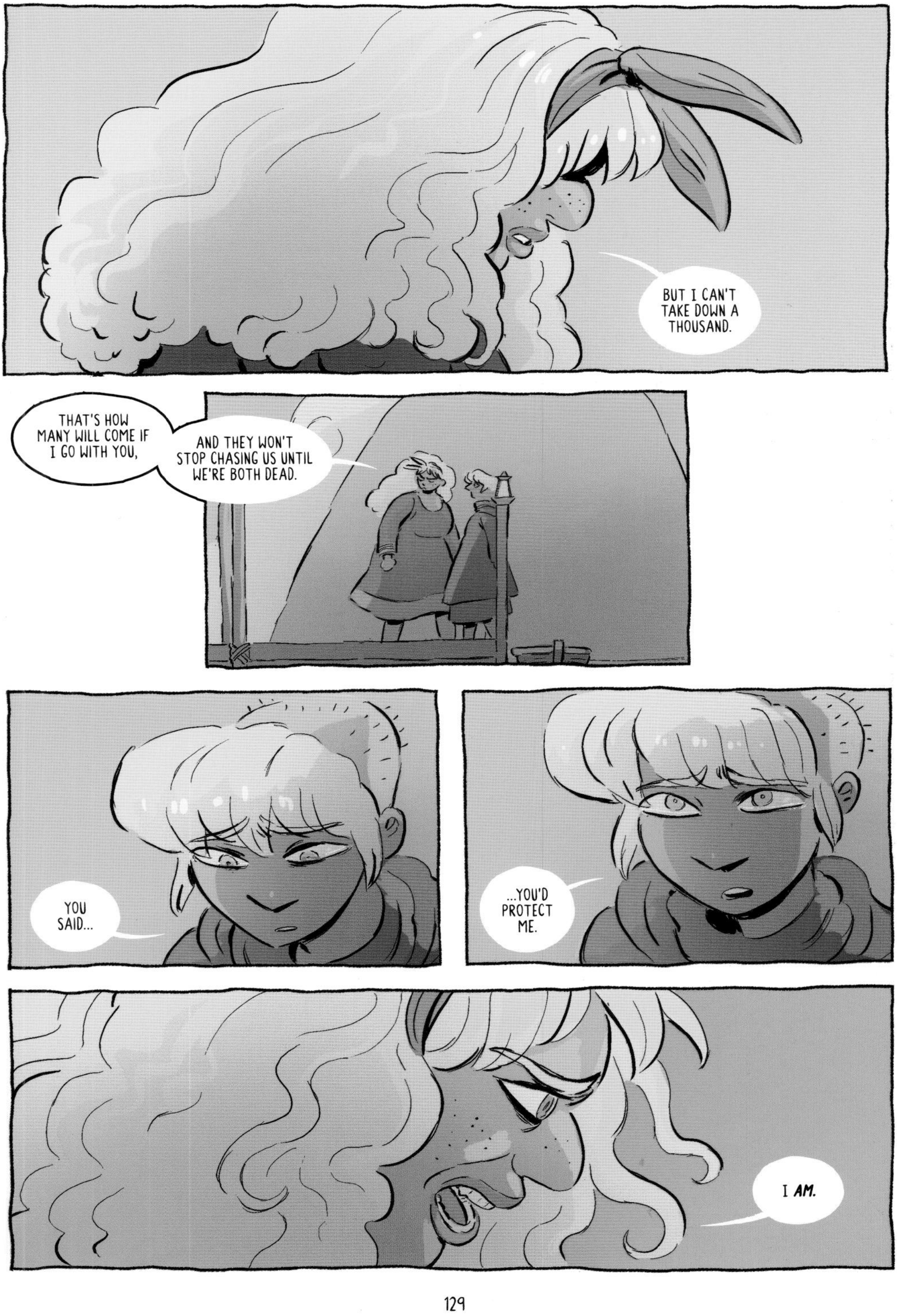
BUT I CAN'T TAKE DOWN A THOUSAND.
THAT'S HOW MANY WILL COME IF I GO WITH YOU,
AND THEY WON'T STOP CHASING US UNTIL WE'RE BOTH DEAD.
YOU SAID...
...YOU'D PROTECT ME.
I *AM.*

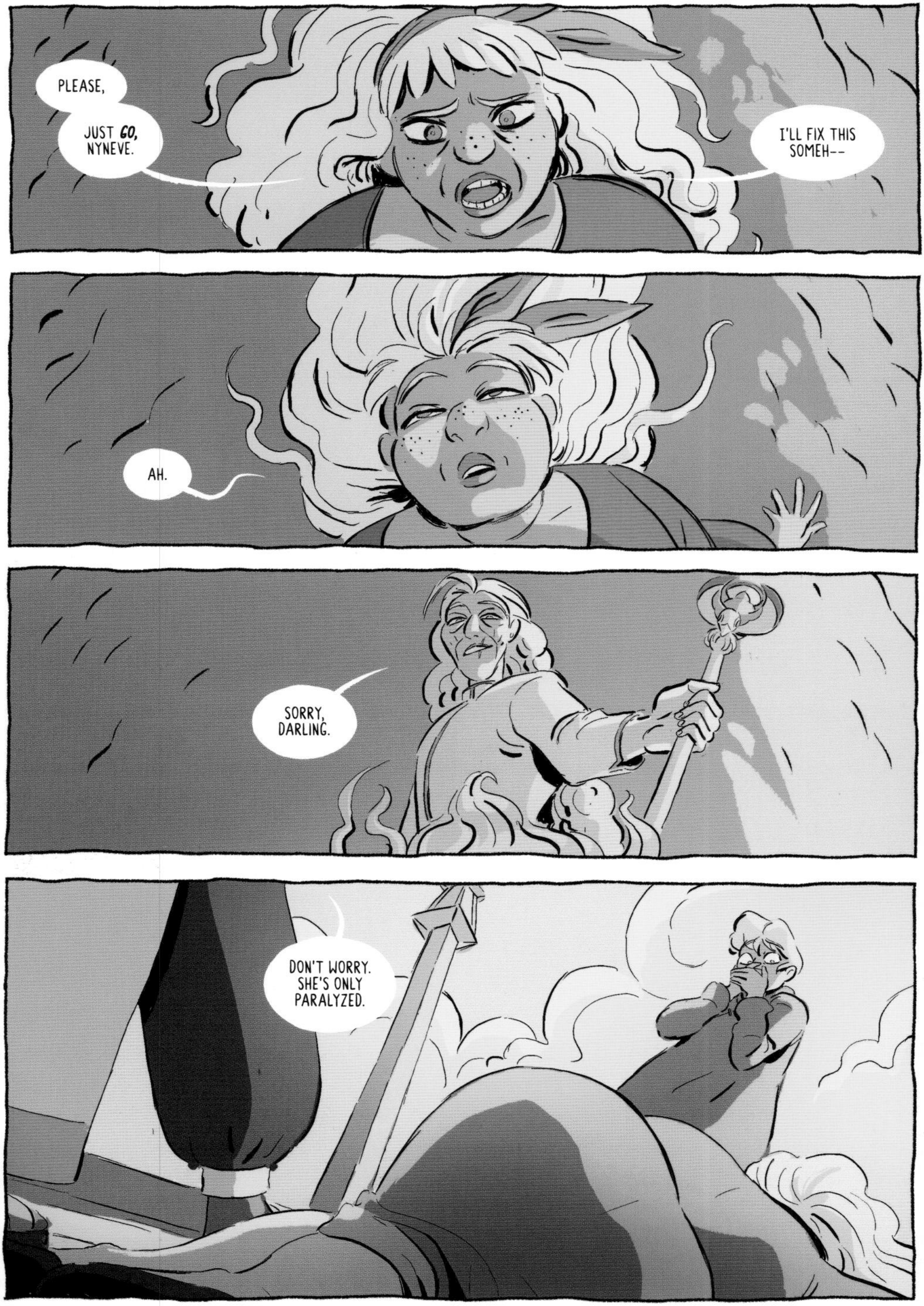
PLEASE,
JUST **GO,** NYNEVE.
I'LL FIX THIS SOMEH--
AH.
SORRY, DARLING.
DON'T WORRY. SHE'S ONLY PARALYZED.

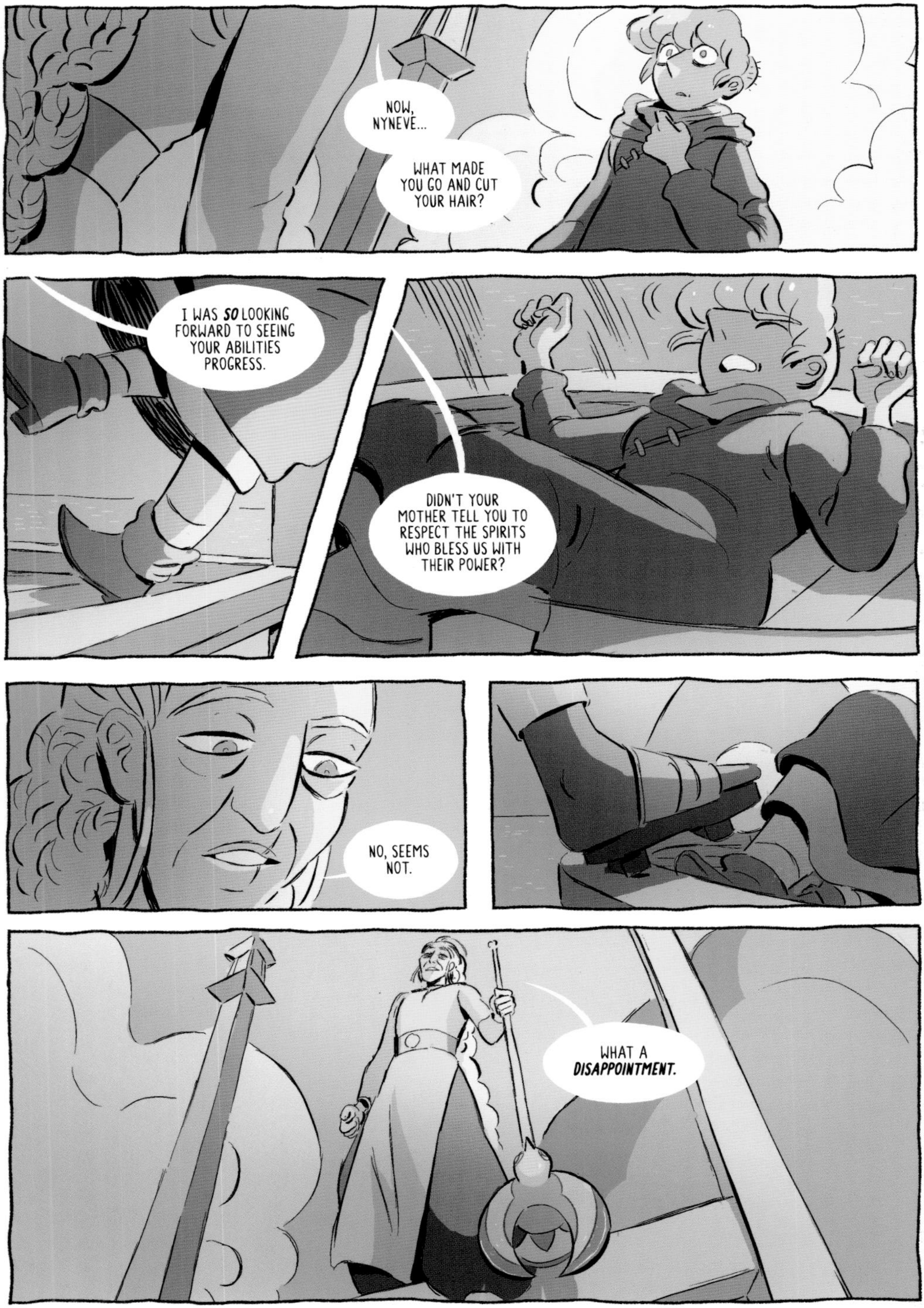
NOW, NYNEVE...
WHAT MADE YOU GO AND CUT YOUR HAIR?
I WAS **SO** LOOKING FORWARD TO SEEING YOUR ABILITIES PROGRESS.
DIDN'T YOUR MOTHER TELL YOU TO RESPECT THE SPIRITS WHO BLESS US WITH THEIR POWER?
NO, SEEMS NOT.
WHAT A ***DISAPPOINTMENT.***

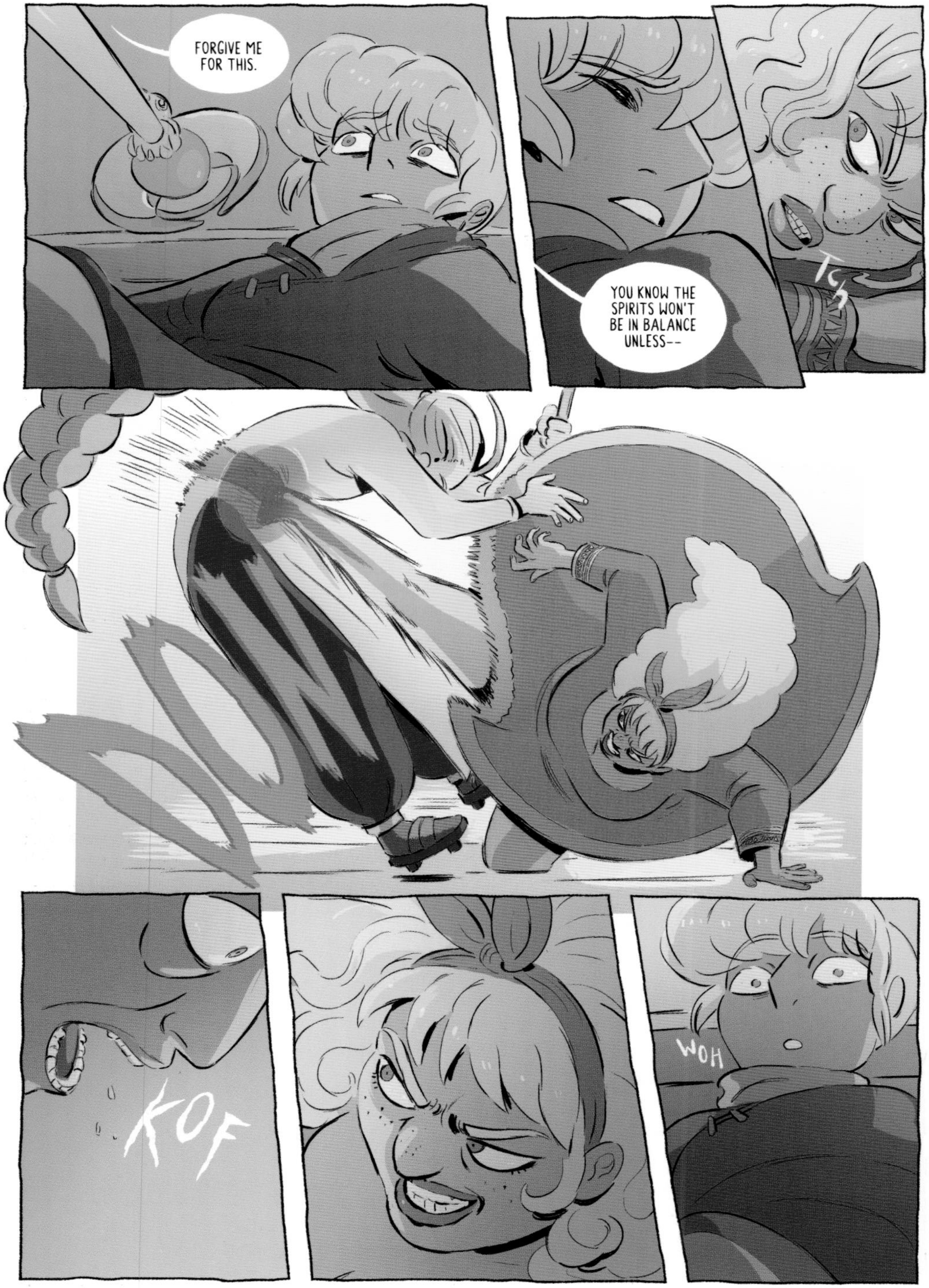
FORGIVE ME FOR THIS.
YOU KNOW THE SPIRITS WON'T BE IN BALANCE UNLESS--
TCH
WOH
KOF

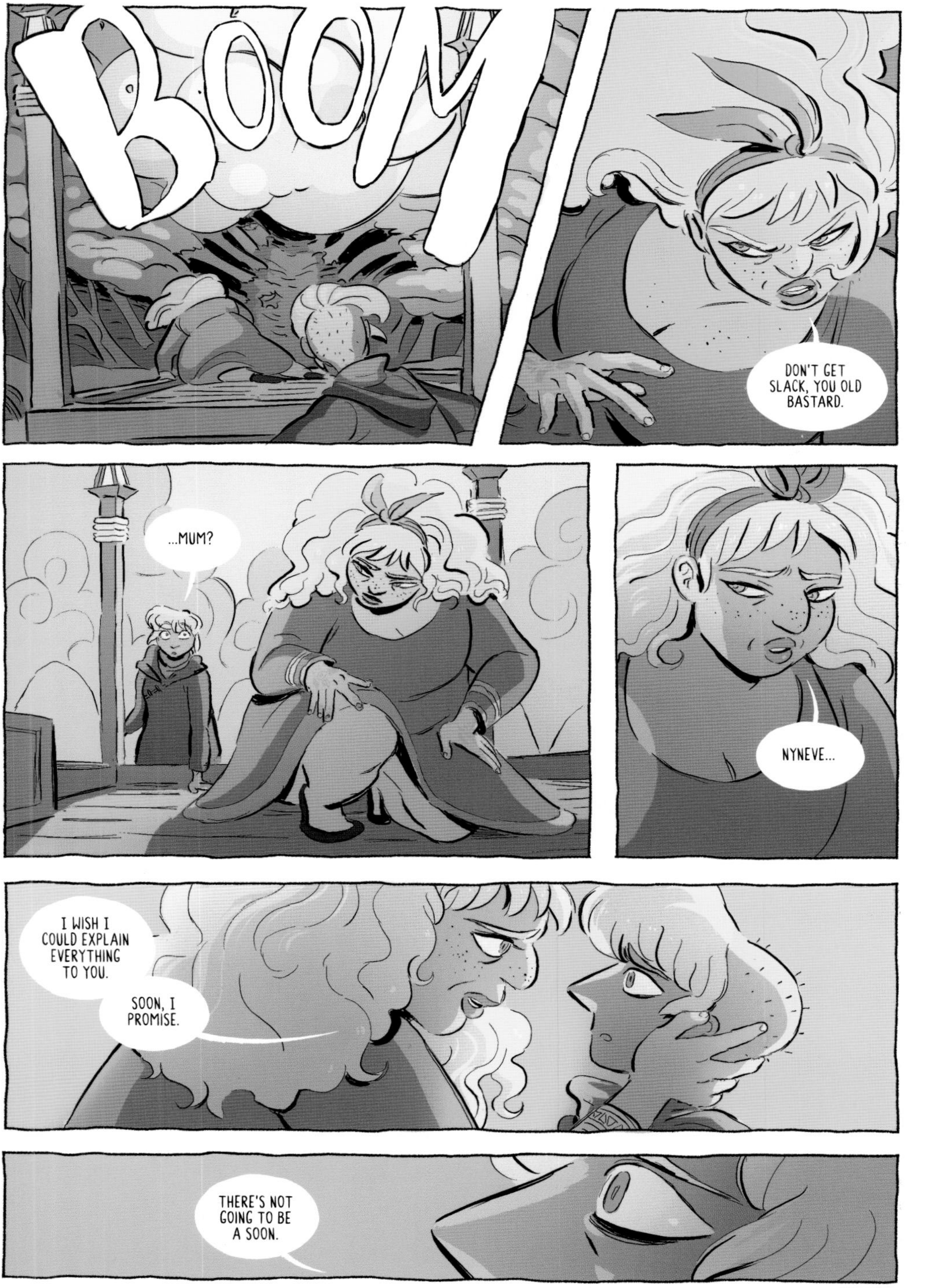
BOOM!
DON'T GET SLACK, YOU OLD BASTARD.
...MUM?
NYNEVE...
I WISH I COULD EXPLAIN EVERYTHING TO YOU.
SOON, I PROMISE.
THERE'S NOT GOING TO BE A SOON.

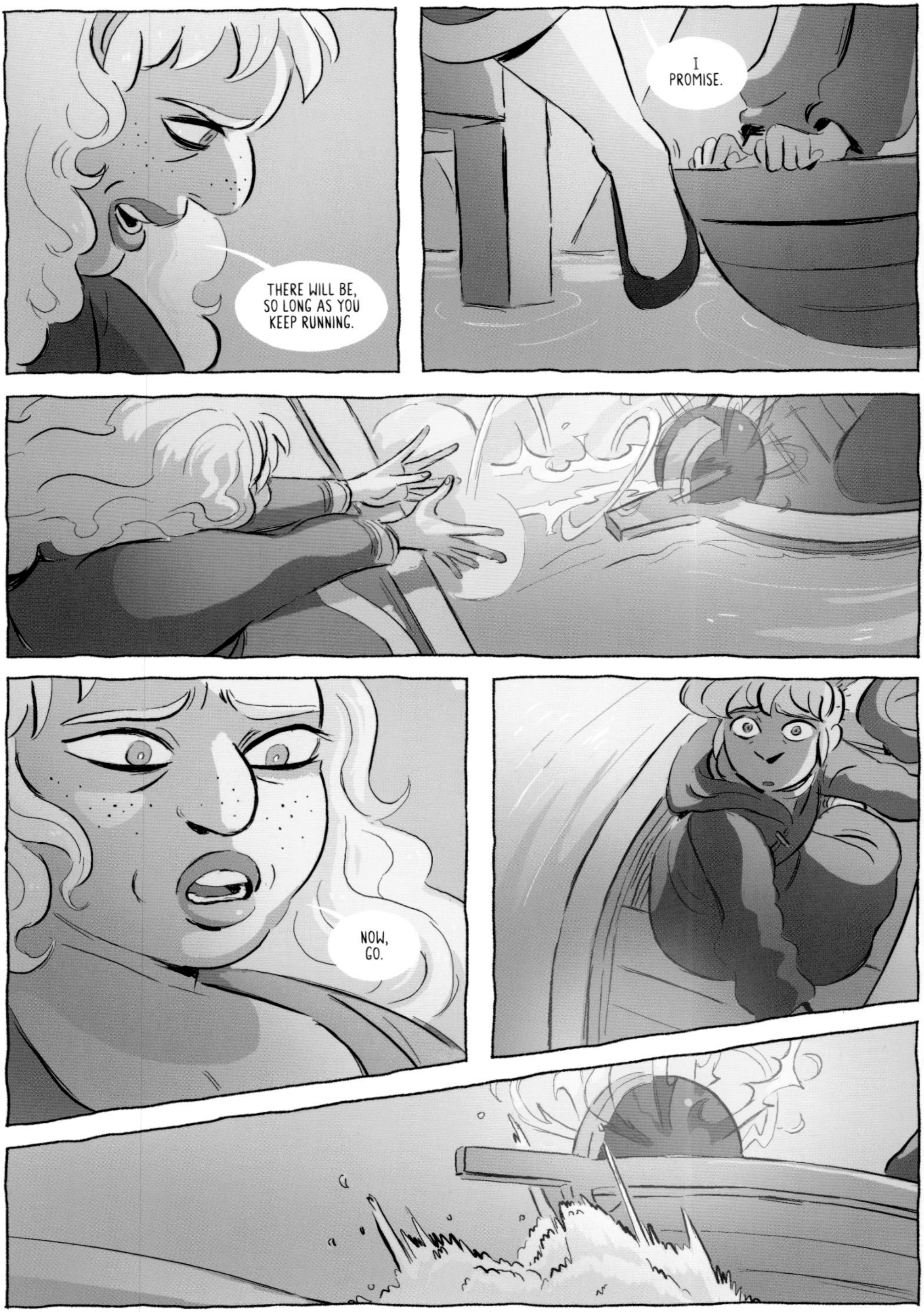
THERE WILL BE, SO LONG AS YOU KEEP RUNNING.
I PROMISE.
NOW, GO.

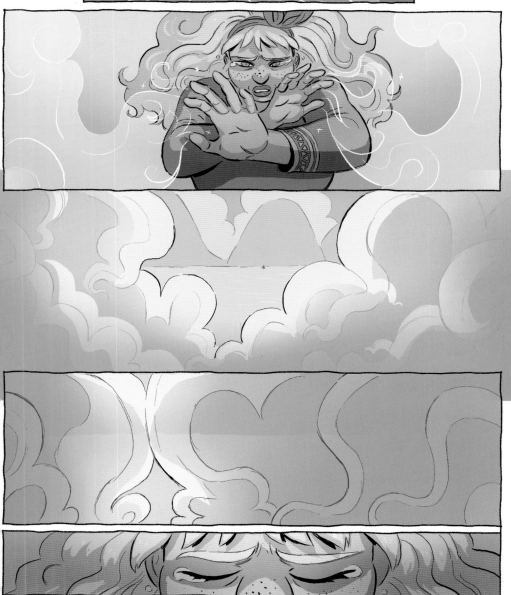

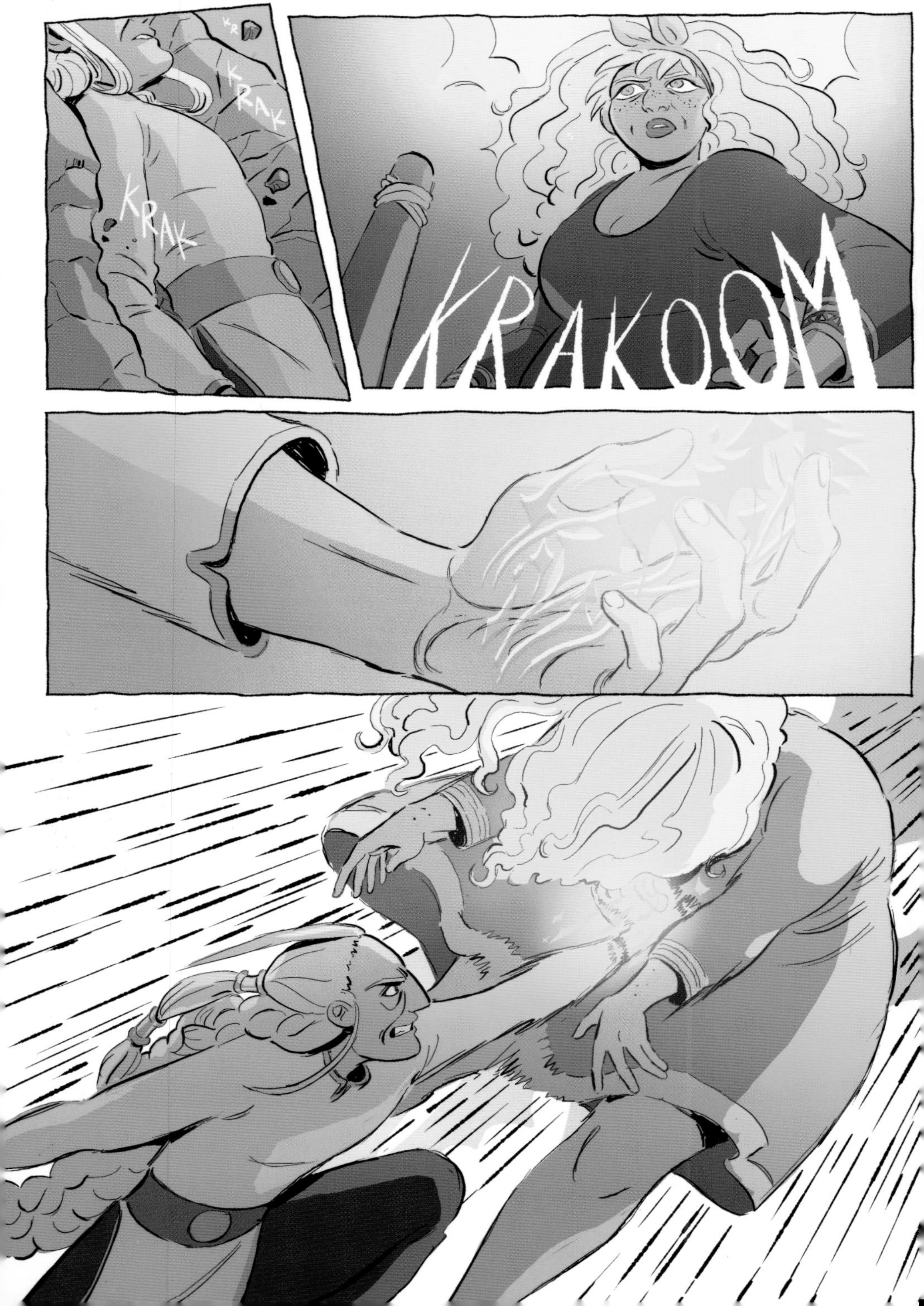

KR
KRAK
KRAK
KRAKOOM

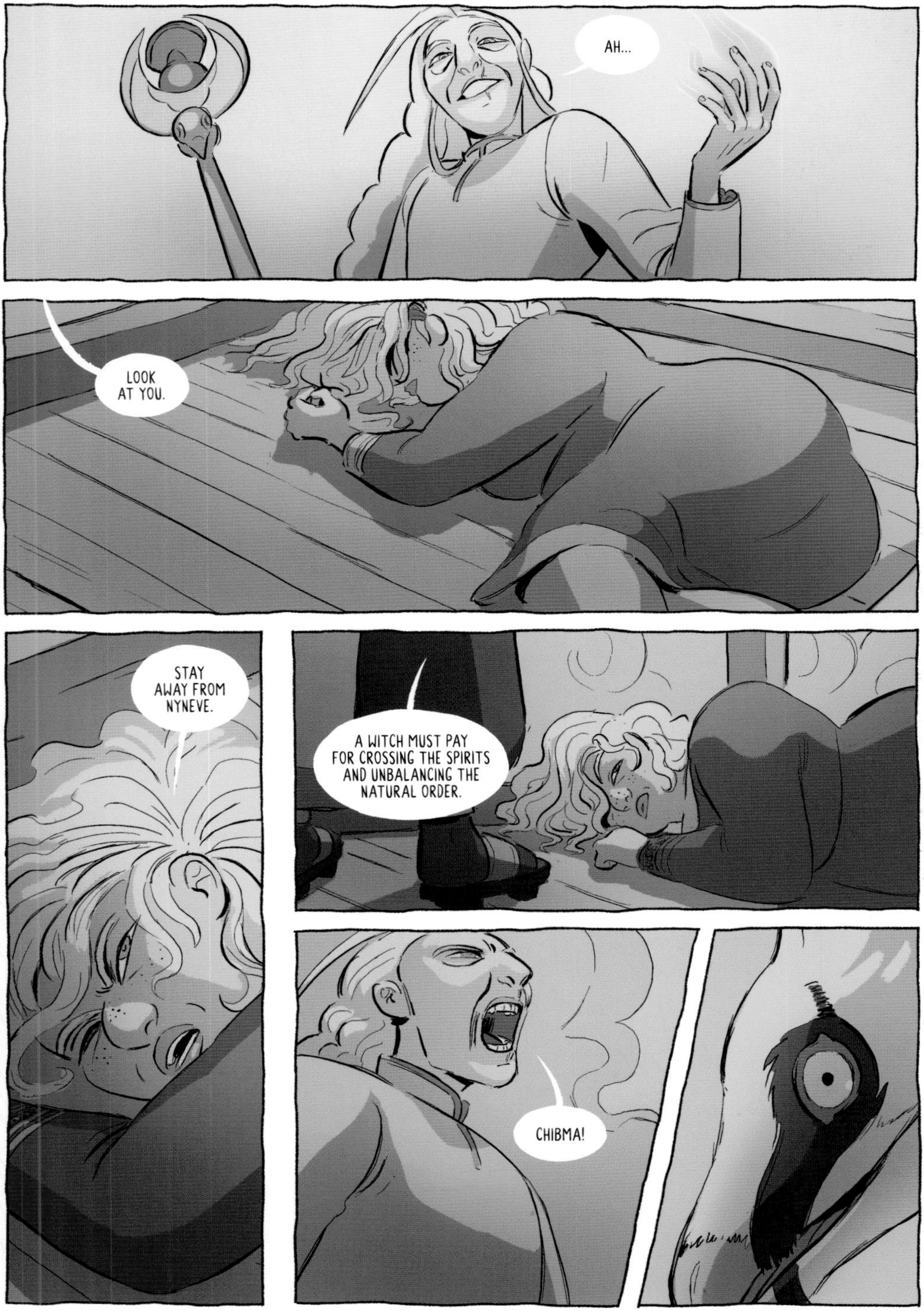
AH...
LOOK AT YOU.
STAY AWAY FROM NYNEVE.
A WITCH MUST PAY FOR CROSSING THE SPIRITS AND UNBALANCING THE NATURAL ORDER.
CHIBMA!

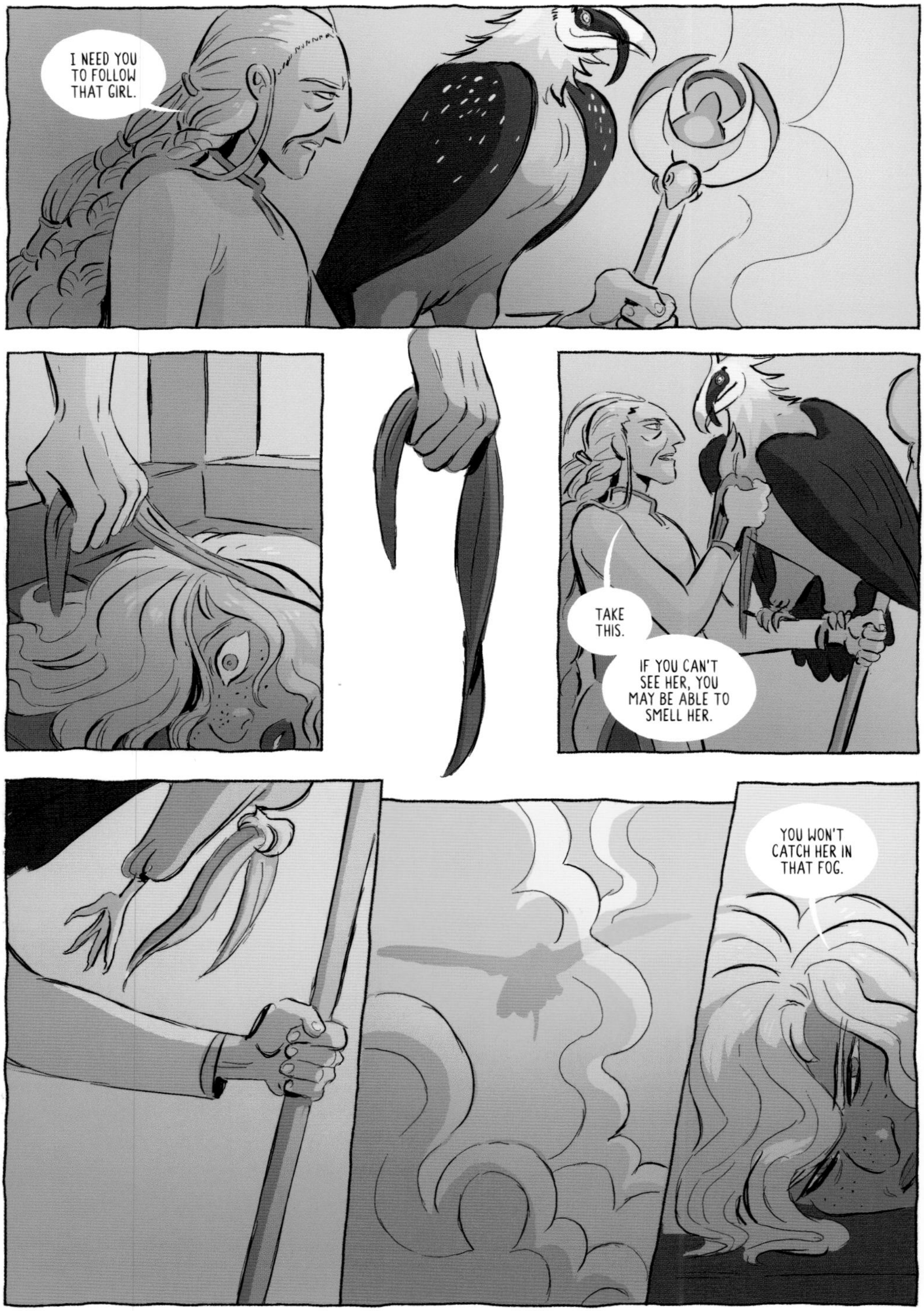

I NEED YOU TO FOLLOW THAT GIRL.
TAKE THIS.
IF YOU CAN'T SEE HER, YOU MAY BE ABLE TO SMELL HER.
YOU WON'T CATCH HER IN THAT FOG.

HA HA.

THAT MAY WELL BE.

BUT TRULY,

HOW FAR DO YOU THINK SHE CAN TRAVEL,

ALONE,

WITH NO MAGIC?

YOU THOUGHT WE'D BE LENIENT BECAUSE YOU DIDN'T GO WITH HER?

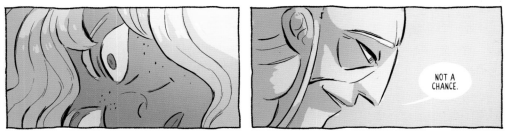

NOT A CHANCE.

YOU DID SURPRISE ME, VEDA.

YOU'RE CERTAINLY STRONGER THAN I THOUGHT YOU'D BE AFTER ALL THIS TIME.

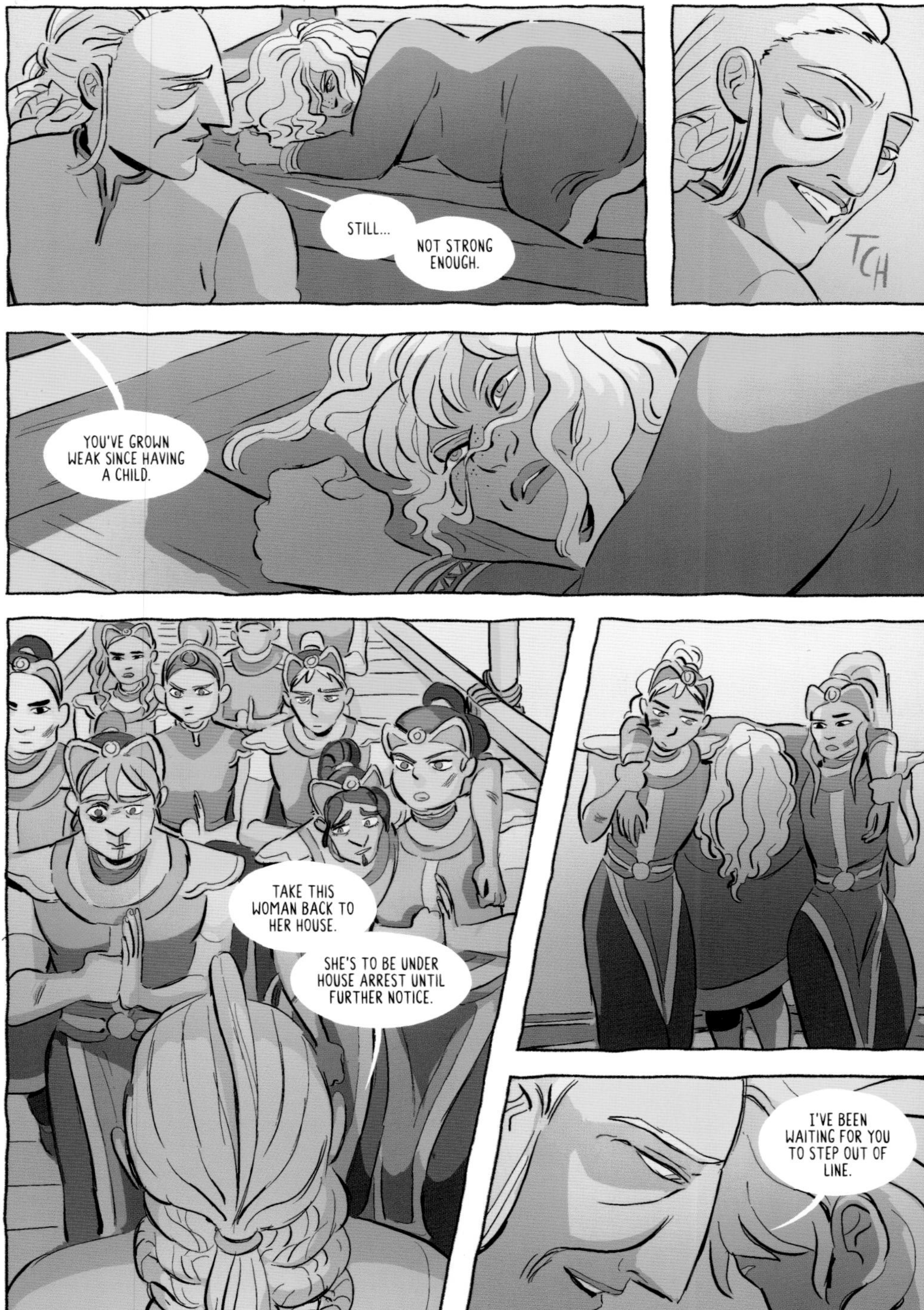
STILL...
NOT STRONG ENOUGH.
TCH
YOU'VE GROWN WEAK SINCE HAVING A CHILD.
TAKE THIS WOMAN BACK TO HER HOUSE.
SHE'S TO BE UNDER HOUSE ARREST UNTIL FURTHER NOTICE.
I'VE BEEN WAITING FOR YOU TO STEP OUT OF LINE.

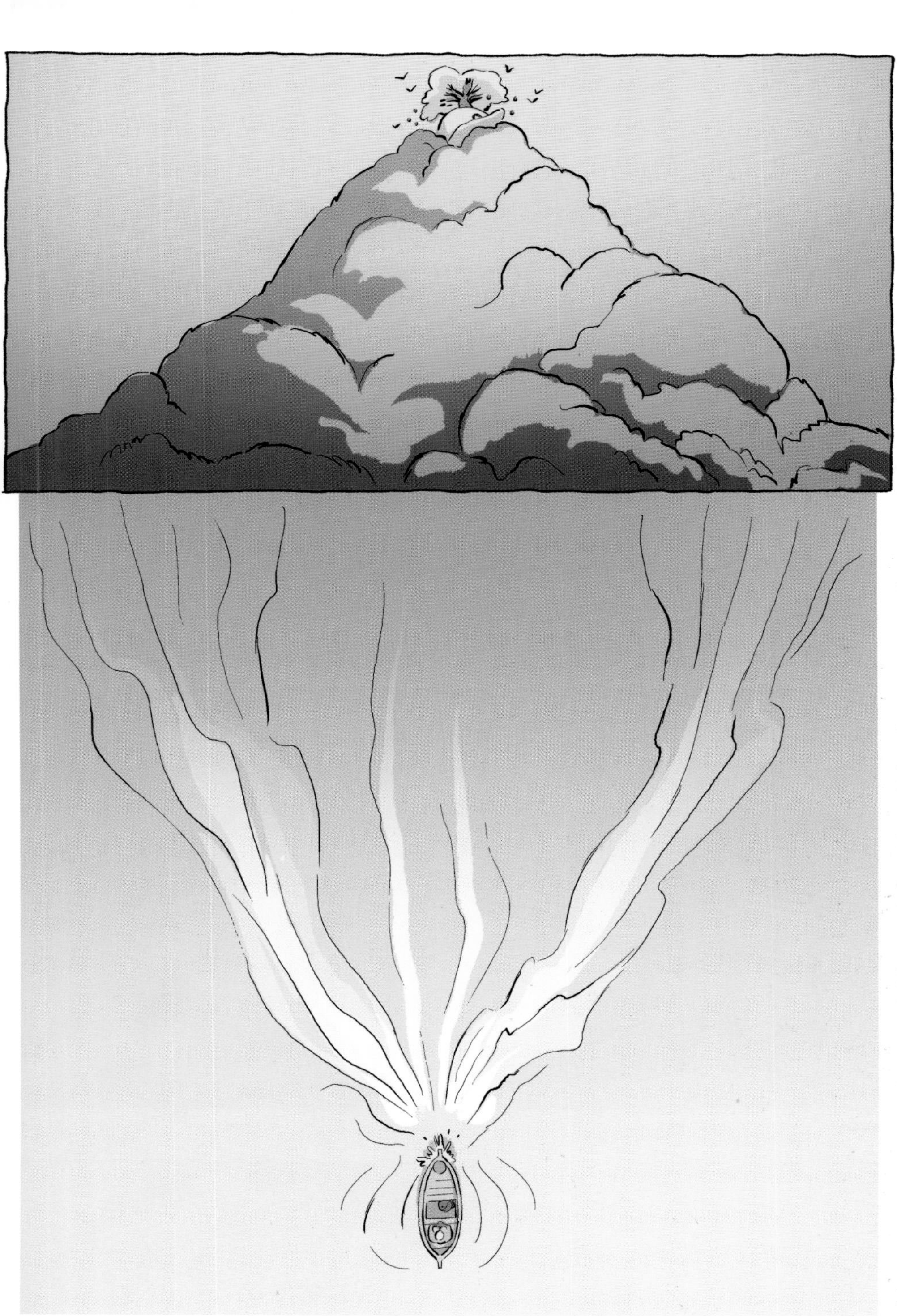

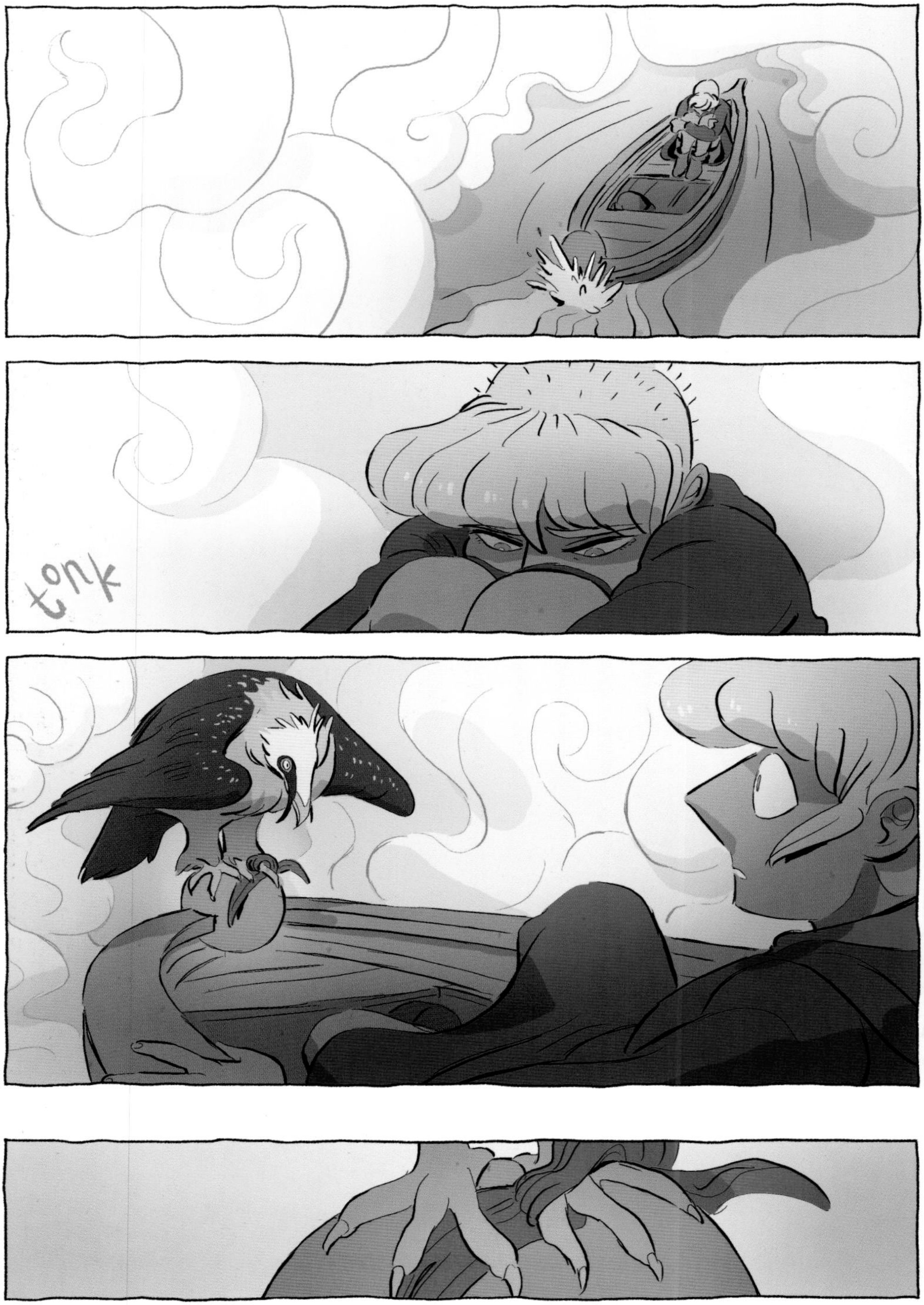
tonk

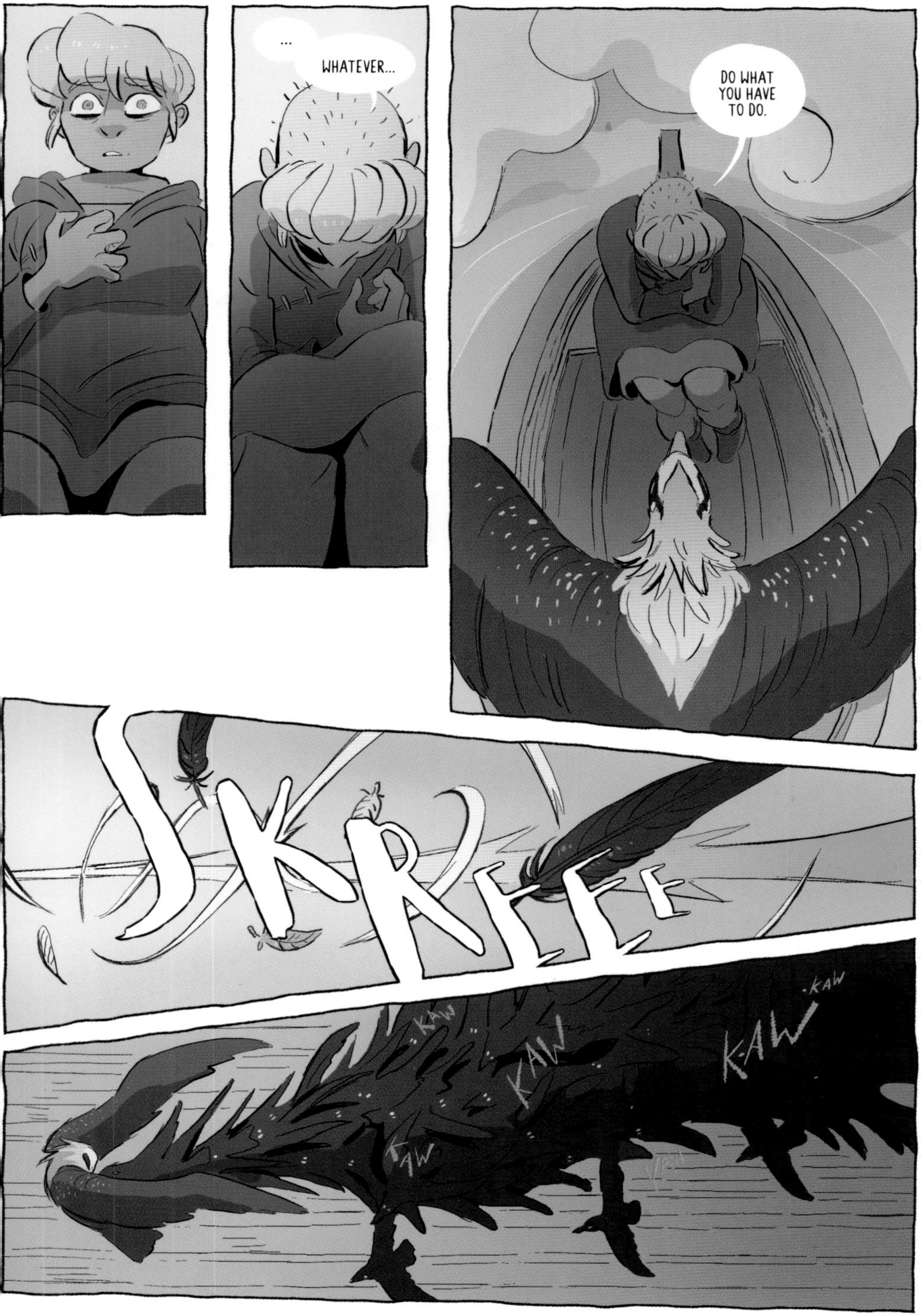
...
WHATEVER...
DO WHAT YOU HAVE TO DO.
SKREEE
KAW
KAW
KAW
KAW
KAW

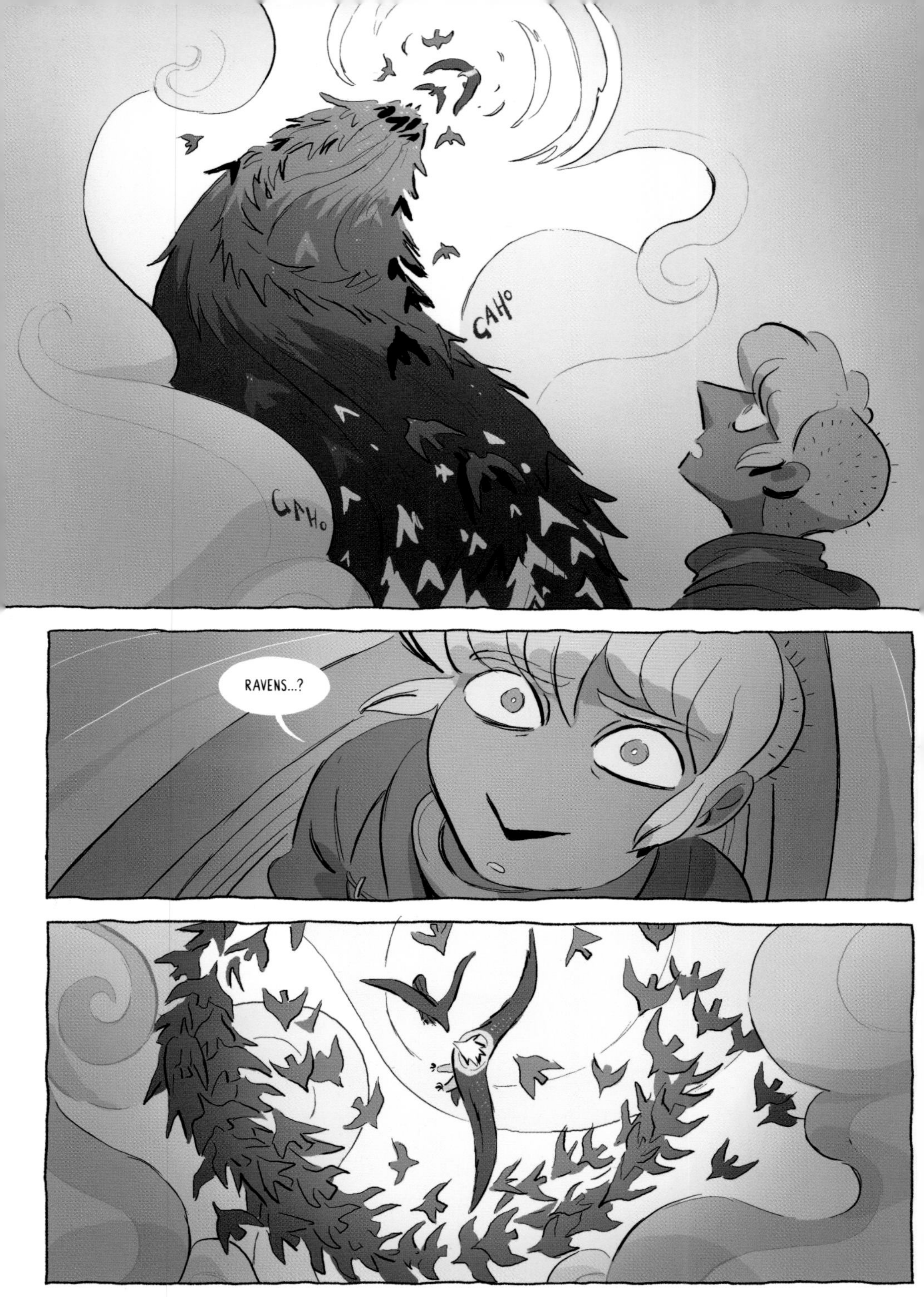
CAHo
CAHo
RAVENS...?

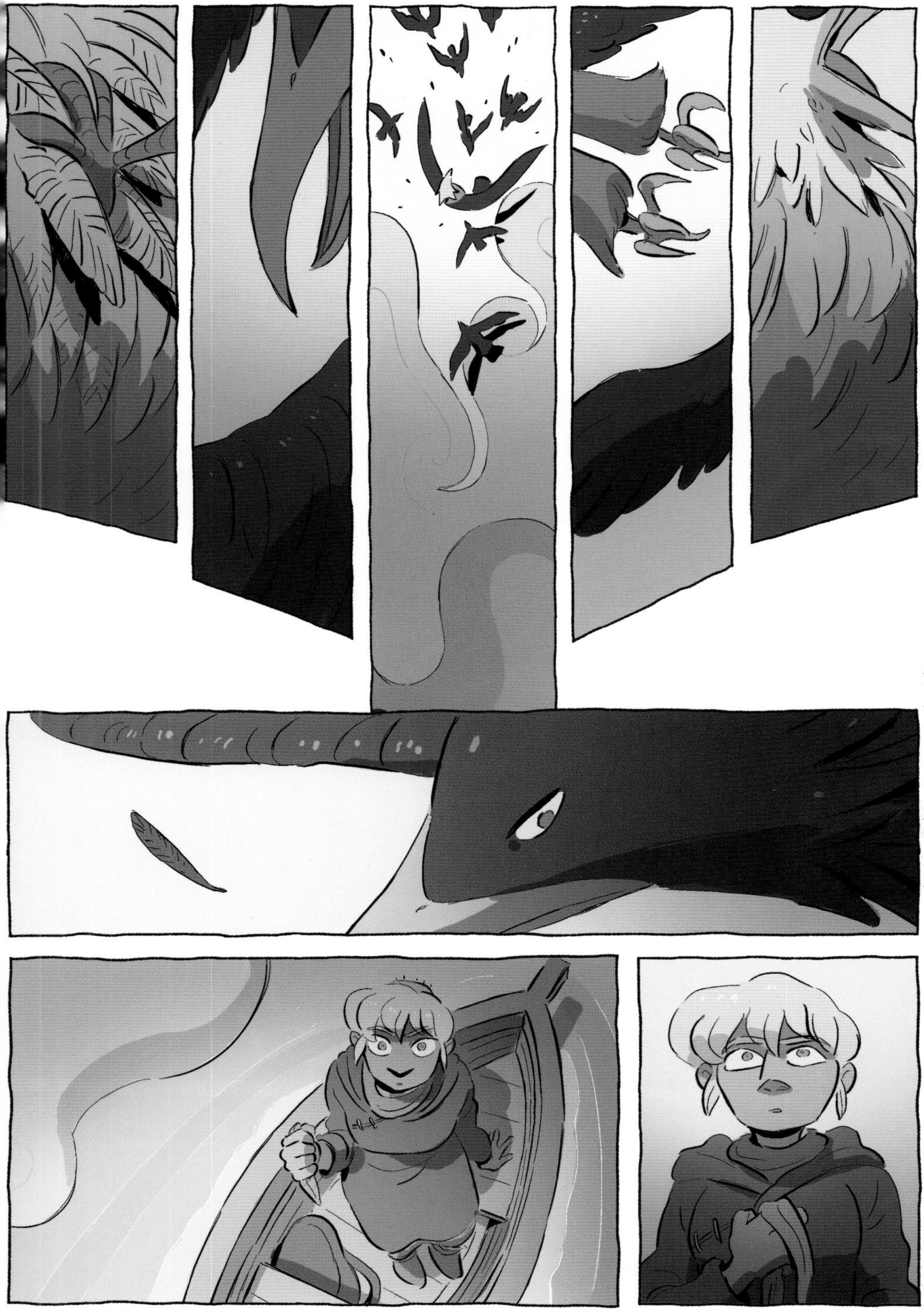

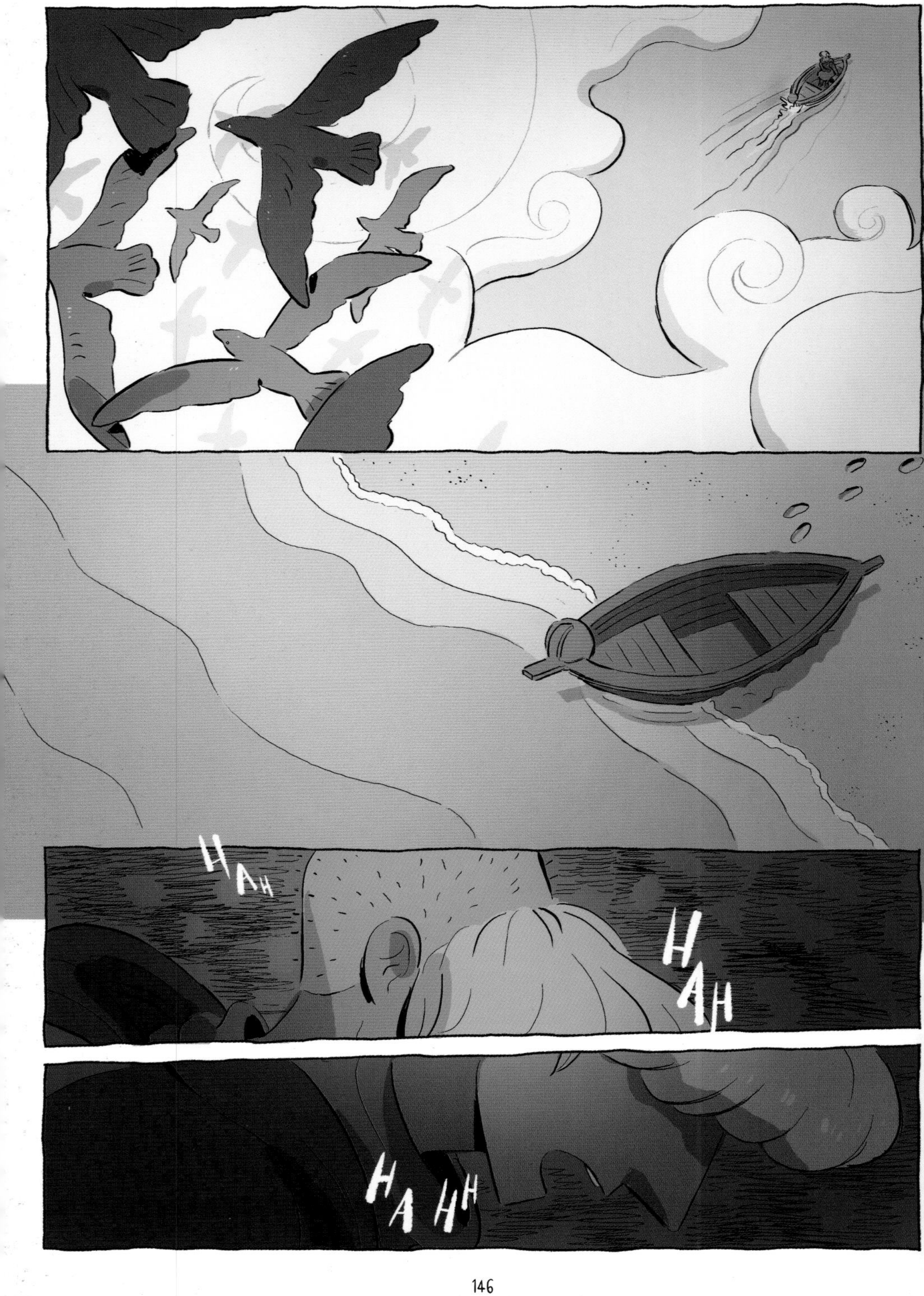
HAH
HAH
HAHH

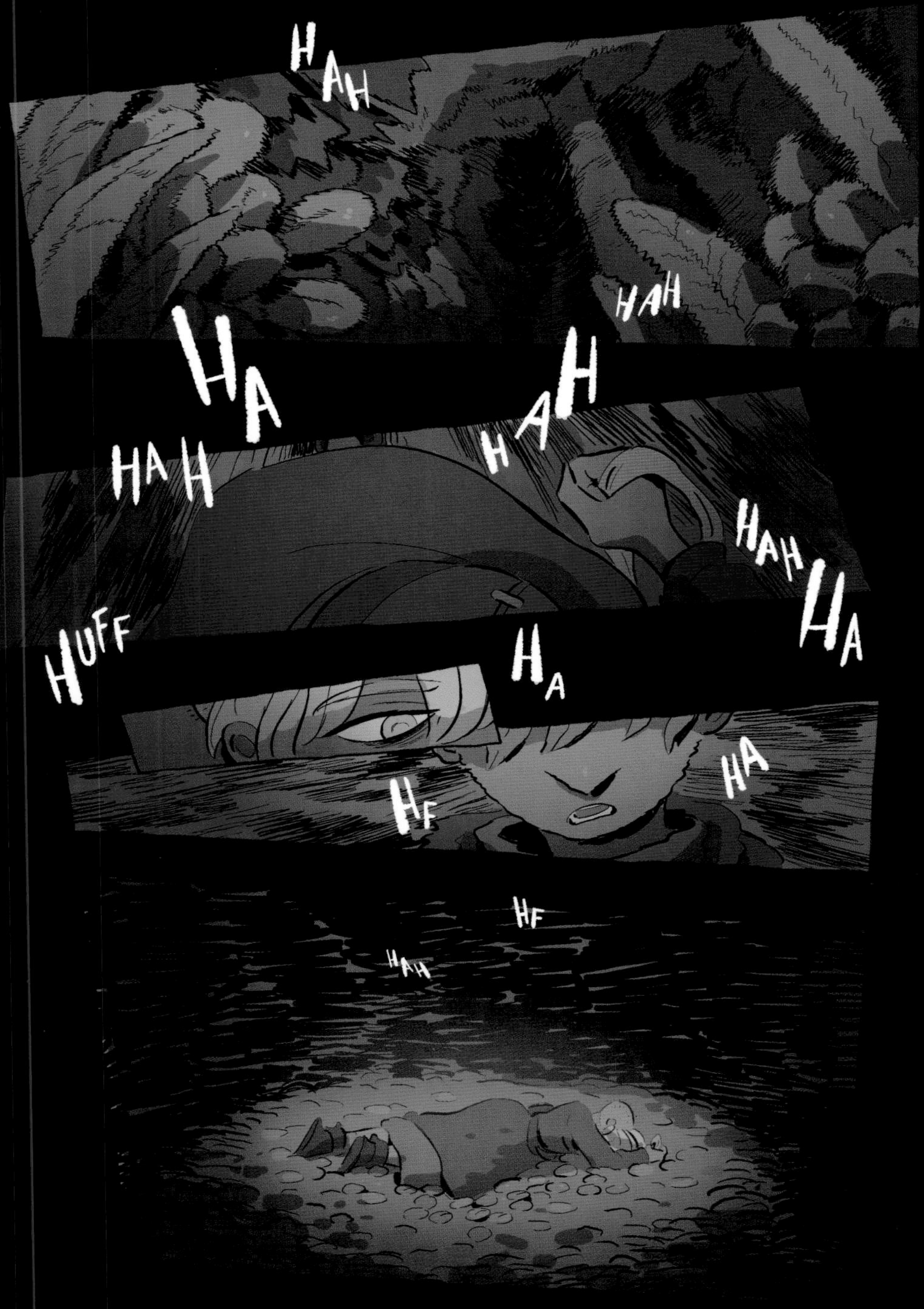
HAH
HAH
HA
HAH
HAH
HAH
HUFF
HA
HA
HA
HF
HA
HF
HAH

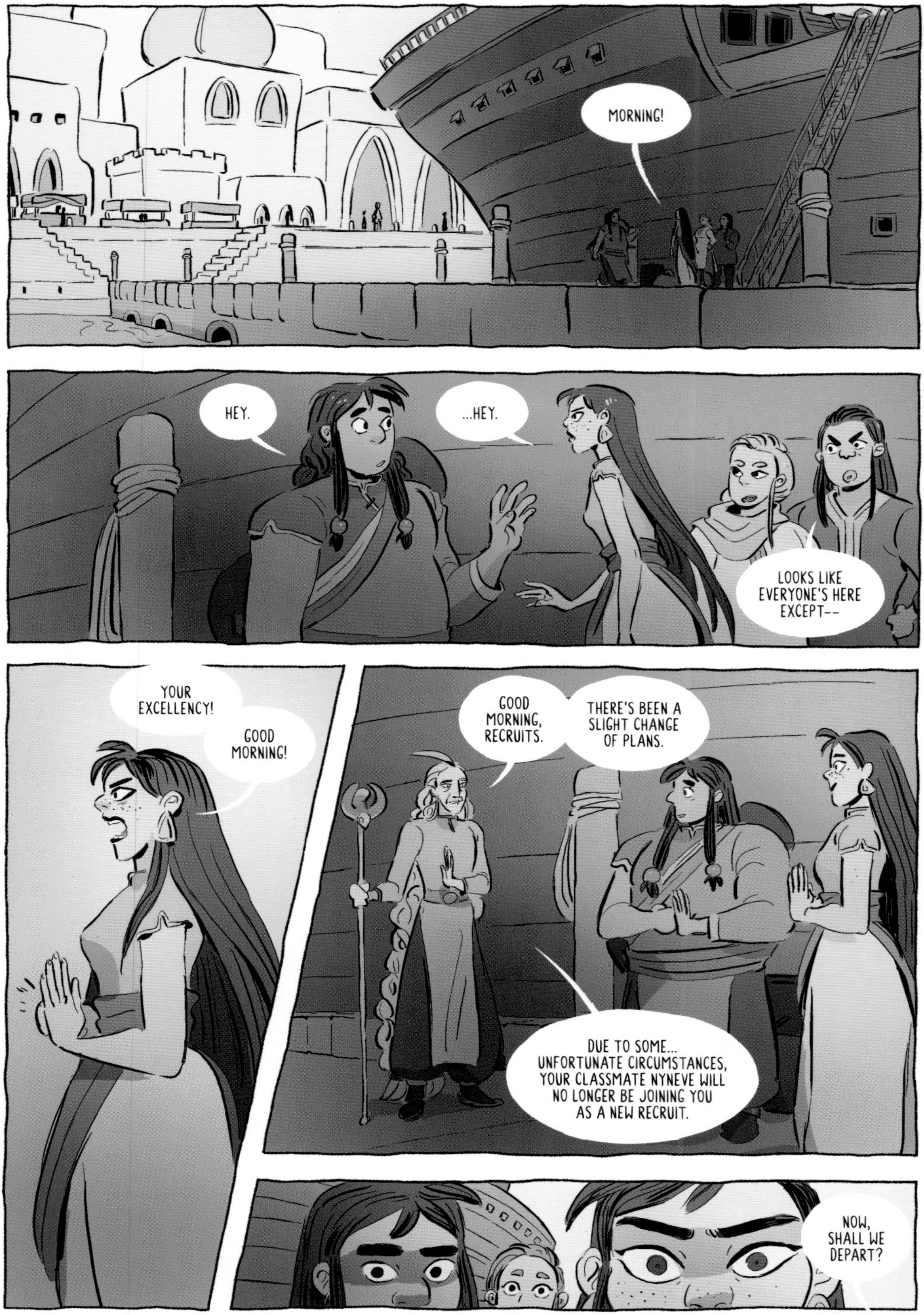
MORNING!
HEY.
...HEY.
LOOKS LIKE EVERYONE'S HERE EXCEPT--
YOUR EXCELLENCY!
GOOD MORNING!
GOOD MORNING, RECRUITS.
THERE'S BEEN A SLIGHT CHANGE OF PLANS.
DUE TO SOME... UNFORTUNATE CIRCUMSTANCES, YOUR CLASSMATE NYNEVE WILL NO LONGER BE JOINING YOU AS A NEW RECRUIT.
NOW, SHALL WE DEPART?

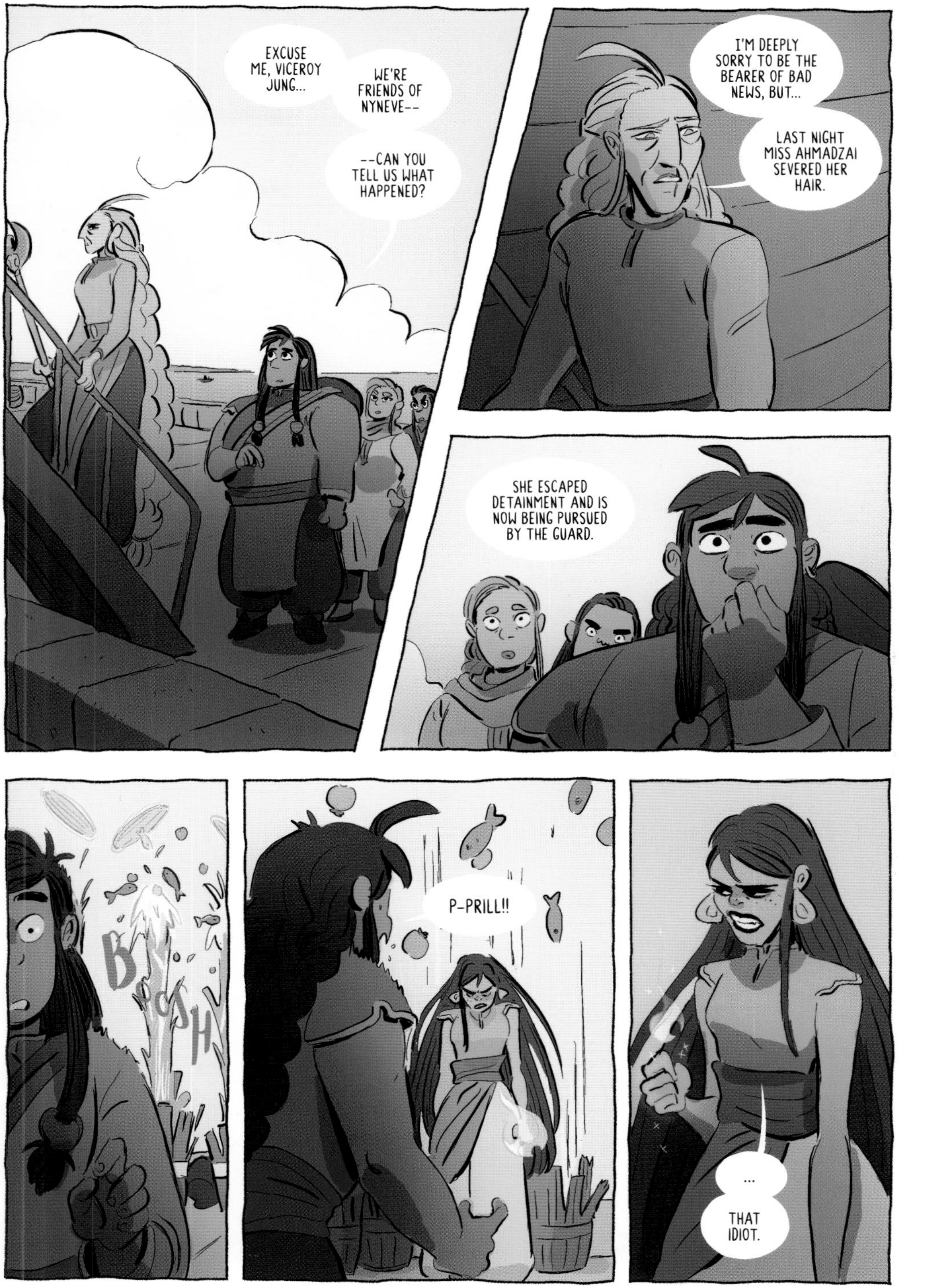
EXCUSE ME, VICEROY JUNG...
WE'RE FRIENDS OF NYNEVE--
--CAN YOU TELL US WHAT HAPPENED?
I'M DEEPLY SORRY TO BE THE BEARER OF BAD NEWS, BUT...
LAST NIGHT MISS AHMADZAI SEVERED HER HAIR.
SHE ESCAPED DETAINMENT AND IS NOW BEING PURSUED BY THE GUARD.
BOOSH
P-PRILL!!
...
THAT IDIOT.

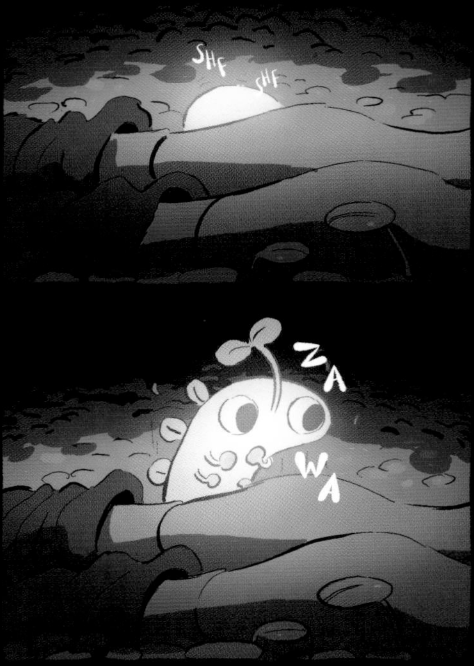
SHF
SHF
ZA
WA

WITCHY
CHAPTER FOUR

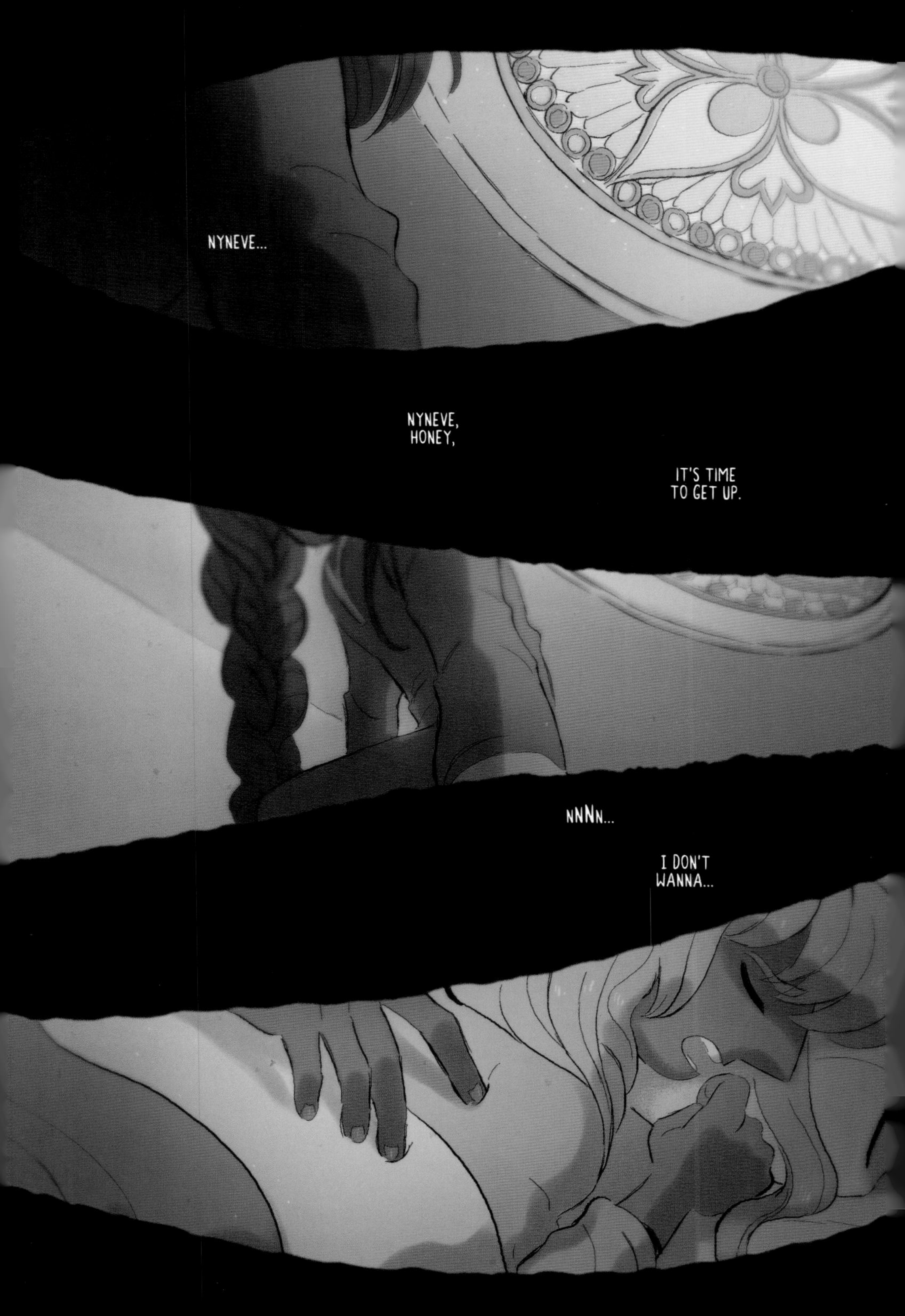
NYNEVE...
NYNEVE, HONEY,
IT'S TIME TO GET UP.
NNNN...
I DON'T WANNA...

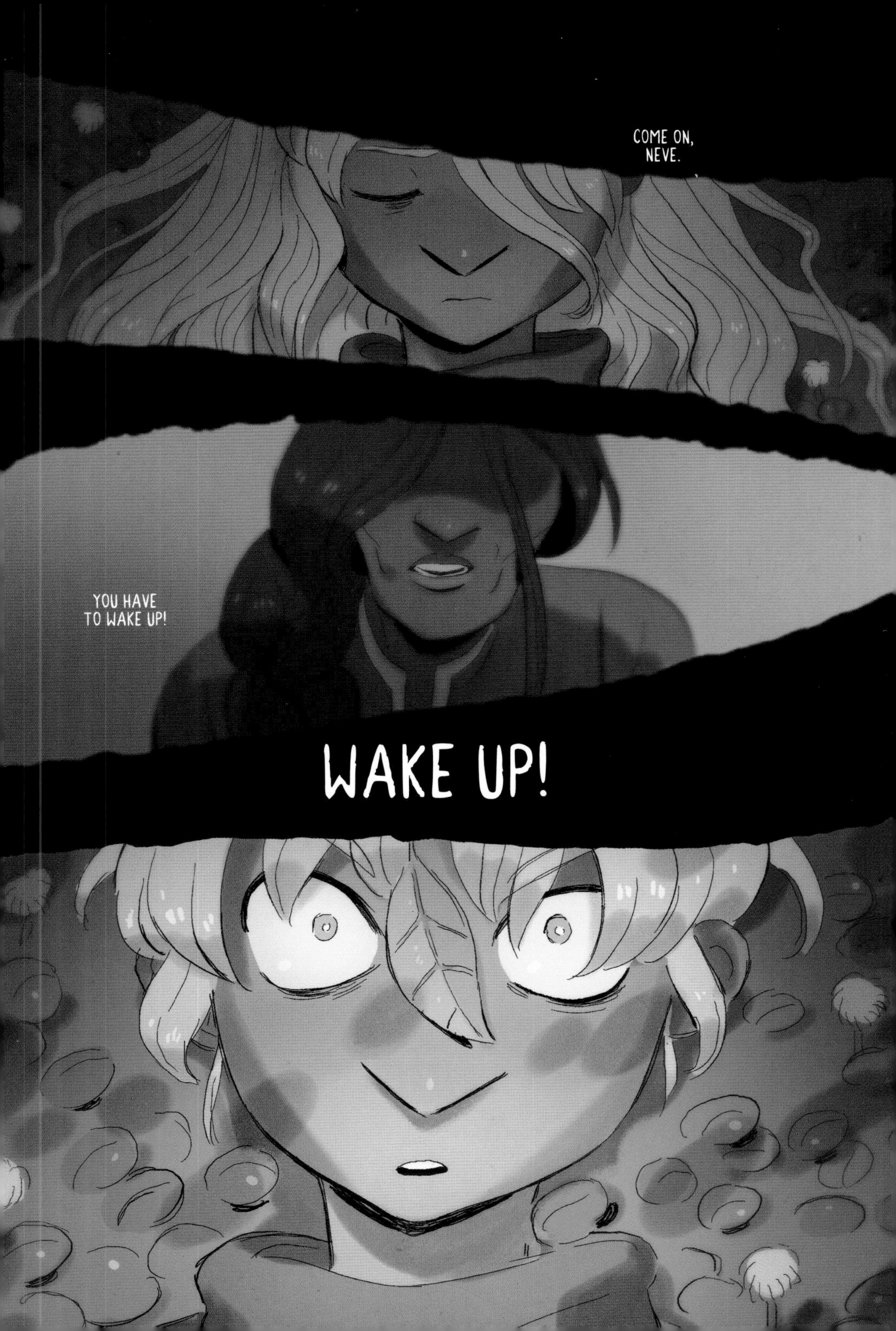
COME ON, NEVE.
YOU HAVE TO WAKE UP!
WAKE UP!

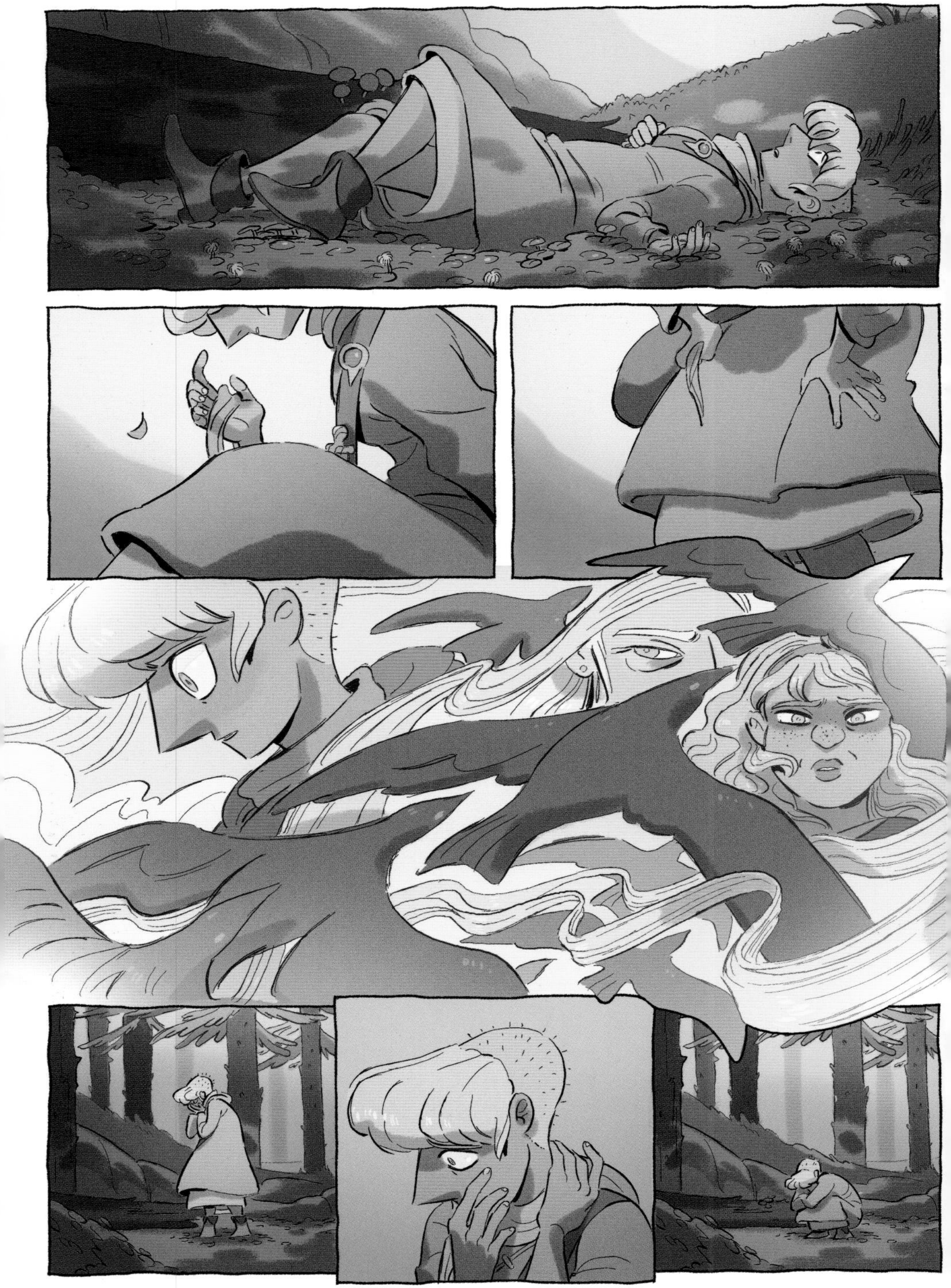

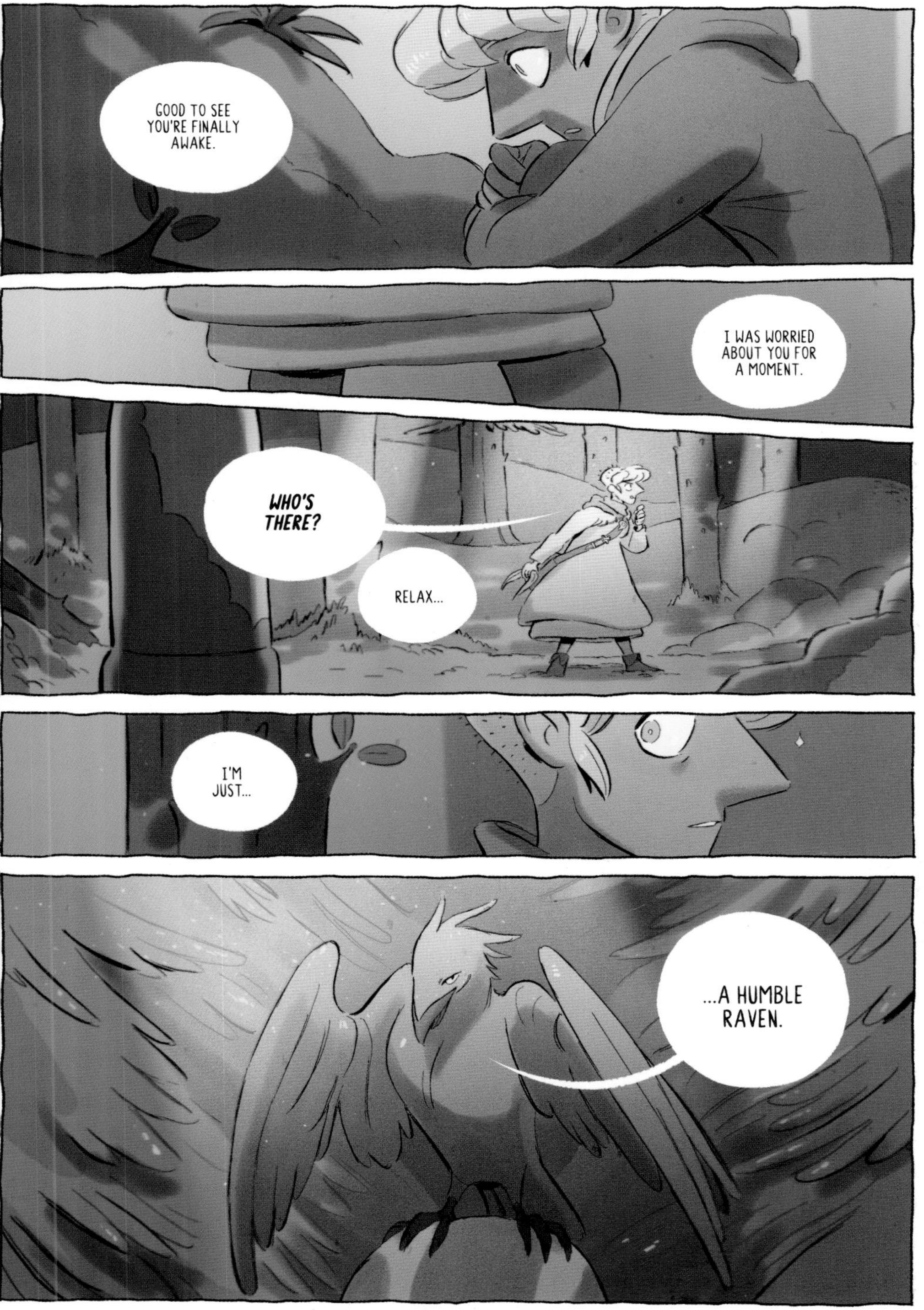
GOOD TO SEE YOU'RE FINALLY AWAKE.
I WAS WORRIED ABOUT YOU FOR A MOMENT.
WHO'S THERE?
RELAX...
I'M JUST...
...A HUMBLE RAVEN.

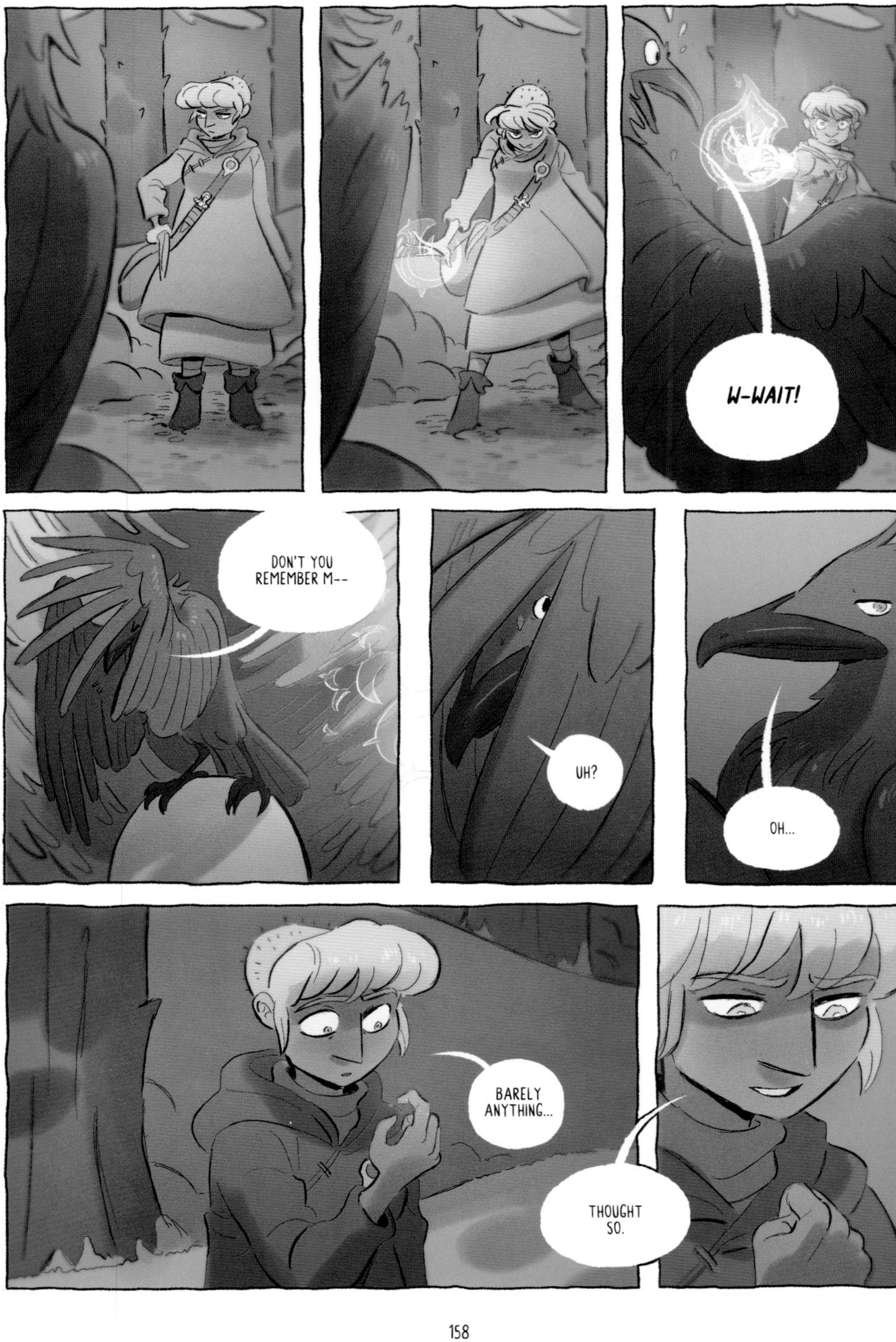
W-WAIT!
DON'T YOU REMEMBER M--
UH?
OH...
BARELY ANYTHING...
THOUGHT SO.

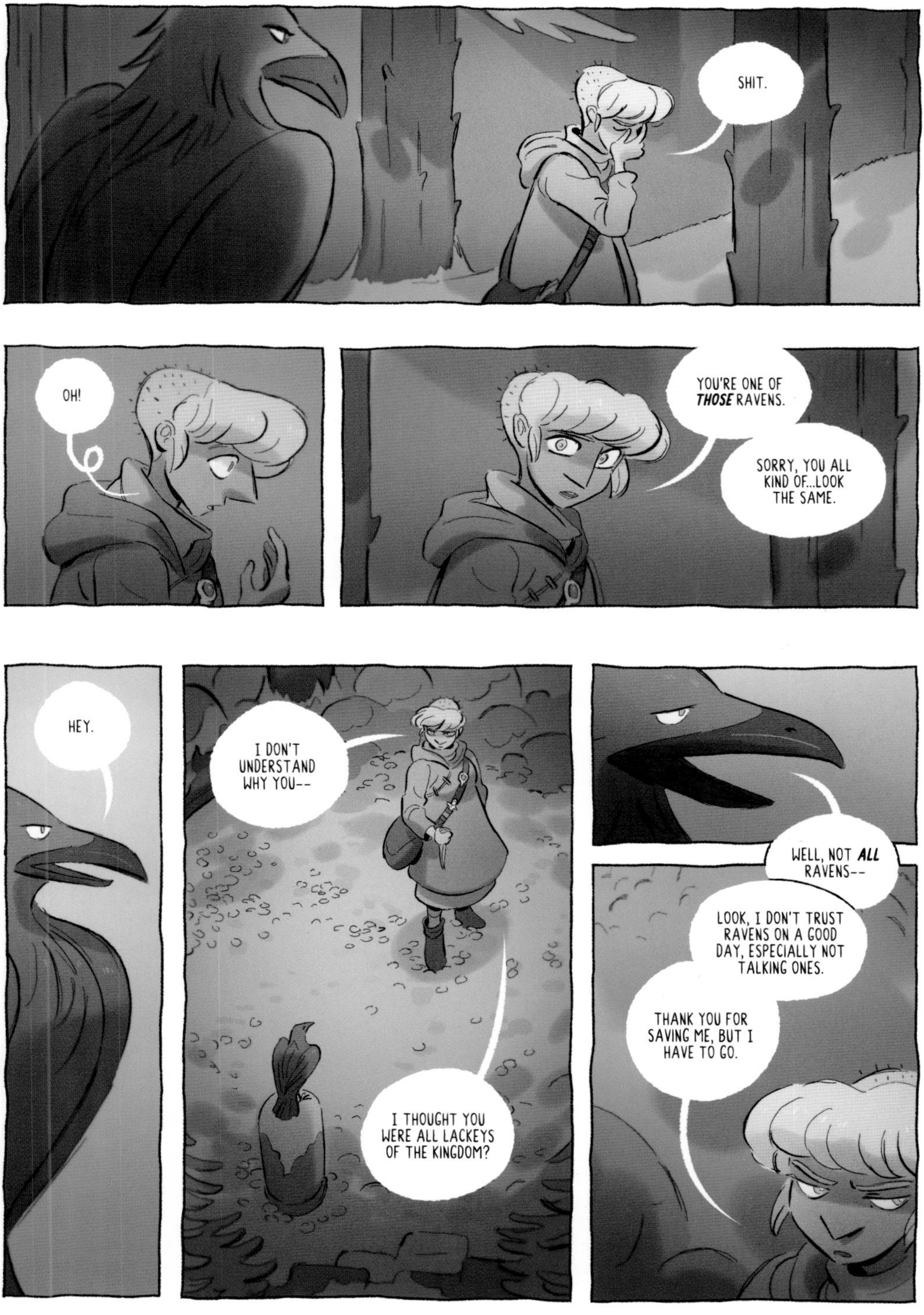
SHIT.
OH!
YOU'RE ONE OF *THOSE* RAVENS.
SORRY, YOU ALL KIND OF...LOOK THE SAME.
HEY.
I DON'T UNDERSTAND WHY YOU--
I THOUGHT YOU WERE ALL LACKEYS OF THE KINGDOM?
WELL, NOT *ALL* RAVENS--
LOOK, I DON'T TRUST RAVENS ON A GOOD DAY, ESPECIALLY NOT TALKING ONES.
THANK YOU FOR SAVING ME, BUT I HAVE TO GO.

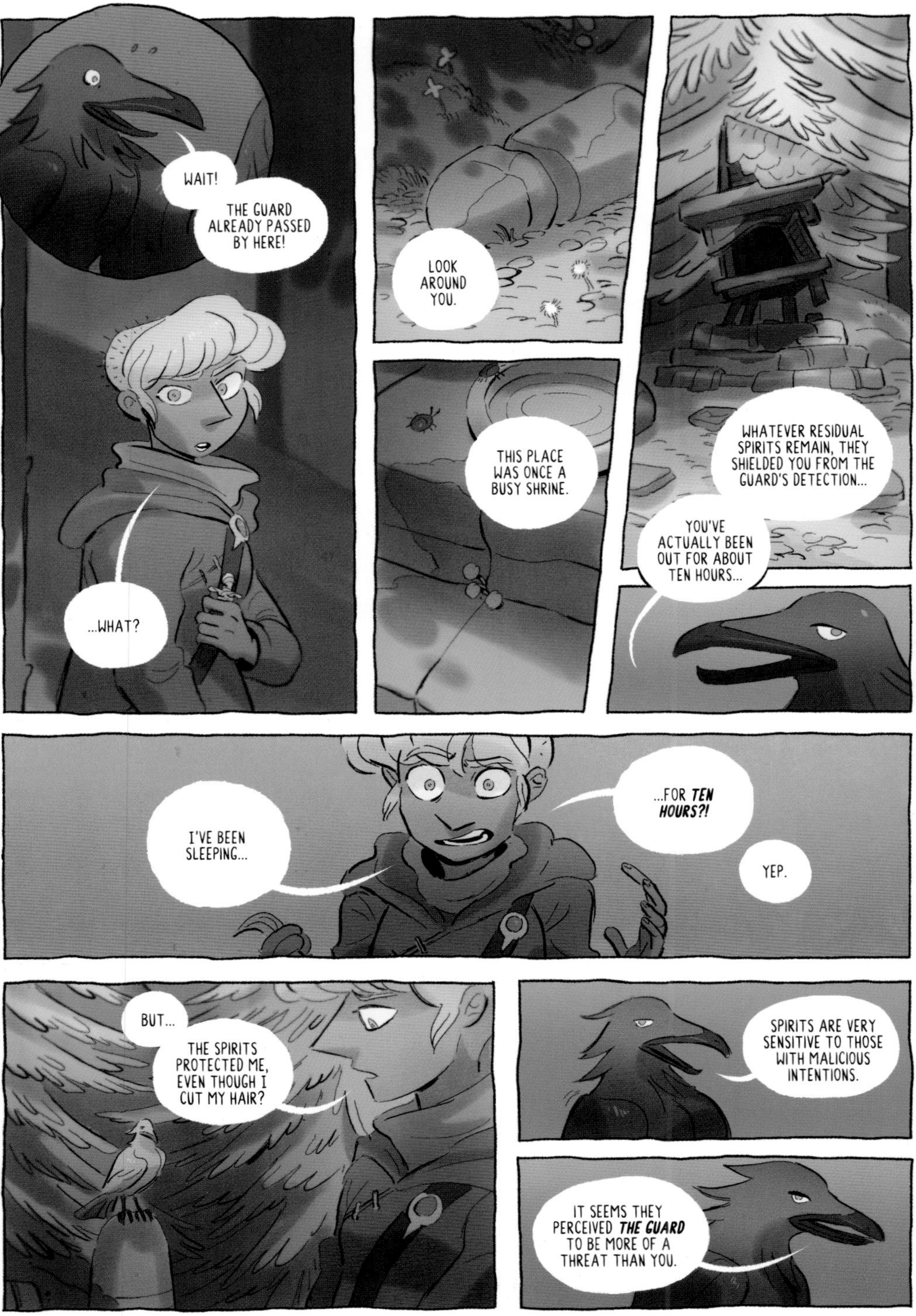
WAIT!
THE GUARD ALREADY PASSED BY HERE!
...WHAT?
LOOK AROUND YOU.
THIS PLACE WAS ONCE A BUSY SHRINE.
WHATEVER RESIDUAL SPIRITS REMAIN, THEY SHIELDED YOU FROM THE GUARD'S DETECTION...
YOU'VE ACTUALLY BEEN OUT FOR ABOUT TEN HOURS...
I'VE BEEN SLEEPING...
...FOR **TEN HOURS?!**
YEP.
BUT...
THE SPIRITS PROTECTED ME, EVEN THOUGH I CUT MY HAIR?
SPIRITS ARE VERY SENSITIVE TO THOSE WITH MALICIOUS INTENTIONS.
IT SEEMS THEY PERCEIVED **THE GUARD** TO BE MORE OF A THREAT THAN YOU.

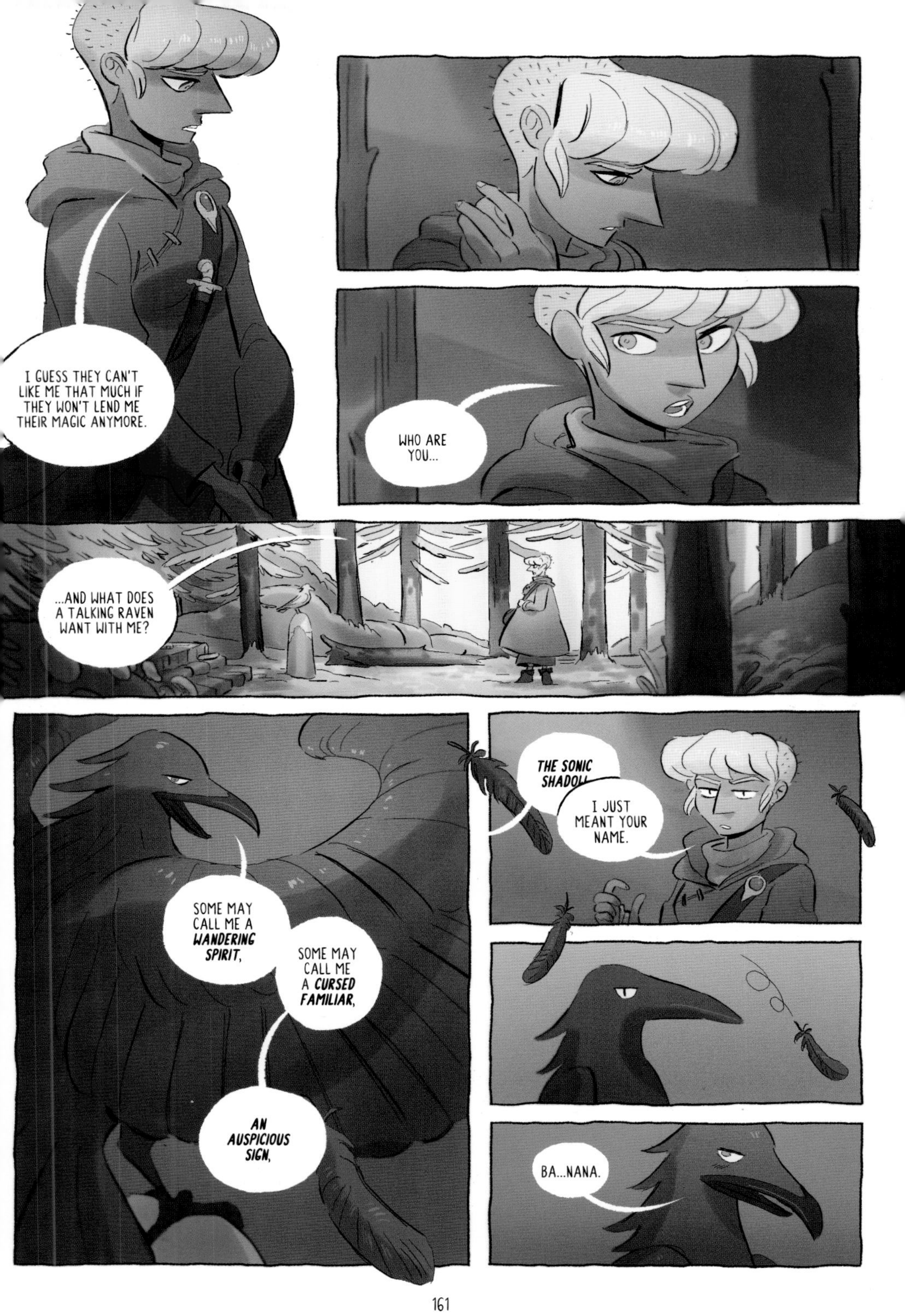

I GUESS THEY CAN'T LIKE ME THAT MUCH IF THEY WON'T LEND ME THEIR MAGIC ANYMORE.
WHO ARE YOU...
...AND WHAT DOES A TALKING RAVEN WANT WITH ME?
SOME MAY CALL ME A ***WANDERING SPIRIT***,
SOME MAY CALL ME A ***CURSED FAMILIAR***,
AN AUSPICIOUS SIGN,
THE SONIC SHADOW
I JUST MEANT YOUR NAME.
BA...NANA.

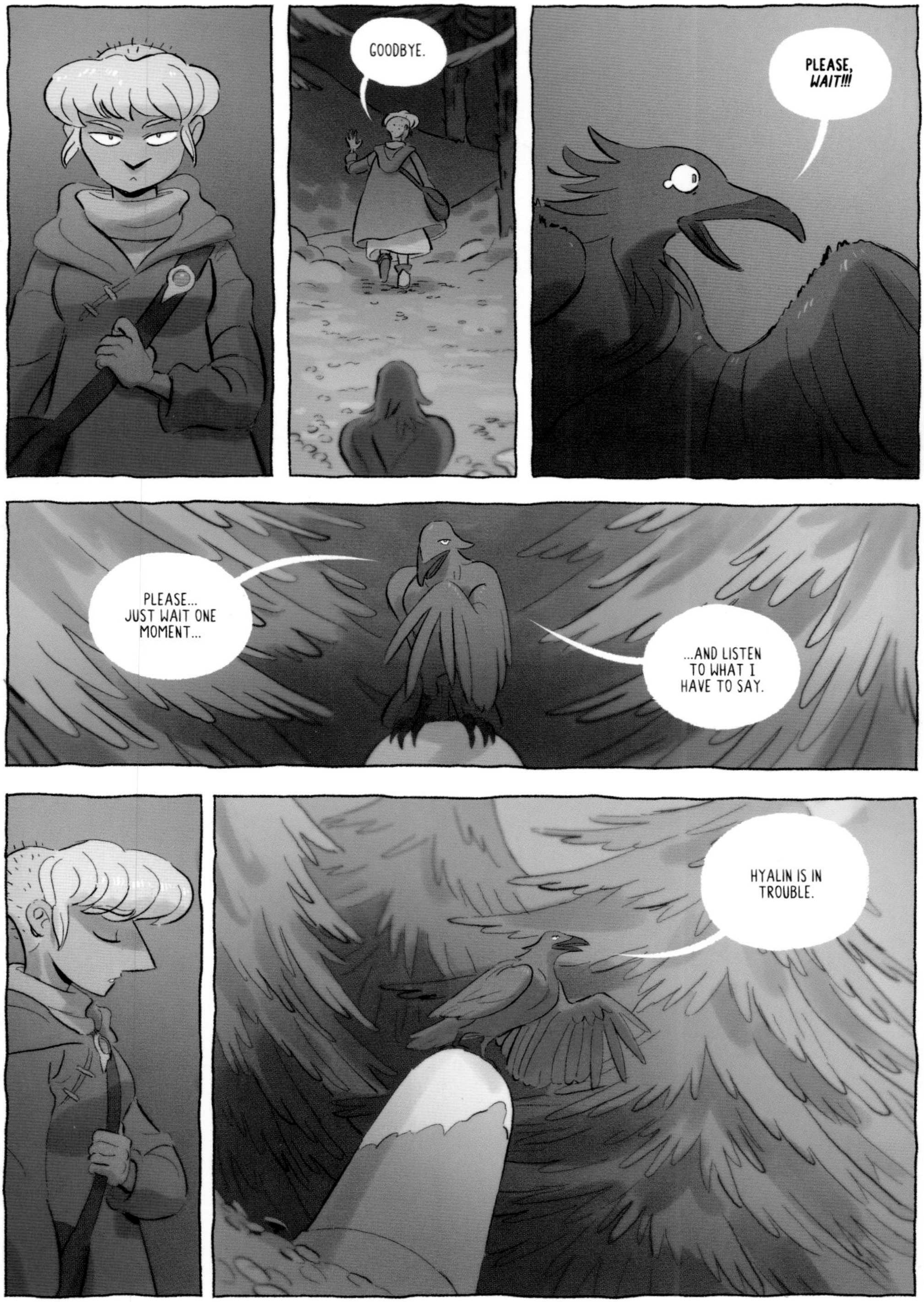
GOODBYE.
PLEASE, *WAIT!!!*
PLEASE... JUST WAIT ONE MOMENT...
...AND LISTEN TO WHAT I HAVE TO SAY.
HYALIN IS IN TROUBLE.

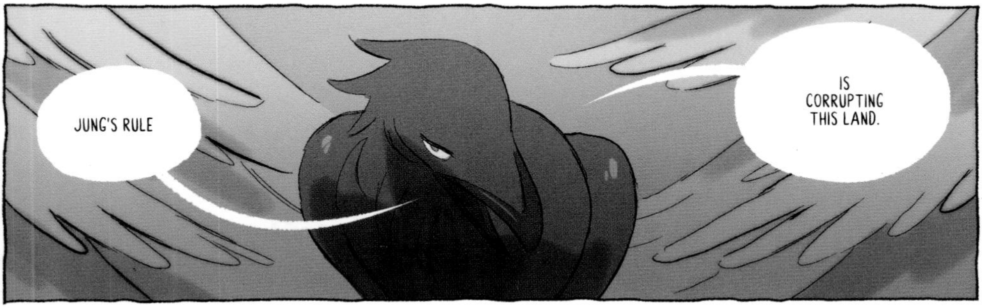
JUNG'S RULE
IS CORRUPTING THIS LAND.

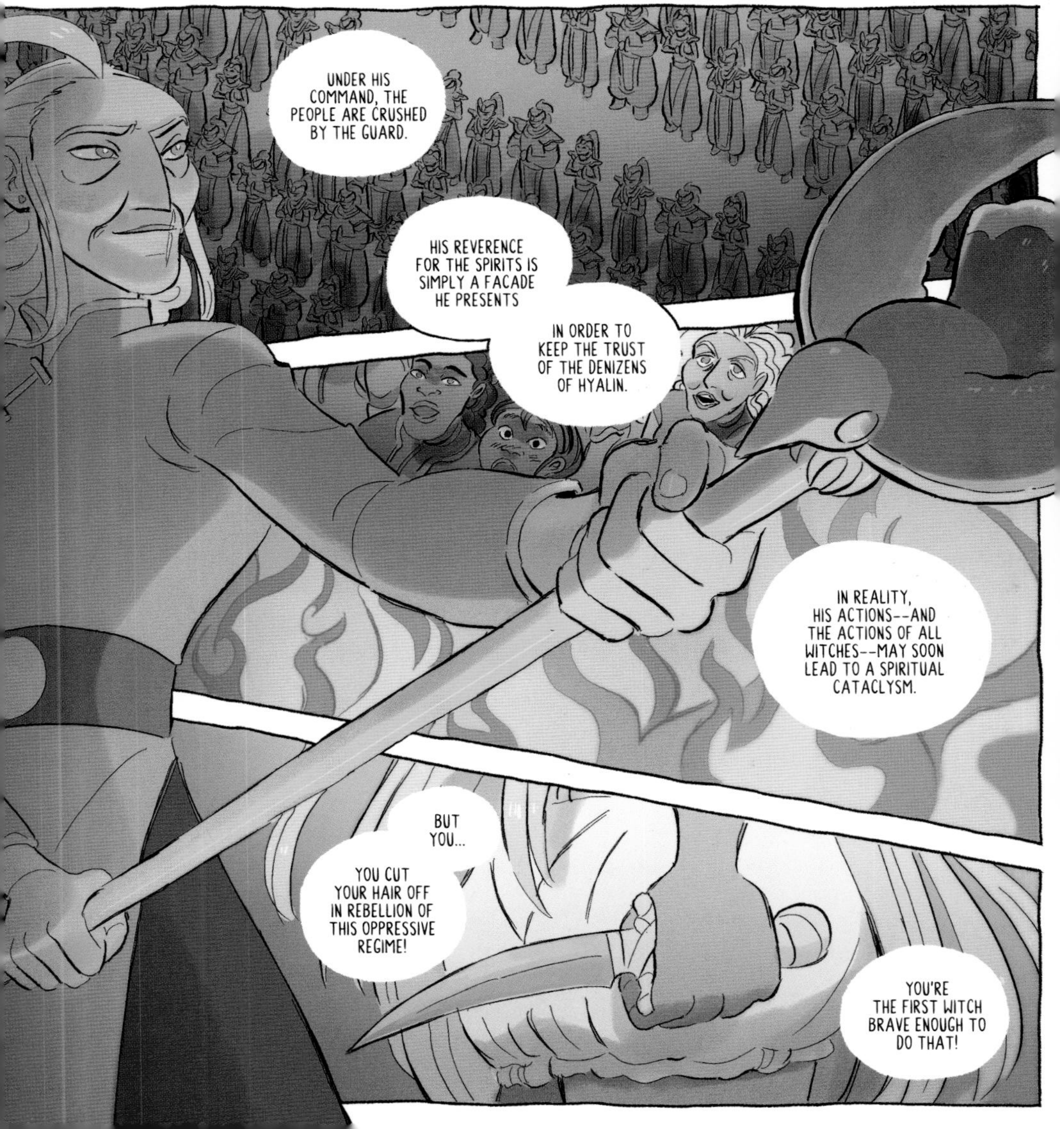
UNDER HIS COMMAND, THE PEOPLE ARE CRUSHED BY THE GUARD.
HIS REVERENCE FOR THE SPIRITS IS SIMPLY A FACADE HE PRESENTS
IN ORDER TO KEEP THE TRUST OF THE DENIZENS OF HYALIN.
IN REALITY, HIS ACTIONS--AND THE ACTIONS OF ALL WITCHES--MAY SOON LEAD TO A SPIRITUAL CATACLYSM.
BUT YOU...
YOU CUT YOUR HAIR OFF IN REBELLION OF THIS OPPRESSIVE REGIME!
YOU'RE THE FIRST WITCH BRAVE ENOUGH TO DO THAT!

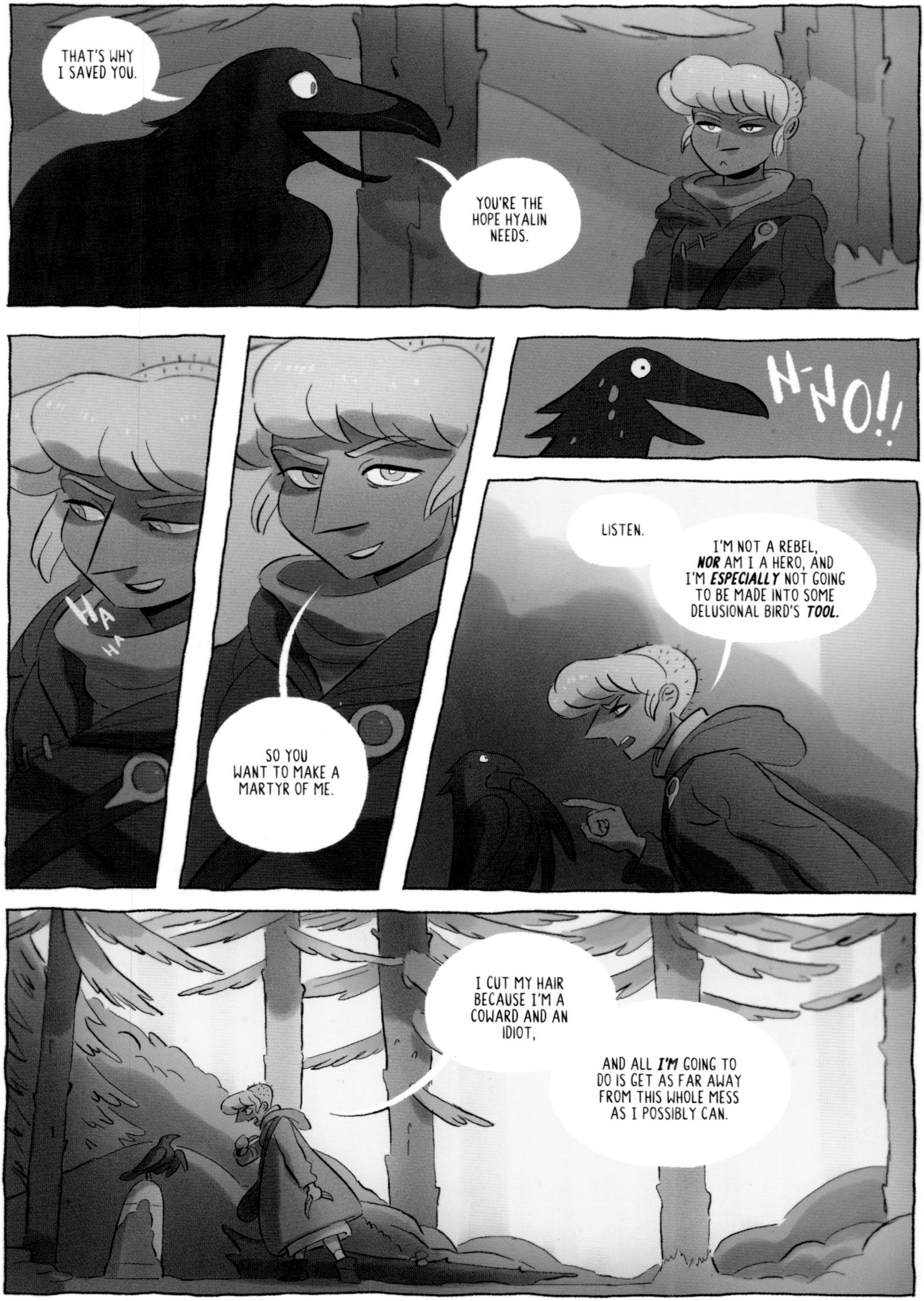
THAT'S WHY I SAVED YOU.
YOU'RE THE HOPE HYALIN NEEDS.
HA HA
SO YOU WANT TO MAKE A MARTYR OF ME.
H-NO!!
LISTEN.
I'M NOT A REBEL, **NOR** AM I A HERO, AND I'M **ESPECIALLY** NOT GOING TO BE MADE INTO SOME DELUSIONAL BIRD'S **TOOL.**
I CUT MY HAIR BECAUSE I'M A COWARD AND AN IDIOT,
AND ALL **I'M** GOING TO DO IS GET AS FAR AWAY FROM THIS WHOLE MESS AS I POSSIBLY CAN.

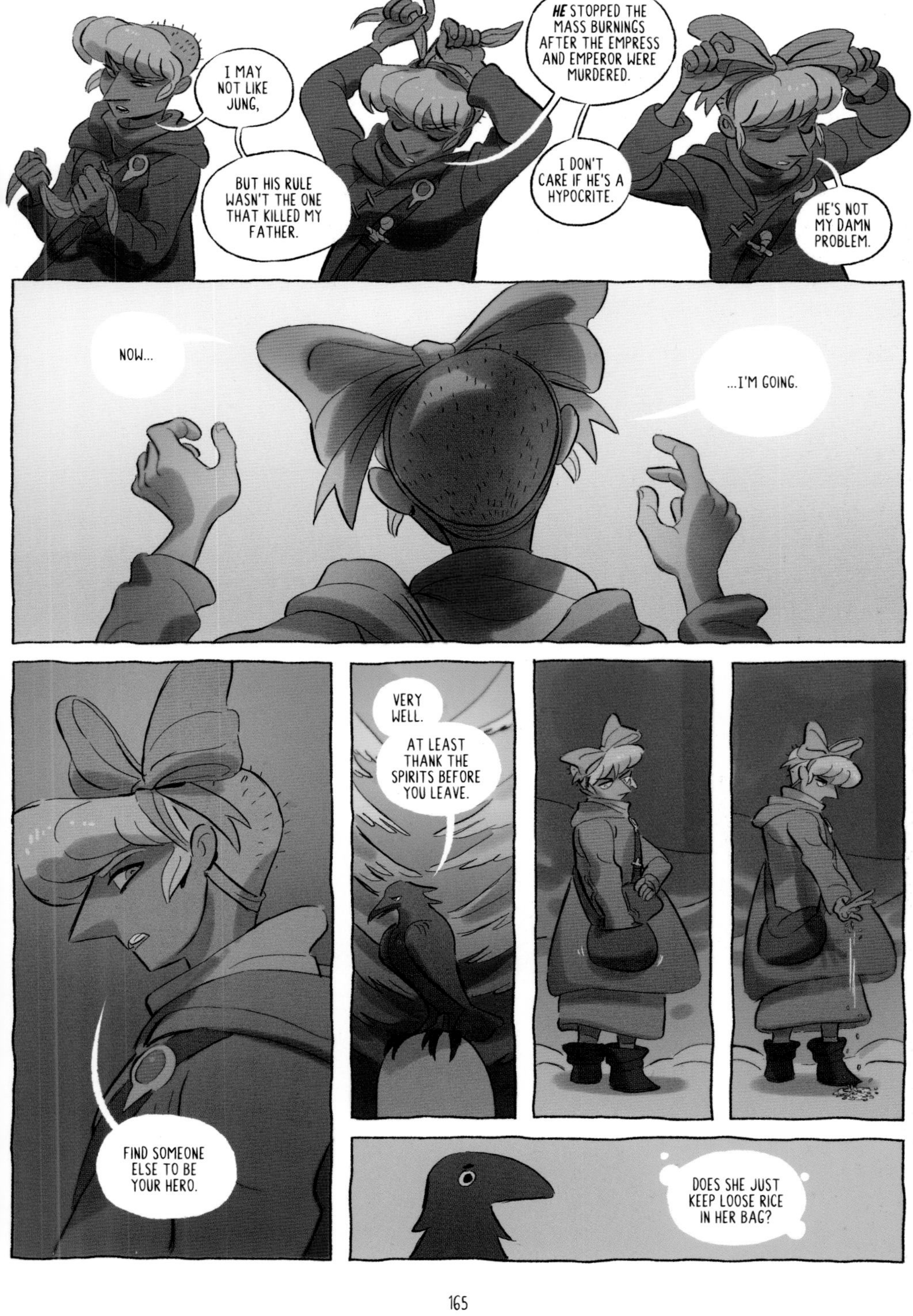
I MAY NOT LIKE JUNG,
BUT HIS RULE WASN'T THE ONE THAT KILLED MY FATHER.
HE STOPPED THE MASS BURNINGS AFTER THE EMPRESS AND EMPEROR WERE MURDERED.
I DON'T CARE IF HE'S A HYPOCRITE.
HE'S NOT MY DAMN PROBLEM.
NOW...
...I'M GOING.
FIND SOMEONE ELSE TO BE YOUR HERO.
VERY WELL.
AT LEAST THANK THE SPIRITS BEFORE YOU LEAVE.
DOES SHE JUST KEEP LOOSE RICE IN HER BAG?

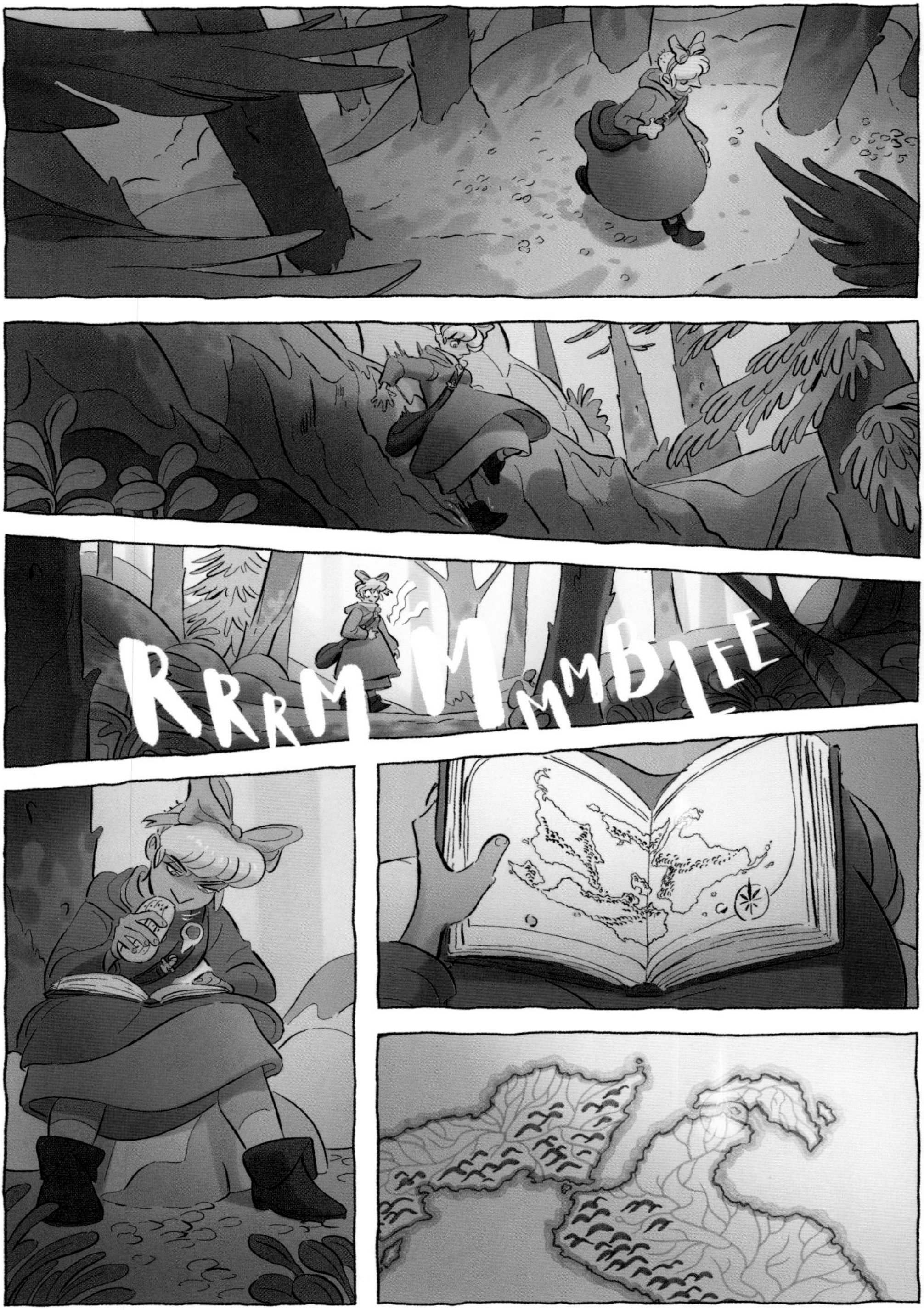
RRRM MMMBLEE

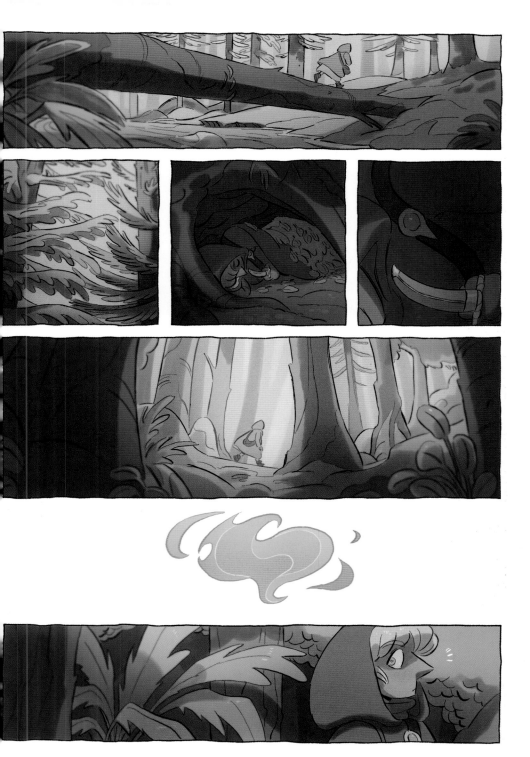

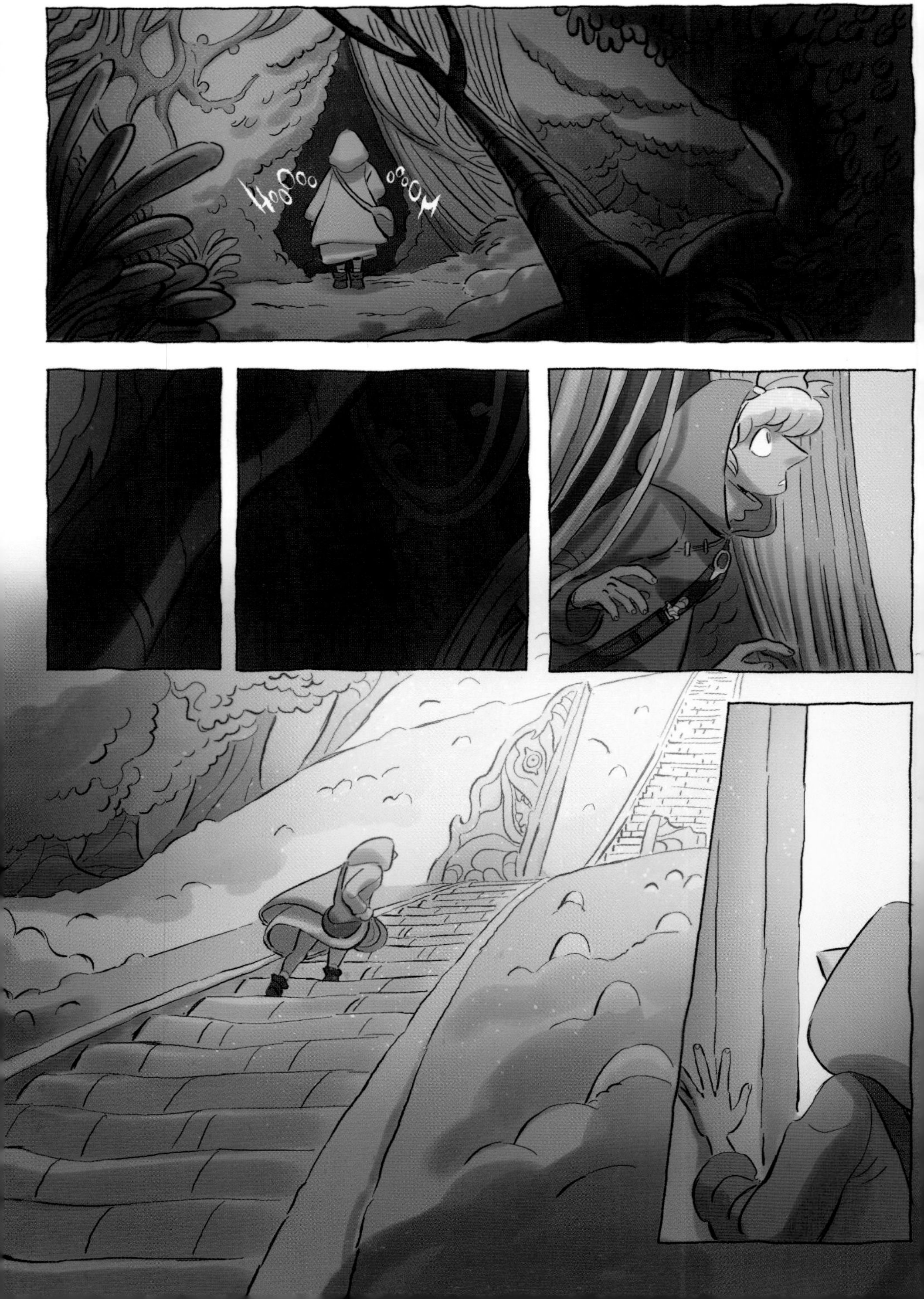
HOOOOOO
OOOOOM

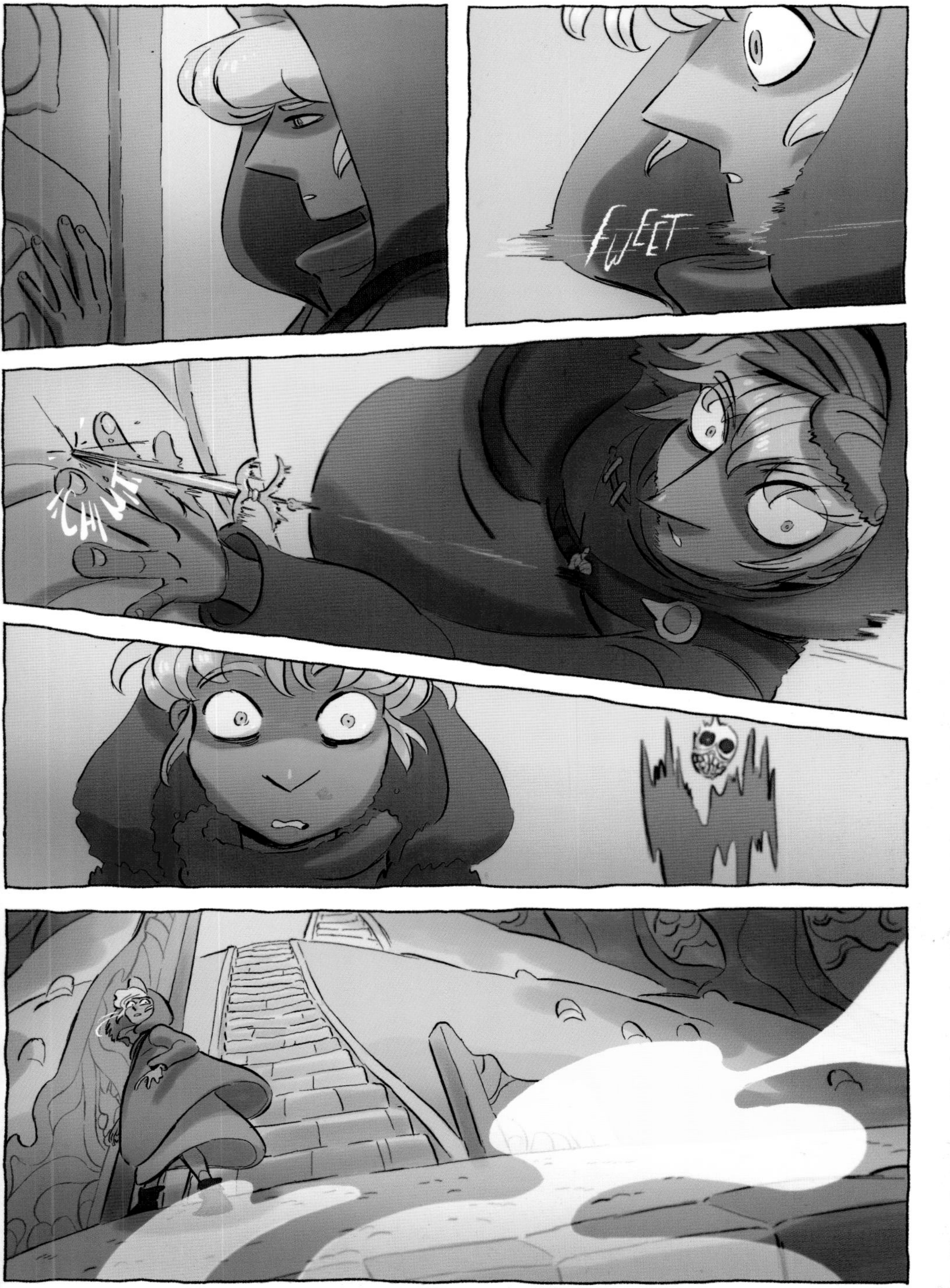
FWEET
CHUNK

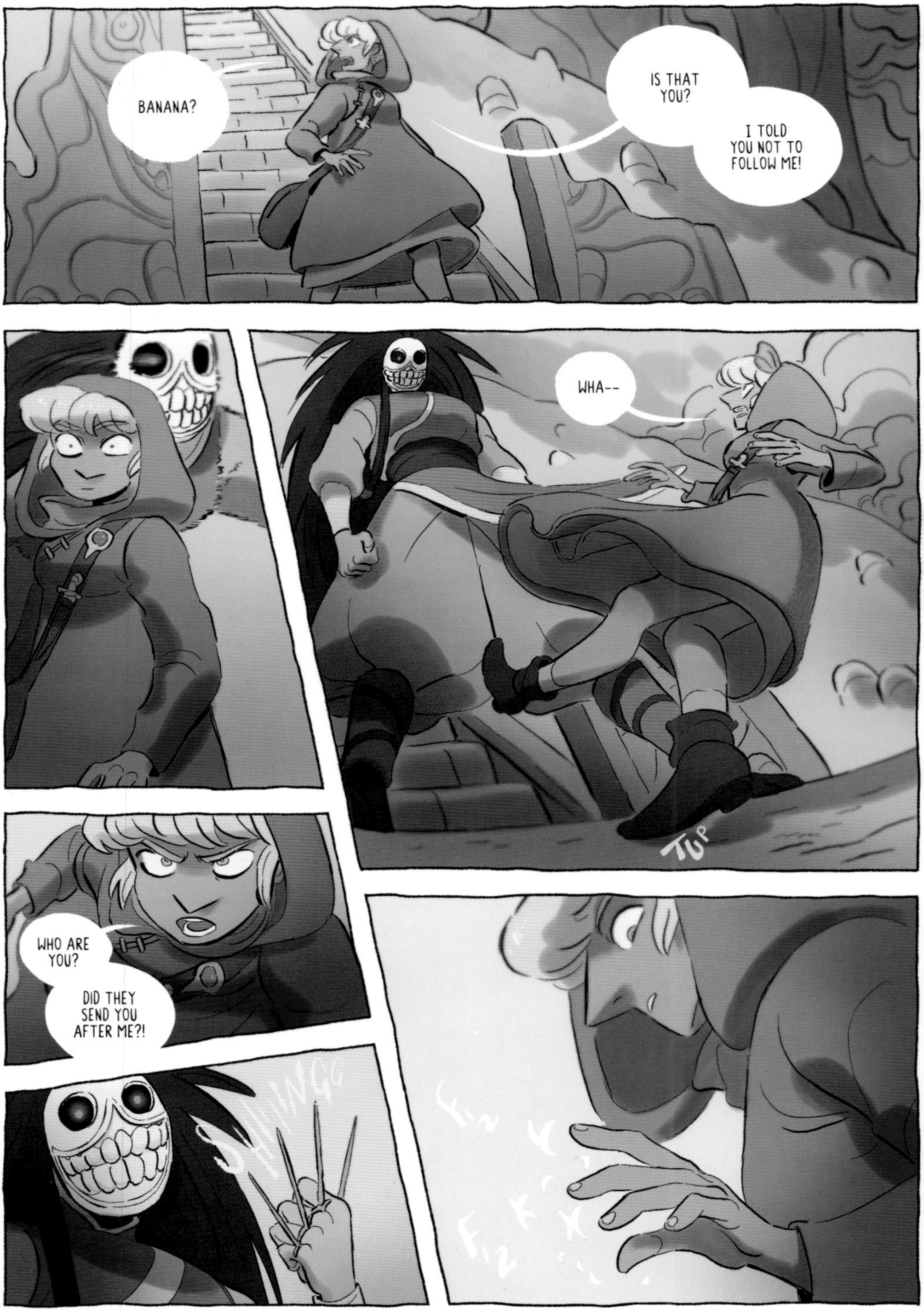
BANANA?
IS THAT YOU?
I TOLD YOU NOT TO FOLLOW ME!
WHA--
TUP
WHO ARE YOU?
DID THEY SEND YOU AFTER ME?!

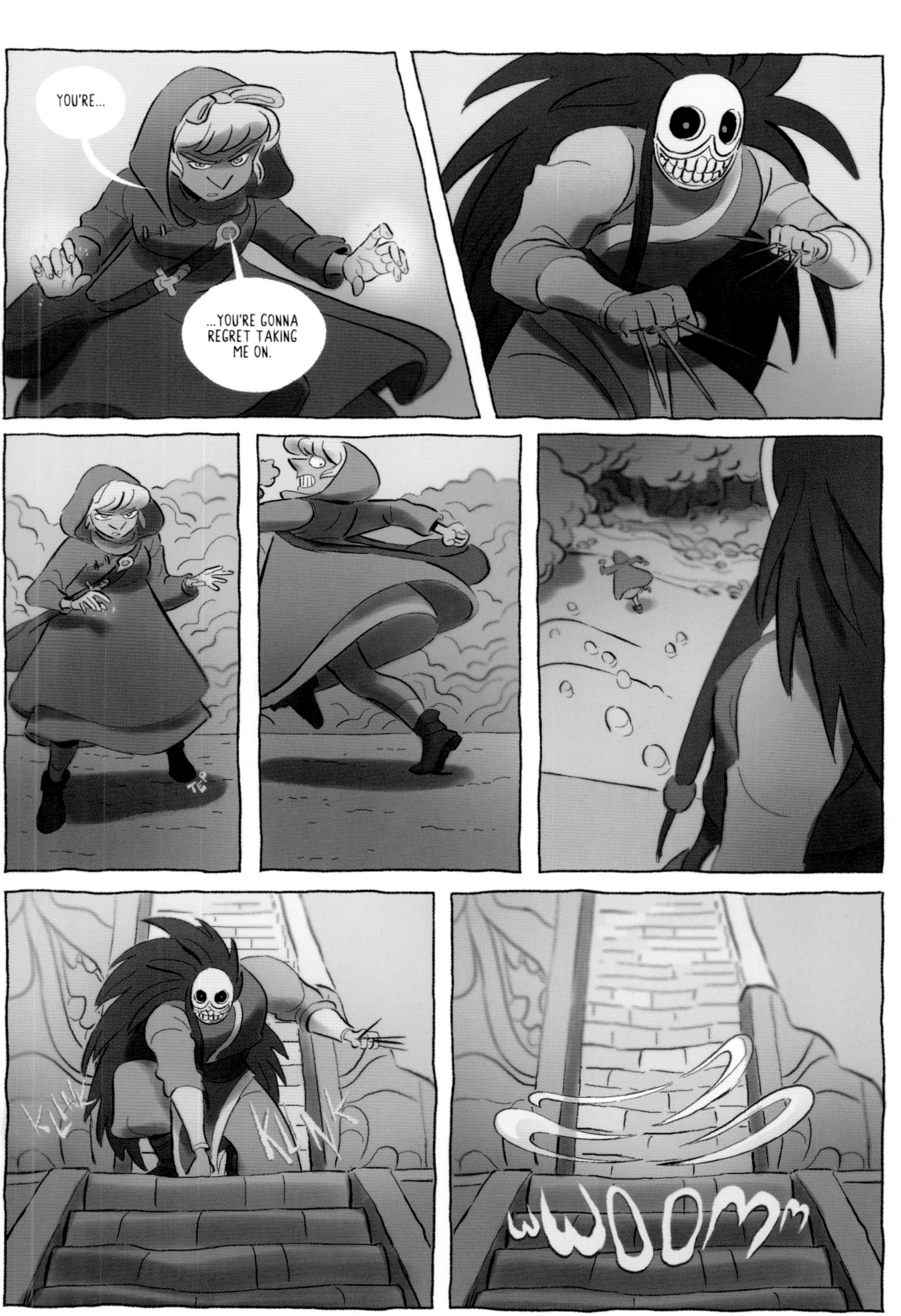
YOU'RE...
...YOU'RE GONNA REGRET TAKING ME ON.
TEP
KLINK
KLINK
wWOOMm

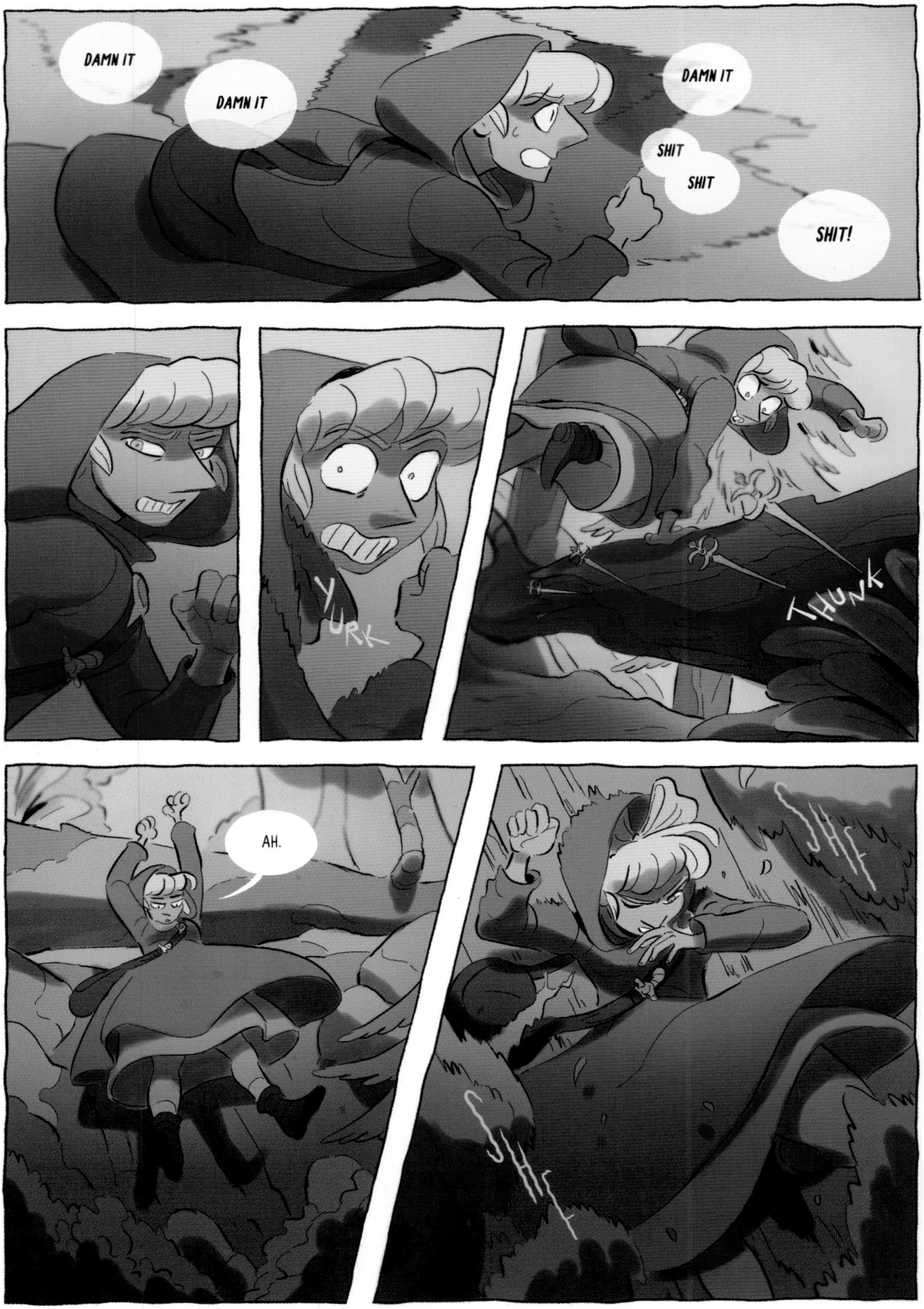
DAMN IT
DAMN IT
DAMN IT
SHIT
SHIT
SHIT!
YURK
THUNK
AH.
SHF
SHF

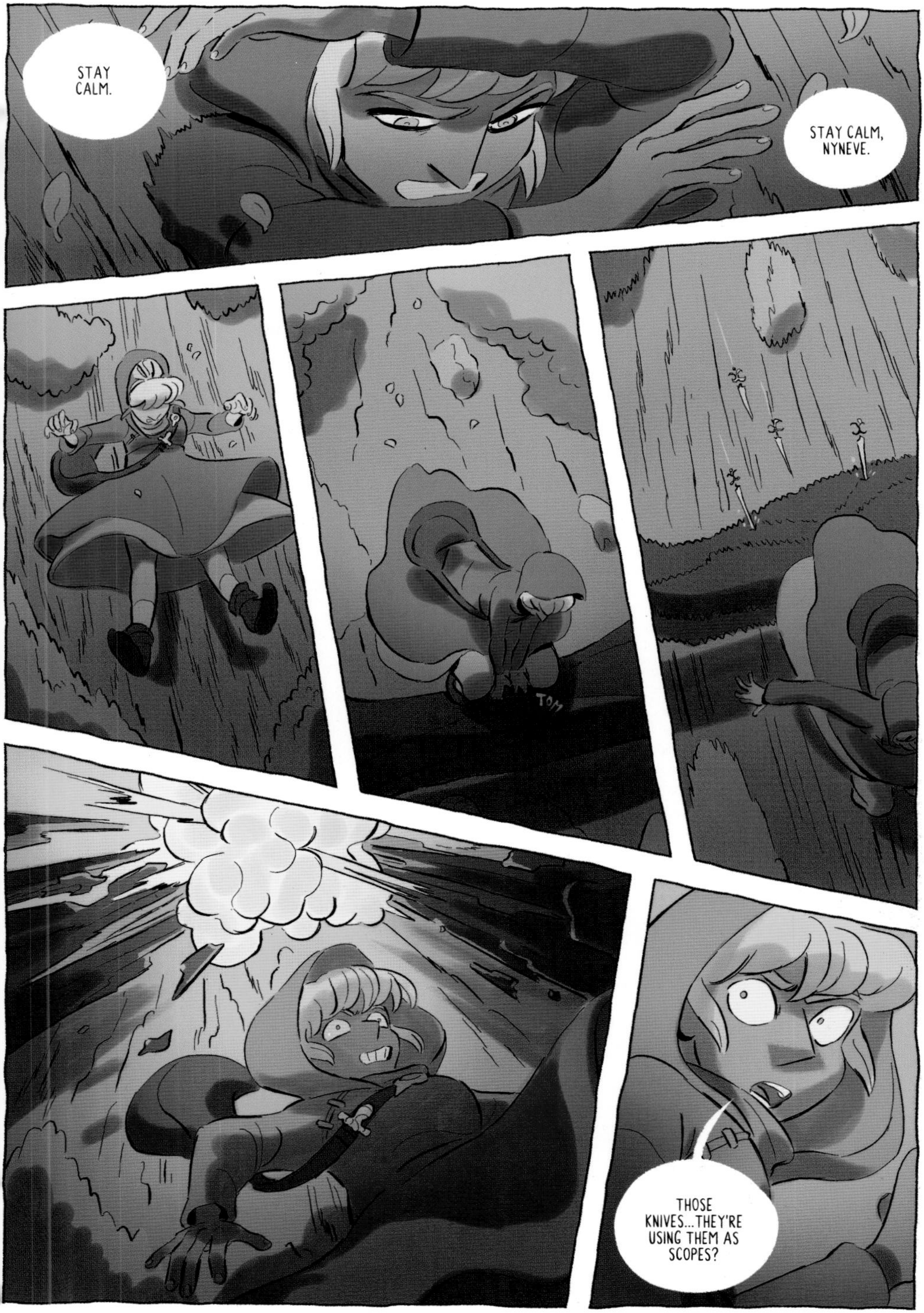
STAY CALM.
STAY CALM, NYNEVE.
TOM
THOSE KNIVES...THEY'RE USING THEM AS SCOPES?

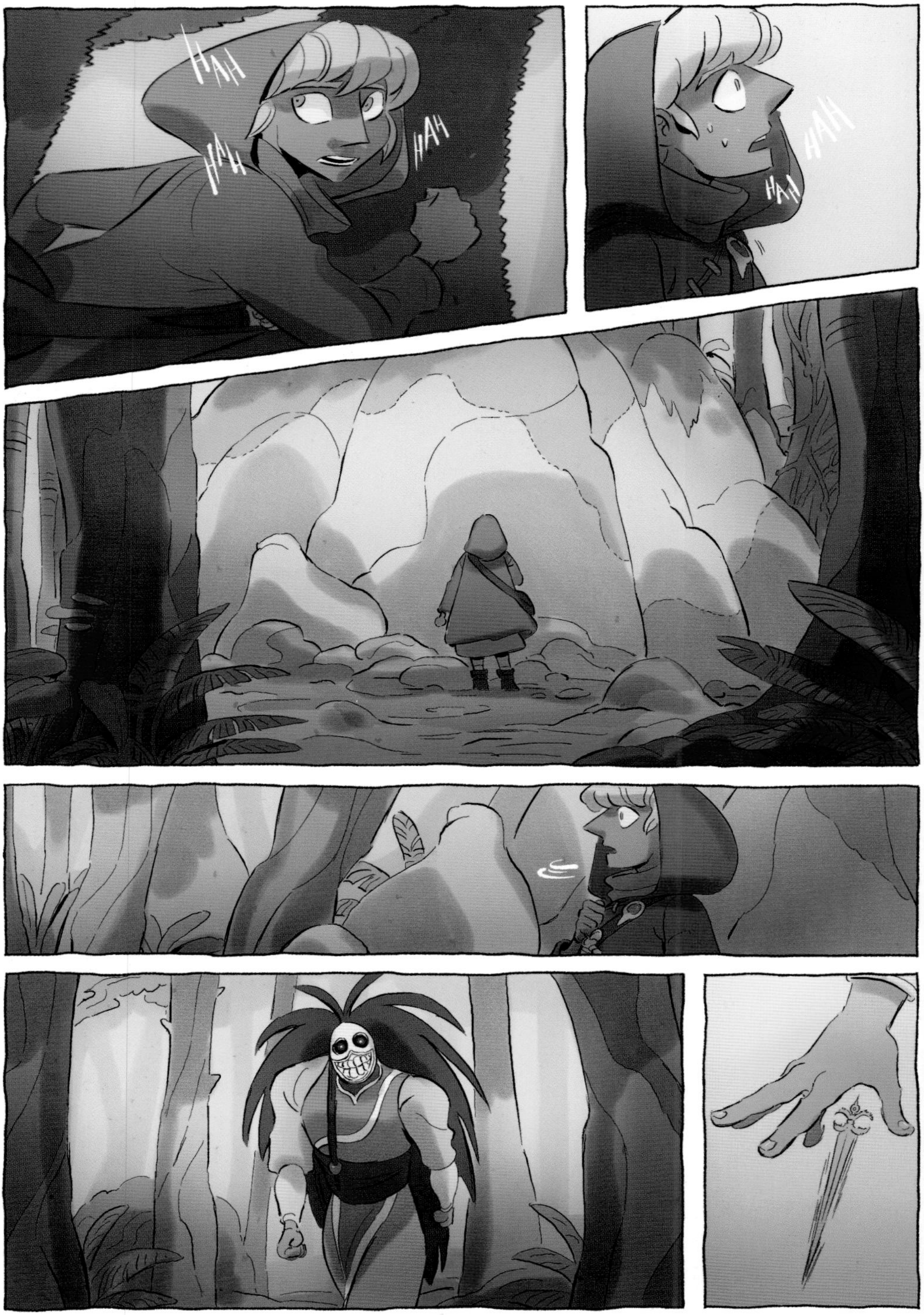
HAH
HAH
HAH
HAH
HAH

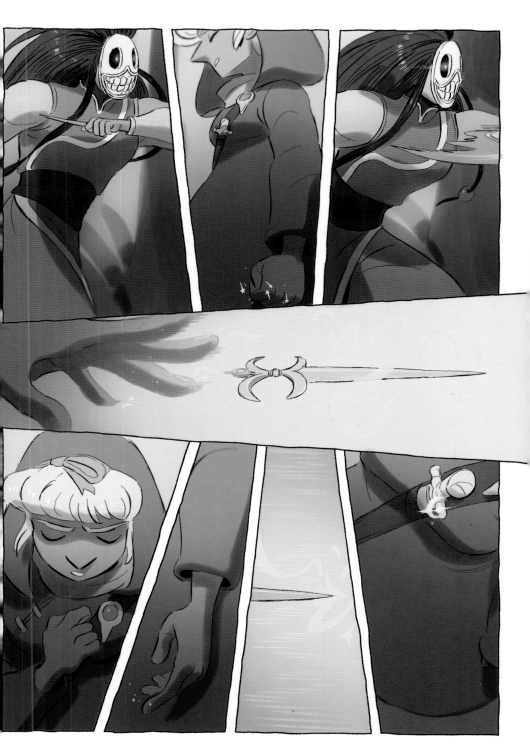

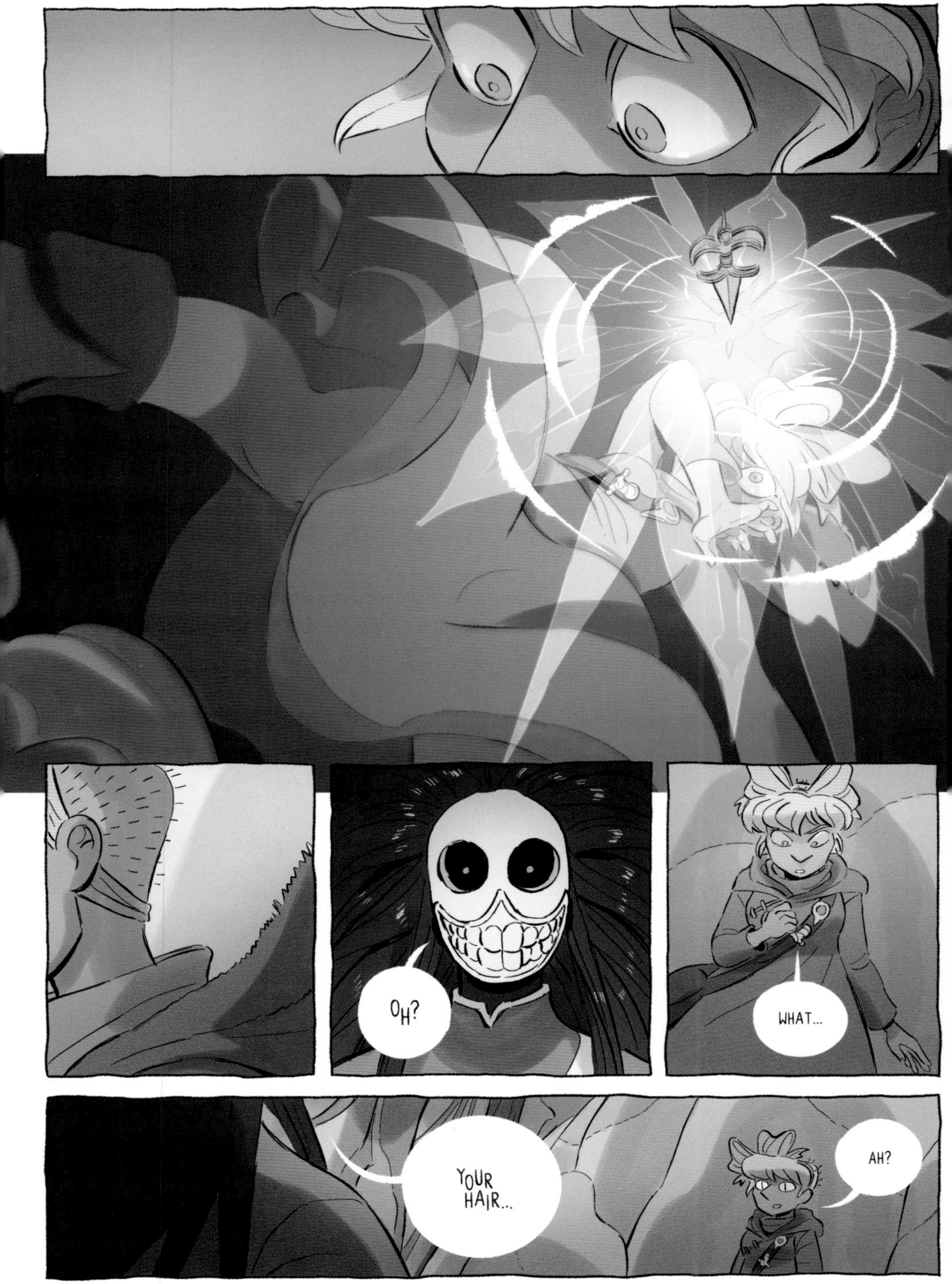
OH?
WHAT...
YOUR HAIR...
AH?

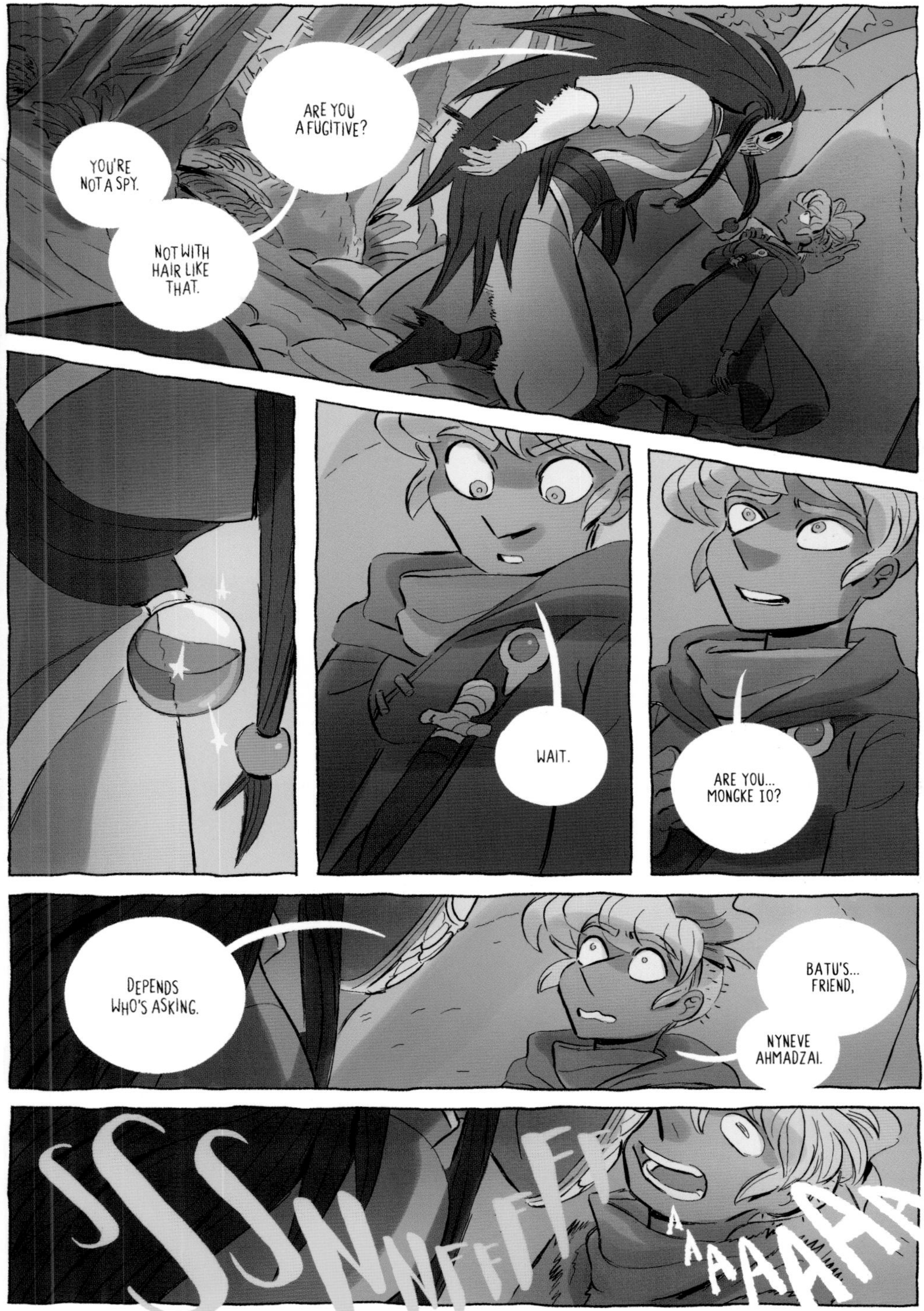
YOU'RE NOT A SPY.
NOT WITH HAIR LIKE THAT.
ARE YOU A FUGITIVE?
WAIT.
ARE YOU... MONGKE IO?
DEPENDS WHO'S ASKING.
BATU'S... FRIEND,
NYNEVE AHMADZAI.
SSSNFFFFFAAAAAA

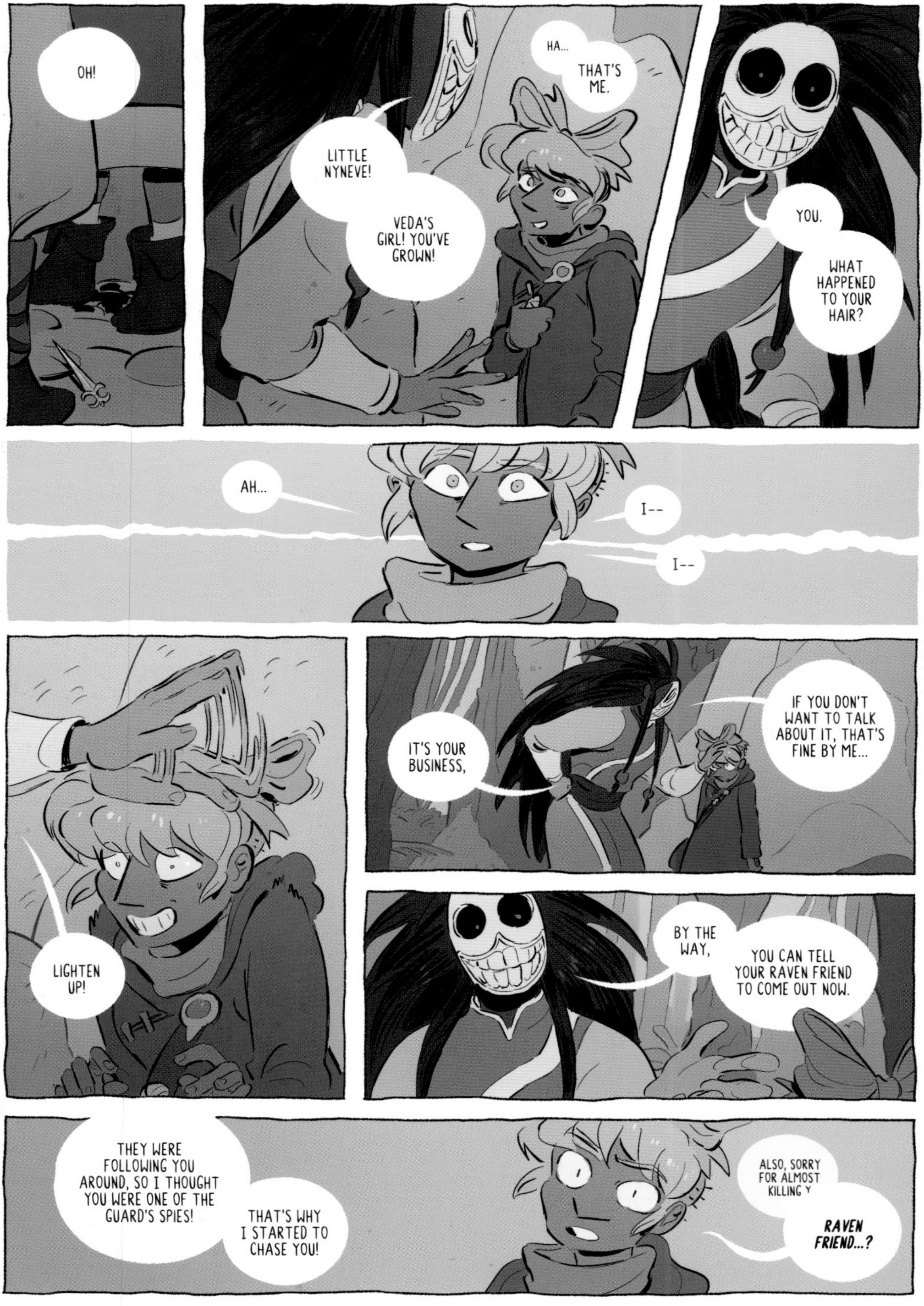
OH!
LITTLE NYNEVE!
VEDA'S GIRL! YOU'VE GROWN!
HA...
THAT'S ME.
YOU.
WHAT HAPPENED TO YOUR HAIR?
AH...
I--
I--
LIGHTEN UP!
IF YOU DON'T WANT TO TALK ABOUT IT, THAT'S FINE BY ME...
IT'S YOUR BUSINESS,
BY THE WAY,
YOU CAN TELL YOUR RAVEN FRIEND TO COME OUT NOW.
THEY WERE FOLLOWING YOU AROUND, SO I THOUGHT YOU WERE ONE OF THE GUARD'S SPIES!
THAT'S WHY I STARTED TO CHASE YOU!
ALSO, SORRY FOR ALMOST KILLING Y
RAVEN FRIEND...?

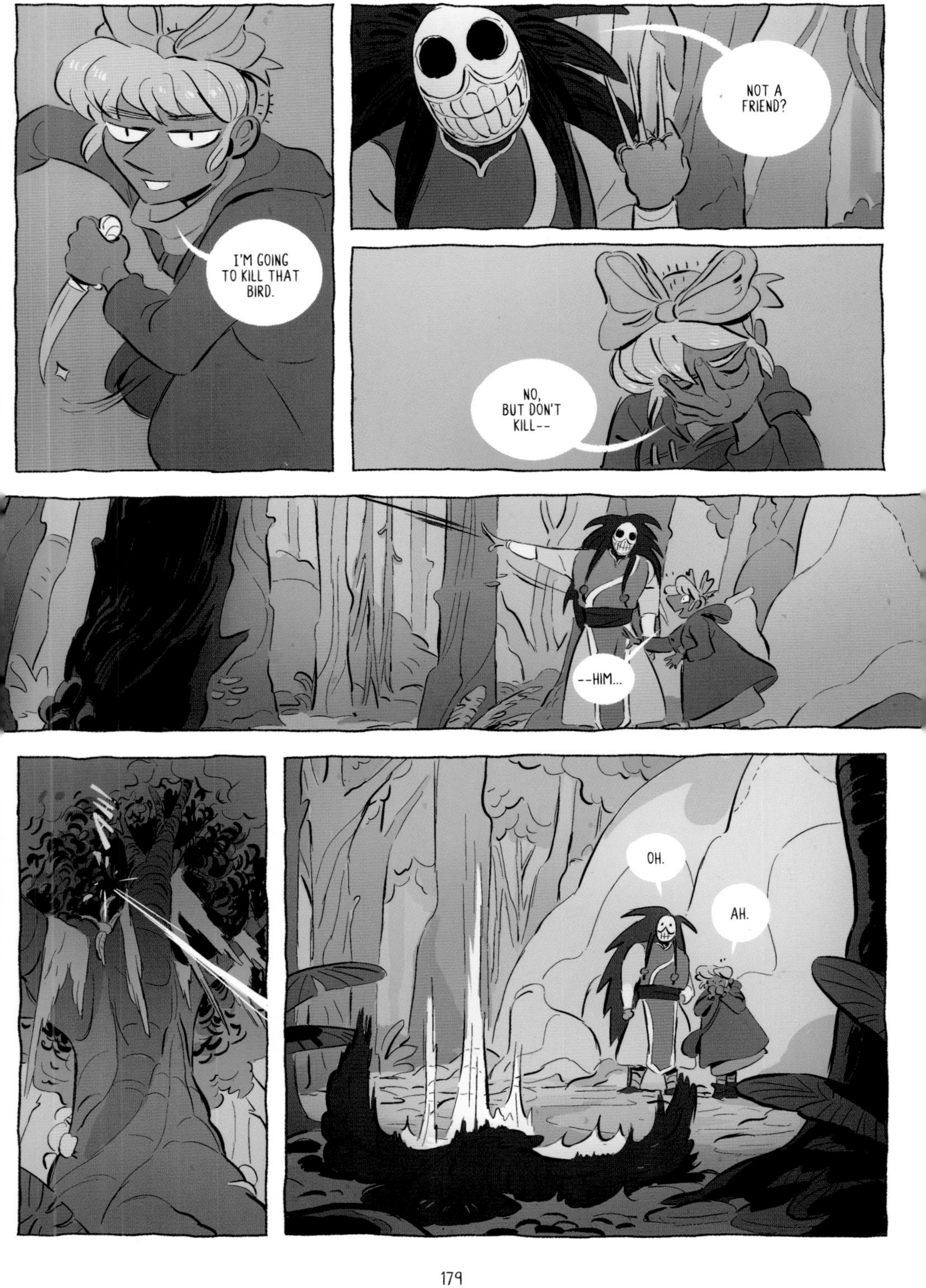
I'M GOING TO KILL THAT BIRD.
NOT A FRIEND?
NO, BUT DON'T KILL--
--HIM...
AHH!
OH.
AH.

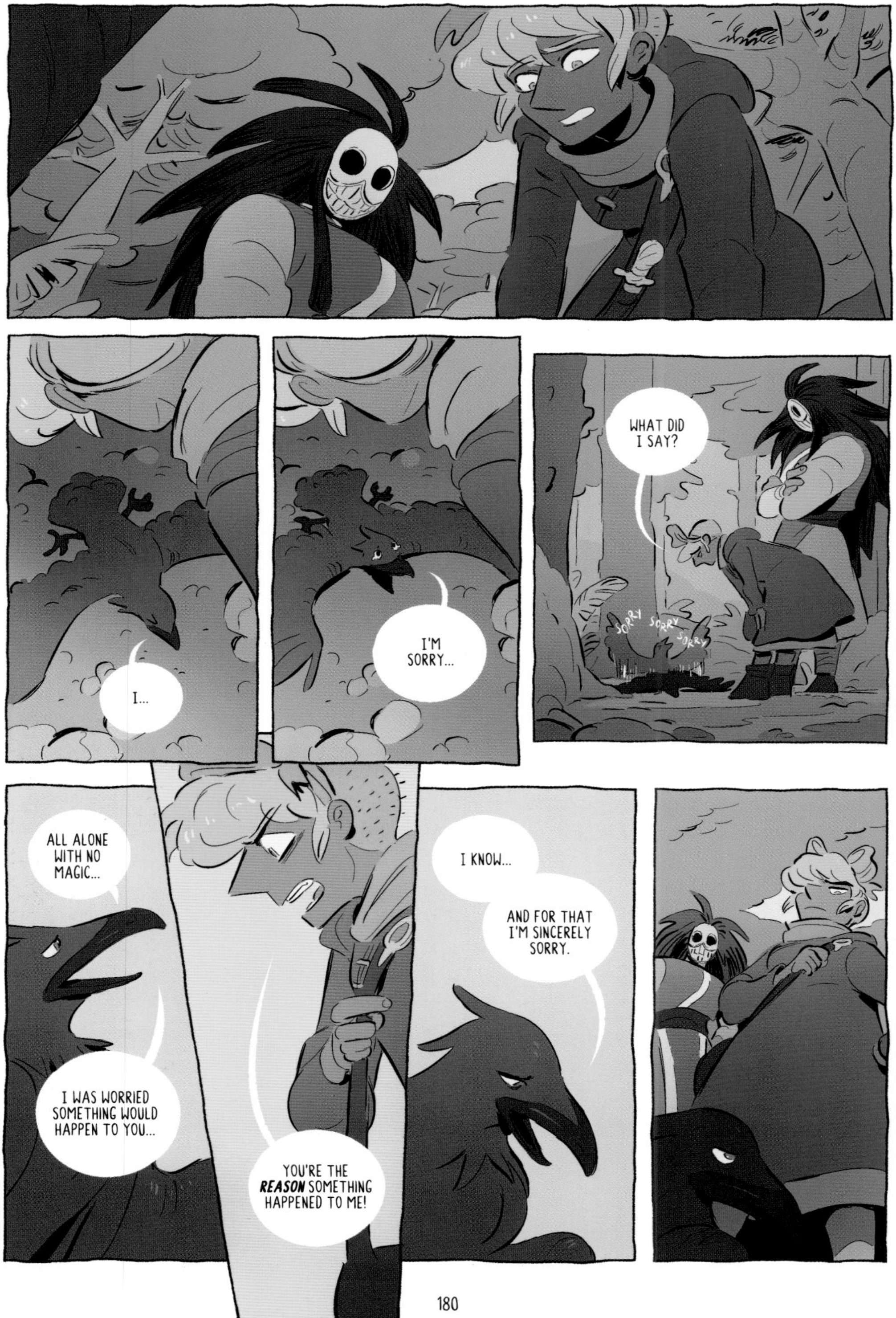
I...
I'M SORRY...
WHAT DID I SAY?
SORRY SORRY SORRY
ALL ALONE WITH NO MAGIC...
I WAS WORRIED SOMETHING WOULD HAPPEN TO YOU...
YOU'RE THE **REASON** SOMETHING HAPPENED TO ME!
I KNOW...
AND FOR THAT I'M SINCERELY SORRY.

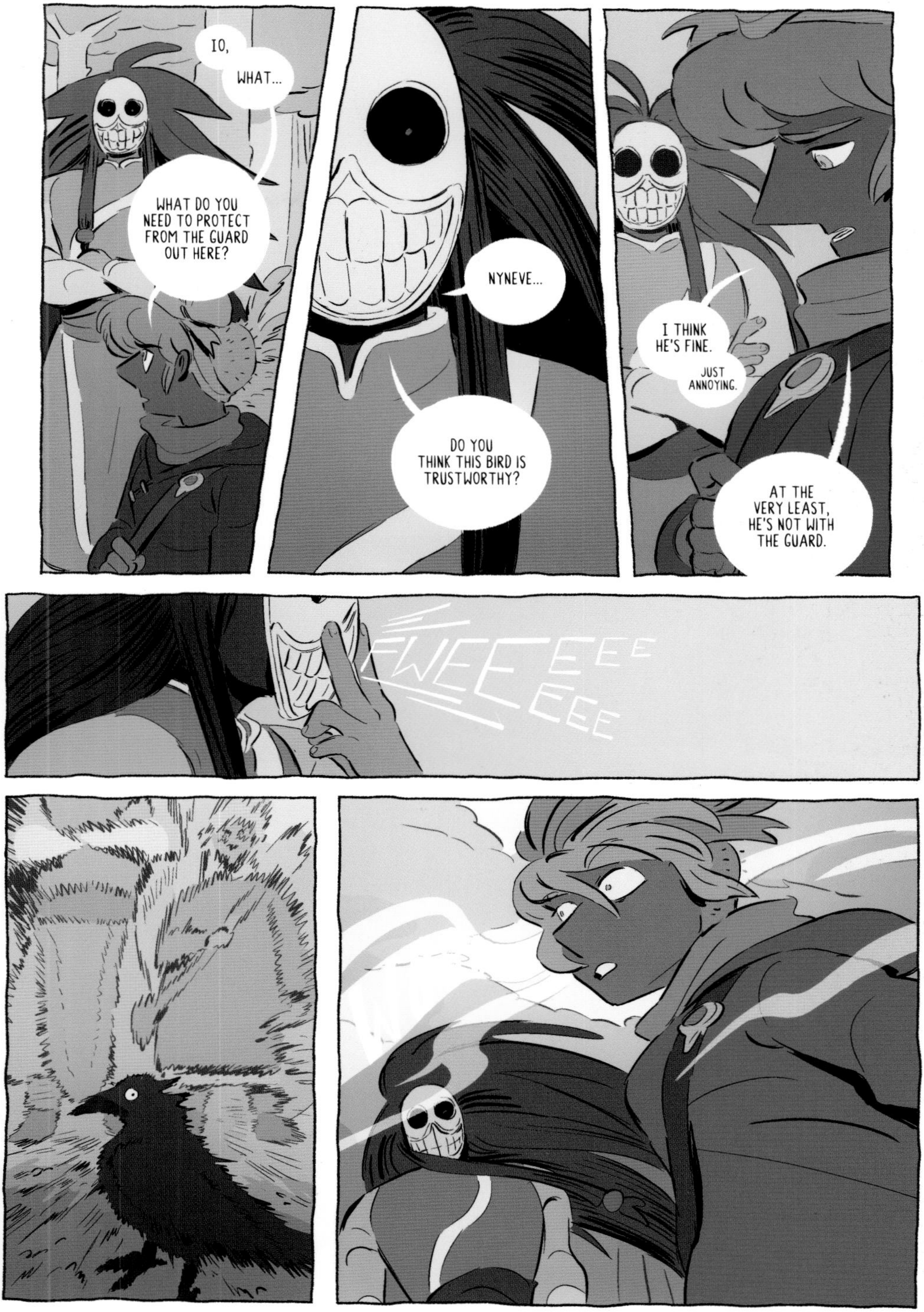
IO,
WHAT...
WHAT DO YOU NEED TO PROTECT FROM THE GUARD OUT HERE?
NYNEVE...
DO YOU THINK THIS BIRD IS TRUSTWORTHY?
I THINK HE'S FINE.
JUST ANNOYING.
AT THE VERY LEAST, HE'S NOT WITH THE GUARD.
FWEEEEE EEE

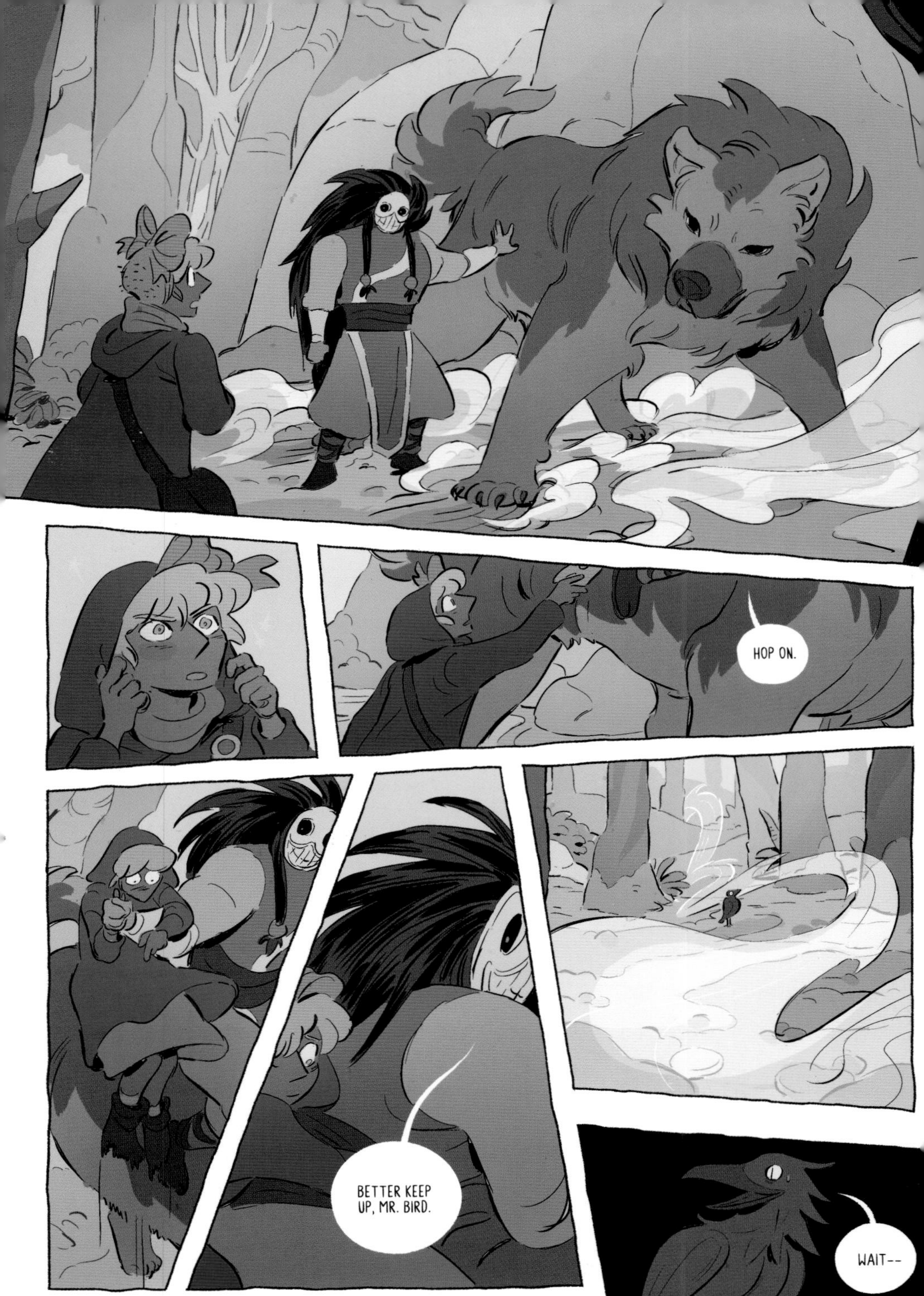
HOP ON.
BETTER KEEP UP, MR. BIRD.
WAIT--

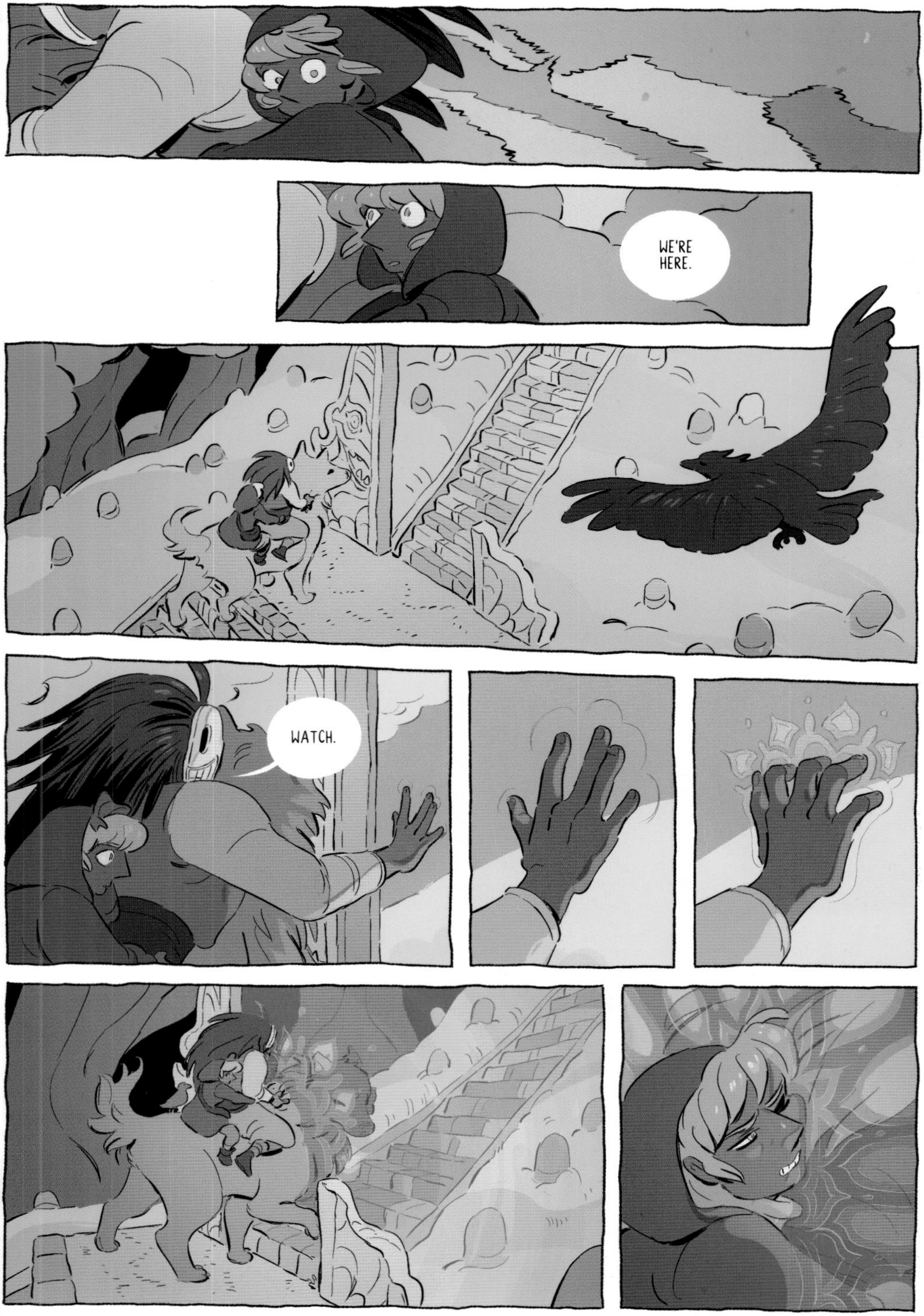
WE'RE HERE.
WATCH.

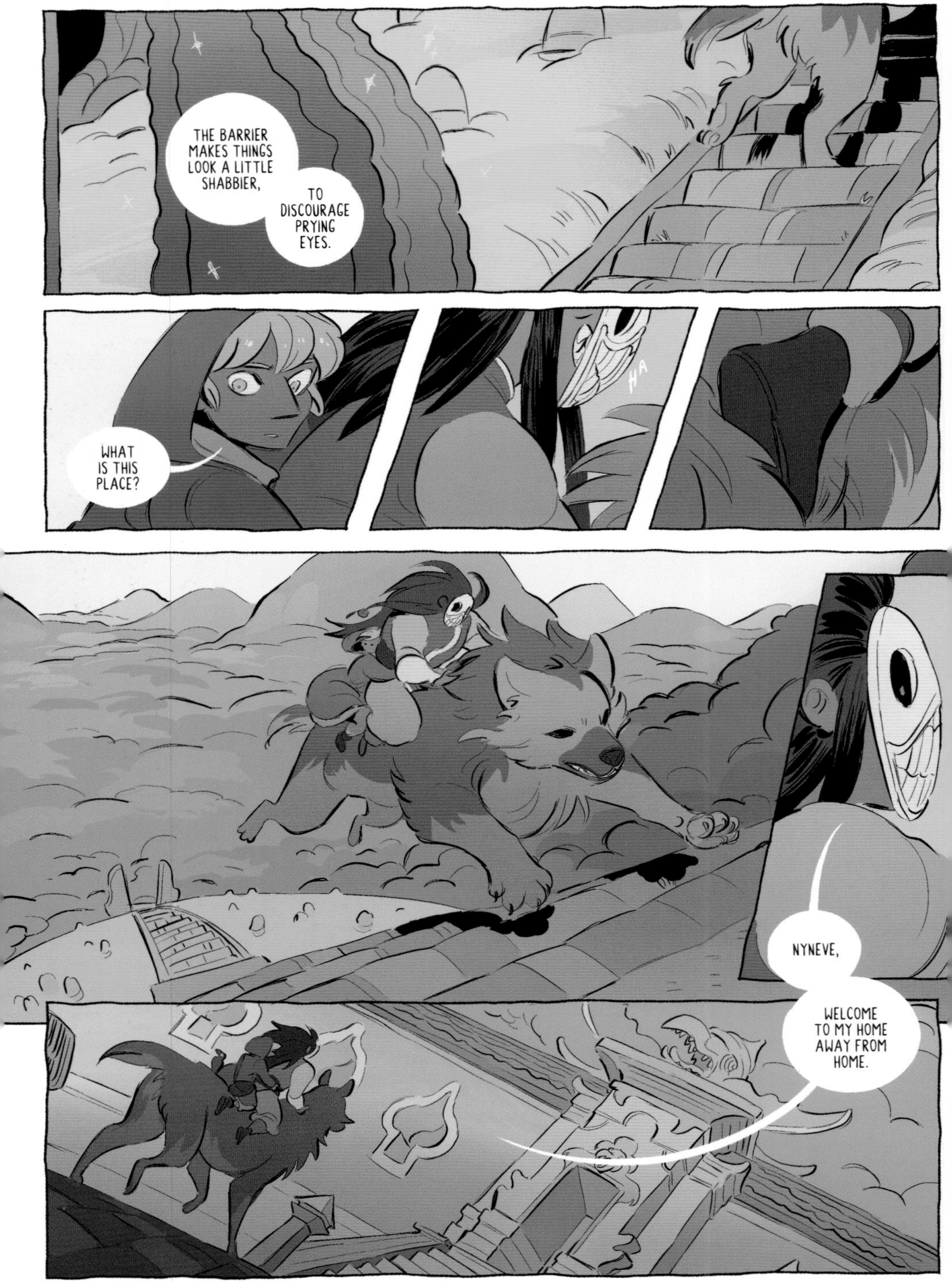
THE BARRIER MAKES THINGS LOOK A LITTLE SHABBIER,
TO DISCOURAGE PRYING EYES.
WHAT IS THIS PLACE?
HA
NYNEVE,
WELCOME TO MY HOME AWAY FROM HOME.

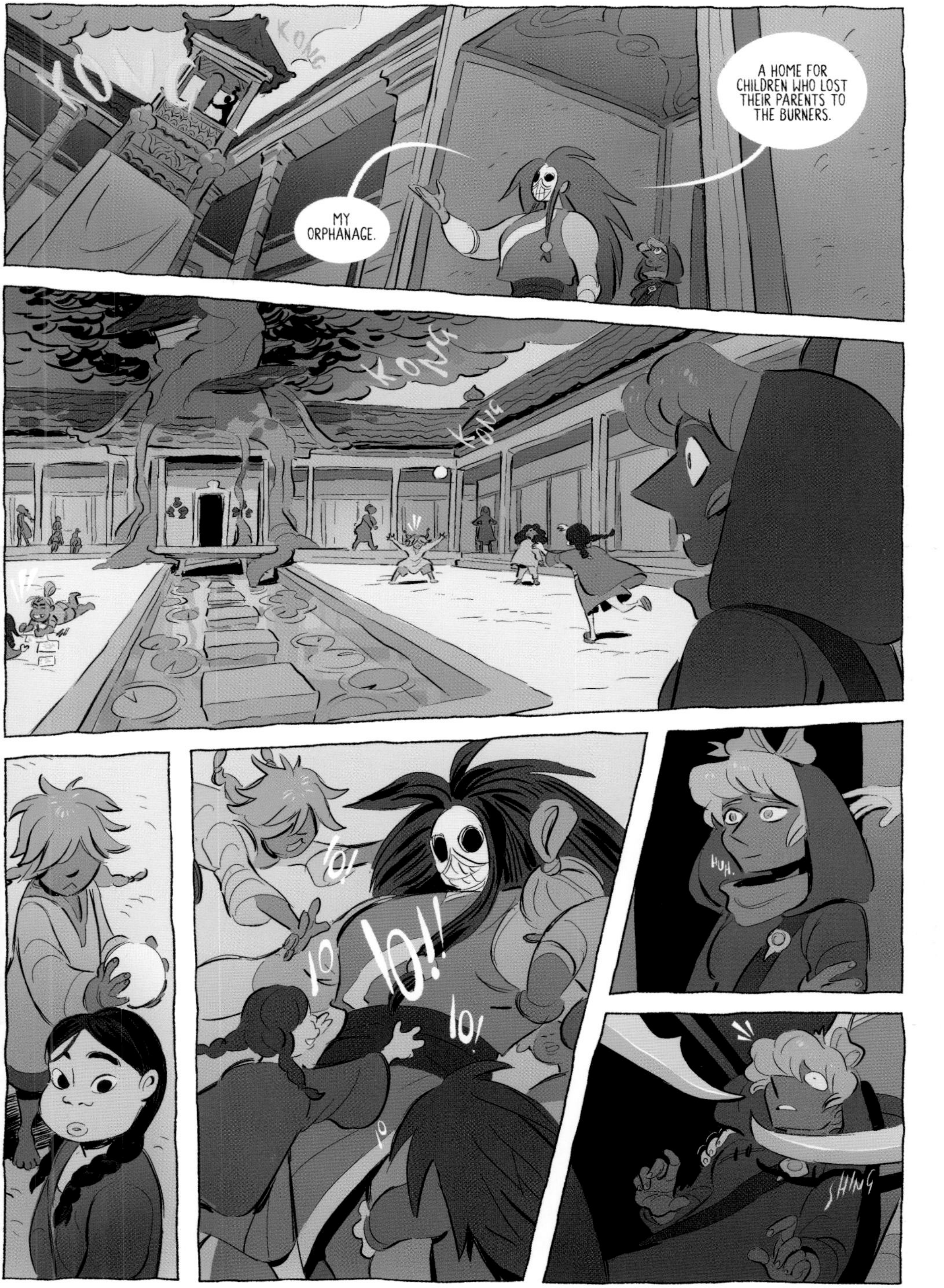
KONG
KONG
MY ORPHANAGE.
A HOME FOR CHILDREN WHO LOST THEIR PARENTS TO THE BURNERS.
KONG
KONG
IO!
IO
IO!!
IO!
IO
HUH.
SHING

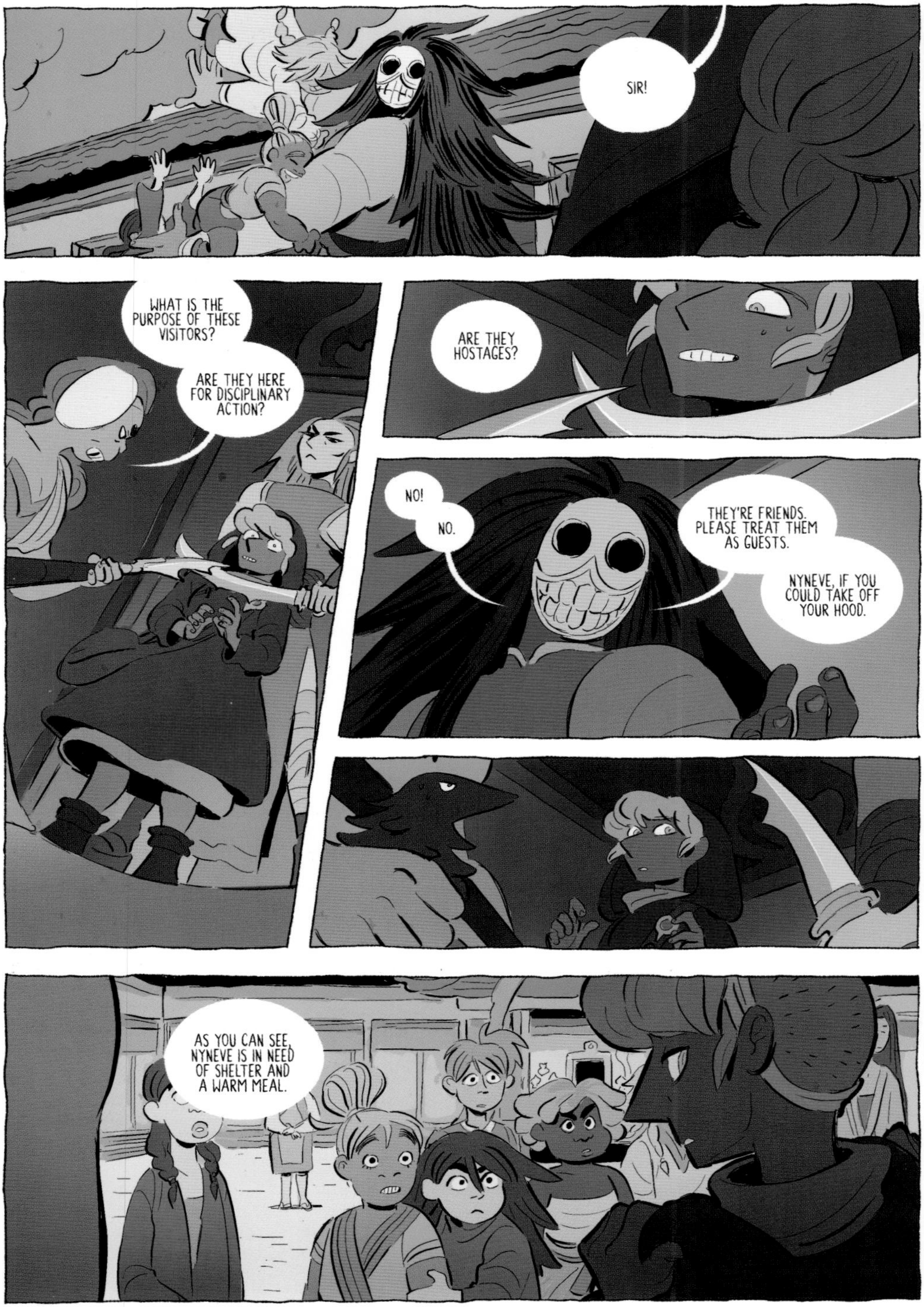
SIR!
WHAT IS THE PURPOSE OF THESE VISITORS?
ARE THEY HERE FOR DISCIPLINARY ACTION?
ARE THEY HOSTAGES?
NO!
NO.
THEY'RE FRIENDS. PLEASE TREAT THEM AS GUESTS.
NYNEVE, IF YOU COULD TAKE OFF YOUR HOOD.
AS YOU CAN SEE, NYNEVE IS IN NEED OF SHELTER AND A WARM MEAL.

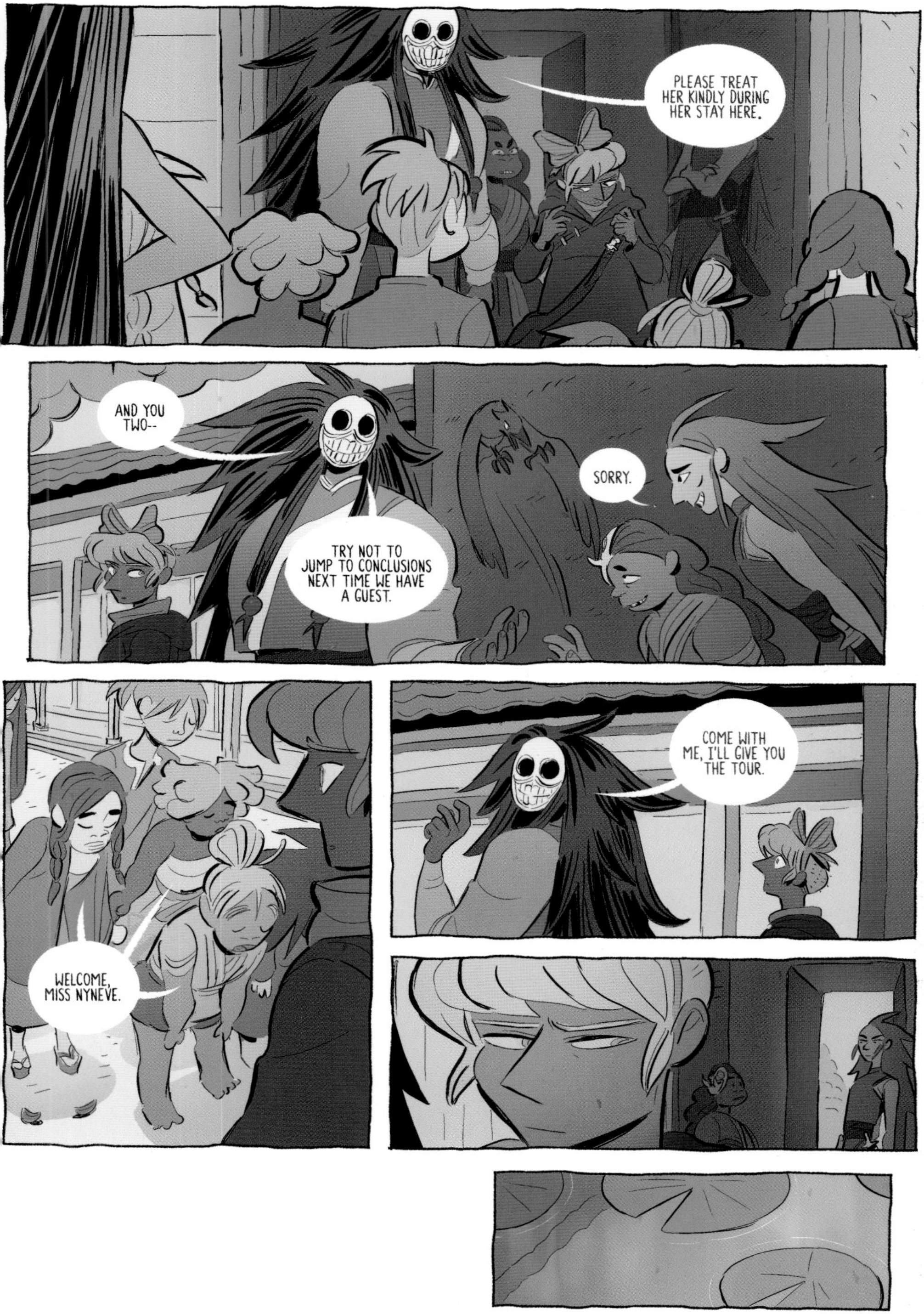
PLEASE TREAT HER KINDLY DURING HER STAY HERE.
AND YOU TWO--
TRY NOT TO JUMP TO CONCLUSIONS NEXT TIME WE HAVE A GUEST.
SORRY.
WELCOME, MISS NYNEVE.
COME WITH ME, I'LL GIVE YOU THE TOUR.

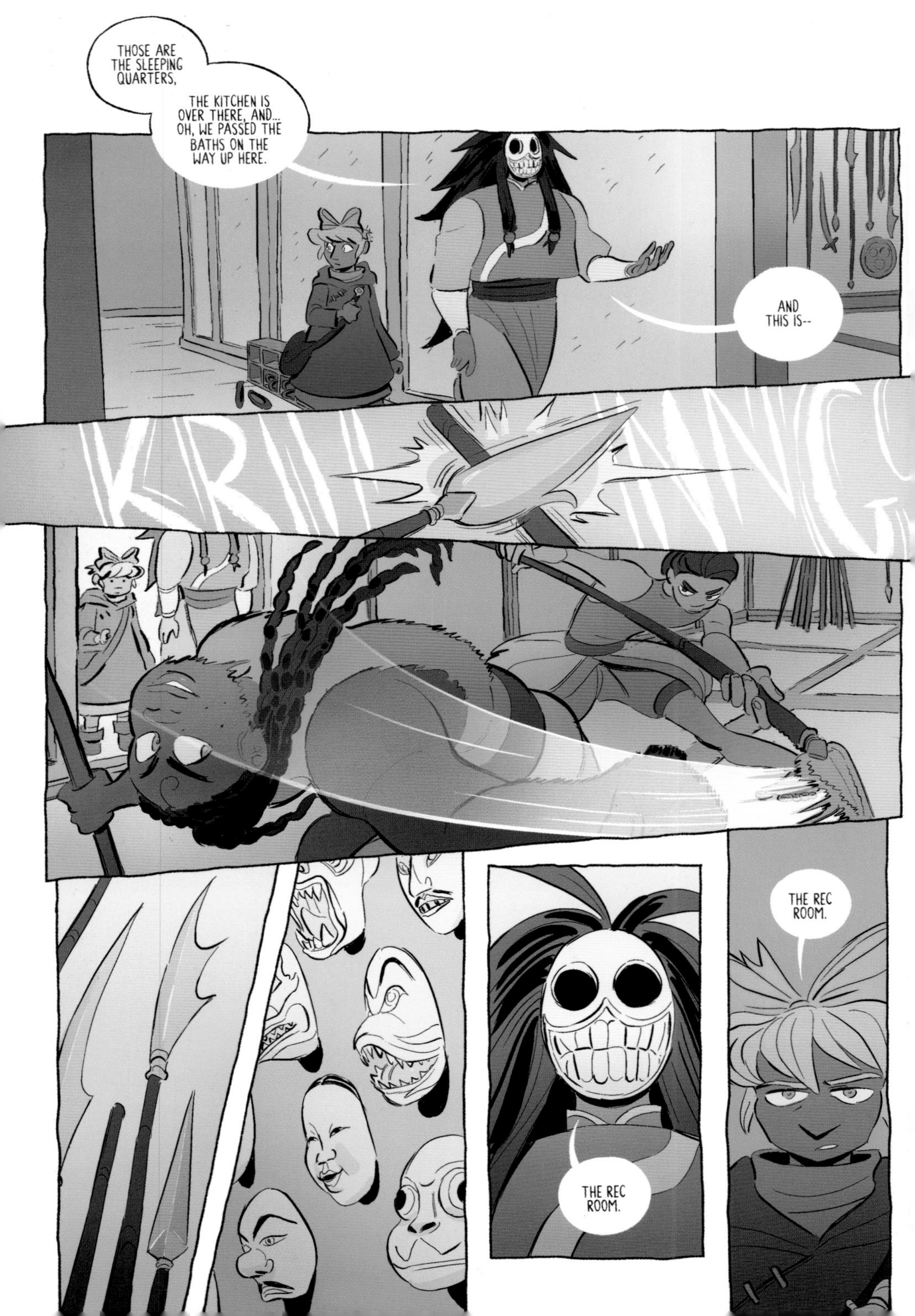
THOSE ARE THE SLEEPING QUARTERS,
THE KITCHEN IS OVER THERE, AND... OH, WE PASSED THE BATHS ON THE WAY UP HERE.
AND THIS IS--
KRIIIANNG
THE REC ROOM.
THE REC ROOM.

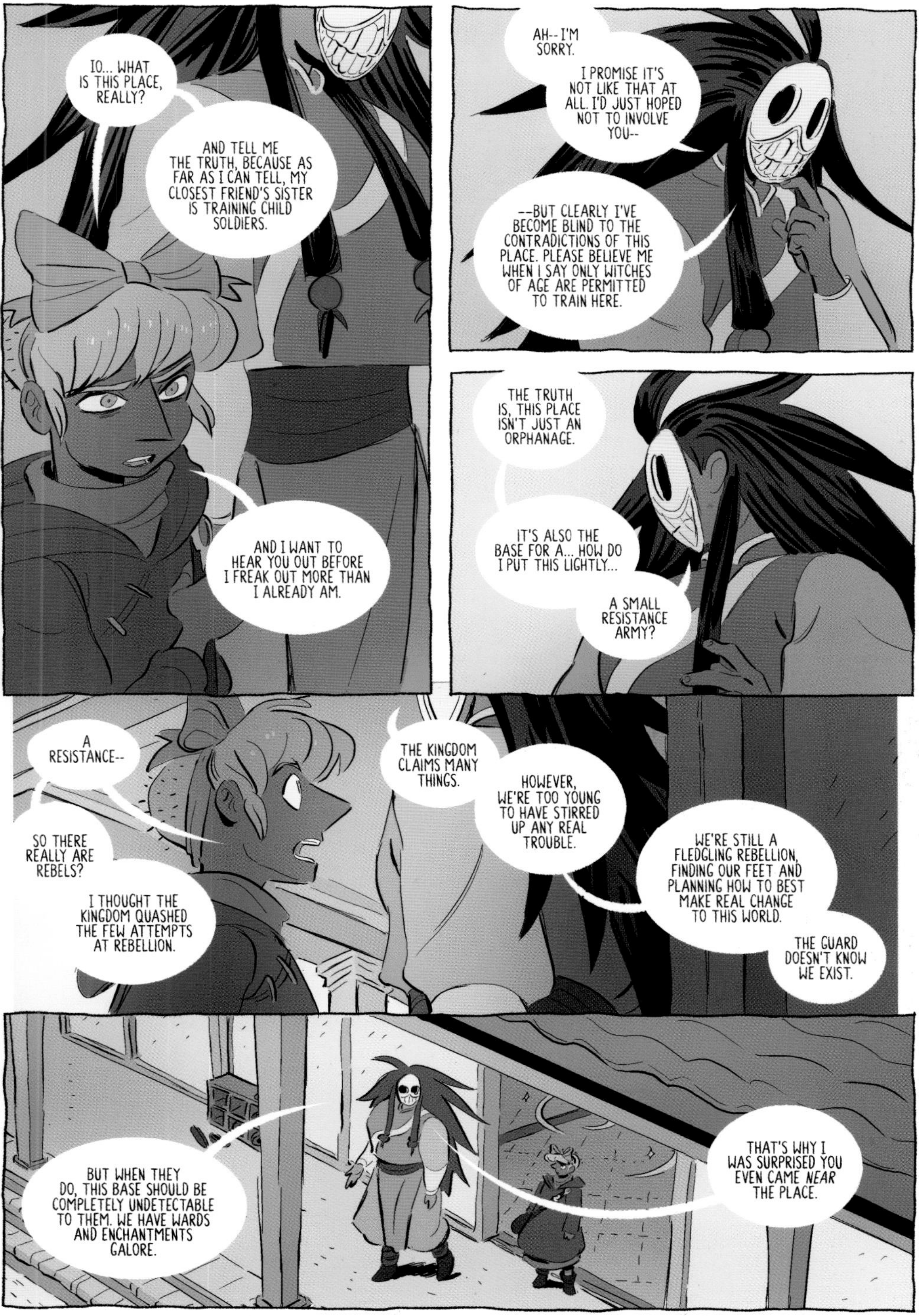
IO... WHAT IS THIS PLACE, REALLY?
AND TELL ME THE TRUTH, BECAUSE AS FAR AS I CAN TELL, MY CLOSEST FRIEND'S SISTER IS TRAINING CHILD SOLDIERS.
AND I WANT TO HEAR YOU OUT BEFORE I FREAK OUT MORE THAN I ALREADY AM.
AH-- I'M SORRY.
I PROMISE IT'S NOT LIKE THAT AT ALL. I'D JUST HOPED NOT TO INVOLVE YOU--
--BUT CLEARLY I'VE BECOME BLIND TO THE CONTRADICTIONS OF THIS PLACE. PLEASE BELIEVE ME WHEN I SAY ONLY WITCHES OF AGE ARE PERMITTED TO TRAIN HERE.
THE TRUTH IS, THIS PLACE ISN'T JUST AN ORPHANAGE.
IT'S ALSO THE BASE FOR A... HOW DO I PUT THIS LIGHTLY...
A SMALL RESISTANCE ARMY?
A RESISTANCE--
SO THERE REALLY ARE REBELS?
I THOUGHT THE KINGDOM QUASHED THE FEW ATTEMPTS AT REBELLION.
THE KINGDOM CLAIMS MANY THINGS.
HOWEVER, WE'RE TOO YOUNG TO HAVE STIRRED UP ANY REAL TROUBLE.
WE'RE STILL A FLEDGLING REBELLION, FINDING OUR FEET AND PLANNING HOW TO BEST MAKE REAL CHANGE TO THIS WORLD.
THE GUARD DOESN'T KNOW WE EXIST.
BUT WHEN THEY DO, THIS BASE SHOULD BE COMPLETELY UNDETECTABLE TO THEM. WE HAVE WARDS AND ENCHANTMENTS GALORE.
THAT'S WHY I WAS SURPRISED YOU EVEN CAME *NEAR* THE PLACE.

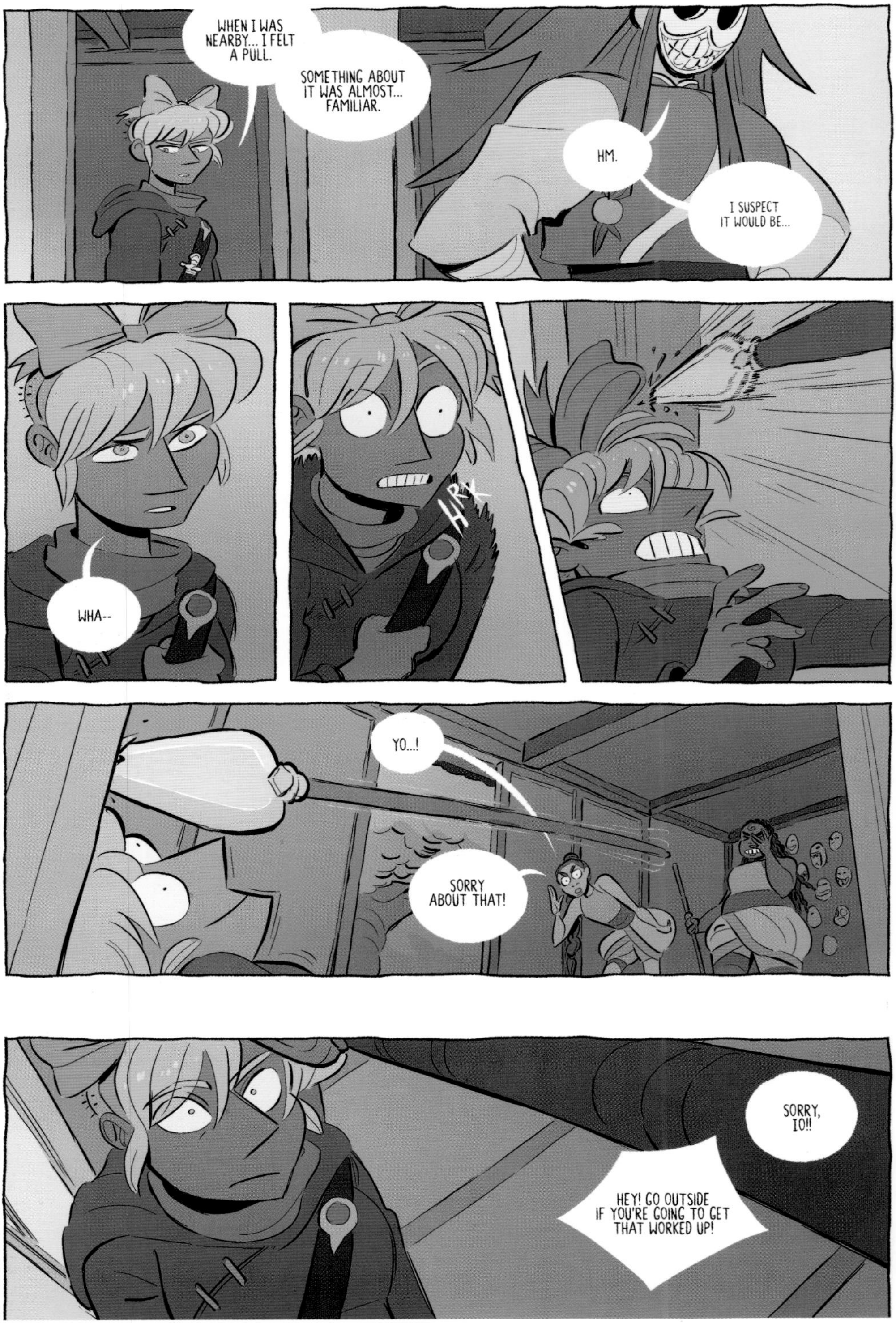
WHEN I WAS NEARBY... I FELT A PULL.
SOMETHING ABOUT IT WAS ALMOST... FAMILIAR.
HM.
I SUSPECT IT WOULD BE...
WHA--
HRK
YO...!
SORRY ABOUT THAT!
SORRY, IO!!
HEY! GO OUTSIDE IF YOU'RE GOING TO GET THAT WORKED UP!

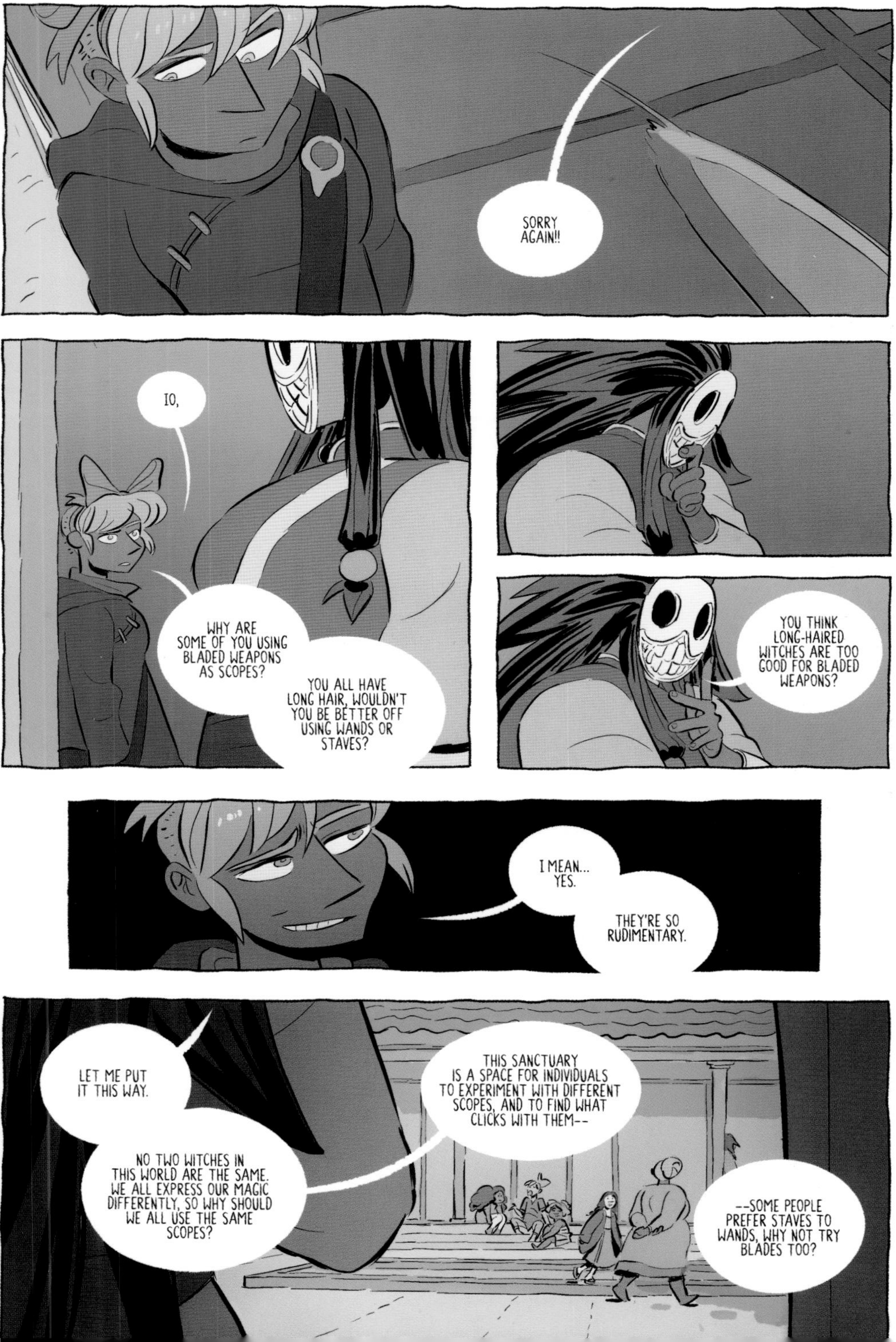

SORRY AGAIN!!
IO,
WHY ARE SOME OF YOU USING BLADED WEAPONS AS SCOPES?
YOU ALL HAVE LONG HAIR, WOULDN'T YOU BE BETTER OFF USING WANDS OR STAVES?
YOU THINK LONG-HAIRED WITCHES ARE TOO GOOD FOR BLADED WEAPONS?
I MEAN... YES.
THEY'RE SO RUDIMENTARY.
LET ME PUT IT THIS WAY.
NO TWO WITCHES IN THIS WORLD ARE THE SAME. WE ALL EXPRESS OUR MAGIC DIFFERENTLY, SO WHY SHOULD WE ALL USE THE SAME SCOPES?
THIS SANCTUARY IS A SPACE FOR INDIVIDUALS TO EXPERIMENT WITH DIFFERENT SCOPES, AND TO FIND WHAT CLICKS WITH THEM--
--SOME PEOPLE PREFER STAVES TO WANDS, WHY NOT TRY BLADES TOO?

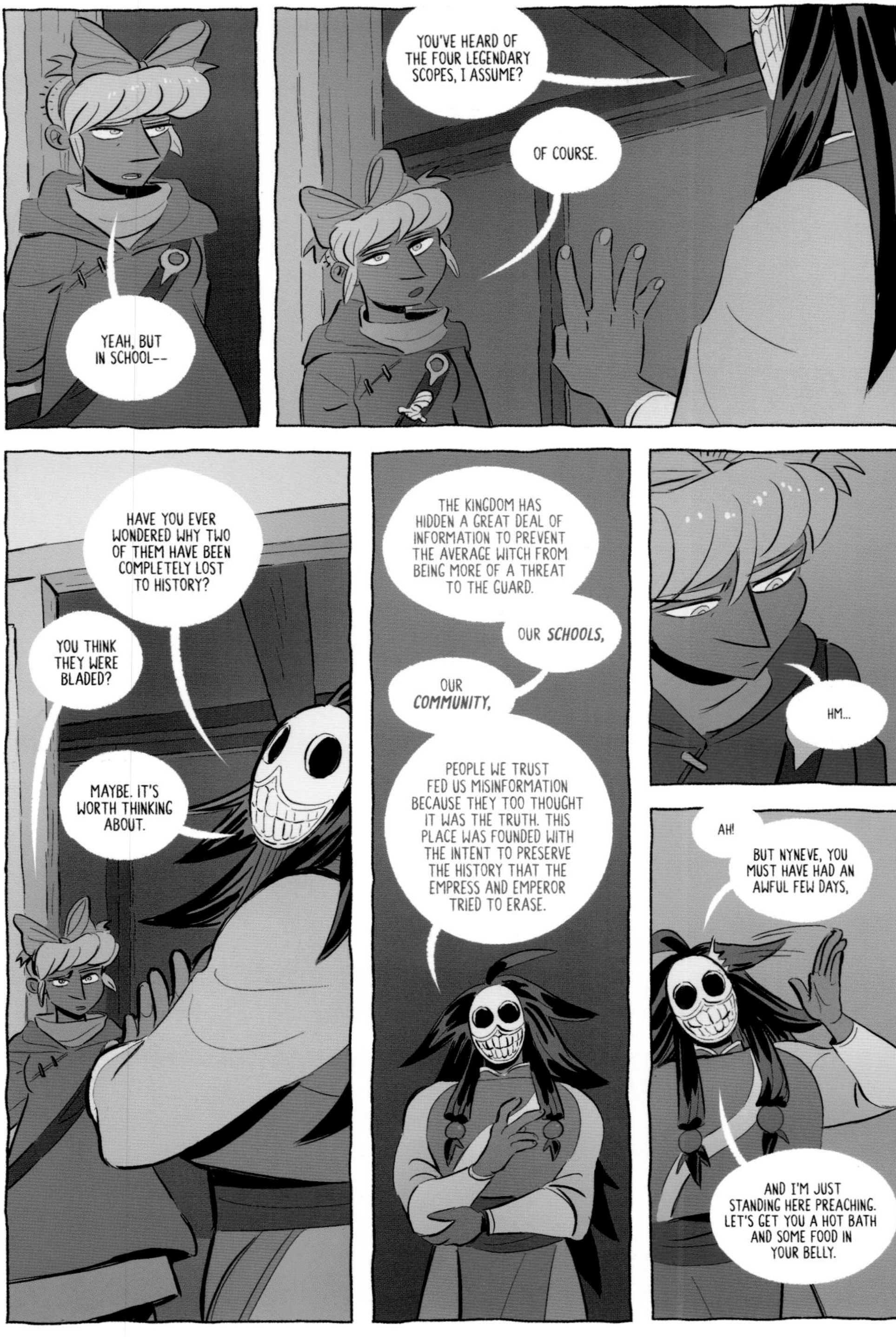
YOU'VE HEARD OF THE FOUR LEGENDARY SCOPES, I ASSUME?
YEAH, BUT IN SCHOOL--
OF COURSE.
HAVE YOU EVER WONDERED WHY TWO OF THEM HAVE BEEN COMPLETELY LOST TO HISTORY?
YOU THINK THEY WERE BLADED?
MAYBE. IT'S WORTH THINKING ABOUT.
THE KINGDOM HAS HIDDEN A GREAT DEAL OF INFORMATION TO PREVENT THE AVERAGE WITCH FROM BEING MORE OF A THREAT TO THE GUARD.
OUR *SCHOOLS,*
OUR *COMMUNITY,*
PEOPLE WE TRUST FED US MISINFORMATION BECAUSE THEY TOO THOUGHT IT WAS THE TRUTH. THIS PLACE WAS FOUNDED WITH THE INTENT TO PRESERVE THE HISTORY THAT THE EMPRESS AND EMPEROR TRIED TO ERASE.
HM...
AH!
BUT NYNEVE, YOU MUST HAVE HAD AN AWFUL FEW DAYS,
AND I'M JUST STANDING HERE PREACHING. LET'S GET YOU A HOT BATH AND SOME FOOD IN YOUR BELLY.

WAIT, I WANT TO HEAR MORE ABOUT THE REBELL--

I CAN ANSWER ANY QUESTIONS YOU HAVE TOMORROW. PLEASE, STAY THE NIGHT AND REST UP.

I'LL MAKE SURE EVERYTHING'S RUNNING SMOOTHLY IN THE KITCHEN. COULD YOU TELL THE KIDS IN THE YARD TO PREPARE THE DINING ROOM?

KIDS?

Y-YEAH... SURE!

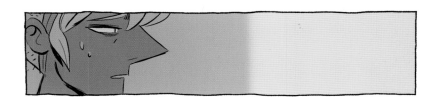

193

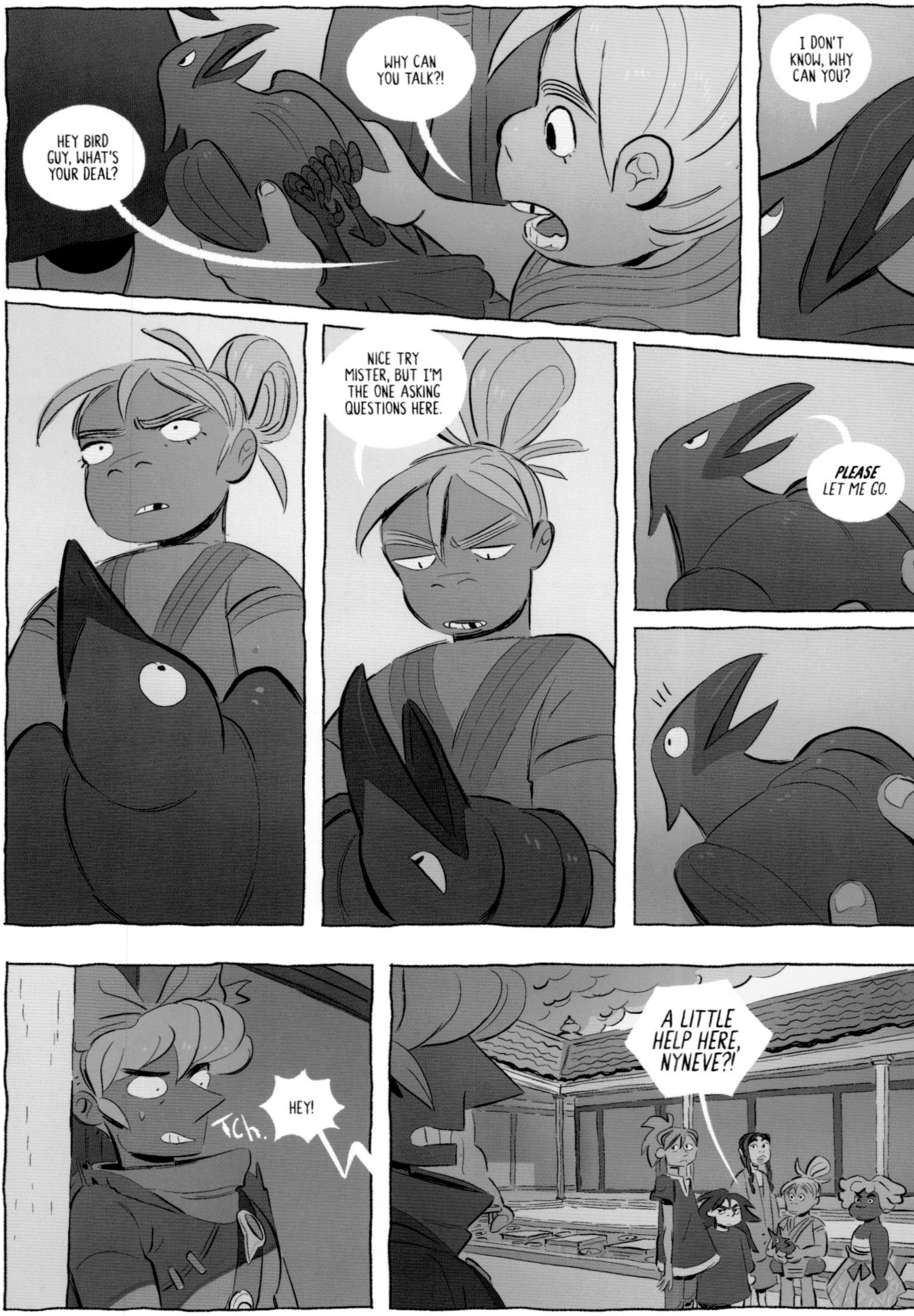
WHY CAN YOU TALK?!
HEY BIRD GUY, WHAT'S YOUR DEAL?
I DON'T KNOW, WHY CAN YOU?
NICE TRY MISTER, BUT I'M THE ONE ASKING QUESTIONS HERE.
PLEASE LET ME GO.
TCH.
HEY!
A LITTLE HELP HERE, NYNEVE?!

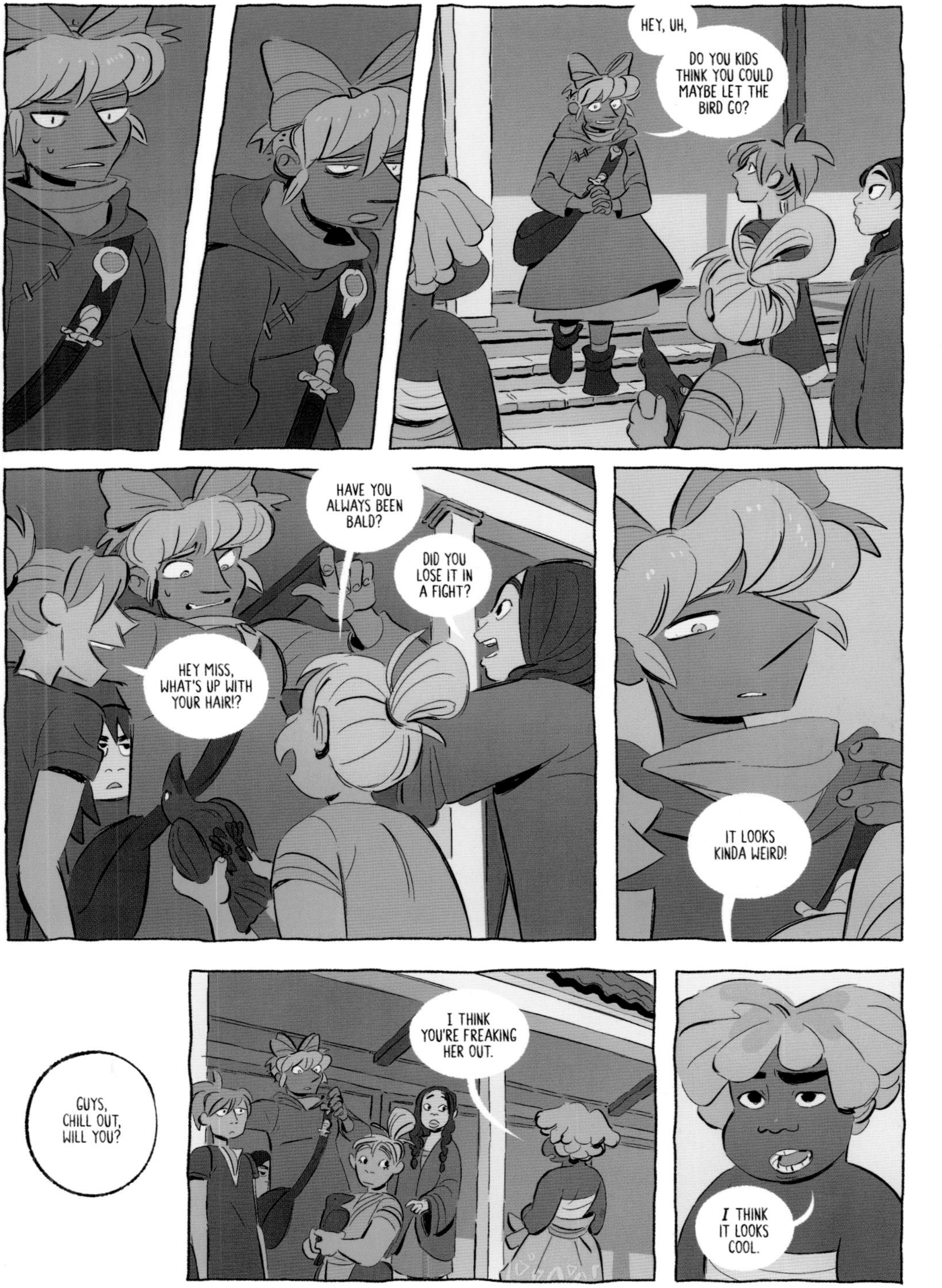
HEY, UH,
DO YOU KIDS THINK YOU COULD MAYBE LET THE BIRD GO?
HAVE YOU ALWAYS BEEN BALD?
DID YOU LOSE IT IN A FIGHT?
HEY MISS, WHAT'S UP WITH YOUR HAIR!?
IT LOOKS KINDA WEIRD!
GUYS, CHILL OUT, WILL YOU?
I THINK YOU'RE FREAKING HER OUT.
I THINK IT LOOKS COOL.

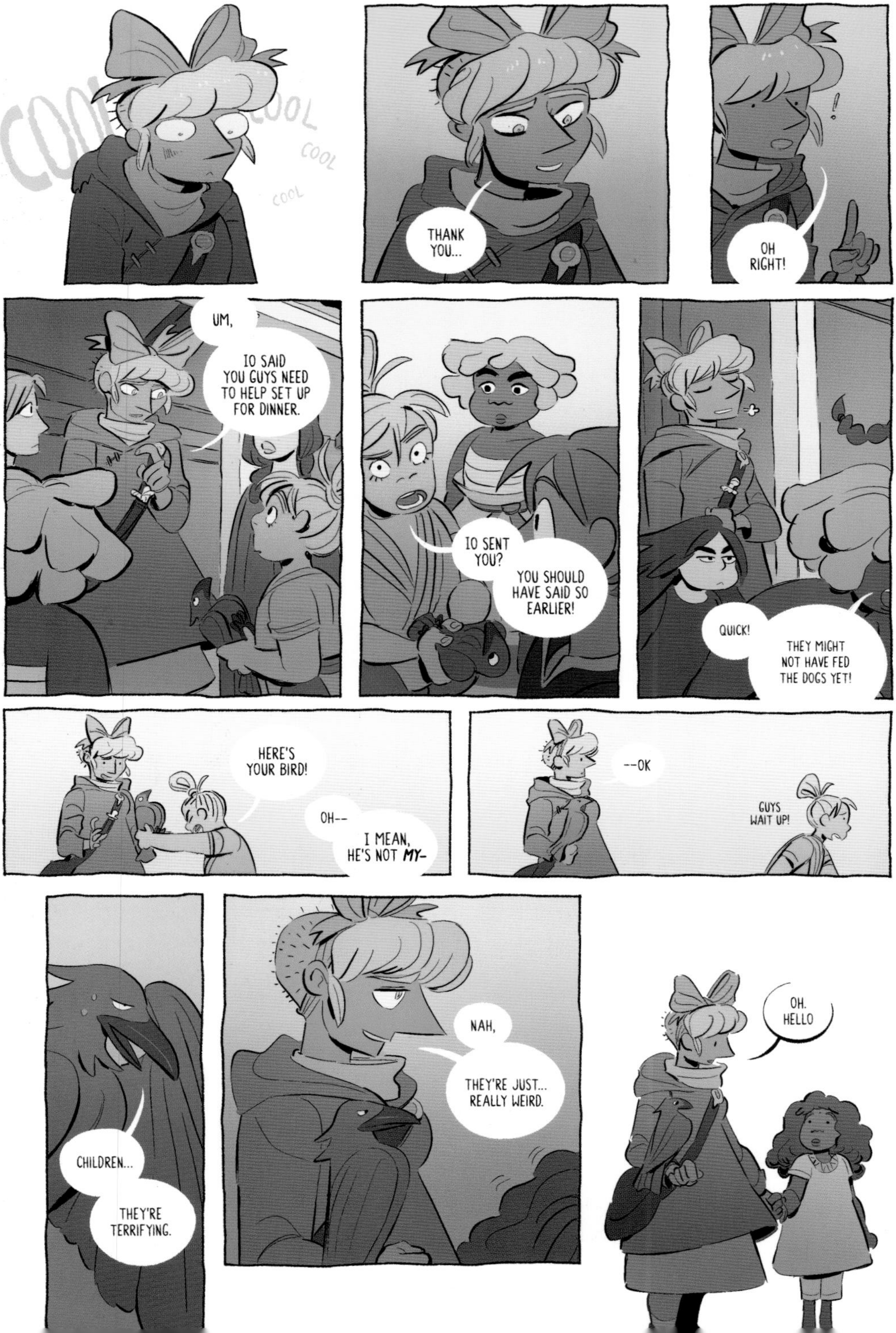
COOL COOL COOL COOL
THANK YOU...
!
OH RIGHT!
UM,
IO SAID YOU GUYS NEED TO HELP SET UP FOR DINNER.
IO SENT YOU?
YOU SHOULD HAVE SAID SO EARLIER!
QUICK!
THEY MIGHT NOT HAVE FED THE DOGS YET!
HERE'S YOUR BIRD!
OH--
I MEAN, HE'S NOT **MY-**
--OK
GUYS WAIT UP!
CHILDREN...
THEY'RE TERRIFYING.
NAH,
THEY'RE JUST... REALLY WEIRD.
OH. HELLO

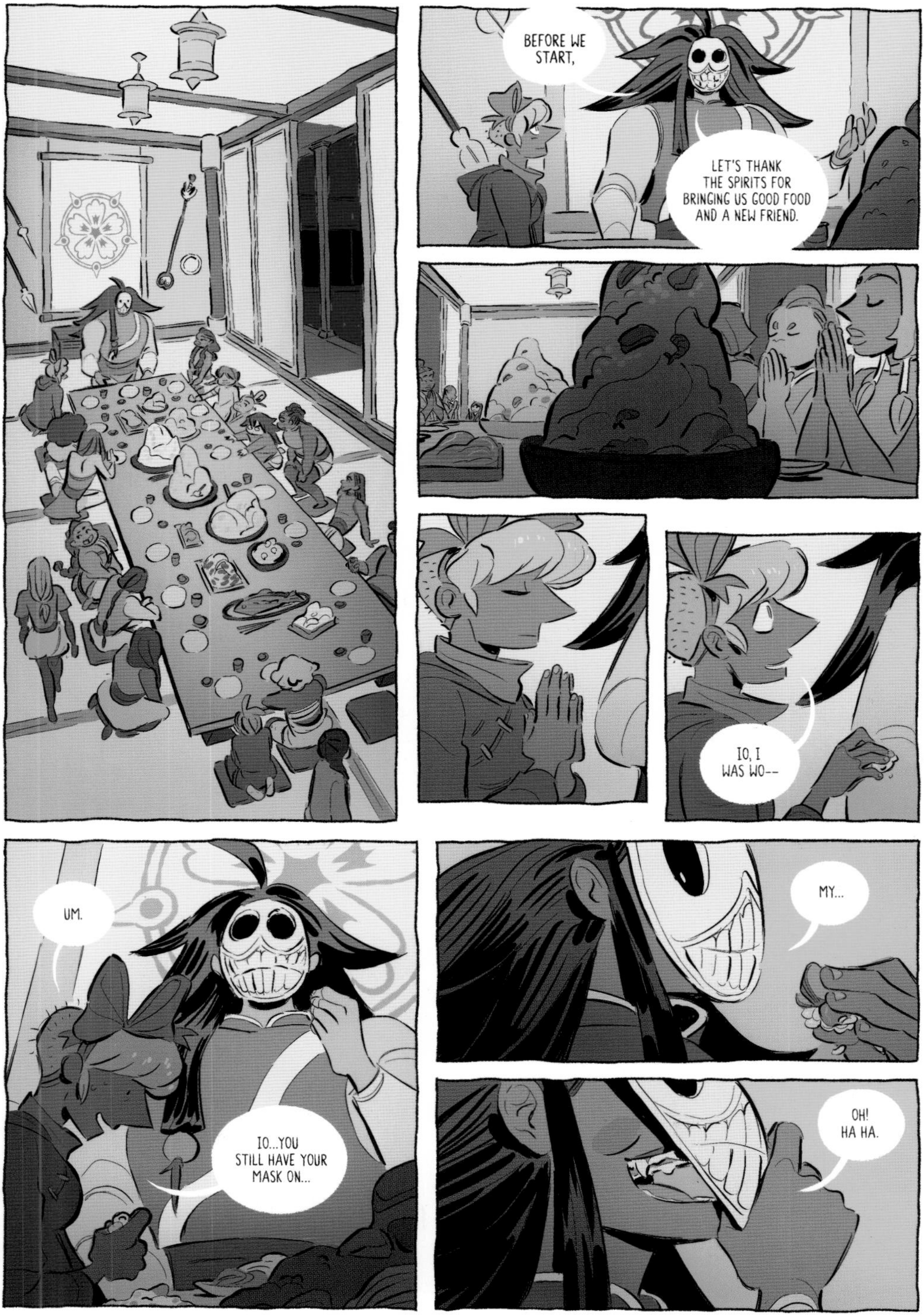
BEFORE WE START,
LET'S THANK THE SPIRITS FOR BRINGING US GOOD FOOD AND A NEW FRIEND.
IO, I WAS WO--
UM.
IO...YOU STILL HAVE YOUR MASK ON...
MY...
OH! HA HA.

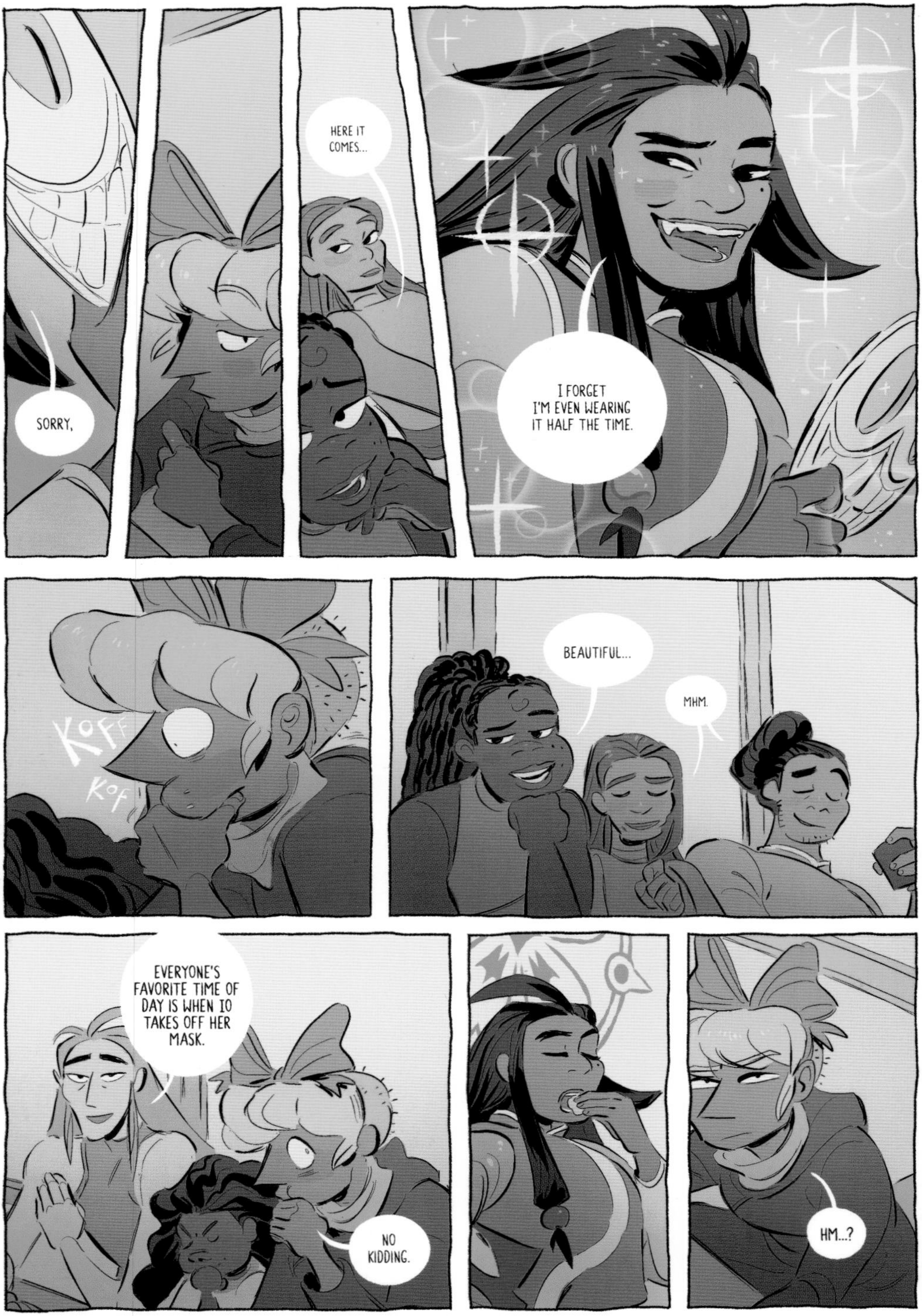
SORRY,
HERE IT COMES...
I FORGET I'M EVEN WEARING IT HALF THE TIME.
KOFF
KOF
BEAUTIFUL...
MHM.
EVERYONE'S FAVORITE TIME OF DAY IS WHEN IO TAKES OFF HER MASK.
NO KIDDING.
HM...?

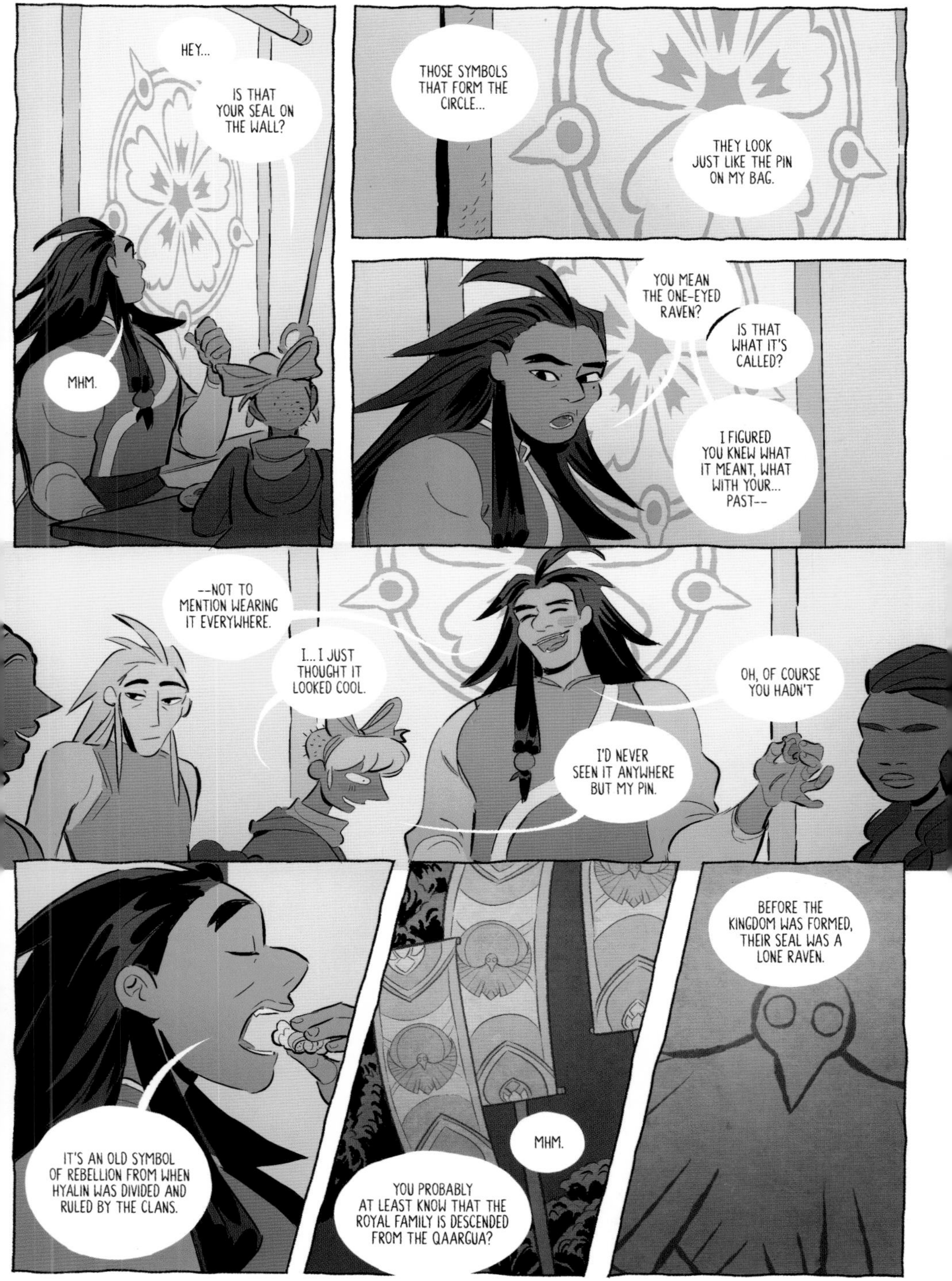
HEY...
IS THAT YOUR SEAL ON THE WALL?
MHM.
THOSE SYMBOLS THAT FORM THE CIRCLE...
THEY LOOK JUST LIKE THE PIN ON MY BAG.
YOU MEAN THE ONE-EYED RAVEN?
IS THAT WHAT IT'S CALLED?
I FIGURED YOU KNEW WHAT IT MEANT, WHAT WITH YOUR... PAST--
--NOT TO MENTION WEARING IT EVERYWHERE.
I... I JUST THOUGHT IT LOOKED COOL.
OH, OF COURSE YOU HADN'T
I'D NEVER SEEN IT ANYWHERE BUT MY PIN.
IT'S AN OLD SYMBOL OF REBELLION FROM WHEN HYALIN WAS DIVIDED AND RULED BY THE CLANS.
YOU PROBABLY AT LEAST KNOW THAT THE ROYAL FAMILY IS DESCENDED FROM THE QAARGUA?
MHM.
BEFORE THE KINGDOM WAS FORMED, THEIR SEAL WAS A LONE RAVEN.

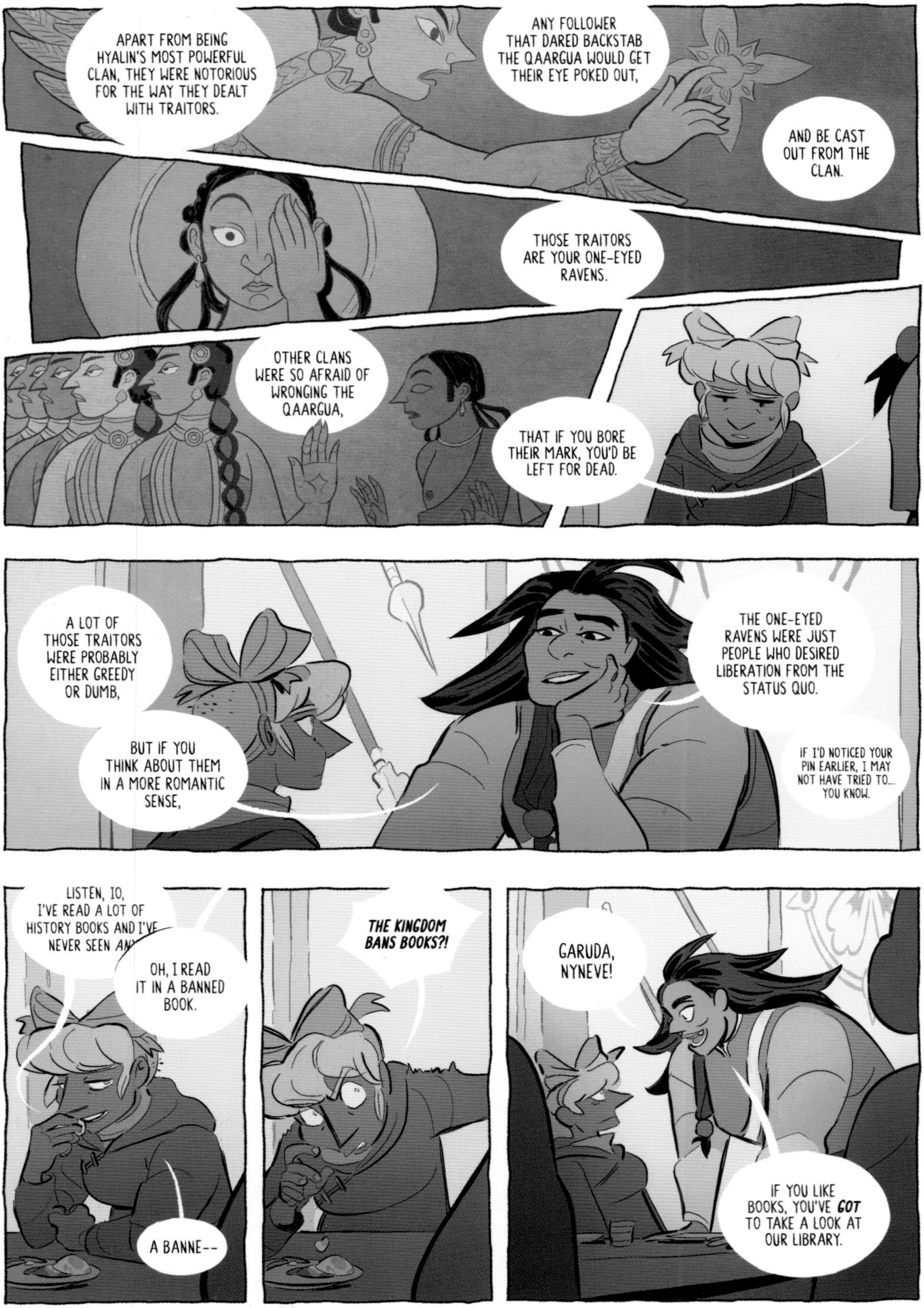
APART FROM BEING HYALIN'S MOST POWERFUL CLAN, THEY WERE NOTORIOUS FOR THE WAY THEY DEALT WITH TRAITORS.
ANY FOLLOWER THAT DARED BACKSTAB THE QAARGUA WOULD GET THEIR EYE POKED OUT,
AND BE CAST OUT FROM THE CLAN.
THOSE TRAITORS ARE YOUR ONE-EYED RAVENS.
OTHER CLANS WERE SO AFRAID OF WRONGING THE QAARGUA,
THAT IF YOU BORE THEIR MARK, YOU'D BE LEFT FOR DEAD.
A LOT OF THOSE TRAITORS WERE PROBABLY EITHER GREEDY OR DUMB,
BUT IF YOU THINK ABOUT THEM IN A MORE ROMANTIC SENSE,
THE ONE-EYED RAVENS WERE JUST PEOPLE WHO DESIRED LIBERATION FROM THE STATUS QUO.
IF I'D NOTICED YOUR PIN EARLIER, I MAY NOT HAVE TRIED TO... YOU KNOW.
LISTEN, IO, I'VE READ A LOT OF HISTORY BOOKS AND I'VE NEVER SEEN
OH, I READ IT IN A BANNED BOOK.
A BANNE--
THE KINGDOM BANS BOOKS?!
GARUDA, NYNEVE!
IF YOU LIKE BOOKS, YOU'VE GOT TO TAKE A LOOK AT OUR LIBRARY.

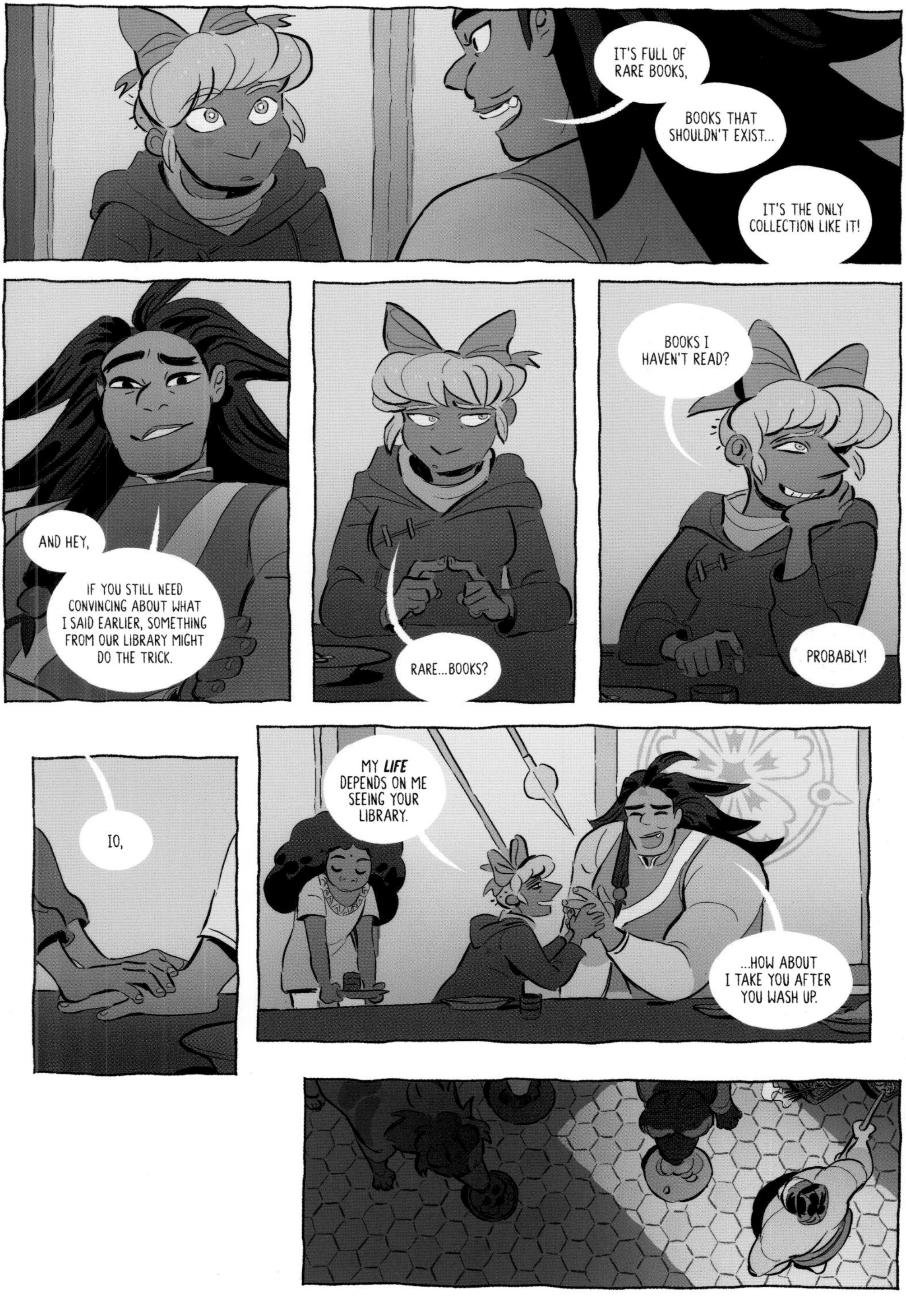
IT'S FULL OF RARE BOOKS,
BOOKS THAT SHOULDN'T EXIST...
IT'S THE ONLY COLLECTION LIKE IT!
AND HEY,
IF YOU STILL NEED CONVINCING ABOUT WHAT I SAID EARLIER, SOMETHING FROM OUR LIBRARY MIGHT DO THE TRICK.
RARE...BOOKS?
BOOKS I HAVEN'T READ?
PROBABLY!
IO,
MY *LIFE* DEPENDS ON ME SEEING YOUR LIBRARY.
...HOW ABOUT I TAKE YOU AFTER YOU WASH UP.

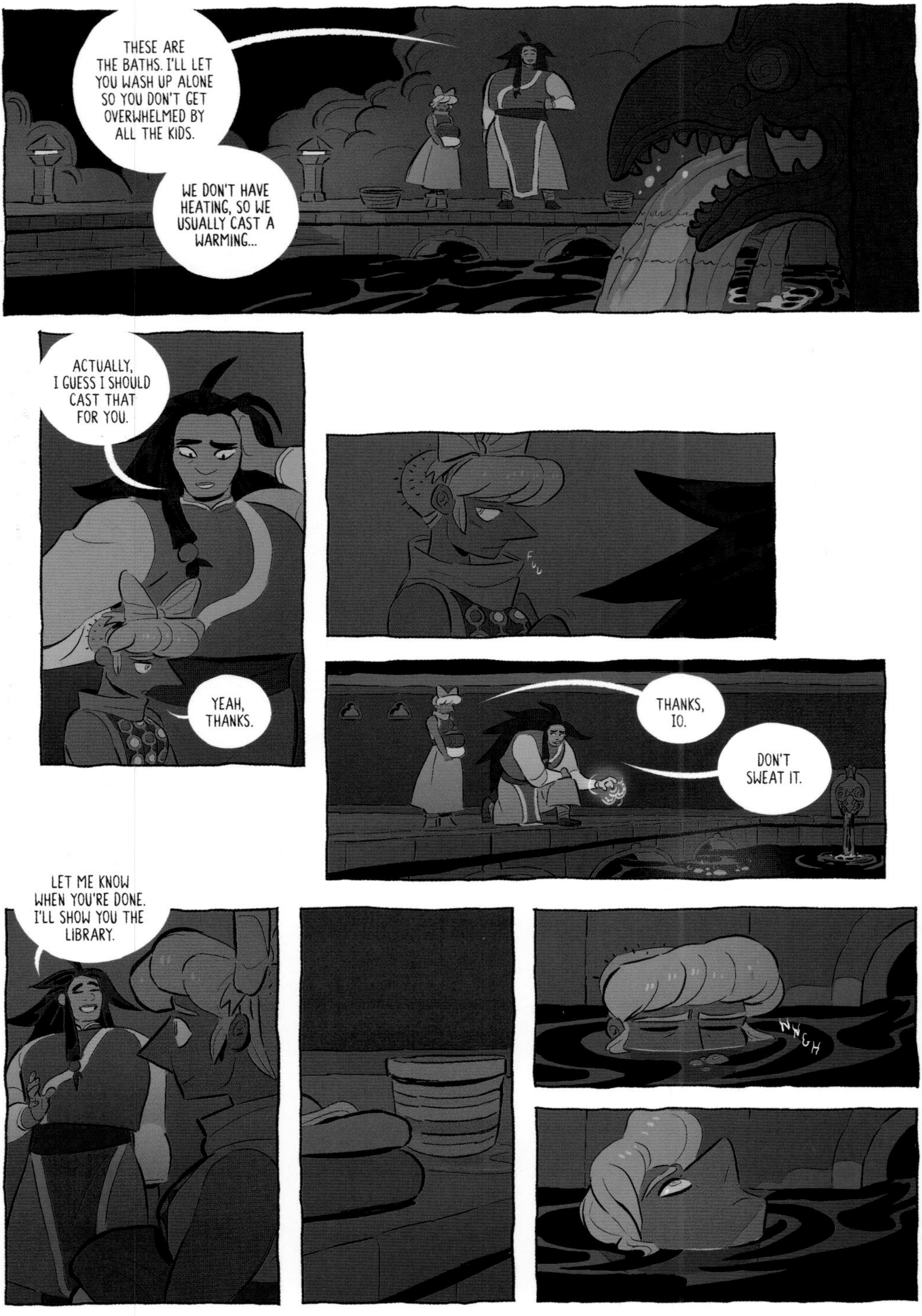

THESE ARE THE BATHS. I'LL LET YOU WASH UP ALONE SO YOU DON'T GET OVERWHELMED BY ALL THE KIDS.
WE DON'T HAVE HEATING, SO WE USUALLY CAST A WARMING...
ACTUALLY, I GUESS I SHOULD CAST THAT FOR YOU.
YEAH, THANKS.
FUU
THANKS, IO.
DON'T SWEAT IT.
LET ME KNOW WHEN YOU'RE DONE. I'LL SHOW YOU THE LIBRARY.
NNGH

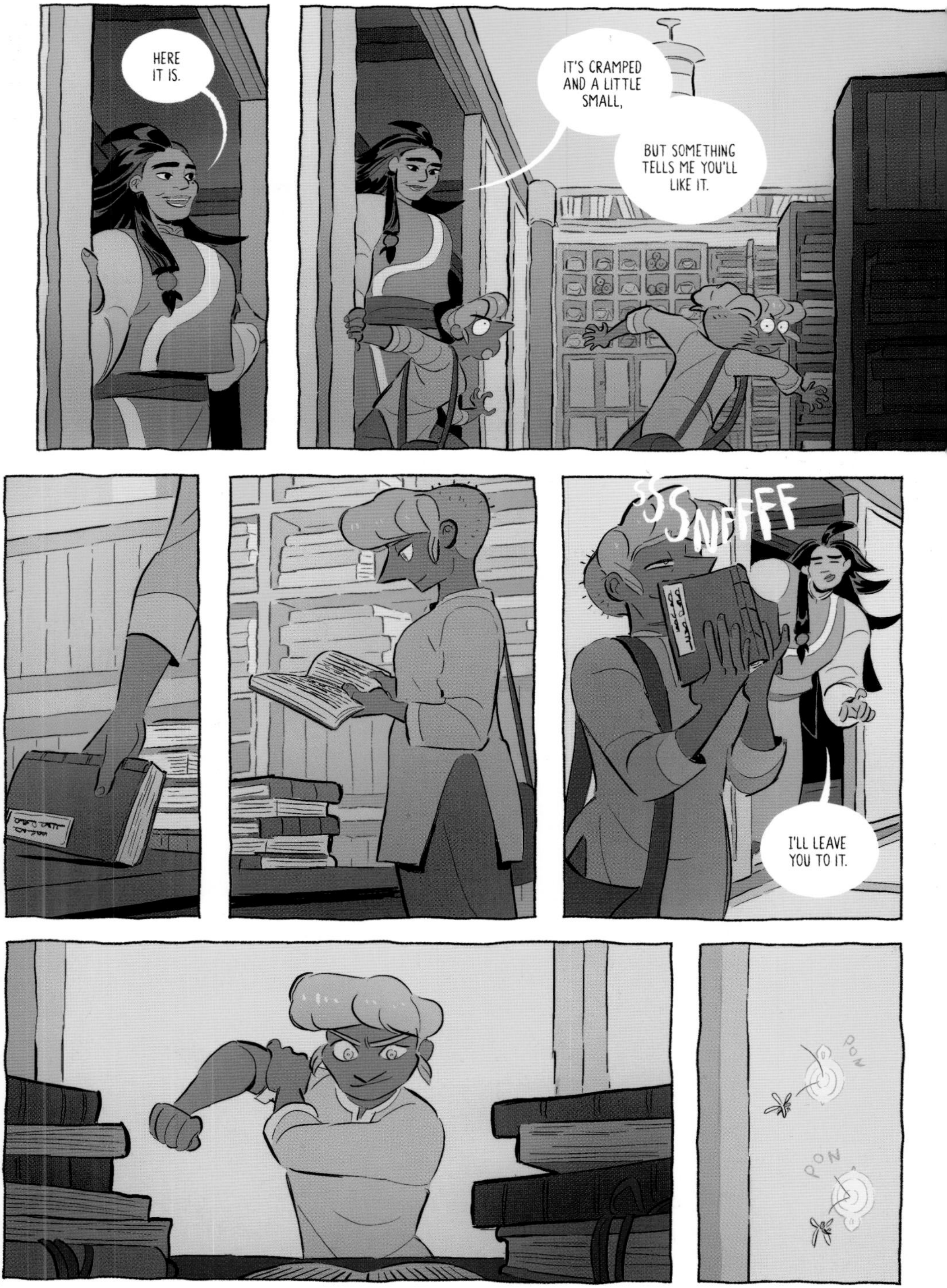
HERE IT IS.
IT'S CRAMPED AND A LITTLE SMALL,
BUT SOMETHING TELLS ME YOU'LL LIKE IT.
SSSNFFFF
I'LL LEAVE YOU TO IT.
PON
PON

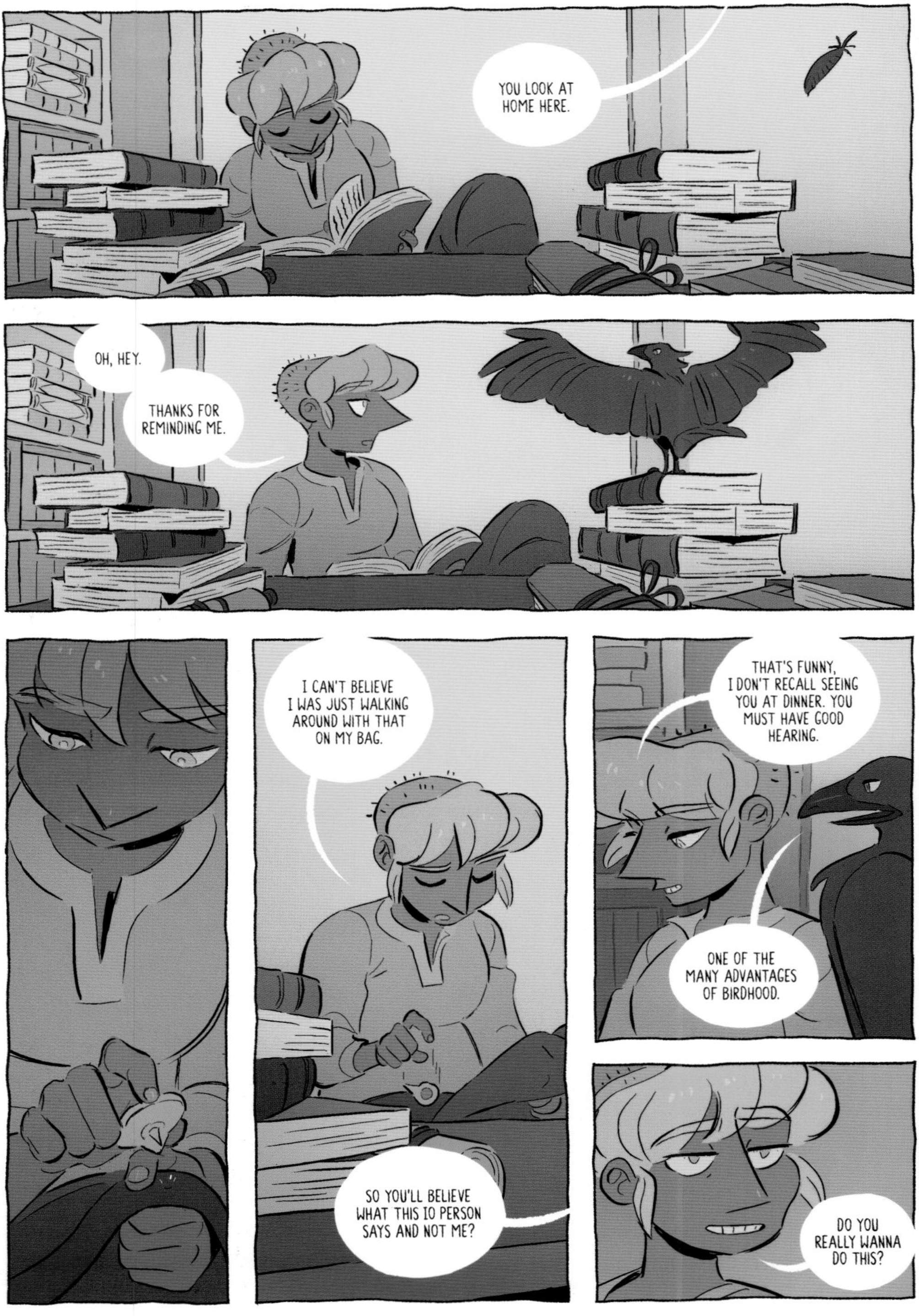
YOU LOOK AT HOME HERE.
OH, HEY.
THANKS FOR REMINDING ME.
I CAN'T BELIEVE I WAS JUST WALKING AROUND WITH THAT ON MY BAG.
SO YOU'LL BELIEVE WHAT THIS IO PERSON SAYS AND NOT ME?
THAT'S FUNNY, I DON'T RECALL SEEING YOU AT DINNER. YOU MUST HAVE GOOD HEARING.
ONE OF THE MANY ADVANTAGES OF BIRDHOOD.
DO YOU REALLY WANNA DO THIS?

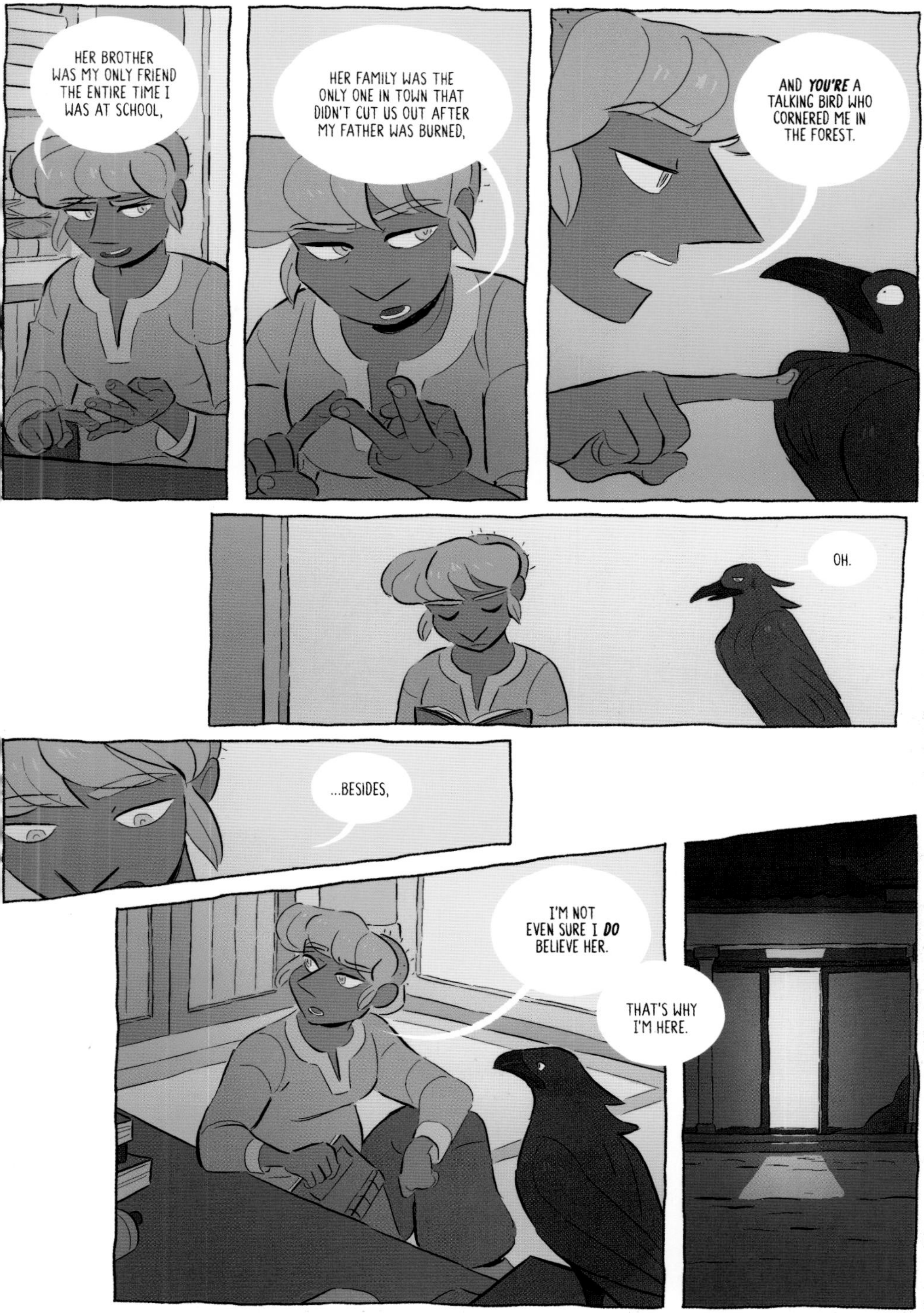
HER BROTHER WAS MY ONLY FRIEND THE ENTIRE TIME I WAS AT SCHOOL,
HER FAMILY WAS THE ONLY ONE IN TOWN THAT DIDN'T CUT US OUT AFTER MY FATHER WAS BURNED,
AND ***YOU'RE*** A TALKING BIRD WHO CORNERED ME IN THE FOREST.
OH.
...BESIDES,
I'M NOT EVEN SURE I ***DO*** BELIEVE HER.
THAT'S WHY I'M HERE.

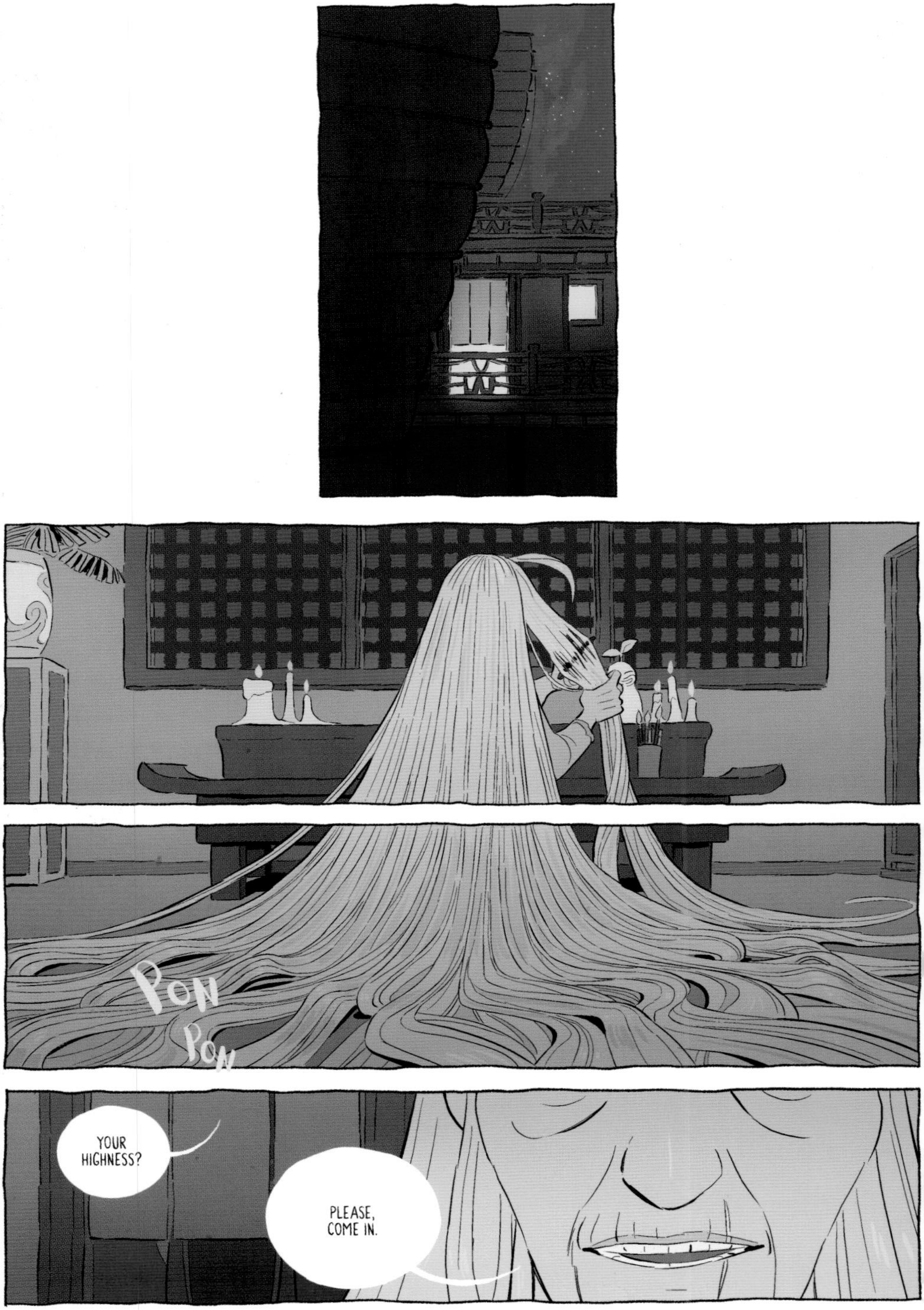
PON
PON
YOUR HIGHNESS?
PLEASE, COME IN.

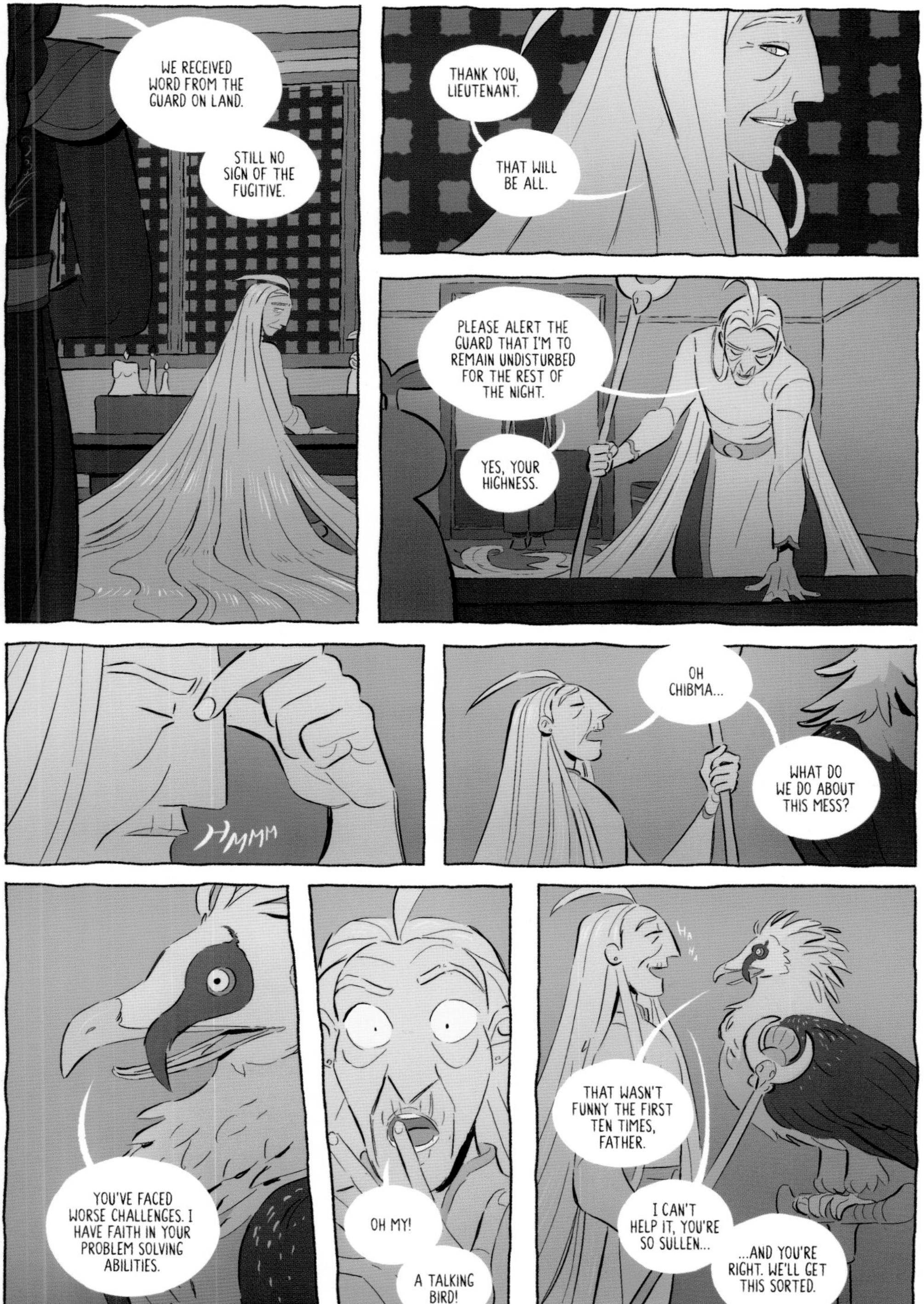
WE RECEIVED WORD FROM THE GUARD ON LAND.
STILL NO SIGN OF THE FUGITIVE.
THANK YOU, LIEUTENANT.
THAT WILL BE ALL.
PLEASE ALERT THE GUARD THAT I'M TO REMAIN UNDISTURBED FOR THE REST OF THE NIGHT.
YES, YOUR HIGHNESS.
HMMM
OH CHIBMA...
WHAT DO WE DO ABOUT THIS MESS?
YOU'VE FACED WORSE CHALLENGES. I HAVE FAITH IN YOUR PROBLEM SOLVING ABILITIES.
OH MY!
A TALKING BIRD!
HA HA
THAT WASN'T FUNNY THE FIRST TEN TIMES, FATHER.
I CAN'T HELP IT, YOU'RE SO SULLEN...
...AND YOU'RE RIGHT. WE'LL GET THIS SORTED.

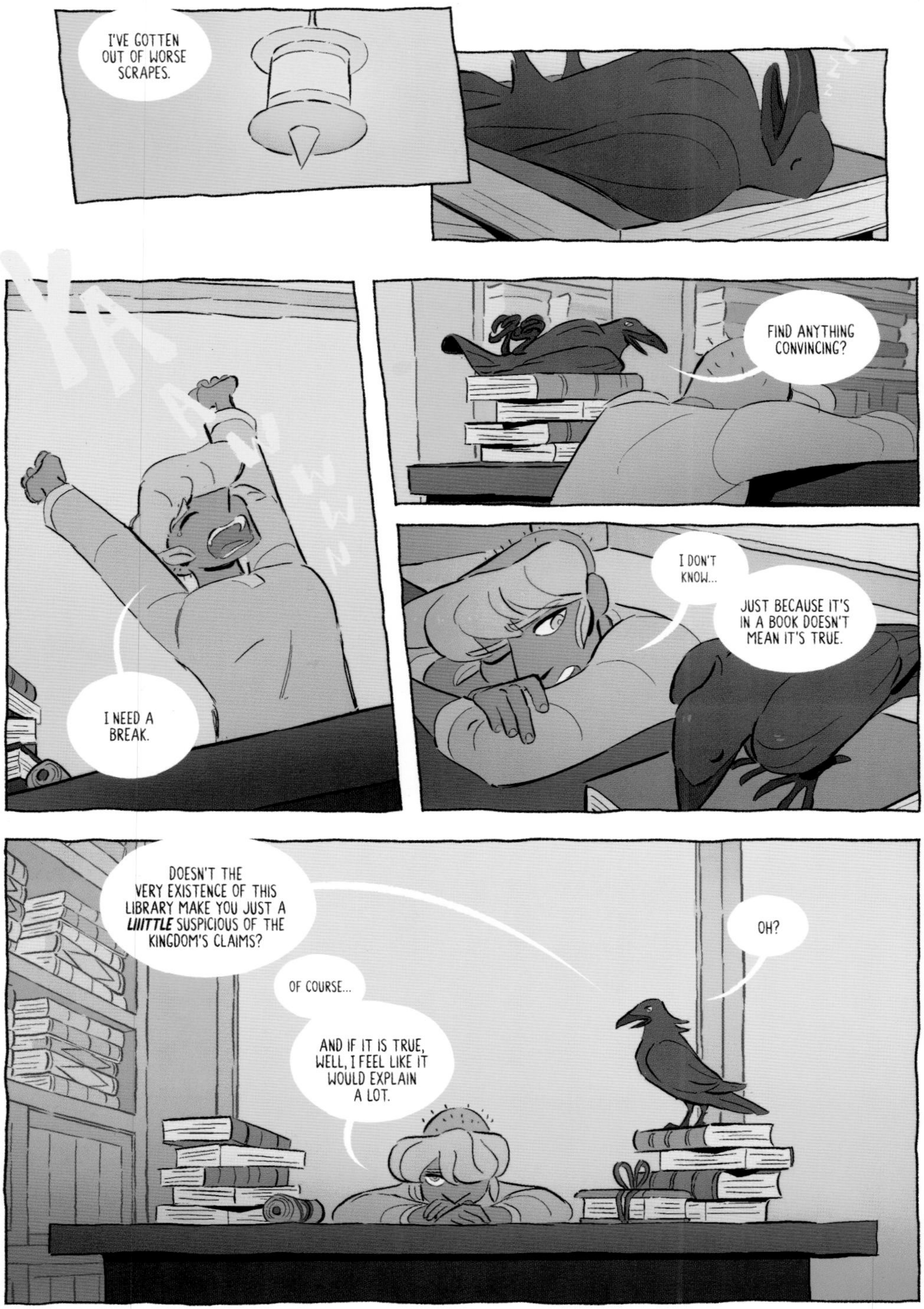
I'VE GOTTEN OUT OF WORSE SCRAPES.
YAAWWWWN
I NEED A BREAK.
FIND ANYTHING CONVINCING?
I DON'T KNOW...
JUST BECAUSE IT'S IN A BOOK DOESN'T MEAN IT'S TRUE.
DOESN'T THE VERY EXISTENCE OF THIS LIBRARY MAKE YOU JUST A LIIITTLE SUSPICIOUS OF THE KINGDOM'S CLAIMS?
OH?
OF COURSE...
AND IF IT IS TRUE, WELL, I FEEL LIKE IT WOULD EXPLAIN A LOT.

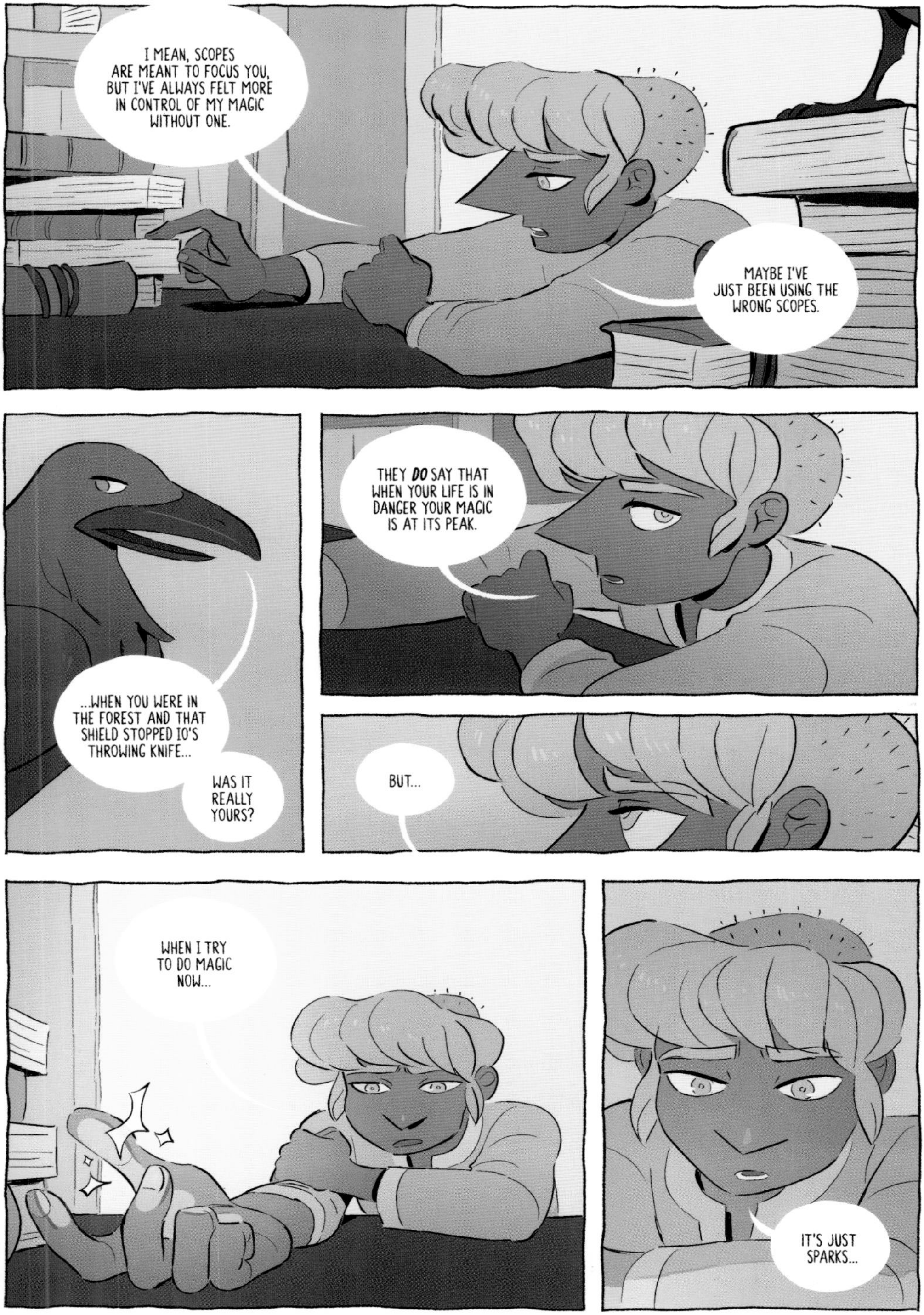
I MEAN, SCOPES ARE MEANT TO FOCUS YOU, BUT I'VE ALWAYS FELT MORE IN CONTROL OF MY MAGIC WITHOUT ONE.
MAYBE I'VE JUST BEEN USING THE WRONG SCOPES.
THEY **DO** SAY THAT WHEN YOUR LIFE IS IN DANGER YOUR MAGIC IS AT ITS PEAK.
...WHEN YOU WERE IN THE FOREST AND THAT SHIELD STOPPED IO'S THROWING KNIFE...
WAS IT REALLY YOURS?
BUT...
WHEN I TRY TO DO MAGIC NOW...
IT'S JUST SPARKS...

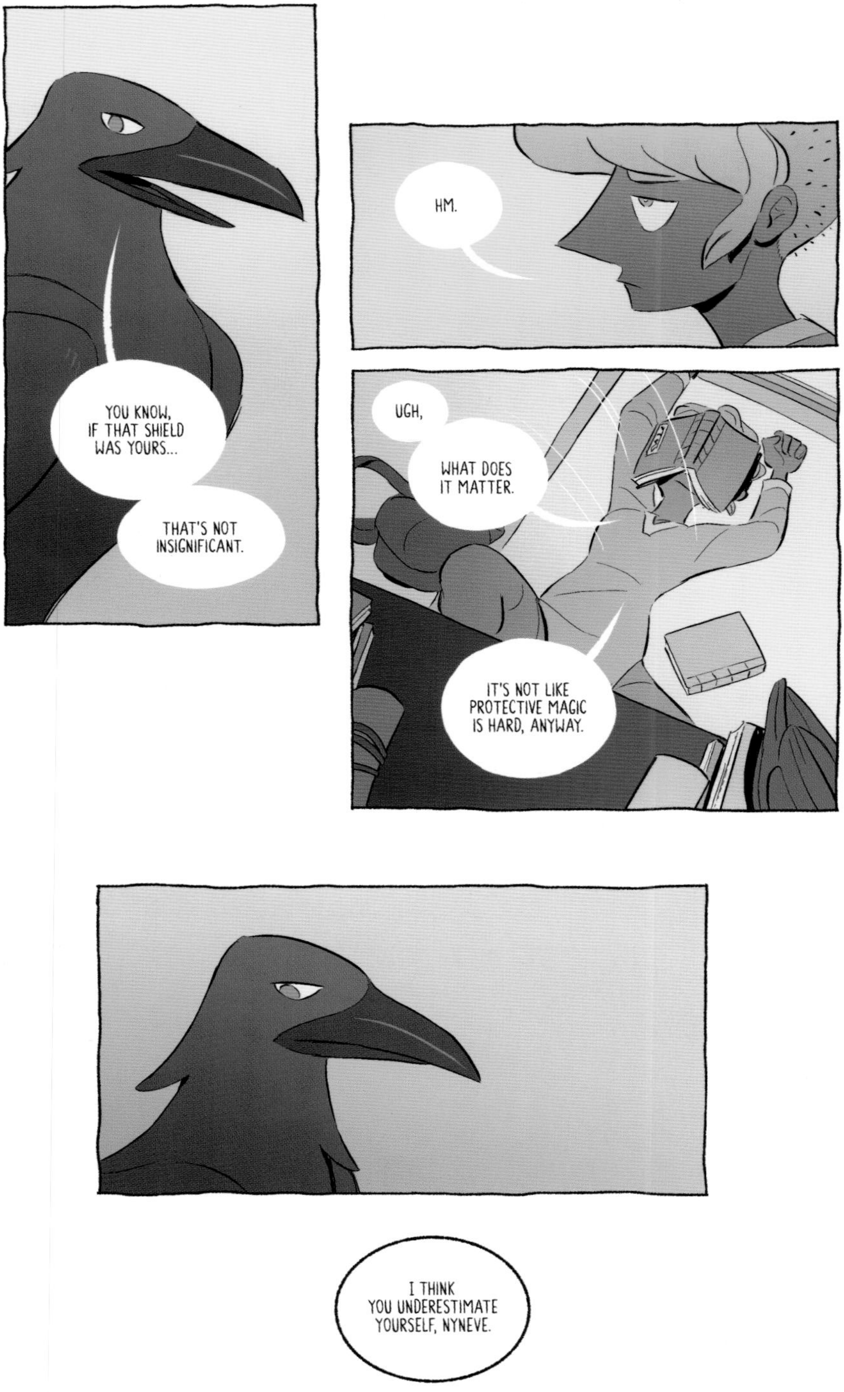
YOU KNOW, IF THAT SHIELD WAS YOURS...
THAT'S NOT INSIGNIFICANT.
HM.
UGH,
WHAT DOES IT MATTER.
IT'S NOT LIKE PROTECTIVE MAGIC IS HARD, ANYWAY.
I THINK YOU UNDERESTIMATE YOURSELF, NYNEVE.

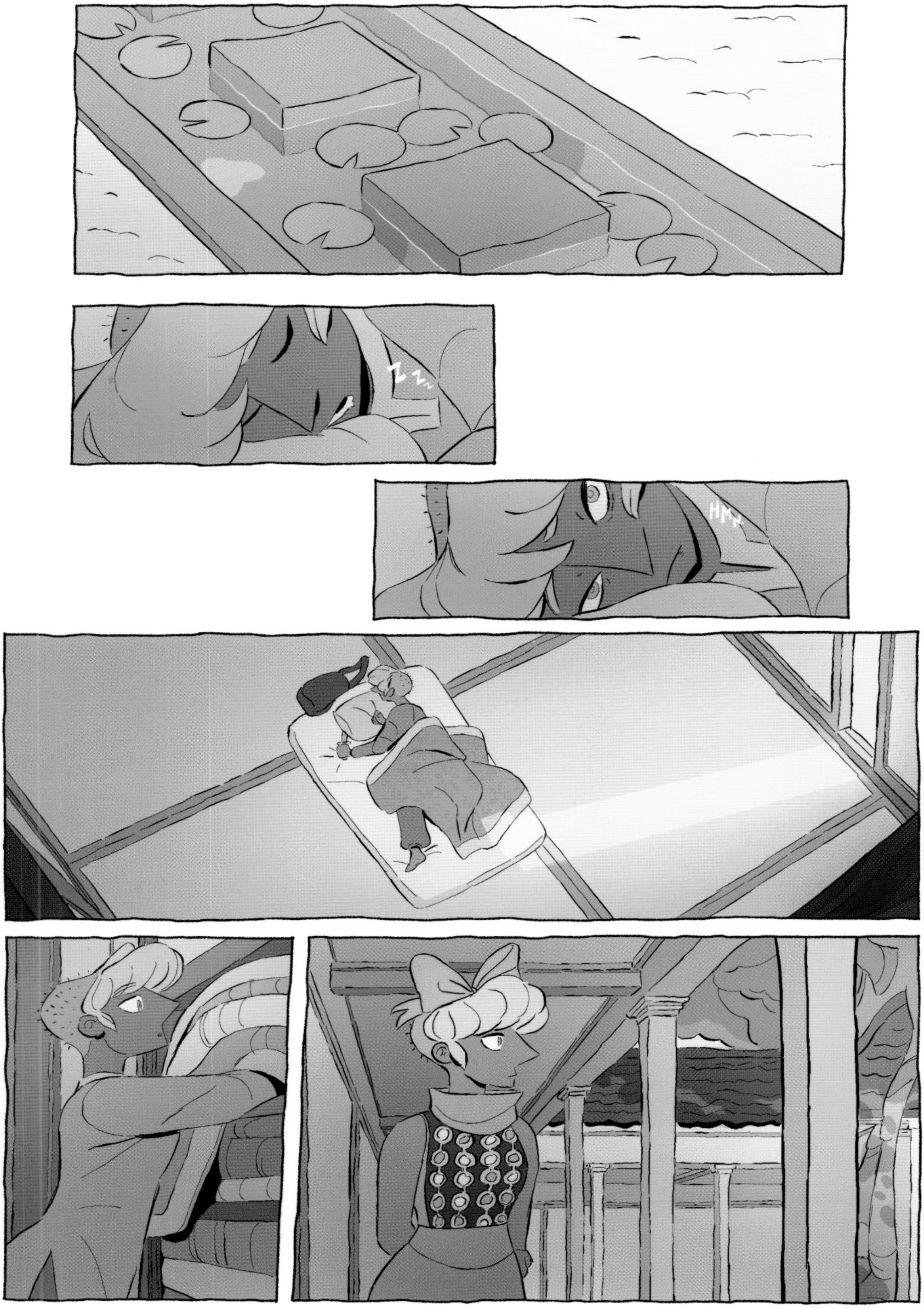
Z Z
HMN.

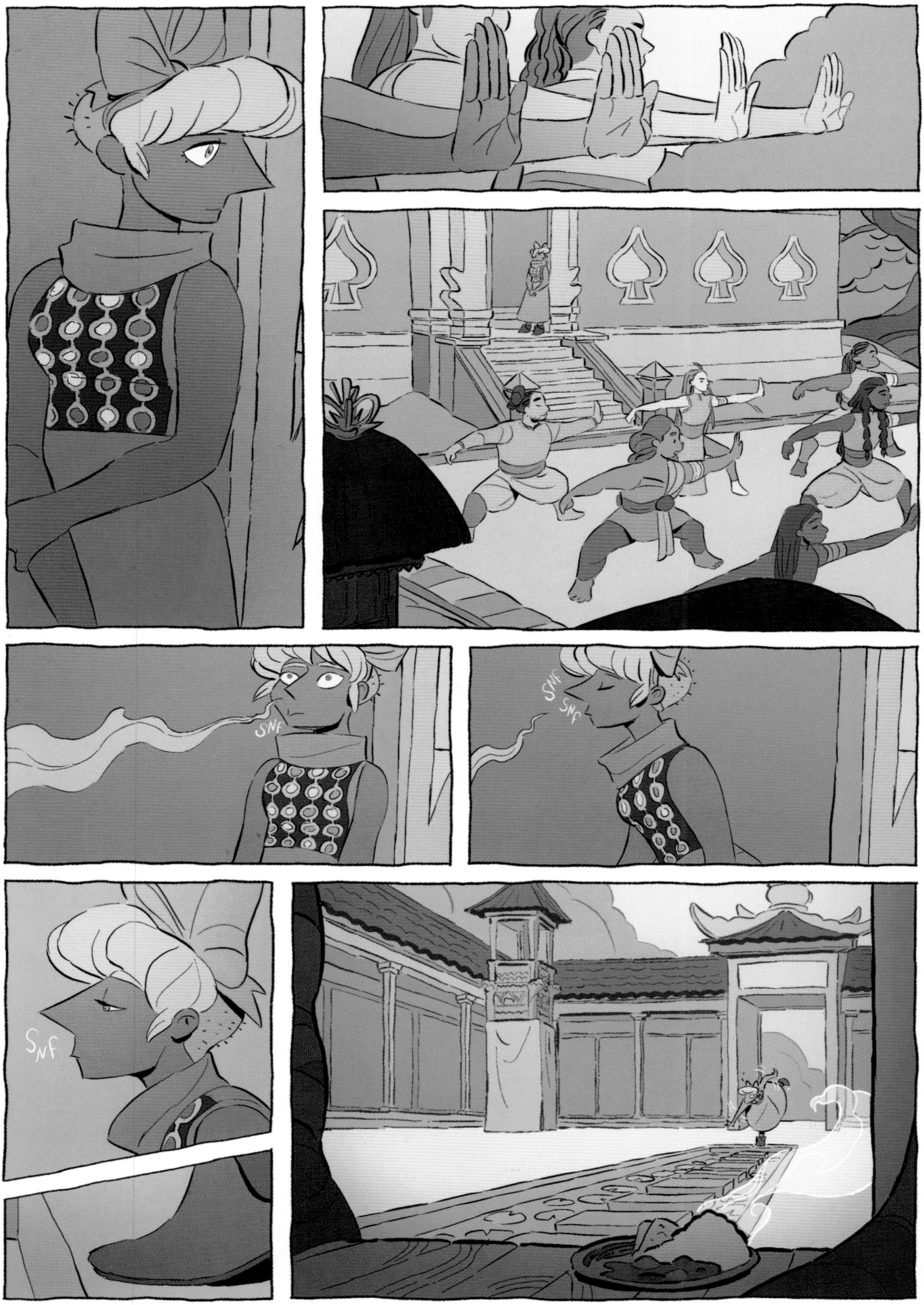
SNF
SNF
SNF
SNF

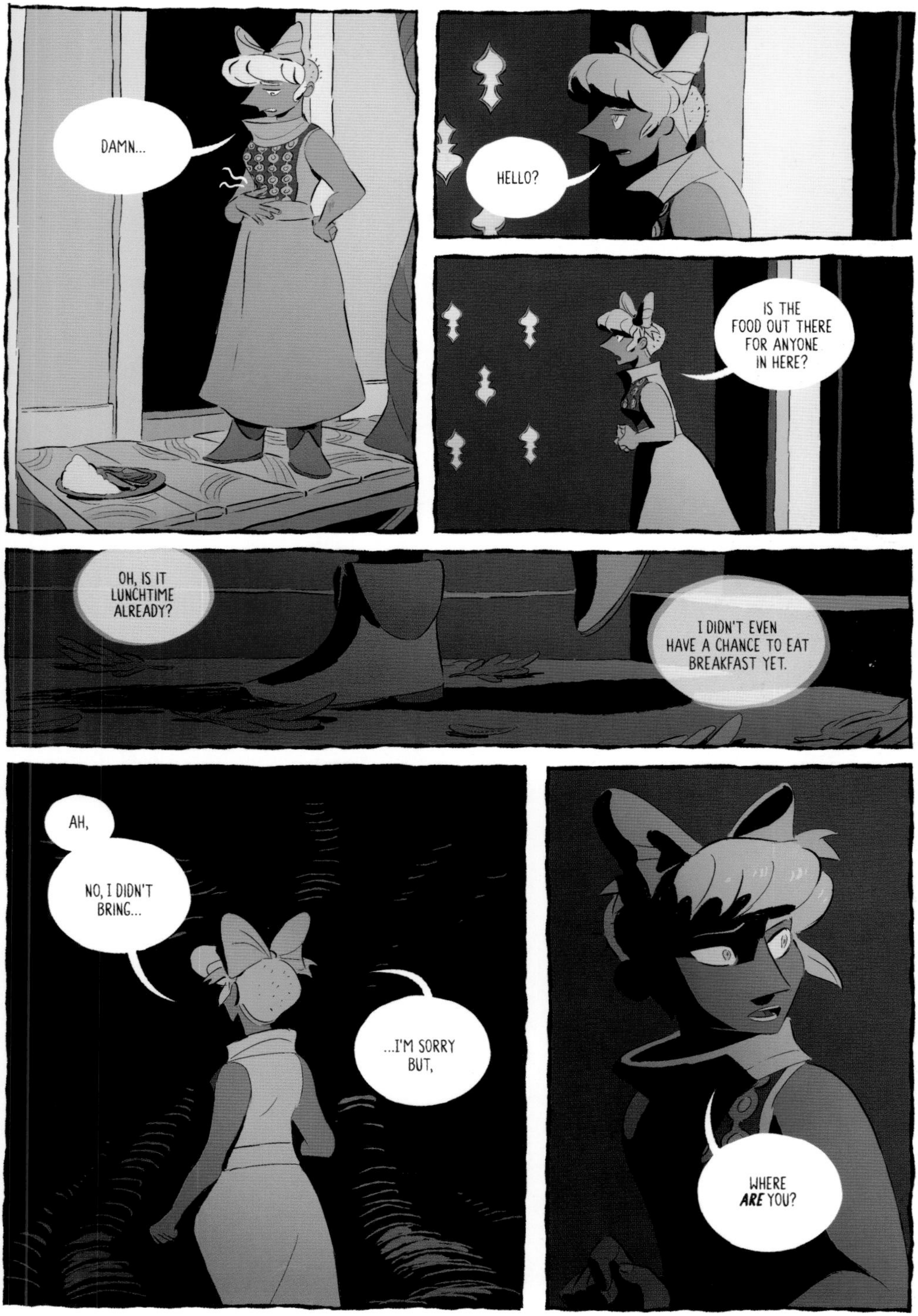
DAMN...
HELLO?
IS THE FOOD OUT THERE FOR ANYONE IN HERE?
OH, IS IT LUNCHTIME ALREADY?
I DIDN'T EVEN HAVE A CHANCE TO EAT BREAKFAST YET.
AH,
NO, I DIDN'T BRING...
...I'M SORRY BUT,
WHERE **ARE** YOU?

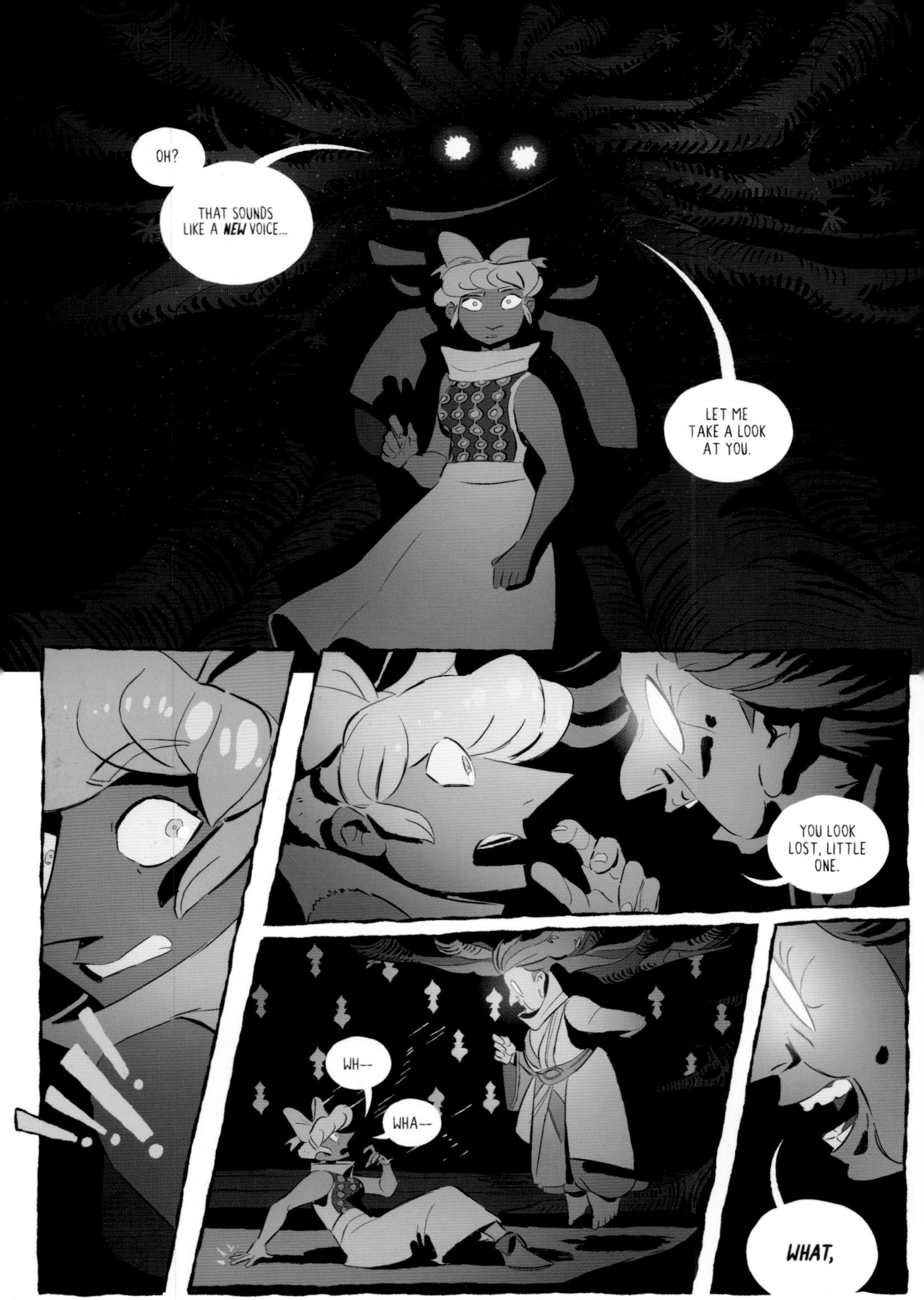
OH?
THAT SOUNDS LIKE A NEW VOICE...
LET ME TAKE A LOOK AT YOU.
YOU LOOK LOST, LITTLE ONE.
WH--
WHA--
WHAT,

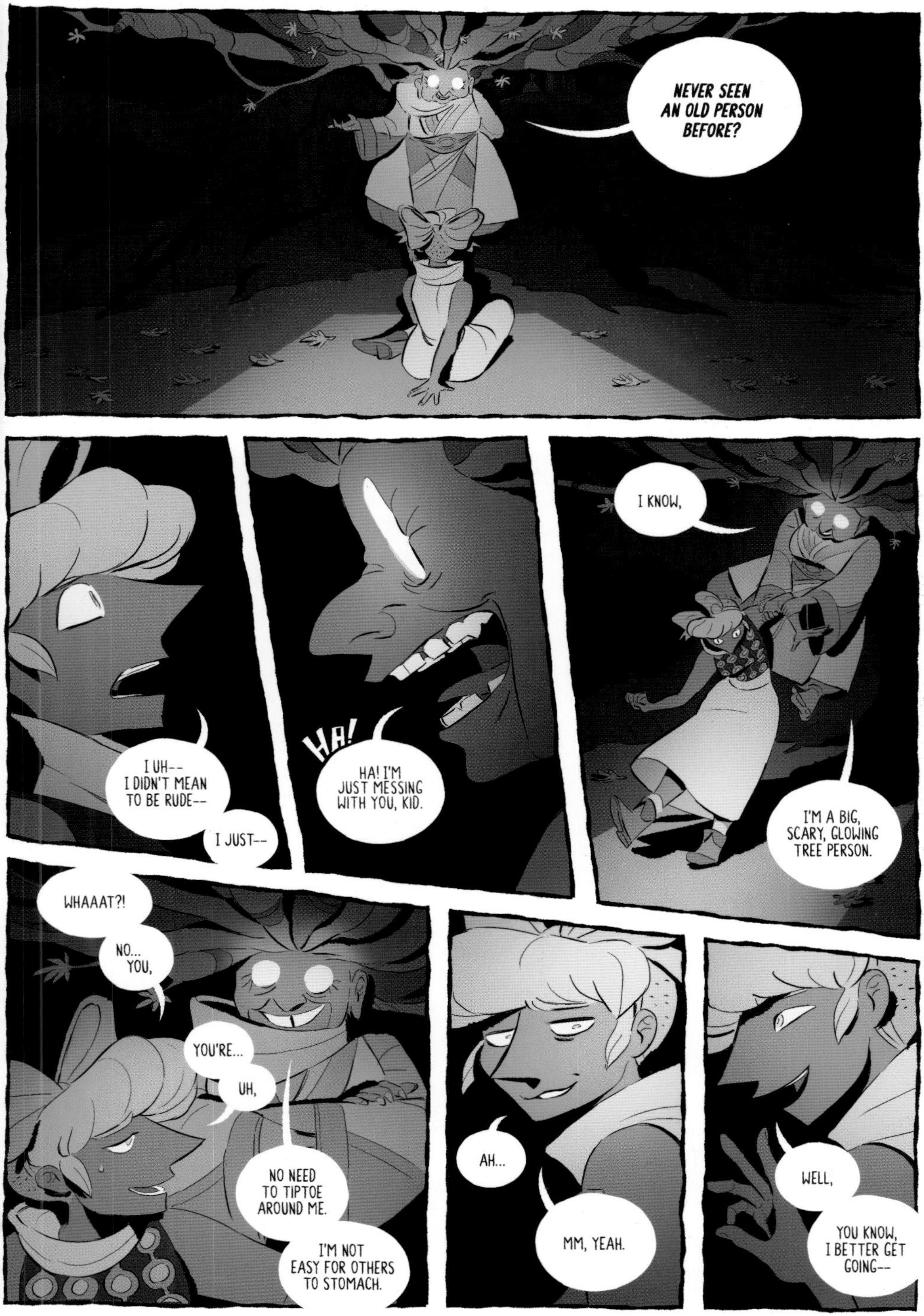
NEVER SEEN AN OLD PERSON BEFORE?
I UH-- I DIDN'T MEAN TO BE RUDE--
I JUST--
HA!
HA! I'M JUST MESSING WITH YOU, KID.
I KNOW,
I'M A BIG, SCARY, GLOWING TREE PERSON.
WHAAAT?!
NO... YOU,
YOU'RE...
UH,
NO NEED TO TIPTOE AROUND ME.
I'M NOT EASY FOR OTHERS TO STOMACH.
AH...
MM, YEAH.
WELL,
YOU KNOW, I BETTER GET GOING--

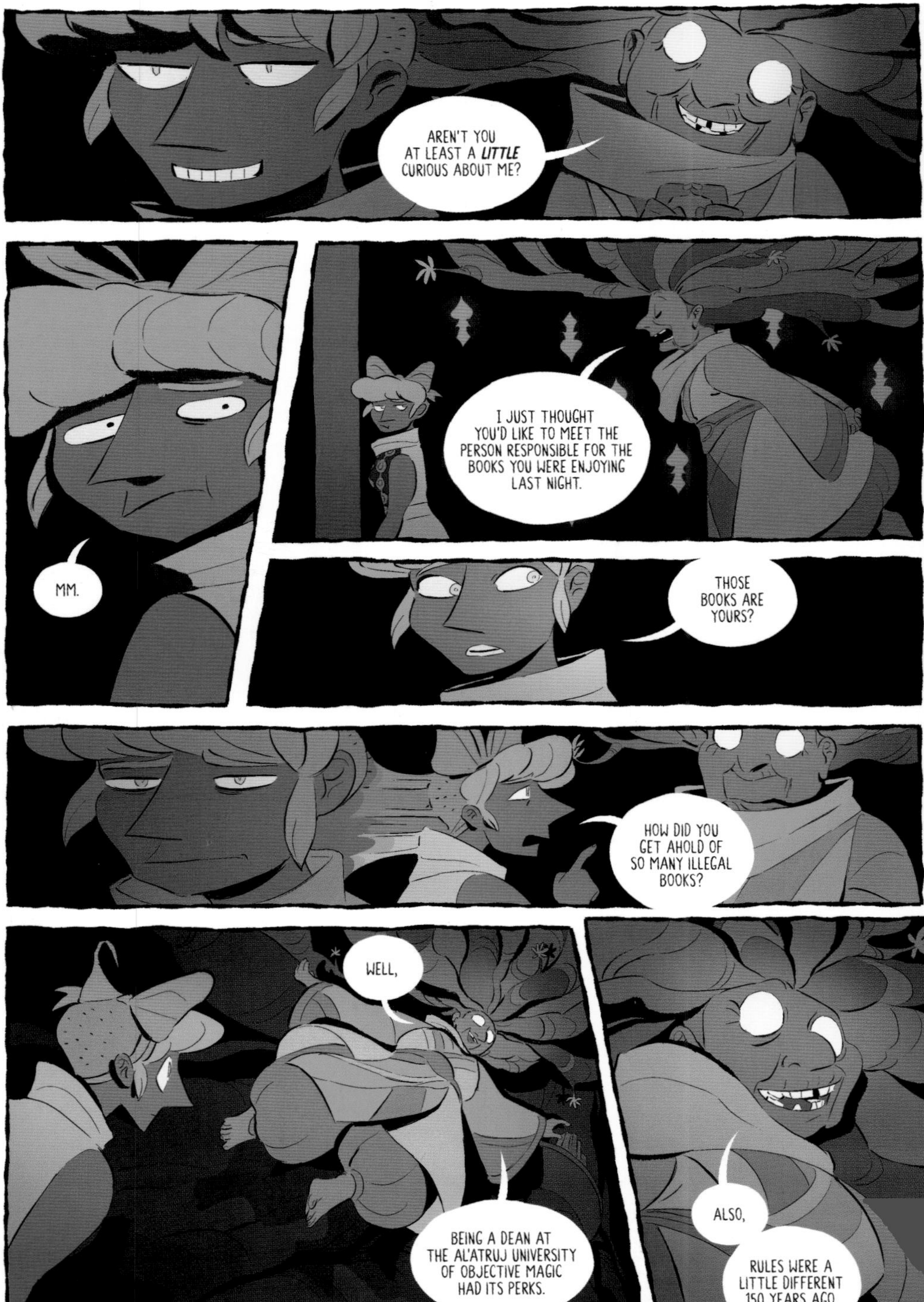
AREN'T YOU AT LEAST A *LITTLE* CURIOUS ABOUT ME?
I JUST THOUGHT YOU'D LIKE TO MEET THE PERSON RESPONSIBLE FOR THE BOOKS YOU WERE ENJOYING LAST NIGHT.
MM.
THOSE BOOKS ARE YOURS?
HOW DID YOU GET AHOLD OF SO MANY ILLEGAL BOOKS?
WELL,
BEING A DEAN AT THE AL'ATRUJ UNIVERSITY OF OBJECTIVE MAGIC HAD ITS PERKS.
ALSO,
RULES WERE A LITTLE DIFFERENT 150 YEARS AGO.

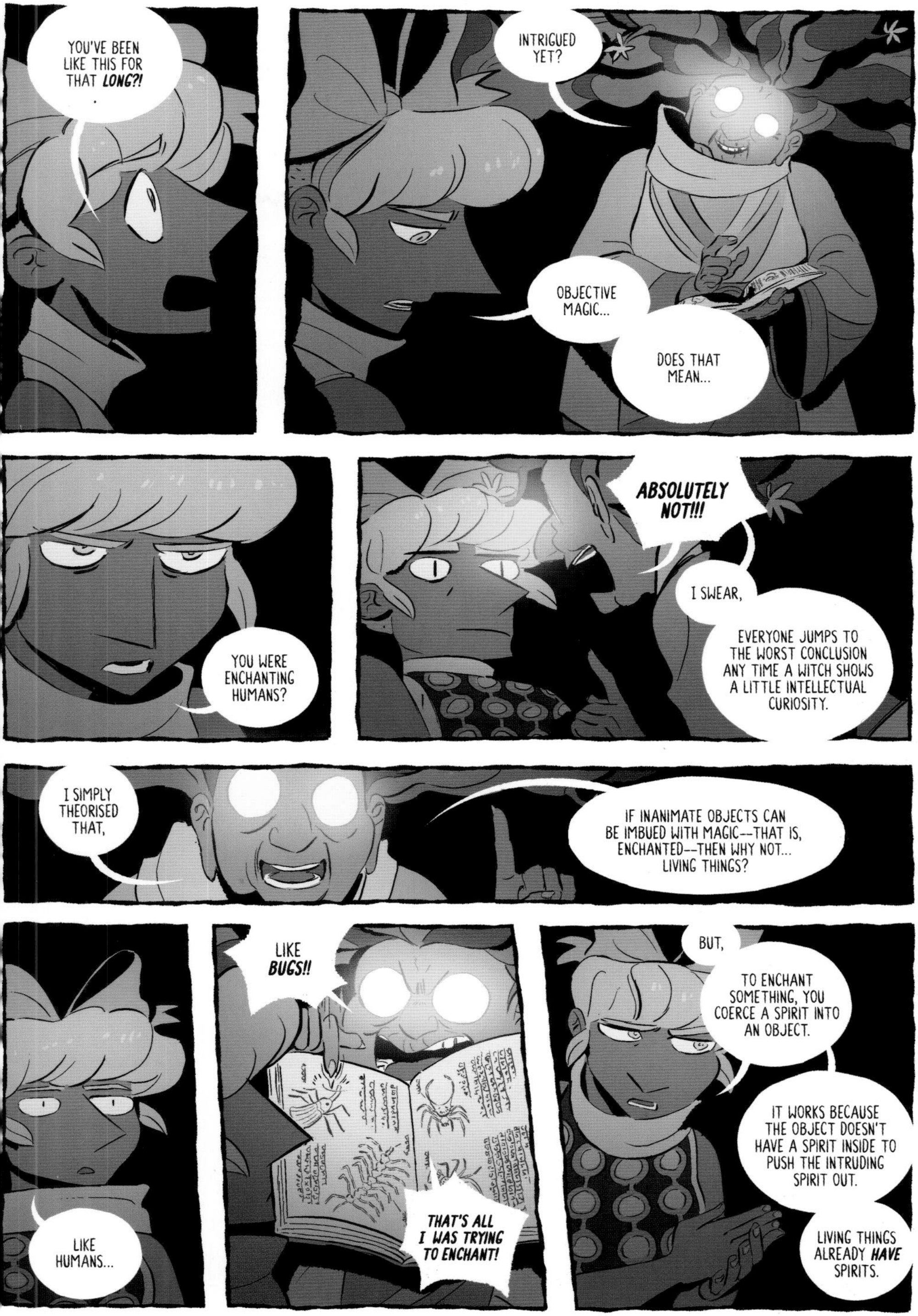
YOU'VE BEEN LIKE THIS FOR THAT LONG?!
INTRIGUED YET?
OBJECTIVE MAGIC...
DOES THAT MEAN...
YOU WERE ENCHANTING HUMANS?
ABSOLUTELY NOT!!!
I SWEAR,
EVERYONE JUMPS TO THE WORST CONCLUSION ANY TIME A WITCH SHOWS A LITTLE INTELLECTUAL CURIOSITY.
I SIMPLY THEORISED THAT,
IF INANIMATE OBJECTS CAN BE IMBUED WITH MAGIC--THAT IS, ENCHANTED--THEN WHY NOT... LIVING THINGS?
LIKE HUMANS...
LIKE BUGS!!
THAT'S ALL I WAS TRYING TO ENCHANT!
BUT,
TO ENCHANT SOMETHING, YOU COERCE A SPIRIT INTO AN OBJECT.
IT WORKS BECAUSE THE OBJECT DOESN'T HAVE A SPIRIT INSIDE TO PUSH THE INTRUDING SPIRIT OUT.
LIVING THINGS ALREADY HAVE SPIRITS.

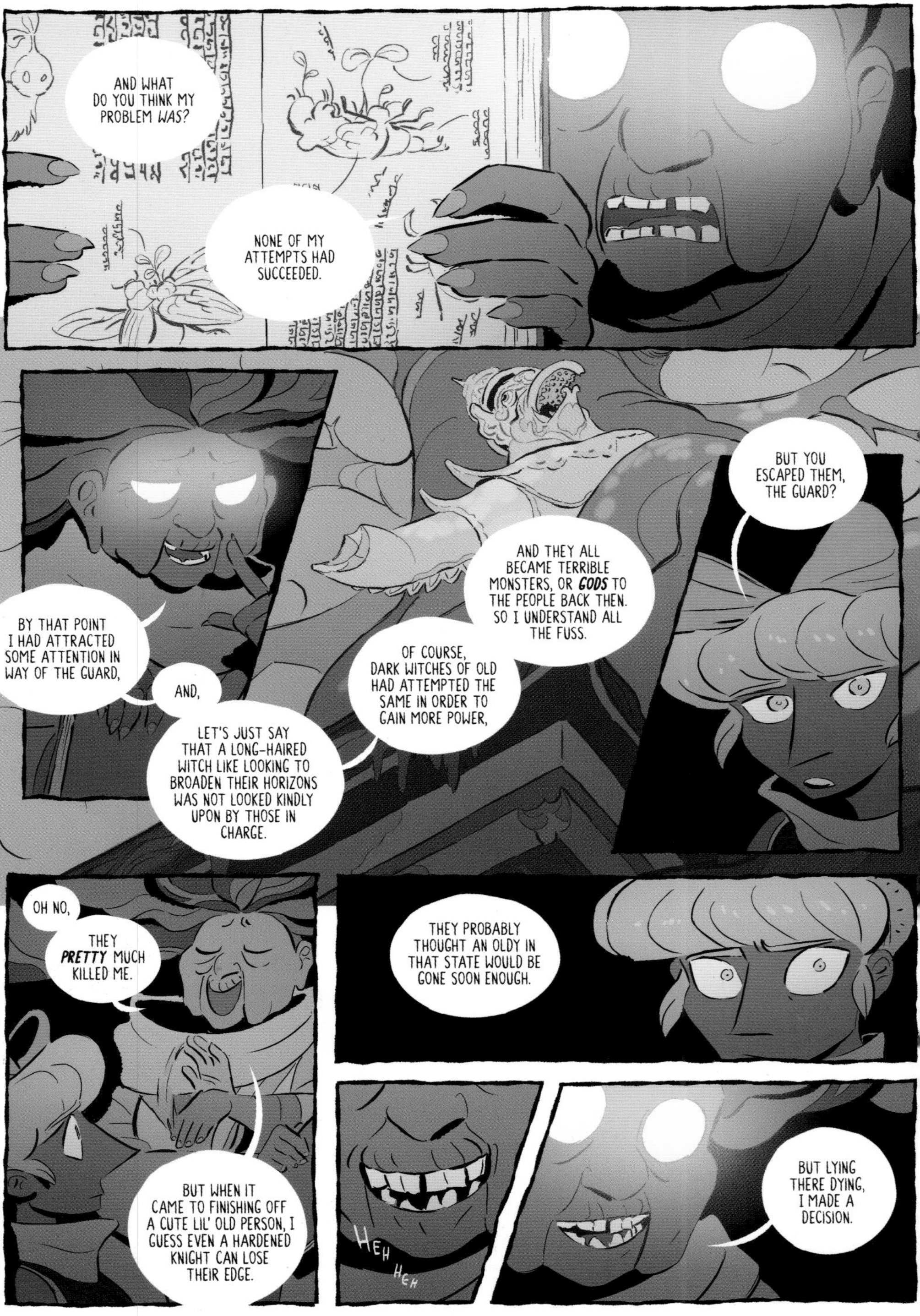
AND WHAT DO YOU THINK MY PROBLEM *WAS*?
NONE OF MY ATTEMPTS HAD SUCCEEDED.
BY THAT POINT I HAD ATTRACTED SOME ATTENTION IN WAY OF THE GUARD,
AND,
LET'S JUST SAY THAT A LONG-HAIRED WITCH LIKE LOOKING TO BROADEN THEIR HORIZONS WAS NOT LOOKED KINDLY UPON BY THOSE IN CHARGE.
OF COURSE, DARK WITCHES OF OLD HAD ATTEMPTED THE SAME IN ORDER TO GAIN MORE POWER,
AND THEY ALL BECAME TERRIBLE MONSTERS, OR ***GODS*** TO THE PEOPLE BACK THEN. SO I UNDERSTAND ALL THE FUSS.
BUT YOU ESCAPED THEM, THE GUARD?
OH NO,
THEY ***PRETTY*** MUCH KILLED ME.
BUT WHEN IT CAME TO FINISHING OFF A CUTE LIL' OLD PERSON, I GUESS EVEN A HARDENED KNIGHT CAN LOSE THEIR EDGE.
THEY PROBABLY THOUGHT AN OLDY IN THAT STATE WOULD BE GONE SOON ENOUGH.
HEH HEH
BUT LYING THERE DYING, I MADE A DECISION.

THE KEY TO ENCHANTING A LIVING THING IS CONSENT.

IN THE END,

THOSE OLD DARK WITCHES WERE RIGHT.

THE OFFER MADE TO THE SPIRITS--

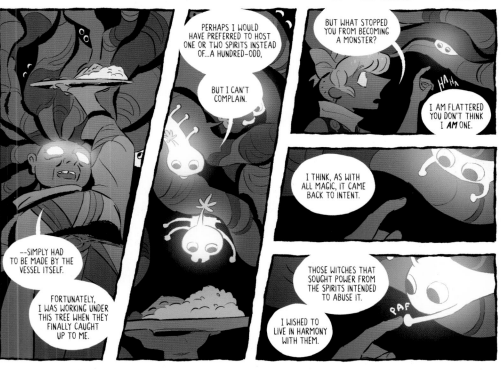

PERHAPS I WOULD HAVE PREFERRED TO HOST ONE OR TWO SPIRITS INSTEAD OF...A HUNDRED-ODD,

BUT I CAN'T COMPLAIN.

BUT WHAT STOPPED YOU FROM BECOMING A MONSTER?

HA HA

I AM FLATTERED YOU DON'T THINK I *AM* ONE.

I THINK, AS WITH ALL MAGIC, IT CAME BACK TO INTENT.

--SIMPLY HAD TO BE MADE BY THE VESSEL ITSELF.

FORTUNATELY, I WAS WORKING UNDER THIS TREE WHEN THEY FINALLY CAUGHT UP TO ME.

THOSE WITCHES THAT SOUGHT POWER FROM THE SPIRITS INTENDED TO ABUSE IT.

I WISHED TO LIVE IN HARMONY WITH THEM.

PAF

AND THEN WHAT HAPPENED?

DID YOU START THE RESISTANCE?

OH, NO.

I ROTTED HERE ALONE FOR A HUNDRED YEARS BEFORE A COUPLE YOUNGINS SEARCHING FOR A SECRET HIDEOUT STUMBLED UPON ME.

THEY BROUGHT ME BACK FROM THE BRINK OF MADNESS, BLESS THEM.

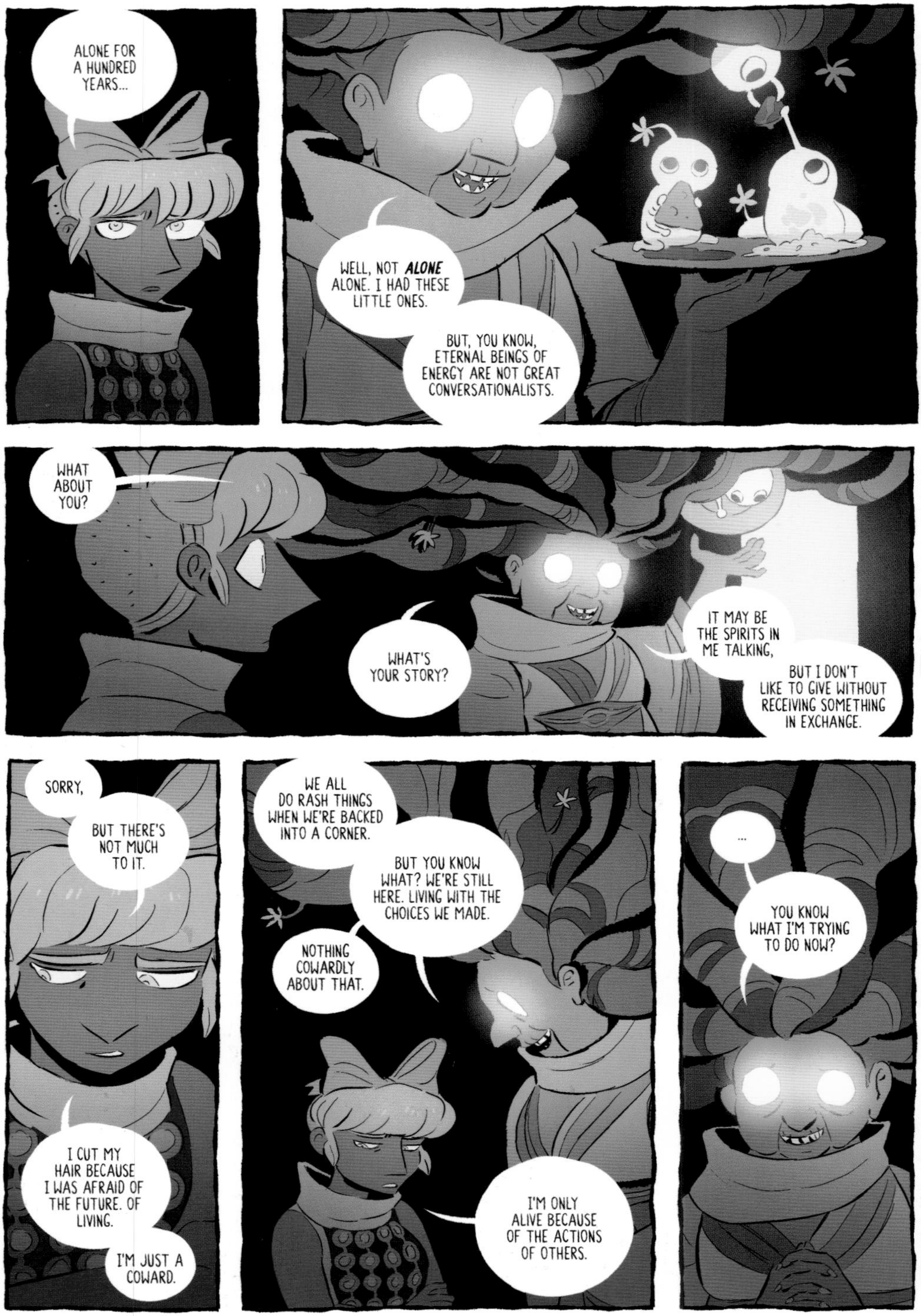
ALONE FOR A HUNDRED YEARS...
WELL, NOT **ALONE** ALONE. I HAD THESE LITTLE ONES.
BUT, YOU KNOW, ETERNAL BEINGS OF ENERGY ARE NOT GREAT CONVERSATIONALISTS.
WHAT ABOUT YOU?
WHAT'S YOUR STORY?
IT MAY BE THE SPIRITS IN ME TALKING,
BUT I DON'T LIKE TO GIVE WITHOUT RECEIVING SOMETHING IN EXCHANGE.
SORRY,
BUT THERE'S NOT MUCH TO IT.
I CUT MY HAIR BECAUSE I WAS AFRAID OF THE FUTURE. OF LIVING.
I'M JUST A COWARD.
WE ALL DO RASH THINGS WHEN WE'RE BACKED INTO A CORNER.
BUT YOU KNOW WHAT? WE'RE STILL HERE. LIVING WITH THE CHOICES WE MADE.
NOTHING COWARDLY ABOUT THAT.
I'M ONLY ALIVE BECAUSE OF THE ACTIONS OF OTHERS.
...
YOU KNOW WHAT I'M TRYING TO DO NOW?

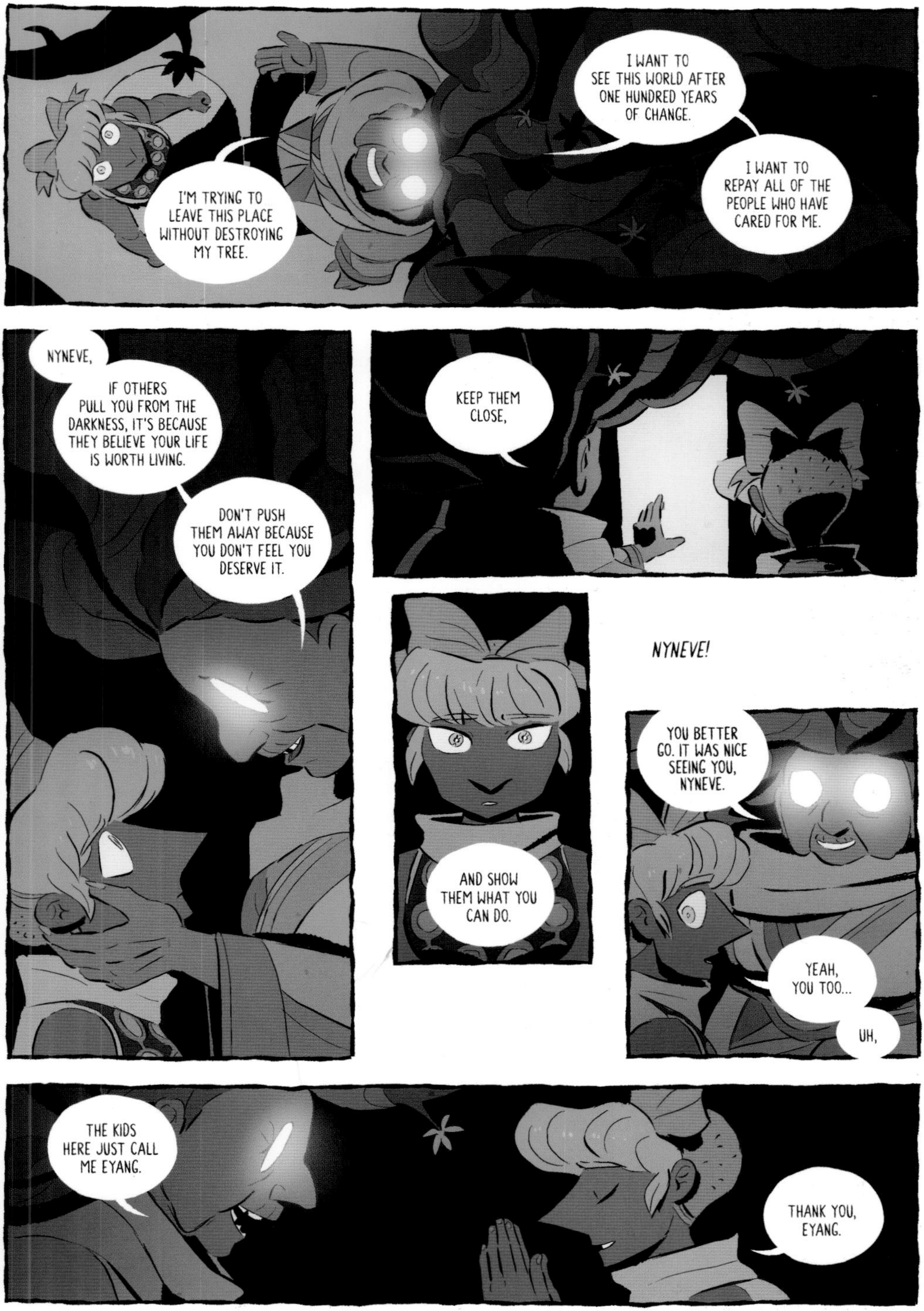
I'M TRYING TO LEAVE THIS PLACE WITHOUT DESTROYING MY TREE.
I WANT TO SEE THIS WORLD AFTER ONE HUNDRED YEARS OF CHANGE.
I WANT TO REPAY ALL OF THE PEOPLE WHO HAVE CARED FOR ME.
NYNEVE,
IF OTHERS PULL YOU FROM THE DARKNESS, IT'S BECAUSE THEY BELIEVE YOUR LIFE IS WORTH LIVING.
DON'T PUSH THEM AWAY BECAUSE YOU DON'T FEEL YOU DESERVE IT.
KEEP THEM CLOSE,
AND SHOW THEM WHAT YOU CAN DO.
NYNEVE!
YOU BETTER GO. IT WAS NICE SEEING YOU, NYNEVE.
YEAH, YOU TOO...
UH,
THE KIDS HERE JUST CALL ME EYANG.
THANK YOU, EYANG.

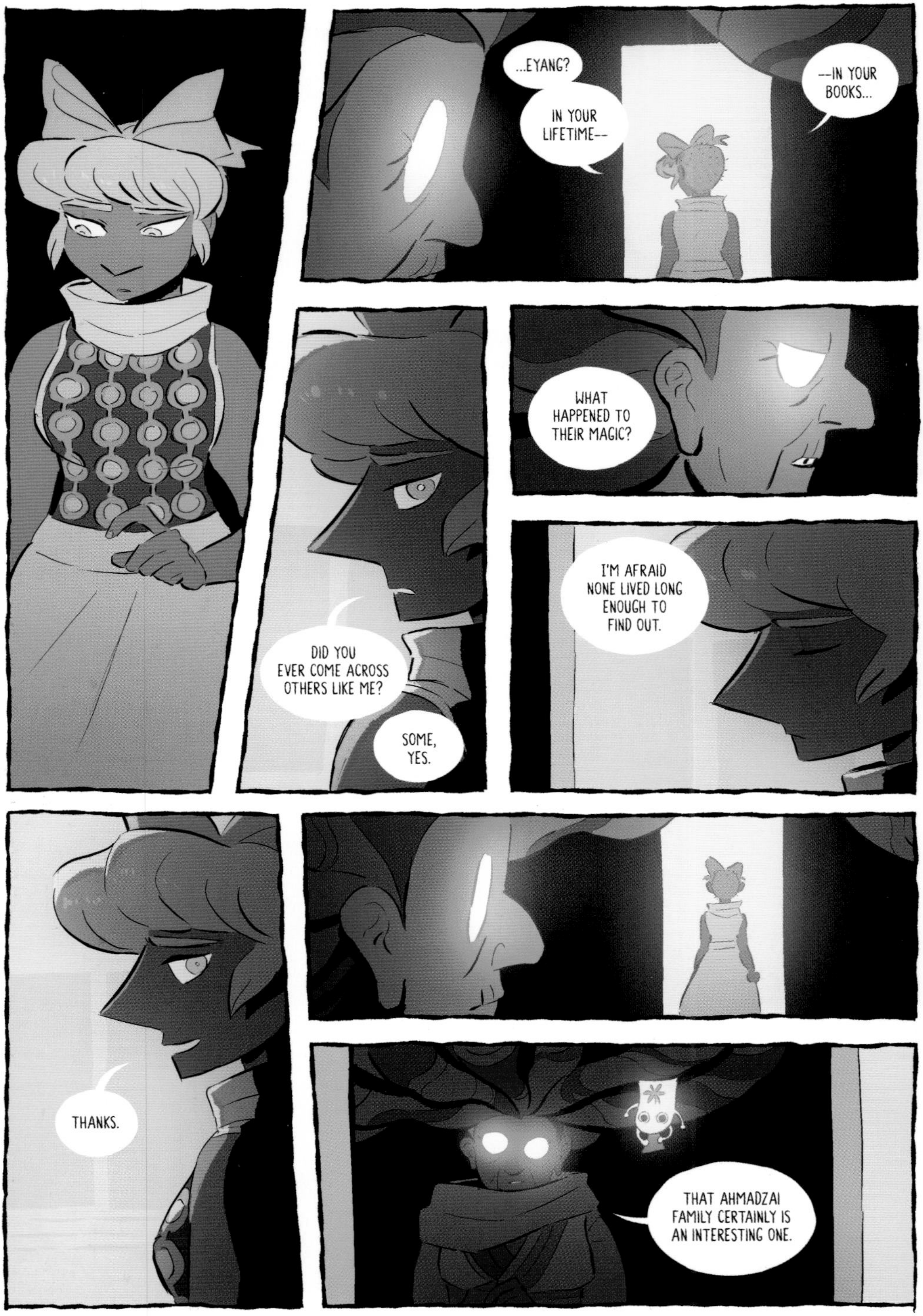
...EYANG?
IN YOUR LIFETIME--
--IN YOUR BOOKS...
WHAT HAPPENED TO THEIR MAGIC?
DID YOU EVER COME ACROSS OTHERS LIKE ME?
SOME, YES.
I'M AFRAID NONE LIVED LONG ENOUGH TO FIND OUT.
THANKS.
THAT AHMADZAI FAMILY CERTAINLY IS AN INTERESTING ONE.

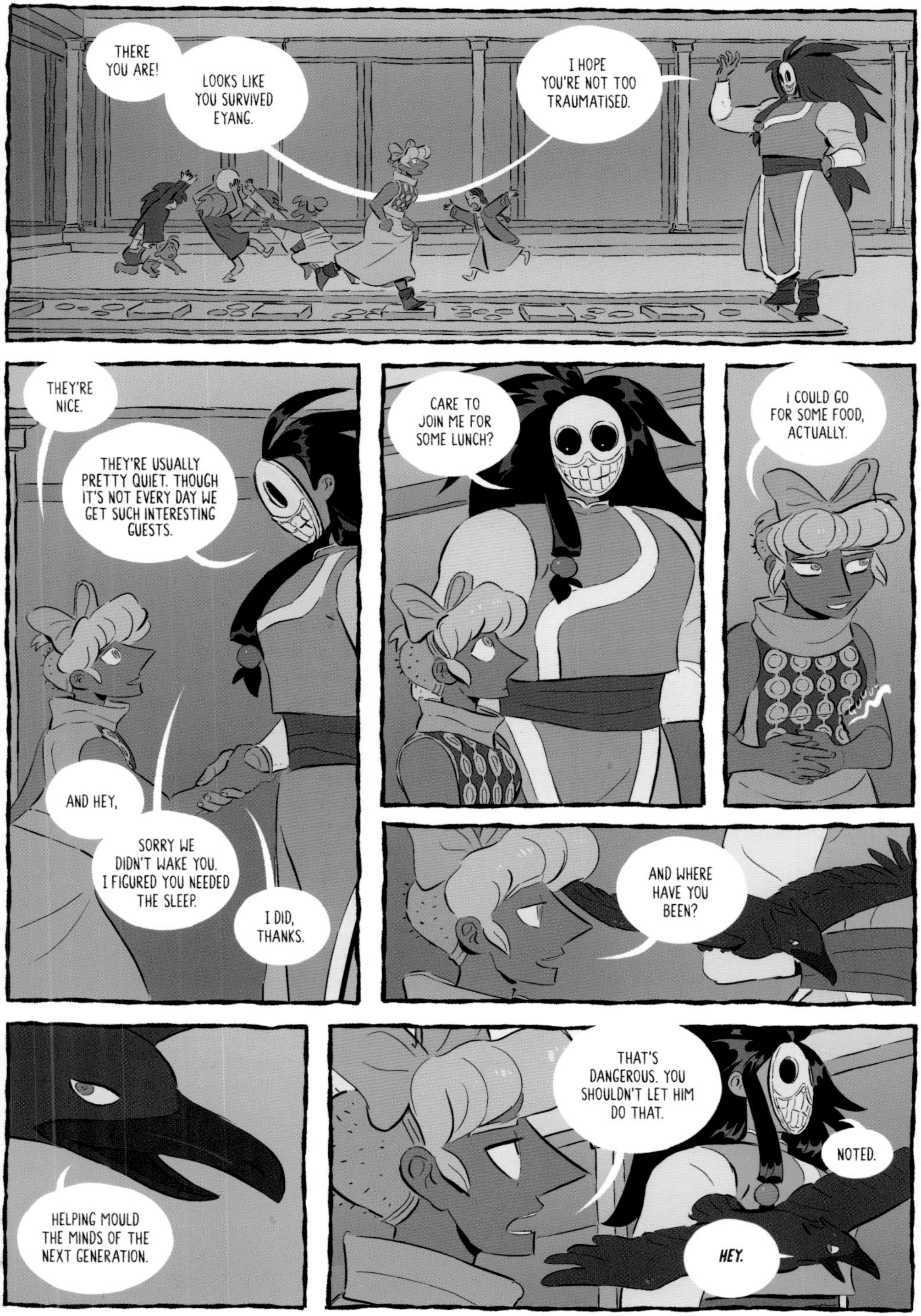
THERE YOU ARE!
LOOKS LIKE YOU SURVIVED EYANG.
I HOPE YOU'RE NOT TOO TRAUMATISED.
THEY'RE NICE.
THEY'RE USUALLY PRETTY QUIET. THOUGH IT'S NOT EVERY DAY WE GET SUCH INTERESTING GUESTS.
AND HEY,
SORRY WE DIDN'T WAKE YOU. I FIGURED YOU NEEDED THE SLEEP.
I DID, THANKS.
CARE TO JOIN ME FOR SOME LUNCH?
I COULD GO FOR SOME FOOD, ACTUALLY.
AND WHERE HAVE YOU BEEN?
HELPING MOULD THE MINDS OF THE NEXT GENERATION.
THAT'S DANGEROUS. YOU SHOULDN'T LET HIM DO THAT.
NOTED.
HEY.

YOU WANT SOME?

PLEASE, IO, I'M A HUNTER.

SPIRIT, SPIRIT, WON'T YOU LEND US MAGIC?

SPIRIT, SPIRIT, PLEAS... ACCE... O... MANG... RIC... COCONU... SNAKE... BREA... OR R...

NYNEVE...

I KNOW IT'S A BIG DECISION TO ASK OF YOU,

BUT IF YOU WANT IT,

YOU SHOULD KNOW THAT THERE'S A PLACE HERE FOR YOU.

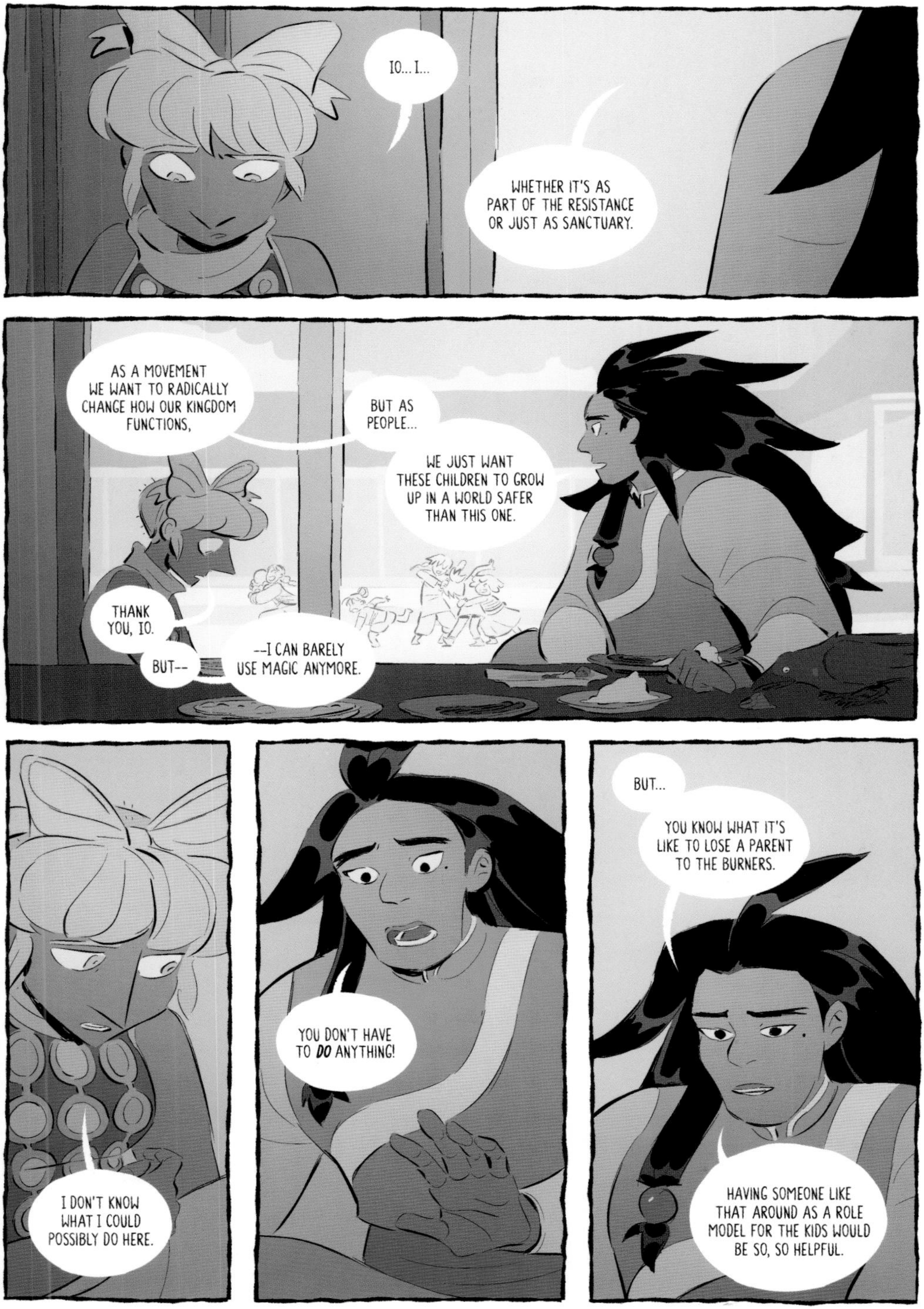

IO... I...
WHETHER IT'S AS PART OF THE RESISTANCE OR JUST AS SANCTUARY.
AS A MOVEMENT WE WANT TO RADICALLY CHANGE HOW OUR KINGDOM FUNCTIONS,
BUT AS PEOPLE...
WE JUST WANT THESE CHILDREN TO GROW UP IN A WORLD SAFER THAN THIS ONE.
THANK YOU, IO.
BUT--
--I CAN BARELY USE MAGIC ANYMORE.
I DON'T KNOW WHAT I COULD POSSIBLY DO HERE.
YOU DON'T HAVE TO ***DO*** ANYTHING!
BUT...
YOU KNOW WHAT IT'S LIKE TO LOSE A PARENT TO THE BURNERS.
HAVING SOMEONE LIKE THAT AROUND AS A ROLE MODEL FOR THE KIDS WOULD BE SO, SO HELPFUL.

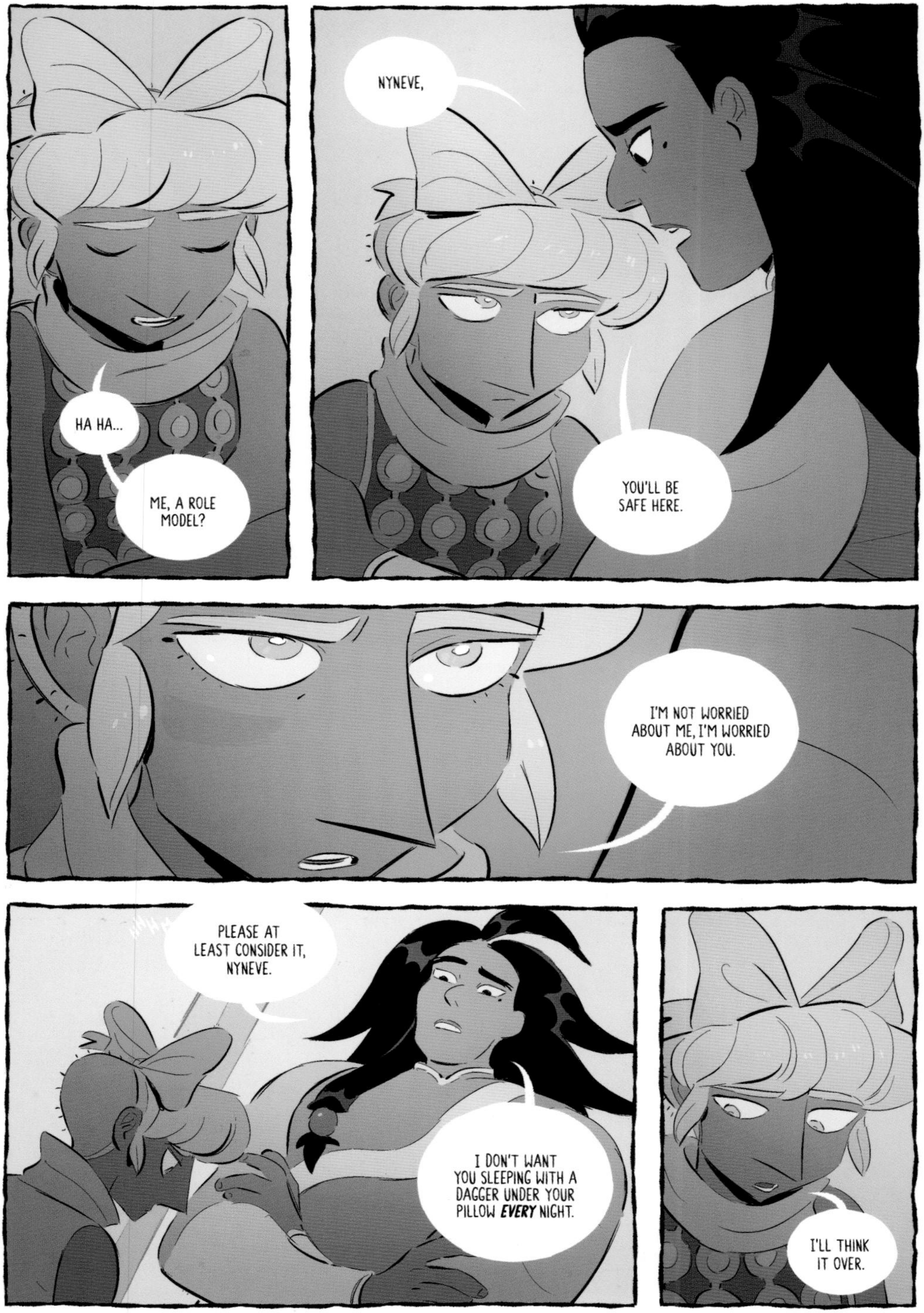

HA HA...
ME, A ROLE MODEL?
NYNEVE,
YOU'LL BE SAFE HERE.
I'M NOT WORRIED ABOUT ME, I'M WORRIED ABOUT YOU.
PLEASE AT LEAST CONSIDER IT, NYNEVE.
I DON'T WANT YOU SLEEPING WITH A DAGGER UNDER YOUR PILLOW ***EVERY*** NIGHT.
I'LL THINK IT OVER.

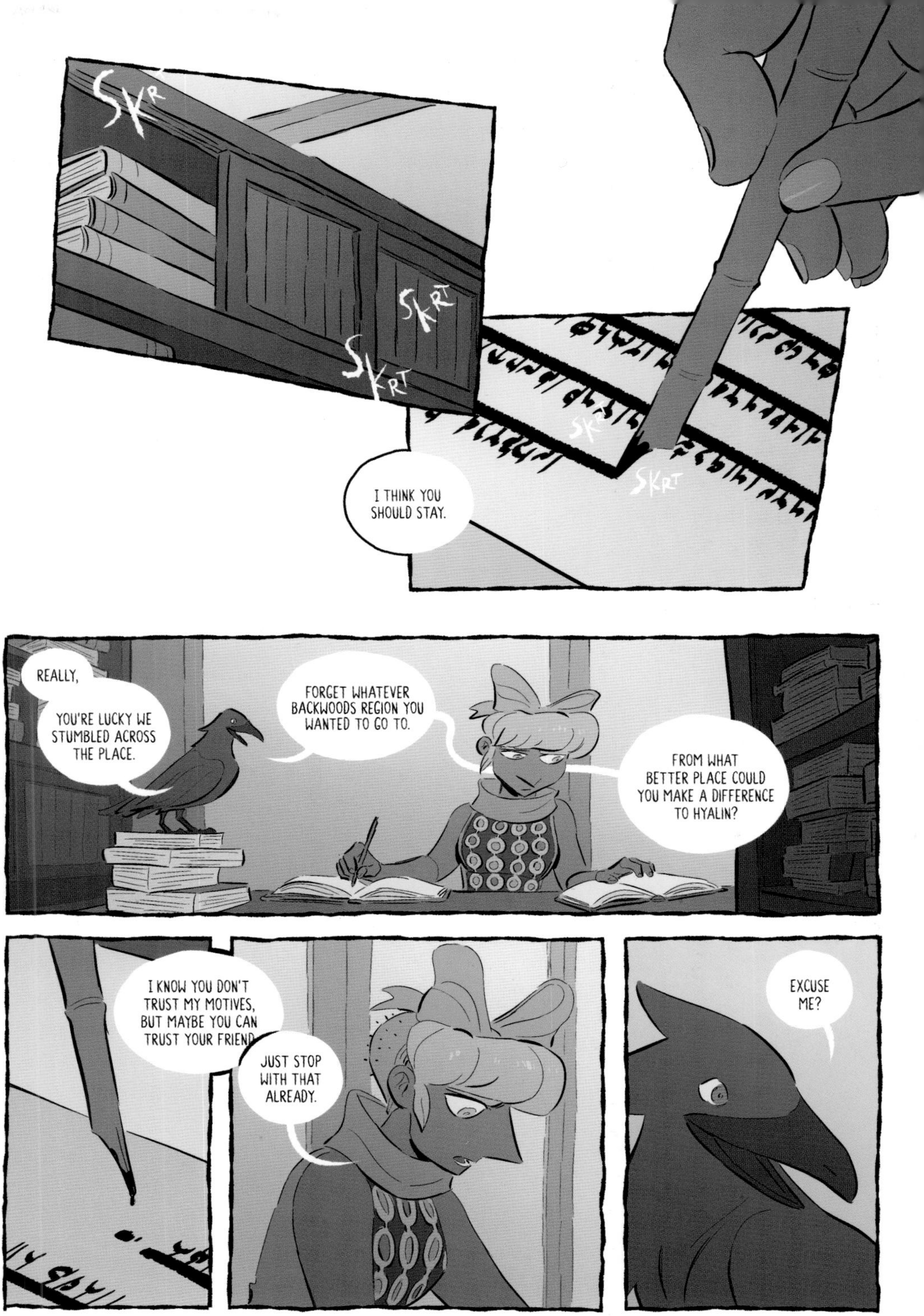
SKR
SKRT
SKRT
SKRT
SKRT
I THINK YOU SHOULD STAY.
REALLY,
YOU'RE LUCKY WE STUMBLED ACROSS THE PLACE.
FORGET WHATEVER BACKWOODS REGION YOU WANTED TO GO TO.
FROM WHAT BETTER PLACE COULD YOU MAKE A DIFFERENCE TO HYALIN?
I KNOW YOU DON'T TRUST MY MOTIVES, BUT MAYBE YOU CAN TRUST YOUR FRIEND.
JUST STOP WITH THAT ALREADY.
EXCUSE ME?

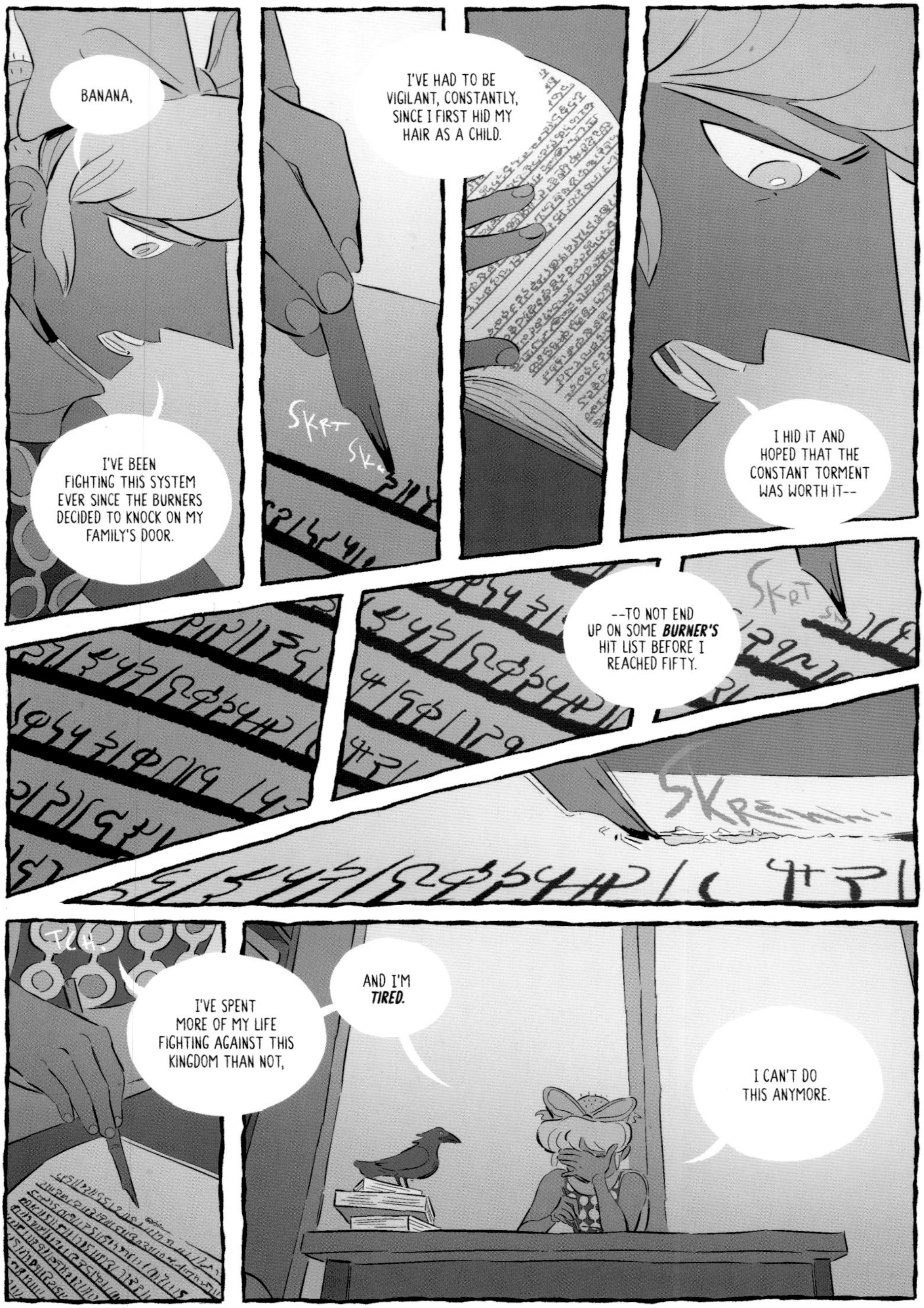

BANANA,
I'VE BEEN FIGHTING THIS SYSTEM EVER SINCE THE BURNERS DECIDED TO KNOCK ON MY FAMILY'S DOOR.
I'VE HAD TO BE VIGILANT, CONSTANTLY, SINCE I FIRST HID MY HAIR AS A CHILD.
SKRT
I HID IT AND HOPED THAT THE CONSTANT TORMENT WAS WORTH IT--
--TO NOT END UP ON SOME **BURNER'S** HIT LIST BEFORE I REACHED FIFTY.
SKRT
TCH.
I'VE SPENT MORE OF MY LIFE FIGHTING AGAINST THIS KINGDOM THAN NOT,
AND I'M ***TIRED.***
I CAN'T DO THIS ANYMORE.

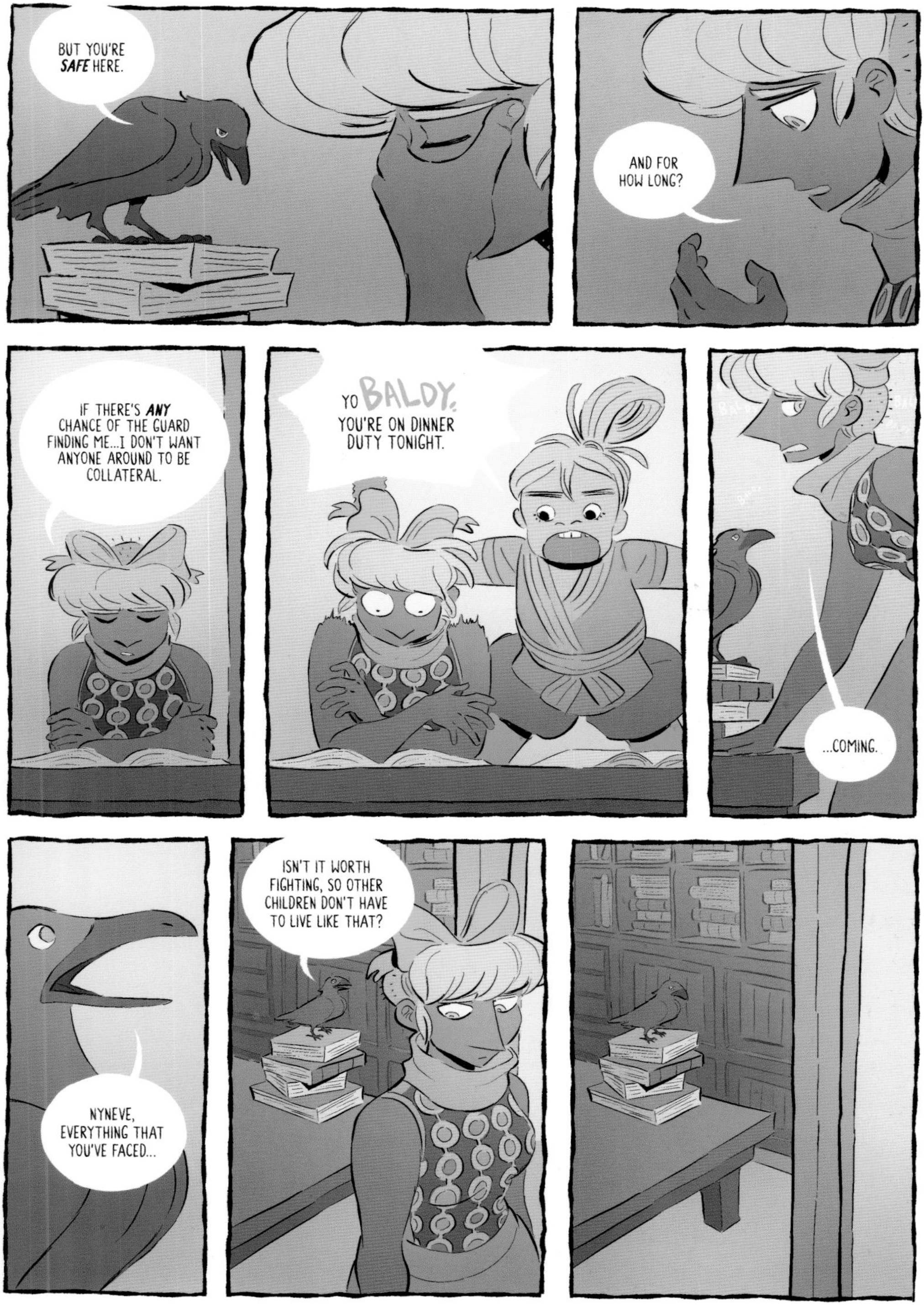
BUT YOU'RE SAFE HERE.
AND FOR HOW LONG?
IF THERE'S ANY CHANCE OF THE GUARD FINDING ME...I DON'T WANT ANYONE AROUND TO BE COLLATERAL.
YO BALDY. YOU'RE ON DINNER DUTY TONIGHT.
...COMING.
NYNEVE, EVERYTHING THAT YOU'VE FACED...
ISN'T IT WORTH FIGHTING, SO OTHER CHILDREN DON'T HAVE TO LIVE LIKE THAT?

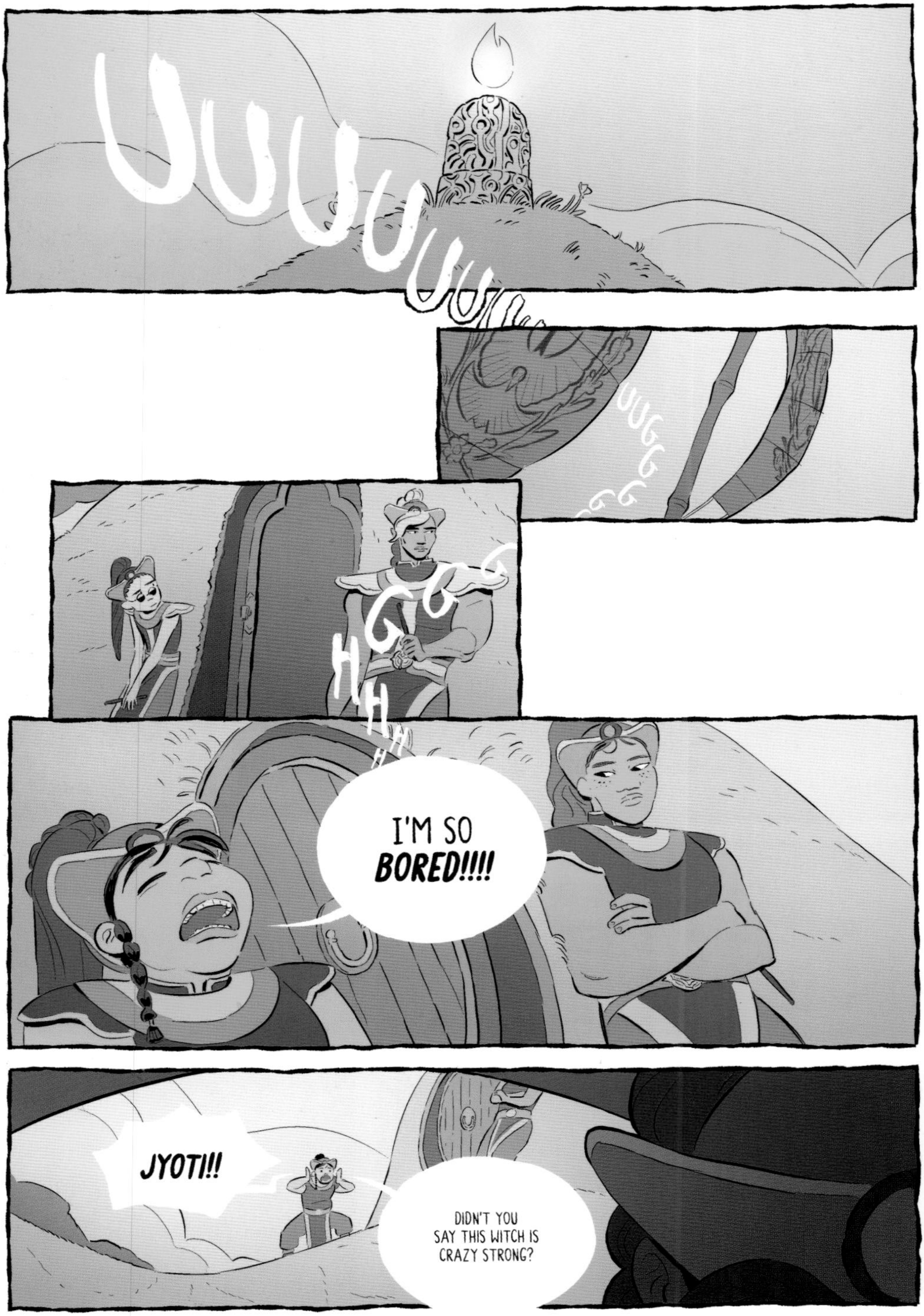
UUUUUUUUUU
UUGGGG
GGG
HHHH
I'M SO BORED!!!!
JYOTI!!
DIDN'T YOU SAY THIS WITCH IS CRAZY STRONG?

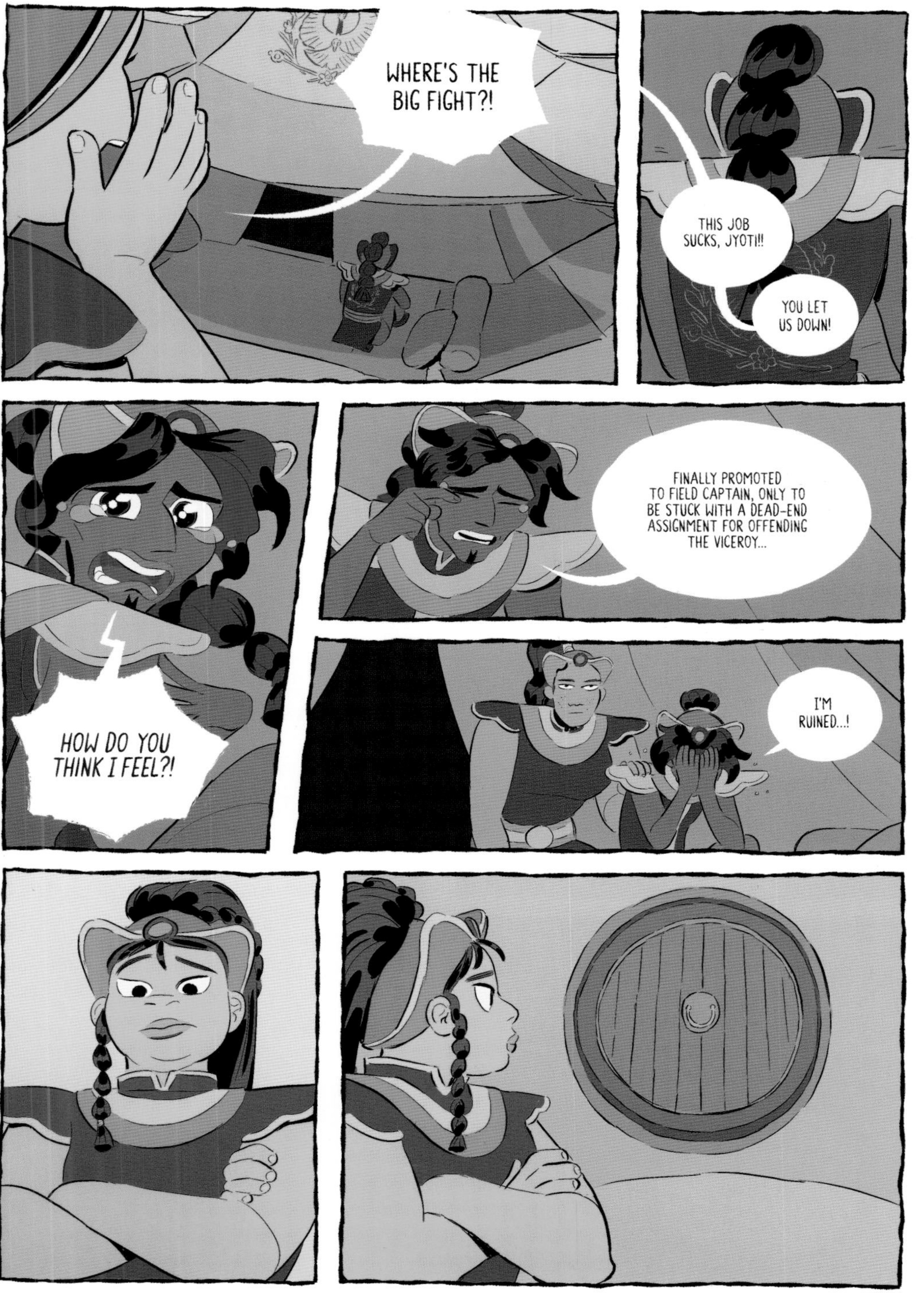

WHERE'S THE BIG FIGHT?!
THIS JOB SUCKS, JYOTI!!
YOU LET US DOWN!
HOW DO YOU THINK I FEEL?!
FINALLY PROMOTED TO FIELD CAPTAIN, ONLY TO BE STUCK WITH A DEAD-END ASSIGNMENT FOR OFFENDING THE VICEROY...
I'M RUINED...!

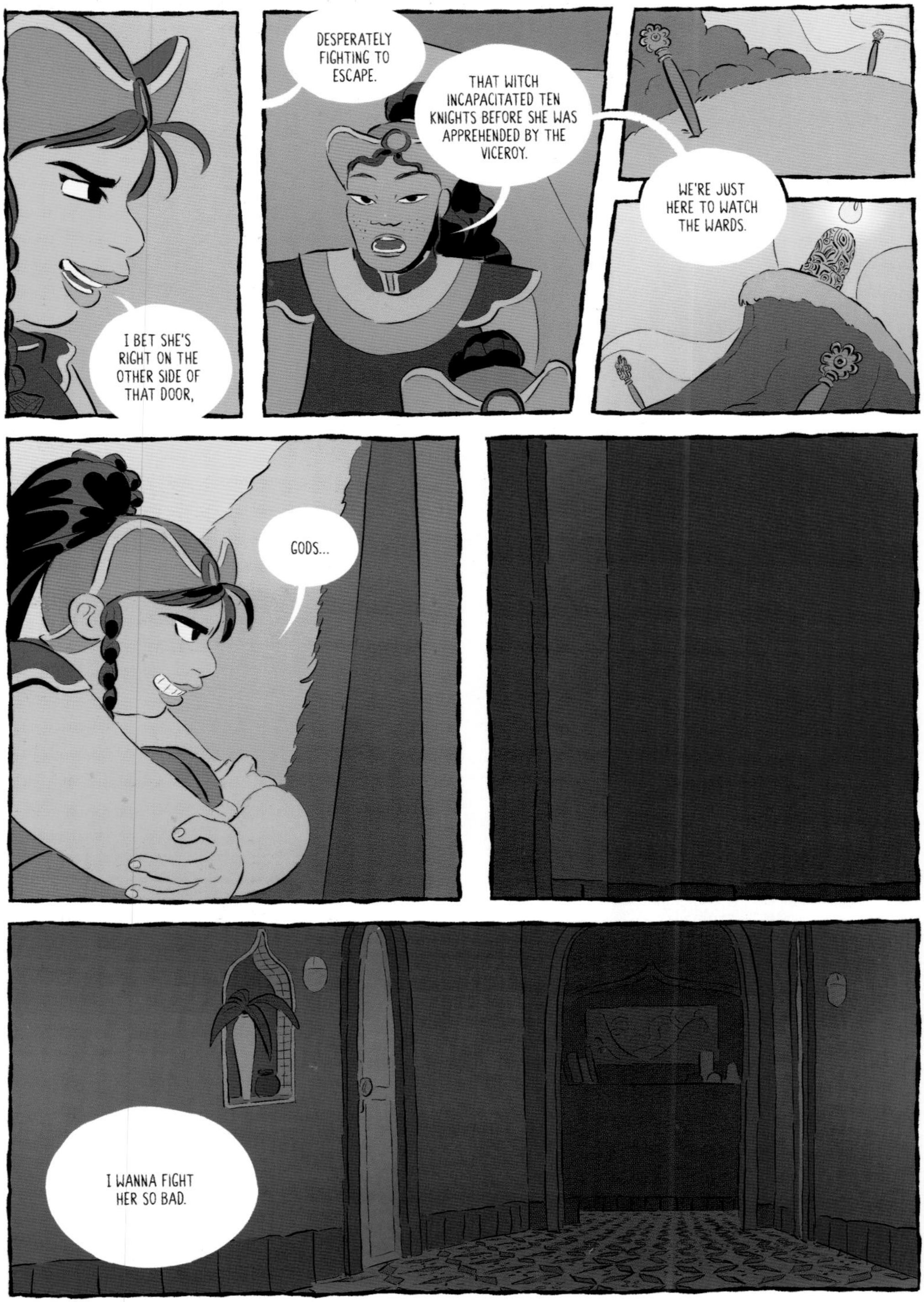

I BET SHE'S RIGHT ON THE OTHER SIDE OF THAT DOOR,
DESPERATELY FIGHTING TO ESCAPE.
THAT WITCH INCAPACITATED TEN KNIGHTS BEFORE SHE WAS APPREHENDED BY THE VICEROY.
WE'RE JUST HERE TO WATCH THE WARDS.
GODS...
I WANNA FIGHT HER SO BAD.

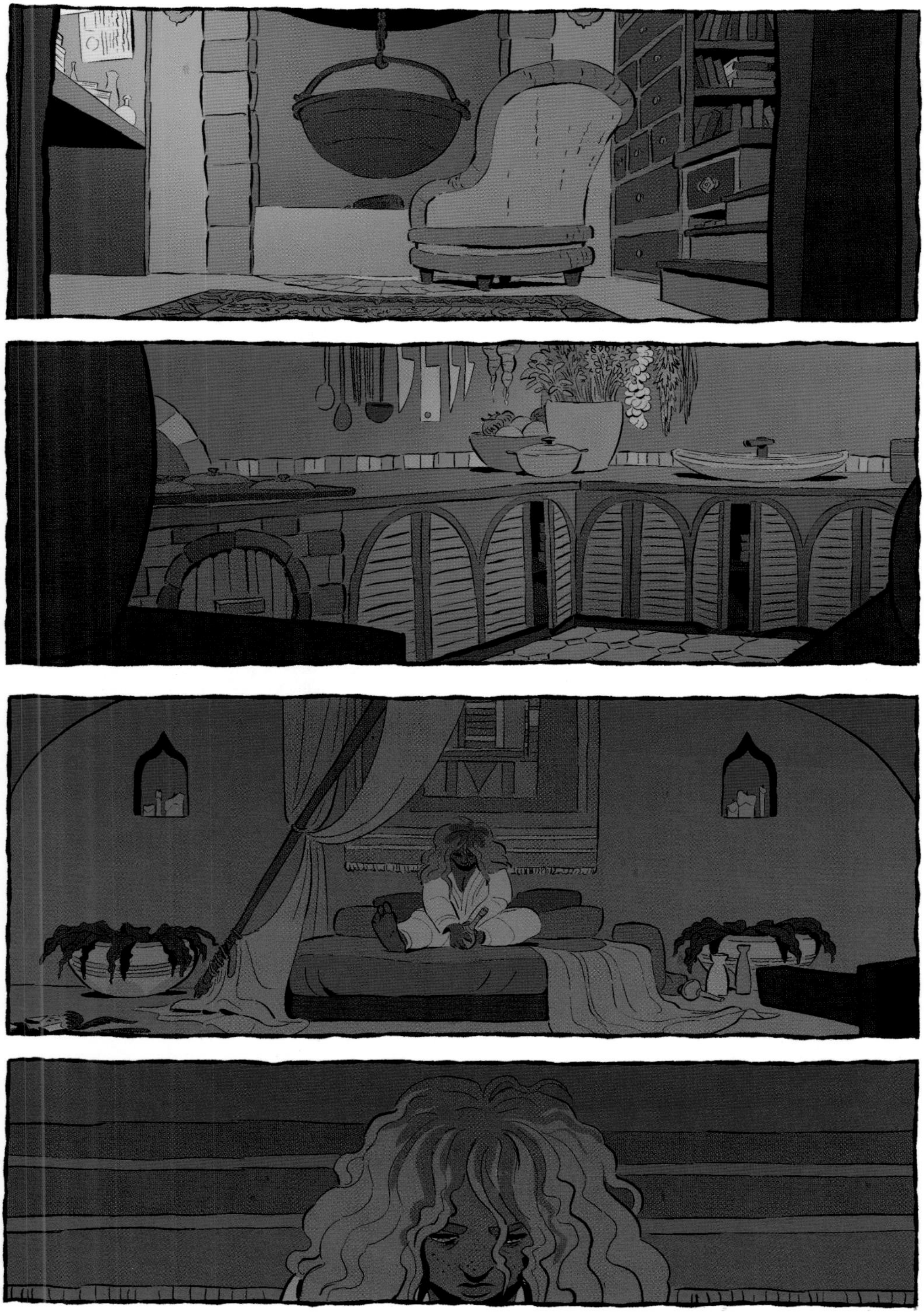

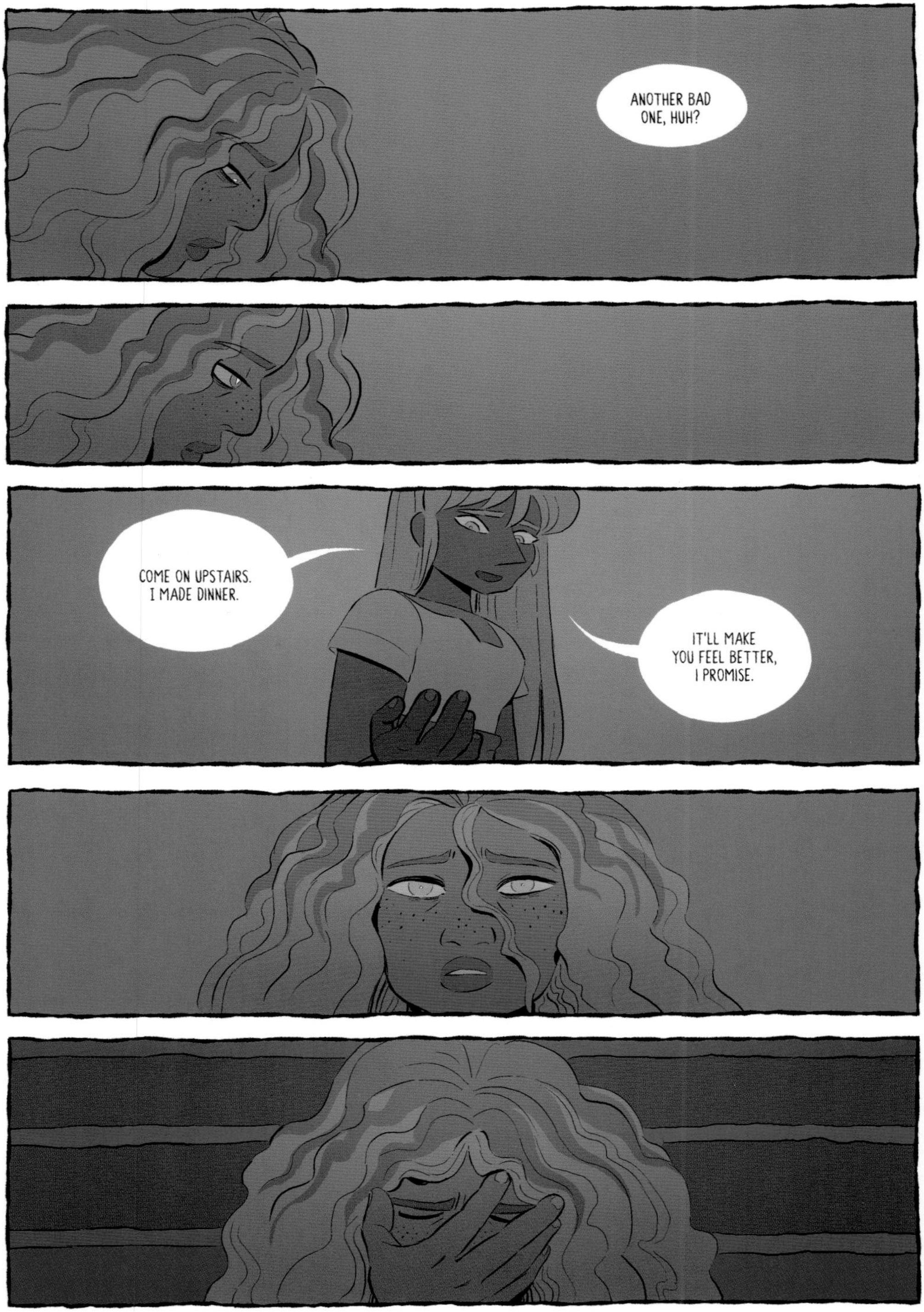
ANOTHER BAD ONE, HUH?
COME ON UPSTAIRS. I MADE DINNER.
IT'LL MAKE YOU FEEL BETTER, I PROMISE.

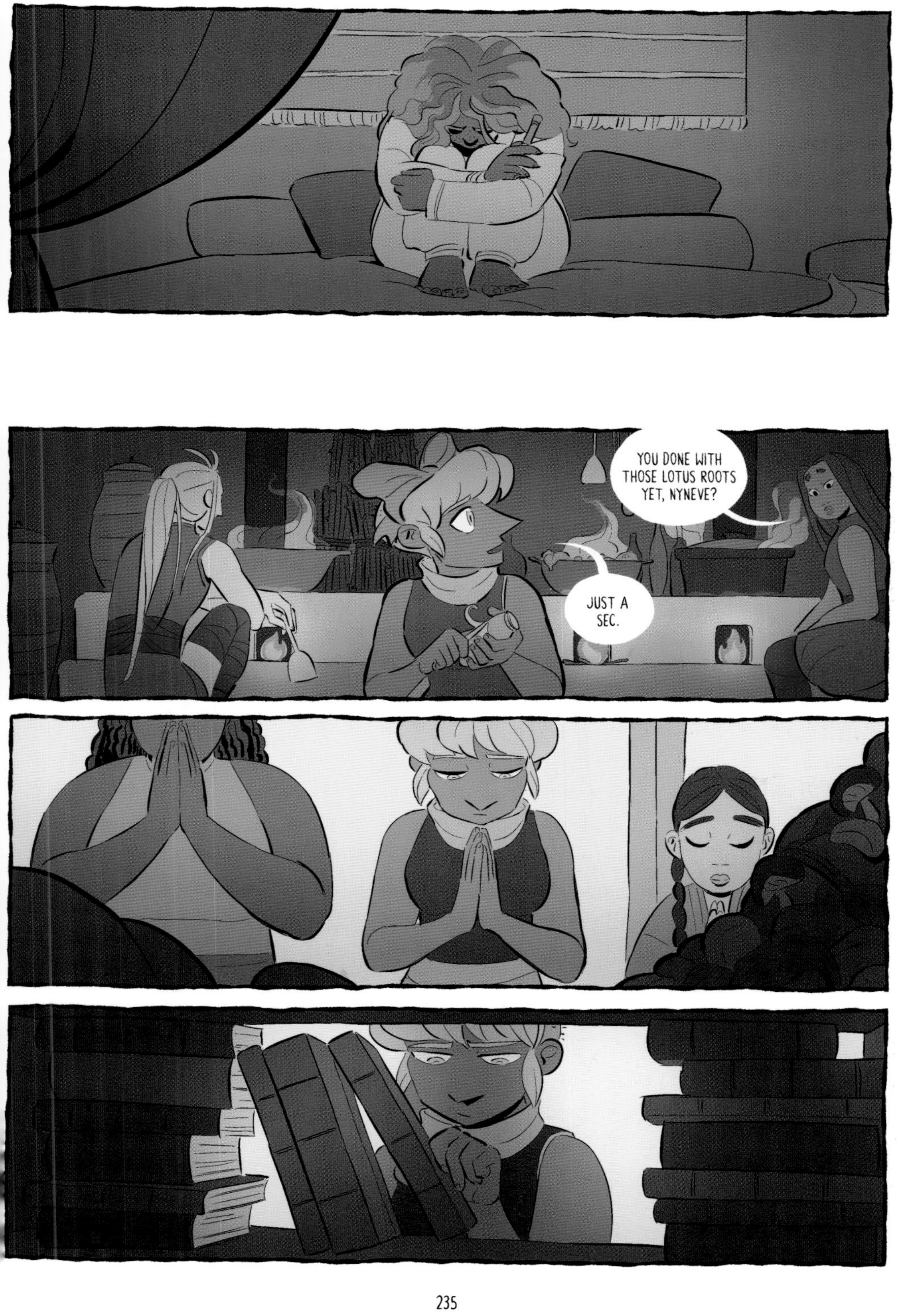
YOU DONE WITH THOSE LOTUS ROOTS YET, NYNEVE?
JUST A SEC.

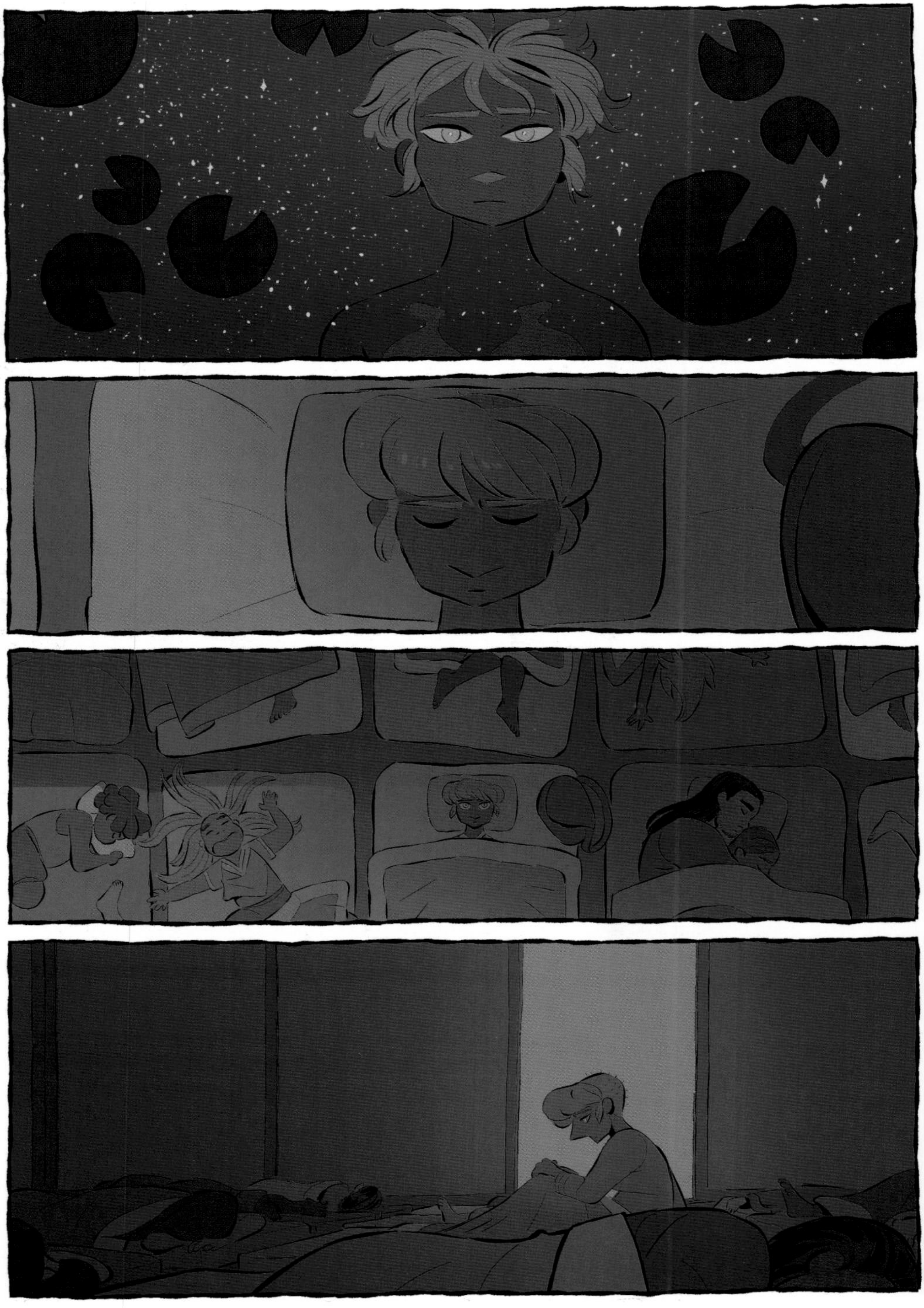

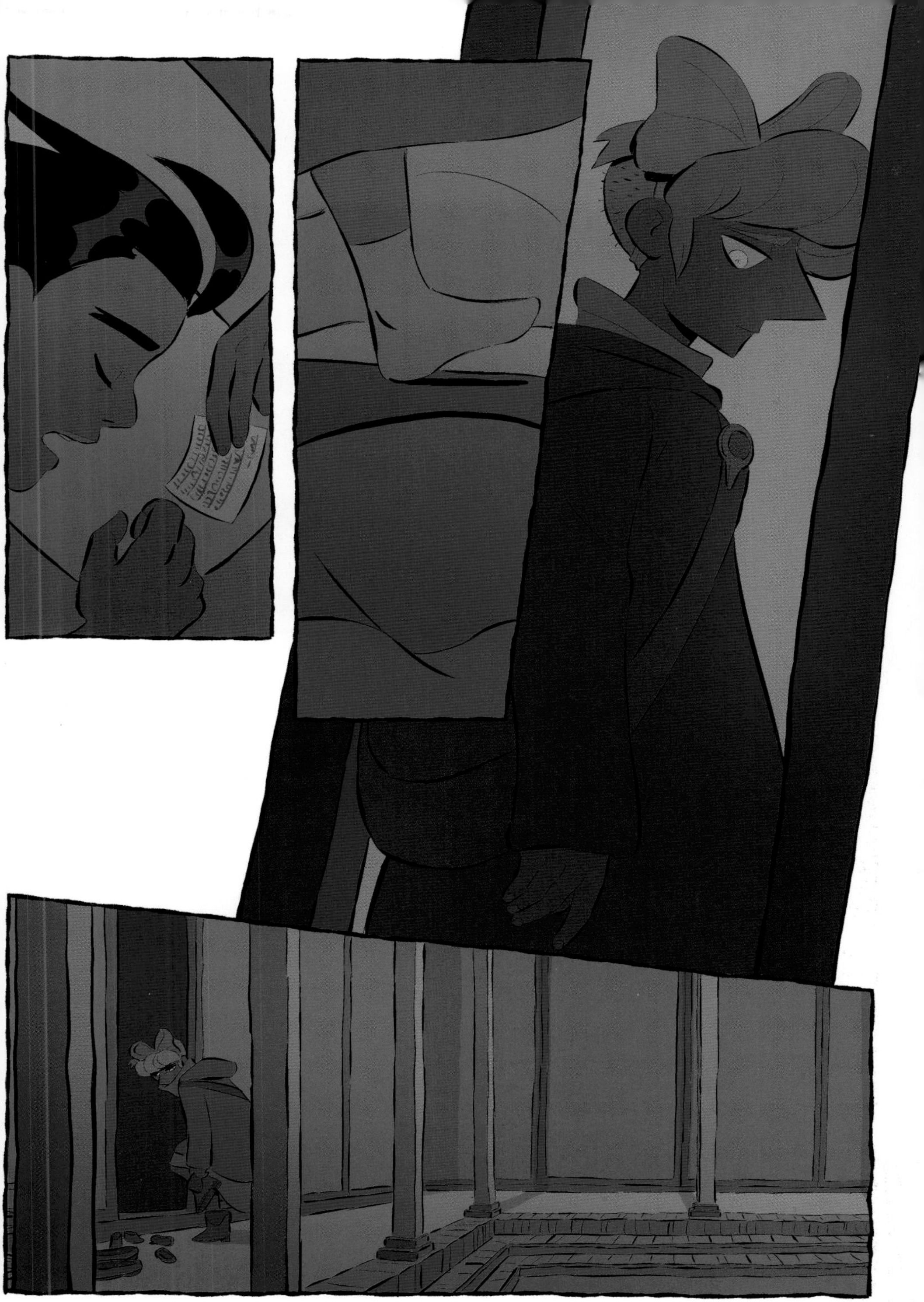

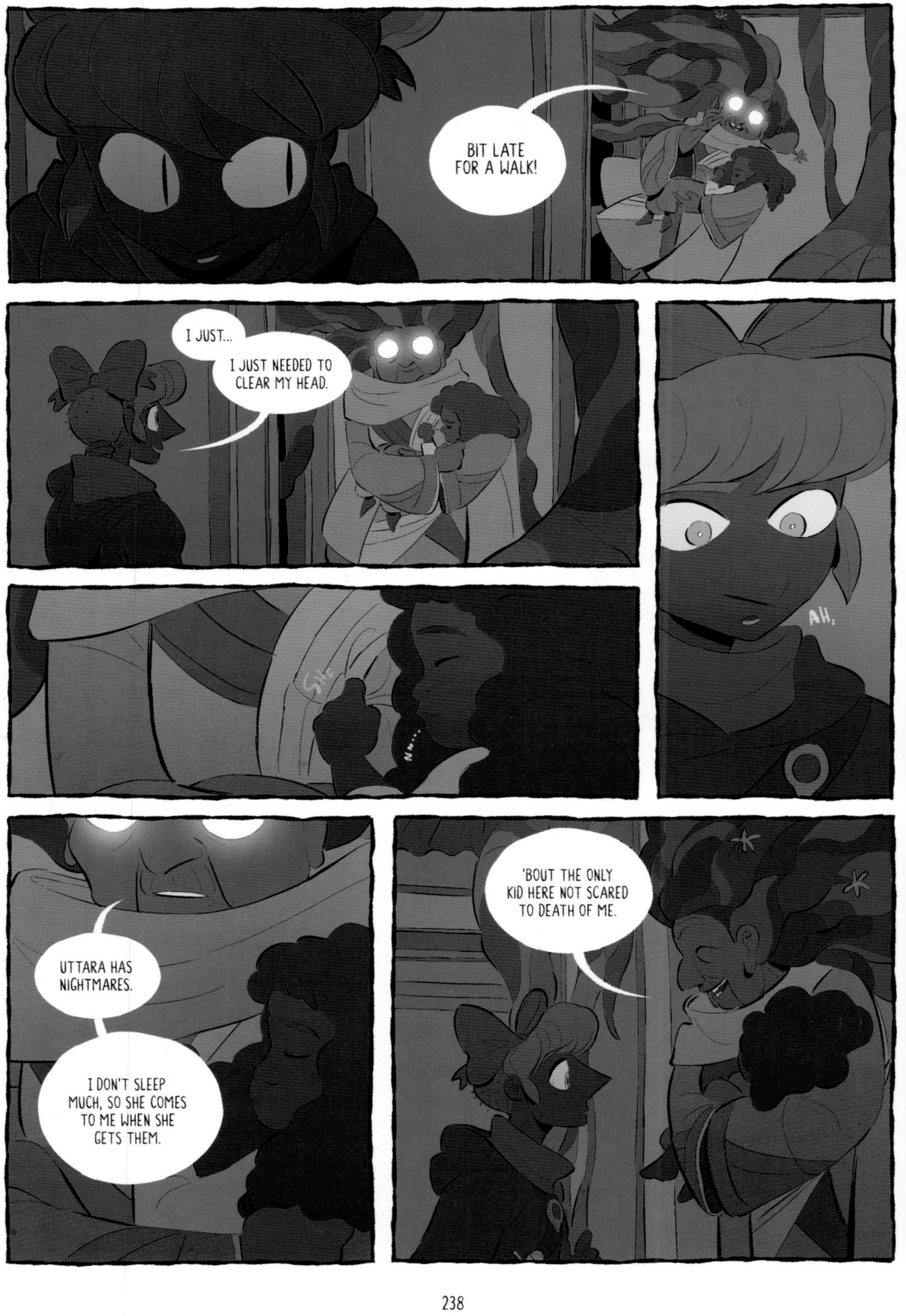
BIT LATE FOR A WALK!
I JUST...
I JUST NEEDED TO CLEAR MY HEAD.
AH,
SHF
Nn...
UTTARA HAS NIGHTMARES.
I DON'T SLEEP MUCH, SO SHE COMES TO ME WHEN SHE GETS THEM.
'BOUT THE ONLY KID HERE NOT SCARED TO DEATH OF ME.

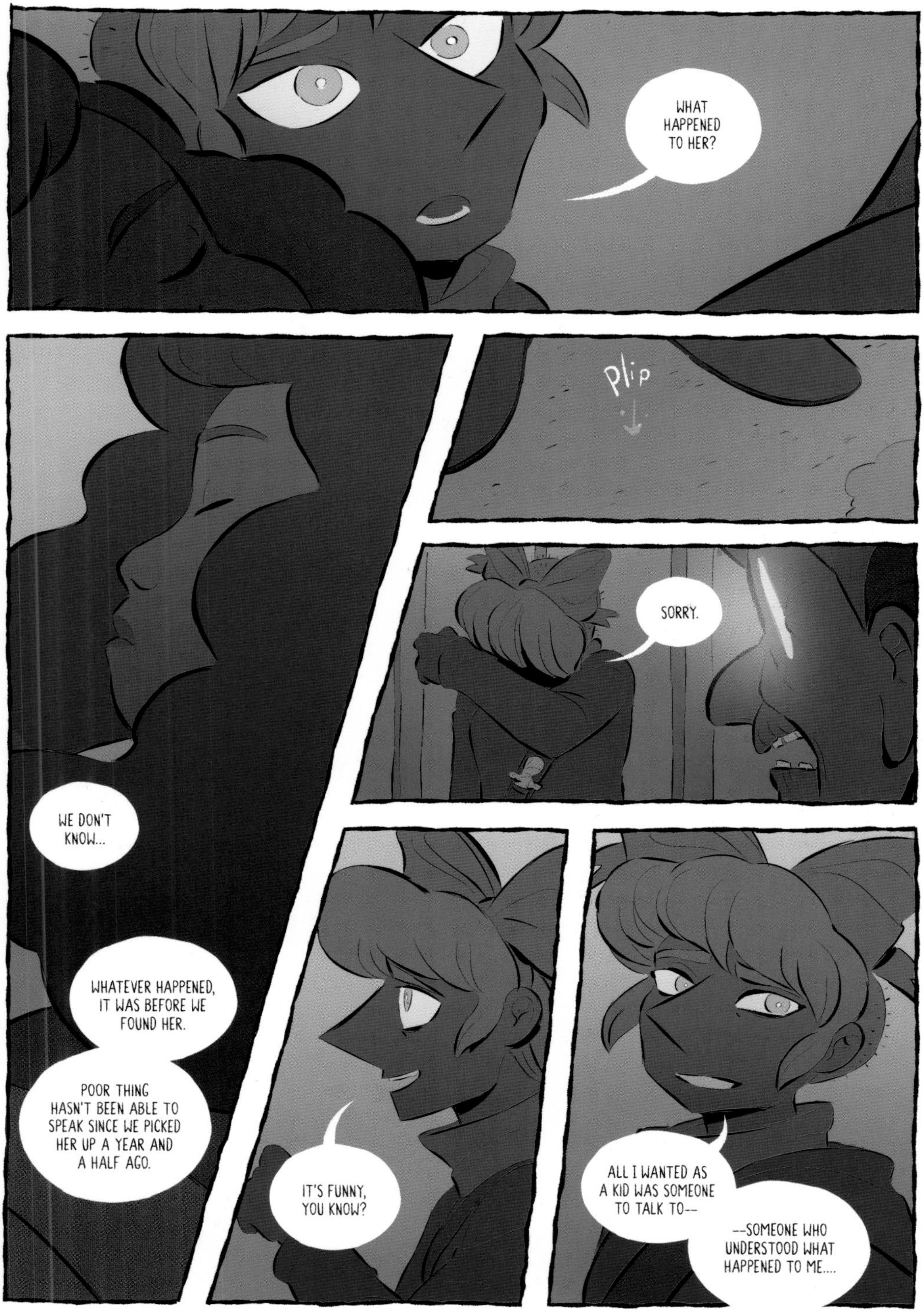
WHAT HAPPENED TO HER?
plip
SORRY.
WE DON'T KNOW...
WHATEVER HAPPENED, IT WAS BEFORE WE FOUND HER.
POOR THING HASN'T BEEN ABLE TO SPEAK SINCE WE PICKED HER UP A YEAR AND A HALF AGO.
IT'S FUNNY, YOU KNOW?
ALL I WANTED AS A KID WAS SOMEONE TO TALK TO--
--SOMEONE WHO UNDERSTOOD WHAT HAPPENED TO ME....

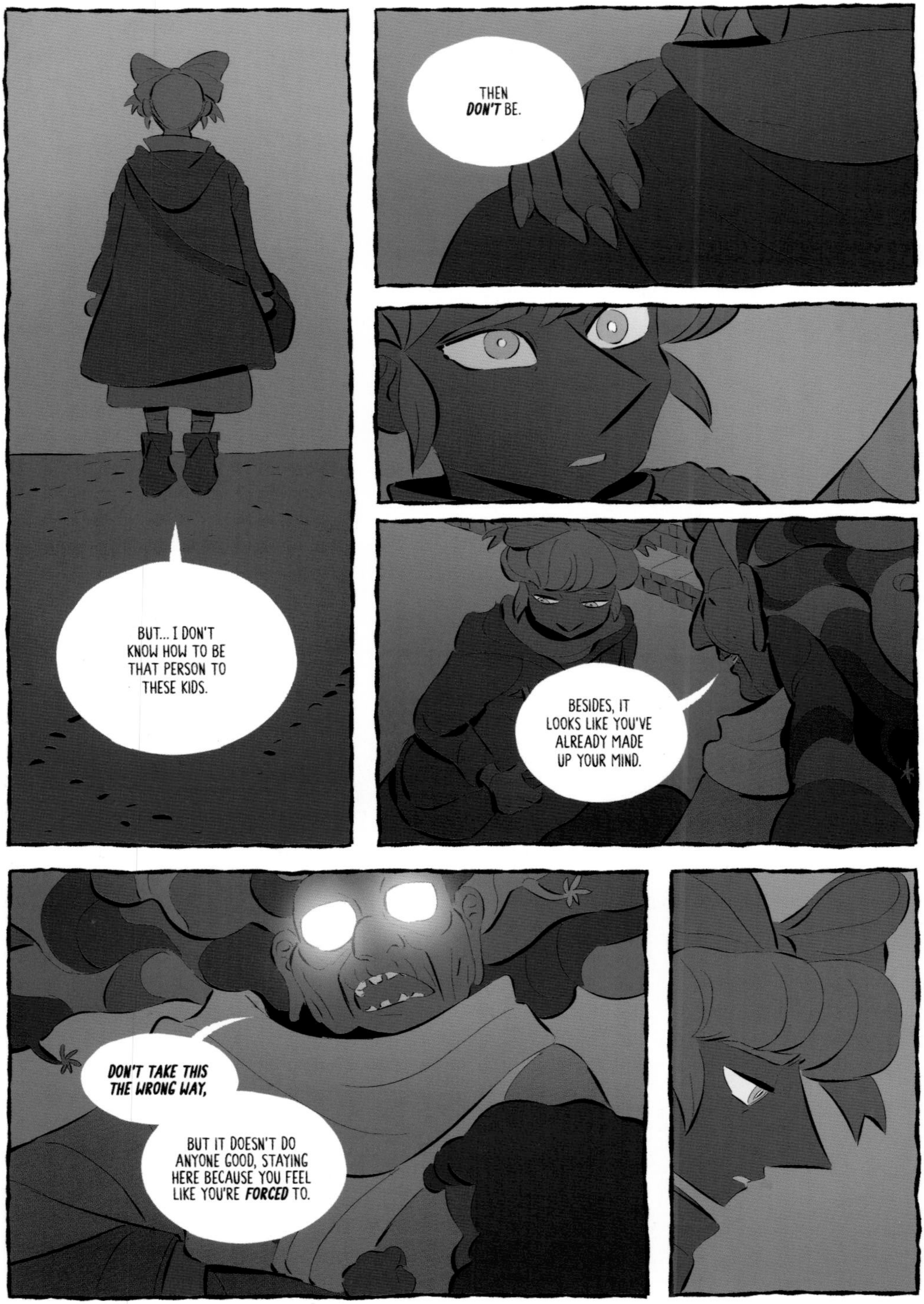
BUT... I DON'T KNOW HOW TO BE THAT PERSON TO THESE KIDS.
THEN DON'T BE.
BESIDES, IT LOOKS LIKE YOU'VE ALREADY MADE UP YOUR MIND.
DON'T TAKE THIS THE WRONG WAY,
BUT IT DOESN'T DO ANYONE GOOD, STAYING HERE BECAUSE YOU FEEL LIKE YOU'RE FORCED TO.

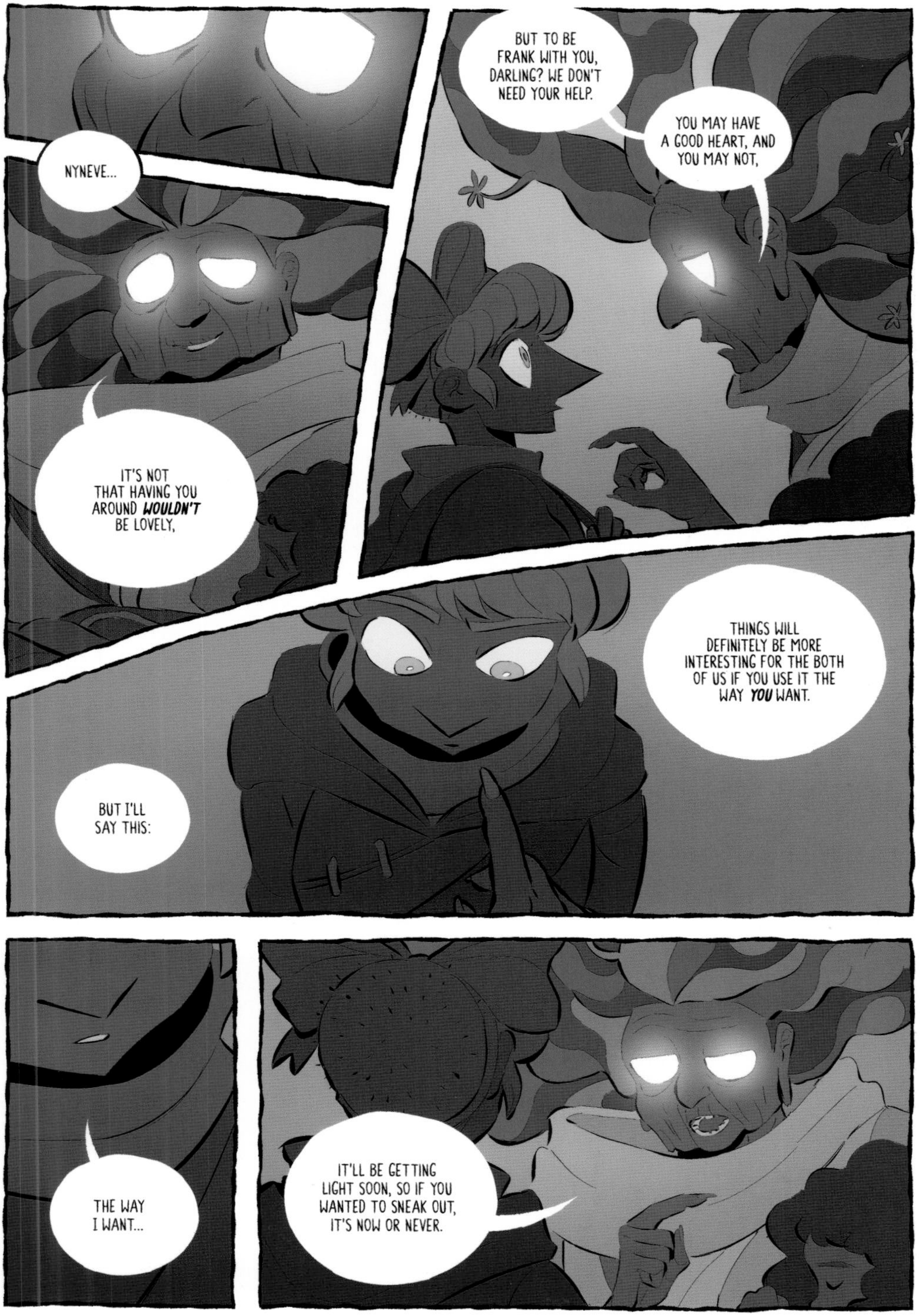
NYNEVE...
IT'S NOT THAT HAVING YOU AROUND WOULDN'T BE LOVELY,
BUT TO BE FRANK WITH YOU, DARLING? WE DON'T NEED YOUR HELP.
YOU MAY HAVE A GOOD HEART, AND YOU MAY NOT,
BUT I'LL SAY THIS:
THINGS WILL DEFINITELY BE MORE INTERESTING FOR THE BOTH OF US IF YOU USE IT THE WAY YOU WANT.
THE WAY I WANT...
IT'LL BE GETTING LIGHT SOON, SO IF YOU WANTED TO SNEAK OUT, IT'S NOW OR NEVER.

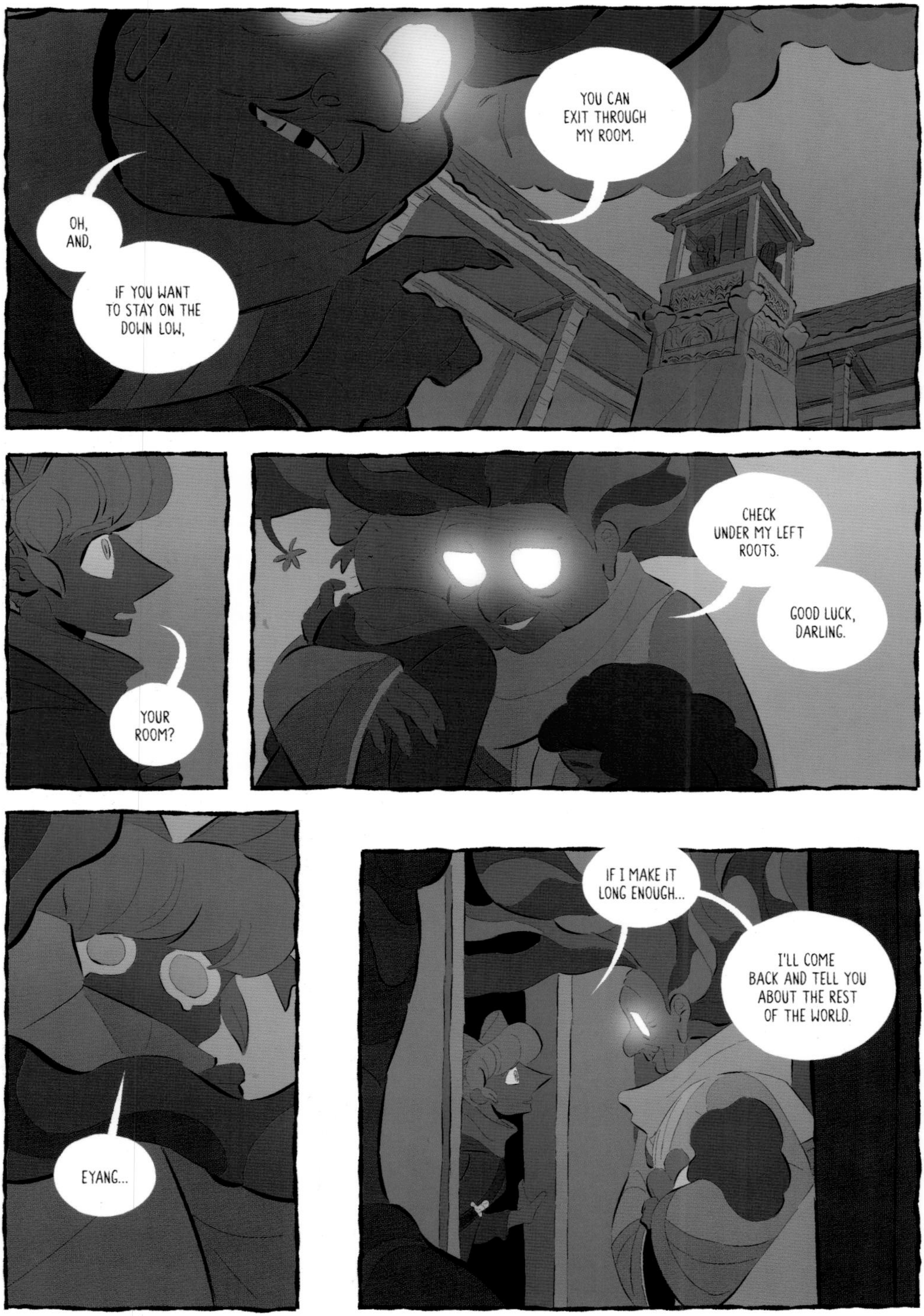
OH, AND,
IF YOU WANT TO STAY ON THE DOWN LOW,
YOU CAN EXIT THROUGH MY ROOM.
YOUR ROOM?
CHECK UNDER MY LEFT ROOTS.
GOOD LUCK, DARLING.
EYANG...
IF I MAKE IT LONG ENOUGH...
I'LL COME BACK AND TELL YOU ABOUT THE REST OF THE WORLD.

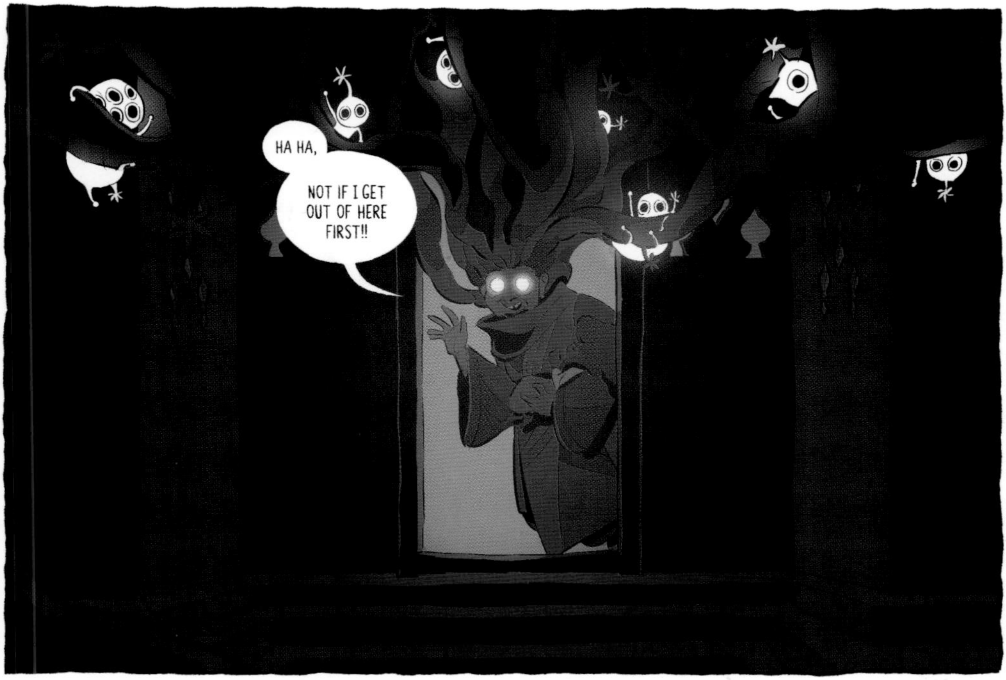
HA HA,
NOT IF I GET OUT OF HERE FIRST!!
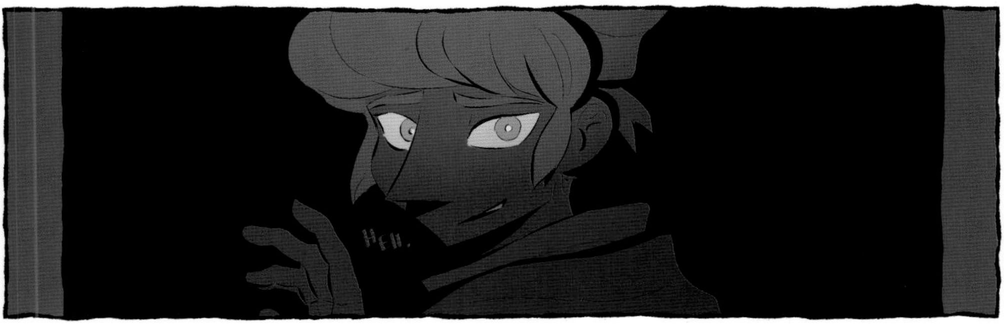
HEH.
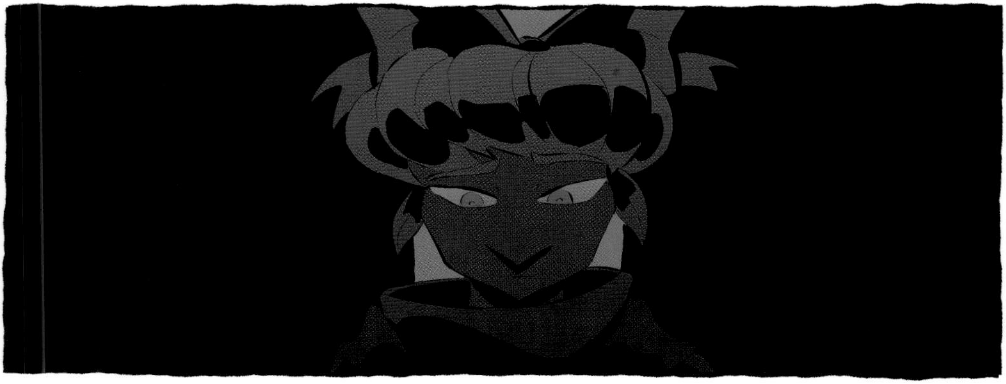

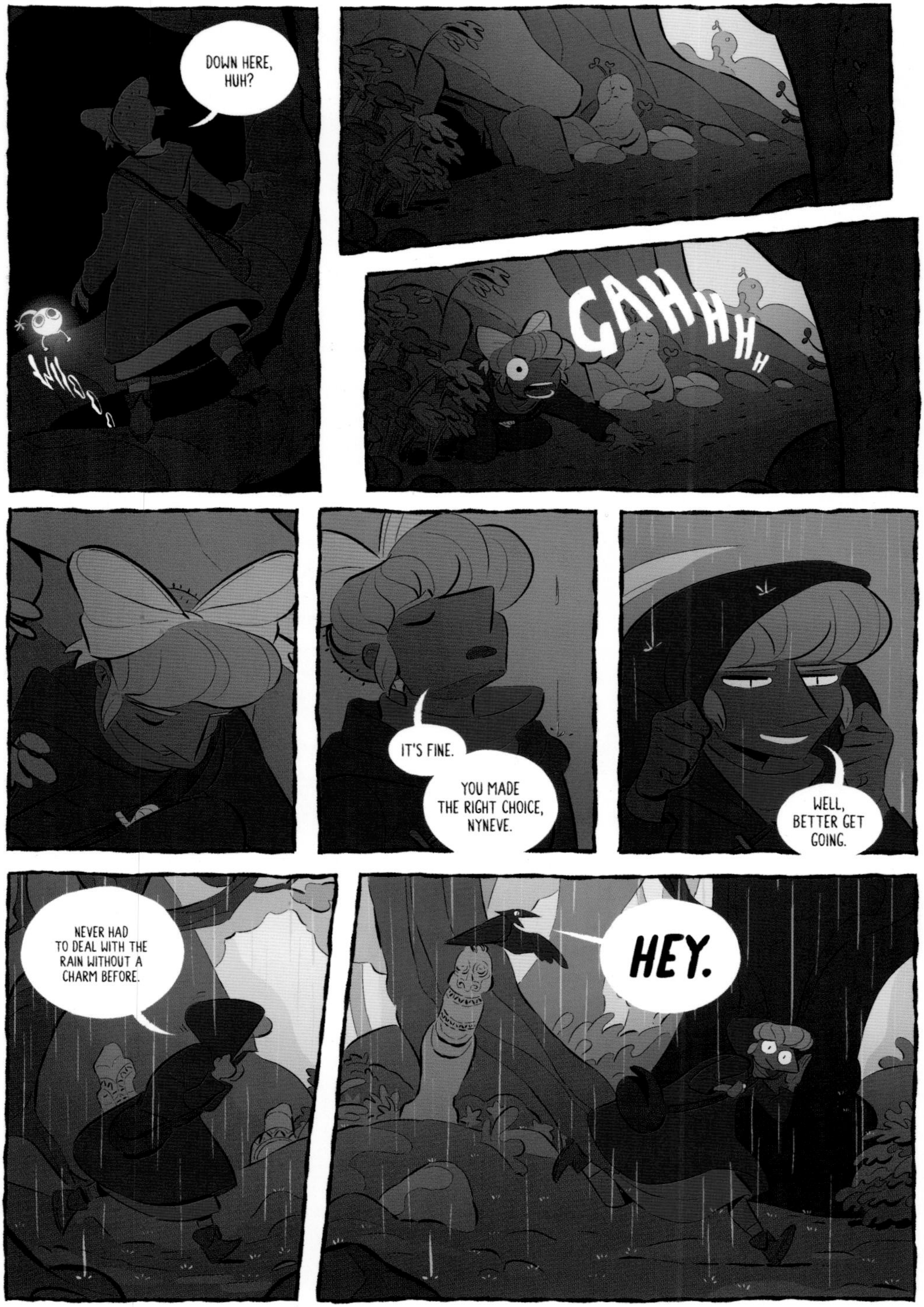
DOWN HERE, HUH?
WHOOO
GAHHHHH
IT'S FINE.
YOU MADE THE RIGHT CHOICE, NYNEVE.
WELL, BETTER GET GOING.
NEVER HAD TO DEAL WITH THE RAIN WITHOUT A CHARM BEFORE.
HEY.

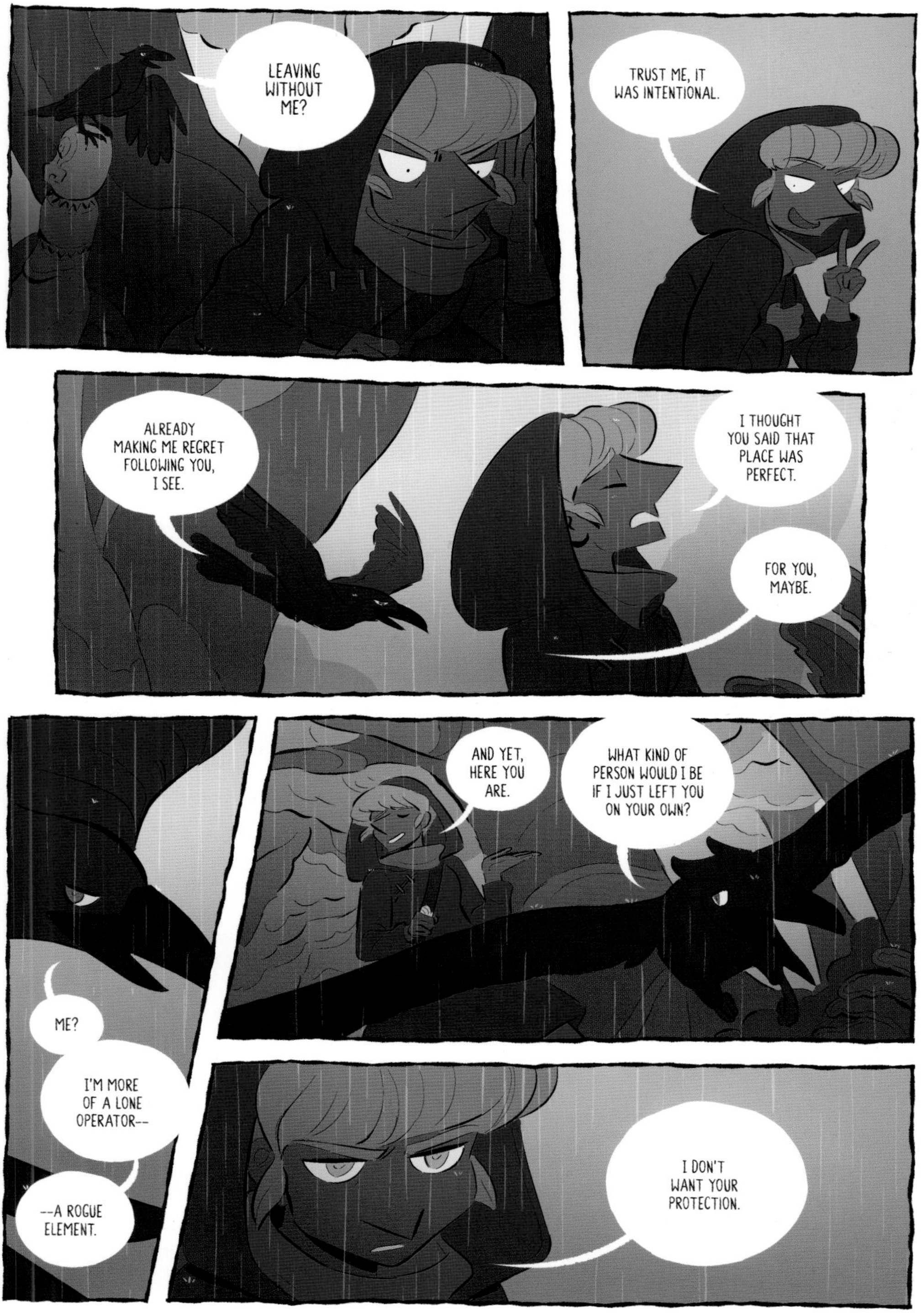
LEAVING WITHOUT ME?
TRUST ME, IT WAS INTENTIONAL.
ALREADY MAKING ME REGRET FOLLOWING YOU, I SEE.
I THOUGHT YOU SAID THAT PLACE WAS PERFECT.
FOR YOU, MAYBE.
AND YET, HERE YOU ARE.
WHAT KIND OF PERSON WOULD I BE IF I JUST LEFT YOU ON YOUR OWN?
ME?
I'M MORE OF A LONE OPERATOR--
--A ROGUE ELEMENT.
I DON'T WANT YOUR PROTECTION.

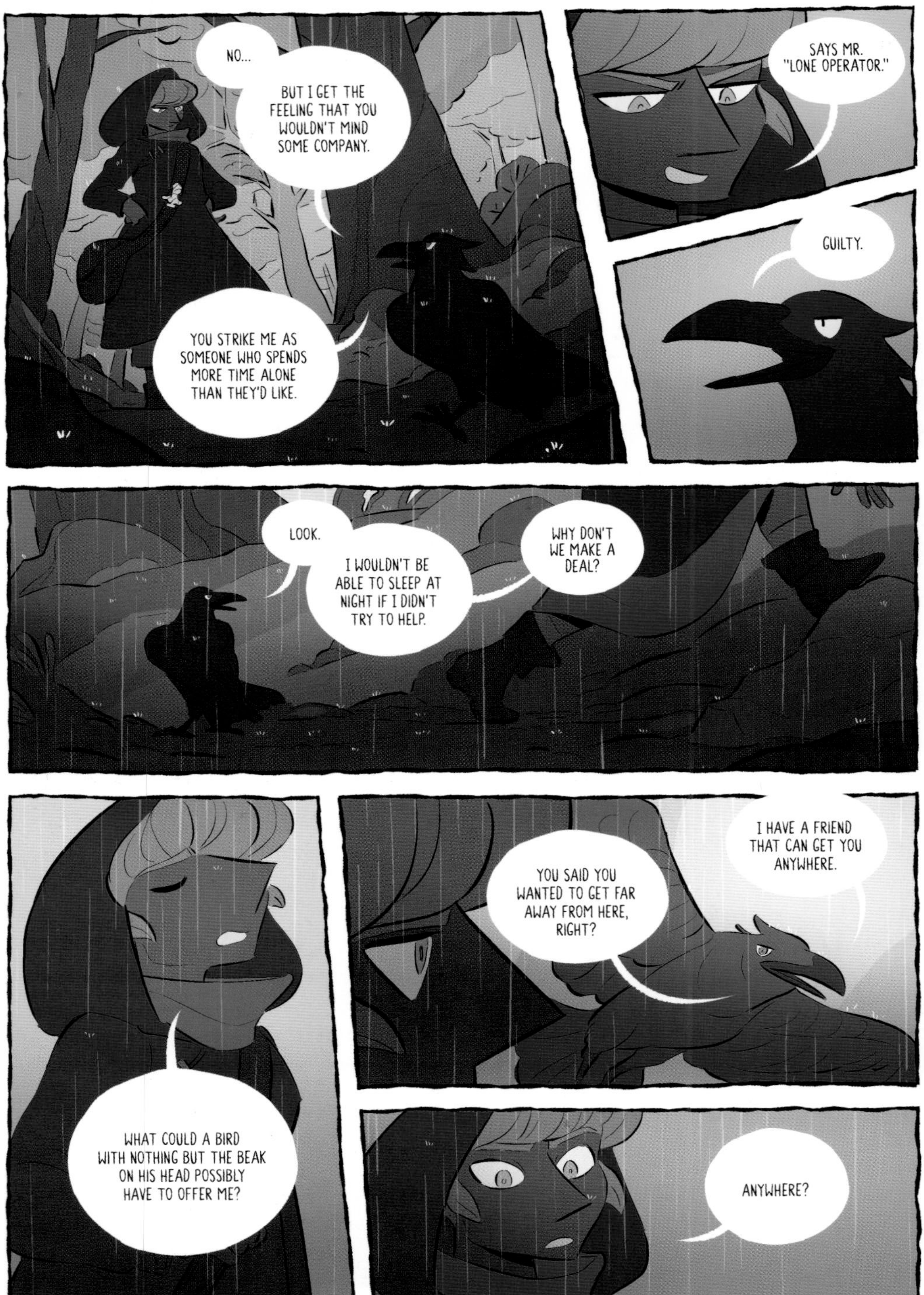
NO...
BUT I GET THE FEELING THAT YOU WOULDN'T MIND SOME COMPANY.
YOU STRIKE ME AS SOMEONE WHO SPENDS MORE TIME ALONE THAN THEY'D LIKE.
SAYS MR. "LONE OPERATOR."
GUILTY.
LOOK.
I WOULDN'T BE ABLE TO SLEEP AT NIGHT IF I DIDN'T TRY TO HELP.
WHY DON'T WE MAKE A DEAL?
WHAT COULD A BIRD WITH NOTHING BUT THE BEAK ON HIS HEAD POSSIBLY HAVE TO OFFER ME?
YOU SAID YOU WANTED TO GET FAR AWAY FROM HERE, RIGHT?
I HAVE A FRIEND THAT CAN GET YOU ANYWHERE.
ANYWHERE?

AND, TO SWEETEN THE DEAL,

I CAN OFFER YOU A VERY DISCRETE POSTAL SERVICE, SHOULD YOU NEED TO,

SAY,

GET SOME URGENT MAIL TO YOUR PAL IO.

KOFF

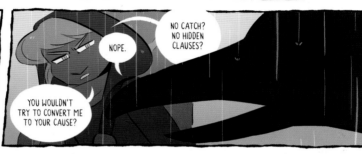

NO CATCH? NO HIDDEN CLAUSES?

NOPE.

YOU WOULDN'T TRY TO CONVERT ME TO YOUR CAUSE?

AND,

THE BEST PART OF ALL—NO EVANGELISING.

ABSOLUTELY NOT!

MY REWARD IS MY OWN EASE OF MIND.

BESIDES,

WHAT'S A BIRD WITH NOTHING BUT THE BEAK ON HIS HEAD GOING TO DO WITH ALL HIS FREE TIME, ANYWAY?

I'D MAKE YOU PINKY SWEAR ON IT, BUT YOU DON'T HAVE FINGERS, SO...

IT'S A DEAL.

YOU'LL JUST HAVE TO TAKE MY WORD FOR IT.

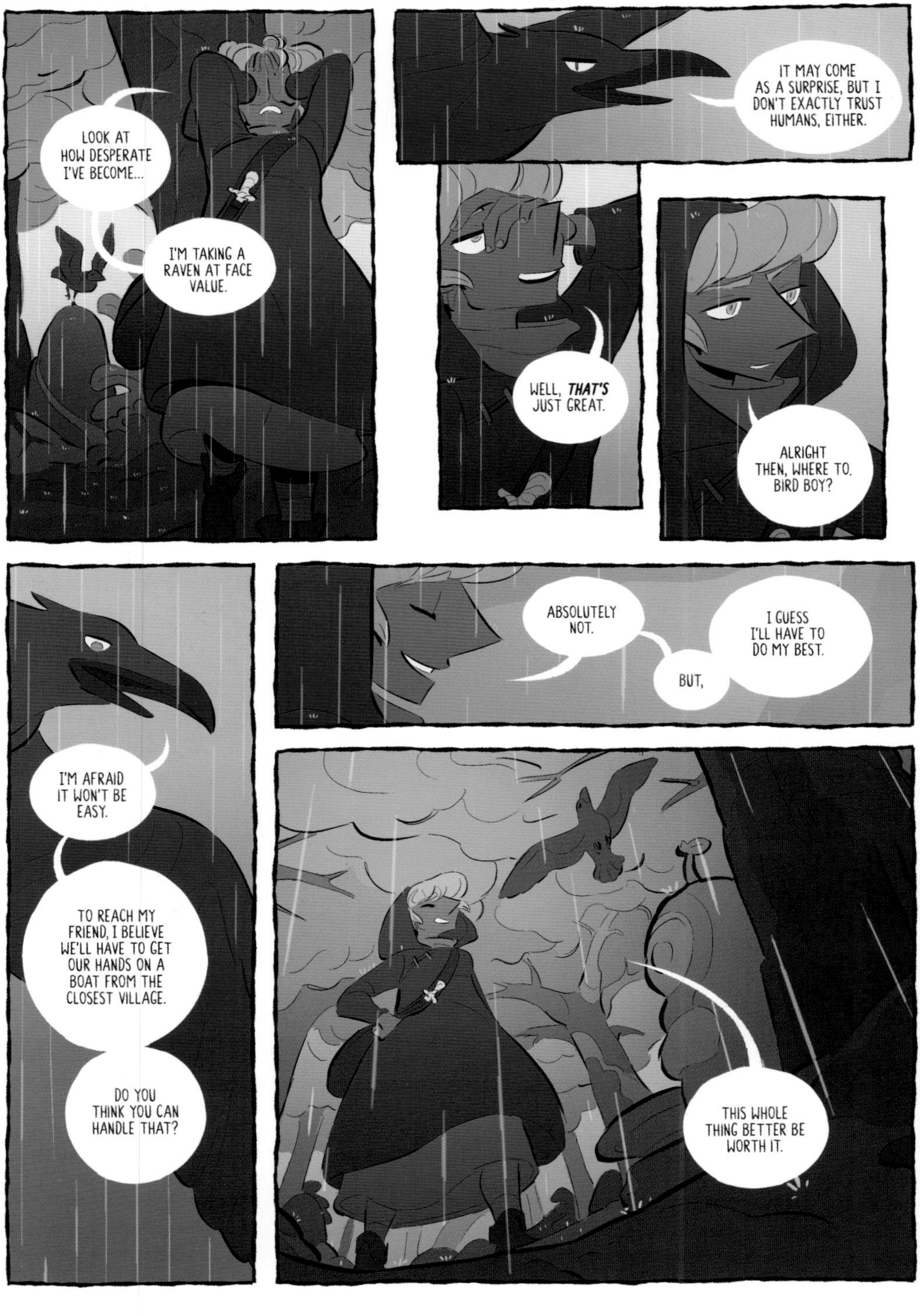
LOOK AT HOW DESPERATE I'VE BECOME...
I'M TAKING A RAVEN AT FACE VALUE.
IT MAY COME AS A SURPRISE, BUT I DON'T EXACTLY TRUST HUMANS, EITHER.
WELL, ***THAT'S*** JUST GREAT.
ALRIGHT THEN, WHERE TO. BIRD BOY?
I'M AFRAID IT WON'T BE EASY.
TO REACH MY FRIEND, I BELIEVE WE'LL HAVE TO GET OUR HANDS ON A BOAT FROM THE CLOSEST VILLAGE.
DO YOU THINK YOU CAN HANDLE THAT?
ABSOLUTELY NOT.
BUT,
I GUESS I'LL HAVE TO DO MY BEST.
THIS WHOLE THING BETTER BE WORTH IT.

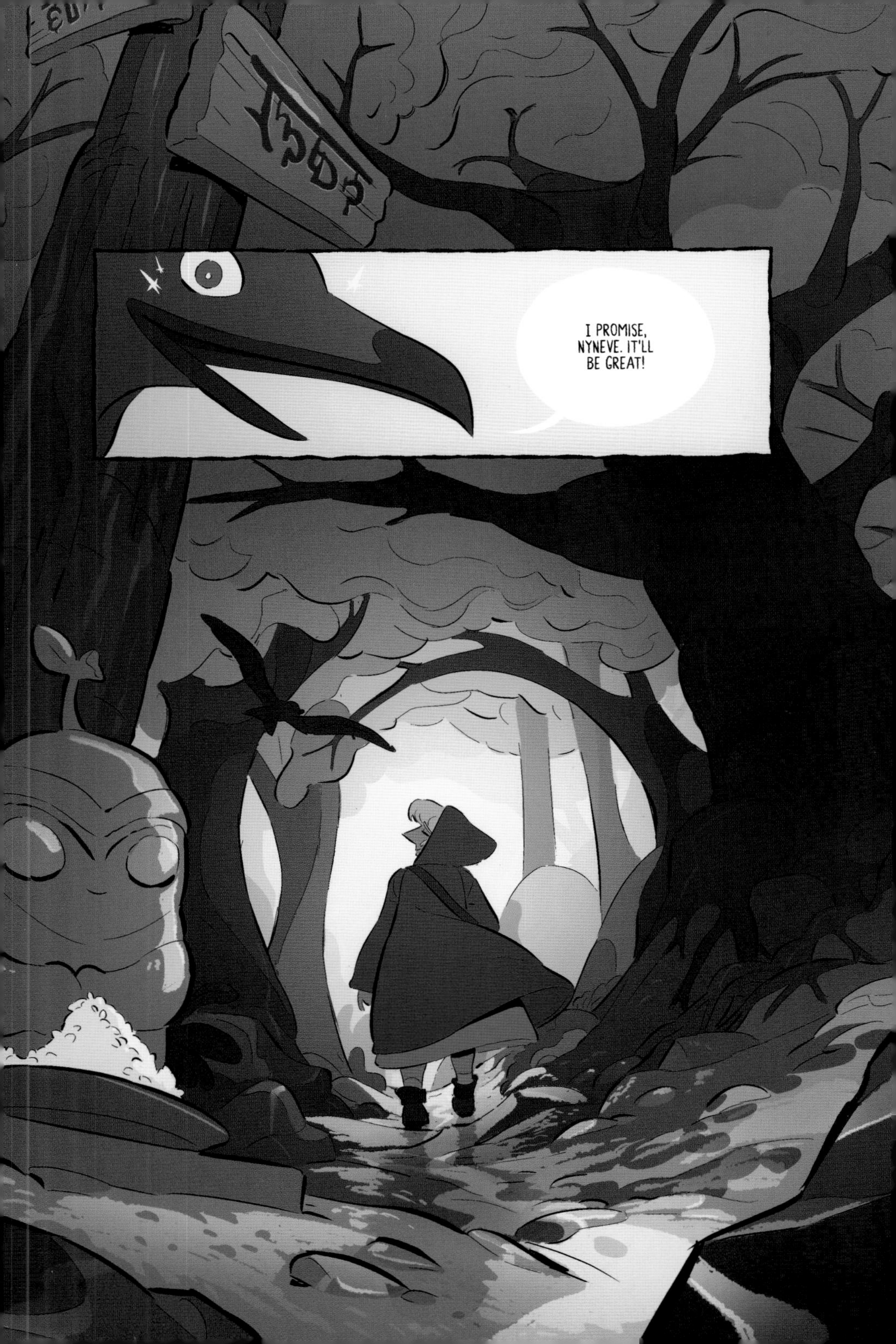
I PROMISE, NYNEVE. IT'LL BE GREAT!

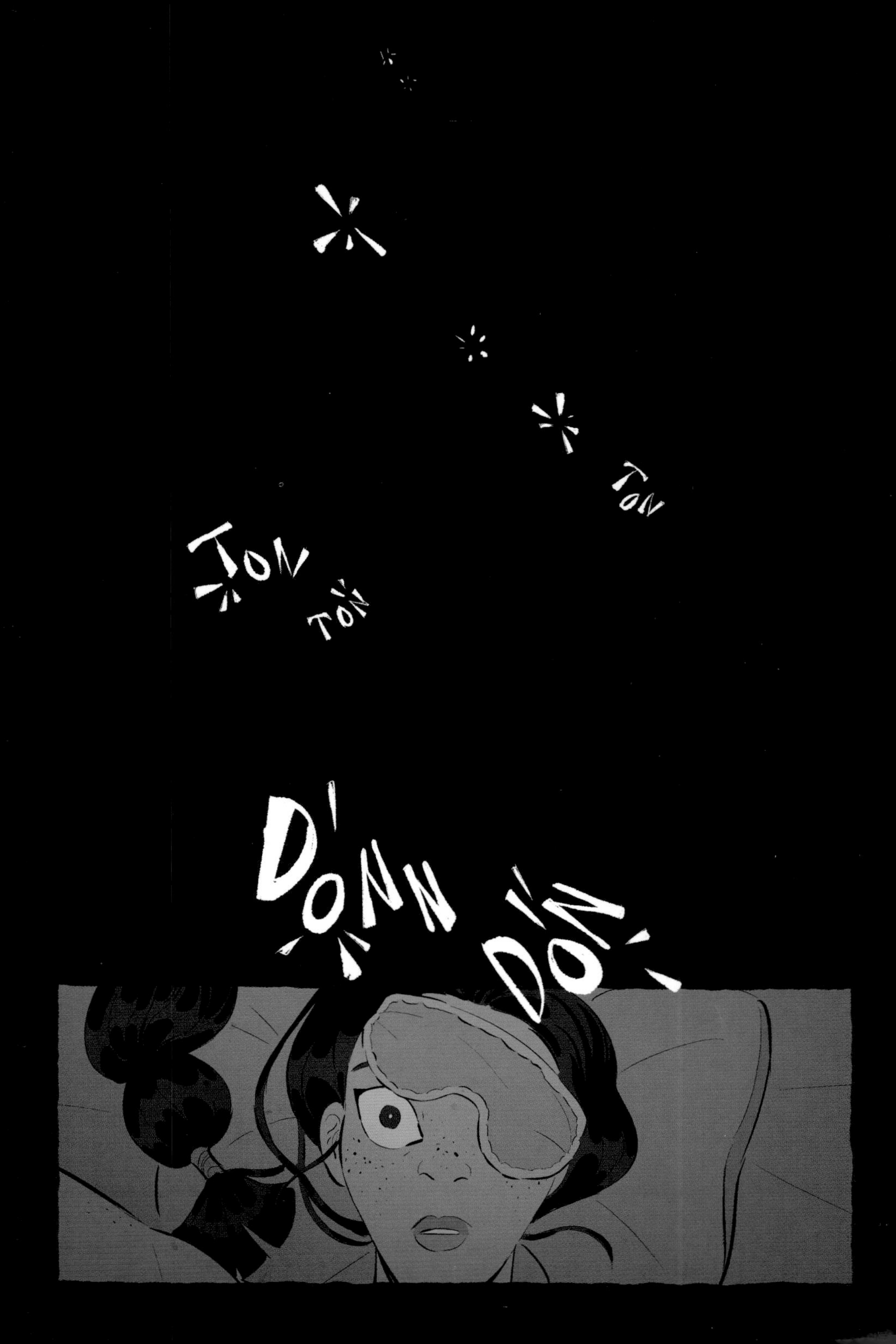
TON
TON
TON
DONN
DON

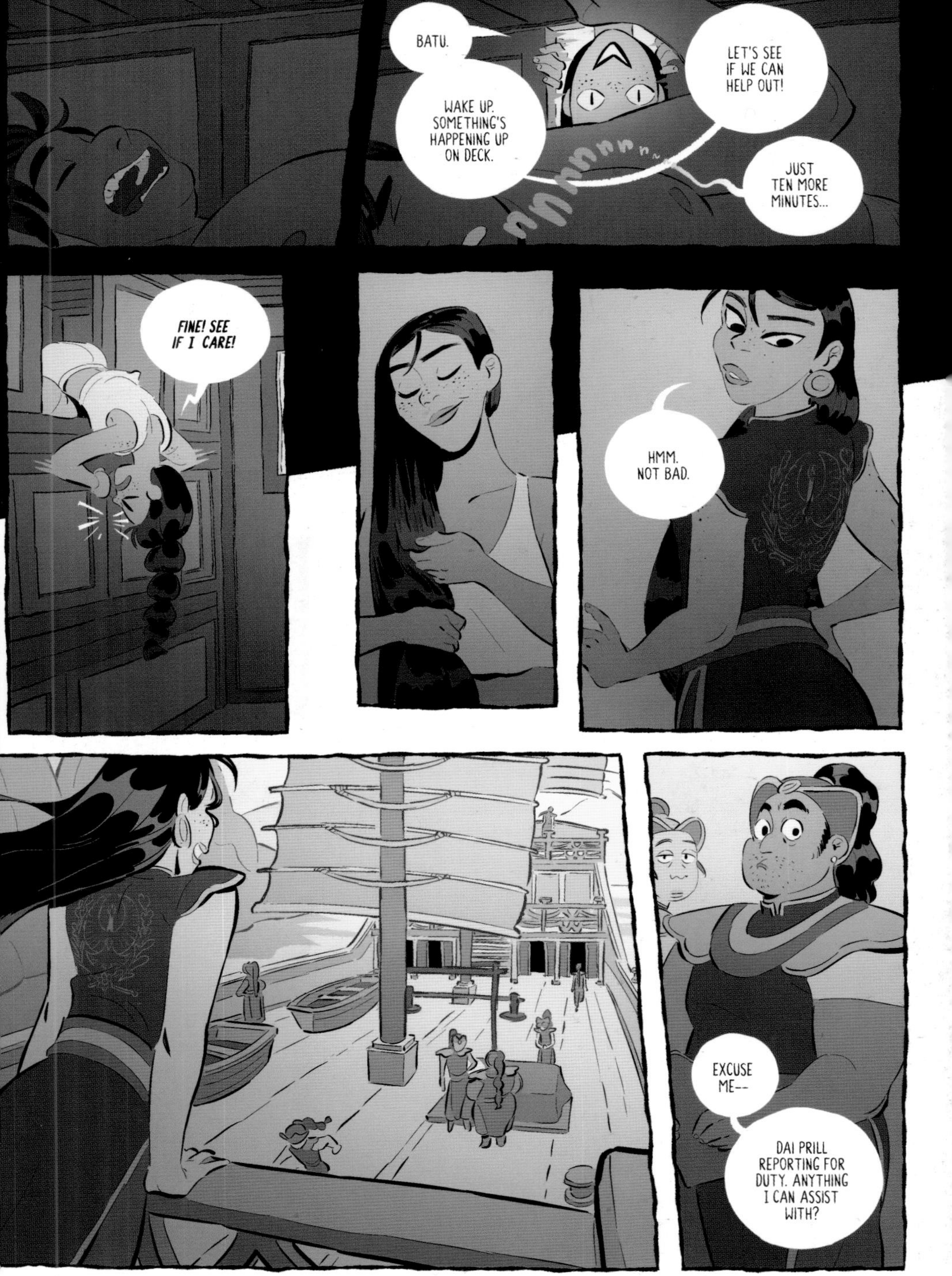
BATU.
WAKE UP. SOMETHING'S HAPPENING UP ON DECK.
LET'S SEE IF WE CAN HELP OUT!
JUST TEN MORE MINUTES...
FINE! SEE IF I CARE!
HMM. NOT BAD.
EXCUSE ME--
DAI PRILL REPORTING FOR DUTY. ANYTHING I CAN ASSIST WITH?

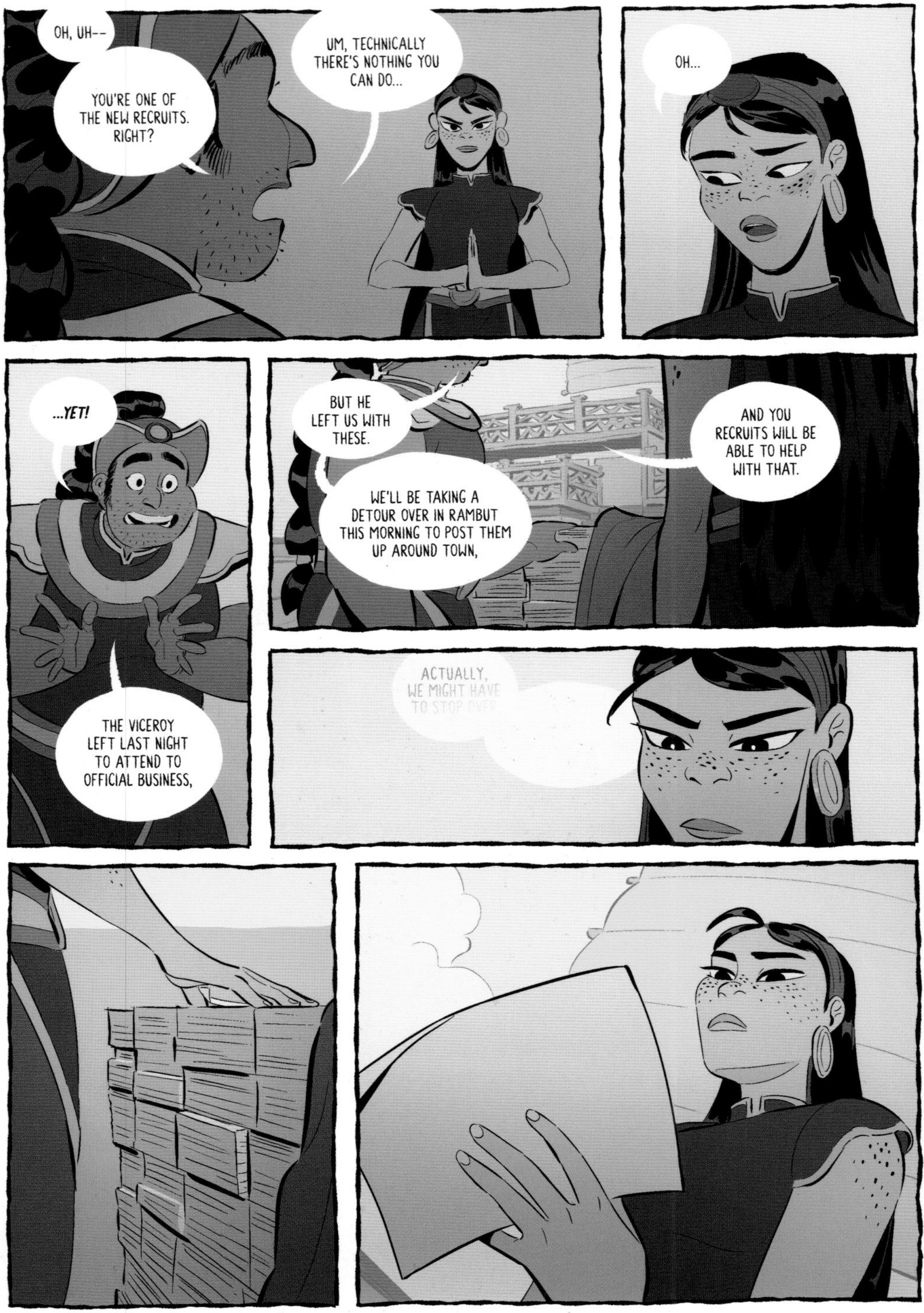

OH, UH--
YOU'RE ONE OF THE NEW RECRUITS. RIGHT?
UM, TECHNICALLY THERE'S NOTHING YOU CAN DO...
OH...
...YET!
THE VICEROY LEFT LAST NIGHT TO ATTEND TO OFFICIAL BUSINESS,
BUT HE LEFT US WITH THESE.
WE'LL BE TAKING A DETOUR OVER IN RAMBUT THIS MORNING TO POST THEM UP AROUND TOWN,
AND YOU RECRUITS WILL BE ABLE TO HELP WITH THAT.
ACTUALLY, WE MIGHT HAVE TO STOP OVER

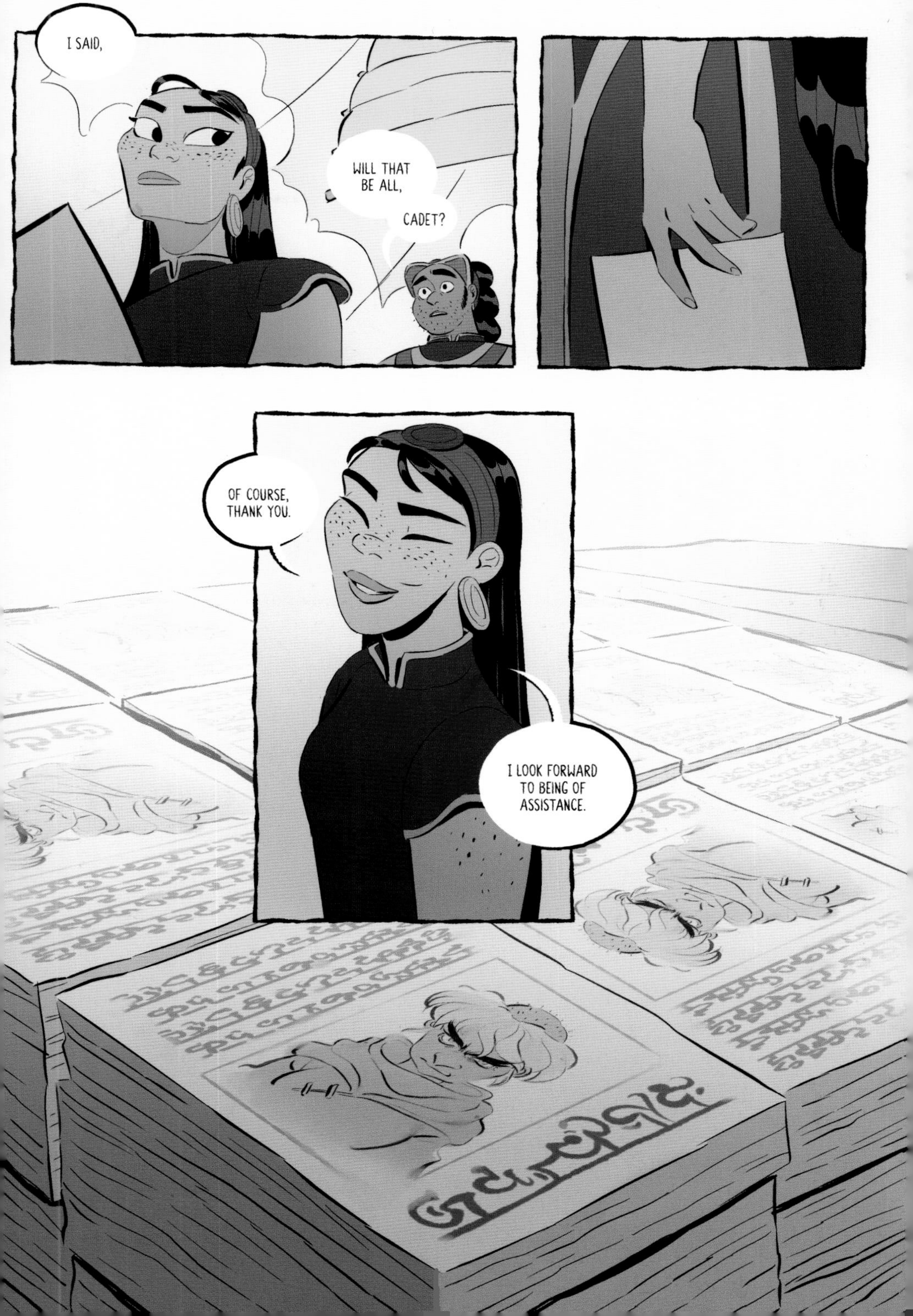
I SAID,
WILL THAT BE ALL,
CADET?
OF COURSE, THANK YOU.
I LOOK FORWARD TO BEING OF ASSISTANCE.

the
making
of
Witchy

Nyneve
Jaga Ahmadzai

After her father was killed, Nyneve and her mother were treated coldly by the inhabitants of Buhok. Remembering the way people treated them then, Nyneve now finds it hard to trust others. Instead of doing things like socializing, Nyneve has always spent most of her free time studying, and damned if she doesn't know she's good at it— although it's maybe not the healthiest way to cope. Nyneve and Veda have a strong bond, which does mean Nyneve can be a little spoiled every now and again. When asked about her hobbies, she may respond; "what's a hobby?" But one thing she'll always enjoy is eating her mother's food.

Veda Ahmadzai

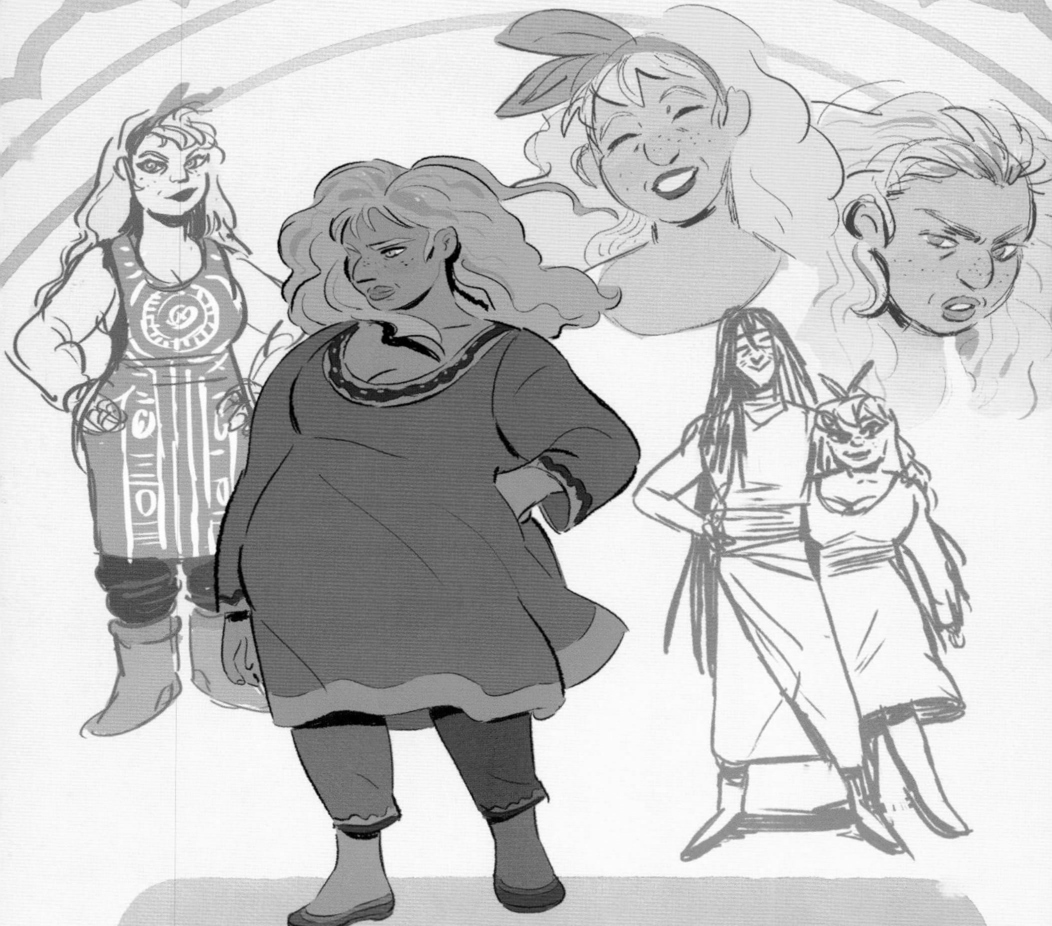

Veda pays the bills as the local apothecary, and she prides herself in her work, even if it's not her passion. She's not been quite the same since Jaga died, and it's clear that beneath the happy facade she projects there lie some repressed emotions. Despite everything, she finds joy in seeing Nyneve grow up, and would do anything for her... except maybe divulging the details of her past. When the working day is done, Veda loves to curl up with a carafe of wine and a murder mystery novel— yes, they have those in Hyalin.

Dai "Prill" Si Yue

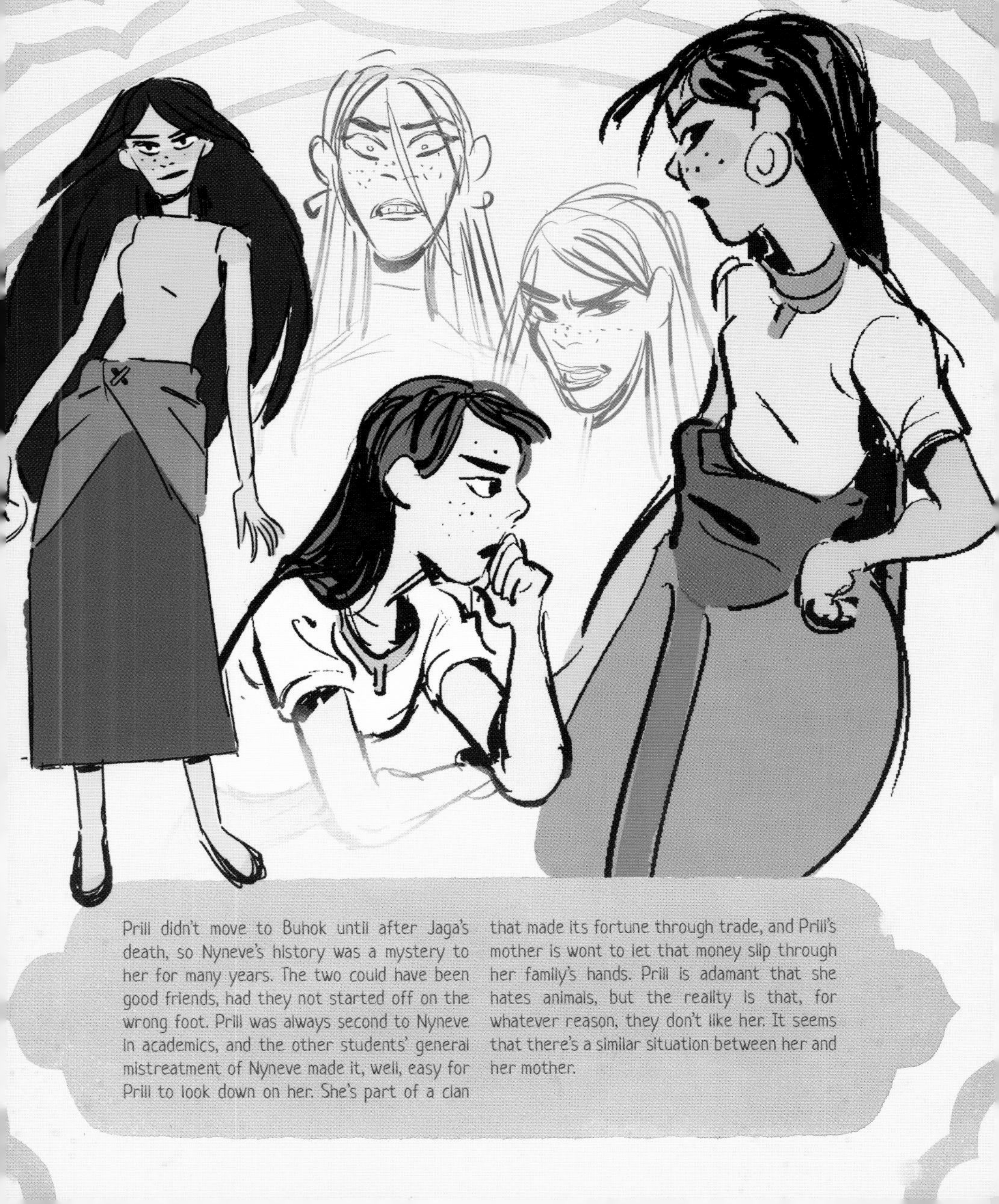

Prill didn't move to Buhok until after Jaga's death, so Nyneve's history was a mystery to her for many years. The two could have been good friends, had they not started off on the wrong foot. Prill was always second to Nyneve in academics, and the other students' general mistreatment of Nyneve made it, well, easy for Prill to look down on her. She's part of a clan that made its fortune through trade, and Prill's mother is wont to let that money slip through her family's hands. Prill is adamant that she hates animals, but the reality is that, for whatever reason, they don't like her. It seems that there's a similar situation between her and her mother.

Mongke Batu

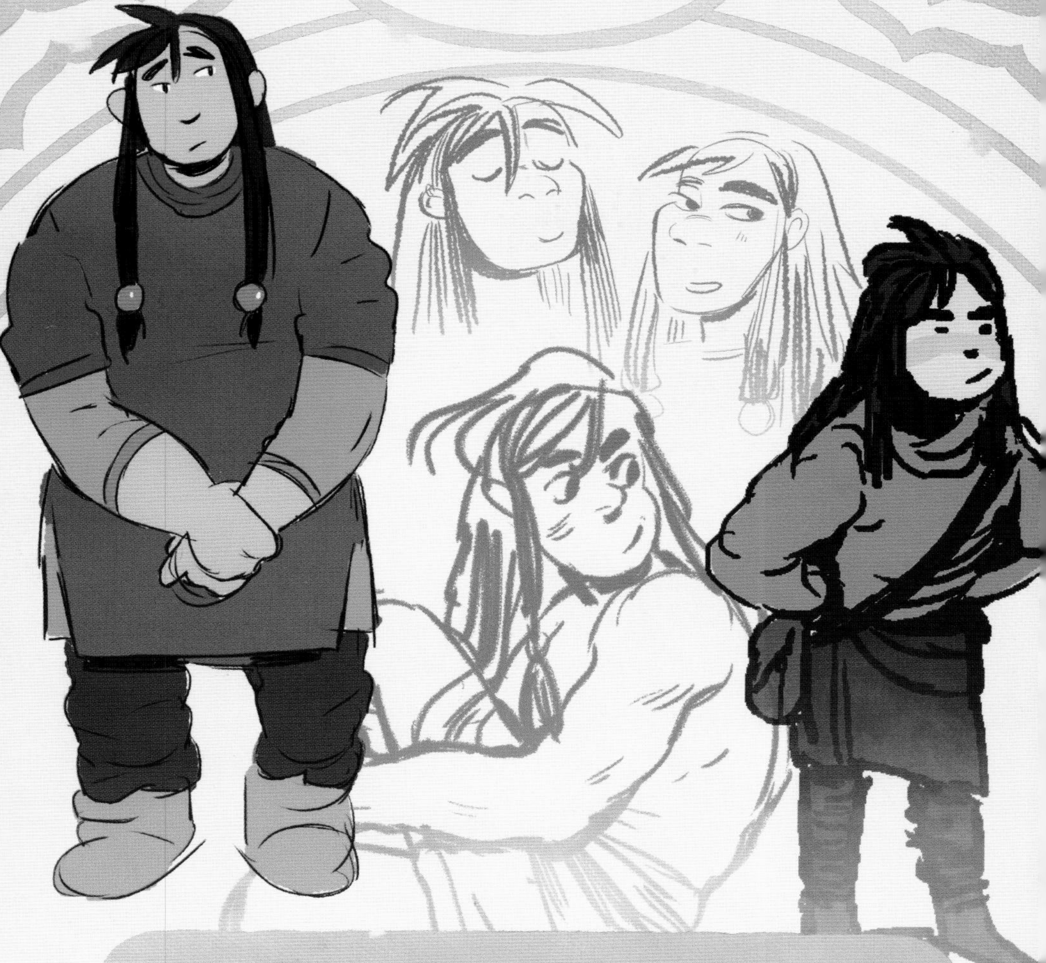

Batu lives on a farm with his family and many dogs. Despite hailing from the Al'atruj mainland, he's a short boat commute from Buhok. He and Nyneve have been friends for what seems like forever. However, Nyneve wasn't always around, so to fill the gap he eventually developed a close friendship with Prill. It's his dream for Nyneve and Prill to get along one day, but that seems like a quickly fading aspiration. Considering his family's ties to the rebellion there's certainly more to Batu than meets the eye, but if it were up to him, he'd probably spend most of his time taking care of his dogs and reading romance novels.

Viceroy Jinheung Nyoto Jung

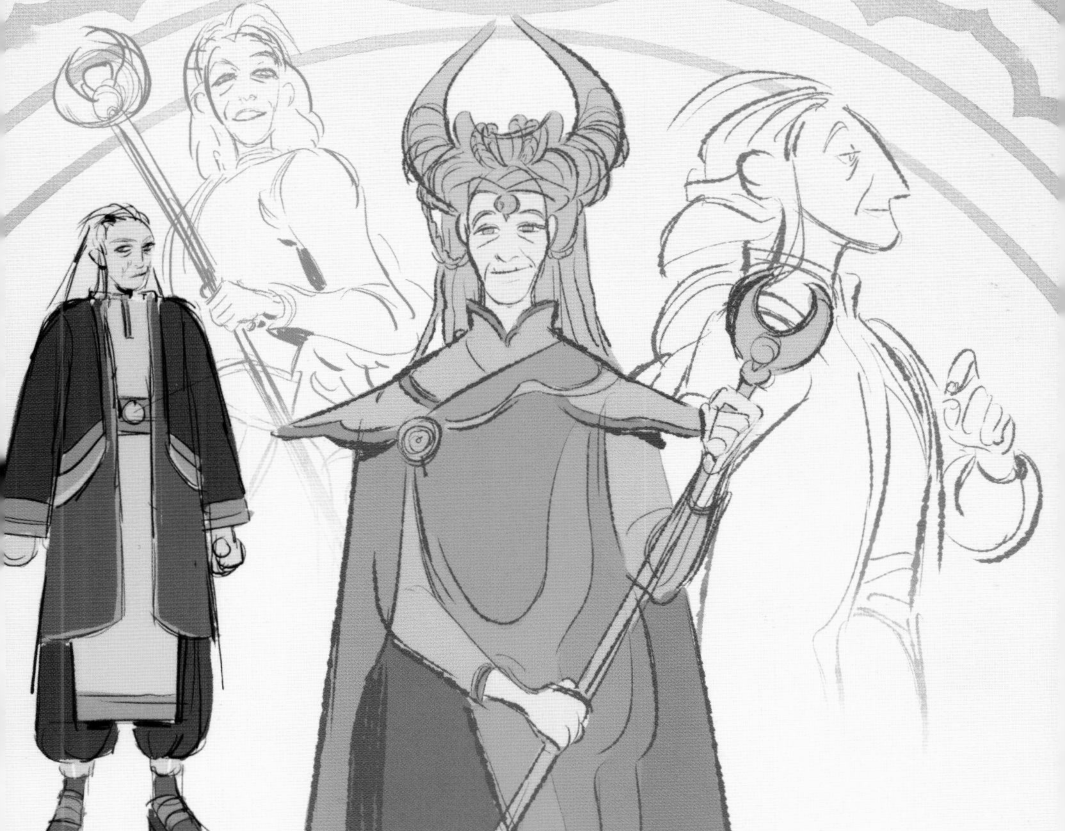

Jung inherited the role of Captain Regent of Hyalin after the tragic deaths of the empress and emperor by the hand of their son, the Rebel Prince. While his leadership of Hyalin is technically temporary, there are no other valid successors to the throne. While his meteoric rise to power earned him many skeptics, he's gradually regaining the respect of the kingdom with his kind demeanor, and enactment of popular reforms. While he cuts a formidable figure, (especially when accompanied by his beloved pet vulture,) he'll be the first to tell you he's just like any other witch; he loves a nice hot bath at the end of the day.

Hyalin

Hyalin was formed in
a tempest of earth and steam and fire, millions
of years ago when the now extinct Gunung Slamet burst
forth from beneath the ocean's waves. In the volcano's wake an
archipelago of over a hundred islands was left behind, each separated
by serpentine river systems and waterways. For this reason the primary
mode of transport in Hyalin are watercraft, and from the ease of travel
provided by these a culture rich in trade was born.

Before magic was widely used, the ancient Hyalinese believed in supreme,
all powerful gods– Early witches who had been corrupted by the power
that harnessing the spirits promised. The crumbling remains of their
statues and temples of worship can still be seen throughout the region.
Modern Hyalinese witches have come to learn that divinity and magic exist
inherent in all that's natural; whether in living beings, the earth, the water,
or the sky. The balance between a witch's own spirit and those found in
nature is integral to the continued existence of Hyalin.

Before the kingdom of Hyalin was established, the region was one
constantly torn by the warring of its many clans. Tired of the endless
conflict, the largest and most powerful of these clans– the Qaargua– set
about forming an alliance with the other clans, with the goal of a just and
unified kingdom. Of course, as this alliance grew, clans who resisted unity
were integrated by force; the units of warriors who strong-armed those
stubborn clans formed the basis of what is now the Witch Guard. This is
why the Guard is so revered today: There is no living memory of another
method through which to obtain peace.

Due to the unification of Hyalin, the kingdom is now the vibrant melting pot
of cultures that exists today. Although some fringe groups still resent the
actions of the Qaargua, the dream of a unified Hyalin has, until this day,
stayed true.

Fanart Selection

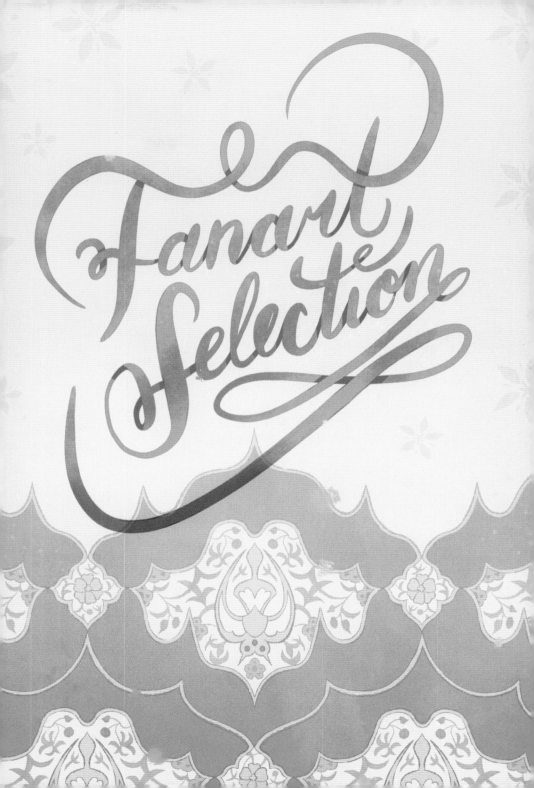

Jake Wyatt

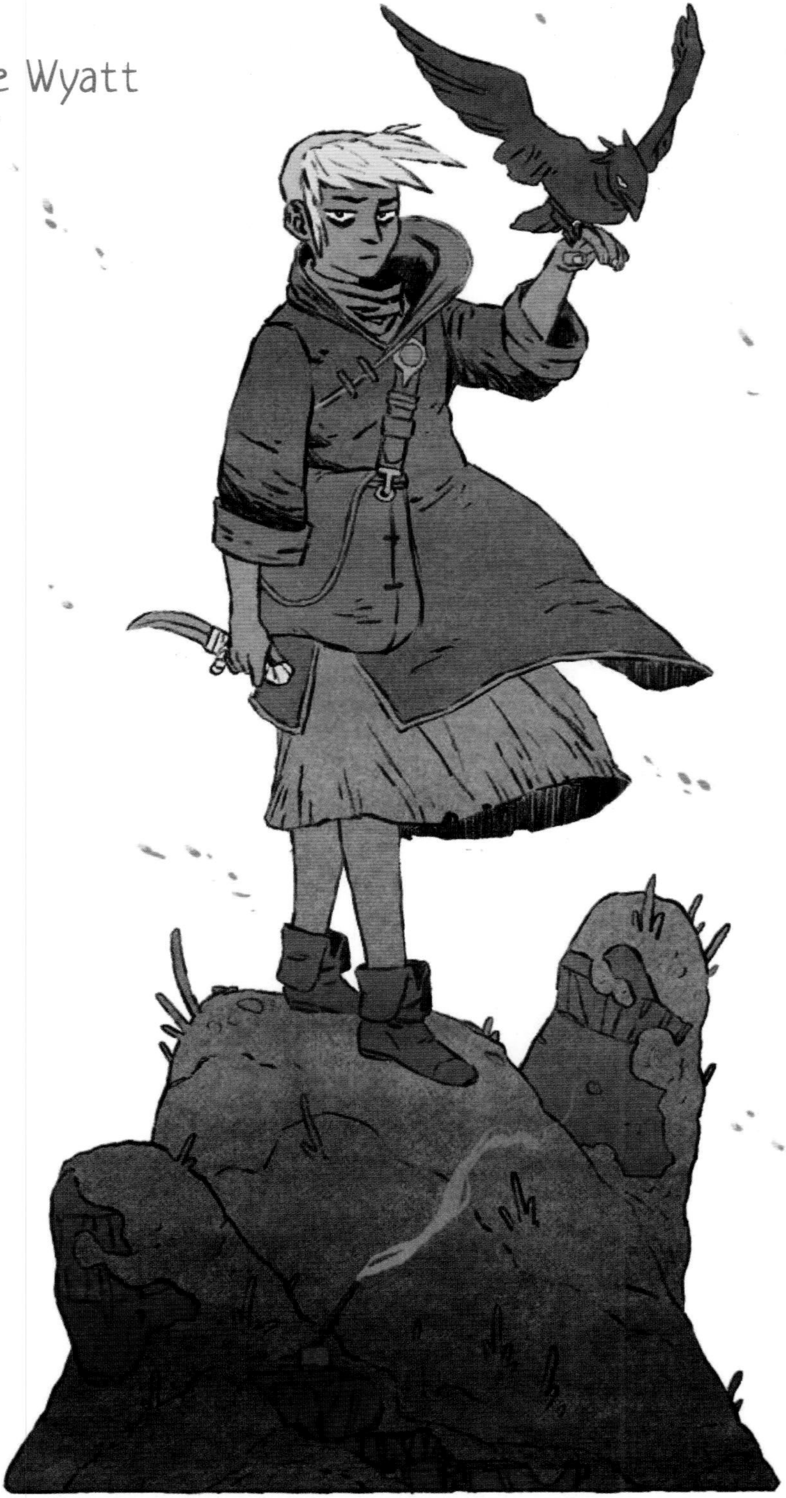

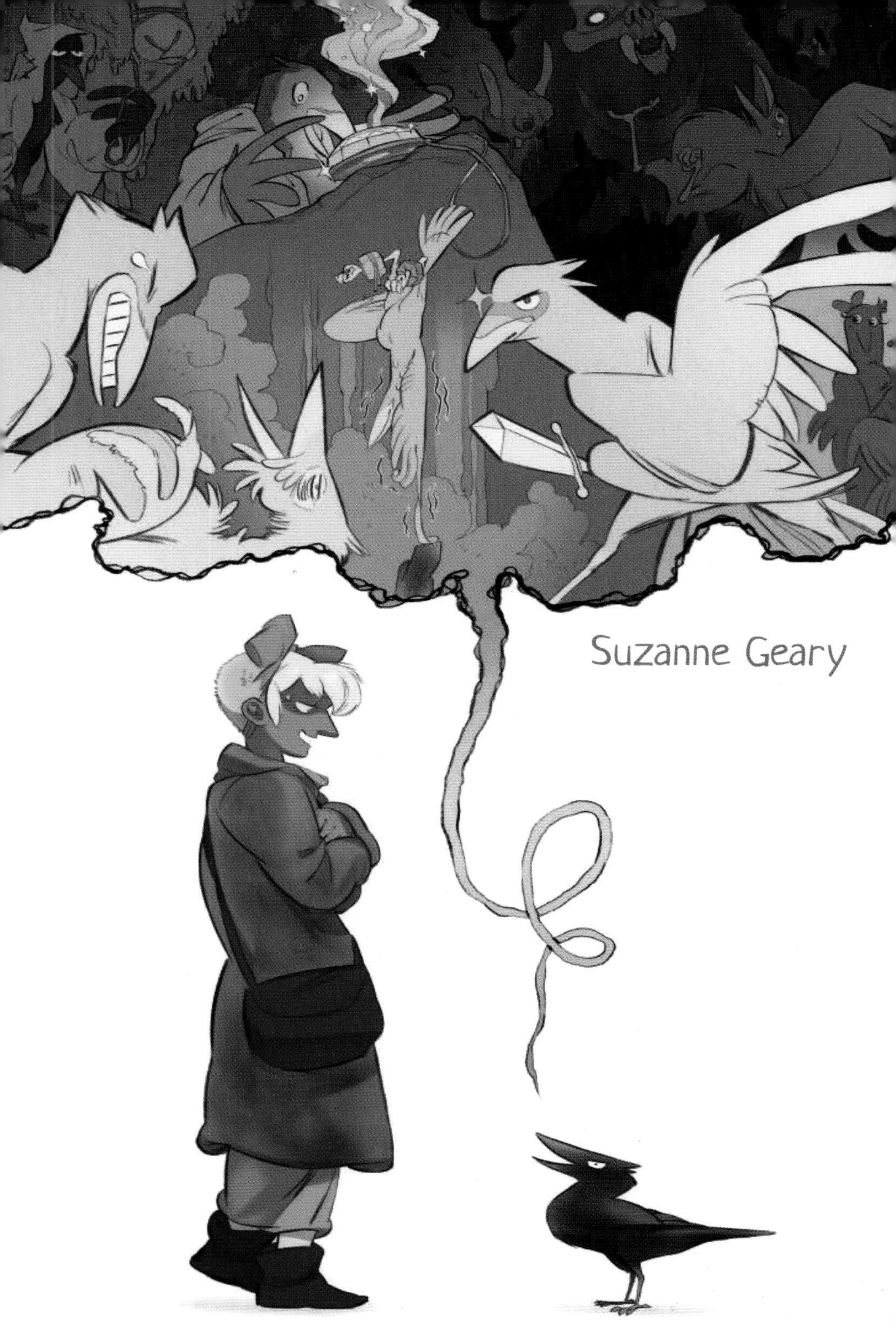
Suzanne Geary

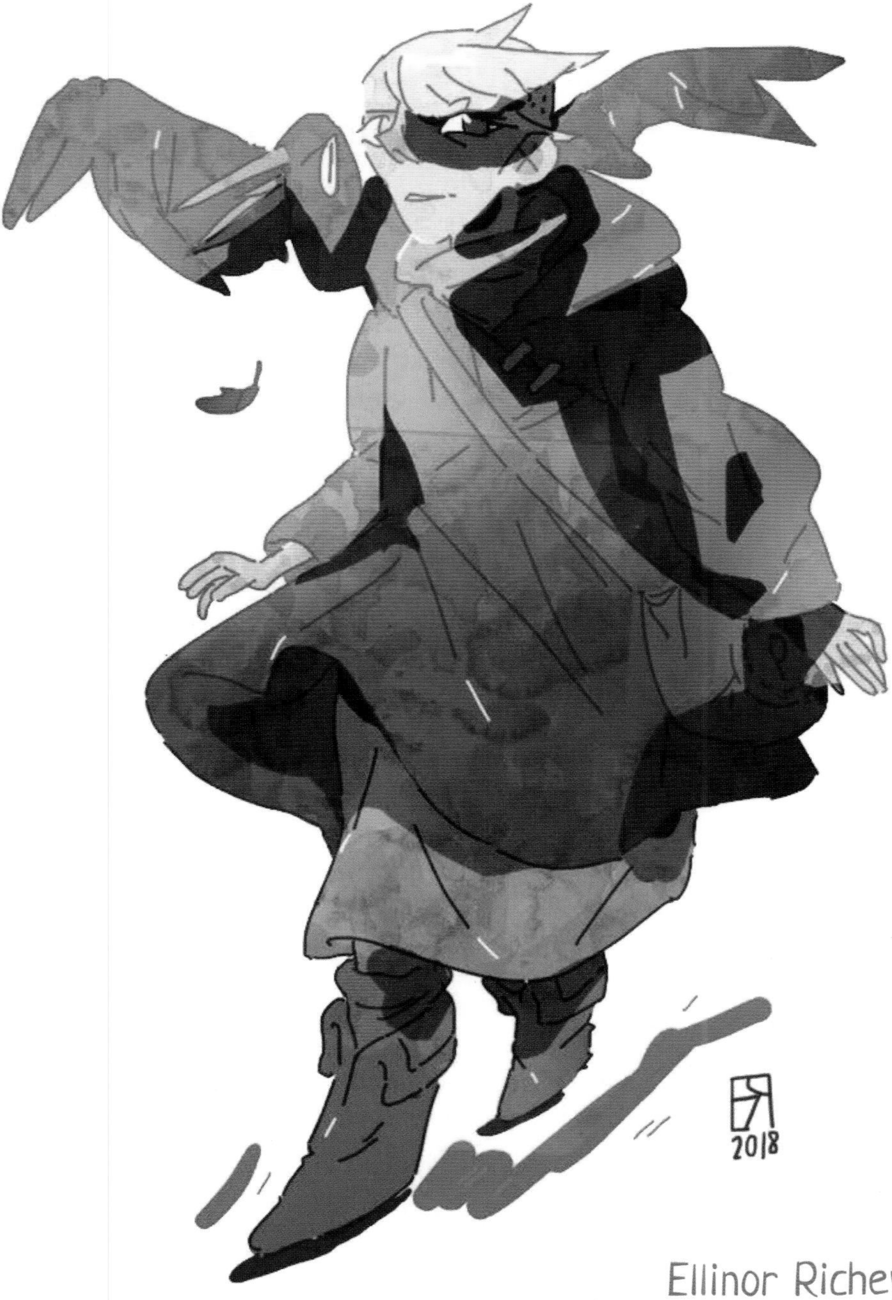
2018

Ellinor Richey

Marta Milczarek

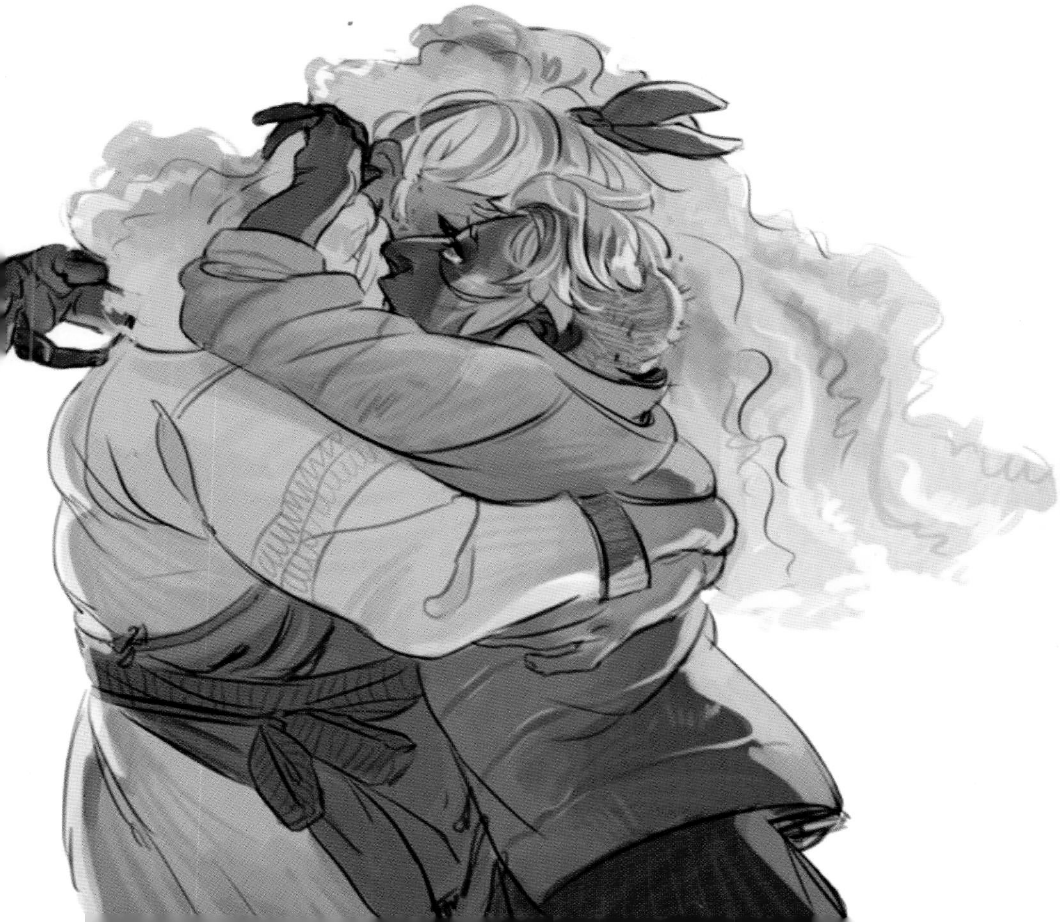

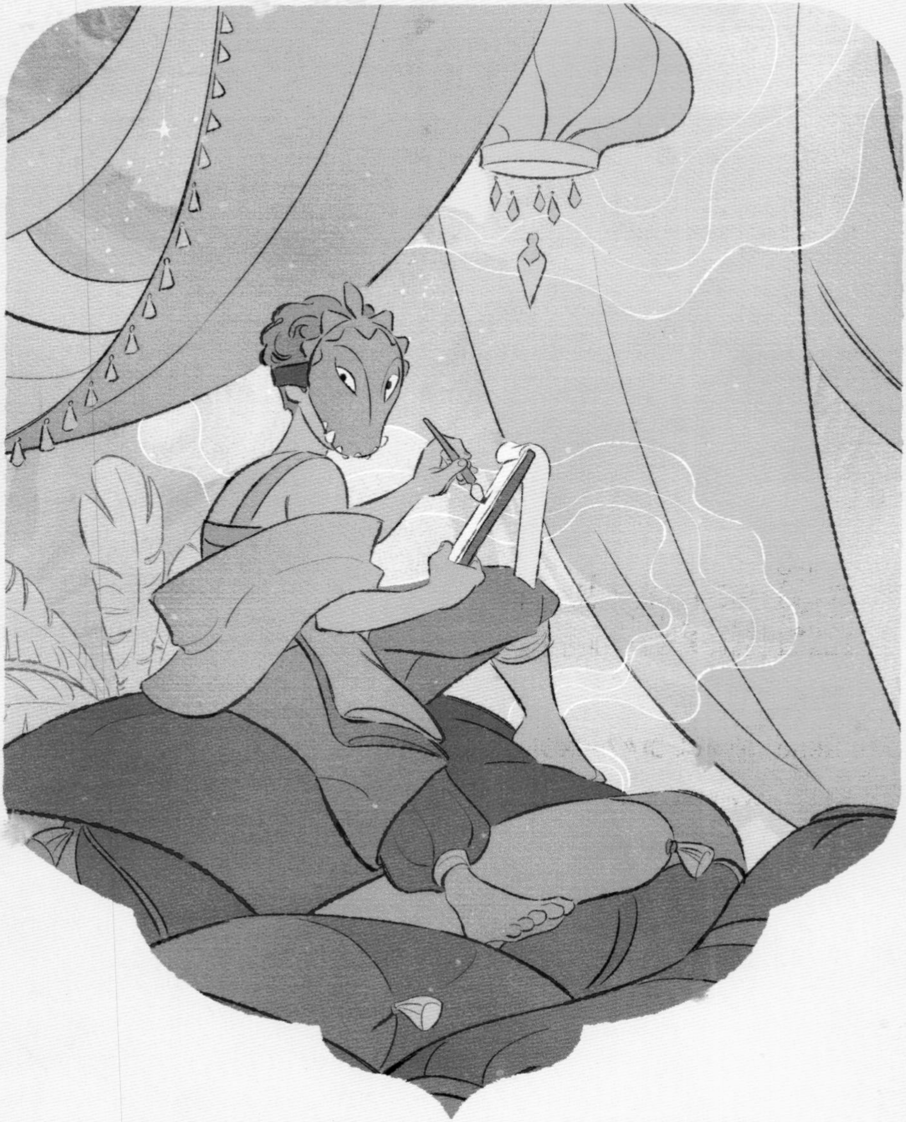

Ariel Slamet Ries is an eggplant fanatic and long-time lover of dogs in snoods from Melbourne, Australia. She studied animation for 4 years before throwing away the prestige and money to pursue comics. She's still waiting to see how that will turn out.